New York Stories

Renald Iacovelli

STONE
TOWER
PRESS

About this edition:

The original edition of this work contained typos and several obvious grammatical errors. Most of these were due to the idiosyncratic blindness any writer is bound to have regarding his own compositions, and on account of which he cannot be effective as a proofreader. As much as possible these errors been corrected in this edition, though no doubt some still remain.

Stone Tower Press
New York, NY

ISBN: 978-0-9852181-0-2
Printed in the United States of America

New York Stories

For

Albert Goldglancz

TABLE OF CONTENTS

JOEY

You no sooner passed through the arch at Station Square and entered into Forest Hills Gardens than you were met with a sign that made it clear you might not be entirely welcome: "WARNING! Entering Private Streets." The word "warning" was in big unmistakable red letters, and the rest of the second line was in big black ones, and beneath that was a single sentence explaining that the area was a "corporation"—a private entity to which no one should think he had some inalienable right as a citizen of the city to walk through or otherwise trespass upon. It was a sign that said in effect: "You can come in and take a look, if you want to—of course, we can't stop you from doing that; but remember you can only look, not stay; so go ahead and walk about, and gawk if you must, but make sure that after you've had your fill you skedaddle back to where you came from, those tawdry outlands of 99¢ stores, greasy fast food joints, and newsstands selling lottery tickets." Pretty much that was the area you had passed through to get here, and if you looked back over your shoulder you could still see it—the rest of Forest Hills with its automobile-choked streets and sidewalks swarming with pedestrians who hurried from one store to another along Austin Street in a frenzied search for bargains. And in turning your head back to this new, better place, you could almost understand how those who lived here wanted to keep it as it was—an oasis of clean gentility amid the madding crowds.

It was an aptly-named area; still more apt was the shortened name it went by—"the Gardens," for there really was, on this June day, much that was garden-like about it. Everything was intensely green, almost lush; there were many trees lining the streets, and hedgerows and shrubs and flowering plants abounded on well-kept lawns. It was delightfully calm and quiet. There was little traffic because motorists generally had no place to park: on every block a few signs warned them that un-

1

less they were residents of the area—unless proper identification was showing on their windshields—their cars would be towed away at their expense. The sidewalks were unpopulated, and so clean and straight that they looked as though they had been painted on a canvas. But most impressive of all were the houses. They would have been big even by rural standards, but here in the city, where most people lived in cramped apartments, they were truly like palaces. Many of them were two stories tall and in a grand Tudor style, with great wooden beams inlaid amid their brick facings, and having high, steep roofs from which chimneys of lighter-colored brick reached upward. They were set back at the end of well-tended lawns, or obscured by high trellises, or hidden completely away behind stone walls. The least of them was worth several million dollars. Their grand, imposing facades helped to set the sober tone of the area: one felt that one had to act more carefully here than on the indifferently crowded streets from which one had come. Back *there* one could run or hop or skip or shout or babble, and people wouldn't notice or, if they noticed, wouldn't care: but here a strict propriety ruled, and if you acted in any way eccentric or disturbed the peace and orderliness of the place you were sure to be visited by the police whom an observant resident would have wasted no time in calling. Such a restrictive atmosphere seemed at first intimidating or oppressive, but in a very few minutes one began to appreciate it, and even to find it refreshing. For while there is much to be said for the freedom to act as one wishes, there is perhaps still more to be said for the immunity from having to endure the freedom of others to act as *they* wish. Given the selfish nature of mankind, some reduction in personal liberty is probably always required for peace and orderliness.

As I made my way into the Gardens, I held a piece of paper on which I had written down the address that was my objective: "21 Tennis Place." At the time I had taken it down I had smiled cynically at its connotation of leisured sport and ease; it seemed just another one of those absurd pretensions one comes across so often in New York City, for instance when someone assures you he's an "executive vice president"—in a company that has two hundred of them—or when the city bolts a few cast iron benches onto a patch of concrete and has the audacity to name it a "park." But with each grand, perfectly manicured street I passed it seemed to me that in this instance the intimation of a better, finer class of life really was in order. There probably *were* private tennis courts somewhere about, and one could imagine that behind one of these houses young men and women dressed in summery white uniforms lobbed balls at one another across a net, getting "a little exercise" while the rest of the world was busy at its dirty, boring, endless labors. I had to ask directions of several people before finding the address, which was at the end of a cul-de-sac. It was a huge house all granite facing, high gables, and fancy quarreled windows. A flagged walkway led from the sidewalk across a long front yard to the front door, which was a marvel of heavy oak planks, thick iron hinges, and a disproportionally small window of thick glass. It reminded me of some immense and heavy door that might have stood at the gate of a medieval castle. Even that door must have cost a lot of money. "Rich," I said to myself, looking to the left and right of me, feeling dwarfed before the great place. I shoved the paper with the address in my pocket and straightened out my clothes a bit. I had worn a jacket and one of the three pairs of pants I owned that weren't made of denim. I trusted that I looked presentable; at any rate, I hoped I did, for I was here for a job.

There had been an advertisement in a local paper for an English language tutor, and earlier that morning I had spoken to the woman who had placed it and she had invited me to come by for an interview. Two months earlier I had been working part-time for an investment banking company, but I had lost the job to globalization, the executives of the company having found some Indian typist in Bombay who would do my job for a fifth of my salary and be glad to survive on curried beans and rice. Since then I had been vainly looking for something of similarly limited hours—and part-time it had to be, for I was also a writer and needed time to write. But in New York part-time jobs are always harder to find than full-time ones, as though the workaday world is determined not to let anyone escape its clutches. That meant I either had to find a regular, full-time job and struggle still harder to write through my exhaustion, or live off my savings till I could find another part-time job and so try to protect and preserve that freshness of mind and spirit without which one cannot hope to create any-

thing vital. In keeping with the reckless tenor of the whole of
my foregoing life, I had chosen the latter—to follow, again, the
perilously narrow, cliff-side path; and hope that I wouldn't stumble and tumble over. But by now I was beginning to worry in
earnest. After two months of unemployment I had very little
money left in the bank. Unemployment insurance had paid me
but a fraction of my already low salary, and after constant with-
drawals from my slender savings account there remained in it
no more than the equivalent of two months' living expenses.
Once that was gone I would be facing ... well, as usual, I preferred not to think of what I would be facing.

I rang the doorbell and waited. When no one came to the
door immediately I wondered if I had written down the right address and scolded myself for my bad memory and sometime lack
of attention to details; it would have been just like me to get it
wrong. "Stupid!" I murmured against myself. But in another
moment the door opened and I stood face to face with a woman
whose smile and air of expectation assured me that I had gotten
it right. In an inquiring tone of voice she said my name, and
when I nodded and replied with, "Yes—Mrs. Larke?" she smiled
a little more comfortably, opened the door fully, and asked me to
come inside, into the foyer, where she shook my hand.

"Did you find your way alright?" she asked, as she closed
the door behind me.

I told her that I had—that I had asked a few people along
the way and they had directed me.

"Good—glad to hear it. Some of these streets are a little
confusing if you're not used to them. Please, follow me: we'll go
out back. We can talk there."

I followed her through her home. To say it was tastefully
furnished would not be saying enough, for what really struck me
was that it was *genuinely* furnished. In an age when so much in
the way of furnishing and architecture was for economic considerations artificial, consisting of veneers and plastics and glass,
here the furniture was of real wood, the fireplace of real granite,
the silver plate in the hutches of real and solid silver—a burglar's dream. Everywhere here the sense of old, solid, beautiful
quality flared out at me, which only goes to show that so long as
one has a modicum of taste even a lifetime of lower middle-class
contentment and pride in faux things is incapable of wiping out

the sensibility that detects the real and better article. The paintings on the walls also impressed me. I am sure that if I knew more about painting I would have found in the signatures at the bottom of those canvases the names of artists admired by connoisseurs. One of them was a full-length portrait of Mrs. Larke and her husband when they had been young, perhaps in their thirties; a large painting of some five feet tall, it dominated the wall it hung upon. Telling from the style of Mrs. Larke's dress and hairstyle it had been painted in the early '60s. Its solid, heavy frame gave it an extra measure of splendor.

We passed through the living room, through a kitchen with a marble floor and sparkling new appliances, and through sliding glass doors to a solarium, an addendum to the back of the house. It was nothing but a skeleton of aluminum beams, for the glass panels they ordinarily held in place had been removed for the summer and replaced with screens. Just beyond it grew banks of flowers: red roses, white and purple lilacs, and deep pink azaleas. They perfumed the warm air, and their brilliant colors lured intermittent bees that alighted on them and probed their meretriciously exposed cups in search of nectar. Beyond this stretched a very green and recently cut lawn interpolated with several large trees whose branches spread out to offer shade to most of the ground beneath them and to host the birds chirping away in their midst. It was almost hard to believe that such peaceful, gracious prospect lay only a few minutes' walk from the car-choked, filthy bustle of the rest of the city.

Mrs. Larke invited me to take a seat at a white wicker table here. Apparently she had been having breakfast when I had rung the doorbell. On the table were an insulated carafe of coffee, a small plate with the remnant crumbs of cake or toast, and her own half-emptied cup. A copy of the New had been hastily thrown aside when she had gotten up to answer the door. She was just about to resume her seat when she hesitated and asked, "Would you like some coffee?"

"That would be great, thanks."

"Let me get you a cup."

She returned only seconds later with a cup and saucer, and poured my coffee for me. It came out hot and steaming from the carafe. She sat down.

"Did you take the train?" she asked.

"Yes. The local, the M train."

"You came from Sunnyside, right?"

"Yes. Right off Queens Boulevard."

"Oh, that's not so far," she said, as though pleased that I should not have had too much inconvenience. "There's the milk and sugar, just help yourself," she said, nodding to them.

I helped myself to each, and marveled at the small ornate ceramic pitcher and bowl in which they were contained: finely made items with little gilt splayed feet and exacting tendrilous decorations that must have taken some time to produce and paint. It struck me how even such small and unimportant articles could be beautiful, and I admired Mrs. Larke for having had the taste to pick out and purchase them, for they made even the otherwise indifferent act of having one's morning coffee that much more pleasant.

"It was pretty easy to get here," I said. "It only took me about forty minutes. I've never been here before. I mean, I've been to Forest Hills before, and I've even walked out this way a little, but never this far back. The houses are amazing."

"Yes, some of them are nice, aren't they?"

"They're amazing," I repeated, putting down the spoon with which I had stirred my cup. "It's like a whole other place—a whole other world. It's like not being in New York at all."

Mrs. Larke smiled in appreciation of this roundabout compliment on her own house.

She was not as I had expected her to look, but then again one always has such strange ideas of how people look by just talking to them on the phone. Earlier that morning I had imagined her to be a woman of perhaps fifty years old, of medium height, with dark features and a plain, kindly face. The only thing I was right about was the kindliness; in all other things not. For she was a tall, slender woman in her late sixties, her complexion fair and her hair dyed to maintain what had once been its natural blonde. She was still attractive "for her age," as the phrase goes, but less because she was well-preserved (to use yet another phrase) than because she had been so pretty to begin with that even age hadn't been able totally to compromise her features, which were still, as they had always been, aristocratically fine and sharp. The nose was small, severely straight, ending in delicate nostrils; the eyes were large, bright, hazel; the well-shaped ears stood close to the head; the lips formed a thin, bowlike curve; and the high cheekbones gave a glamorous curve to her face when she turned it ever so slightly this way or that. Her hands were remarkable for the long, slender, elegant fingers ending in short, polished, tapered nails. That morning she was wearing a light-colored, summery, cotton outfit of slacks and blouse. She wore no jewelry aside from a pair of tiny diamond-studded earrings. In her movements, in the way she looked at you, in the way she nodded slightly when you spoke as though agreeing with you, everything about her was quiet, refined, and—one felt—sympathetic. She spoke good English, enunci-ating her words precisely. She seemed to be fairly well educated. There was no question in my mind that she had had a charmed, privileged life. She had undoubtedly seen a lot of the world, had stood amid the famous, storied places the likes of which someone like myself had only read about. My sense was that if she didn't "go anywhere" these days it was only because she had already gone everywhere worth going to. I remember suddenly hoping that she wouldn't ask me whether or not I had "traveled," had visited Europe, say, or the Far East, or knew German or French, for that line of questioning would have soon enough revealed to her how circumscribed my life had been.

Despite my insecurities I was also sensible that she was respectful, even somehow deferential, toward me. And I knew the reason for this. It was because I had published a few novels, a fact I had disclosed to her earlier that morning when, during our initial conversation on the phone, she had asked me for my credentials. That had been the first time I had ever tooted my horn about my "accomplishments," and I had only done so in the hope that it would help me land the job.

"So, you have a few books out," she said, smiling, leading into the subject that had most recommended me to her. "That's very nice. I checked on the computer"—she meant the Internet—"and saw them listed on a few sites. Very impressive. I'll have to get them."

I thanked her for the kind remarks even as I hoped she didn't expect me to talk about my books. For the first had been published by a small company of questionable repute, and two more had been published at my own expense. And yet the fact remained that my books were available to the public and had even been stocked by a few public libraries. If someone were to ask me why none of my works had been published by a large, well-established company and in a big way, I could only have replied that it hadn't been for want of trying. For almost two decades I had tried to place my work with mainstream publishers, only to have it consistently returned unread, or under-read. (I knew this, by the way, because in those days I used a simple but infallible method by which my returned manuscripts always revealed the extent to which they had been handled.) In the meantime I had watched and wondered at men and women of lesser ability having their inept or moronic scribbling spread across the country, across the world, and give them some kind of income and notoriety, while my efforts left me as anonymous and poor as ever. Constant disappointment is a harsh taskmaster;—eventually it whips the naiveté out of you. I had come to understand that the literary world could be ruthlessly hit or miss, and that someone with the title of "editor" could very well be a dunce. And in general the world is less eager to recognize and promote talent than to applaud that which has already somehow made its way. In light of this reality one sees that the only door likely to open for you is the one that you yourself kick in; and even then it will probably not open more than a crack. At any rate, I had never made any real money with any of my books. The proceeds from my latest novel—the work of a year—had enabled me to buy a pair of shoes, and not an especially good pair at that.

I thanked her for her compliment, and added, by way of humility and truthfulness, that the sales rankings for my books were all low. "Nobody buys them," I said.

"Oh? Well, I hope you haven't gotten discouraged," she said, kindly. "I read parts of them on the computer and they seem very good, very well-written. I'm sure you're talented. You know, when I was younger I was a writer myself—a journalist."

"Really?"

"When I left college—oh, a long time ago now!—I was hired by the Boston *Herald* as an assistant editor and helped to write articles. I could have had a career in journalism, I suppose. But I met my husband ..."

Her husband, as I would later learn, had come from a wealthy family, from "old" money, and at only twenty-six years of age had been through his family's connections comfortably ensconced in a well-paying position in a large bank, the first of many powerful positions which would result in his becoming a chief executive in a major Wall Street firm in which his responsibilities were indeed weighty but recompensed by a yearly salary of tens of millions of dollars. After marrying him there had no longer been a financial reason for Mrs. Larke to work, and she had been too intelligent to buy into the notion that there is something intrinsically noble in pursuing a "career" when one could be pursuing life itself. Undoubtedly too her five-month stint as a reporter-in-training had been enough to convince her that having one's nerves rattled into wakefulness by an alarm clock each morning, then having to knock oneself out eight to ten hours a day for only enough money on which to survive, wasn't exactly a civilized way to live. Instead she indulged in her love of reading, she traveled, she learned of the world firsthand and enriched her life. She had a child, a daughter, whose son it was that now lived with her and for whom she was seeking a tutor.

"I've often thought of taking up writing again," she continued. "Actually, I think I'd like to write my auto-biography. I've seen some interesting things in my life—done some interesting things—met some interesting people."

"You should, then."

"Oh," she said, modestly, shaking her head, "I'd probably botch it up. You just can't sit down and start writing like that."

"It's true that you can't do it all at once. But you can do it little by little—a paragraph, a page at a time. You'd be surprised how much you can get done in a couple of hours a day so long as you're consistent. Just take your time. You'll see—you would get it done. It might be very good. It might be wonderful."

"Who would publish it?" she asked, in a way that was, I felt, fishing for information.

I told her that that was always the hardest part, but if she had something to say, and it was unique, or even just uniquely expressed, it wouldn't matter whether or not it was published in a large or a small way. Books were strange things, I said; if

they were worthy, they had a way of taking on a life of their
own. There were obscure books that had survived for centuries,
revered by a small discerning audience, while the majority of
the bestsellers of the day made their world-rattling splash and
seemed to be in the hands of every other person, only to sink
into obscurity in a few years, and be utterly forgotten by the
next generation.

"Just write it and see what happens," I said.

She smiled appreciatively at my encouragement and no
doubt too at my confidence in her literary ability. Like so many
people who have been blessed with wealth, she wanted to believe that there was something about her—in herself and apart
from her financial standing—that made her special and worthy.

We began talking again about the area. Or rather, I
brought it up again, mentioning again how impressive it was.

"Actually it's ironic you say that," she responded. "It's gotten pretty bad over the last ten years or so. Not around here so
much, maybe, but you know—out *there*," she said, moving her
head in a way that was almost a nod, as though to say every
other place round about this one. "I used to enjoy going shopping so much, not even to buy, especially, but just to get out—to
look, to walk. Now, I go out there and"—she shook her head—"I
can't stand it for more than a few minutes at a time. I don't
like what I see and hear. People aren't ..."—she struggled for
the words to express precisely what she wanted to say; and, not
finding them, settled on the general and tepidly imprecise explanation—"... they aren't *nice* anymore. Do you know what I
mean?"

I nodded. I knew what she meant. She was referring to
the rising tide of vulgarity which had over the last few decades
begun to overwhelm New York. What had once been only scattered, clearly-defined pockets of the utterly benighted and violently coarse had metastasized even into areas once considered
"good" and "safe." For a long time things had been changing in
the city. To a large degree the traditional middle class, which
had always been the backbone of the city's social stability, and
had infused it with an ethos of politeness and law-abidingness,
had vanished—run off to find their cleaner, safer American
Dream in the suburbs of Northern New Jersey or Long Island,
where they could at least raise their children without having to

worry about them being shot on the street, stabbed in their schools, or associating with hoodlums. All that remained were those who were either too poor to move, or could find work nowhere else, or who still clung to the belief—this despite the evidence of their own eyes—that New York City was the "greatest city in the world." And yes, there was one more group that had remained: the wealthy. They could live anywhere they wanted, and they lived in New York only because they did not have to live in it the way everyone else did. Their home was some luxury condominium on Park Avenue, guarded by doormen round the clock, or a house in some exclusive borough enclave, such as Forest Hills Gardens, and wired with an alarm system that went directly to the local police station. They rarely if ever rode the subways, and their pampered skins crawled at even the thought of taking a cab, its back seat the site of unimaginable tawdry events or persons, and its driver perhaps an aromatic fellow from a place where American notions of personal hygiene (a daily shower and underarm deodorant) were regarded as ridiculously degenerate.

Mrs. Larke frankly mentioned how she too had wanted to flee New York. She had wanted to buy a home upstate, perhaps in the Adirondacks, in some beautiful place where merely looking out of one's window was a pleasure. But her husband had always kept her in the city on account of his job, though repeatedly assuring her that they would move out "soon." Yet even after his death she had remained in New York. Probably she hadn't moved for the same reason that most of us stay where we are: because we convince ourselves that things aren't so bad after all, or because we have learned through experience that every place has its drawbacks and that in moving to escape one set of problems we find we have only exchanged them for another.

We finally got around to the reason why I was there. She spoke to me about her grandson for whom she wanted to find a tutor. She said that he was her daughter's son and that she had taken him when her daughter had died five years earlier.

"I'm sorry to hear it," I said.

She smiled sadly and nodded in thanks for the condolence. She went on to mention that the boy's father was "out of the picture"—alive but (to tell from the whiff of contempt with which she mentioned him) extremely persona non grata. Obviously there had been in this family, as there are in so many others, great and irreconcilable rifts. It was not my place to inquire into them, though these too, in time, would become known to me.

She got up from her chair and walked a few steps into the adjoining kitchen from where she called out, "Joseph! Joe! Joey, dear, where are you?"

Very faintly, from elsewhere in the house, a boy's voice responded that he was "up here."

"Come down here! I want to see you!"

She glided back into the solarium and resumed her seat with the slightest of embarrassed smiles, as though to apologize for having raised her voice before me. In another minute her grandson was standing before me

Let me confess that I spotted it at once in the boy: the inherent, the essential, the (one might as well be blunt about it) genetic and therefore irretrievable vulgarity. Nature had stamped it unmistakably on his frame and face. Everything about him was thick, clumpish, coarse. Easily twenty pounds overweight, his face was round, his forehead sloping, his jaw prognathic, and he had full humid lips of the sort that never come together and therefore give their unfortunate possessor an expression of stupid wonder. His small dark eyes were dull, sluggish, and unresponsive. As it was summer he was wearing short pants, a short-sleeved shirt, and sneakers. His heavy thighs touched each other long before they reached his torso, and the lower part of his legs looked a little bowed and ended in large, floppy-looking feet. He was carrying a basketball.

"Darling, come here!" Mrs. Larke said, waving him over.

He duly entered, keeping his eyes on me all the while. He stood beside his grandmother and, in doing so, presented such a complete contrast to her that one wondered how it was possible for them to be so closely related.

"This is Mr. Sullivan," she said, introducing me to him. "He's a very nice man. He answered the advertisement I put into the paper about being your tutor and he might be helping you with your English lessons!"

She had spoken enthusiastically as though she were doing him a great favor, but the last thing a child wants to hear about after the almost mortal tedium of a school year is that he will, no matter to how small a degree, be plunged back into hateful studies. Moreover the boy was understandably appre-hensive about a stranger who had been foisted upon him without his consultation. It wasn't just that I might become his tutor (with all its onerous implications) but that I was, just as regrettably, an old man with whom he could have nothing in common. For he was a boy of thirteen and I was thirty-five years old, and I have never been so divorced from my childhood as not to know how children regard grownups—as creatures fundamentally apart from themselves, and with whom they can never have important things in common.

"Go on, Joey," she told her grandson, "shake Mr. Sullivan's hand!"

He would have preferred to keep his distance, but he did as he was bidden, putting his basketball under his left arm, then reluctantly leaning his body forward and extending his right hand.

"Pleased to meet you," I said, shaking his hand.

He nodded and uttered a begrudging, pro forma, "Me too."

Shifting my eyes to his basketball, and wanting to make a connection with him on some personal level, I said jovially, "So, you like basketball!"

He nodded again and after the slightest hesitation ventured, "Yeah ... do you?"

I didn't—I loathed it—but out of deference to his interest in the sport, and wanting him to like me, I temporized by saying that only times I had ever played the game were in high school during gym class, and that since then I hadn't really followed it. The boy indifferently accepted my indifference and proceeded to tell me about his favorite teams. There were two of them, he said—one from New York and one from Chicago. His eyes took some light, his voice became animated, as he told me about the games they had played the night before. He had watched one on television while he had recorded the other. He mentioned half a dozen names of basketball players, whom he described as "awesome." He used the same word (it was one of his favorites) when he related how they had played—how they had eluded the "blocks" of this one, "passed" the ball to that one, "sunk the ball" from a great distance, or had "flown" up to hoop despite several members of the opposite team crowding in on them and trying to claw them down. He related how "at least five guys" were "all over" a particular player who had nevertheless "sunk the ball" after freeing himself from an impetuous congress of the opposing team. (I could just imagine the frenzied collision of sweaty, evil-smelling armpits.)

"You should have seen it!" he exclaimed. "It was awesome!" He had taken the basketball out from under his arm and was passing it from one hand to the other.

Mrs. Larke had been smiling politely as the boy spoke, but there was something in the way she avoided my eyes—in the way she resolutely kept them on him—that told me she was conscious of how looking at me at that moment might betray something she would have been embarrassed to let me see. I knew what it was, even then. For though she didn't look at me, I now and then glanced at her, and her expression of grand-motherly tenderness was incapable of fully masking a tinge of disappointment. She knew as well as I did what a bad impression the boy made—she for whom impressions were so impor-tant, so much an indication of who and what one was. After he had gone back to his room, she resumed her easy and gracious manner and began telling me all her grandson's good points, all his "talents." He drew pictures, she said—wonderful pictures; and for the next two minutes she recounted half a dozen exam-ples of his wonderful imagination. To hear her speak of him one might have thought she had a little Leonardo on her hands. I smiled, nodded, uttered the occasional "Ah!" and "That's nice!" as though there were no question about the accuracy of her glowing assessment of her grandson's abilities. But I had begun to sense that she didn't believe her own words and was saying such things because she felt she *ought* to say them. A grandpar-ent's bragging about her grandchild is always excusable and charming—that is to say, so long as there's some, even the smallest basis for the boast. But in Joey I had seen none, and I suspected that she didn't either.

"Unfortunately," she said, "he's not doing as well in school as he should be. This year he did especially badly—they wanted to hold him back, again," she said, the word "again" coming out after what was almost a hesitation, a kind of embarrassed catch in the voice, as though it had slipped out just before her better judgment could keep it in. "I'm sure it's just a matter of his not having good study habits. The problem is that he doesn't apply himself. He has too many distractions. You know how kids are these days, with all the games and computers and TV shows they have—they just don't concentrate. That's what it is. He pays attention to everything but his books. But I told him that this was it: no more fooling around; that I wasn't going to toler- ate him wasting away his summer with nonsense, and that he would have to study during his vacation, and that's that. And I'm sure with a private tutor he'll do a lot better. You know how these schools are—even the good ones—and he goes to a good one—they all have large classes, and teachers just can't give kids the kind of personal, one-on-one attention they need sometimes. With a private tutor, with someone who can spend time with him, I'm sure he'll do a lot better. I specifically want to make sure he does better with the basics, you know? Read- ing, writing, math."

This mention of math alarmed me. She had not mentioned it in her advertisement for a tutor, nor had she said anything about it in our telephone conversation. But nothing could have been more impractical for me to do. I have always been bad at numbers. They confound me. They get me mixed up. I blun- der at the simplest addition and subtraction. I sat there with the rising sense that I had wasted both her and my time. Yet the consciousness of my fast-dwindling bank account urged me to act to act as though I were capable of teaching the boy any- thing he needed to know. I reckoned that it would take her at least a couple of weeks to figure out that I was a mathematical dunce, by which time I would hope to have made *some* money— and some is always better than none. But in the end I decided that it wasn't a gamble worth taking because it wasn't likely to work: the boy himself was bound to give me away after our first session, if only to get rid of me and have more of his summer vacation to himself while his grandmother found a replacement.

"Mrs. Larke," I said, tentatively, "about the math part ... I have to tell you that I might not be the best choice for that. I'm not very good at it. I can do basic addition and subtraction, I guess, but anything more than that ..."—and I shook my head, looking at her apologetically and preparing to get up and leave.

She smiled a little as though she regarded my confession as

nothing more than a too-modest protestation of abilities that were in fact entirely acceptable. Then I thought she was going to believe me, but not let me go without mildly berating me for having misrepresented myself and wasted her time. Instead she returned brightly: "Oh, but you're not going to be teaching him that. Did you think I wanted you to tutor him in math, too?" And she watched me with some amusement.

"I wasn't sure."

"Not at all," she said, graciously. "I've already hired a math tutor for that. He's a very nice man. He's a retired school-teacher. He used to teach at Forest Hills High School."

"Oh ..."—relieved.

"Believe me, I'm not so great at mathematics either," she said, giving a little, self-deprecating laugh. "My husband—he was the whiz at that stuff, not me. But anyway, what do you think? Does the job interest you?"

"Very much," I said. I doubt whether in all this time she had had any idea of how anxious I was to have it.

"Well ... I've only seen one other person so far—you're the second—and another person called me about the job, and she's coming by tomorrow. So why don't we do this: I'll let you know by the end of the week if I decide to go with you. Fair enough?"

"That's fine."

She showed me to the door and in taking leave of each other we shook hands, she thanking me for coming by, I thanking her for having seen me, but even as I turned away and walked off I resented her for not having hired me then and there. What was there to wait for, to see another person for, after all? It seemed to me that she must know whether or not she wanted me. This attitude was childishly unfair of me, and arose out of frustration at not having found—yet again—gainful employment.

When the end of the week, Friday, came, and I hadn't heard from Mrs. Larke, my hope of being employed by her faded and I was back to scanning the Internet for job openings, sending out my resume, and calling placement agencies. The responses were always the same: in so many words, "Sorry, but we have nothing available ..."

As I mentioned earlier, I only had the means to afford another two months of rent and utilities. There began to spring up in my mind a vision of hardship that could no longer be dismissed as absurd, as the ridiculous fruits of a neurotic imagination. The economy was getting worse with each day; the news reports were full of stories of banks closing, of stores going out of business, of companies laying off more and more employees; it was getting so bad that perhaps I wouldn't find work for a long time; and then what? True, my landlord wouldn't be able to throw me out of my apartment immediately, but even supposing I'd have a roof over my head for several months after my last rent payment, the warrant of eviction would eventually go through and soon enough a few burly city marshals would be pounding at my door intending to haul me and my stuff out onto the sidewalk. And even before that happened, how was I going to pay my electric bill, or buy food? I didn't mind so much sitting in the dark at night, but going hungry was another matter. There appeared before me a worst-case scenario in which I skulked around fruit stands, grabbed an apple or a bunch of grapes, and made a run for it ...

The good thing about placing oneself in a worst case scenario is the relief you feel when, for the time being at least, you realize it won't happen to you. Later that day my phone rang and it was Mrs. Larke calling to tell me that she wanted to hire me as a tutor for her grandson, and was I still interested in the job?

"Yes, of course," I said, closing my eyes in gratitude.

"Good. I'm glad. So I was thinking three days a week—how about Monday, Wednesday, and Friday?"

"That sounds fine."

"Good! So what if we start, say ... this coming Monday? At eleven o'clock?"

"I'll be there," I said.

II

These days hardly anyone remembers the Kranzler murder-suicide case, but that summer it was big news in the city—one of those stories that captures the public's imagination, or at least its prurient interest. Walter H. Kranzler had been an immensely wealthy self-made man, the head of Kranzler Associates, an architectural firm that specialized in designing and

building airports. He had lived on Long Island's North Shore—
the so-called "Gold Coast" famous for its mansions and history of
wealthy inhabitants such as the Vanderbilts, the Roosevelts, and
J. P. Morgan. He had seemed to have everything: good looks,
an immense fortune, a beautiful wife and children, an easy work
schedule. Then one day he had come home from work, shot his
family to death, and turned the gun on himself and blown his
head off. Adding to the sensationalism of the case was his good
reputation. By all accounts he was an entirely sane and charming man, a loving husband, and a fair-minded, even altruistic
businessman. For weeks the local news carried a nightly report
about the case—even if it was to report that nothing new had
come to light. The reporters would stand before the Kranzler
mansion, looking with their usual assumed expressions of intense seriousness into the camera as in consciously-cadenced
voices they "filed" their reports. Most of the time they ended
with the same question, the question "everyone is asking—why?"

"Why? They want to know why? Puh! It don't take no
rocket scientist to figure that one out! The man was crazy,
that's why!"

—So my neighbor, Mr. Hecht. He was eighty-seven years
old and looked every year of it. Short, sunken, white-haired, severely wrinkled, his face was covered in age spots and he
walked with a cane in a slow, painful shuffle. The poor fellow
had become so frail and tired that he didn't leave his apartment
much, though he always came out once a day to check his mailbox in the lobby. He was a veteran of World War II and used
always to wear on his lapel or jacket some pin or sigil of his service or patriotism, though for some time now he had ceased to
do so. On the Monday that was to be my first day tutoring Joey
I ran into him while waiting for the elevator. After we had exchanged a few words about the weather, the Kranzler case
somehow came up, bringing a cynical sneer to his face and evok-
ing the quote transcribed above. He continued by saying:

"You know what the problem is? No one has any pride in
themselves these days. That's what the problem is. Everything's
gone upside down in this country."

By what process of deduction he made such a sweeping conclusion, or even what specifically he meant by it, was a mystery
to me. He didn't bother to expatiate on it, and it seemed more

an outburst of geriatric grumpiness than anything else. I just shrugged and nodded as though I agreed with him. We got into the elevator together and he asked me about work. He remembered our last chat and how I had told him that I had been laid off. I told him that I had found a temporary job as a tutor.

"I knew you'd get something," he said. "You're a smart young man."

His use of the word "young" made me smile. "It's only for the summer," I said.

"Ehhhh, don't worry about it. You'll find something else."

Why is it that people who no longer have to worry about meeting their living expenses are so often breezily certain of the same security in others? Do they really believe what they are saying, or is it merely a mechanism by which they save themselves the discomfort of thinking about another person's misfortune?

When we got down to the lobby I held open the door for him and he shuffled off to get his mail. I watched him move on and pitied him. At his age, in his condition, manila envelopes must have consumed him. Every stage of life has its own worries.

On that first day I was to tutor Joey I got to Mrs. Larke's house ten minutes early. She invited me into the living room to have a seat and wait till the math tutor, Mr. Miller, had finished. He was scheduled to tutor Joey on the same days I did, only an hour earlier. At precisely eleven o'clock I heard muffled voices from upstairs as he took his leave of the boy and then the sound of his feet on the stairwell. When he had descended into the living room Mrs. Lark introduced him to me. He seemed a pleasant enough old fellow. In his late sixties, of medium height, trim, his thinning hair white, his complexion wrinkled and rosy, he smiled a great deal and had quick, youthful mannerisms. In our short introductory chat I learned that he lived in Kew Gardens, "not far from the courthouse." He had taught at Forest Hills High School for forty years and had retired two years earlier. Like so many mathematical and scientific people there was about him something that I can only describe as shamblingly intelligent—that is to say, he was casual to the point of near sloppiness; which is further to say that he was just eccentric enough to be interesting

"How did everything go?" Mrs. Larke asked him.

"Oh, fine, fine," he said cheerfully, looking at his employer with a bright, contented optimism as though it could not have gone any other way. "Today I just wanted to get a feel for where he left off in school and to give him a few things to do for Wednesday."

Mrs. Larke thanked him for his time and walked him to the door, and I watched his shambling figure leaving the room with a sense of pity. Was he tutoring because he needed the money too? Of course he was, and that was sad for him, and hopeless for me: for it only went to show me that a man could work all his life—spend the best energies of his youth and manhood in making a living and "planning for the future"—only to have the future refuse to cooperate with him. Mr. Miller had had a long career as a teacher, was probably collecting a pension and most certainly a government stipend, yet he still felt it necessary to "get out there" and make a few more dollars. When did it end? Was there every any rest? For average men like me and Mr. Miller, did the long, weary, and sometimes desperate search for "security" ever stop short of winning a lottery or dropping dead?

When Mrs. Larke came back to me, she offered to escort me up to her grandson's room. Together we ascended the stairs, not speaking, she a step or two in front of me, I trailing behind her with a sense of expectation and some anxiety. On the second floor we walked down a hall about twenty feet and came to her grandson's room. The door was closed and she knocked on it lightly, saying, "Joey? Mr. Sullivan's here!" And though there was no answer, she pushed in.

He was sitting on the edge of the foot of his bed, a few feet away from his desk on which rested, among other things, his computer. The chair to the desk was pulled out somewhat and apparently this was where Mr. Miller had been sitting. On one side of Joey lay an open math book (Mr. Miller had brought it), and, on other side of him, several stray sheets of paper and a spiral-bound notebook in which calculations had been scratched out. The expression on the boy's face was unforgettable: one of agitated bewilderment. His open, humid lips were farther apart than ever and his small unblinking eyes betrayed distress as though he had been forced into a situation he didn't know how to handle or get out of.

"Mr. Sullivan's here, sweetheart," Mrs. Larke said, smiling; and to me, "Well, I'll just leave you two alone."

"How did your math class go?" I asked, after Mrs. Larke had left the room.

He shrugged. "Okay."

"Wasn't too hard was it?"

He shook his head, no, but my sense was that it had been hard for him—impossibly hard.

"Well, I'll let you in on a little secret: I'm not the best mathematician in the world myself."

The boy smiled faintly, tentatively, hopeful that I wasn't going to be as unpleasant as he had found Mr. Miller to be.

I looked about the room. It was no different from what one might expect the room of any boy his age to be, with this all-important difference: it was fuller of those things that other boys his age were generally not fortunate enough to have. On his desk was a new computer with an oversized monitor. Against the wall opposite his bed stood a bureau on which bulked a large flat screen television. Beside this was a unit that enabled him to record any of the hundreds of cable channels that came into his room. On the night table by his bed were a new camera, two handheld devices that played videos and music, along with a few crumpled twenty dollar bills—these the indifferent excavation of his pants pockets. Posters, held up by tape applied across their four corners, covered a large portion of the painted walls. Some of them were for sci-fi movies and showed futuristic space ships or absurd monsters in postures of imminent destructive fury. These were naively fantastic and therefore charming. But some of the other posters evoked in me an opposite sentiment. They were of the musical idols of the day—at least, the ones Joey was interested in. In every one of them the face of a stupid- and vicious-looking thug stared out at me. Some of them stood with arms crossed and smirking heads thrown back in an attitude of contemptuous hostility, as though they would as soon plunge a knife into your back as say good morning. A few of them were loaded with jewelry; thick, gaudy gold and diamond-encrusted rings, chains, and watches, inferring some connection between their gangsterism and their glitz, their proclivity to violence and their possession of wealth;—a

strange confounding of the repugnantly vile with the conventionally admirable.

"Who the heck are *they?*" I asked, nodding to them.

Joey laughed at my ignorance of these "celebrities," who
bulked so large in his world and informed so much of the content of his mind. He couldn't imagine how someone might not
know who they were. He told me their names, or rather their
stage names—all of them ridiculously strange or silly or willfully
illiterate. He asked me if I wanted to hear their music. As we
only had an hour together I didn't want to waste time doing
that, but then thought that it would probably be in my and his
best interest to do so for a few minutes, if only to start off our
relationship on a friendly footing. For the next ten minutes he
played me his favorite songs. Each one was worse than the
next. The overall impression was one of rank savagery—a complete and utter break from any civilized sensibility.

"Enough!" I said, after he had played ten seconds of the second "song."

"Don't you like it?"

I told him that there was little to like. There was no real
music to speak of; no lovely or even interesting melody, no har-
monies, no especial musicianship, above all no vocal ability;
nothing but steadily pounding drums and percussion, with
booming bass lines and a few electronic trills and whirrs thrown
in along the way to accompany doggerel rhymes shouted in
stupid-sounding voices about low subjects. "What's 'doggerel'?"
he asked. I told him, and suggested the names of a few contemporary bands and singers whose work was listenable. He had
heard of some of them, he said, but didn't know their music.
"Well, when you get a chance look them up," I suggested; "you'll
like them."

One of the first things I found out from Joey was what he
had been doing in school before summer vacation—in particular,
what reading or writing assignments he had done, and what
books he had used. It happened that he and his class had only
been using one book, evidently a standard textbook for his age
range, though he had also had to read novel of his choosing.

"What was it?" I asked.

He mentioned a science fiction title about a robot.

"Did you like it?"

"Well"—he shrugged, looked at me a little apologetically—"it was okay, I guess. I didn't really get to finish it all."

"Why not?"

"It was kinda long."

"How long?"

"Like, almost a hundred pages!"—and he rolled his eyes and let out a huffing breath as though to say anyone who would write a book more than a hundred pages long had to be almost as crazy as someone who would actually read it.

"Well, we won't be doing anything that long," I told him. "In fact, the things we'll be doing are going to be very short. Let me show you what I brought."

In the shoulder bag I carried with me were two manila envelopes, which I now brought out, handing one to him. Each contained copies of poetry and prose scanned from an English literature anthology into my computer and then printed out in a large, accessible, serif font. There were poems by Chaucer, Keats, Byron, Swinburne, Hardy, and Yeats, and prose passages (never more than a paragraph or two long) by Hume and Robertson, Carlyle and Ruskin, Dickens and Eliot, Conrad and Woolf. Excising such small sections from larger works would be taking them out of context, but my intention was not polemical so much as artistic: my idea was to present to Joey, perhaps for the first time in his life, great literature. He would be exposed to the richness of language, of *his* language, which was a birthright of great value. I didn't expect him to understand or even like everything that I had put together for him, but there were bound to be a few pieces that kindled his interest, that nudged into a little life an aesthetic sensibility hitherto dormant. To my mind it wasn't so important that he knew grammar, or even read certain books; all that, and more, would come in time if only someone—I—could fire his interest in letters. It seemed to me that the mistake traditional education made was that it sought to "teach" students when it ought to have inspired them to teach themselves. And so it was my intention to inspire the boy. I would show him the great things he had missed out on, the things he had never suspected. His eyes would be opened and he would be changed.

He took up the topmost page from out of his folder and looked at it blankly. Another boy might at least have flipped it over to see what was on the other side or what lay beneath, but Joey only turned his eyes back up to me with an air of uncertainty as though he weren't sure what he was holding or what he was supposed to do with it.

It was a selection from Ruskin, one of those crafted passages of English prose that quicken the hearts of poets and which the dullard minds of journalist-critics decry as unbearably purple. He looked down at it and his eyes quickly scanned from left to right, not reading so much as looking at the words and letters.

"This comes," I told him, "from a book called *The Stones of Venice*. It was written more than a hundred years ago by a very great man. It's about the old palaces and great churches in Venice, which is in Italy—how they were built and why they were built as they were."

He was still looking down at the page filled up with large text. I didn't expect him to see anything in it at first; he had to *hear* it for himself. I read it over to him in an easy, conversational tone of voice, always, however, conscious of the rhythms of the prose; conscious too that the boy was looking at me as I read. When I had finished, I asked him, "What did you think?"

He hardly knew where to put his eyes. He looked off to one side of the room, then down to the floor, then back up at me. He knew that I was expecting from him a certain kind of response, but he wasn't even sure what kind it should be. He shrugged.

"Did you like it?" I asked.

"I don't know. I mean ... I guess so."

"Well ... what did you think about the way it was written?"

"I don't know."

"You understood it, didn't you?"

His thick, humid lips were open as usual and his uncertainty seemed to increase. He shrugged.

Before I read it over again I asked him to stop me if I spoke any words he didn't understand. As every word in the passage was of the simplest kind, he heard me out again without interruption. I also hoped that though he might not have grasped the ideas in the passage at the first reading, he would surely do so after the second, and be more confident about having an opinion about it. But once again I raised my eyes to see him looking at me expectantly, waiting for me to explain to him what it was all about. I did my best to do so, but I was aware of doing him a disservice by paraphrasing something that could not have been better expressed.

Next, we read together a lovely lyric from Thomas Wyatt, about animals taking bread from his hand;—then a magical speculation of Swinburne's, about the gods and the feet of the years;—then something by Yeats, about the wild flappings of the wings of swans. Joey always watched me read with his lips apart, his eyes dull and inquiring, as though he couldn't make heads or tails of what I was saying. Now and then he glanced down at his own text and squinted at the words; for a few seconds a look of hard concentration would pass over his face; but as though he were incapable of maintaining that kind of exertion, he would in another few seconds pull back and look up at me with patient, or rather longsuffering expectation. The more enthusiastically I touted the wonders of these short passages, the more he fidgeted, frowned, and heaved impatient breaths. He kept looking at me in a way that was half bewildered, half wondering, as though no one could possibly expect him to make heads or tails of any of it.

What astonished me most of all that first week with the boy was how little he had learned in school. He could barely read, and still less write. That he had "passed" his reading classes and graduated year after year into the eighth grade mystified me till Joey himself told me that he had had to "stay back" two times—repeat the fifth and seventh grades. In both instances he had done no better the second time around than he had done the first, but the school authorities had graduated him anyway, probably because he had been growing rapidly, was large for his age, and would have been a distraction to the other students in his class. Perhaps they also hoped that he would "catch up" once he was placed among children closer to his age.

Nevertheless during those first two weeks my enthusiasm remained high, for I was excited and even proud about my position as a tutor, and was convinced of my own insightful ability in that way. It pleased me to think I would have an important influence in a child's life, that on account of my efforts he would grow into a finer, more enlightened human being. I imagined him one day looking back on our sessions together and saying to himself gratefully, "That's when things changed for me!" As we

read together, discussed the ideas we read, I always expected to
see some glint in his eye, some flash of a smile or a sudden,
gleeful impetuosity in his manner indicating that the words had
bypassed the groping intellect and gone straight to heart, that
the revelation of the joy of language had effloresced within him.
But the weeks passed and it never happened. Instead he would
sit beside me, the text in his hand or on his lap, reading it with
a slow, fumbling uncertainty. His homework assignments were
to practice reading these passages so that the next time we met
he would be fluent in him. He was also to write a short "essay"—no more than a page long—about any thoughts he might
have on what he had read. But he was never any more fluent
at our next session, and his written assignments were ridiculously unacceptable. His handwriting was atrocious, a run of
barely-legible scratches and dots which, once you interpreted
them, turned out to be full of misspellings (usually phonetic).
There was no logical cohesion to his statements; he flitted from
one thought to the most disparate next. The notion of elaborat-
ing on a subject, of concentrating on a thought and explicating it
to its finer, fuller, more intricate end was alien to him. He re-
belled against that kind of precision, saying:

"But people know what I'm talking about."

"Well, maybe they do and maybe they don't, but with a little more effort you can make sure that they do."

And when on another occasion I encouraged him to develop
his ideas more fully:

"They wouldn't want us to do all this in school."

"On the contrary, I'm sure they would."

He shook his head, no. "My teachers always say keep it
short and to the point."

"You can keep it short and to the point," I said, "the next
time you're giving a presentation with bullet points to a business meeting. But this is your writing assignment. I want you
to develop your opinions, not truncate them. If your teachers
don't understand that keeping something to the point doesn't
necessarily square with keeping it short, then they're idiots."

He laughed appreciatively at my criticism. After looking at
me uncertainly a few moments he asked, "What's 'truncate'
mean?"

He employed any number of "tricks" (as he probably considered them) to make his homework look more substantial than it was. For instance, he would write in a large hand and copy lines out of what he had been given to read, then, just below them, give his "commentary," which however was nothing more than a rambling free association, as inane as stream-of-conscious prose usually is. I would spend some minutes with him trying to find out what he had wanted to say, only to learn that he himself wasn't sure; he had just been babbling in prose—filling up a page for the sake of filling it up and having something to show me.

"Joey, please," I told him, in our sixth session together, holding up his homework assignment which I had just read, and which again didn't make much sense; certainly it had nothing to do with the any of the texts we had gone over together. "You can do better than this. What is this? You didn't even think about what we were reading."

"Yes I did," he said, simply.

"I don't think so. This doesn't address any of the ideas in it. It doesn't have anything to do with it."

He looked at me a little sullenly.

"I'll tell you what," I said. "You don't have to write about the excerpts if you don't want to. Write about whatever you want—just give me a page or two. That's not a lot. But I want you really to think about what you're writing—that's all I ask."

He was rich in manipulations to distract me from our lessons. Knowing that we only had an hour together he would try to use up as much of our time as possible in conversation, which he rather skillfully initiated through some subject suggested by the reading material. This would always give his questions an air of legitimacy, though they would soon enough branch out into wholly unrelated subjects. If in our first few sessions I let him get away with this time-wasting ploy it was because it had at least had the benefit of allowing us to get to know each other better, to make him more comfortable with me. I will never forget one such conversation for the disconcert-ing insight it gave me into the boy's character. He had asked me about the background of the writer we happened to be reading, and, after my telling him all I knew, he informed me—in a way not entirely sequitur—that his grandmother had bought "all" my books. The way he said "all" amused me, and I said with a laugh, "There aren't that many, Joe."

(By the way, if Mrs. Larke did buy my books I never saw them in her house, and she certainly never approached me with any of them in hand. And I am glad of that. It would have been embarrassing for me to have thanked her for buying books which she would never have heard about if their author hadn't come knocking on her door looking for a paycheck.)

"What do you write about, anyway?" he asked.

"Nothing in particular. It's mostly fiction. You know," I added, when he seemed uncertain of what the word meant, "— stories."

"Stories about what?"

"Anything."

"Like what?" he insisted.

"People. The situations they get into. How they live and how they react to one another."

He looked at me a moment and twisted up his mouth a little as though in consideration; then he heaved a great bored breath. He would have liked to utter some expression of how disagreeable all that seemed to him, but he had enough sense to know that it would be rude. "What else do you? What do you do for fun?"

"That is what I do for fun."

"No, really."

"Yes, really."

He just shook his head, slowly, and looked at me with wonder.

"It has its own rewards, Joe. Actually, it can be quite exciting. Who knows—one day you might be as excited about it as I am."

"But you haven't made any money from it."

"How do you know that?"

"Because you're here doing this."

He didn't mean to be insulting; he was just stating the most obvious of facts. But for that very reason it was the more withering to me. He might have been a boy, and maybe he couldn't read and write well, but he had a damn clear insight into the purely financial considerations that made the world tick.

"You're right," I said. "I haven't."

"How much?" he asked, naively, purely curiously.

"You're not supposed to ask people how much money they make. It's not polite. Let's just say I haven't made much."

"Then why do you do it?"

"As I said, it can be exciting. For me it is."

He almost sneered but again he caught himself and just looked away from me. He seemed to consider whether there could be any truth to what I had said. Deciding that there couldn't be, that perhaps I was testing his common sense, and wanting to me to know that he was no fool, he announced:

"Well, I wouldn't work hard at anything unless I could make a lot of money at it!"

My indulgent smile camouflaged two things: my contempt for his crassly commercial attitude, which was especially unbecoming in a child whose innocence, one would think, would have inclined him to a grand and impractical idealism; and my envy for what was his already ruthlessly clear-sighted understanding of the financial practicalities of life. That he *could* be so ruthless at such a young age was nevertheless distasteful, and momentarily forgetting about our lesson for the sake of improving his morality I sought to show him that he couldn't mean what he said.

"You like basketball and baseball, don't you?" I asked. "If you had the chance to play those games, to be in a stadium full of people watching you, rooting for you, wouldn't you do it, even if you weren't paid very much for it?—even if you weren't paid anything for it?"

"Hell no!" he said, at once.

"Nonsense. Of course you would. You *know* you would. You love that stuff, don't you?"

"Yeah, but ... "—and he shook his head.

"But what?"

"But I'm not gonna do something and not get paid for it. That's just stupid!"

—Which I couldn't help feeling *was* a roundabout insult to myself.

"Well then you obviously don't like sports as much as you say you do," I said.

"I do like them," he countered, "but I'd rather make a lot of money than do something and not make any money."

"Making a lot of money isn't everything, Joe."

"It is to me."

"You think so?   And what would you do with all that money?"

"Everything!"

"Such as?"

"Buy a new Corvette!"

"And after you've bought that?"

"A jet airplane!"

"And let's say you bought that, and everything else you could think of buying. Let's say you had everything you wanted. Then what?"

He considered for a moment, then opened his mouth as though to say something, but nothing came out as he realized that he didn't have anything cogent to say; and then just shrugged his shoulders and admitted, "I dunno."

"Exactly. You *wouldn't* know. But you'd still have to do something with your life—something that you felt was important, that gave your life meaning. Otherwise you'd get bored and you'd be miserable. In itself, Joe, life doesn't mean very much. It has no inherent value. It's only what you do with it that counts."

"But you can't do anything without money!" he said, suddenly confident again and regarding me with a challenging air.

"Well, of course we all need money to live."

"Not just to live. If you want to do things, you need money. I'm gonna do a lot of things when I get older—anything I want! You know why?"   He didn't give me a chance to answer the question before he announced: "I'm gonna be rich!"

"Really?"

He gave a definitive nod. "Sure. One day I'll have all the money my grandmother has. And she's got millions and millions!"

So there it was. Joey might not have been a good student; he might have been "slow"; he might not have cared a jot about reading, writing, and arithmetic; but he understood that one day a great fortune would fall into his hands like the sweetest of all the world's plums. One could only hope that his grandmother would make—had already made—arrangements for him to receive the greater part of his inheritance only when he was well

into adulthood and had reached the years of at least some discretion; but even then he was likely to consume much of it in
the most wasteful extravagances. Just the thought of how much
he would spend on, say, front seat tickets for baseball and basketball games, adding his shouts to those of the thousand dolts
around him, slightly nauseated me.

"Well, Joe, that's a long, long way off yet, and in the meantime there's a lot to be learned, so ..."—and I held up the pages
we had been reading as though to say that we ought to be getting back to them.

But he was interested in carrying on the conversation and
said, "It's not a long way off. My grandmother's pretty old. She
can't last forever."

"Joey!" Even as I exclaimed his name I barked out a
laugh—a nervous reaction to the terrible thing he had said.
That any child should regard his loving parent or grandparent
as some sort of obstacle to the rest and better part of his life
was unspeakably monstrous, and yet the boy had spoken it out
with such a happy anticipation that in that first moment it
seemed almost comical. But then the mercenary crassness, the
cruel thoughtlessness of it, angered me, especially when I
thought of how concerned his grandmother was for his sake. I
looked at the boy with a reprimanding shake of my head and
told him gravely, "That's a horrible thing to say, Joe."

He shrugged and frowned in a retiring, apologetic manner,
and as though to show me that he wasn't so calculating—that
he had merely spoken an a-moral fact of life—he said, "But she
is old."

"So what? What does that have to do with anything? And
for your information, she's not that old. Old is when you're
eighty and ninety and a hundred, and she's not. And in the
second place, Joe, your grandmother takes care of you—she does
everything for you. Don't you understand that? She *loves* you."

He was a little surprised to see how warmly I had defended
his grandmother, but those last words had no sooner left my
mouth than he sat up a little straighter, looked at me with the
superior, self-possessed expression of better knowledge, and
said:

"Not the way you think."

"What do you mean?"

"She don't like me."

"That's ridiculous. Of course she does. She *loves* you."

He shook his head, no, and gave me the half-pitying, half hopeless look of someone who knows that he has on his side of the argument the trump card of an irresistible fact. He said:

"Yes, but she don't *like* me."

Only because he insisted on the distinction this second time did I understand him, and, in doing so, felt suddenly sorry for him: first, that he should think such a thing; then, that he was probably right. I recalled the first interview I had had with his grandmother and how in introducing him to me she had worn a set, somehow forced expression of pride. If this was apparent to me, who was a stranger to her, it must have been more than obvious to the boy who lived with her and knew all the subtleties of her manner. Joey had long seen that his grand-mother's love for him was of the pro-forma kind—genuine insofar as it went, but never going far in the way it *should* have gone. She loved him because she felt she had to, because a sense of her duty as a grandmother compelled her to make a show of affection; but it was something she never had and perhaps never could feel. She herself had to be aware of this and must often have felt guilty about it. Thus she tried to compensate for what seemed to her an unnatural lack of affection by going out of her way to do the right things for the boy—by calling him "dear," "darling," "sweetie," or some other proud endearment, and by getting him the expensive toys he wanted or giving him a generous weekly allowance. But of all pretenses the show of love is the least likely to succeed. For the nature of love is instantaneous and expansive, while that of pretense is studied and after a while strained. The dichotomy between Mrs. Larke's words and behavior, and what she really thought, was too great, too antagonistic and irreconcilable, not to show through. Joey probably never exchanged with her so much as a look or a word without sensing her fundamental, if subtle, antagonism toward him.

That the boy knew he wasn't wanted by the one person whose affection for him ought to have been unconditional saddened me, and then aroused in me a rather paternal urge to protect him. I did this first, in a rather reflexive way, by assuring him that he was mistaken and that his grandmother loved him a great deal. And yes, I knew even as I said it that it probably wasn't true. But so what? Why should the truth always, in every instance, be best? Are there not in life worries enough, and disappointments enough, and heartbreaks more than enough, that we cannot give ourselves and others a break by foregoing a bootless honesty in order to believe in a brighter, sweeter, however less accurate view of things?

But I was mistaken in thinking he needed this kind of re-assurance or support. I had undercalculated the coarse clay of which this pot was made. Another, more sensitive child would have been stricken to the core to think himself unwanted, but off Joey's tougher psychological skin it bounced without leaving more than a slight mark indicating the curious point of impact. He accepted it the way he might have accepted an old basket-ball score: as something vaguely interesting, perhaps, but so far in the past, so much a done deal, that there was no point in wasting much time over it. With the most innocent and indif-ferent of smiles, he told me again that he knew his grand-mother didn't "like" him but that it didn't matter because he wasn't "crazy about her either."

"Well, I think you're wrong, Joe," I said. "One day you'll see. Now, c'mon," I continued, "let's get to the lesson ..."

III

It happened that one morning a few weeks after I had been tutoring Joey I walked toward Mrs. Larke's house and saw parked in the cul-de-sac before it a small truck. On the door of the cab was emblazoned the name "Union Contracting" with an address somewhere in Long Island City. A middle-aged man wearing denim overalls and a blue shirt that somehow looked to be part of a uniform was walking slowly along the facade, carrying a clipboard in one hand, a pen in the other, his eyes turned upward to eaves as he searched for something. Every now and then he jotted something down. He was so engrossed in his work that he didn't see me coming up the walkway and ring the doorbell. Mrs. Larke opened the door for me. I stepped inside and mentioned the man outside her house.

"It's one of the contractors," she said.

"Doing something to the house?" I asked, thinking she might be adding to it in some way.

"I'm not sure yet," she said.

She explained that she had called them to examine her house because she was concerned about cracks in some of the walls and parts of the ceiling. They had been there for years, she said, but recently they had been getting much more notice-able—longer and deeper, and hinting at some serious, underly-ing problem. Just as she said this there was the tramping sound of heavy, booted feet coming up from the basement. In another room a door—the door leading to the basement—opened and shut, and in a few seconds another one of the contractors stepped into the living room. Like his colleague outside, he was in his late forties or early fifties and wore "work clothes": a blue shirt with the sleeves rolled up to the elbows, jeans, and beige work boots. Mrs. Larke turned to him with somewhat anxious eyes that asked, "Well?"

The way he looked at her in response was not encouraging; it was one of those half-sympathetic, half regretful expressions that herald a begrudging message of bad news. "These cracks you're seeing inside—like over there and over there," he said, pointing them out to her, "are stress cracks from the torsion of the major support beams. Apparently there's some shifting go-ing on."

"Shifting?" she asked, looking bewildered. "What shifting?"

He said that it all had to do with the foundation: either it hadn't been properly built given the type of soil beneath it and was therefore less stable than it should have been, or one or more walls or main beams of the house were defective. He said that to find out precisely what the problem was, to fix it, would be a "big job." Cement walls downstairs would have to be bro-ken into, the main beams examined and, where necessary, rein-forced or replaced. Possibly even new concrete would have to be poured. "It's a job," he said again, and seemed hesitant to offer his own services as though the project would entail more work than he could or wanted to do.

Mrs. Larke looked taken aback; she had evidently thought there could be nothing seriously wrong with her house because it wasn't old, having been built only fifty years earlier. She turned to me a pair of inquisitive and vaguely distressed eyes as though she were seeking my advice or was asking me if what the contractor was telling her could possibly be true, but I only shook my head, giving her to understand that I had no idea about such things. Perhaps too she was put off by the notion that whatever was wrong with the place was going to cost a lot of money to fix. But in the next few minutes she learned that she didn't have much of a choice in the matter. Standing before her with a hand casually on his hip, the contractor told her in a simple, straightforward, and somewhat gruff way that if she didn't take care of the problem now it could only get worse and then she'd wind up with something "really serious"—a wall collapsing or even the ground floor falling in. It was that bad.

Just then the math tutor, Mr. Miller, came downstairs, in his usual way, with his usual smile. At the scene of Mrs. Larke, the contractor, and myself, he blinked quickly a few times, not especially curiously. Mrs. Larke excused herself from us and showed the old math teacher to the door, asking him along the way, "How'd everything go?"—to which he gave his usual, quipping answer: "Oh, fine, fine." When she had bidden him goodbye, she returned to the living room. It seemed that even in the few seconds it had taken to show Mr. Miller out—in the few feet she had traversed to the front door and back—she had made up her mind about what she had been told, for coming back to us she said:

"Well ... if it has to be done, I guess it has to be done."

"You can get a second opinion if you want," the man said. "In fact, I suggest you do, just for peace of mind. But I think you'll find they're gonna tell you the same thing."

"Well ..."—shaking her head, looking about her a little helplessly—" ... I'll let you know. I mean ... do you have any idea how long something that would take?—how much it would cost?"

He said he wasn't sure how long it would take because he wasn't sure exactly what was going on, but he was able to give her a rough estimate if the worst should come to the worst: if he should have to shore up the foundation and replace main support beams. The sum was enormous. If he had been speaking to me I probably would have passed out. But to Mrs. Larke, while it might have been an unfortunately large amount, it was something she could easily absorb, and so she resigned herself to it. She thanked the man and told him that she would let him know.

I went up to Joey's room. The door was closed and I knocked lightly on it. Joey called out for me to come in. He was sitting at his computer. As soon as I walked into his room he said enthusiastically:

"Hi. Wanna see something cool?"

"If it'll take less than two minutes, sure."

I stood over him as he sat at his computer and began looking for something. Beside his keyboard was another one of his drawings. They were always of cars that had flames shooting out from behind as though to indicate a powerful, perhaps rocket-fueled propulsion system. Like all his drawings this one too was crude and unimaginative: a two-dimensional, elongated rectangle on two wheels with blacked-out patches indicating windows.

"Here it is," he said, pressing a key.

It was a horror movie he had been watching for the third time and he forwarded to the part that he thought would especially impress me. A group of young women had taken refuge from a storm in a lonely hotel. They had no sooner turned into bed than their rooms were broken into by psychopathic killers who murdered them by hacking them apart. There was a great deal of screaming and gore and crazed satisfaction on the part of the killers, and these outrageous scenes had been manipulated through lighting, camera angles, and special effects to look as realistic as possible.

It was appalling. To my generation, which after all wasn't so far before the boy's, the "horror" of a movie derived from a sense of the eerie, the otherworldly, of inexplicable and perhaps threatening things that lurked among shadows in cobwebbed basements and attics; but to his generation it meant something else, something violent, painful, revolting: the limitless exhibition of gratuitous suffering, the orgiastic display of innocence ravaged by sadistic bloodlust, of scene after scene in which people were hacked apart, their limbs severed or torn out of their bodies, their flesh stabbed or seared or mutilated as they writhed and screamed in the extremity of human suffering. It wasn't "scary"; it was just obscene and degrading. My irritation was evident as I told the boy:

"Joe, that's really disgusting."

His face dropped and he turned off the movie, then peered

at me uncertainly. He really had wanted to please me with a moment of exciting terror.

"You didn't like it?" he asked, his grin fading.

"Why would I like that? It's not 'scary,' Joe. It's sadistic. Do you understand the difference?"

He looked at me uncertainly.

"It means when people enjoy seeing other people in pain. It's the worst thing in the world, Joe. Absolutely the worst. There's nothing scary about that. It's just horrible and degrading and disgusting."

He seemed uncertain what to say. Then he shrugged and said, "It's just a movie."

Of course I understood that, too, and on some level I was a little relieved that he had made that comment, since it showed he was clearly aware of the distinction between reality and a criminal fantasy. But even now I am dismayed to think that such things are routinely regarded as "entertainment," for surely where people are entertained by fictionalized images of blood-letting they are bound to be desensitized to the reality of it, and when they can sit in a theater munching candy and popcorn while images of writhing agony are flashed before their eyes, they have already gone a long way toward losing a sense of distress at the thought of another's pain, and which is the first, most basic element of decency.

For this day's session we were to go over Mansfield's "Cargoes," which he was to have read for his homework assignment. We had in fact read it together just before our previous session had ended, but he was to have read it again and written something about it. But when he gave no answer to my question, "What did you think about it?"—it was clear to me that he hadn't looked at it in the interim. I was irritated to think that he had been unwilling to exert himself even to read over the few lines of the poem, but rather than question or reprimand him I merely suggested we go over it again together. "Read it out," I told him; "let me hear you." He did so, falteringly; mumbling out every word as though it were an individual entity without reference to the word that had gone before or which followed behind. As he mumbled and fumbled his way through the text I got up from the desk and, as I sometimes did, walked back and forth in the room, my head bowed, listening, waiting to correct him or prod him along. I stopped at the window and looked out at the lovely, park-like back yard. Straight below were visible the blue and white irises before the screened solarium on the ground floor, and which I had noted in my first interview with the boy's grandmother. To the left was visible, over a high fence, the next door neighbor's large pool, surrounded by several lounge chairs and tables shaded by great yellow umbrellas. A maid in a uniform puttered about there, tidying up the area and wiping already clean surfaces a little cleaner. The neighbor's yard to the right was, like Mrs. Larke's, grassy and treed, but also contained a picnic table. A boy was sitting at it. He looked to be about Joey's age. He was setting up a telescope, looking back and forth between its component pieces and a manual that he had laid out on the table before him. As Joey continued in his halting recitation, his voice receded in my consciousness as my whole attention was focused on that boy next door. There was something touching about his solitary pastime there. Only some half a minute after Joey had finished reading the poem did I realize he was watching me, waiting for my reaction. In a half-embarrassed, half-amused way I alluded to what had captivated my attention by saying:

"I see your neighbor down there."

Joey bounded off the edge of his bed, stood beside me, and followed my line of vision over to the yard to the right, to the boy at the picnic table. In a bored, smirking tone of voice he said:

"Oh ... yeah."

"Is he a friend of yours?"

"Hell no! I wouldn't be friends him."

"Why not?"

" 'Cause he's a jerk."

"Why do you say that?" I asked, laughing a little.

"He just is."

I looked over to the boy again. Even from this distance I could see that everything about him was different from Joey—indeed, he was the opposite of everything Joey was. He was slender, slight, delicate. He had fair hair and a long, sensitive, intelligent face. He wore round wire-framed glasses: a style that adults would probably think eccentrically charming but which children his own age (somehow I knew this) would think absurd.

Just then, as I watched him, a young woman, a woman in her thirties—his mother—came toward him holding a plate of sliced fruit of some kind, either cantaloupe or oranges. She put it down on the table and said something to him. Without looking at her he nodded. She smiled widely, proudly, lovingly, and in a quick, irrepressible, gesture reached out to him and affectionately mussed up his hair a little before turning around and heading back to the house. —It was all very immediate and sweetly human.

"Little boy has to have his *mommy* feed him!" Joey said, with a sneer; adding, "I can't *stand* that kid."

"Why not?" I asked, a little taken aback by the hateful vehemence of Joey's disdain.

" 'Cause he's real dweeb," Joey said.

"What's a 'dweeb'?" I asked;—but in the next second I realized I hadn't had to ask: the pejorative meaning was clear by the sneer of its utterance.

"You know, a *dweeb*—a dork, a nerd, a geek, a goofball."

"He looks like a nice kid to me," I said.

Paying no attention to my opinion, Joey asked, "He's so stupid that he's making a telescope in the daytime!"

"It looks like he's just putting it together. One has to put it together some time, after all. Besides, you can use a telescope in the daytime."

Joey considered; continued to look; then added:

"Guess what his name is?"

I shook my head. I had no idea.

"Octavian," Joey sneered.

"Wow!" I said, impressed.

"You *like* that name?"

"It's a great name! It's Roman ... *Divi Filius* ... it's so ... noble!"

Joey wasn't quite sure what I had meant by that but he sensed that it was the opposite of what he thought, and so he was a little taken aback. He continued, "He goes to my school. Know what we call him? 'Dirty Laundry'!"—and he gave a single, almost forced laugh as though to show that he still found the pejorative funny.

"Why do they call him that?"

"One day in the lunchroom some kid threw soda at him

and his shirt got all messed up and he started crying."

I shook my head and frowned. Joey laughed, and said:

"Crying cause his shirt got dirty! How stupid is that!"

"Why did that kid throw soda at him?"

Joey shrugged. "I dunno. Just did." And he added, "Last year he got beat up."

"Who beat him up?" I asked, alarmed.

Joey shrugged. "Some kids."

"Why?" I asked.

" 'Cause he's a dweeb!" Joey said, as though that explained everything.

"That's horrible," I objected. "I hope *you* didn't have anything to do with that!"

Joey shook his head quickly, no, and left my side at the window to return to the lesson.

But later I saw through the matter more clearly. Call it an inspiration, some mystical, time-shifted insight into the past, but I just knew that Joey had had a hand in beating up the boy next door. Perhaps he had even been the leader of the wolf pack. He and his tough friends had lain in wait for the fine smart boy and confronted him; pushed him about, from one to the other, mocking him as they did so; and finally pounced on him. No doubt they had left him bruised and crying, in shock and trembling like a leaf, his round spectacles broken or smashed; and all because he hadn't been as big and strong as his attackers;—all because the most despicable human creatures are never so degraded but they are able to perceive their superiors, the very sight of whom is a constant reminder to them of their own inadequacy, and whom therefore they hate and try to destroy. During my next lesson with Joey I ambled again to his window, looked outside, and remarked that the boy next door was nowhere to be seen. Before Joey could say a word or make a move I added:

"Imagine anyone wanting to beat up that poor little kid? Who could be so rotten? Whoever those kids were that did that to him had to be the scum of the earth. Right, Joe?"

For a fraction of a second he looked at me blankly; then— some faint glimmer of shame rising up in him—turned his eyes away, and nodded.

—And so was I hopeful that I had had some influence in

protecting the noble Octavian!

On Monday of the following week I came to the house promptly as usual at a few minutes before eleven o'clock and saw again the truck from "Union Contracting" parked in the cul-de-sac. As soon as she opened the door for me, Mrs. Larke regretfully informed me that Mr. Miller had started fifteen minutes late, apologized for him, and asked me if it would be possible for me nevertheless to spend a full hour with her grandson. I said that of course that was not a problem.

In the meantime she invited me into the living room, bade me have a seat, and asked me if I would like some coffee or tea or juice, but I declined everything, saying that I had had a good breakfast. I sat before her with an uncomfortable sense of anticipation, anxious that she might ask me how her grandson was doing—what progress he had been making. I didn't want to have to lie and tell her that for the last three weeks not much progress had been made. I sought for a diversion from that topic and found it in the large painting of herself and her husband hanging on the wall behind her. She was a great beauty there: slender, elegant, her hair full and yellow; staring out at the world with an expression of complete contentment as her husband, standing just behind her and a little off to the side, wrapped his arms around her, she holding both his hands at her waist.

"That's quite a painting," I said, nodding to it.

She turned around to it briefly, then back to me. "Oh, yes. We had that picture taken in 1964."

"Picture?"

"Yes, they took a picture first and they painted the portrait from it. We had that done in Manhattan—a place on 22nd Street, I think. I've forgotten exactly where. My husband was so handsome when he was young, don't you think?"

I nodded, yes, though, strictly speaking, Mr. Larke had been quite average in appearance. "Has he been gone a long time?"

"Six years. It's so strange, it seems longer. He was going to work one morning when he had a heart attack in the car."

"I'm sorry."

She accepted the condolence with a nod and a faint smile, and continued, "It was so hard at the time—those things always are. But I've come to be grateful about the way he went: so quickly. That was a blessing. Garret always hated being sick— he couldn't stand even having a cold. He would have been a miserable patient."

"How old was he?"

"Young. Sixty-one." She smiled at me a little knowingly, almost mischievously, and continued, "'Young!' Isn't it strange how our notions of 'young' change as we get older? I guess I should have said he wasn't 'very old.' Anyway, he didn't look his age; he looked ten, fifteen years younger. I just wish he could have stopped working a little earlier so that we might have had more time together. But he was one of those men that can't stop. His work was his whole life. That's all he thought about. He was never happy unless he was working. So I never said anything. But believe me, if I had known how little time we had left, I would have made him stop—I would have been selfish and insisted on it, and gotten my way. But we always think we have time, don't we? And of course we never do."

Just then a tremendous bang shook the house, as though something of great weight or power had smashed into it. Both Mrs. Larke and I started, sitting up suddenly straighter and turning our heads as though to locate the source or cause of the shock. It had come from below, from the basement, and it was followed in quick succession by three more bangs, though these were less impulsive and loud. Mrs. Larke put a hand to her head and looked to me with an expression of apology and impatience as she said, "Oh, there they go again!" She explained that the building contractors had started working downstairs. They had been making a racket since they had gotten there. "I'm sorry about the noise. I know it's loud, but I hope it won't bother you too much—"

Again, a bang that made the whole house shake.

Mrs. Larke looked at me apologetically.

"I had to have the work done," she said. "I didn't have any choice." She explained how she had gotten a second opinion about the matter, and it had confirmed the first. Indeed the house was in worse condition than any of the contractors had initially thought. When the men had started working the day before, they had brought her down into the basement to see for herself what they had discovered: cracked main beams, rotting cross braces, foundation walls flaking and crumbling after forty years of water damage. They held a level against several surfaces to show her far how off true they were. All of this had mortified her. She had always been quietly proud of her house, one of the grandest in an exclusive area, and now she had learned that its impressive appearance hid an inherent, rotten reality.

"It shouldn't be too loud upstairs," she said.

"It won't bother me," I said, more hopefully than anything else.

The doorbell rang. Mrs. Larke looked a little surprised as though to ask, "I wonder who that is?" and excused herself to answer it. In another moment I heard her talking to someone— greeting someone—at the door, and she came back into the living room followed by a woman whom she introduced to me as Hope Peaview, her neighbor who lived next door. She was not however the woman I had seen a few days earlier, bringing her son a plate of fruit—she wasn't Octavian's mother. She was the other neighbor, the one who lived in the house with the fenced-in property, the pool, and the maid. She was about forty-five years old, below average in height and was pretty with even, pert features. She was well-dressed and wore a lot of jewelry— diamond earrings, various necklaces and bracelets, and a sleek Movado watch. A folded newspaper was tucked under one arm, a Louis Vuitton pocketbook slung over one shoulder, and she was carrying a briefcase. She might have been some professional woman on her way to work but somehow I knew that if she did work it was at no conventional job—nothing that forced her to be at a specific place, during specific hours, or even made her accountable to anyone. After shaking my hand and saying how pleased she was to meet me, she sat beside me on the couch and placed her newspaper on the coffee table so that it opened up to its front page; there, a screaming headline proclaimed another tidbit of information about the Kranzler murder-suicide case.

Like everyone else in the city Mrs. Larke had been following the case, and she had her reasons for having a deeper interest in it than most people. It wasn't that she had known the Kranzlers—she hadn't—but her experience in life had made her sympathetic to the kind of life they had led, which after all wasn't so different from her own. Moreover she had friends and acquaintances who lived on Long Island's North Shore. She and her husband had gone to any number of parties given by people who "had homes" there: fabulous parties on summer nights, out in the open, out in the air kissed and cooled by the waters of the Sound, and attended by beautiful, well-dressed people who chatted with one another, laughed with one another, sensible of their exclusive good fortune, of their freedom from care, of the rarefied atmosphere in which they moved. Those enjoyable evenings were still more memorable, more wistfully touching to her in retrospect, now that her husband was gone and her life was so different from what it had been in those days. When she saw and read the headline, she shook her head over it and murmured what a pity it was—what a terrible, terrible thing.

"Oh, that, yes," Hope Peaview said, glancing at the paper. "Terrible. Obviously the man was sick—mentally ill. Really, to have so much going for you and to think it's not enough or to be unhappy about it, well, you just have to be out of your mind. What gets *me* angry is the selfishness of it all. I mean, why did he have to kill his whole family too? Those poor kids. They were innocent. If you're unhappy, if you hate yourself and you want to kill yourself, well, then, go right ahead, but leave the rest of us out of it!"—and she looked to me as though to get my opinion either of the case or of her reaction to it.

"I guess when you're a sick person you don't see things logically," I said.

"I guess not," she said.

BANG! BANG! BANG!

The house shook enormously. Hope Peaview almost jumped out of her seat. Her eyes darted questioningly to Mrs. Larke, who explained:

"I have some men doing some construction in the basement."

"What are they doing?"

"Fixing," Mrs. Larke said. She pointed out to Hope the cracks in the wall and ceiling and repeated what the contractor had told her about the faulty foundation.

"Sounds serious!" Hope said.

"Well, they're going to fix it," Mrs. Larke replied.

Hope gave a sympathetic shake of her head, as though

sorry to hear that her neighbor had to put up with such distractions, then got down to the purpose of her visit.

She was canvassing for the incumbent Congressman, Antoine Benedict. She had "just" been going through the neighborhood to let everyone know how important it was that he be reelected. He had won reelection for the last three terms, but this time, she said, he faced stiff competition from the opposing candidate, Adam Jones, who of course would be just terrible for Queens, for all of New York, and "in fact for the whole country."

"This jerk wants us to go backward," she said, referring to Jones. "Backward! But we *can't* go backward. We have to keep moving *forward!*" In saying this she had used a variation of the campaign slogan that her candidate and party had latched onto, and which was one of several by which they presented their platform in an aura of glowing advancement and progress. Hope Peaview had unconsciously absorbed these slogans and catchwords. Whenever political discussions came up she advocated and argued using the very phrases that she read in party pamphlets and heard in the speeches of Antoine Benedict. "We've made so much progress in the last few decades that it would be a *disaster* if someone like Jones came along and tried to undo everything that we've worked so hard for! He's wrong on every issue: taxes, education, law enforcement, foreign policy—you name it. It's probably because he's not originally from New York that he's got everything backwards. He's originally from Nebraska, you know. Nebraska! What do people know *there?* I'm sure that *we* wouldn't want someone like *that* to represent *us*. This is New York! We do things differently here!"

She opened her briefcase and began taking out various printed sheets and glossy pamphlets, the "literature" she had been handing out to prospective voters, and which in brief or in detail presented Representative Benedict's achievements and the things he was "fighting'" for. In themselves all of these things sounded and were admirable. There would be better education for "our children"; better jobs for "our workers"; better health care for "our seniors"; better opportunities for all people of every background and belief. The have-nots would finally be on a par with the haves, and the haves would happily live among those who had formerly been the have-nots; and, in

short, everyone would co-exist happily in a world finally made
bright and peaceful and clean. She rattled off these generous,
high-sounding talking points with great enthusiasm. Clearly,
they made her feel good just to speak them out, rather in the
same way the formula of a prayer might ease a distraught
spirit. But never once did she specify how these lofty goals were
to be reached; what efforts or sacrifices would have to be made,
how much and by whom; nor take into consideration that human nature itself might be at odds with her most basic assump-
tions. It was as though it were enough for her to bask in the
warmth of ideals whose implications she had never understood
or looked too deeply into.

     She was especially earnest when speaking about the need
to reduce poverty. It was, she said, getting worse and worse in
New York according to "statistics," and she happened to have
these statistics printed on blue sheets of paper, which she proceeded to whip out her briefcase. As she did so the band of her
Movado caught on one of the clasps of the briefcase and came
clear off her wrist. In that split second her chatty poise was instantaneously overcome by a panicky lunge to keep the watch
from falling; with the instinctive, lightning-quick reflex of a pan-
ther pouncing on prey she managed to catch it just in time.
"Whew!" she said, a little breathlessly, "that's all I need is to
break *this!* I just got it!" She secured the watch to her wrist
again, then held it out a little to ensure that it hadn't been damaged, and resumed her earnest advocacy of taking care of "less
fortunate New Yorkers."

     As she handed us the poverty statistics she also talked
about the city's woeful housing shortage ("We have to start revi-
talizing our neighborhoods!"), the upsurge in crime ("Our children need extracurricular activities to keep them busy!"), and
her and her candidate's commitment to "diversity" ("In today's
global world it's imperative for us to be exposed to different
kinds of people!") Then she asked me:
     "Are you voting this year?"
     "Maybe," I said. In fact, I had no intention of doing so, for
I had lived long enough to know for sure two things: first, how
to keep out of doing jury duty and a judicial system in which
lawyers were less concerned with justice and the public weal
than with making money and gaining reputation; and, second,

that American politics had become so corrupt that voting for one of the two major parties was in effect choosing either side of the same corporate coin.

"Well, if you do," she said, "I hope you'll consider voting for Antoine Benedict. He's really the only candidate out there. Where do you live, by the way? Are you in the neighborhood?"

"No, I'm in Sunnyside."

Her eyes darted to Mrs. Larke, then turned back to me. It was a gesture of only a second; yet despite its brevity it bespoke volumes of discomfort and disapproval the likes of which she herself seemed to be unconscious of and which was apparent to me only in the brief chilliness of her smile as she said:

"Oh! Sunnyside. Well. That's nice."

"He's tutoring Joey," Mrs. Larke interjected.

"Oh, that's wonderful!" Hope Peaview said, her words, her manner, now again impeccably easy and natural.

There was the sound of a door closing upstairs and then of footfalls on the stairway. Mr. Miller, the math tutor, had finished his lesson and was on the way downstairs. Mrs. Larke stood up and went to him, to show him out. At the sight of me and Hope Peaview he nodded a hello. I heard Mrs. Larke asking her usual question of how everything had gone, and he gave his usual answer of, "Just fine." When she had shown him out the door, she came back to the living room, and I got up from the couch.

"Well, let me go upstairs," I said.

I told Hope Peaview it had been a pleasure to meet her and walked out of the room sensing that I had barely escaped having a political pamphlet pressed into my hand.

Another round of loud banging from the basement followed me up to Joey's room.

The noise of construction was to be the bane of the rest of my time with the boy. If I had told Mrs. Larke that it wouldn't bother me, it was because I had assumed—hoped—that it wouldn't be too noticeable up on the second floor. But as much of the construction work affected the main beams and supporting walls of the house, the racket spread instantaneously to all parts of it. The hammering, drilling, and sawing seemed at times to come from just outside the closed bedroom door. After fifteen minutes I would begin nervously to fidget with irritation.

Sometimes a minute or so would pass in silence—a silence the more glorious for the noise that had preceded it and the promise of continued quiet; but just when it seemed I could relax, another hammer blow or tearing whir of a power saw would make every muscle in my body tense. It was my habit to use earplugs when out in the streets or riding the subways, and I was tempted to put them in now, but decided against it because Joey was sure to report it to his grandmother, who might think it an eccentricity in me.

The boy himself wasn't bothered at all by the noise. Even when an especially loud bang shook the walls and made me jump, he smiled or laughed at my reaction as though it were ridiculously disproportionate to the cause. A hand grenade might have gone off beside his head and the most he would have said was, "Wow, that was a loud one, wasn't it?" The pounding reverberated around us as he held in his hand the poem we had been reading and his voice droned uncompre-hendingly on:

"But now I only hear
Its melancholy, long, withdrawing roar,
Retreating, to the breath
Of the night-wind, down the vast edges drear
And naked shingles of the world."

—When he got to the word "naked" he looked up at me with something of a leer in a foolish attempt to divert the sense of the word to its lascivious connotations. But seeing I was unresponsive to this silliness, he became a little more serious and asked, "What's 'shingles' mean?"

"The small stones and shells that you might find on a beach."

"Oh. Well ... why don't he just say it?"

"He is saying it. That's what the word means."

He made a sour face.

When he had finished the poem he said he couldn't make anything out of it. He said this evenly and simply, without the least bit of anxiety as though there were no more point in struggling to understand the thing than there would have been in trying to flap his arms and fly: it just couldn't be done. "Why do I have to know this?" his eyes always seemed to ask me. "What is the point of it all? Where does it get me? Nobody knows this stuff—why should I?"

It did no good to assure him that there *was* a point to it all—the point of improving himself. He didn't understand that kind of improvement. The only improvement he understood was running faster, jumping higher, or "scoring" in some absurd ball game at a park where he would go with his friends.

By the way, these friends of his didn't come from the neighborhood. They did not come from his own privileged background. They lived outside the Gardens in the innumerable hive-like apartment buildings of Forest Hills or Kew Gardens or Rego Park. They came from middle- and lower-middle class families. They never came to the house, for over the months or years they had received a too-chilly reception from Mrs. Larke, who indeed didn't like them because she regarded them as a bad influence on her grandson—the "wrong crowd" who could only lead him down a delinquent path toward which he might already be predisposed. More than once when coming downstairs I saw her standing at the front window, peering out from behind a curtain at a group of boys, all in their early teens, who were loitering across the street, waiting for Joey. She regarded them with the same kind of suspicion that settlers of the American West probably felt on seeing Indians gathering on the horizon.

I learned from Joey that she had adjured him to befriend local boys whom she knew and who apparently met her standards. They were children who undoubtedly came from "good" families, who had been raised in "professional" households, who had been "well" brought up—that is to say, taught to be polite, to respect learning, to have an interest in, or at least some exposure to, cultural things. Given Joey's attitude toward Octavian it wasn't hard to imagine what his response to his grandmother's suggestions and pressure in this matter had been: making him that much more inclined to ignore it, to go against it, to do the opposite and rebel the more entirely.

And I can't say that I myself saw anything wrong with these friends of his. I had been their age, and I knew what that was and meant. They were at that time of life when the greatest vitality is combined with the most naive adventurousness—and this must necessarily result in some reckless behavior.

Probably they experimented with tobacco and alcohol, talked lasciviously, and indulged in pranks that just verged on breaking some law. And so what? What boy didn't—what boy shouldn't? I would have been a lot more concerned had it been otherwise. For there's nothing sadder and even a little repulsive than a child, and a boy especially, who, on the verge of adulthood, remains entirely passive and obedient;—who never tries to test the limits of authority, or never wants to try something other than what he has been told he should want;—who isn't curious, isn't skeptical, isn't willing to take a chance, isn't willing to test himself physically;—who dutifully, unquestioningly goes along with the mores and morals of those who have raised him but who in the end may not be worthy of emulation. Such a human creature isn't "good" so much as pitiably effete: a born loser and slave.

On the other hand I also understood Mrs. Larke's concerns. She knew that it is always easier for children to be brought down by bad influences than to be raised up by good ones—just as falling is always easier than climbing. And there was no question in her mind that Joey's friends *were* a bad influence on him, to tell from what behavior she had seen. They could be offensively loud and were often violent: pushing one another, pummeling one another, tripping up one another, all the while shouting obscenities with complete indifference to (or, what was worse, unconsciousness of) the offensiveness of their language. Mrs. Larke might have been able to overlook boyish horseplay, but her naturally aristocratic instincts recoiled at its vulgarity, which after all *did* bespeak a low mentality and even something of an evolutionary retrogression. Yet she knew that in trying to prevent Joey from associating with these boys she would only envelop them with an alluring aura of the forbidden. And so with all her energy she would restrain herself from upbraiding him about them. But sometimes, when she was irritable, she couldn't help criticizing them and warning him that they were the "wrong crowd" who weren't going "to do anything" for him.

Joey would listen glumly; resent the advice, which he thought baseless and unfair; and of course go his own way.

IV

Whenever I showed up for Joey's lessons the construction was in full swing in the basement. Pulverized brick and cement and fiberboard, having filtered up into the rest of the house, would hang in the air as a fine mist, which turned any stray sunbeam slipping through the curtains or blinds into a sharp-edged sword of light. Now and then one of the workmen would come upstairs bleached with dust and wearing a paper mask over his nose and mouth. He would tramp through the living room in order to fetch something from the truck outside. Mrs. Larke would watch him pass with compressed lips and a barely-restrained protest against the tracks he made on her carpet. Eventually she finessed this part of her frustration by placing a vinyl runner from the kitchen to the front door.

The loud pounding, sawing, and tearing would begin gnawing at my nerves from the moment I stepped into the house. Perhaps my anticipation of having to endure them made them seem that much worse, but as the minutes passed my good cheer gave way to quiet solemnity, then to nervous impatience. My legs would jitter, and I would find myself consciously stifling a curse at having to endure the audile torture.

My irritation was enhanced by Joey's dogged lack of progress. Even after six weeks of repeated exposure to many of the same poems and prose extracts he was not reading or comprehending them any better than he had at first. On some of these we had spent so much time—whole hours—that it seemed impossible he couldn't remember or have any insight into what they were about. But information of that kind apparently went into one of his ears and came out of the other with nothing in between to absorb it or slow it down. Whenever, in some frustration, I would remind him of the discussions we had already had about the texts, he would only look at me with his small, vacant eyes, open his mouth a little, and say, "Well ... I forgot." But his problem wasn't a bad memory. On the contrary he had wonderfully good memory for the innumerable foolish things that interested him. If that ability could only have been turned to meaningful account he would have done very well. It occurred to me again how my job was to arouse his interest in reading, and so whenever I introduced him to something new it was always enthusiastically, with a promise of pleasure; only to see his increasing silent distrust of me and the material as though he were never more sure he would dislike something than when I talked it up.

Yes, it was getting hard for me. It was getting hard for me not only to convey to him any delight in literature but even to maintain it for myself. I realized that my pleasure in it and teaching it were very different things. Pieces that I had selected for our use, and which once had made me jump a little for their lapidary precision or gorgeous nebulousness, became flat and lifeless under our trudging, dissecting, defining, interpreting scrutiny. The fact is that one can never examine too closely or too long any work of art and know it in the way it is meant to be known. Just as the impetus behind its creation is immediate and essentially spiritual, so one's own spirit must be affected by it in an immediate, essential way. Everything else is ancillary— a reading into, a groping that tends to chill, adulterate, suck the life out of the thing. But no matter how often I tried to inculcate into the boy that there was nothing hidden or abstruse in our lessons—that he had only take these texts and their meanings and face value for complete understanding—he never once seemed receptive to them.

"Good God, he can't be serious!" I would think to myself, with growing frustration, when he haltingly uttered the words of the simplest poem or the most straightforward prose, and at the most beautiful images or phrases merely shrugged his shoulders, saying, "I don't get it."

"There's nothing to 'get,' " I would tell him, forcing myself to ignore the banging and hammering that came up from the basement and reverberated around us. "It means just what it says."

"Well, what does it say?"

"It says what you just read."

"Well, I ..."—and he would look down at the words and shake his head again.

And we would go over it for the second or third or fourth time, word by word, idea by idea, till all the soaring sweet life of the thing had been pounded into dead flatness.

What with the interminable racket of construction and the continued thickness of my student, it was inevitable that my once-positive attitude should sour.   What had been smiling, leisurely corrections of his mistakes became even-lipped, curt injunctions to repeat what he had not read correctly before. The boy's halting, monotonous, soporific-yet-irritating droning made me impatient for the lesson to be done, for my whole tutorship with him to be finished. I began to feel that he had become the bane of my existence, like some chronic, stabbing pain that makes it impossible for you to enjoy anything. He noted this change in my attitude, and was intimidated by it. He no longer greeted me with his animated chatter but instead, when I entered his room, sat looking at me silently, curiously, trying to gauge my mood. For a moment I would feel guilty to think he had to be on his guard around me, and I would try to be my old pleasant self again ... only for the construction noise and his tedious slowness to irritate me all over again, and make me more irritable than ever.

Nevertheless later, in the restorative peace and quiet of my apartment, I would reflect on the day and find myself making excuses for Joey's poor performance. I remember how once I went so far as to consider how even geniuses in art and literature gave no indication as children of their future brilliance; how in fact they sometimes seemed more than commonly obtuse.   But immediately afterwards I chuckled in disdain to think that my charge belonged to that rare tribe—that he was some little Michelangelo or Proust in the making. It was really too absurd! It may be true that the child destined one day to draw, compose, or sculpt magnificently might seem unexceptionable, but in fact, to the eye keen enough to perceive it, there *will* be something to give away the fact that here is one not made of common clay. Perhaps he will be a dreamer; perhaps he will be silently observant; perhaps he will shun the crowd, or command it; or talk about and try to fashion strange mechanisms; or have a quick, an insightful, a sharp tongue;—but always there will be *something* a little out of the way, a little unexpected and delightful or alarming, about him, and which retrospect will discover as the telltale sign of what grew into the later remarkable ability. But the only telltale sign I ever saw or rather heard in Joey was the remark he sometimes made a few minutes to twelve o'clock, just as our lesson was ending:

"I could sure go for some potato chips."

Of course I was disappointed in myself too. I had failed to inspire in him any interest in reading or writing, and I couldn't imagine what else I might do to make the boy's lessons easier or more interesting. I thought on the matter a long time and several things occurred to me to account for my failure. The first was the relaxed nature of my relationship with the boy. Perhaps we had been too chummy. There had not been between us that psychological distance which would have made him respect me enough—yes, even fear me enough—to want to avoid my disappointment or censure. If most teachers were aloof from their students, if they didn't engage in any personal conversations or exchange extracurricular points of view, it was because they understood that an emotional distance helped to guarantee the discipline necessary for effective teaching and learning. But even more important than this was the content of our lessons. It had been wrong in me to expect him to appreciate things he would not ordinarily been exposed to till his high school or even college years. I should have recalled that at his age literature had been the furthest thing from my mind or interest, and no teacher, no matter how impassioned or interesting, could have brought me round to it. There were things for the appreciation of which one simply had to reach a certain level of maturity and understanding, as well as to have a certain natural proclivity. Equally misguided had been my intention to arouse in him some life-altering love of literature. For what if I had succeeded in doing that? What if I had really lit that fire in him? Would it have "helped" him? On the contrary, it would have been a disaster for him. It would have led him off life's beaten path, which, thanks to the countless feet that have trodden it before, is the only one that is really smooth. The boy needed to be made competent in the most basic reading and writing—not to be turned into some impractical, starry-eyed, angst-ridden poet. I was there to make his life easier, not harder. And so in a flash of revelation I saw the error of my ways and vowed to change. Another six, perhaps seven weeks remained for me to tutor the boy: just time enough for an entirely different, more conventional method to be employed, and get the basic results I was getting paid to deliver.

I remembered the name of the textbook Joey had once told me he used in school and found a copy of it online and ordered it—paying the extra charge for an express, next-day delivery. The cover showed several young teens happily sitting around a table talking to one another while the title of the book—"Reading, Listening, Speaking"—hovered over their heads. It was printed on heavy, semigloss paper, and it was full of pictures relating to the large-sized text around them. The book was written in the most basic style imaginable: short sentences of no more than eight or ten words. Most of them had no punctuation except for a period. A few others might have the minimal punctuation of a comma, or even a semicolon; but of the latter there couldn't have been more than a dozen sentences in the entire book. Each lesson consisted of about ten pages with large, widely-spaced text, at the end of which were about ten questions requiring written answers, or, in some cases, a single command to write an essay about a given subject. It was all very straightforward and basic.

Joey was surprised when I showed up without any new texts to offer him and told him that we were going to try something "different." When I pulled out his old textbook, he smiled at once and exclaimed, "Heyyyy!"—reaching out for it and enthusiastically taking it into his hands. He turned it over a few times. "Where'd you get this?"

"I found it online. We're going—"

The house shuddered; a high-pitched drilling sound from below filled the room, swept around us a vortex of deafening sound. "What the heck is that!" I exclaimed, rather than asked.

"From downstairs," Joey said evenly.

"Was that going on this morning with you and Mr. Miller?"

He shook his head, no. Just my luck!

"Alright. Listen," I continued, "we're going to be using this book from now on. Do you remember where you left off this year?"

He opened the book in the middle and began flipping through the pages, trying to find the last chapter-lesson he could remember having read. As he did so I felt a flush of relief to think that I had, just in time, done the right thing by him; that now, with that particular book and my help, whatever he had learned in school would be reinforced, and that together we would go beyond it in preparation for the coming school year.

Often having to stop, to compose myself amid the whirs

and booms of the construction going on in the basement, I told Joey we were going to do one lesson per session—there was just enough time in the hour to do it—and his homework would be to do the exercises and essay questions at the back and read over the succeeding lesson for our next appointment.

"That's a lot," he said, looking up at me a little uncertaintly; and for the first time sensing that lessons drawn from a familiar schoolbook might not be any easier or enjoyable than our previous ones had been. "That's like ..."—he thumbed through the book, through the lessons in question, his eyes making a quick calculation of the pages involved, and said: " ... twenty pages!"

"Actually it's ten," I told him, without a hint of humor, with only an adamant expectation that he would do it. "And the text is spaced out a lot, so it's really like four or five pages in a regular book. You can certainly do that in a half hour, let alone a whole day. And the exercise questions in the back shouldn't take you more than fifteen minutes. But I'm telling you right now, Joe, I don't want any slapdash work: I expect you to write out all your answers to the questions, and then there's an essay I want at least two pages of writing from you."

"Two pages? Heyyyy ... I don't have *time* to do all that!"

"If you have time to spend your day watching movies and playing video games, you have time to do that. It won't take you long."

"But it's ..."—he just shook his head, exasperated, bewildered, quietly overwhelmed by what seemed to him an impossible avalanche of work.

Of course one of the most disagreeable traits a person can have is volatility. To be cheerful one day and morose the next, where it is natural to a person, bespeaks a severe flaw in character, even a mental derangement, or, at the very least, a repulsive social moronism. From such loose cannons one would always do well to keep one's distance. I wanted Joey to know that the change in my behavior wasn't of this loathsomely unreasonable kind, but had a definite and considered cause. Before leaving him that morning I told him how disappointed I had been in his progress so far. He had, I said, gotten away with too much, and I went over the catalogue of his remissness: the assignments never or ill-done, the vocabulary not learned, the texts never even partly mastered. I told him that it wasn't all his fault, that I was partly responsible for having given material that might have been inappropriate for him, which was why from now on we would be using his school textbook. But time was running out, I said, and in the next month and a half we had left we had to make up for the foregoing fruitless weeks. We were going to work hard.

For a while he tried engaging me in his usual, time-wasting small talk, but now I didn't respond to it. I would smile briefly, comment curtly, and in the next second return to the lesson at hand by blurting out a quiet, serious-sounding, "Let's get back to this." These repeated, subtle rebuffs eventually had their effect. He no longer tried to engage in friendly conversation with me. He saw the hopelessness of trying to waste time. When I entered his room he would utter a begrudging hello and, at my injunction, silently and with an air of resignation open his lesson book. For the next hour he would drone on as stumblingly, as uncomprehendingly as ever;—and the pounding of the construction work in the basement would reverberate around me, chipping away at my composure;—and I would quietly correct him when he mispronounced a word, gritting my teeth in irritation at his absurdly basic vocabulary;—and I would tell myself that "that was that," that I couldn't take it anymore, that this boy really *was* ineducable, and that my own peace of mind depended on getting away from him as soon as possible.

The upshot of it all was that I began to despair of teaching Joey anything. My characteristic self-doubt had inclined me to believe that I was the problem, that my methods were wrong, my objectives inappropriate, but there had come a point at which even I had to admit that this wasn't entirely true. The boy simply wasn't absorbing *any* of the information I had to give him. Still worse, he had no sympathy for it. "I can't relate to it" was the phrase he used. That had seemed to me just another one of his excuses for laziness but in looking back on it I realized how entirely it summed up his and my predicament. The last thing in the world for which he had any aptitude was the written word. There is an essential humanity in literature that requires a corresponding degree of humanity for it to be appreciated. If one doesn't have it, or has it in too small a degree, then the most wonderful writing will seem indifferent or tedious; and as far as Joey was concerned, it was more than just tedious—it was entirely intolerable.

V

In my ideal world no one would ever hold against me the sorry state of my wardrobe. I could go about in my few, comfortable, worn (but always clean) clothes, and never receive an askance look. My winter coat, which is twenty years old, and my spring jacket, which is fifteen, wouldn't incline any eyes to linger superciliously on their frayed collars or sleeves. My sneakers and "dress" shoes—the only two pairs I own—wouldn't elicit the disapproving glances of those who put stock in fashionable, or at least relatively intact, footwear. Shoes, by the way, were always the first items of clothing to wear out for me. They never lasted for more than a year on account of my walking the city streets for sometimes miles a day. Yet even when they became extremely slipshod my tendency was to hang on to them, telling myself that they were still good for another week or so;—which had a way of turning into a month, and then another month, and then another. But one morning I noticed Mrs. Larke glancing at my feet and was suddenly mortified to think my shoes were as bad as all that, only to look at them more objectively and to see that the heels had indeed worn half off. And so new shoes became the order of the day. Besides (I told myself in justification of the expense) a new pair would be necessary for any job interviews I went on.

There were three shoe stores in my Sunnyside neighborhood. Two of them were owned by Romanians, and one of them by a Turk. These fellows had the strangest notions of fashionable footwear: shiny buckles, pointy or square toes, slanting high heels, faux white alligator leather, and elaborate stitching. They were shoes designed to add the perfect finishing touch to a polyester suit and gold-plated chains jangling against a hairy chest. But they weren't at all appropriate to a less ridiculous American sensibility.

Having recalled seeing shoe stores on Austin Street not far from Mrs. Larke's house, I decided one Thursday to do my shopping there. It happened that while waiting to cross 71st Street I came upon Mr. Miller. He didn't notice me as we both waited for the crossing signal. I bent forward a little, and then took a step yet closer to him so that he might see me from the corner of his eye. He finally turned to me and we greeted each other. He himself had been shopping in the neighborhood, for he held a cream-colored bag bearing the name and logo of a nearby chain bookstore.

"Buy a book?" I asked.

He looked down at the bag and lifted it a little as he said, "Oh, no. A map."

He reached into the bag and pulled it out: a laminated, folded, map of Maine.

"Taking a trip?" I asked.

He nodded. "A permanent one. We're moving—my wife and I."

"Oh ..." I wasn't sure whether I ought to congratulate him or ask him the reason for the move. Instead I just remarked, "It gets cold up there, doesn't it?"

"Yes, the winter is very cold. But then we're missing out on the horrible New York heat in the summer."

"Why Maine?"

"I've been up there a few times and kind of liked it. And the cost of living is something we'll be able to deal with. And we just wanted to go somewhere ... you know ... civilized."

"I would think that if it's civilization you're after, you'd stay here in New York."

He laughed lightly. His eyes glittered at me. He smiled widely, somehow tensely and impulsively: it was clear that something, a retort, had occurred to him and he was restraining himself from blurting it out. But in the next few seconds the temptation proved too great to resist, and he said:

"How very New York of you! You know, years ago an acquaintance of mine told me that the most narrow-minded people he had ever met lived between the Hudson and the East River—and by way of extension, in the boroughs as well. At that time I thought he was just trying to be witty or cynical. Since then I've come to see he was entirely right."

Was that meant as a jab at me? But it was hard to take it personally when his tone of voice was so pleasant, his address so friendly.

"Are you buying a home there?"

"No, I'm afraid we don't have the money for that. We'll be renting. But there you get a lot more for your money." He put the map back into the bag and began, "So tell me—"

A burst of pounding, thunderous sound interrupted his words: a cacophony of savage drumbeats and barked-out, obscene, violent rhymes. It was the same kind of music that Joey had once made me listen to. It came upon us suddenly and was so loud that it made the air vibrate as though some enormous machine were pounding the earth itself. Everyone on the street stopped and turned around to see where it was coming from: a car full of four young people, three men and a woman, who had stopped at a nearby traffic light. They were talking or rather shouting above the deafening noise. The men had coarse faces and their female companion presented the repulsive image of a woman who despite her rouged cheeks and jewelry was anything but feminine. It was a wonder that they could have tolerated, much less enjoyed, the volume of that music so close to their ears; and, in fact, they did not really enjoy it—at least, not for its own sake. Rather, they reveled in its volume, in its offensive and barbaric percussiveness, only insofar as it was a weapon, a means of assault, against the people on the street.

Mr. Miller looked at them with a hard, disapproving, even an angry expression as though by looks alone he might force them into more sociable behavior. But they didn't heed him, any more than they heeded the dozens of people who gave them similarly dark and disapproving looks. One old lady on the sidewalk called out to them, "Turn it down!" They shouted back at her to shut up and mind her own business, and the woman among them stuck out a middle finger at her and laughingly hurled an indecent insult. The light turned green and the car zoomed forward, spreading its pandemonium into other areas.

Mr. Miller and I, and everyone around us, watched the car drive off, heard its audile barbarism dying away. We shook our heads at one another in a kind of sympathetic sadness at our powerlessness to do anything about such things. We all felt the same thing: the great pity of it all—that somehow, in some fundamentally important way, something had gone wrong with the world.

Mr. Miller turned his eyes to me significantly, wearily. He looked very old at that moment, as though he had fought a long, brave fight—a fight of a lifetime—but in the end had lost. "As I say," he continued, the obnoxious noise fading still more in the distance, "we're going somewhere civilized ..."

We walked across the street together and continued side-by-side. I mentioned to him that I was in the neighborhood to buy shoes. He suggested a few stores down the street and said there were also good stores in the mall on Queens Boulevard. Then he said, "So tell me, how is it going for you? With Joey, I mean."

"Alright, I suppose."

"Really?"

He stopped walking and looked at me with a strange expression, smiling yet kowingly doubtful: the kind of expression people give you when they know you aren't being honest.

"Yes, why?"

"It's just that I find our little Joey a rather tough nut to crack."

"How so?"

"How so?"—again that look, as though I knew precisely what he meant. "He's not learning. Anything."

"Maybe he's not mathematically inclined."

He looked away from me, to the street, saying, "Yes, of course, that's it," but there was an unmistakable intimation in his voice—the intimation being that the boy couldn't possibly be doing any better with me. And there was more to it even than this, as he was about to let me know, for then he turned back to me and said, "Let's be honest: that boy isn't going to be learning anything this summer from either one of us."

"Why do you say that?"

He came right out with it. "I don't think he can."

"What do you mean?"

"I don't think he can," Mr. Miller repeated.

"I think he can do anything he wants to if he just applies himself."

That elicited a chuckle from the old teacher, who looked at me now with an air of disappointment as though I had somehow betrayed his trust. "You know that's not true," he said. "The fact is"—and now he became very serious—"our little Joey is stupid."

He waited for my reaction to this (as he himself knew it to be) shockingly blunt pronouncement. I wasn't sure what to say in return. I couldn't agree to it—that would have been a kind of betrayal of my tutorship. Nor could I defend the boy's progress with some vigorous and outraged counter-statement, for that would have sounded ludicrously false even to myself. I responded with a simple but drawn-out, "No"; but whether this were meant as a rejection of Mr. Miller's pronouncement, or as an expression of a sad acceptance of an unhappy fact, would have been hard for an objective hearer to tell.

"Listen," Mr. Miller continued, "I'm not saying that to be cruel. I'm saying it because it's the truth. The boy's stupid. Period. He'll never learn anything with us, or with anyone else. And I know what I'm talking about. I was a teacher for forty years. I've had some experience with children."

"Then why did you tell Mrs. Larke that everything was fine? I heard you tell her that more than once."

"Did I? I don't remember. Well, if I did, you took it too literally, because that boy never makes progress. I was probably just being polite. Why not? I don't want to hurt the woman— she's a nice lady. Besides, I really am doing the best I can—the best anyone could do. But she might have hired Einstein and it wouldn't have made any difference. And I have as much a right to make a little money as anyone else."

"So you're duping her, is that it?" I asked.

And now whatever friendliness he had had toward me disappeared entirely; in an instant he had relegated me to, if not the status of an enemy, then to that of someone undeserving of his confidences.

"Aren't *you* duping her?" he returned.

"Not at all."

"Oh, I see. He's doing so *well* with you!"

"I didn't say that either."

"Then what?"

"He's trying."

"Is he? Really?"

"Yes," I said, not without the sense of telling a lie.

"Alright. Good for you! But let me tell you something. I've seen thousands of kids in my time—tens of thousands. I've learned something about them. Most of them are just average, the way most people are just average. A certain smaller percentage are a little quicker. They're the ones who do well, get good grades, and have nice careers in front of them. A still smaller percentage are brilliant—gifted. They may fail in every subject they're taking, but you look into their eyes and hear the way they talk, and you know you're dealing with a mind that's a cut above the rest. They're the ones who go on to do great things and give people like you and me the things to teach—if they don't go crazy first. But there's an equally small proportion on the opposite end of the scale: the ones who are stupid. It's not their fault and it's nothing they can change; it's just the way they are. They always have the same way of looking at you—the way a cow looks over a fence: vacantly. When I first started teaching I used to think it was my duty to make every stupid kid smart, to bring him 'up to par,' as the school authorities used to tell us; but over time I saw how ridiculous that notion was. If you came across a coach or a physical trainer who told you he could turn every boy or girl into a good athlete, you wouldn't believe him; and why not? Because you know very well that not everyone *can* be a good athlete no matter how much they may want to be one or how hard they may train. They either have the physiological makeup to excel in that way or they don't; and obviously a lot of people don't. But we always refuse to believe that the same thing might be true for brains. We never want to admit that some people are a little slow upstairs, any more, I suppose, than we like to admit that we ourselves might be a little slow compared with others. I'm afraid Mrs. Larke falls into that category where her grandson is concerned. She insists on believing that he can be something that he can never be. It's her fixed idea—see? She wants to make him worthy of herself, of her family, of what she knows to be admirable. But she's not delusional, either. She knows what the story is with her little Joey. She *knows*—see? You and I are just a diversion for her. We're the straws she's giving herself to hang onto so she won't have to face up to the fact that it is as it is—that it's all fallen apart—that her family's come down to this—to him."

I couldn't look the man in the eye. Just then he struck me as repulsively insincere and scheming—a man too capable of

harboring one set of sentiments while expressing those of an opposite kind. I was just about to wish him a good day and move
on when he continued with:

"Boy, oh, boy, I wish I could tell her! I wish I could just sit
down with her and talk to her honestly, and just tell her the
way things are: that her grandson's a big dope and the best he
can hope for is a job one day at a restaurant washing dishes."
He smiled ruefully as he looked at me with eyes full of a sad
better knowledge. "But I guess neither of us are about to do
that—right? It would put a stop to the cash flow—right?"

Did he expect an answer? Or had the question been posed
as a subtle attempt to highlight what he regarded as my
hypocrisy, as though to say that no matter what airs I assumed
we were really in the same boat?

But I wasn't in the same boat with him and I didn't want
to be. Just then he reminded me of so many old people whom I
had met and known—people who had become bitterly, selfishly
indifferent to everything but their own welfare and comfort.
How often I saw such characters in New York! They had started
out in life with youth's beautiful starry-eyed optimism, believing
in good, hoping for love, planning great things, impatient for
glory; but with each little defeat and disappointment, with each
love gained and lost, each ambition checked or subverted, each
expectation dashed or placed beyond reach, they had become a
little less lighthearted, a little less magnanimous, a little more
calculating and suspicious, till by the time they were middle-
aged, and certainly by the time they were "seniors," they were
the monstrous opposite of their youthful selves, their once sweet,
pellucid spirit having grown dark and poisonous, and coloring all
their thoughts and actions with its vitiating hue. They shuffled
morosely down city streets; they waited with huffing impatience
in grocery store lines; they sat on park benches and scowled at
the younger world going by. As surely as a coin is stamped by a
die, so were their faces stamped by the angry disillusionment of
their lives: their mouths contorted downward into an expression
of perpetual disgust. They no longer had any joy of life. Their
sense of humor—if they had ever had one—was gone.   They
could no longer burst out into one genuine, free-spirited bout of
laughter.   They no longer listened to music.   They no longer
read novels. Art meant nothing to them. Politics and current

events left them cold, unmoved: there might have been a war raging on the borders of their own country, and they wouldn't have cared so long as their Social Security checks kept coming in. For they had lost even a sense of honor. Honor? What was "honor" compared with eating the next tasty meal? And as they wallowed in this miserable degeneration of mind and spirit they flattered themselves that their attitude was merely "realistic," the result of "having lived," of having "seen" the world, of finally knowing "what was what." But it was nothing of the sort. It was just the opposite of that. It wasn't knowledge that had turned them into what they were but rather six or seven decades of unrelieved ignorance. Having drudged and blundered their way through the pitiably narrow channels of their personal lives or professions; having been averse from the work required to gain knowledge, and the discomforts of introspection which alone yield insight; having spent the best and most vigorous years of their youth and maturity in trying to "get ahead," in trying to "secure" their future, in dreadful competition with millions of others who were clawing just as desperately and often more successfully for the same things; they had found out too late the hopelessness and false promise of that contest, which had left them old and empty and beaten and befouled, the exhausted, resentful inheritors of a sterile ideal.

—All this I saw in old Mr. Miller as he stood before me with his self-satisfied simper, almost as though he were happy to have found in Joey and Mrs. Larke another confirmation of his cynical view of humanity: another reason to get for himself as much as possible "while the getting was good."

After I had said goodbye to him on the street I resolved never to talk to him again. I didn't like his brand of "wisdom." And as I've said earlier life is usually too filled with unpleasant things to do or think anything that would add to their number. I didn't need someone like him to bring me down—I was usually depressed enough. I resolved that if we should ever meet again I would, at most, be polite to him, and hurry away from him as soon as possible as though he carried the plague.

As for his proclamation of Joey's stupidity, that was something that for the rest of the day I kept trying to discount to myself—in vain, however. As a man, as the embodiment of a "philosophy" or point of view, Mr. Miller repulsed me; but the messenger and the message were two different things, and there was no getting around the fact that he might have been—no, probably was—right: the boy *was* stupid. In my mind's eye Joey's face appeared with a new and still less flattering objectivity: the large jowls, the somewhat heavy-lidded eyes, the humid, ever-open lips;—yes, such a face was the very image of stupidity; of, even, something more disconcerting than this—of a kind of human retrogression. For the first time there dawned on me a sense of the hopelessness of trying to teach him. He would never catch up to other children his age and whose bad academic performance—when it was bad—was attributable merely to distraction or laziness. Those things could be corrected, could be made up for; and even where they couldn't be at any one time there was still always the potential for excellence on account of an intrinsic integrity. But where there was *no* potential?

Well, but nothing is more changeable in me than despair and a sense of defeat, and so before the day was over my resignation to Joey's failure had morphed into something hopeful and positive. Surely (I now thought) he was capable of at least *some* improvement. Even if he was slow—very slow— he could surely make some small advance in his language skills. And learning was relative: so long as one learned something it was a net gain. The best way to ensure this, it seemed to me, was to increase the tempo of his lessons and the amount of homework he was expected to do. If more was expected of him he would never be able to give me less; and the more he did, the more likely some of it was bound to stick to him. Thus during our next session, before taking leave of him, I doubled the amount of his usual homework: he was to read not just the next chapter, but the next two; and he would have to write an essay at least five pages long.

"What?" he asked, his tone of voice astonished and protesting. He looked at me as though I must have misspoken, and when he said that I hadn't, "Nooooo ..."

"What do you mean, 'no'? That's your assignment this time."

He looked away from me and heaved a loud resentful breath. As he did so, the pounding from the basement—which had never once entirely stopped—became especially loud and

frequent. I made a conscious effort to ignore it, to keep its cacophony at bay from my nerves, as I said:

"Listen, Joe, here's the way it is: we only have a few more
weeks together. We *really* have to start working on this stuff. I
want you to be able to read well and easily, and to understand
what you're reading. But reading is like anything else: it takes
practice. The more you do it, the better you'll get at it, and the
better you get at it the more you'll like it."

"But that's *too much*."

"You can do it."

"But I can't—"

"Uh!"—raising my hand, a finger, to him, stopping his
protest mid-speech. "It's not too much. You can do it."

"But I have other stuff to do!"

"Like what?"

"Like the math. Mr. Miller gives me a lot of homework too.
That takes time."

I barely tamped down an irritated outburst against the
ridiculosities of Mr. Miller's equations. The last thing in the
world the boy needed was to have his already unfocused brain
further scrambled by involved counting exercises. It occurred to
me to speak to Mrs. Larke about getting rid of the math tutor
altogether; setting out to her a case of why, in the general
scheme and scale of things, it was a hundred times more important for her son to be able to receive and to think clearly about
ideas than it was for him to calculate numbers, a task for which
he could just as easily buy a two-dollar calculator. But in the
end I decided against this because she might think that I had
something against Mr. Miller (which in fact I *did*), and second
because it seemed mean-spirited of me to try to undermine another man's livelihood, though, strictly speaking, his main
source of livelihood came from elsewhere. As the pounding from
the basement, I couldn't help saying to the boy:

"Math isn't as important as reading and writing."

"Mr. Miller says math is the most important thing ever."

My right leg jittered in pure impatience to tell the boy that
Mr. Miller was a fool. Instead:

"Well, reading and writing are just as important, if not
more so. So for the next few weeks, Joe, we have to work a little harder at them, alright?"

He couldn't bring himself to assent even out of politeness. Glumly, he looked away from me and said:

"We don't have time for all that. We can't even do one lesson in an hour."

About that he was right: there was no way we were going to get through two lessons in a session when we usually didn't even get through one. Our time together would have to be extended at least another hour. But as I was descending the stairs to leave the house and talk to Mrs. Larke about spending more time with Joey, the prospect of making such a request embarrassed me. Perhaps she would think I was angling for more time because I wanted more money. Even if she believed the impartiality of my request, even if additional money wasn't mentioned or I insisted on forgoing it, she, who was so conscious and punctilious about propriety, would be placed into the uncomfortable position of allowing me to work for nothing. And so rather than propose a definite extension of my time with her grandson I mentioned to her in an offhand way that henceforth I might need "a few more minutes" with him just to "wrap up."

"That's fine," she said, simply, appreciatively.

Joey showed his disappointment when at the end of our next hour together I remained seated at his desk and told him that we were continuing. It was the last thing I wanted to do. The pounding, gnawing, irritating noise of construction had been especially loud and incessant that morning, having hardly let up for a minute at a time, and it was a little warm in the room, and my head was beginning to hurt with headache, and the boy's droning had made me irritable. I was ready to snap at him if he objected. But he did not. He seemed to expect that we would be spending more time together. Perhaps his grandmother had mentioned to him what I had told her. And so he droned on in his reading for another fifteen minutes, his mumbling, stumbling voice sometimes hard to hear amid the loud knocks and bangs coming from the basement and filling the house. We finally turned to his homework assignment. As usual it was a mess. I had gone over it with an unprecedented and ruthless scrutiny, and with a red pen had underlined, circled, and placed imperious exclamation marks—like so many scolds—next to all the errant things. Sometimes my marginal notes took up half as much writing as his own did. We went over it line by line. In the end I told him he would have to do it over again.

"But I already *did* it!"

"Next time you'll do it better."

"I can't do it any better!"

Bang!—bang, bang, bang!—went the pounding from the basement.

My jaw tensed. My head was hurting me. The boy looked at me with his small, dull eyes and his lips forming an upset pout.

I took a deep breath and consciously told myself to relax, not to let the morning's irritations overcome me;—not to give way to an unkind outburst which I would only regret. I spent a few seconds composing myself and managed to tell the boy in a quiet voice:

"You can do better. You'll do better next time."

With Joey one needed a stick as well as a carrot. The carrot was my approval. As for a stick, the only one I had had so far was my reprimand, and that hadn't been very effective. It had occurred to me to hit him in the pocketbook. I was going, I said, to talk to his grandmother about connecting his allowance to the progress he made in his studies. No progress, no money.

"Heyyyyy, you can't do that!" he said, and though he smiled in wonder at my audacity in making a threat that would affect his personal life, he was clearly worried it might be carried out. The sensitive nerve had been hit.

"Oh yes I can," I said. "And I will. And your grandmother will listen to me. I'm not fooling around, Joe. I'm serious. You're not putting enough effort into this."

"But I *am!*"

"Put in more."

He gritted his teeth and looked at me resentfully.

Would I have actually gone to Mrs. Larke and told her to cut him off? Only if he had challenged me to do so. But he didn't. He took me seriously. He felt the intended pressure, and relented. Or at least, I believe he did. I believe he began to make a real effort. He would tell me how he had spent an hour a night on his lessons and had taken his time with his written assignments, and certainly they were longer and written in a more careful hand. But this didn't mean they were any

better; their length was but an increase in the amount of mis-
spelled rambling. For fifteen minutes at a stretch we would go
over this work and I would, pointing out his vague phrases or
imprecise colloquialisms, insist that he specify what he had
meant—insist that he be clear about what he wanted to say.
He would grit his teeth with the effort to do so, and his new
phrasing was never any better than before.

Really, by this time I couldn't sit patiently at the desk in
Joey's room for more than ten minutes without getting up out of
nervous impatience at the pounding noise of construction in the
basement and at the boy's hopeless mumbling. I often stopped
at the window and gazed outside, invariably turning my eyes to
the right in the hope of seeing Octavian again. I never did, but
the memory of that shy, delicate boy sitting out there with his
telescope persisted wistfully in my memory like the image of a
promise. If only *he* had been my pupil! Everything would have
been different, then. *He* would have learned everything there
was for me to teach him. The only problem of course was that a
child like him didn't need the tutoring, or, if he did, it wouldn't
in the long run have made much of a difference in his life. He
was among those children who are destined to find their own
way and rise above, no matter how many schoolyard bullies beat
them down, no matter how much of the world's stupidities they
have to struggle against. Between a swift noble Octavian and a
lumbering clump of a Joey—what a world of difference!

BANG!

—The enormous noise brought me back to the moment and
Joey looking silently down at the text in his lap as he tried to
pronounce another one of the simple words unknown to him.
With each half-attempt to mumble it out he would look up at
me as though for help, only to see me shaking my head with an
unamused smile as though to say, "No, no—you try to pronounce
it," and only giving in—only quietly telling him how to say it—
when he seemed to be getting a little frustrated and it was clear
he never would get it on his own.

"I don't get it," he complained. "Why don't they just use
simple words. Wha'd'they gotta use words like that for?!"

Bang! Bang! Bang!

"It is a simple word, Joe. Plenty of people use it."

"Well, nobody I ever knew used it."

Bang!—BANG!

I pressed a few fingers against my forehead as though to push back the throb of another headache, and said calmly:

"You'll hear it and see it a thousand times, so it's good for you to know."

He returned to the book looking down at it for almost a whole silent minute; then, letting out an impatient breath, he shook his head and said, "This is hard stuff!"

The house rumbled a little from something heavy being hauled or pulled in the basement.

"As I've told you four-hundred and seventy-four times, if you read a little more every day it wouldn't be hard."

"I'm already reading."

"Not enough."

He huffed. He flipped a few pages further into the book almost as though with impatience to get to the next lesson but really in order to express his impatience with the present one. With each page he turned—with each of his gestures or looks of feigned interest—a great concussion reverberated throughout the house as something in its foundation fell or split or shattered.

He fumbled over the next half a page, fidgeting as he did so.

"Read it over again," I told him.

Bang! Bang! Bang!—came the sharp, smashing percussions from below, shaking the house.

Joey heaved a few impatient breaths; tried again; got it all wrong—everything wrong.

"One more time, Joey."

BANG!

He sighed.

"Go ahead," I urged.

BANG! Bang, bang!

"Uh!" he said, frustrated.

"What is it?" I asked.

"It's just ..."—staring down at the page, shaking his head.

Bang!

"Try."

"I am."

"You're not."

"I *am!*"

Bang-bang-bang! Zzzzsssshhhh! Vrrrrrrr!

—Both Joey and I raised our heads at this latest, loudest, most powerful-seeming series of noises;—the sounds of hammers and drills, both manual and powered, tearing away at, boring into, or ripping apart the most fundamental structures of the great house.

"This is hard!" the boy said.

"Joe, *what* is?"

Despite myself I asked the question with some harshness, narrowing my eyes on the boy. For I really *did* want to know what he had thought was so difficult in the text which in fact was composed of the simplest words and in the simplest, most direct sentences.

He shook his head. A part of him must have known that there was no reason for him to find anything difficult about it. He kept staring down at his book, mouthing words, then saying with a shake of his head:

"I don't get it."

"Just take it for what it is, and you'll have it."

BANG! Bzzzzzzz! —The latter was high-pitched, enormous, piercing, as though some gigantic dentist's drill were boring into the walls.

The boy looked up, cocked his ear.

"Forget about the noise," I told him.

"But it's distracting," he said; not because, for him, it was, but because he knew that it was for me, and hoped to gain my indulgence through pretending that he was equally irritated by it.

"Concentrate," I said.

When he had finished mumbling and bumbling through the last few short paragraphs of the reading material, I asked him for his homework. He handed me the several sheets of paper filled with his large, childlike writing. In the past I had merely taken his paper and shoved it into my shoulder bag intending to read it over, consider it, at home, and bring it back with the inevitable corrections and suggestions, but this time I began reading it right in front of him. He watched in silence as I took up a pen and began marking up his work. Often, for effect, I shook my head and let out an impatient, almost angry breath—I wanted to intimidate him a little. In five minutes I shoved the paper back at him, saying, "No good."

"What's no good?" he asked, as some sort of electronic hammer used in the basement made the house shudder steadily.

"Everything. My comments are there."

In silence he looked down at the marked up paper, his eyes glossing over my impulsive and, frankly (so impulsively had they been scribbled), rather illegible comments.

"You have to do it over," I said.

"But I did it," he mumbled.

"Not well enough. Do it again."

He said nothing; he was not looking at me, either in embarrassment or in anger at what was really my first harsh scolding of him. He sat on the edge of the bed with the schoolbook lying on his knees. His expression was sullen. His thick lower lip trembled, which made me think, mistakenly, that he was on the verge of tears. In fact his frustration with his own lack of progress, with his difficulties, real or imagined, with the subject, had reached a breaking point. His complexion reddened, his lips tightened, his legs fluttered restlessly up and down as nervous tension swept through and overcame him. He took a few deep breaths and, as the pounding from the basement came up to the second floor—as a new, yet louder round of banging shook the whole house—he threw his book on the bed and jumped up, facing me with a flushed face and glaring eyes, and nearly shouted:

"Leave me alone! What do you want me to do! Don't you understand? I *can't* do it! I *hate* it! I *hate* it! I can't do it if I *hate* it!"

The suddenness with which he'd leapt off the bed and faced me, the loud frustration in his voice, above all that expression of his—those glaring, hateful eyes, as though he would have liked nothing better than to strike me down;—it all took me aback for a few seconds and I looked at him in astonishment. Then, collecting myself, and in an attempt to attenuate the explosive passion of the moment, to becalm him, to lower his voice so that his grandmother should not come rushing upstairs to find him in such a state, I held back a few moments before saying quietly:

"Joey, I didn't mean to get you upset. I don't want you to

get upset. I'm only trying to point out to you that you have to be willing to make an effort at this. We don't have many more weeks together. I'm here to help you. I want you to do well in school. Don't you understand that?"

"But I hate it! I hate all this stuff !"

"There's no reason to," I replied, calmly, quietly. "Why would you hate it?"

"Because it's stupid!" he said, his voice still loud, still angry, though now the intensity of his tone had lowered somewhat and a note of pleading had entered into his manner as though he realized he had to give some sort of explanation for his outburst. "Why do I have to know this stuff! What difference does it make! No one knows this stuff—no one cares about this! I hate it!"

"Alright, listen," I said, my voice still low, soothing, "if this is too hard for you, maybe we can find something else, something you might like, something easier."

"There *is* nothing easier!"

"Sure there is," I assured him. "There are so many different kinds of things—"

"No! There isn't! I don't like any of it! I just can't *do* it!"

It was then that from the basement came a great shearing sound as something heavy and hitherto immovable gave way, followed by a deep, thunderous boom and crash. A wrecking ball could not have been louder or more destructive. The whole house shuddered. Pictures rattled on the wall, and items on tables or shelves jumped and slid. There was an ominously loud creaking just beneath the floor as though it were about to give way. To this enormous and, frankly, frightening event, Joey paid no mind in his emotional upset; he continued standing in front of me as angry, frustrated, and adamantly resistant as ever.

To his perfect confession of frustrated inability—to that irrepressible, explosive outburst of thorough despisal—what was I to say? He knew himself better than I did, and for me to have gainsaid or contradicted him could only have added to his seething frustration a rank hatred toward myself for not having respected him enough to take him at his word. I realized I was faced with the dilemma of either ignoring his outburst and continuing with the lessons, or admitting the truth of what he had said and resigning as his tutor. Resignation however was not an option. It was too late in the season for that. We had but two more weeks together—six more sessions—and a week later he would return to school, and it was unlikely that in so short a period his grandmother could hire another tutor, or that another tutor could make much difference: what had not been done in nine weeks could not be done in two.

The result was my acceptance of having failed him. I told myself that I had done the best I could and none could have done better—even if my conviction about this sometimes wobbled in the face of my characteristic self-doubt. At any rate I never again became agitated when Joey mispronounced words we had gone over two dozen times, or when he bumbled his way through some simple passage of his lesson book. Even the construction noise no longer bothered me so much because I had decided to wear my earplugs after all. Just as I'd suspected, Joey reported them to his grandmother. The next time I came for lesson she brought up the matter immediately, saying that she had had no idea the noise had bothered me so much, and that she was very sorry for it. It had been driving her crazy too, she said, and after apologizing again, offered, "If you want, I can tell the men not to work while you're here."

I told her that that wouldn't be necessary. Now that I was wearing earplugs the noise wasn't nearly so irritating.

"But can you still hear what Joey is saying?" she asked, still very politely, but expressing what was really her first concern.

"Of course. The earplugs don't block out sound completely. They just muffle it. Believe me, I can hear every word he says."

"Well ... I am sorry," she said.

"Don't be."

And so I continued tutoring Joey in a semi-bliss of both reduced noise and indifference to his progress. The fact was that I had crossed a psychological dividing line with him. It was undoubtedly the same line that had been crossed by his teachers in school and the school authorities themselves: an understanding that one's best efforts, in his case, could have but a fraction of the intended results, and one had to be satisfied with that. Try as you might, you couldn't spin gold out of a block of lead.

My new indifference wasn't lost on the boy. Yet again he

saw and heard another change in me, and this time one that was more baffling to him than any of the others. Whereas once I had interrupted him with cheerful corrections or encouragement, or later quipped out dour reprimands or expressed irritated disappointment, now I sat with him largely in silence, waiting till he had finished reading before mentioning to him—in a quiet, distant tone of voice—what he might want to keep in mind. The homework assignments I returned to him were sparsely commented on, and I handed them back to him with a simple, "Here you are." During these last sessions he often looked at me curiously, almost regretfully as though he knew what had happened—knew that I had given up on him—and wished for a return to our old, strenuous, sometimes confrontational footing. But on the whole his attitude was one of relief. Demands were no longer being made on him. He knew that whether he worked hard or not at all would no longer have the least consequence to himself so far as I was concerned.

In our last three sessions I merely corrected him succinctly, or nudged him along quietly. I would sit or stand or pace the room, apparently listening to him but really thinking of the day, fast approaching, when we would spend our last hour together, and I would once again be free. The prospect of that freedom would fill me with warm impatience—but only initially, only till its consequences became a little clearer. For it would be freedom for what? To be unemployed again? To start worrying again? Undoubtedly again to find another job as uncertain, as sparsely compensated, as all those that had gone before, and which, in its clockwork regularity and alienating mindlessness, would resume the process of demoralization that throughout my working life half the energies of my soul had struggled to keep at bay. As for the salary Mrs. Larke had paid me, it had been generous, but it had never quite covered my expenses: it had only enabled me to hold on a little longer to what was left in my savings account. It had postponed, not obviated, the day of reckoning.

When the last minute of our last hour came and passed, I stood up and smiled and said simply, "Well, that's it, Joe."

He watched me as I slipped my pen into my shirt pocket, then lifted my shoulder bag and slung it over my shoulder. He was sitting on the bed and didn't get up. He just looked up at me, a little apprehensively.

"Good luck with everything," I told him, my slight, forced smile not varying a centimeter. "Try to go over your lessons when you get a chance. You can keep the book. Try to do a little reading every night. When you don't know a word, Joe, look it up and make sure you get the pronunciation right. Alright?"

He nodded. I put out a hand to shake his, which he offered so indifferently, so much as a matter of concession and without an iota of regret or affection, that it felt like a limp fish in my hand, and I rather regretted having offered this gesture of polite leave-taking. When I left his room I closed the door behind me. I had only gotten to the end of the hall when he, holding a basketball, came zooming out of his room and flew by me saying, "See ya!" His heavy legs and big feet pounded the steps as he hurriedly descended them.

Mrs. Larke had been sitting in the living room and stood up at the sight of first Joey then me. To her grandson who was hurtling out of the house she called out, "Darling, where are you going?"

"Outside!" he said only; and in an instant was gone. Gone— to bounce a ball, to dream of emulating one of his idiot heroes, who, even if they all were a thousand, a million times better than they were at what they did would not and could not (O Isocrates!) advance mankind so much as a micron forward.

Mrs. Larke shook her head with indulgent amusement at the thought of her grandson's childish eagerness to go outside, then turned her attention to me and, all smiles, said, "Well! This is it—eh?" As always she had my payment ready in a plain white envelope. She held it at her side in her right hand. As I came toward her she continued, "Really, I can't tell you how much I appreciate everything you've done for me—for us. You've been such a great help!"

Poor deluded woman! She held out the envelope with my pay.

Just then bits and pieces of Mr. Miller's conversation with me on the street a few weeks earlier came back to me, especially that question, "Aren't *you* duping her?" A sense of honor told me not to take the money. But the proximity of her cheerful, confident smile embarrassed me out of the boldness of refusing it—at least, at first. I took the envelope and held it uncomfortably, looking down at it, not feeling too good about myself.

"Well, thanks again," she said. "I hope you'll keep in touch!"

I nodded. I wanted to say something. I didn't know what. Then I noticed that the sounds of the construction had stopped totally and said, "It's quiet."

"Oh, the men took a lunch break. Thank God! But believe me, they'll be back."

I didn't start out. I didn't want to "dupe" anybody, least of all her. And damn it, I wasn't Mr. Miller! I hadn't become like him—not yet.

"I was wondering," I said, "do you have a few minutes? I wanted to talk to you about something."

"Oh? Sure! Come—sit down."

She put out a hand to the couch even as she stepped to a chair opposite and sat down. Her expression was light-hearted, smiling, inquisitive, encouraging as I sat opposite her. She waited for me to speak.

There was a coffee table in front of us and I set down on it the envelope containing my payment. Her eyes followed my hand as it did this.

"I wanted to talk to you about Joey," I said.

"Sure"—there was a hint of concern in her voice and manner. She watched me more intently, waiting.

"I just wanted to say ... that over the last couple of months he's really tried to do his best."

"Oh. Alright."—nodding, waiting, waiting, knowing that I couldn't have wanted to tell her only that.

I realized that I had to be more forthright. What I wanted to say couldn't be spoken through comfortable euphemisms or disguised by circumlocution. I didn't want to dupe her. I wasn't Mr. Miller. I didn't want to be like him, ever.

"I think that in a lot of ways he's done his best," I said. "It's just that his best ... might not be enough."

"What do you mean?" she asked, her smile fading a little.

"I mean that I really haven't been able to teach him as much as I had hoped. In fact, I'll be honest and say that ... I don't think I've taught him much of anything."

She wasn't sure what to make of that. She couldn't or

didn't want to take the statement at face value. "I don't understand," she said, inclining her head slightly forward. "Why not?"

I hesitated as though I weren't sure of what my own statement had meant. At that instant I was satisfied that at least I hadn't duped her and had told her the truth. I saw no reason to spin out that truth to the last of its most hurtful details. But when I didn't elaborate, she leaned forward, looked at me the more expectantly, and reminded me:

"You always gave me the impression he was doing well."

"Well ... maybe because, sometimes, I thought he was. I thought he had to be making progress. We were going over the same things so many times that it seemed to me it had to be sinking in. Maybe some of it has—I don't know. But not much."

She sat watching me, waiting for me to go on. So far what she had heard wasn't an explanation, and she wanted an explanation.

"The thing is," I continued, "Joey doesn't *want* to learn. He doesn't have an interest in it, and he doesn't have an interest in it because ... well, he just doesn't."

She shook her head a little, as though she didn't understand what I was getting at.

"Mrs. Larke," I said, "I don't think he can do it."

"What do you mean? Do what?" she asked quietly, staring at me.

"I mean that I don't think he's cut out for academics," I said.

With her head tilted slightly to one side she looked at me with a curious, uncertain intensity; she wasn't, even then, quite sure what I was getting at. Uncomfortably I continued:

"You know, everybody's different. Everybody has things they're good at, and things they're not so good at. I don't think Joey's meant to be a good scholar, or even a mediocre one. It's not who he is. But," I said, consciously putting a lighter, more encouraging tone into my voice, "I'm sure he has talents in other areas. It might be better in the long run to try to find out what those are, and encourage them. School might not exactly be the right way for him. I mean, in the future—after high school. I think that expecting him to go beyond that might make him very unhappy."

"I can't believe you're saying that," she said, though she did not sound genuinely surprised. "He has to go to college and get a degree and—make something of his life. What are you talking about?"

"I'm just saying that even getting his general education is going to be difficult for him—maybe more difficult for him than for others. In that case ... in my opinion ... he shouldn't be forced to go to college if he doesn't want to. There are other things that he might want to do that don't require a college education, and which he might good at."

"Like what?" she asked, with something of a challenge in her voice.

"Well, I don't know, offhand—"

"Maybe he could be a street sweeper? Oh, I know: I'll enroll him in car washing school. Is that the kind of thing you think he can do?"

(I was reminded of Mr. Miller's cynicism, "... the best her grandson can hope for is a job one day at a restaurant washing dishes.")

I looked away from her and felt my face warm with embarrassment. Out of the corner of my eye I saw the white envelope still on the coffee table and had a new sense of having lost it—of having forfeited that week's pay, since there was no way I would be able, in good conscience, to take it. A part of me was grateful for not having had this conversation with her before today, and so having lost that much more income.

"That's not what I mean, Mrs. Larke," I said. "But like everyone else, he has to find something he's good at, something he wants to do and has a natural aptitude for. Maybe he could ... "—I stopped and fumbled internally for some example of what her grandson might be good at, but each time a career occurred to me it was dismissed as ridiculously unlikely given the limited capacities of the boy. Under the pressure of having to say something, I recalled Joey's drawings and ventured, "Maybe drawing. He likes to do that. It comes naturally to him. Perhaps he could be a painter, an artist—"

"Please!"

—The expletive exploded from her lips with all the force of insulted high pride, with an almost shocked surprised at having been condescended to. She leaned back a little in her seat and half-smiled, half-sneered as she considered the audacity of anyone trying to convince her of her grandson's artistic talent. But no doubt recalling how she herself had once extolled Joey's drawings, she could not carry her resentment too far—certainly could not accuse me of trying to make a fool of her—and was perhaps angriest at the thought of my having, as it were, used her own weapon against her. Her lips compressed and she looked at me narrowly before saying:

"His drawings are ridiculous and you know it!"

"Well ... he's only a boy. Maybe if he were to go to art school or something he might—"

"I said, his drawings are ridiculous," she repeated, interrupting me imperiously. "He has no more talent for art than you do for laying down railroad tracks. An 'artist'! Please!"

—And she looked at me hard, silently demanding of me not to add insult to injury by trying to pull over her eyes some preposterous length of wool.

And I realized that that was just what I had done. In order to spare myself the discomfort of telling her a hard truth I had (Mr. Miller, there you go: you old, cynical goat, you win after all!) tried to "dupe" her.

Only, there was no real duping her anymore. She was too experienced in life, in the ways of world, to allow her trust to be taken advantage of. She set on me a pair of eyes that were calm, hard, strangely unyielding; they seemed to pin me to my seat, to constrain my person till I had given way and done what she insisted I do: drop every pretense and be completely, unabashedly honest. I told myself, "Yes, tell her the truth. Why should you lie? She's a nice woman, a good person; she's always done right by you. Don't lie to her." And so I said:

"Well, I don't know, then. I don't know what he might be good at."

Oh, yes, there's a great deal to be said for straightforwardness, for total honesty, for telling it "like it is." But at what cost? And when is the cost too much? Mrs. Larke was willing to accept the sad truth about her grandson, but I could see how much it hurt her to hear it spoken of by another, by a stranger, whose much more objective opinion must demolish whatever particles of hope she clung to for the future prestige of her family. The light seemed to go out of her eyes, which shifted away from me. I felt very bad for her just then. In an access of pity I sought to reassure her, to raise her spirits, and continued in a fumbling way:

"You know, books and schooling aren't everything. I mean, it's great to learn and know things, but there's more to life than that.... A lot more. That kind of stuff doesn't really make much difference in the real world. I mean, just look at *me*. I've spent a lifetime in books, trying to learn things and ... *do* things ... and where has it gotten me? Half the time I'm scrounging around for work, and then when I do manage to get a job it's one that I despise and get depressed over, but that I can't leave for the sake of keeping a roof over my head. It's not a very pleasant way to go through life. But that's what it all comes down to for practical purposes, knowing the kinds of things I know ... the things I think you want Joey to know. In the everyday world they don't amount to a hill of beans."

She seemed surprised at my having injected so personal a note into our talk. Her eyes passed over my person in one quick, critical sweep: over the shirt that was faded from having been washed too many times, over the baggy pants bought three years and ten pounds earlier, over the "new" shoes that were new and shiny in the cheapest, most plastic way. In me she was confronted by the way most people lived, and perhaps for the first time in a long time she understood what it meant not to have money—to be insecure, to spend one's life negotiating a tightrope of uncertainty. It must have occurred to her that however disappointed she was in her grandson, she would not have been especially satisfied if he could only have met her expectations by having to live as I did. Or at least it seemed so, for there was something conciliatory in her voice as she said:

"It's not just how well he reads and writes. It's not even whether or not he finishes school. Maybe you think I want that just out of some conventional notion of what one is supposed to do—because I'm a stickler for degrees and titles. But that's not it. I want him to get a good education because I want him to be able to think for himself. I want him to be able to talk to people, and have a good sense of things, and to be respected and .. ."—she left off as though with frustrated inability to articulate what she could only feel to be the deeper truth of the matter. She looked down to the carpeting, then off to one side, then her eyes rose to the wall and fixed themselves on the portrait of herself and her husband as they had been when they were young and happy. Her stern expression gave way a little before good memories that filtered into her mind at the sight of him, at the remembrance of those not-so-distant times when her world had been a different, sweeter place. She returned her eyes to me and said: "Joey has to complete his education. As much as possible, and whether he likes it or not. I won't allow him to be ... vulgar."

So there it was, the real truth, the ultimate admission. In speaking it out to me she must have felt vulnerable and exposed, but I certainly didn't see it—she had had a long lifetime of experience in maintaining a proper outward show. I felt impelled to say something to alleviate her gloomy view of her grandson. I knew what I *wanted* to tell her. I wanted to tell her that practically speaking Joey was the luckiest of boys because in the end it wouldn't matter what he knew or didn't know, or whether his address was fine or rough, for he had a grand inheritance coming to him, and would always live well and make a good show of things. So far as most of the world would be concerned he would be anything but vulgar, and the Larke name would suffer no loss of reputation. —These were the things I would have liked to say, but in the end I only said:

"I wouldn't worry too much about him. Everything will work out alright for him."

"Yes, I'm sure he'll come around," she said, intentionally or not mistaking my words. "It'll just take some time. He's young; just a child. He'll learn. I'll just get others to help him out— others who are qualified and know what they're doing."

That was a jab at me of course, but I took no offense at it. If anything, it seemed to me that it was the least that I deserved. I had let her down. I hadn't fulfilled her reasonable expectations of me. She had paid me a good salary for not many hours work, and she hadn't gotten what she had paid for.

"I do have a suggestion," I said.

She didn't say anything to this; she just looked at me as though she didn't have any choice but to sit there and hear whatever unpleasant thing I would say.

"I don't mean to get involved in your family's personal affairs, but I've been seeing Joey for almost three months now and I think I have a sense of who he is and what might be good for him. Like all kids, he needs guidance ... someone to look up to, take direction from. Someone that can be an example to him. I know you've done the best you can, but sometimes a boy needs someone with whom he has something in common ... you know, a male influence. I was thinking that maybe if he had more contact with his father it might be a good thing for him."

Mrs. Larke stared at me hard for an instant as though she couldn't believe what she had heard—the impertinence of someone, a stranger, daring to get involved in her personal business. But this emotion gave way to a still stronger one as, apparently recalling Joey's father, she exclaimed:

"It's his father that's responsible for everything!"

She looked at me as though it had to be obvious what she meant by that; and seeing that it wasn't, she hesitated between the impulse to explain herself and a proud unwillingness to expose more of her family's private and, as she considered it, checkered past. But then she must have seen that my suggestion about the boy's father had been only well-intentioned and made in complete ignorance about any reasons she might have for despising him. Her challenging posture relaxed and the fire of irritation that had leapt up in her eyes died down a little. She shook her head a few times as though to apologize for her outburst, and looked away from me, looked into the past, and said in a calmer, reflective voice:

"You don't understand. Joey's father isn't ... right for us. He never was. He wasn't ... *like* us. I knew it the minute I saw him—that stupid face of his. No brain, no manners, no sense of dignity; nothing." She said that she had always wondered how her daughter could have found anything even remotely attractive in such a man, especially in light of the fact that the men she had had dated before him had never been good enough for her: she had always found something wanting in them, even in the ones who were handsome, came from good families, and had wonderful prospects for their future. Mrs. Larke painted Joey's father as an obtuse blockhead, as a man not much more refined than a hulking gorilla, and when, seeming to recall his expression more particularly, she mentioned that he would "look at you like a stupid ox" I couldn't help immediately associating that description with Joey's own frequent expression. "I suppose my daughter thought him somehow charming," she said. "Some women are like that, you know.   They see some horror of a throwback and think that's what a man is supposed to be—that *that's* the way men are—and they never think what that might mean for the future, for their children.   How a woman couldn't take that into consideration I will never understand.   I mean, I suppose I can understand how some women have no choice ... how their options for marriage might be limited, and they get lonesome or desperate and so settle for whatever they can get. But my daughter didn't have to 'settle' for anything, ever.   She had everything going for her: she was beautiful.   She could have had anyone.   She could have had the most beautiful—"

She stopped, catching herself from finishing the sentence that would have been the most direct expression yet of her essential contempt for her grandson.   She looked startled, caught off guard, embarrassed by an indiscreet slip.   She knew I knew what she had been about to say.   Another woman would have colored to her roots.   But that grand sense of herself, of her family, her ideals, her pride, held Mrs. Larke in good stead: her poise didn't falter.   She hemmed lightly, nonchalantly, and continued:

"You know what it was—ultimately?   My daughter didn't appreciate what she had.   She wasn't proud of who she was. She was too quick to discount where she had come from, her own way of life, in deference to that of others.   I don't know what made her so insecure like that.   I'll never understand it. She didn't get it from me or my husband, I can tell you that.   It was her own self-doubt that was the end of her."

She paused and watched me for a few seconds.   She heaved a deeper breath and shrugged her shoulders.

"But it's all in the past," she said.   "The best we can do is try to right the wrong—to make things better."   She hemmed again lightly, and sat up a little more stiffly, and seemed to come still more to herself, and continued, "Anyway, I don't give up so easily.   In fact I don't give up at all—ever. Joey will be just fine.   As long as he has the right teachers, the right environment, everything will work out for him.   Because that's what it is, you know: it's the way you're taught—the environment you're in.   *That's* what it is.   And that's why he'll be just fine.   I *know* he will be."

It was as though, after having poured her heart out in a

few minutes of painful honesty, some dearly-held, comforting self-delusion had returned to her. Suddenly I had the mental image of a frail old woman attempting with her last, failing, pitiable bit of strength to hold shut a fortress door against which a horde of powerful barbarians were pounding away with a battering ram: a resistance impossible, utterly hopeless.

I got up to leave. She followed me to the door and I said goodbye to her. She didn't deign to answer; she only nodded and closed the door behind me. For a few seconds I stood there with a sense of regret—for not having helped Joey, for Mrs. Larke and her disappointment in life, and then for myself, who was again faced with unemployment and the ever-present prospect of scrambling to make some kind of living. I started down the flagged walkway to the street but had only taken a few steps when I heard the door open behind me and Mrs. Larke calling my name. She stood behind the screen door, her face shrouded in the shadow, though not so much that its unhappy expression was totally obscured. I feared she was going to give me another piece of her mind—fling at me some final scolding. But when I reached her she merely opened the door and held out the envelope I had left on the coffee table.

"You forgot this," she said.

"No I didn't."

At first she seemed confused: then she understood, and some of her hard disappointment in me seemed to dissipate. In a quiet voice, in which some of the old kindliness seemed to have returned, she said:

"Don't be silly. Take it." And when I didn't at once reach for it, she lifted it a few inches higher as though to prod me on. "Go on. You worked for it."

I was grateful for that last remark, as though it were a concession by her that I had done the best I could do.

"Thanks."

She nodded and stepped back and closed the heavy wooden door. A moment caught me wondering whether I might not speak with her again—perhaps make an offer to continue helping her grandson during the coming school year, even doing it for free; something, anything that would make up for the things I had said not too many minutes before. But I knew that it could only lead to more disappointment for her and Joey and me. I turned around and started off.

Just as I reached the street a familiar truck pulled up and
parked a few feet away: the one belonging to the construction
contractors.   The workmen were coming back from lunch.   I
didn't know any of them by their names, and they didn't know
mine, but over the previous few weeks we had seen one another
in the house and exchanged nods of recognition.   So now, too,
the driver, as he got out of the cab, looked to me and called out,
"Hey, how ya doin'?"

"Good, how about you?"

"Good."

He and two other men, who also acknowledged me with
nods of the head and brief hellos, opened the back of the truck.
One of the men hopped inside and began rummaging about for
tools.

"How's the job going?" I asked

"Oh, it's going!"

"Will it be alright? The house, I mean."

"Ohhh, I think so. In the short run. In the long run ..."—
and he put up both hands in a gesture of uncertainty. Then he
turned back to getting his tools.

I headed toward Station Square and passed under the arch
on my way to Austin Street. I noticed political posters in store
windows and taped to light posts. Those for Antoine Benedict
far outnumbered those for his opponent. No doubt Hope Peaview had put up some or even most of them, and had thus occupied herself in a way she never could have done where she
chose to live, in the "Gardens," where such posters were not permitted. But here among the common folk—among the people
who, so unlike herself, scrabbled for a living—she had been as
busy as a bee. Yes, there he was, her candidate, Representative
Benedict, on a dozen posters: the incumbent of a dozen years;
dressed to impress in his expensive, impeccable, somehow
Mafia-don tailoring; looking out at the world with a white-
toothed, suntanned, smiling face; an American flag patriotically
standing behind him; while over his head and in quotation
marks floated the campaign slogan that had helped to convince
people to vote for him time and time again:

"Building a Better Tomorrow!"

It was just after noon and the sidewalks bustled with

crowds. Taking advantage of this human traffic a Peruvian vendor had set up a cart selling skewers of suspicious meat he was cooking on a grill of questionable cleanliness: from his cart rose huge curdles of black smoke carrying the sickly-sweet odors of seared flesh. A little further on the owner of an Indian restaurant—it had once been a pizzeria—was putting out a sign announcing the daily buffet: all you can eat for a moderate fixed price. On the same block Koreans who owned a cheese shop were taking a delivery from a Russian carrier and apparently there was some discrepancy in the bill of lading because they were engaged in an animated dispute, though apparently neither of them knew much English and half their animosity toward one another was owing to the fact that each side was misinterpreting what the other was saying. At a greengrocer young Mexicans stocked fruit, their radio, set atop a bin of oranges, blaring out Mariachi music broadcast from a local radio station to accommodate an ever-growing audience. A couple of short, squat women from some Central American country went by pushing baby carriages, surrounded by four of their children. They came up just behind an old, white-haired American couple who, at a street corner and beneath the smiling eyes of Antoine Benedict, pressed themselves against a wall in order to let the young family pass them by.

SUCCESS

For Elena Frasheri, the decision to come to America had in many ways been forced upon her by circumstances. Albania was in an economic slump, and in her town of Kashnjet, some thirty miles outside Durres, things were even worse. Every day she saw jobless men roaming the streets or sitting despondently outside their small, ramshackle homes, unkempt, unshaven, awaiting better times and thinking up new ways to make the remnants of their money last just another week longer. Her own father, now sixty-two years old, had lost his job, and her mother made precious little money in a shirt factory. "Elena should come to America," Marta told her parents in a telephone call. She was Elena's older sister and had emigrated to the United States five years before. She had always kept in touch with her family, calling her parents at least once every couple of months to let them know how she was doing and to find out the latest news. "There is nothing in Kashnjet for her. Why don't you ask her how she feels about it? She's already told me she'd like to come here. She could stay with me. And I could get her a job; she can work with my company. Our boss Mr. Brozi is Albanian and he owns the company so just about everybody I work with is Albanian, with the exception of a few Poles and Russians. Believe me, she'll be better off here! She can make up to $500 dollars a week here, and the work isn't so hard." When Elena was given this option she decided that she would take it: she would leave her parents, her town, her life as she had known it; she would make a new, better life for herself in America, in New York City. At the very least it would relieve her parents from the burden of supporting her, over which she felt particularly guilty since she was twenty-five years old now and should have been making her own way. Though her parents objected that they would lose both their children if Elena left them, they did not, in fact, put up much resistance. They knew as well as Elena herself that her prospects in Albania were limited. Elena assured them, moreover, that she would come back often to visit. And so it was that six months later she arrived at Kennedy Airport, falling into the arms of her waiting, older sister whom she had not seen in four years.

She had brought with her three large suitcases stuffed to the hilt and containing all the clothing and personal items she had, after days of consideration, settled on as things to take with her. And yet there were two items that she had not brought for herself but for her sister: a couple of jars of their mother's homemade pilav—grape leaves stuffed with a tasty concoction of rice and onions flavored with pine nuts and parsley and peppers and dill. It was food they had grown up with and adored, and which Elena had recalled Marta telling her that she could never find quite the same thing in America. Marta gave a little shriek of delight when her sister presented these to her. They opened one jar that evening and had it with dinner, Marta never taking a forkful of it without closing her eyes, luxuriating in its taste, and sighing as though for the land and the life from which she had come.

Her whole first week in the city had been spent in a kind of daze, as though her brain were incapable of taking it all in. Such immense buildings, so many different kinds of people, and everyone, everywhere, always hurrying, always in a rush! People walked on the sidewalks here at a pace that would have been considered back home a slow run. Countless thousands of cars and trucks zoomed back and forth on the highways day and night. The honk of horns, the wail of sirens, the thunder of airplanes flying overhead formed the cacophonous but fitting soundtrack to the endless commotion and bustle and energy of the place. When she had for the first time walked on Fifth Avenue amid the lunchtime crowds, she had felt breathless with the sense of riding some gigantic wave of humanity bearing her away despite herself; indeed, she had been a little frightened of so massive a congress of people and had veered off into a less-populated side street in the same way that someone borne along a fast-flowing stream might lunge at a low-hanging branch by which to pull himself to the safety of the tranquil banks. And the stores! There were so many of them, offering everything in the world. She had never suspected how rich the world was in fine and beautiful things till she had walked into Macy's at Herald Square or Saks Fifth Avenue or Bloomingdale's, or strolled into the specialty shops, or lingered before the jewelry stores on 47th Street, there to gaze upon gems fit to emblazon queens. Lovely, fine things; and expensive, of course. Such things would make her dream gorgeous dreams of a sort she had never known before.

Just as Marta had said, she got Elena a job with the same company she worked for, Decco Services, which was in the business of cleaning office buildings. She was given a light blue uniform emblazoned with the Decco Corporate Services logo at its breast and sleeves. The work was not very hard, as Marta had said, though the hours at first took some getting used to, since she had to start at seven in the evening and work till two in the morning. The building to which she was assigned was a skyscraper at 50th Street and Broadway and she was responsible for cleaning three floors: the 35th, 36th, and 37th. At first she had quailed at what had seemed an impossibly gargantuan task. Three whole floors of a sky-scraper?—to be cleaned every night? Marta assured her that the work was not half so extensive as she imagined. "In the first place, you don't have to worry about the desks. Never, ever mess with anything on people's desks, because that's their work and you don't know what those papers mean. So right there, half the floor you don't even have to worry about. The main thing is to keep the rest rooms and the pantries clean, to empty the trash cans, maybe dust off the computers, and vacuum any large spaces. And you don't even have to vacuum every night—you can do it every other night. So you see, it's not so bad."

Elena quickly discovered that her older sister was right about all this: after a few weeks, it was nothing for her to finish a whole floor in a couple of hours and move on to the next one; and depending on how conscientious she wanted to be, she could even save time by dusting and scrubbing a little less thoroughly and have everything done by midnight. By that time she would need the rest, for her feet and legs would be sore from hours of moving about. She would help herself to a cup of tea from one of the pantries and relax for fifteen or twenty minutes in one of the deserted conference rooms. There, sitting in one of the large, comfortable chairs, she would bring the cup to her lips, take a sip, and look about her at the room with its corporate artwork, its grand polished table, its air of rich importance; and think of how different all this was from what she had known back home. Truly, it was a different, grander, more polished and powerful world, this America, this New York!

In order the better to fit into this new, great country, she was determined to learn English. When she and Marta were home in their Queens apartment, Elena would summon up all her attention to listen to the words her sister tried to teach her: "Television ... lamp ... table ... carpet ... wall ... me ... you ... window." Marta would say the word, each time pointing out the object, and Elena would repeat it, more or less correctly, and often with a giggle. How droll English was! But it was the language of a great country, of a great and powerful people, and she was determined to learn it.

"It's a hard language to speak, believe me," Marta said, a little despairingly. "So many rules! So many words! And so many of the words, when you look at them, don't look they way they sound! It's just crazy. And the people here talk so fast! Bla-bla-bla-bla! They jabber at you like chimpanzees! You can't make out half of what they're saying. But you'll learn—you'll learn. It just takes time." In fact her own English was of the most basic and stumbling kind even after four years, and though she had thought about taking classes and learning it properly, she had always resisted doing so, in part because it would have been another expense that she could ill afford, and in part because she was so tired from her job that she naturally wanted to spend any time off in resting.

As it happened, there was no very great pressure on Elena to learn English at work, since so many of the women she worked with were also Albanian, as were a few of the men, who also were employed by Decco. One of these, Thoma, she met on the second week of her assignment, he having just been transferred to her building. He was in his twenties, was tall, good-looking, with a trim mustache, a straight nose, a cleft chin, and a full head of thick black hair. His smile showed a perfect set of very white teeth. They would sometimes meet in the elevator and would strike up a conversation.

"How long have you been in America?" he asked her, the first time they had spoken.

"Only four weeks," she said. "You?"

"Oh, I've been here for five years now."

"Really? You must speak English well, then."

"Oh, I can speak it alright," he said, with a modest shrug, and displayed his ability by babbling off, "'Good morning,' 'How are you,' 'Get lost,' 'Take it easy.'" He smiled widely at having uttered these phrases, and Elena smiled back, her eyes wide with both amusement and an impressed sense of his accomplishment; and she was doubtful about whether or not she would ever have that kind of—as she took it to be— amazing fluency.

Elena knew that Thoma liked her; she had always been able to tell. And she liked him as well because, after all, he was so tall and handsome and sweet. One evening she accepted his offer to eat with him during his dinner break, which like many of the cleaning staff he took at ten o'clock. When she appeared at the empty conference room on the 35th floor, where he had asked her to meet him, she saw him sitting at the long, polished table poring over a menu. "No, no," he said, shaking his head, glancing at the bagged food she was holding and which she had taken from home, "let's order out. My treat. This place has great food"—shaking the menu. "Come here— see what you'd like." Of course, she couldn't read the menu, but he interpreted everything and ordered for them both on the telephone. Once again, she listened with envy and admiration to him place the order in English.

The food was delivered in a large white paper bag and contained in several Styrofoam containers. Thoma took these out and set them down on the table, opening each one, peeking in, and saying, "This one's yours ... mine ... yours ..." Then he opened the cellophane packages containing the paper napkins and plastic spoons and forks, and set them out for himself and her. As they sat there eating and talking, she often noticed his arms and hands, for he wore his shirt with the sleeves rolled up above the elbows. Strong, muscular arms, and his hands large, not too rugged-looking, his nails clean, tapered. The sight of these things filled her with pride, as though she owned him.

"How long have you been working for our company?" Elena asked him.

"Only a few months."

"Where were you working before?"

"Another cleaning company," he said. "I was there for more than three years."

"Why did you leave?"

"Well, I didn't leave, exactly," he said. He hesitated before he admitted, "I was let go."

"Oh. Why?"

Thoma smiled and shook his head, as though he knew she was not likely to understand his reasons. "The boss and I just didn't get along," he said. "He was an American and not very fair to me—not that Americans aren't fair, you understand, it's just that he wasn't to me. Why? Who knows? Some people just don't like other people, I guess. He didn't like me from the first—I could tell. Anyway, that was his prerogative. But I didn't have to put up with it. So one day he started up with me again and I just told him where to go." Unconsciously he had made a loose fist with his left hand and given the table a little pound: a gesture which hinted to Elena that the incident had been far more urgent in nature, and his part in it far more dramatic, than was conveyed in his calm retelling of it. That his charming and good-humored exterior might hide a hot temper gave her some pause even as she admired him for it. "He's so typical," she thought, thinking of the men she had known back home, "so proud, so jealous of his name and image of himself." She was not sure that this was a good thing; like many women she had her reservations about men's notions of honor, which struck her sometimes as boyishly foolish. On the other hand she could see in this behavior a dignity apart and above that of women, and which spoke to and aroused her feminine soul.

They had been eating and talking and laughing for some twenty minutes when Thoma, after a nervous pause, asked, "Listen, there's a movie I wanted to go see this weekend. I was wondering ... how about coming out with me to see it this Saturday?"

Elena accepted. Why not? She had not really taken advantage of the many things to do in New York, and it would be so much more pleasant to do them with someone she liked. Her easy acceptance aroused a smile and sense of relief in Thoma. When they parted that evening she noted with satisfaction and pleasure that in addition to saying goodbye to her he looked at

her with a solemnly hopeful expression and even touched her
arm with gentle affection. She thought of him all the rest of
evening, and the more she thought of him the more happy she
became. She wondered how long it would be till they kissed, for
she was certain that they were going to have a romantic union.
"He's so beautiful!" she exclaimed to herself, reflecting on his
noble features, his tall, lean body, his flashing smile. She imagined herself being held by his strong arms, firmly, protectively.
Her heart was full.

"Oh, why did you do that?" Marta asked her sister, when
she heard about the date she had made with Thoma. "There's
someone I wanted you to meet on Saturday."

"What? Who?"

"One of Victor's friends," Marta replied.

Elena had of course met Victor, who was Marta's boyfriend.
He was also Albanian and was the head waiter at one of the
most exclusive restaurants in the city. He was planning to open
a restaurant of his own in the next few years. He always spoke
of his plans to Marta, who admired him for his industry and
ambition.

"Who is this person?" Elena asked.

"His name is Mendu. He's from Tirana. He's very nice;
you would like him. He works for Unity Financial Holdings
Corporation. Do you know what that is? It's one of the biggest
financial companies in New York—in the world! He works with
the big, big executives. He drives them to their meetings, in
limousines. It's an important job! And," she added, with especial emphasis, and now looking at her sister with the intensity
of an important prognostication, "he's starting his own limousine company. He's a great businessman. He's doing very, very
well even now, but in a few years? Ouf! He'll have everything!
You really should meet him, Elena. He's the kind you want to
meet."

"What's he look like?"

Marta hesitated ever so slightly before saying. "Oh, you
know, kind of average—but he's very, very sweet! You would
like him, believe me."

Elena shrugged almost indifferently. She had no objection
to meeting him, in part because she could not help valuing her
older sister's opinion about men but also because, though she

liked Thoma very much, she had not known him long enough to feel it a betrayal of his trust to go on a date with someone else; and after all, just one date would mean nothing. But she could not go out with Mendu on Saturday, she said; they would have to make it for another time. A half hour and a telephone call later, Marta told her sister that the time had been set for Sunday night.

When Sunday came Elena was in the best, most elevated of spirits, for she had had a good time with Thoma the evening before. The movie they had gone to was a romantic comedy, and though she had been incapable of enjoying it on account of the language barrier it had been exciting for her to sit there in the darkened theater with Thoma beside her. She had thrilled each time he had leaned close into her to whisper in her ear some translation of the dialogue. Later, they had walked hand-in-hand down Second Avenue and stepped into a small pizza restaurant to have something to eat. There, sitting under rather harsh fluorescent lights at a small wooden table that wobbled unevenly beneath them, they happily enough had their meal, talking, laughing, sometimes falling into silences during which they would look into each other's eyes only to turn away with some embarrassment but also with hearts brimming with the anticipation of a closer and more fulfilling union. At the end of the evening, Thoma accompanied her back home on the subway and walked her back to her apartment building. He asked her out again for next week, smiled gratefully when she accepted, and, before leaving, kissed her goodnight. It was hard for her to sleep that night for thinking about him.

But now Sunday was here, and she was to meet Mendu. As she prepared herself for doing so she smiled and laughed a little to think of how busy her personal life had become. Quite the popular one, she! Finally enjoying herself, going out, having fun! And there flitted through her mind, with a joy so keen it was almost painful to consider for more than a few seconds at a time, a life with Thoma, as his wife; she, a married woman, with a husband she loved, a home, children, happiness forever after ...

Victor and Mendu were to arrive at six o'clock, but at a quarter to seven they had not yet shown up. Elena had not eaten anything since noon in order to build up an appetite for this evening but she was so hungry that she told Marta she had to have a little something or she would get a headache. She remembered one of the jars of pilav had not yet been eaten, and she decided to have a little of it—no more than a few mouthfuls—in order to quell the worst of her hunger pangs. But when she opened the jar she smelled a foul odor, and when she tasted its contents she at once spit it out. The once fresh, delicious food had spoiled.

"The air must have gotten into it," Marta remarked, shaking her head as she took the jar from her sister and threw it into the trash can. She encouraged Elena to hold out just a few more minutes with, "They're bound to be here soon. Just be a little more patient."

No sooner had she spoken than the buzzer for the front door sounded, and a few minutes later the men entered the apartment, offering apologies for their lateness.

At the sight of Mendu Elena was taken aback and gave her sister a glance of alarmed accusation as though she had been misled. For Mendu was certainly not what she had hoped to see. Standing just under medium height, his torso seemed a little too long for his short legs, and he had something of a belly. His face was round and chubby, his eyes were too close set, and his complexion was pale and somehow effete. His ears protruded strangely, the tops and bottoms sticking out and creating a weird concave shape. Not only was he not good looking but he was also considerably older than Elena: she could see at a glance that he had to be at least ten years her senior. Compared with Thoma, this Mendu was absurd!

And yet no sooner had she perceived his diminutive size and ill-favored features than her disapproval was mollified somewhat by the succeeding impressions of his dress. For his clothes were of the very best cut and kind. The jacket, of English fabric, looked soft and expensive even from across the room; and his pants were made of a material of corresponding fineness, and draped perfectly over his shoes, which were new and shiny. Of course none of this made him one whit taller or better-looking, or hid the disproportion of his pear-shaped body, but no one with two eyes in her head could ignore the rich luxury of those clothes. When introduced to Elena, he drew up his small person with all the pride of a soldier receiving a medal of honor and said in an easy tone of voice how much he had been looking forward to meeting her. He stretched out his right hand to take hers, and as he did so Elena noticed the elegant gold bracelet peeking out from beneath his cuff. He smelled ever so faintly of fine cologne.

"Yes, nice to meet you too," she said, politely enough.

They all went to a restaurant in Soho, a new place that had opened only six months before and had earned rave reviews in the New York *Times*. Mendu had heard about it from one of his "clients." He also mentioned that many celebrities went there and that perhaps tonight they might see one. The lighting throughout was invitingly subdued; the tables, covered in white linen and set with fine china and sparkling crystal wine glasses, were spaced far apart among large potted plants which gave the place the feel of some exotic outdoors; and this delightful ambience was furthered by a brass and marble fountain set in the middle of the space and whose tinkling waters created a soothing audible backdrop. The maître d' led Mendu and his "party" to the table he had reserved. As she was escorted through the dining area, Elena noted with pleasure the aura of sophistication and refinement of the people dining here. The young women were pretty and elegant, wore fine clothes, and comported themselves with an air of proud glamor; and the men, dressed in formal attire, looked as though they had high positions in the world. This was especially true of the older gentlemen, who, despite their age, looked so well-scrubbed and fresh; —yes, on account of their grooming even more attractive sometimes than men half their age;—and who in every instance sat across from a woman much younger than themselves, and pretty. Elena wondered who all these people were and what their lives were like.

It was a lavish dinner, with one expensive course after another. Elena had never seen food prepared so ornately, each element of it set perfectly on its plate and served by a smiling waiter who treated her as though she were royalty; saying, as he set down a plate before her, or filled her glass with wine, "Ma'am." Mendu was talkative and charming. As he spoke he leaned back and put an arm over the top of his chair and looked about him easily, assuming an air of total confidence and control. To Elena he seemed to fit right in to this place; he was just like one of those other men at all the other tables, well-dressed, confident, sophisticated; a man who had done important things, or would do them, and who wanted and knew how to enjoy the best things in life. She was the more confirmed in this idea of him when, during dinner, Mendu spoke of the places he usually went to, the people he had seen: the Waldorf, the Plaza, Trump Tower—Mr. Lawrence R. Fisher, who had just closed this multi-million- dollar deal, or Mr. Barry S. Graves, whom he had driven to the airport for a flight to Japan, where he was to meet that country's Minister of Finance. He dropped one name after another and it was obvious that his job brought him into contact with important people from all over the world. Marta, Victor, and Elena listened intently to these stories. He often directed his words to Elena, smiling widely. She noticed that his teeth were small and, on the bottom, crooked.

When dinner was over Mendu insisted on paying for everyone. Marta, Victor, and Elena objected, but he would hear none of it. "It was my pleasure, my pleasure!" he insisted, waving away their continued pleas that he let them chip in. He took out his wallet and Elena could not help noticing the thick wad of cash in it—all fifty-dollar bills! But he did not pay with cash, for that wallet also held a collection of credit cards, each one in a plastic sleeve and overlapping the one beneath it. He flipped through a few of these till he found the one he was looking for: it was impressively platinum-colored, with, at its center, an intricate portrait of the sort one might find on currency itself. Magnificent was the indifference with which he slid so important-looking a card out of its holder and placed it in the leather fold in which the waiter had brought the check. He handed the fold back to the waiter with a jovial, "Here you are!" A few minutes later, when the waiter returned with a receipt to be signed, Mendu reached into an inner pocket of his fine jacket and brought out a gold-colored pen with which he scratched out his signature with quick authority.

Later that evening, when Marta and Elena had returned to their apartment, Marta told her sister:

"Mendu liked you very much. Victor told me. He wants to see you again."

"Oh, I don't know," Elena said. But in fact she was secretly flattered that he wanted to see her. She was hardly thinking now about how short he was, or his little belly, or how far his funny-looking ears stood out. On the contrary, over the course of evening she had come to like him more and more. He was so charming, such a good conversationalist, so good-natured! —qualities, surely, that were much more important than mere physical appearances. And so it was that when her sister insisted that she go out with him at least one more time, Elena, with but little hesitation, nodded an assent and said, "Alright."

For the next month she dated two men simultaneously, not letting either of them know about the other. But there was no longer any question in her mind about whom she wanted to be with. Thoma was certainly a very sweet man, and tall and handsome, with a wonderful sense of humor and, she sensed, a great fund of tenderness; but when she would see him in the building, pushing his huge cleaning cart in his light blue overalls, she would at once compare him with Mendu, who, what with his impeccable clothes, his half dozen credit cards, his important job, his confident air and the assurance of an easy if not resplendent future, seemed to her so much more attractive despite his obvious physical shortcomings. She told herself that it was not just a matter of money or status that made her prefer Mendu, but rather the character or personality which had enabled him to acquire such things. That was a fine, even a sophistical distinction, but Elena convinced herself that it was legitimate and absolved her from any unattractively mercenary motives. On the other hand she had to admit to herself that when she would see Thoma she would feel a kind of breathless admiration and longing of the kind she did not and could not feel with Mendu; but she always made a conscious effort to tamp down this reaction, telling herself that it arose from a foolish and superficial immaturity. For surely looks weren't everything! Surely they weren't even so very important! Surely it was more important that a man had "character," had made something of himself in the world, that he was, as she had begun to think of Mendu, "successful."

One evening when Elena and Thoma were eating together during their dinner break, he suggested that they go out again this coming weekend. Elena told him that she couldn't do so because she had made "other plans." He asked what those plans were. She answered vaguely, off-handedly, saying with a shrug,

"Oh, there are just some things I need to do." But something in the way she said this—in the way she blinked, smiled quickly and falsely, and then turned her eyes away—made him suspicious. He had in fact noticed over the last few weeks a certain cooling in her attention toward him. He asked her outright if she was seeing someone else. Elena's first reaction was to shake her head and utter not a denial so much as an expression of surprise at his inquiry. Then it occurred to her that she ought not to feel any guilt over wanting to date Mendu, for there was no real commitment between herself and Thoma, who would have to be told sooner or later. She managed her disclosure in the gentle, roundabout way typical in such cases; saying that as a matter of fact she was seeing someone else—nothing serious, mind you—he was just a friend—they just spent some time together—they enjoyed each other's company so much— they liked doing things together—it was nothing serious—she was single, after all ...

With eyes downcast, Thoma listened expressionlessly. He understood at once what the word "friend" meant in this instance. "Who is he?" he asked, looking back up to her and managing a smile as though he had calmly accepted her commitment to someone else. "Is he an American?" For he could almost understand how she would have preferred to him an American, someone who was born here, who was established here, who was accepted entirely, and under whose aegis, as it were, she might be made to feel more comfortable in this new country.

Elena shook her head. "No, he's not American. He's Albanian."

"Oh," Thoma said, genuinely surprised. "Where did you meet him?"

"He's a friend of my sister's."

Pride prevented Thoma from expressing his disappointment, and a reasonable understanding of the shortness of his association with Elena restrained his impulse to blame her for infidelity. He knew that he had no real claim on her. Their relationship had been incipient, inchoate; headed, undoubtedly, toward something more serious—if this had not occurred. His spirit sank a little but he was able to summon up an appearance of happiness for her as he said, "Well, then ... good for you.

He's a lucky guy."

Elena was relieved at having told the truth to Thoma; now she would not have to make excuses about why she could not see him on this or that day. At the same time she lamented the fact that she had had to make a choice between him and Mendu. If only the good points in each of them could have been combined in one of them!—that would have been perfection in her eyes and her choice would have been easy and immediate. As it was, she quickly, even as she sat there, tallied up what she was losing in letting Thoma go and what she was gaining in throwing in her lot with Mendu, regarding whom in the end she could only tell herself with weary acceptance, "It's just that his character is better." Yet a part of her doubted her own conviction.

One weekend Mendu planned to take Elena out to Long Island, to Oyster Bay, for a fishing excursion. He assured her that even if she didn't fish, she would enjoy the boat, which was large and comfortable. However, the night before he received an unwonted weekend assignment of picking up one of the company's top executives from Newark Airport and driving him to his Park Avenue apartment. "It won't take more than forty-five minutes, maybe an hour," Mendu told Elena. "Why don't you come with me? Once we drop him off at home, we can just head out to Long Island. We'll save some time that way." Elena happily agreed.

The man they were to pick up was James T. Huntington II. He had appended the "II" to his name when, at twenty-five years of age, he had been hired by Unity Financial Holdings Company, for he was sure that it made him sound as important as he hoped one day to be. Of course, this affectation had been sneered at behind his back by his coworkers and managers who, among themselves, laughingly referred to him as "Henry VIII." Only when, after two decades of tireless work and slow promotions, he had risen into a position of high pay and power did his self-styled eminence take on a patina of legitimacy, at least by those who worked under him and on whose good graces their own futures in large measure depended. Ordinarily he was a polite man, if rather on the quiet side, but this latest business trip had worn him out. It was one of ten that he had had to take in the last three months. In fact he had been working twelve-hour days for the last two weeks and his nerves were worn to a frazzle. To make matters worse, he was going through what is commonly referred to as a "mid-life crisis," which in plain English means that he had come to see with despairing and almost frightening clarity how far below his youthful dreams of happiness his life had turned out to be. For there he was, forty-four years of age, single, empty inside, without a sense of real accomplishment, knowing that he had never done anything especially exciting or memorable, and hating the job that had extorted the best and most vigorous years of his life in exchange merely for the ability to buy the expensive things he did not even have the time to enjoy. His despisement of what his life had become poisoned his view of the world. As often happens in such cases, he blamed others for the unhappiness that arose out of his own shortcomings. Chief among these was his having come to take seriously the corporate notion of "excellence," that is to say, an excruciating and inhuman attention to the most petty details. Thus he was wont to say that while he did not "suffer fools lightly" he never ceased running into them because their natural indifference to minutiae seemed to him proof of a despicable inability. Such a man was bound to find the grossest, most intolerable flaws and errors everywhere in the happenstance of daily life, just as someone who wears dark sunglasses is bound to see the world in muted shades. At work he gritted his teeth in irritation at some underling who had, say, made a mistake in a document or report, even if it were only the infinitesimally small one of an inconsistent space between one footnote and another. He had fired more than one secretary for having taken a message for him on a miscellaneous piece of paper rather than on a message pad. He mumbled imprecations against his dry cleaner if there was a crease in the paper sleeve over the returned shirt or jacket; he breathed impatiently at whoever was running the local grocery store if the selection of produce was not what he expected; and if a bus or a subway train came late, he would stomp his feet and swear to himself that someone was going to pay for it—that he was going to call someone and make sure someone got fired. Some nights after a long day of tolerating a hundred irritations he would lie in bed and feel his limbs tingling nervously. In the last few weeks he hadn't been able to sleep well; he had woken up repeatedly in the middle of the night, bothered with bad dreams. He was a time bomb waiting to explode, each check and setback in his life, however small and either real or imagined, another tick forward to the moment of combustion.

When he got into the limousine that was waiting for him at the airport, he said not a word, merely nodding to Mendu who opened the door for him and greeted him with a deferential, "Hello, sir, how are you this morning?"

"Who's that?" the executive asked, noticing Elena in the front seat.

"Oh, a friend of mine, sir," Mendu said, cheerfully. "After we take you home, we're going out to Long Island."

James T. Huntington II sat in the back seat with a tight-lipped expression. After getting behind the wheel Mendu glanced up into the rearview mirror and could see that his passenger was irritated—whether or not because of Elena's presence he couldn't tell.

Now, no roadways are more notorious for traffic and unexpected delays than those going into the city of New York. Though ordinarily the traffic going into the city from North Jersey was light on a Sunday morning, today there had been an accident along the route: a tractor trailer, hauling fuel oil, had overturned. The police had managed to clear only one lane and traffic was backed up. Mendu, Elena, and James T. Huntington II became part of this traffic. After he had stopped for ten minutes and then went forward at a crawl, Mendu noticed in the rearview mirror how his passengers would look up impatiently from the papers he had spread out on the briefcase lying on his lap. "What's going on?" he asked, craning his neck a little as he looked through the windshield.

"Oh, traffic, sir," Mendu said easily, though he was a little nervous to see that his passenger was fidgeting. He turned to Elena and smiled with a reassurance he himself did not feel.

With each minute in traffic, the executive in the back seat became more restless. He looked at his watch or shifted his gaze down to his paperwork, which he would shake brusquely, and which he regarded for only a moment before turning his eyes away, outside the windows, as though to see if there had been any change in the pace of advancement, only to find that there was none, and to let out quick, deep, exasperated breaths.

He shifted in his seat. He mumbled impatiently to himself, "What's going on out there?" Mendu said to himself in the American vernacular he had come to learn so well: "He's pissed."

For forty minutes they crawled along, and for most of that time James T. Huntington II was becoming more and more irritated. "This is ridiculous!" he kept muttering, shaking his head. "People! People! On a Sunday! Ridiculous!"

Though she did not understand what he was saying, Elena could tell by the tone of his voice that he was upset. She glanced at Mendu, who glanced back at her with an uncomfortable smile before quickly returning his eyes to the road. She could tell that Mendu was tense and preferred that she not ask him any questions or even speak to him.

The traffic finally started moving again. As soon as Mendu reached the scene of the accident, and then slowly passed the policeman who was waving the cars along, he accelerated quickly and drove toward New York City as fast as he dared, at almost 70 miles per hour. A wave of relief passed over him to think that this more normal pace had assuaged the frustrated passenger behind him. But as he neared the Lincoln Tunnel going into Manhattan, there was another delay, although not quite so bad as the one he had just left. The traffic moved steadily but slowly. James T. Huntington II, in addition to continually looking up, snapped the papers in his hands and now and then stomped the floor. "Damn it!" he said, under his breath.

Once they had entered Manhattan, they ran into still another problem. There was a parade down Fifth Avenue and many of the side streets had been blocked off or detours had been set up. The traffic was heavy. Cabs seemed to be everywhere, honking furiously and always trying to nudge their way before other vehicles. Mendu, in an effort to get his passenger home as quickly as possible, drove more recklessly than he otherwise would have done. He squeezed his limousine between cars, accelerated swiftly, and in a few instances drove right over curbs in order to beat out a traffic light about to turn red. On account of the parade the city was especially crowded with pedestrians, who in New York seem to delight in taking suicidal chances with oncoming vehicles. Mendu repeatedly honked his horn at them, and in one instance he had to come to an abrupt halt when a bevy of young women, holding flags from Honduras, ran out a hundred feet in front of him to cross the street. With each red light he came to—with each street he sharply turned into—he could hear his passenger mutter something under his breath. Indeed he dared not even look in the rearview mirror anymore, for he could feel the tension rising in the back seat.

But finally they were on Park Avenue, and James T. Huntington II's building was only ten blocks away. Mendu accelerated toward it. A few times he could not beat the traffic light turning from yellow to red and had to stop short; and each time this happened he himself let out a deep breath, as though of frustration. Elena noticed that he was tapping his left foot nervously.

The building in which the executive lived was grandly imposing with a marble facade, a palatial foyer, and a doorman who wore a uniform that looked like some extravagant military costume: it was green with gold braiding, gilt buttons, and tassels hanging at the shoulders. For the people who lived here paid huge sums of money for their apartments, and they expected their doormen—just as they expected the carpeting in the lobby or the sconces in the hallways—to display some correspondingly obvious degree of splendor.

Just as Mendu was turning in toward the sidewalk in order to let off his passenger, a white van, which had seemed to be parked, speedily pulled out in front of him, cutting him off. Mendu braked hard to avoid a collision and beeped his horn impatiently. The driver of the van, a young, coarse-looking man, leaned out of his window and yelled an obscenity at Mendu, at the same time sticking out his hand with an extended middle finger. But far more disconcerting was the fact that the sudden stop had sent James T. Huntington II lunging forward so that the papers he had been reading and collating went flying onto the floor, and he himself hit his head on the back of the driver's seat. He nearly scrambled on the floor as he grabbed up his papers in movements so fast and abrupt that it seemed he was clawing to hold on to life itself. Mendu was worried that he had injured himself and asked, "Are you alright, sir?" But there was no answer. The executive continued to grab up his papers with grunts of effort, and when he finally got them all in the briefcase he slammed it shut. His nerves, already stretched their uttermost for the last forty-five minutes, if not, indeed, for the last few months, had finally snapped.

He slid over to the door and flung it open with such force that there was a sharp *"crack"* as though one of the hinges had broken off. He jumped out of the back seat, violently pulling out his briefcase after him, then slammed the door shut so fast and hard that it sounded like a gunshot. Mendu and Elena jumped in their seats. He took a single long stride up to Mendu, who lowered his window despite his foreboding of something bad about to happen and looked up meekly into a furious, empurpled face. The veins on the executive's forehead were standing out as though they would burst; the muscles of his neck bulged and corded; his brows were knit tightly over eyes intense, even fiery with a rage that had been years in the making and was now given a loose.

"What the hell is wrong with you!" the executive screamed, bending his body forward, and almost choking on the volume of his words. "What the hell are you doing! You drive like shit! Did you know that?—you drive like shit! You're worthless! Worthless! A worthless piece of shit! Oh, I can't stand this anymore! I just can't—I can't! That's it! The end! What's your name! I swear to God, I'm going to do something about this! I swear to God I am! What is your name, I said!"

"What's my ... my name?" Mendu stammered.

"What the hell is your name! What is it! I want to know what your name is, and I want to know it NOW!"

"My name is ... Mendu ... Mendu Varoshi ..."

James T. Huntington II stomped his foot and slammed his briefcase against the door of the limousine with a force and malevolence that seemed to dare the driver to get out of his seat and expose himself to a direct assault. He heaved his breaths as though he had just run a quarter of a mile; his whole frame shook with nervous energy. "Mendu!" he shouted. "Mendu? Mendu? What? What the hell kind of a name is that! What the hell is going on with this country! No one's an American anymore! Stupid foreigners! That's all I see around me! Idiots! Idiots! Why do they send an idiot piece of shit like you to pick me up! I can't stand it anymore. It's too much! Too much! Why don't you go back to where you came from and *let me alone!* You're a worthless piece of shit! Worthless! You should all drop dead—all of you! ALL OF YOU!"

—And with that mad exclamation, that explosive outburst that could have been heard for blocks away, the executive stormed off, taking long, stomping strides, expectorating curses as he went, and disappeared into the entrance of his building even as the liveried doorman, who held the door open for him, watched in blank amazement as he passed by.

Mendu sat behind the wheel of his limousine with his eyes fixed on the dashboard in front of him. He seemed stunned, frozen, as though he were a shell-shocked soldier in a battlefield. Elena had not understood what the enraged man had shouted, but she had understood that he had abused Mendu vilely, and she herself was shocked to dumbness by the ferocity of the attack. She watched as Mendu slowly and calmly opened the door and stepped outside. He stood there for some moments gazing down at the door of his vehicle and assessing the damage that had been done to it. Then, just as slowly, as though he were moving in a dream, he got back into the limousine and sat with his hands on the wheel.

Elena was not sure where to turn her eyes. She dared not look at him. She could feel his humiliation; it emanated from him in waves. She merely listened as he placed the car in gear and turned the wheel in order to pull out into Park Avenue. For some time they drove in a painfully awkward silence. She made no effort to speak to him because unsure of what she should say. She knew that if she mentioned what had happened it would only deepen his humiliation, while on the other hand if she tried to lighten the atmosphere by talking about something else she would only highlight the matter in trying to avoid it. All she could do, she felt, was to wait till he said something and then follow his lead. She was prepared to commiserate with him, or excoriate with him, or to speak of something that had nothing to do with the man they had left behind; —anything to dissipate the oppressive awkwardness that hung over them.

Only when they had left Manhattan, and had been riding eastward on the Long Island Expressway for some fifteen minutes, did Mendu speak. Elena turned to him at his first word and was surprised to see that he had regained his wonted easy demeanor and smile. Considering what had happened to him not too long before, this change in his behavior and attitude was remarkable. She knew that she ought to be grateful for this because it would help to retrieve the rest of the day, but a part of her regarded it with a sense of weary resignation.

"After we get off the boat we'll have lunch at the Fisherman's Café," he was saying, his voice as chatty, as cheerful as ever. "Let me tell you, the food is excellent there—a bit on the pricey side, but really excellent. We'll have lobster. We'll order a nice bottle of champagne. I'm sure you'll like it. A lot of important people go there. It's a very exclusive place—very!"

POISON

Every woman in New York City knows how easy it is to find a man, and how almost impossibly hard it is to find a good one, for the good ones are always taken or otherwise unavailable: either married, homosexual, or dead.

For Melissa Adler there were times when she had thought she'd never find a good man, the right one whom she had dreamed about, whom she would love with her whole heart and want to marry and start a family with. But finally here she was, thirty-three years old and dating the prince who had shown up after she had kissed so many frogs.

His name was Colin and he was thirty-five years old, though he looked much younger; frankly, he looked younger than she did. He was a chemist who worked for a pharmaceutical company a few miles outside of Hoboken, to which he commuted each day from his apartment on the Upper West Side. He had a lot of other things going for him other than good looks, mature youth, and a secure, lucrative job. He didn't have the "baggage" of ex-wives or children, and promiscuity had never been a part of his character. He was a good lover and a good friend.

She had fallen in love with him hard and fast. After only a month of dating him she was sure that he was "the one"—the man she would marry. Of course she dared not tell him so; she knew men generally were scared off by emotional commitment. Instead she played that shrewd game of making herself indispensable to him by satisfying him physically and offering him the comfortable and sometimes necessary refuge of a trusted confidante. She introduced him to her family, her mother and brother, who liked him. Indeed Mrs. Adler did all she could to further the relationship. As a doting mother she had always been critical of her daughter's boyfriends, for who could be good enough for her darling daughter, her precious gem, her little angel? But lately even she had begun to see how that angel's wings were looking a little the worse for wear—how the gem had lost some of its sparkle owing to a certain age-related patina—and realized that it would be in her daughter's best interest not to criticize but rather to advocate for her daughter's boyfriends, and so help along an overdue marriage. Thus not a breath of negativity escaped her lips regarding Colin; on the contrary, she praised him to the skies. "Now *that's* what I call a good man!" she told Melissa from the first, her eyes bright, enthusiastic, entirely pleased. "He's beautiful! What a sweetheart! Oh—I love him!" She would hug her daughter as though in congratulations at having finally found someone worthy of her.

Colin lived on West 77th Street just off Broadway in a prewar building whose lobby was a glory of polished marble, mirrors, and art deco coffers. He had a large apartment with three bedrooms, one of which he had converted into what he called his "lab." The first time Melissa stepped into this room she was astonished at how completely appointed it seemed to be with technical paraphernalia. A low table extended three quarters of the way around it and was loaded with all kinds of receptacles and instruments. There must have been tens of thousands of dollars worth of equipment there. The room had an odd chemical smell even though the window was always kept a little open for ventilation. Various cartons were stacked against the wall, and on the face of some of these were labels in large red letters spelling out the word "WARNING" or, still more disturbing, the image of a black skull and crossbones set within a yellow diamond shape beneath the word "POISON."

"What do you do in here?" she had asked him, gazing from one mysterious item to the next.

"My work."

"You take work home with you?"

"No, no: this is my *own* work—my own project."

"What is it?"

He laughed. "I'll tell you one day."

"Why not tell me now?"

"It's just experiments," he said in a dismissive tone of voice.

In part because she sensed he preferred not telling her about what he did in this room, and in part because science was alien to her in the same way that a masculine interest in machinery or astronomy might be, she accepted his essentially noninformative answer as sufficient.

Yes, Colin was the most perfect man imaginable except that he was also one of the most secretive. He was not just secretive about the "work" that he did in his home laboratory but also about his past generally. Everything she had ever learned about his parents and brothers and sisters, about the place where he had grown up, the school he had gone to, or the major events in his life, she had had to ask him about with some insistence, to dig and dig until he had relented his bits and pieces of information. His unwillingness to be candid about these things irritated her. She had always been frank with him about everything, even about the most intimate experiences of her life. She regarded his unwillingness to be equally forth-oming as a frustrating, demoralizing sign of some lack of trust toward her; and how could their relationship ever hope to grow with such an obstacle before it? But one evening after dinner they went back to his apartment and drank a bottle of wine together, and without any prompting he talked candidly of his past.

He hadn't, he said, always wanted to be a chemist. When he had been a child it had been the furthest thing from his mind. In those days he had wanted to be—if she could imagine it!—the captain on a submarine. The notion of diving to the bottom of the sea, and finding in its cold dark depths all kinds of marvels, had fascinated his boyish mind. Slowly he had grown out of that infatuation, and now, of course, he would no more want to dive to the bottom of the sea in a submarine than he would want to stroll through Central Park at two in the morning. In maturing his interests had become much more mundane. He had become interested in chemistry. He had found that subject endlessly fascinating. By the time he was in college it was the only thing in the world he was interested in. He had studied the subject with an intensity that delighted his professors and worried his parents, who, while proud of his enthusiasm, thought they saw in it a certain unhealthy single-mindedness of purpose. They often counseled him to get his nose out of his large, heavy chemistry books; to go out, "clear his head," have some fun. They wanted him to have a more balanced life. But the only balance he was interested in was the one wholly tilted toward that one side in which his passions lay. He graduated from Cornell University with top honors and easily found his first job with the chemical conglomerate where he had worked for eight years before assuming a more lucrative position with his current employer, of whom he always spoke disparagingly.

"The pay is alright, I guess," he said. "But it's so much time! I never have time for myself!"

"You work five days a week like everyone else," Melissa said.

"Well, yes, but ... five days is too much! That only leaves me two on weekends, and whatever vacation time I get, and ... well, that's just not enough."

"So take some days off," she suggested.

He regarded her with the grateful but pitying indulgence one shows toward someone who has made a well-intentioned suggestion about something they know nothing about.

"It wouldn't be enough," he said.

Apart from his secretiveness there was one other characteristic of his that continually disheartened her. He was completely, almost bewilderingly indifferent to the conventional expressions of romance she had come to expect. Valentine's Day came and went without a bouquet of flowers or a box of chocolate. When she mentioned it to him he apologized, said he had forgotten, and made it up to her the next day; by which time of course it no longer meant anything. Again, her birthday came and went, and that too he had apparently forgotten. She didn't remind him of it; she didn't want him to think she was fishing for gifts. She would have taken deeper umbrage at these things if in other ways he was equally thoughtless, but whenever she was with him he was attentive and affectionate. It was enough for her—for now at least—to feel that he returned her affection.

She stayed at his apartment three nights a week, but on those days she remained home she reflected on how their relationship had settled into a routine of having dinner and sleeping together at appointed times. Was she only to see him on Mondays, Wednesdays, and Fridays, with a Saturday or Sunday thrown in at some distant interval along the way? She couldn't help feeling that she was being used, was becoming a commodity to be partaken of when he felt the need, with no consideration of her own desires. On the other hand she feared that to protest against this so soon in their relationship would make her seem demanding or, worse, nagging. She told herself that with Colin, as with anyone else, she had to take the bad with the good, and further consoled herself with the thought that in time, as they drew still closer together, she would be with him much more. One Thursday morning as they both left his apartment building to go their different ways to work, he gave her a quick kiss goodbye with, "I'll talk to you later! We'll get together again Friday!" She smiled, nodded, and seemed as cheerful as ever; but just then her resentment flared up. Throughout the rest of the day the thought of having become a convenience for him rankled in her proud soul. The more she considered it the more unfair it seemed to her. She called him at work, intending to discuss the matter with him, even to castigate him, but at the sound of his voice she thought better of it and referred to the matter with a gentler, "You know, Colin, I was thinking ... we're only seeing each other three days a week. I'd really like to see you more than that."

"I'd like to see you more too!" he said, cheerfully, wholly oblivious to the fact that her apparently casual suggestion arose from a deep and considered anxiety. "I wish I could! But I have so much work just now."

"And just what is it again you're doing?" she asked, fidgeting as she spoke, continually having to tamp down her annoyance.

"I'll tell you what," he said, "I'll explain everything to you the next time I see you—how's that?"

"You can't explain it over the phone?"

"Oh, I guess I could. But it'd be better to show you. Besides, it'll be a big surprise."

"I hope it'll be a good one!" she said, laughing.

"It's a great one!" he assured her.

He met her at eight thirty on a Friday night at a restaurant on West 66th Street. It was a small, elegant place that once had been a basement apartment—one had to open an iron gate at street level and step down into it. The dining area contained eight linen-covered tables on which tea candles flickered in red bowls. A small but well-stocked bar was located at the back of the room. The waitress was a young woman who was the daughter of the cook-proprietress, and who, after seating Colin and Melissa, suggested the special—tonight's was clam spaghetti—and a wine to go with it. They ordered both and she came back almost at once with the wine and poured it for them, leaving the chilled, napkin-wrapped bottle on the table.

Colin raised his glass to Melissa and said, "You look beautiful. To everything you want."

"To you too," she said.

They clinked glasses and drank.

"You look tired," she said, after she had put her glass down.

"A lot of work," he said, shrugging.

"So," she said, "what've you got to show me. Remember? You said you were going to show me something."

He smiled in that somewhat tense way people do as they prepare themselves to admit something they would prefer to keep to themselves. Then, taking a deep, resigned breath, he glanced about him to make sure he was not being watched by any of the other diners and reached into an inner pocket of his jacket and extracted something. It was a plastic bag. He unraveled it and took out a small glass vial. It was an inch and a half high and had a black plastic cap. He held it close in to his body, between the thumb and forefinger of his right hand, and said in a low, surreptitious voice, "Here it is."

She looked at the vial, then back up at him, and said, uncertainly, "Okay ... and that is ... ?"

"Well it's part of what I do, what I'm working on. It's just a small part. I have a lot more of this stuff back home. You'll never guess what it is."

"You're right, I won't," she said. "It looks like ... water."

"Water," he repeated, smiling almost to himself at what he took to be a charmingly naive answer. "Not quite. I'll give you a hint: it's not something you probably ever came across before because it's kind of hard to get. And yet you've heard of it."

She shook her head, shrugged; she had no idea.

"And," he said, slowly tilting vial this way and that so that it caught and reflected the light of the candle, and glittered, "it's very, very dangerous."

"Dangerous?" she asked, her smile fading a little as she knit her brows, focused in on the substance within the vial, then raised her unsure eyes back to him. "Why would you have something dangerous?"

"Well, when I say dangerous I mean that's how a lot of people would regard it. Of course it *isn't* dangerous—as long as it's in this vial. As long as you don't come into direct contact with it. And it does have its legitimate uses—industrial uses—though not many people know much about those. Most people only think about its more sensational history."

For the first time since she had known him, Melissa thought he was talking circles around her.

"Really, Colin, I have no idea. You'll have to tell me."

"So, you give up?"

"Yes, I give up."

"You're sure?"

"Yes, Colin, I am sure."

He seemed to take a little boy's pleasure in having stumped her. He looked about surreptitiously as though to make sure no one was within earshot, then leaned still further toward her so that the flicker of the candle cast waves of yellow light on his face, and he said in a low, confidential, conspiratorial voice that was barely above a whisper:

"Cyanide."

"What?"

"Cyanide."

Melissa's mouth opened slightly. "Cyanide?" she repeated.

"Actually, potassium cyanide. In its raw state it's dry and white and looks like salt or sugar, but I made a solution out of it."

"Isn't that poisonous?"

"Oh, I'll say! You say 'poisonous' like you're talking about a mushroom or something; but it's a lot more deadly than that! Cyanide stops the very cells from functioning; it inhibits their use of oxygen, and of course without oxygen ..."—he shrugged. "Know what happens when you get poisoned by this stuff? You can't breathe—you have seizures—your heart stops. Anyway, this is just a little bit; it's nothing compared to what I've got at home, in my lab. I've got big bottles of it there, along with some other really dangerous stuff: amatoxin, strychnine, even ricin. Between you and me, I'm glad no one else in my building knows what's going on in my apartment because if they did they'd probably call the cops on me in a minute."

For a few seconds her eyes seemed glued to the vial; her mouth was open; her breathing seemed to have stopped or slowed; and finally she managed to ask, "What are you doing with it?"

"I use it in my lab at home. In my work. I've discovered that cyanide is a necessary part of the process."

"Part of ... what process?"

He enfolded the vial in his hand and said with an especially intense expression:

"Did you ever hear of ... alchemy?"

"What?"

"Alchemy, Melissa. It's the process by which base metals are turned into more precious substances; in particular, gold."

She wasn't sure how to react. Her uncertainly in this respect didn't arise from any doubt she might have had about alchemy and its definition; she had heard Colin plainly enough; but in those first moments she couldn't bring herself to equate the quiet and perhaps too-reserved Colin with the extravagant notion of trying to create gold.

"So what are you saying?" she asked. "That you're making ... gold?"

"I know it sounds impossible," he continued, "but I've already done it. Granted, so far it's only been very small quantities—a few particles here and there, and even that's taken an immense of work—but the point is that I *have* done it; and what I can do in small quantities I'm sure I can do in larger ones so long as I keep going, keep working, and don't give up or get discouraged. Oh, I know, I know," he said, watching her intently and misinterpreting her mute wonder for cynicism, "it sounds impossible. People told me all my life that I couldn't do it. I know scientists at work who tell me that the only *possible* way it could be done was through some billion-dollar super-collider that could swap out protons from other elements. But they're thinking too conventionally. They think about things the way they learned them at school, as though the physics of today is infallible, when of course a few hundred years from now people will look back on us and wonder how we could have been so stupid. The thing is, they don't use their instincts about things, Melissa—that's what it is. And maybe they don't use their instincts because they haven't got them. But I've always believed that the transmutation could be done chemically and cheaply, because after all what are chemical reactions if *not* atomic reactions? It just a matter of getting the right reactions going. Nor do you need millions of dollars' worth of equipment and immense quantities of energy because the energy is already there, in the stuff you're using, and it's just a matter of releasing it, of unlocking it, of chemically influencing it to act in a specific way. You have no idea how many substances and processes I've experimented with: hundreds—thousands! And then one day I got this hunch about it because it occurred to me that whenever I seemed to make a step forward it was only after I had been using dangerous or volatile substances. That prompted me to overcome my hesitation to using cyanides, which I had suspected might have just the right properties I needed. And that's when the real breakthroughs started to happen. The thing is that it's all so counterintuitive. From a straightforward chemico-molecular point of view it doesn't make sense, though when looked into a little more deeply you can almost begin to perceive the means by which it works. Anyway, I don't claim to know *exactly* how it works—at least, not yet. I'm still studying it. On the other hand, it *does* make a strange kind of philosophical sense when you consider that anything as valuable and rare as gold *should* require some correspondingly obscure, difficult, or dangerous process, otherwise it would have been discovered a long time ago and everyone would be doing it. Yes," he said, shifting his eyes to the vial, which he somewhat hid in his half-clenched hand, "it seems to be a kind of law of nature that you don't make any great strides without taking great risks. And of course I am aware of the risks. I know that what I'm doing is dangerous. Why, even the cyanide in this little vial—do you know how many people this could kill? Probably a hundred. It could! If this ever got into the hands of a crazy person he could murder a hundred people, maybe more. It wouldn't be hard for him to do, either. All he'd have to do is go to a salad bar or something, and just sprinkle it on the tomatoes and onions. No one would suspect a thing. In only minutes you'd have a dozen people jittering on the floor in death convulsions."

"But why are you carrying it around?" she asked in a whisper, hearing her voice, her question, almost as though it were coming from someone else because so large a part of her mind was occupied with the struggle to make sense of what he had told her, of what it told her about him.

"For inspiration," he said.

"I don't ..."—she shook her head, not knowing what to make of such an answer. Her eyes shifted to the glimmering, lethal liquid in the glass vial.

"Inspiration," he said again. "I don't know how else to explain it. But when I'm carrying this stuff around, it does something to me ... it's hard to explain ... it gives me all kinds of ideas that wouldn't ordinarily come to me. Maybe it's because even when I forget that I'm carrying it around my unconscious mind knows that I am and is busy working out the problems connected with it. Anyway, a few times I experimented with leaving it behind—putting it away—but the result was that when I went back to my lab I didn't have a single new idea about how to continue with my work: I would just sit there, stymied, drawing a blank. It was very frustrating. Yes, it's quite amazing when you think about it," he said, gazing thoughtfully on the vial and tilting it slowly this way and that, "the effect something like this can have on you, something so dangerous, so harmful, so close to your breast, your heart."

In another moment he snapped out of his own fascination with the vial, slipped it back into its little plastic bag, and returned it to the interior pocket of his jacket. Only then did he notice that Melissa looked upset. Her large gray eyes looked at him in a half accusatory, half questioning intensity as she shook her head a little in a gesture of distressed incomprehensibility. It occurred to Colin that she hadn't really understood what he had told her, otherwise her reaction would not have been so negative; at the very least she ought to have given him the benefit of her doubts by regarding him as a professional chemist, a man who quite knew the properties of potentially dangerous substances and how to handle them safely. Or perhaps—he thought—it wasn't his possession of the cyanide that bothered her so much as his absolute conviction of the reality of the alchemical process. She was an intelligent woman and it probably struck her practical, level-headed sensibilities as fatuous. Seeking to reassure her on this point he continued:

"As I said, Melissa, I've had some success. I'm on the brink of a breakthrough—I'm sure I am. I just need to work harder, that's all. And of course I'll have to get my hands on more cyanide, since I'm running out of it."

"Colin ... do you mean to tell me that ... you always carry that around with you?"

"Well, no—I haven't always carried it around. Only for the last couple of years. But don't worry," he hastened to add, seeing that she seemed disturbed by his answer, "it's in a vial, and that's in a plastic bag, so it can't hurt anyone. I mean, it could—but only if someone were to put it into your coffee or something like that."

Her eyes opened a little wider at him; her lower lip dropped ever so slightly. She crossed her arms as though she were suddenly chilly.

"Are you alright?" he asked her. "You look a little pale."

"No ... I mean, yes. I'm fine."

She considered it fortunate that just then the waitress arrived with their food and gave her something with which to feign a blithe distraction. She leaned back in her chair a little as a large, white, oval plate of steaming clam spaghetti, garnished with mussels, parsley, and Romano cheese, was placed before her. She took up her napkin, placed it across her lap, then lifted a fork and focused on her food, not raising her eyes from it as a dozen upsetting thoughts and feelings tumbled through and addled her mind. She poked at the strands of spaghetti repeatedly and even managed to utter a happy-seeming, "Looks great," but her appetite was gone and in its place churned a stomach uneasy with anxiety. She heard Colin saying happily how he had always wanted to try this place and was glad that they had come here. She could not but note how already the matter of the cyanide he kept in his pocket was a matter of complete indifference to him.

For the rest of the evening she tried to forget about his disclosure. But she was too old and wise to ignore the red flag of warning that had begun to wave in her heart. There was something wrong here—something very wrong. She recalled with a despairing, almost angry disappointment the boyfriends in her past who had always seemed at first to possess every good quality a woman could want only for this veneer to fade or peel away and reveal the unsightly interior. Now it seemed that Colin was falling into the same category; indeed, in his case it was worse than any of the others because his failings were more than merely moral—they were downright psychological. No matter how she tried to make excuses for him she couldn't rationalize away his carrying a deadly poison with him. Who would do such a thing? As for his carrying it for the sake of "inspiration" (whatever *that* meant!);—as for the whole notion of making gold;—well, none of this mattered to her, none of it excused his behavior or attitude. For what was gold? She didn't care about it. She didn't care about money. Sure, it was always better to have money than not to have it. But she was a woman with a big heart; sensitive in her way; perhaps something of a romantic too; and had never believed money could make you happy. She had dated men whose wealth had never made up for their unattractiveness or coarseness or lack of humor. Besides, the great dream of her life had never been a life of pointless ease but the life of an average wife and mother with all its quiet joys and sorrows and sacrifices. But how could you be the wife of a man who was apparently infatuated with poisons that could kill a hundred people at a time? It was ridiculous—preposterous. More than that—it was mad.

Suddenly it struck Melissa that all this while Colin's cheerful, lovely personality had been but one side of an essentially dark and disturbed character. Granted, she didn't know anything about chemistry and therefore could not, strictly speaking, know that his goals were absurd; but her instinctive sense of the thing was that no one could "make" gold, and that a poison gray as cyanide could have no place in it. She recalled that Colin himself had said that the use of cyanide was "counterintuitive"—but she wondered if he had said that only to throw her off track and better gain her trust. Yes, what if he *was* mad? Just the thought of it, later, had her pacing her apartment. She couldn't help her suspicion. She had lived in New York too long not to be distrustful even of people she had known a long time and who seemed to be normal. She recalled any number of news stories she had heard over the years about wives whose husbands were living a secret, criminal life—who during the day were kindly, cheerful, devoted husbands, then at night or on weekends ventured solitarily out into the world on murderous sprees.

"What if he's crazy and he's planning to kill me?" she asked herself.

But she had no sooner asked herself that question than it struck her as ludicrous; she even laughed a little to herself. The same instinct that told her base metals couldn't be turned into gold also told her that Colin, while he might be many things, was harmless. There was only one way to find out if he was telling the truth about why he carried the poison. She would have to see the results of his so-called "work."

The next time she stayed at his apartment she asked him to show her the gold he had made. Hadn't he said he had made some? She wanted to see it. Colin did not receive the request eagerly. He told her that there wasn't much to see—he was still trying to perfect the process. When he had made more—when he had accomplished something substantial—then, he said, he would be happy to show her, but right now there was so little of it ...

"It doesn't matter, I want to see it," she insisted.

"But Melissa it's hardly anything."

"That's fine. I still want to see what you have."

With begrudging concession he led her into his laboratory. The sickly-sweet chemical smell in the room, which she had the first time noted only with curiosity, now seemed to her disagreeable, even disgusting. She glanced uneasily at the ominous warning labels on the various containers stacked here and there.

Colin walked over to a rack of test tubes and lifted up first this one, then another, searching for, and finally finding, a particular one: a dark, burnt residue lined its bottom. He scraped up some of this with a long, narrow metal instrument and placed it on a slide, which he brought over to his microscope. Sitting before it, he looked through the binocular eyepiece for about twenty seconds, all the while adjusting the slide beneath the lens till he had positioned it to reveal whatever it was he had been looking for. Then he pushed back his wheeled chair, got up, and told her, "Okay, you can look."

She sat down and looked into the microscope. She wasn't sure what she was looking at because she only saw rough-surfaced particles of various sizes and degrees of darkness. "What am I supposed to be seeing?" she asked, not raising her eyes to him.

"Don't you see them? Those flecks of yellow? It's gold. Actually, they're so small that they don't quite look yellow—they seem to be more gray than yellow. But if they were larger or there were more of them their color would be more apparent."

"Oh yes, I see them," she said. She looked for a few more seconds before pulling away from the microscope, then leaning over to look directly at the slide, which to her eye seemed only to have a smudge streaking across it. "Is that it?" she asked, turning to Colin.

"What do you mean?"

"I mean is that all the gold you've made?" She asked this with apparent sincerity, but in fact she suspected that what she had just been looking at wasn't gold at all.

"Melissa, you say that as though it's a snap of the fingers. Do you know how hard it's been even getting that?"

She got up from the chair and looked around her again. The hollow sockets of the skull and crossbones warning labels stared at her with a ghastly warning of menace. She felt a sudden chill to think of her proximity to so many things that were potentially so dangerous. She recalled Colin telling her how even the small amount of cyanide he carried in his vial could kill dozens of people. How many thousands could be killed therefore with the great quantity of poisons stocked here? She turned her eyes to him and in that instant, as he stood there with his hands folded before him with a pleasant, nonchalant smile, she saw him with a stark, unflattering objectivity as a man who spent hours alone in this wretched, stinking, dangerous room, and his strange and dangerous isolation struck her powerfully, as though with a flash of unerring insight, as impossibly abnormal. All she had ever wanted was a normal life—a life with a regular guy who would be a regular husband and a regular father and a regular companion throughout a blissfully regular life. But here she was again confronted by another man whom she didn't understand. Indeed, he was worse than all the others who had gone before!

"What?" he asked, seeing the strange, self-occupied look in her eyes.

"Nothing," she said.

"Anyway, as I say, it's not a lot right now," he went on

comfortably. "But I'm getting there. I know I'm on the right track. As you can see," he said, noticing the way her eyes kept shifting to the supplies stacked against the wall, "I use a lot of stuff."

"Yes. I see."

She wanted to tell him then and there that he had to stop what he was doing; that it made her uncomfortable; that somehow it wasn't right. But what was the point? She knew he would brush off her concerns and marshal to his defense a dozen reasons why he had to continue his work.

"I've seen enough," she said, managing a smile and leaving the room.

She didn't sleep very well that night with him in his apartment. Always in the past his touch, his embrace, had filled her with a sense of complete contentment, of euphoric satisfaction; but now, for all its warmth, it left her a little cold, and colder the more she concentrated on it, so that she often awakened from her sleep and, at the touch or nearness of his person, moved away from him.

And yet she loved Colin as much as ever, for where love is real it does not and cannot end in a day. At times she told herself that she could change whatever the problem was; that as his girlfriend and future wife she had over him a power which he himself was unaware of. Of course she would have to go about it discreetly. She couldn't come right out and make demands on him—insist that he change his ways; she couldn't even show him how upset she was. Intuitively she understood the independent nature of men and of how so much of their pride is bound up in their notion of doing things their way and not as others wish. She had to be discreet and bend him almost unknowingly to her will. Thus for several days she didn't say anything about what he had shown her in his laboratory, nor did she say anything about his carrying a vial of cyanide on his person. Then one evening she casually broached the matter. She asked him how his "work" was coming along, and when he replied with a rather indifferent shrug that it was going along "as usual" she asked further, "And are you still carrying around that cyanide?"

"Oh, always!"—cheerfully.

"Are you sure that's such a good idea?"

"Of course it is. I'm telling you, really, Melissa," he chattered on, "carrying it around has a way of changing one's whole perspective on life. It makes me value it more—enjoy it more. I see how important it is to live each day to the fullest, and to work, to work as hard as I can before ... well, before the end. Are you okay?"

"Yes. Why?"

"You look a little pale again. You know, you haven't been yourself lately. I can tell. Are you sure you're feeling alright? When's the last time you went to a doctor for a checkup?"

She just shook her head and looked away from him.

"You really should get a checkup, you know. At least once a year."

"There's nothing wrong with me," she said, a little testily, suddenly irritated by his incomprehensible unconsciousness of why she might, as he had put it, look a little pale.

"Alright," he said, a little timidly, surprised by her strangely hostile reaction to his concern.

"Well, there *is* something wrong," she said then.

"What?"

"Colin ... I have to tell you something ... I don't like what you're doing."

"What am I doing?" he asked, apparently having no clue of what she was hinting at.

"That poison you're carrying around. I don't like it."

He hadn't expected that. He might have expected it when he had first shown it to her, or even that evening when she had shown her his laboratory and she had seen how much poison he had stocked. It seemed to him pettishly arbitrary of her to bring up the matter now when it was the furthest thing from his mind. He was thinking of something to say when she continued with a seriousness and determination he had never heard in her before:

"I'd like you to get rid of it, Colin. It's not a good thing to be carrying around."

"But I thought I explained it to you."

"What you told me isn't an explanation," she said. "It doesn't make sense."

"It makes sense to me," he ventured.

"It doesn't to *me*," she returned, with still a greater edge in her voice. "I don't like it. It makes me *very* uncomfortable. So I would like you to stop carrying it around. Is that such a big thing to ask?"

On the face of it, he knew that it wasn't. What could have been easier than to leave the vial at home, stored away in his lab? But a small, internal, knowing voice within him whispered that to do so would deprive him of the (as he had called it) inspiration without which all the dogged application in the world could not avail him in his particular quest.

"So you'll do that for me, right?" she asked.

Ignoring the voice of his conscience, he said, "Sure."

"Promise?"

He smiled quietly. "Of course."

Melissa relaxed; she let out a breath of relief. She told herself that yes, it would not be so hard after all to "train" him, to turn him into the man she wanted and knew he could be. Her eyes softened as she regarded him with renewed affection. It seemed to her in that moment that a great disappointment in her life had been averted. The future, once again, looked bright and comforting. "I knew he would be fine," she told herself.

A few days later when they embraced in meeting she was sure that she felt something through his jacket, something small and hard: the vial of poison. She said nothing at the time. She didn't want him to think she was suspicious, nor did she like to think he had lied to her. She told herself that it could very well have been something else: a pen, a roll of mints, maybe a pair of sunglasses. But the moment she had the opportunity to check— he had taken off his jacket, left it on the couch, and walked out of the room for a moment—she couldn't help herself and lunged at the jacket and stuck her hand into the interior breast pocket, only to pull out the plastic bag and vial. She was so hurt and angry that in those first few seconds she wanted confront him with his lie. But then, thinking that it would be wiser not to do and say anything in the heat of the moment, she returned the poison to the jacket. When he came back into the room she tried to act as normally as possible, but she knew he could tell that something was wrong, though he didn't ask her what it was.

In the days that followed she regarded her discovery of the vial of cyanide as more serious than she had at first supposed.

It came to represent to her more than an odd stubbornness on Colin's part: it amounted to nothing less than a breach of trust: the proof that ultimately he either didn't love her enough to care what she thought or wanted, or that he was possessed of a mania beyond reason. And even if, somehow, he had been able to reconcile in his own mind the carrying of the poison with the promise he had made to her not to do so—well, wasn't that just as worrisome, just as unacceptable, since it showed he didn't even reason the way she or most people did?

She wondered if she should confront him about it; but what would have been the point of that? The issue wasn't that he had broken a promise but rather in what lay beyond that, in his thinking that his word meant nothing. She was too old and experienced not to understand what unflattering volumes it spoke about his character, and consequently about the kind of relationship he was or rather was not capable of having. The next time they met it was impossible for her to hide her disappointment in him; she was uncommunicative and morose. He asked her several times what was the matter, but she, filled with a sense of the hopelessness of again bringing up the reason for her behavior, only shook her head and said nothing. When the evening drew to a close she declined to go back with him to his place; she said she was tired and wanted to go home.

"Something is wrong. What is it?" he asked her.

But again, what was the point of telling him he was a liar?

"Nothing. I don't feel well. I just want to go home."

She did not see or call him for the next three days. On the telephone she told him that she wanted to be alone for a while. She told him that she needed some time to think things through, and when he asked, "What things?"—she was angry that he could even ask her such a question and said through her pain and anger only a quiet, "Things."

"Don't be stupid," she said to herself. "He's lying to you already. He's a liar. If he's lied to you about this, he'll lie to you about anything. You can't trust a liar—ever. He may be a nice guy—in some ways—and maybe you've had good times with him, but he's not good for you ... you know now it can't go anywhere ... cut your losses ... don't waste your time."

It was remarkable that she could be so clear about the matter in one minute and so painfully confused about it the

next.   Her mood shifted with each hour: she could be quietly
confident about never seeing him again at three o'clock only, by
nine, to be pacing her apartment, tearfully telling herself that
she didn't want to live without him. When she was out in public,
when she was at work or with friends, she tried to put on a
show of normalcy.   But she wasn't a good actress, and people
saw through the pose, even though they might not have said
anything to her about it.

Mrs. Adler, her mother, certainly saw through it. She was
fifty-eight years old, and had already begun that descent into
dowdiness by which an aging woman shrugs her shoulders at
the sight of dyed hair showing gray at the roots, or of a
wardrobe ten or fifteen years behind the times. Only one thing
had grown stronger and surer about her with the passing of
years: her devotion to her children. In this she was as ancient,
as timeless, as unexceptionably noble as Motherhood itself. Her
daughter and son were the lights of her life; their happiness,
worries, successes, and failures she felt as her own. She was
naturally more concerned and worried for her daughter's sake,
for she knew that the world was often a hard place and therefore especially antagonistic to a girl's softer nature. Secretly her
heart had ached to think that Melissa had not the comfort and
satisfaction of a husband and family of her own.   For some
weeks she had seen the sad worry in her daughter's eyes and
knew something was wrong. She had asked Melissa about it
only to receive the dismissive, offhand response, "Everything's
fine, Ma"—making it clear that inquiries in that direction would
not be welcome.   But Mrs. Adler was unable to bear seeing her
baby so unhappy and when Melissa, looking worse than ever,
next came to visit her, she could not forebear from finding out
what the problem was. At once she zeroed in on the only thing
it could be by asking:

"Is everything going alright with you and Colin?"

"Yes." —But the anxiety in the eyes belied the confidence
from the lips.

"Oh!" Mrs. Adler exclaimed softly yet forcefully, as though
surprised that her intuitions had been so accurate. She looked
at her daughter with eyes that drilled unerringly into the pools
of worry in her daughter's soul. "Melissa!" she said, "I hope that
guy's treating you alright."

"Everything is fine," Melissa said.

"No it's not. I can see it's not. Honey, what's going on?"

Melissa only shook her head glumly.

"I knew it," Mrs. Adler said. "I knew it for a while now. Well, what is it? Tell me. I want to know." And when her daughter still remained silent: "That bum! I hope he's not doing anything wrong by you!"

"He's not a bum, Ma," she said, gently. "Don't say that. He's a good guy. He's just ... caught up in something."

"Something like what? What are you saying?" Mrs. Adler's worried mind jumped to the most extreme conclusion. "Is he involved in drugs or something?"

"Nooooo," Melissa said, letting the word out within an elongated, morose, yet somehow amused tone of voice as though nothing could have been more preposterous than the notion of Colin as a drug dealer or addict.

"Is he in trouble with the law?" Mrs. Adler persisted.

"No, he is *not* in trouble with the law."

"But something's up," Mrs. Adler said, provoking her daughter to confide in her. Then, after a moment, her whole body sagged and she looked at her daughter with an expression of heartbroken resignation, which in only a few seconds changed again into anger as she said, "Ah! He's cheating on you, isn't he! That bum!"

"No, Mom, he is *not* cheating on me," Melissa replied, a little impatiently; adding, "If anything, I'm the one who's going to be cheating on him!"

"Why?"

And Mrs. Adler waited. She would not press anymore for information; perhaps because she knew her daughter was ready to confess everything. Melissa told her mother about the laboratory in Colin's apartment, how it was filled with dangerous things, and how he carried a vial of cyanide in his pocket. To all of this Mrs. Adler had only one impulsive response:

"He's out of his mind!"

"He says he needs it for his work."

"He's out of his mind! Cyanide? Poison!"

"He says it can't hurt anyone because he keeps it in this little bottle."

"He's nuts! Oh, my God!"

"I told him I didn't like him walking around with it. I told him a dozen times already. He just won't get rid of it. He says that he needs it, that it helps him think."

" 'Think'! Think about *what?* Oh my God ... he's crazy!"

"About some work he's doing on his own, at home. I don't know. It has something to do with gold." She turned to her mother a pair of eyes now frankly displaying the worrying sadness that had clamped around her heart for the last week. "He thinks he's making gold, Ma. He showed me some stuff that he made that he said was gold. I don't know what it was. He made me look at it through a microscope ... I didn't see anything ... I don't know ..."

"He's nuts," Mrs. Adler said quietly.

"Don't say that," Melissa said, her voice low, almost pleading.

"But what kind of man does such a thing? That's not right. Cyanide? And now he thinks he's making gold? Honey, that's *crazy.*"

"He'll stop it," she said.

"What do you mean? When?"

"When I talk to him."

"You said you already talked to him."

"I'll talk to him again."

Mrs. Adler just shook her head, and only a sense of not wanting to add to her daughter's pain prevented her from repeating that Colin was out of his mind. Nevertheless, the maternal urge to protect her offspring, to guide her into a better path, overcame any scruples she might have had about saying more on the subject, and she added:

"Melissa, darling, listen to me. I didn't want to say anything all this time because I know you don't want me to get involved in your business, but you're my daughter and I love you and I want the best for you, and I am telling you, I knew it—I knew it—I *knew* there was something wrong with this guy. He never treated you right. I *knew* he wasn't right for you. You think I didn't notice what went on? Honey, I notice *everything.* When holidays came around, or your birthday, or special occasions, did he do anything for you?"

Melissa turned her eyes away from her mother, and remained silent.

"Your birthday this year," Mrs. Adler continued. "Did he ever get you anything or even take you out for a nice dinner, or anything?"

Melissa continued silent.

"And did he ever talk about taking you anywhere, or going on a vacation with you, or anything?"

Melissa breathed deeply, heavily, her lips set, her eyes thoughtful, sad, beneath this bombardment of what after all were undeniable instances of Colin's indifference to the things—"the nice, little things," as she thought them—that a man ought to do for his girlfriend. She had always made excuses to herself for his thoughtlessness, telling herself that it wasn't important if he forgot a special anniversary or even her birthday, for the bond between them transcended any such paltry conventions and considerations. On the other hand she understood that if he was remiss in doing these things now, how much less attentive was he bound to be years down the road when the familiarity of marriage took the bloom off their first and strongest affection and made them that much less likely to want to please each other? Perhaps it was inevitable that even the best, most loving relationship degenerated and fell apart, but for now she demanded the pleasure of its illusion. And it was in part out of a desire to hang on to that illusion—an unwillingness to relinquish its pleasure—that she now tried to excuse his thoughtlessness by saying:

"He just forgets a lot."

"Forgets? Is that the excuse he gives you? No, no," Mrs. Adler said, shaking her head, "he doesn't 'forget'! He knows what he's doing. And if he *does* forget—well, what does that mean? He's not *supposed* to forget things like that. What kind of man doesn't at least bring his girlfriend something on Valentine's Day? Pfuh! It's ridiculous."

A few hours after speaking with her daughter, Mrs. Adler might have been seen in her apartment talking to her son, Aaron. She went over with him the gist of the conversation she had had with her daughter. "I knew it!" she was saying. "I knew there was something wrong with that guy! I knew something wasn't right!"

"I thought you liked him," came the much calmer voice on the other end of the line.

"No, no, I knew there was *something* up somewhere," she insisted. "I just didn't say anything."

Aaron smiled as his mother said this, amused at her characteristic but baseless insistence on her prescience.

"You should see your sister, how miserable she is!" Mrs. Adler said. "She's very, very upset."

Aaron breathed evenly, a little wearily, his mood wondering and indecisive, not sure of what it was his role to do or think in this situation. Aaron had met Colin several times and had regarded him as a likeable enough fellow, having no strong feeling about him either one way or the other. Their conversations had always been friendly, cheerful, and superficial: the small talk of people who meet infrequently and sociably catch up on what the other has been doing since last seen. This comfortable indifference was understandable given their different personalities and vocations. Science and chemistry were after all the last things in the world of interest Aaron, whose mind was always on either his family or his business. He was married with two small children and also owned two men's clothing stores: one on Madison Avenue at 48th Street, and another on Second Avenue at 50th Street. Neither was doing well on account of a sinking economy, and the overriding concern in his life these days was the possibility of having to close one of them. As for his sister's problems with her boyfriend, well, he couldn't help think it entirely her business. Of course he wanted the best for his sister—the last thing in the world he wanted was to see her unhappy—but his instinct was to shy away from her personal life and problems. On the other hand, he realized these must be unprecedentedly extreme if his mother was discussing the matter with him. He was the surer of this when in another few minutes, after lamenting Melissa's unhappiness, Mrs. Adler said:

"Listen, Aaron, why don't you talk to him."

"Me?"

"You're friendly with him. You're both men. Talk to him. For Melissa."

"Ma, I don't think she'd want me interfering in her life like that."

"Who's interfering? You're *helping*. Your poor sister is a nervous wreck! You should see her."

Aaron breathed deeply, uncertainly, and murmured, "That's

not really my place, Ma. I mean, unless Melissa asks me, that's different."

"She's not going to ask you to do that. She doesn't want you to know her problems."

"Yeah, exactly. She doesn't want me to get involved."

"It's not to get 'involved,' Aaron. It's to *help*. It's to set this guy straight about what's going on. He's carrying a big bottle of cyanide with him, for God's sake! He has it when he's with your sister—don't you understand that? What is that supposed to mean? Who the hell knows what's in his mind? He might be planning to kill her, for all we know! Do you feel comfortable with your sister going out with a guy who's carrying a bottle of cyanide? Do you?"

"I never heard of such a thing—"

"Exactly! It's crazy. I'm telling you, I don't trust him—no, no, I do not trust him!"

'But why is he doing that? What does he say about it?"

"How should I know? It has something to do with gold. He told your sister he's making gold. I'm telling you, the guy's nuts! I want you to talk to him and get it through his head that he's got to cut it out, that we don't tolerate that kind of stuff in this family. You're a big guy," she continued, in this hinting that she had no qualms with her son using physical intimidation, "you meet him face-to-face, and lay it on the line with him. You let him know!"

"I don't know, Ma ..."

"What's to know? Just *do* it. Call him. I have his number—I want you to call him. You go and talk to him. Go in person. Just tell him you want to talk to him. You're a smart man. You know what to say." —And she proceeded to order her son to get a pen and paper and take down Colin's telephone number, which she repeated three times over before her son interrupted her a little impatiently with:

"Ma, I have it—I *have* it."

If ever Colin had received a phone call from out of the blue it was this one. He was at work when his phone rang and heard a man on the other end of the line saying hello, it was Aaron.

"Aaron? Aaron who?"

But when he realized it was Melissa's brother his reaction

was a joyously loud, "Oh, *Aaron!* How are you?"

Colin's first thought was that Aaron was calling to tell him some bad news; for why else would he call? When in the next few minutes he realized the call was—or at least seemed to be— purely social, he was pleasantly and naively surprised to think that Aaron was more disposed toward him than he had thought. But after thirty seconds of the kind of aimless small talk that had always characterized their conversation, Colin heard Aaron's voice take on a more serious tone as he asked, "Listen, Colin, do you think I could stop by and see you today? There's something I wanted to talk to you about."

"Sure," Colin said, knowing now for sure that something was amiss. "Maybe we could go out for a drink or something ..."

"Well ... how about if I just stop by your place—say, seven o'clock or so? Will you be home then?"

"Sure, I'll be there."

"And what is your address again?"

Colin gave it, not without a sense of misgiving.

When Aaron arrived a little after seven o'clock that evening at Colin's door he was looking a little worse for wear. He had the slightly ashen, hangdog, wrinkled look of a man who has used up entirely, and then some, the stock of freshness, vigor, and hope with which he awoke that morning. It wasn't easy running a business in a flagging economy. He had taken off his jacket, which was draped over one arm, and he had also re- moved his tie so that his collar was open at the neck. The two men shook hands and Colin happily invited him inside, bidding him take a seat. Aaron walked into the apartment, looking about him with a quiet yet thorough intensity as though he were trying to extrapolate meaning from every smallest object he saw. "Nice apartment," he said; but the compliment was rote, insincere. His own home in Westchester was a lot more spacious and tastefully decorated, and when he looked out his windows he didn't see buildings of pollution-stained brick but a living, green, inspiring vista of lawns and trees. He wondered why people lived in the choking, dirty city if they didn't have to.

"Would you like something to drink?" Colin offered. "I have some beer in the refrigerator."

"No, thanks. I have to drive."

"Soda?"

"Sure. That'll be fine."

"Be right back," Colin said, as he went into the kitchen. He came out of it with two tall glasses filled with ginger ale and handed one to Aaron, then sat in an armchair opposite him.

"You look tired," Colin said.

"Yeah ... it's been a long day."

"How's business?"

Aaron shrugged, shook his head as though to say, "Not so good."

"Have you had dinner? Do you want to go out and get something to eat? There's a nice restaurant on the corner. The food is good and it's not expensive."

"No, Colin, that's alright. I'm sure my wife's prepared dinner for me. Actually ... I came by because I wanted to talk to you about something."

"Sure, what?"

"I got a call from my mother the other day. She was upset about Melissa. Apparently Melissa is upset about something you're doing. Do you know what I'm talking about?"

"Oh," Colin said only, lowering his eyes.

"What's this I hear about ... cyanide?"

"I think I explained all that to Melissa," Colin said.

"Yeah, well ... it's kind of confusing us." Aaron took a long drink of his soda, finishing almost half the glass, then hemmed a little as though to clear his throat, and said, "Is that true that you carry a bottle of cyanide around with you?"

"What?"

"Is it true that you carry a bottle of cyanide with you?"

"Well, no, of course not. I mean ... not a *bottle!*"

"But you carry *some* with you—right?"

"Well ... but it's not a *bottle*. It's just a little vial."

"I see." Aaron said, nodding a few times. "So ... you *do* carry cyanide around. Colin, I'm confused. Why on earth would you do that? What is that about?"

"I explained all that to Melissa."

"Explain it to me. I'm interested."

"It's just ... something I do. It's really a non-issue."

"A 'non-issue'? Maybe to you. But not to Melissa. And frankly, not to me either. Do you think it's normal to be doing that—to be carrying that with you? Doesn't that strike you as the least bit strange?"

"I never said I didn't think it was strange," Colin replied. "I can see how people could think it's strange. That's why I never said anything about it to you or anyone else. And I didn't even tell Melissa about it for a long time either. But, after all, strange is a relative term. I'm a chemist, remember? I deal with chemicals all the time."

"Oh, I see, so because you're a chemist that makes it alright for you to be playing with cyanide," Aaron said, frowning, almost mocking. "That's like saying because somebody's a construction worker it's okay for him to be carrying around sticks of dynamite."

"Well, I think that would be illegal," Colin noted.

"How do you know that carrying cyanide around isn't illegal?"

"Because it's not. It's just not. It would be illegal if I put it into somebody's coffee or soda—sure." (Aaron glanced at his soda.) "But I'm not doing that. I'm just carrying it."

"But *why* for God's sake! What's the point?"

"It helps me think about my work."

"How is that?"

"It just helps me to focus on what I'm doing. I have a lab there, in my extra bedroom," Colin said, nodding toward the other side of a room, toward a hall that led to the rest of the apartment. "I do some ... work there."

"Oh, yeah? What kind of work?" Aaron asked.

His question was of course disingenuous, for he had already heard from his mother about how Colin was trying to "make gold." But he suspected the accuracy of his mother's report—it would have been just like her to exaggerate something out of all proportion. If, on the other hand, it were true, and Colin was really trying to do such a ridiculous thing, Aaron wanted to hear about it firsthand; and so he asked, almost provokingly, "What could you possibly be using cyanide for?"

"It's kind of hard to explain. It's ... kind of involved."

"I don't need all the details," Aaron returned in an easy, inviting voice. "Just give me the basics."

"Well, alright ... I've discovered a process that can change the molecular structure of several common elements into the structure of a much more valuable material. Cyanide is part of the process."

"What does that mean?"

"It means ... I've found a way to change several everyday materials into ... gold."

Outwardly Aaron gave no indication of how this revelation, or rather confirmation, affected him, for he was held in a stasis of uncertainty by two opposite and equally strong urges. On the one hand he conceded to himself that he didn't have the kind of scientific knowledge Colin must have, and that he was therefore incompetent to judge against the practicability of such a goal; while, on the other hand, common sense told him that he had just heard something very foolish. And so in a voice which was neither doubtful nor impressed he said:

"Gold, eh? Well ... that's very interesting. I'd like to see that."

"Oh, but I haven't been able to make much."

"How much? A few ounces?"

Colin, who all this time had been deferential, serious, even timidly apprehensive, pulled back his head and laughed as though he had just heard something very funny. "Oh, I wish!"

"How much, then?"

"Just"—shrugging, a little helplessly—"a few particles."

"Particles? What do you mean?"

"I mean ... particles. You know: tiny amounts."

"What's 'tiny'?"

"Well ... microscopic."

"What!"

"What?"

"Microscopic?"

"Yes."

"You're kidding me!"

"Why would I kid you?"

"Isn't that a little ridiculous?" Aaron asked, suddenly a little brusque, as though discovering he had just been had. "What's the point?"

"Well"—Colin seemed genuinely taken aback by the question—"because I can."

"Because you *can?*"

Colin nodded, yes.

"Colin, I can go jump off the freakin' Brooklyn Bridge but

that doesn't mean I should do it."

"Well, that's not really a fair analogy, Aaron. Jumping off the Brooklyn Bridge wouldn't get you anywhere—doesn't help anyone or prove anything; but what I've done is an achievement."

"Ohhh, 'achievement'—please!" Aaron said, his irritation now getting the better of him. "If the only gold you've made is 'microscopic,' that's hardly an achievement."

"If you knew how difficult it was, and how long I've been working on it, you wouldn't say that."

"Yes, I would, and I *am*. Listen, Colin," Aaron said, putting his drink down on an end table and getting up from the couch. "I'm going to be honest with you. You always seemed like a nice guy, and I have nothing against you. But this whole thing, with you carrying around cyanide—it's very bizarre, it's really not good. It's not *normal*, my friend! People don't *do* that. They just *don't*. So I think—I'm going to ask you to stop it. For Melissa's sake."

"But I explained everything to her—"

"Yes, and that's why she's upset. Look, I might as well ask you this and cut to the chase. What are your intentions toward her?"

"My intentions?"

"I mean, what is your long-range plan. Is this just a dating thing or ... what?"

Colin looked a little bewildered for a few seconds before saying, "I love Melissa. I would like to get married to her."

"Fine. That's great. So that means you can't always do the things you want to—get it? No engaged or married man can. Marriage is a compromise, and usually it's the woman who gets the compromise she wants. Melissa doesn't want you dealing with cyanide or anything else that's dangerous, not while you're at home, anyway, not while you're around her, and I don't blame her, so"—he raised his hands, palms upwards, in a gesture indicating the obviousness of the matter—"that's it. That's the way it is. You have to stop it already with the cyanide. You shouldn't have anything to do with that stuff. It's too dangerous."

"I'm very careful with it—"

"It doesn't matter. It's too dangerous. Just forget about it.

Just"—Aaron put up his hands and shook his head a little as though the matter were really as simple as that—"*forget* about it."

Colin was silent as he thought of things he might say to exculpate and defend himself; he could have said dozens of things. But he knew that Aaron, like his sister, would not be sympathetic to them; rather would probably be further irritated by them; and so in the end he only said, haltingly:

"It's just not as easy as that. I've been working on this a really long time. I don't think I could just give up like that, especially now. The thing is, I'm really getting somewhere now. I know it may not seem like a lot to you or Melissa, but it really *is* something. And if you don't mind my saying so you're focused on the wrong thing, and so is Melissa: the cyanide, I mean. The cyanide might be a part of it, but it's not the most important part. It's the result you should be focusing on."

Aaron had listened; and he had tried to understand; but he didn't. Suddenly he slapped his thighs and assumed a tight smile in which decision combined with disapproving indulgence.

"Well!" he said, "it's up to you, my friend. You have to decide what you really want in life. Melissa's not going put up with the way you've been acting. She's very unhappy right now. *Very* unhappy. I just wanted to tell you that. It's upsetting the whole family. So you have to make a decision. It seems to me the choice is pretty clear, but if you can't see how clear it is, if you want something else ... well, maybe it's just not going to work out between you two, that's all. I'm sorry to have to say that. You seem like a nice guy, Colin, you know I have nothing against you, but there's obviously a problem here. I don't know what else to tell you except ... it's up to you. That's all."

The two men left each other with a lot less good will than they had met. Colin followed, rather than showed, Aaron to the door, and rather than say goodbye to each other they merely exchanged solemn nods.

Aaron had been right in thinking that his sister would regard his visit to Colin as interference. Colin left a message on her answering machine, telling her about the visit, though he had watered down the tense mood of the interview, saying only that Aaron had told him how upset she was "about things," that he was sorry for it, and that he wanted to talk to her. He ended the message by saying, "Call me."

Instead she called her brother to find out what had happened. Initially she challenged his for his presumption; then learned that it was their mother who had put him up to it. Despite her irritation with this meddling in her life a part of her was grateful for it: she had been at her wit's end, and her brother had championed her cause. "So what did he tell you?" she asked. "What did he say about it all?" And after Aaron had given her a direct, honest, and therefore unpromising version of his conversation with Colin, she asked, "So what do you think?"

"You mean what do I think about your continuing to see him?"

She hesitated a moment out of a prescient fear of what he would say, then bravely answered, "Yes."

"I don't know, sweetie," he said, not wanting to disappoint her, wanting to seem neutral, to legitimize the hope he knew she was still clinging to, even as his better judgment told him that that was precisely what he had to discourage so that she might sooner find someone more appropriate. "You have to do what you want, Melissa, but ... really?—if you want my opinion? I don't think it's good. The guy's obviously got issues. I mean real issues. I mean really ... cyanide ... which is such a dangerous poison ... and thinking he can make gold with it ... it's really nutty. You know, I gotta tell you something: when I was over there he gave me a soda and I was afraid to drink it."

"Oh, Aaron, he would never do anything like that."

"Well, I don't trust anyone carrying cyanide around, and neither should you. I'm just telling you how I feel about it. So if I were you I would really, *really* think hard about this one. That's all I have to say about it."

It was the first time her brother had ever said a negative word about someone she was dating. She realized that only an ultimate concern for her welfare had enabled him to risk causing her pain by suggesting she end her relationship with Colin. As much as she tried to dismiss his opinion, therefore, she could not do so, knowing how it arose, solely and purely, from an interest in her welfare.

A few hours after she had spoken with her brother she worked herself into such a dark, self-pitying mood that she wept a little; but only a little—no more than a minute. She pulled herself together quickly. She told herself, "Well—so much for that!"—and resolved to end her relationship with Colin. And somehow she knew that she had crossed an emotional Rubicon and that henceforth it would be easier, if not easy, never to see him again.

If it were asked how she could so quickly decide to break up with a man to whom she had only a few weeks or days before been so passionately devoted, the answer would be that a reasonably attractive woman does not remain single to the age of thirty-three in New York City without having gone on enough dates, and been in enough relationships, and had her hopes dashed enough times, not to see with ruthless clarity that she must quickly cut the bonds between herself and the object she knows will only again waste her time or break her heart.

But mornings have a way of making us rethink our resolves of the night before. The next day Melissa told herself that she would give Colin one last chance. She would give him an ultimatum. It was either his "work" or her; either that crazy, impossible, pie-in-the-sky quest for gold, or a relatively fulfilled and happy future as her husband. For the first time in a week and a half she called him and said she wanted to see him. He was overjoyed at her call—poor deluded man, who knew not the real reason for it. When they met he hugged her wildly but his arms dropped to his sides when she did not respond. She delivered her ultimatum in a manner that had something bizarre about it, for while she spoke in a quiet, smiling voice there was nevertheless something steel-hard in her demeanor. Indeed the incongruity between the politeness of her words and her adamantine manner made him wonder. It was a side of her personality he had never known or suspected. He could only liken it to having come up against a brick wall, which all the pushing in the world could not budge. Colin reacted to it with another fumbling explanation about the importance of his "work," of how he was coming closer to his goal each day, but she stopped him even before he had finished his first sentence, saying, with the same easy steeliness of tone:

"No, no. No, Colin. I'm sorry. I won't talk about it anymore. You just let me know what you want to do—it's entirely up to you. It's your decision to make. It's either yes or no. It's either me or your so-called 'work.' One or the other. Not both.

You let me know."

Three days passed and they did not speak to each other. She waited for him to call, waited for him to relent. Her telephone remained silent.

Her mother assured it was for the best. "It just goes to show he didn't really care for you after all," she said.

Melissa didn't want to believe that, but a cold, obvious logic forced her to concede it. Nor did she give in to an intermittent impulse to regard him sympathetically and make excuses for him. That was the kind of weakness she might have given in to ten or even as little as five years before; but not anymore. Perhaps some people really did die of broken hearts, but she knew she would never be one of them.

The first three days of not speaking to him, of coming to terms with the end of their relationship, were hard on her. She worked as a loan officer in a bank and her separation from Colin troubled her all day. She missed him horribly. As people in her situation are wont to do, she was inclined to remember the happy times she had spent with Colin and to forget the intolerable conditions that had brought about their separation. All of her coworkers noticed that something was wrong with her. Most of them did not ask her about it, sensing it was a personal matter and not their place to inquire into it; and the few who did so were answered with a patently false but brave, "Oh, it's nothing. I'm fine! Really."

Time enabled her to accept the end of her affair with Colin. After two weeks of not seeing and speaking to him, and constantly telling herself that she had to go on with her life, she accepted that she was again a single woman; and if on the one hand she felt as though she had been used and had wasted her time, she felt, on the other, that she had gained a little more wisdom about people and would not be similarly befooled or misled in the future.

She lived on East 51st Street off Second Avenue in an apartment building characterized by the boxy, white-brick, unadorned "modern" style that dominated so much of the architecture of the mid-1960s. She had just gotten home and was finishing her dinner when her buzzer rang and the doorman announced she had a visitor—"His name is Colin." A combined thrill of hope, dread, joy, and nervous anticipation swept through her. After a moment's pause and somehow against her better judgment she told the doorman to send him up. But rather than utter some word of acknowledgment and do as he had been told, the doorman, unprecedentedly, asked in a lower, more confidential voice, "Are you sure, Miss Adler? I think, uh . .. you might want to come down here first."

"What's wrong?"

"Uhhh ..."—the voice lowering to a whisper, as he turned his head away still further from the visitor—"... well ... I think you might want to come down first."

This time she heard the friendly warning in his voice. "I'll be right down," she said.

A few minutes later the steel doors of the elevator opened to the lobby and Melissa stepped toward the entranceway of the building, a compartment between two glass doors and in which the liveried doorman was standing at his tall, narrow desk beside another man whom she didn't recognize. Then she saw it was Colin. He looked worn and shabby. He hadn't shaved for several days and his face was dark with an incipient beard. His tousled hair was unclean, his face drawn and sallow, and dark rings encircled his eyes as though he were ill or hadn't slept. She had never seen him looking so ragged and her first thought was that she hadn't heard from him because he had been sick. The thought that he had been lying in bed at home, alone, feverish, in pain, with no one to look after him, gave her a little stab of pain as though she had been derelict in some sacred duty. She greeted him with an uncertain, "Colin?" and he, in turn, smiled eagerly and with relief as though, now that she were here, he could relax because he was safe.

"Melissa, I need to talk to you," he said. "I have something to show you!"

"Are you alright?"

"Yes, I'm fine—better than ever!" He glanced uncomfortably at the doorman then back to her. "I need to show you something! Just for a minute!"

"Come here," she said. She led him to far side of the lobby, beside the elevators, where she looked at him more closely, and was still more disturbed to see how worn he looked.

"You look like hell," she said.

"Oh, I'm okay," he said, and added hurriedly, "there's something I want to show you." He reached into the pocket of his coat and brought out a folded piece of dark blue cloth. As he opened it carefully he glanced up at her a few times with tense lips as though in happy anticipation of her pleased reaction. There, within the dark folds, lay a few specks of gleaming yellow, of no more mass, taken altogether, than a tiny pebble.

"Look," he said. "Gold."

She was speechless. What was he expecting her to say, how to react, over those tiny bits of yellow?

"You see, I finally did it, Melissa. Finally! I knew I could. You have no idea how hard this was—how I worked and worked on it. I didn't go to my job—I couldn't. I needed the time. Time! That's always been the problem. So I called in sick. You should have heard what I told them! I told them I broke my wrist and would be out for two weeks. Two weeks!" He started laughing, and a note of hysteria entered into his laughter, for he seemed unable to control himself, his whole body shuddering as his reddened eyes moistened, but his laughter subsided suddenly, he composed himself and went on with a new, intense seriousness: "I guess when I go back I'll have to wrap up my wrist and tell everybody how much it hurts. But so what? I'll tell 'em what I have to. That job that I have is so stupid, so meaningless. Those people I work with—what do they know about anything? Just for once I was going to do what I needed to do. And look!—See? I was right!"

"Colin ... you look so terrible ..."

But he seemed not to have heard her and continued:

"You know what the trick was, Melissa? It was ... *lots of poison!* See? That was the thing! I wasn't using enough. I had always been afraid to use too much. I had always been too careful—always holding back—afraid that if I used too much it would ruin everything, when in fact I *had* to ruin everything, had to change the compounds entirely, for them to begin transmuting into something better, more valuable; into the gold. It's so, so counterintuitive! But I'm telling you, *I'm telling you,* that's what the real secret of it is! And you want to know what's really funny about it all? You'll never guess, Melissa—never guess," he said, swallowing hard as he looked at her with a dire intensity. "I almost can't take credit for it. Because it happened by accident. It's true! I was working with a ricin solution ... ricin, you know what that is? Oh, it's so dangerous! Worse than cyanide! Just inhale a whiff of it and you're done for! Just a little of it can kill a dozen people—easy. Anyway, I was pouring it from a bottle when it slipped out of my hand. I don't know ... maybe I was tired. I'm sure I was. I don't know. But it fell and broke on the table and went all over the place. I had to run out of the lab pretty quick! If I hadn't run out of there fast enough, I'd've been a goner! They'd've found me in that room a month from now dried up like some old mummy, and you would have heard about it on the news. Thank God I had enough sense to buy a gas mask and a protective suit. I wore them while I flooded the whole lab with water and bleach—threw pails and pails of it all over the place to neutralize the stuff. My God, it was like a bathtub in there! It's a wonder it didn't leak through to the people downstairs, and maybe some of it did, I don't even know. It took me hours to clean up: four in the morning, and there I still was, still throwing bleach and mopping up and then doing it all over again! And who knows? Maybe I did expose myself to some of it. Maybe I *am* poisoned. I've been feeling nauseated and sweaty and dizzy for a whole day now. But it doesn't matter. I don't care. I don't care what happens to me at this point, Melissa, because you know what?—I *did* it. I found the way. And there's only one way. And it has to do with *quantity*. You have to have a lot—*a lot*—of poison to get anywhere."

As she stood there listening to him, watching him, the attention she had been paying to his words shifted to something else, to something behind the words, something visible in his face, in his eyes, in the sudden, impulsive way he leaned forward and the way his lips trembled on the verge of an irrepressibly euphoric smile. It was the kind of immediate, overwhelming, urgent excitement she had never seen in him before, and her first astonishment at it subsided beneath the bitter sense that never once, in all the time she had known him, had he greeted or regarded her with a similar enthusiasm, even after long absence. She concluded that he himself was unconscious of how utterly he was giving himself away—of how eloquently, though without a specific word spoken, he had just stated the unwavering priority in his life. She knew there was no point in trying to make him understand how little she thought about his mania (as she saw it), but she wanted to make one point absolutely clear lest there be any doubt about it in his mind.

"You don't understand, Colin," she said, her eyes almost softening with the pity superior understanding sometimes bestows on ignorant innocence, "you could have brought me a truckload of gold, and it wouldn't have mattered to me. I don't care about that. I never cared about that."

"I know you didn't. But Melissa, it's not just the gold, it's the ... the ... "—he struggled to find the right words

"The what?"

" ... it's the doing it—to be *able* to do it."

And even though she understood what he meant by this, it seemed to her more than ever how far his values were removed from her own. "I don't care about any of that," she said.

Colin put down the hand that had been holding up to her the bits of gold. They both felt the impasse they had come to. A few seconds passed in silence.

"Are you still carrying the poison with you?" she asked.

His silence confirmed her suspicion.

"Figures," she said. "You'd better go home and sleep, and clean yourself up. You look terrible."

She turned to leave.

"I'll call you," he called out.

She stopped at the sound of his voice but didn't turn around to him. "Don't call me, Colin," she said. She got into the elevator and went back to her apartment.

It was the last time they saw each other.

Six months later Melissa Adler met the man whom she fell in love with and married. He was tall, handsome, two years younger than herself, and, though divorced, had no children and was eager to start a family. His name was John and he did everything right. He brought her flowers and chocolate on Valentine's day, took her to dinner on her birthday and the anniversary of their first date, and was always affectionate. He loved going to movies and watching television; invariably in the evening they were wrapped in each other's arms on the couch watching the news, movies, or situation comedies for hours, quietly, contentedly exchanging comments, chuckles, and intermittent kisses. He was a great sports fan—he and his friends (he had twelve of them) regularly attended baseball games. He always invited her to go with him to these events, and she did so now and then, though she had to make an effort to appear to be interested. They bought a house in Westbury. It was a ranch-style house with three bedrooms, two baths, and a back yard where they had barbecues in summer and kept their dog year round (Melissa would not allow the dog in the house). Eventually they had three children: Jane, Tom, and Barney. For each of them they set up a college fund, determined that their children should grow up to be well-educated, professional people with some guarantee of a good life. And these plans panned out: Jane became an insurance adjuster, Tom the owner of a lucrative car dealership, and Barney entered politics and won election as the comptroller of a Long Island county. Melissa was very proud of her children and they were very proud of her. They always honored her on Mother's Day—sending her cards and flowers, taking her out to dinner, and telephoning her with avowals of their love and congratulations. She would protest against all this as unnecessary, as a foolish waste of time and money, but in fact all of her children saw how she delighted in being made a fuss over.

As for Colin, Melissa came to regard him as just another (albeit vivid) affair of her "youth." Sometimes the thought of him would cross her mind and she would wonder at how stupid she had been in those days ever to have become emotionally involved with such a man. She would wonder what had happened to him, and almost chuckle when she recalled his crazy quest for making gold. "What a nut he was," she would think, sardonically. It wouldn't have surprised her to learn that he had succeeded in discovering some process to make it in large quantities. Who knew?—perhaps he was swimming in gold! She smiled faintly and shrugged. Even now—especially now— she couldn't have cared less.

SING

In its twenty-year history, Angie's Place, a bar in the Green-point section of Brooklyn, had gone through several transformations. It had started out as an Austrian restaurant, then an Italian had bought it and turned it into a pizza restaurant, then an Irishman bought it and turned it into an Irish restaurant, and after he went bankrupt (the food was overpriced and there were "issues" with the Department of Health), yet another Irish person took it over. She was a relatively young woman in her late thirties with a stocky body and a girlish Irish face. Her name was Angela but her friends called her Angie, and she named the bar after herself. How she had come into enough money to buy a business on a main thoroughfare was a matter of neighborhood speculation; perhaps a parent or other relative had died and left her a bundle of cash. At any rate she had a better business sense than all the foregoing owners combined. She knew that the bar was the main thing, the place where the real money was made, and that it behooved her to make it as inviting as possible. She entirely renovated that area. What had been a narrow, stained, distressed, cheap-looking wooden counter became a long, wide, heavy, traditionally elaborate bar of stained oak with a wide, polished, sloping edge against which patrons might comfortably lean their forearms as they sat on cushioned stools and drank. What had been paltry selection of liquor had become a large collection of the world's best and well-known wineries and distilleries: almost two hundred bottles of wines, vodkas, gins, and whiskeys rose tier on tier within great, arched, mirror-backed recesses, and were illuminated from beneath with soft blue and white lights that made them glow magically. As for the room itself, its merely painted walls were replaced with wood paneling on which hung large oval mirrors and framed prints whose themes were the speakeasy days of the '20s and '30s. Four cream-colored globe chandeliers, equidistantly spaced throughout the length of the bar area, shed a soft, dim, yellow light. A string of tiny, star-like bulbs of the sort used on Christmas trees festooned the area just below the ceiling and over the top of the cabinetry of the bar. And of course there was television: two large flat-screen sets perched in the corners at either end of the main room. For at least fourteen hours a day they were tuned into sports stations showing a baseball or football game: grown men chasing or throwing balls, and stadiums full of people working themselves up into a lather of idiotic passion over a home run or a quarterback whose neck had nearly been broken. Yet even with these distractions the bar had the subdued, comforting ambience of a place safely secluded and apart from the glare and bustle of the incessant, exhausting rush of the outside world. Here one might sit, think, be sad or cheerful, and drink away one's worries for a while. A new, simplified menu offered a dozen items among which were burgers, french fries, stuffed potato skins, and salad.

This latest incarnation of Angie's Place did well from the start and became a favorite watering hole in the neighborhood. Almost as soon as it opened at eleven in the morning a few old alcoholics would stop by for their first lonely drinks; then, in the afternoon, a younger, working crowd came in, and might spend their lunch hour here. It was essentially the same crowd after five o'clock when people stopped by after work, or when, still later in the evening, they decided to leave their apartments to "go out" for a while. But it wasn't till the weekends that the place really got busy—very busy. On Friday, Saturday, and sometimes Sunday nights it was packed. Word of mouth of its popularity had even reached Manhattan and on a Saturday night the devoted bar flies of that borough would overcome their sniffish cynicism about taking a train across the river and see for themselves what all the fuss was about. They came, they saw, and they realized that the fuss wasn't about much that they couldn't get in their own neighborhoods; and soon they stopped coming. After a very profitable run of about four months Angie's Place began to lose business as the novelty wore off. The owner came up with any number of gimmicks to try to entice new customers: happy hours, two-for-one nights for ladies, buffets, birthday specials, and so forth, but none of these were sustainable because none of them substantially increased the profit margin. She tried raising the price of drinks, but since they had already been no bargain this only had the effect of chasing more people away, and she quickly enough brought the prices back down to their former, regular levels. She resigned herself therefore merely to making a living and hoping the economy stayed healthy, since when things were going well people were more inclined to go out and spend money. Whereas once on a Friday or Saturday night the place bustled with a crowd so dense that one had to squeeze through clusters of hot bodies to walk a few feet in any direction, there were now never more than a couple of dozen customers, and most of these were local men. Half of these were men in their fifties and sixties, stout, ill-shaven, shabbily-clothed, who sat for hours at a time staring up in glum silence at the sports events on the televisions—empty-headed, lost souls for whom all the mystery, richness, and romance of life, if they had ever known it, had died away with their wasted youth.

One afternoon a rather striking-looking man stepped into Angie's Place. He was about forty-five years old, slender, and wore sleek clothes and blue-tinted sunglasses. His long, graying hair was combed back and bound in a short pony tail. His taut, punctilious appearance made him look out of place in this working-class neighborhood where most men his age were paunchy and shambled about indifferent to their appearance. He looked about him with the analytical air of a tax assessor, examining the lighting, the seating, the layout of the tables, and paid particular attention to the bench-seated alcove in the wall opposite the bar. Then he strode up to the bartender and asked, "Is the owner here? Could I speak with him?"

"It's a her. Yeah, she's here. What's it about?"

"Business."

When she came out to him he introduced himself as "Mr. Entertainment"—chuckling as he said the name, as though he knew how ridiculous it sounded, and quickly adding that that was just his "business name" and that she could call him Tony. He handed her a business card showing a black silhouette of a man singing into a microphone with dashes raying out from his head as though to show his voice booming forth. Above this figure floated the words "Everyone Is a Star!" with musical notes floating on either side. In the center of the card was the proclamation, "Karaoke by Mr. Entertainment," with, below this, the man's real name, Tony Guenser, and his telephone number and email address. At the very bottom edge of the card ran in small print the following exclamation: "Get the party started, let the good times roll!"

He explained that he had happened to drive by Angie's Place and wondered whether or not she offered any "entertainment"? No? Ah, well, she really should consider it! Did she know that by having a karaoke show on a Friday or Saturday night she could increase her business by at least one hundred percent? It was one of the surest ways to get a crowd. People these days, he told her, no longer went to bars just to drink; after all, they could do that at home, and a lot more cheaply. No, they wanted to be entertained; and what better entertainment than to have people get up and sing? After all, everyone liked to sing, he said, and laughed in his soft little way: "Hahahaha." He also assured her that he had a "following." He had been in "the business" for ten years and during that time he had come to know hundreds of people who attended his "shows." Of course he couldn't guarantee that they would all come; but a certain proportion nearly always did, and those who didn't would be more than made up for by new patrons who had a secret itch to perform. She needed only to put up a sign in the window that there would be karaoke on this or that night, and she would see—people who ordinarily passed by the place without a second thought would make a point to stop in. As for his rates, they were extremely reasonable, only three hundred dollars for five hours worth of music, fun, and—most importantly for her—increased business.

The proprietress had listened with growing interest, though she pulled back a little when he mentioned the cost. It was not that three hundred dollars was an especially large amount of money, but what if she had to pay it out and Mr. Entertainment didn't deliver the crowd? On the other hand, she knew that she had to do something to drum up business, and having a karaoke night seemed as good an idea as any. She agreed to try him out on the forthcoming Saturday night. There was no written contract—it was enough that they shook hands on the deal. Happy at having made a sale, and saying he would be right back, Mr. Entertainment hurried out to his car and came back five minutes later with a poster to be placed in the window and which announced the event. "You'll see," he said. "You'll get a lot of people in here just from seeing this!"

Six months later the karaoke show was still going on at Angie's Place; it had become a regular event starting promptly at nine o'clock every Saturday night. It always drew a crowd, and the crowd was always very different from the usual one that on every other day or night came here to eat or drink.

At eight thirty Mr. Entertainment would enter, or rather barge into the place, carrying his sound equipment. This consisted of a CD player, a mixing unit, an amplifier, several microphones, and two large, bulky speakers, one of which he set on the floor while he placed the other on a nearby juke box. With the use of telescoping wand with a clasp at the end he attached to the ceiling a self-adhesive spotlight, which was small, battery-powered, and shone bright light down onto the area where the singers would stand. He was assisted by his wife, a woman who wore jeans, a sweater, thick glasses, and who looked for all the world as though she had just come off the line at some factory job. In her case looks were deceiving, for while one might at first have been put off by her homely inelegance she was rich in a cheerful personality and, more than her husband, was responsible for keeping the show going—greeting people she knew, cajoling those she didn't into singing, and generally making good cheer. But at this point she was just a quiet, rather frumpy woman who efficiently heeded her husband's instructions to tilt one of the speakers a certain way or to unwind or plug in a cable. She then distributed the songbooks. These were large, three-ring binders divided into two sections: the first listed names of the songs, the second the names of the artists who had originally done them. Each listing was followed by the number of the CD on which the track was located. Mr. Entertainment's wife placed these songbooks throughout the bar along with small sharpened pencils and narrow slips of paper on which to write one's name and song selection.

On this evening she happened to place one of these books before two men, both in their sixties, sitting at the bar. Neither of them had been here for several months on a Saturday night and so didn't know what was going on. Neither of them had noticed the sign in the window announcing tonight's karaoke show. One of them was a retired fireman and the other a retired shopkeeper. Each was ill-shaven, stout, and well on his way to developing an old man's gruff intolerance to anything he deems nonsense. They had been sitting side-by-side for the last hour without giving each other more than a begrudging glance. Each of them would have liked to talk to somebody but neither ventured to make an overture to the other. Something prevented them from doing so—some force or fear that stood watchful over the companionable parts of their nature, and kept it suppressed, whipped back into its distant, hard shell. With their drinks before them, they sat with their heads tilted up to the same television set on which a baseball game was being shown: just now a batter stepped up to home plate, spat on the ground, and lifted his bat. They had intermittently looked over to Mr. Entertainment as he had set up his equipment. They supposed he must be some kind of musician.

When Mr. Entertainment's wife slid a songbook on the bar next to them, saying, "Here ya go, gentlemen!" the fireman leaned back a little and looked at her with knit brows as though she were out of her mind. Then he looked down at the songbook and mumbled, "What the hell is *this?*"

He turned his eyes to the shopkeeper beside him as though for an answer, but that man only shrugged vaguely and returned his eyes to the television screen.

"Foul ball!" cried the announcer.

The fireman looked to the bartender, a tall, slender man in his early thirties, an immigrant from Ireland who spoke with a brogue. Thinking the old fellow wanted another drink, he strode over to him.

"What's goin' on?" the fireman asked, nodding to Mr. Entertainment's wife, who was continuing to the scatter the songbooks.

"Oh, they're having karaoke tonight," the bartender said.

"Carry-what?" the old man asked, knitting his brows and looking hard at the bartender as though he couldn't have meant what he just said.

"Karaoke. You know: singing. You get up there and sing, if you want."

"You gotta be kiddin' me," the old man said, and his lips

puckered as though someone had stuck a lemon in his mouth.

"No, that's what they're doing." The bartender put a hand against his chest and shrugged: a defensive gesture that said as clearly as words could, "Hey, listen, it's not my idea."

"Jesus!" the old man mumbled, then bunched his lips up into an expression of disgust.

He glanced again at the shopkeeper beside him, and who had heard this interchange, and there passed between them a vibration of shared disapproval. They both scoffed at the idea of people, ordinary people, getting up and trying to sing a song. That was just damned ridiculous! And embarrassing! The fireman felt that he would be embarrassed just to sit there and listen. And who on earth would do such a thing anyway? Could people really have the gall, the lack of shame, to stand up in front of strangers and sing! Not all the beer in the world could have gotten him to do that. Even when he had been a young man he had had more sense than to do something so foolish. And damn it, why did this have to happen tonight when *he* was here! He had come to the bar to get out of the unbroken silence of his apartment, to sit and get a good buzz and allow his thoughts to wander as he stared unseeing at a baseball game— not to hear some fool "singing"! He wondered if he should leave. Well, maybe he would ...

People who were coming expressly to see or be part of the show began arriving. Among the first were two young women in their late twenties. They were both fat and unattractive. As soon as they stepped into the place they said hello to Mr. Entertainment, which made it clear that they were acquaintances of his. They took a seat at a table and when the bartender came over to ask them what they would like they ordered vodkas with cranberry juice. The first thing they did was reach for a songbook and start flipping through its pages. They were oblivious of everything else. When they paid for their drinks they did so with an air of impatient resignation as though they really would have preferred not to pay at all.

Other strange characters followed quickly. The old fireman and shopkeeper never saw these newcomers enter but with the surprised awareness that these were not the kind of people they were used to seeing in bars. In most instances there was no question but that they were oddballs. For instance, in came a man with a perfect rug of a toupee: it was so thick, so black, so obviously *plopped* on the fellow's head that it looked as though he had cut out a wedge of his living room carpet and glued it to his head. ("What the *hell?*" the shopkeeper mumbled, staring.) Next came a very short, nerdy-looking fellow wearing a business suit complete with a gold tie clip and polished patent leather shoes—he looked like a pixie dressed up for a business meeting. Then lumbered in a fellow with a dark, exotic face and deep-set, dark eyes. Then came two middle-aged men, one of whom was bald, the other of whom had a hairline starting halfway back on his head, and both of whom—to tell from the way they giggled and whispered to each other, and touched each other's back in gestures of exclusive confidentiality—were obviously "together." ("Jesus *Christ!*" the fireman said to himself, "look at *that!*") Another remarkable person was a woman who could only be described as an Amazon. She was big and powerful. She stood six feet, three inches tall, and her bare arms were startlingly muscular: she had the biceps of a bodybuilder. On account of her fair complexion and even features, it was, perhaps, understandable how someone might have considered her attractive, at least from the neck up; but the average man shuddered to consider her as a whole: all that muscular, powerful bulk in a feminine wrapping. She could have beaten up half the men in the place, and, likewise, half the men in the place said to themselves, "I wouldn't want to get in a fight with *her!*" Oddly enough she was accompanied by a young man of stick-like thinness and butterfly delicacy. He wore the tightest of blue jeans and a torso-hugging knit sweater that highlighted his bony, fragile form. He carried a dainty shoulder bag and seemed to tiptoe as he walked.

By nine thirty Mr. Entertainment had finished setting up his equipment. As his wife puttered about him, looking over two large cases filled with song track CDs, he picked up a microphone, tapped it lightly, and spoke into it, "Check ... check, check ..." His voice boomed out above the television announcer declaiming a home run. He made several adjustments at the mixing console and added a tad of reverb to the input. "Check ... check ... check." He looked over to the bartender and nodded affirmatively, quickly, as though to say, yes, he was ready. The bartender turned down and then off the volume of the television sets even as a blast of loud music emanated from Mr. Entertainment's loudspeakers, and in another moment he was holding a microphone and announcing enthusiastically:

"Good evening, ladies and gentlemen and welcome to Angie's Place! My name is Mr. Entertainment and this is Karaoke Night! That's right, this is the place and now is the time when *you* get to be a star! Just take look a through one of our song books, pick a song and write it down on a slip of paper, and bring it to me, and we'll get you up here in no time! Don't be shy! Once you get hold of the mic, you won't want to give it up!" He pressed a button on one of his audio components and the music blared out: a horn-heavy, big band introduction to "On a Wonderful Day Like Today," and in the next moment he was belting out the peppy lyrics.

—And so he kicked off the show, filling the bar with music and his voice, and not only singing but also animatedly, unabashedly performing. He held the microphone with his left hand as with his right he made delicate swirls in the air, and stepped briskly this way and that, and made faces in time to the music. To see the verve and animation he put into his performance, one might have thought he was not in some obscure bar in Brooklyn before a half a dozen old sots and another two dozen strange-looking patrons but rather in the middle of Madison Square Garden entertaining an audience of thousands of cheering, adoring fans.

The old fireman and shopkeeper at the bar stared at him with blank faces and open mouths as though they had just been transported into a new and bizarre world. Sheer embarrassment formed a large part of their unblinking astonishment: they couldn't believe a grown man could have so little self-respect as to interrupt the sedate honor of the place—as it were—and start dancing and singing as though he were hopped up on drugs. Granted that he had an acceptable voice and was clearly comfortable performing, the fact remained that it was all just "too much." Neither of them had any inkling that however preposterous Mr. Entertainment seemed, he was to be the least remarkable of tonight's performers.

As usual the evening started off slowly and Mr. Entertainment was the only one singing. He belted out another two songs, each of which was met by the pitiably hollow and somehow insulting sound of applause that comes from but a few pairs of clapping hands—for at this early hour the bar was but sparsely populated. This didn't faze or embarrass him, for he didn't regard himself as a singer. He only sang because it was a part of his responsibility as the host, because it set the musical tone to the evening and encouraged others to come to the microphone. He always worried about "off" nights when only a handful of people showed up and the establishment made so little money that his fee seemed unacceptably exorbitant. Two such weekends in a row were sufficient to have an owner calling him over at the end of the night and telling him that his show was canceled until further notice. The only possible hedge against this was to ensure that patrons who showed up got into the spirit of things—had a good time—and stayed as long, and spent as much, as possible. And so from the first he repeatedly urged everyone to sing, to fill out slips with their selections and bring them up to him. "Don't be shy," he coaxed, his voice booming over the speakers, "we're all friends here, no reason to hang back. Just come on up! We're all waiting to hear you!" In making this latest appeal he happened to look to the bar, to the old fireman, who turned his head away and mumbled gruffly:

"Yeah, right!"

The shopkeeper beside him gave a single, low, bark of a laugh, but said nothing in return as he reached out for another swig of his scotch.

It happened that this evening Mr. Entertainment would not have to worry about having a crowd. It slowly but surely materialized, and became evident especially after ten thirty. People came singly, or by twos, or in little groups of three or four. Some of them were people he had had invited via an email list, while others were neighborhood folks who had seen the advertisement in the window.

As they entered Angie's Place and sat at the bar or at one of the high, square tables throughout the floor, the old fireman was more certain than ever that there was something "wrong," something strange, about them. It wasn't just the way some of them looked, though, to be sure, some of them looked odd; no, it was something else, something in their aura—in the tentative, suspicious energy they brought with them. They did not walk in naturally and comfortably, with the easy, confident gait of people who went to a bar as easily as they went to a supermarket, but rather with a surreptitious, apprehensive uncertainty, as though someone or something had pushed them through the threshold against their will and they had entered some kind of lion's den.   They would make a beeline for an empty table or some unoccupied space at the bar, order a drink, and either guzzle it down in a matter of minutes, as though quickly to numb themselves to some unpleasant task, or hold it in their hands with the awkwardness of people who never drink but feel compelled to make a show of it.   Then they would reach out for a songbook in a leisurely, offhand manner only to become instantaneously engrossed in it, gazing down on the lists with the same singleness of purpose with which a seminarian might examine a passage of Scripture. When they eventually wrote down their selections, they would consider what they had chosen and seemed unable to decide which song they wanted to sing first, which second, which third; or whether they would sing any of them and ought to look for something different. When they had made their selection, however, they would leave their table or bar stool and with a discreet, self-effacing air hand their slip of paper to Mr. Entertainment or his wife who, with a smile of thanks, would dutifully take it and place it in the queue.

The first singer of the evening was one of the two fat girls who had come earliest into the bar.   Mr. Entertainment introduced her as Carol. "Let's give Carol a big hand, c'mon now!" he said, himself leading off the applause. Most of the newcomers clapped politely, and there were one or two people who knew Carol through evenings such as these and whooped or whistled encouragingly: offering her the "support" of one performer to another.

The old regulars at the bar however did not clap and only looked on more surprised than ever at this obese young woman whose bottom was as wide as a refrigerator and who, now, forthrightly stepped into the spotlight shining down from overhead, thus baffling the dictates of propriety and personal dignity. For, really, why on earth would you be so eager to show yourself off when you looked like that? Then again, perhaps she was conscious of possessing a talent so immense and unique as would cast even her disproportionate physique into a better, more attractive light. One wondered; it seemed the only logical conclusion. The music began and Carol raised the microphone to her mouth and started to sing.

She had chosen a ballad of love and longing, originally recorded and made famous by a singer who had risen to fame on account of the bell-like quality to her tone. But the voice that now boomed out over the loudspeakers was anything but that. Though it was never off-key it too often rose into an ear-splitting shriek that sent a half-shocked, half-fearful shiver down one's spine.

The old fireman looked about, first to the shopkeeper whom he had been sitting beside all evening and hadn't said more than two words to, then to the bartender; and to each of them his eyes seemed to ask, "This is a joke, right? She can't be serious, can she? Tell me this is a joke!"

Of course it wasn't a joke and the young woman was as serious as cancer. She had been trying to be a professional singer for several years. She regularly performed in karaoke and piano bars. She was sure that if only she could get a "lucky break," if only she knew the "right" people, she could be a sensation. She had sometimes thought about auditioning for television talent contests, but a remnant of common sense reminded her that she didn't fit the expected, desired mold—that she was "a little heavy" and didn't have the model good looks that popular singers, in this visual age, were expected to have. At other times she would think that this didn't matter; that she had more than enough talent to make up for that superficial shortcoming: the quality of her voice would bewitch an audience into overlooking her appearance and rouse up in them a clamorous appreciation. She often went over in her mind all those singers who were neither slender nor especially attractive—even if these exceptions to the rule numbered no more than half a dozen in the last twenty years, and even though, however unkind age had been to their looks, they had been, in the first flush of notoriety, slender or somewhat attractive. But her dream of becoming a famous singer burned in her like a low, steady flame. It gave her the strength to get up in the morning and face each day of her real life, which was that of an obese twenty-six year old woman who had never had a man—who feared she never would have one—and who drudged her way through five days a week at the front desk of a Social Security

Office, trying to assist the old, sickly, or indigent wrecks of America. "One day I'm gonna make it big," a voice in her head would reassure her throughout her long, tedious, alienating days; and fame, money, and love would all be hers, and her life would become the opposite of all the hateful things it now was.

For the past two years she had been especially fond of performing at the shows hosted by Mr. Entertainment because his song selection was extensive and featured many of those by her favorite singers. He also had a better sound system than most: as she told her friends and other people she might talk to during the course of an evening, "You can really hear your voice here. There are other places that it gets all muddled up with the music." Little did she suspect that that was, if anything, a point against her. For in fact she had mistaken an ability to sing forthrightly for the ability to sing well. She mistook loudness for fineness of tone. The only thing that made her stand out from other singers was the ability to fill a room with large unlovely sounds. When she reached for a high note she always wound up screaming it, her voice assuming a hard, harsh, drilling quality that made people turn to one another wide-eyed as they gritted their teeth in plaster smiles. And so tonight as she ended her song—the first of several she would sing—she threw back her head, elevated the microphone to her mouth, and put all the power of her heavy being into maintaining a roar not unlike what one might expect to hear from a water buffalo into which a lion has just sunk its fangs. She emptied her lungs so completely that her face turned red, then purple, then an ashen gray.

"Let's hear it for Carol!" Mr. Entertainment enthusiastically announced.

Polite applause broke out. Amid this small acclaim the fat girl blushed for pride, then with little tiptoeing steps wended her way back through the crowd to her table—feeling once again, as she never did at work or in her personal life, some smidgeon of reassurance that she was worthy of people's positive attention.

At the bar the old fireman blurted out, "Jesus Christ!" He looked about him again at the strange crowd, at all these weird people who sat or stood looking at songbooks, intending to sing, and became a little agitated, fidgeting in his seat with an ex-

pression that vacillated between anger and distressed resignation, just as one might expect a man to look when he discovers
he's just been robbed. He waved over the bartender.

"How long is this supposed to go on?" he asked.

"Whatd'ya mean, how long? It's all night."

"Jesus Christ!"

The bartender laughed. He understood why the old timer
was irritated, but already he had made a lot more money on
tips than he usually did by this time, and he was happy to
think of how much he would make before the evening ended.
Moreover he had come to know many of the people who came
here to sing, and though he would have agreed that many of
them were a little strange, he also knew that they were harmless, bought liquor, made the bar money, and gave him tips.

"I gotta get outa here," the old man grumbled, half to himself, half to the shopkeeper he was sitting beside, and who now
actually said something in response:

"I don't blame ya."

"This is ridiculous."

"Yeah. Ridiculous."

"Can't even go out to watch a freakin' game in peace!"

"Yeah. Can't even watch the game."

"Sheesh!"

The other shook his head.

They both half turned in their chairs and looked over their
shoulder when Mr. Entertainment called up the next singer:

"Frankie Cadenza! C'mon, Frankie, get up here!"

There strutted up to the microphone the short man in the
business suit. He was only a little over five feet tall. The suit
made everything about him look miniature with the exception of
his head, which, on account of its thick curly hair, looked disproportionately large. His real name was Bob Krankenhauser—
which simply would not do as the name of the singer he wanted
to be. His secret ambition was to be a romantic crooner; he had
been told and believed that he had a "smooth" sound; consequently, he invariably sang American standards, and now as
the opening strains of a lush orchestration for "Come Rain or
Come Shine" filled the air, he took a dramatic stance, putting
his legs a little apart and holding up his right a little as though
he were about to conduct members of a sixty-piece orchestra

who were playing for him. Just as he was about to start singing
the first words, however, his nerves—the nerves that always
caused him to guzzle three drinks in forty minutes so that he
would have the courage actually to sing in front of people—got
the better of him. His throat was so nervously tight that the
first few words of the song came out as a rasping croak. He
tried to act as though it hadn't been a croak—as though it had
just been a catch in his breathing or perhaps a slip of the
tongue—but everyone knew it was a croak, just as they heard
his voice getting worse as he went on. Beads of sweat popped
out on his forehead as though someone had sprayed him with a
water pistol.

"Oh, Jeez!" the old fireman muttered. He slapped both
hands down on the bar. "That's it! I'm outa here!" He got off
his stool, looking to the bartender with a reprimanding sneer as
though to say, "My whole evening has been spoiled! You've lost
my business!" He walked through the bar glancing to either side
of him at what was now a bigger crowd, and a larger collection
of misfits, than he had bargained for. He strode out the door, no
sooner gaining the sidewalk and the open, cool night air than
drawing a breath of relief, swearing to himself that he would
never come back to Angie's Place when it was having such an
annoying event. Karaoke? Kara-foolishness!

As he stood there a cab pulled up to the curb and two
women in their fifties emerged. They were "dressed up" in accordance with their rather old-fashioned notion of that phrase:
wearing new or just-pressed slack suits, high heels, carrying
pocketbooks, their dyed hair carefully coiffed and sprayed stiffly
into place; everything about them neat, proper, presentable. The
old fireman watched them as they paid the cab driver and with
a shared girlish giggle started for the front door. As they approached him his eyes took on a piercing intensity as something
within him stirred, some sudden flame of lust from out of the
smouldering embers of lost sensuality. For a few seconds he
was no longer the old, paunchy, alcoholic of sixty-one who had
seen it all, done it all, been defeated by it all, and trudged out
his days in solitary, snarling cynicism, but rather the young,
slender, vigorous, wide-eyed, hopeful youth of twenty-five who
had a hundred plans and dreams, and for whom a woman's favor—the approbatory smile, the whispered word of acquies-

cence—held all the good the world could give.   Just as the
women reached him, and almost despite himself, he reached for
the door and opened it for them, putting out his free hand as
though to guide them inside, saying with solicitous, flattering
gallantry, "Ladies!"

The two women passed him with the most begrudging acknowledgment it is possible for one human creature to give another and still be said to give it: the faintest nod of the head,
the most fleeting, resentful half-glance of recognition that politeness can extort from despisement. Without a thank you, with a
new hurry in their step as though to flee from an unpleasantness in their path, they passed through the door, sweeping by
him royally.

The old fireman at once felt the intended insult.

"Ahhh!" he growled, letting go of the door. Anger flared up
in him, directed less at them than at himself for having been
hoodwinked (as he now saw it) into a belittling act of deference.
He strode off. The little flame of hope had already gone out of
him, had withdrawn into the spent, charred embers of his soul.
In its small way the incident was but another confirmation to
him that the only things a man could count on not to let him
down, not to betray their promise, were a good meal and a stiff
drink.

The two women were Estelle and Dora. They lived in the
area and had been coming to Angie's Place "off and on" since it
had had a karaoke night, and they had met here. Over the last
few weeks they had been coming every Saturday night to Mr.
Entertainment's shows.   Estelle was fifty-five and Dora was
fifty-nine. Aside from their age they had little in common, but
that had proven to be more than enough on those evenings
when they found themselves to be the only older women in the
place. Neither of them had children and both of them had been
married more than once. In each case their husbands had been
unfaithful or treated them cruelly.   Their experiences had
soured them to men generally, but that had not made it any
easier to do without them, for the alternative was a slow, sad,
lonesome decline into withered, celibate senescence; into becoming the sexless old women they had in their younger years despised.   This was their greatest fear, and each of them had
vowed never to let it happen to herself insofar as she could help

it. That was why they had another thing in common: the reso-
lution to date only younger, much younger, men. In conversation
with other women they would expatiate on how, for them, there
was no point in going out with a man close to their own age because he wouldn't be able to "keep up" with them. Oh, believe
them, they knew what they were talking about! They had yet to
meet a man over forty-five who wasn't washed up, worn out,
wrung dry, and just plain "no fun." And *they* weren't like that!
Why, they were the same now as they had been at twenty-one!
They wanted to go places, to see things, to enjoy life! Go dancing, go to restaurants, travel overseas—live, live, live! Thus
they were always flirting with men who might have been their
sons or—depending on how late the evening had gotten, and
how much they had drunk—their grandsons.

Of the two of them Dora went further out of her way to
look attractive. She always wore short skirts and tended to sit
a little off to the side so that she might cross her legs freely.
She would dangle her high-heeled shoe from the toes of the foot
of her upper leg. While she sat at the bar her general demeanor
was quiet and restrained, but her eyes belied her desperate lookout for potential romance. And however much she seemed
coldly unapproachable to men she wasn't interested in, she
would become aggressively seductive when her young ideal happened to be within striking distance. If a young man stepped
up to the bar beside her for the sake of ordering a drink, she
would turn to him, catch his eyes, flutter her eyelashes de-
murely or part her lips suggestively, and let him know in a
dozen subtle and not-so-subtle ways that she was "interested" in
him. Invariably the reaction she got was the same: a tight
smile, a suddenly galvanized rigidity, an icy, defensive aloofness.
Perhaps he would give her a nod of recognition or say hello, but
as soon as he had his drink in hand he would hurry away as
though having barely escaped a grisly trap. If he had come
with friends he would mention to them with a roll of the eyes or
a relieved guffaw how some old bat at the bar had tried to pick
him up. Dora would always be hurt, flustered, frustrated by the
rejection; but ultimately unfazed. She knew the power of alcohol on the locomotive libido of youth. She knew that one who,
in the beginning of the evening, had given her the cold shoulder
might very well, if he drank long enough and had had no luck

with women his own age, rationalize to himself an anonymous, secret, one-night stand with her—"just for the hell of it." The only problem for her was that by the time his thinking ran in that vein he would be so drunk, so unaware of what he was doing, that his receptivity to her really amounted to a desperate self-immolation, and thus his murmured, leering, slurred, graphic suggestions of intimacy were, each of them, only so many backhanded insults. She would become disgusted with him, with herself, with the way her lonely life had led her here, to this seat, this bar, talking to this young man drunk out of his mind, and she would stiffen, grow silent, distant, hostile, barely looking at him, making it clear to him that she wanted him to get away from her. It was a rare night indeed when she ever went home with anyone.

When she was not amused by them, Estelle was secretly embarrassed by Dora's overt attempts to meet men. She told herself that she could never be so forthright; *she* had too much class for that. Her method was more cerebral, if perhaps more mercenary and no less dishonest. She used her surname of Carnegie as a conversation-starter and lure, for she would always introduce herself with both her first and last name. "Hello," she would say, putting out a hand in a polite handshake, leaning forward slightly, her manner suddenly gracious, obliging, "I'm Estelle *Carnegie.*"

Invariably the bait was taken. "Carnegie?" people would ask. "Are you related to *Andrew* Carnegie?"

Assuming a somewhat embarrassed air that she had practiced so often it was impossible to distinguish it from the real thing, she would explain that yes, yes she was, she was related to that renowned magnate, and would proceed to exaggerate and embellish a genealogy that was in fact so distant and convoluted that for all practical purposes she was no more akin to Andrew Carnegie than she was to King Tut. Nevertheless she made it sound as though he had been her great grandfather whose wealth, power, and prestige had directly devolved to her. Most people accepted her introduction at face value and looked duly impressed, and not because they were entirely naive or gullible. For in New York one might very well walk down the street and run into some notable politician, entertainer, or other public figure, so that it wasn't outlandish at all to suppose one might find oneself rubbing shoulders with a Carnegie in a bar on a Saturday night.   Sometimes however the person she had just introduced herself to would be more cynical than most, doubt her pretension, and skirt impoliteness by inquiring into it, asking for specifics, for names and dates and locations; whereupon she would nip that conversation in the bud with an impatient, "Yes, yes, but I really don't like to talk about all those things!"—making it sound as though her reticence arose from the humility that would not allow her to flaunt her privilege in the face of the less-fortunate.

Estelle didn't sing. She knew she couldn't. No matter how drunk she became, some lingering trace of dignity, some shred of self-respect, always prevented her from attempting it. Moreover it would not have been consistent with the staid, established, superior image of a "Carnegie" that she cultivated to be stepping into the spotlight and trying to entertain a roomful of anonymous "little" people. She almost had no choice but to sit as a spectator with an aloof and somewhat unapproachable air.

But Dora had no such self-imposed limitations. On the contrary she looked forward to singing. She liked to sing and she was sure that she did it fairly well. Besides, it was very tiresome for her to sit at the bar for hours, drink, and listen to other people, especially "little girls"—women in their twenties or thirties—get up there in front of everyone, thinking they were so special. She, Dora, could show them all a thing or two about how to sing and perform a song! After the second drink, and certainly during the third, she would start telling Estelle the same thing she always told her when they came here:

"What these kids don't understand is that *anybody* can sing. So what? The thing is to *entertain* people. Yeah ... yeah . .. that's the thing. To entertain 'em. Know what I mean? Sure. Pfuh!" she would subtly exclaim, looking about the room at the young women who, even when they were unattractive, still had what she did not have and for want of which a core of bitterness expanded yearly within her: the freshness of youth, its potential for growth and improvement. "They don't know a thing about it! They're just *kids*. What do *kids* know?"

Another drink later and she would casually glance about for one of the songbooks, and finding one nearby (there was always one nearby), she would take it up, telling Estelle, "I think *I'll* sing something!"

Estelle would titter, sip her drink, shake her head as though Dora had said something amusing or naughty, and say encouragingly, "Go ahead!"

And so Dora filled out one of the slips of paper with the name of the song she wanted to sing. Estelle didn't bother asking her which one it was. By this time she knew it was one of the three songs that Dora always sang.

By midnight Angie's Place was full. Every seat at the bar was taken, and dozens of people were standing. At the small square tables intended to accommodate two or three persons were gathered five or six who had been drawn together for lack of seating; and though initially uncomfortable sitting with one another they had, after the first few drinks, become bright-eyed and chatty and the best of friends. There were people of all ages. Dora and Estelle were hardly the oldest. There were also two men in their seventies. They were both Italians and one of them sang a spirited, quaint "traditional" Italian song that left the audience sitting with sickly smiles and wishing the old goat would finish as soon as possible. There was also a woman who was eighty-four years old. She didn't sing. In fact, she could barely walk. She had been escorted into the place by her Jamaican caregiver who followed at her side with one hand beneath a shivering arm in order to catch her if her frail steps should falter. She sat at one of the tables in the booths beyond the bar and ordered a ginger ale and whiskey—insisting that it have only a little whiskey, only a few drops, only a touch; and even then she took but two small sips of the drink. She sat there tapping out of time to the music on the table with gnarled hands, and after a half hour, feeling exhausted, she left, her caregiver—a woman of infinite and angelic patience—once again leading her out gently through the crowd.

Generally the older people left early, before midnight or a little after, and the young were always a little relieved to see them go. For no matter how egalitarian they wished to be they could not help feeling that there was something inappropriate in people over a certain age attempting to mingle with them, to insinuate themselves into younger life with its rough and tumble, its carouse, its overtly verbal and sometimes raucous sexuality. There was a time and a place for everything, and the old had

had their day; for them the present ought to have been characterized by a smarter, quieter existence. Besides, their presence
had been to the young a nagging, half-conscious reminder of the
brevity of their own lives. It brought home to them again the
understanding that they too would "get there"—that no matter
how bright, vigorous, or exciting their lives now were, they too
were headed toward the inescapable catastrophe.

One might not have noticed it but all along people had been
going up to Mr. Entertainment and handing him slips of paper
with their names and song selections; he had a fifteen people in
the queue, awaiting their turn in the spotlight. He would duly
hand these off to his wife, who kept track of them, setting them
down neatly in an ordered row, the newest ones topmost and
further away from her, and no sooner getting in one CD sound
track disk than beginning the hunt for the next one, so that
there should never be a pause between singers.

"Gertrude!" Mr. Entertainment called out, scanning the
crowd. "C'mon up, Gertrude!"

She was the large, powerful, hulking Amazon who had entered the bar with her delicate, pencil-thin consort. As though
they were inseparable, he even now followed her as she made
her enormous way through the crowd. As she stepped under the
spotlight and took the microphone, he stopped a few feet away
from her, leaning against a table, folding his arms, and gazing
on her with a slight, reassuring smile. His last name was Finny,
and he was known by his nickname of Fin. He was more than
just Gertrude's friend; he was also her—manager. That anyone
should need a manager to sing at some anonymous bar in
Brooklyn, or that any performer would think she needed it,
would have seemed to most people laughably absurd. But
Gertrude and Fin were not most people. They lived in a world
different from that of the rest of humankind. It was a world of
their own making, their own interpretation; it arose from the
unique personalities they were, and consequently adhered to a
physics different from that which governed the rest of the world.
They had met each other two years earlier and had been drawn
to each other by a sympathetic understanding of shared pariah-
dom. As sometimes happens in nature, where the existence of
one kind of creature is dependent on that of a wholly other kind,
so here an equally strange symbiosis had occurred, and two en-

tirely opposite types had become the closest of friends, each of them reinforcing and sustaining the other's peculiar self-conceptions. Gertrude's kernel of an idea that she should be in show business had been carefully cultivated by Fin, who had convinced himself that he could guide, nurture, and promote her talent to the eventual splendor of worldwide acclaim and his own financial security. Thus he dragged her through the city every other night to appear at places that had an "open mic." He had her singing at piano bars, restaurants, jazz clubs, even if they had to wait all night, till minutes before closing time, for her to do a three-minute song. He had had her take head shots and make demo recordings. He pushed her to audition for Broadway and off-Broadway shows, for television talent contests, for cruise ship revues, even for garage bands in Queens and Long Island. "Hey, you gotta start somewhere," he would tell her, whenever they came away from a basement in which she had stuck out like a gigantic sore thumb among a group of teenagers who had hardly been able to play, so speechlessly entranced had they been by the weird presence of this duo. Fin wasn't blind to her intimidating appearance, but regarded it as part of her uniqueness. He calculated that while she would have to create the taste by which she was appreciated, her ultimate success would on that account be the larger and more lasting. Of one thing he was entirely correct: Gertrude's appearance was an effective gimmick for getting attention. Standing head and shoulders above every other woman and most of the men, she drew all eyes to herself. She stood there a hulking giant, her shoulders slightly stooped and hunched together, her long, styleless, and somewhat greasy-looking brown hair hanging forward on either side of her down-tilted head as she prepared to sing, She held the mic not at her mouth but close to her chest. The prelude to a pounding rock song began and she started singing exactly on cue. Her voice was powerful, impulsive, and so deep that it sounded like the angry snarling of a Rottweiler or a Bullmastiff. She did not sing so much as bark out lyrics with an occasional, and precarious, holding of a note. With every other word she rocked back and forth, massively, impulsively, stomping her right foot as though she were smashing the head of a foe she had just overpowered and thrown down in mortal combat. Her limp hair swung back and forth, slapping against her face.

The diminutive Fin watched her with an ever-increasing exhilaration. A look of wild, loving wonder came into his eyes. It was clear that he was thinking and feeling:

"Amazing! Amazing!"

The rest of the audience also thought she was amazing—though for a very different reason. They were appalled. Men shuddered to see her huge, powerful stomping body, to hear her tenebrous growling, while the women sat with open mouths, then turned to one another with incredulous eyes and set lips as though they were trying not to laugh or had become suddenly nauseated. But after their initial amusement or revulsion had passed a gentler sentiment often succeeded as people realize what a tough hand this woman had been dealt in life. It couldn't have been easy for her, looking as she did, the antithesis of everything feminine, and having, too, evidently, no sense of how utterly talentless she was. It was one thing to be unattractive and a bad singer; quite another not to know it—to think, indeed, that one was the opposite of all this and unwittingly drag one's dignity through the muck of public ridicule.

Her song ended with a rising trill of guitars, a growing volume of drums and cymbals. When it reached its final, explosive chord she dramatically, violently, brought her hand down with the swiftness and power of a railway worker smashing sledgehammer down on a tie; and so brought her performance to an end.

People applauded, sparsely. What else were they going to do? She had been a horror or, at best, a curiosity—yet one had to be polite.

Little Fin was ecstatic and clapped with swift little claps as he jumped up and down a few pert times, his whole skinny, taught, delicate body quickened with pleasure, with confirmed admiration at what he had heard. Gertrude's saw his enthusiasm and she smiled faintly at his "support."

But someone else was evidently just as pleased. A whistle of immense, shrill volume cut through the dying applause like a rapier-slash. People turned in the direction from where it had come, wondering who could be so enthusiastic about something so excruciatingly bad. They saw a middle-aged man who had put his fingers in his mouth to produce the overwhelmingly loud sound. Somehow that vulgar pose and act did not suit him, for what with his graying hair, bowtie, and wire-framed glasses he looked bookish and intelligent, as though he were a doctor or a professor. In fact, he was: he taught Sociology at Brooklyn College. He had been sitting in a darkened corner with the satisfied smile of a man who serendipitously finds himself in circumstances both entertaining and professionally instructive. He had been amused by the singers, but it was the audience's reactions to them that fascinated him, finding in these a kind of microcosm of the world of human interaction. He had been noting every detail of the events around him, and a few times had reached into a vest pocket, extracted a pen, and jotted down notes on a napkin. Always he was on the lookout for how something he saw and heard might be used in the book he was writing. It was to be his fourth book and he had been writing it for the last eight months, for upwards of six hours a day, much of which time was spent flipping through reference books filled with all kinds of tables, charts, equations, and minutely-printed footnotes. His book had been consuming so much of his attention that a few times in the last week he had woken up in the middle of the night, his head pounding with headache as a particular set of statistics had taken on an insidious life of its own and octopally infiltrated into the remotest corners of his brain, squirming naggingly there. His book was tentatively titled, *A Postmodern Analysis of Impactful Divarications Among Key Occupational and Societal Trends*—a title indicating how entirely the professor's brains had been scrambled by academe. It also perhaps hinted at the incipient insanity that would in another year cause him to be committed to an insane asylum. But for now he was rather lucid and enjoying himself hugely, if, as always, solitarily. As for his whistling, he had meant it satirically; and indeed only alcohol had enabled him to express himself so forthrightly. But he had no sooner drawn attention to himself than he quickly took his fingers out of his mouth and with a blush of embarrassment, and a shy lowering of his eyes, took another swig of his second pint of Guinness.

One o'clock in the morning was the bewitching hour for Angie's Place, as it was for so many bars throughout the city: that magical time when the crowd was largest, the liquor flowed most freely, and the last inhibitions had been tossed aside. A loud hum of conversation, punctured with bursts of wild laughter, formed the aural backdrop to the loud music. Often passersby outside would glance through the window, see the crowds and hear the music, and be drawn inside. Sometimes they stayed, but more often than not they turned around and walked out. This was especially true of young people who had been barhopping all night in search of a "hot" crowd and the potential of picking someone up. If they were young men they would no sooner step through the door than see that all the women here were too fat, too old, too dowdy, or otherwise too unattractive for them to want to go to bed with. If they were young, good-looking women, they would see just as quickly that the men here were not what they wanted—were too shabbily blue collar and incapable of providing the kind of "security" that they believed their beauty could command. In either case there would be a period of about thirty seconds during which they would stand just inside the door, looking over the patrons, assessing the atmosphere, then consulting with one another about what to do:

"You don't want to go in *here*, do you?"

"Hell no!"

"Isn't there any other place to go around here?"

"I don't know, but I don't want to stay *here!*"

"Yeah, this sucks."

"Let's go."

—And out they would walk, disappointed in having wasted the time and effort to investigate a place they might have heard about and the good reports of which had proven to be unfounded, and conscious that the evening was running out for them—that in just a few more hours they would have no choice but to return home, alone, and have to wait another whole week before once again making the rounds in search of the Hot Chick or Mr. Right.

Well, Mr. Right might not have been here, but Mr. Entertainment assuredly was. He had kept the show going for over three hours already. Even those patrons who had regarded him and his karaoke show as an unwelcome interruption to their evening had entered somewhat into the spirit of it—helped along with copious amounts of alcohol. To be more precise, they had drunk themselves into that altered state of mind in which one can accept almost anything. If an earthquake had occurred they would have calmly looked about themselves and, with a good-humored smile, have asked their neighbor, "Mmmm—what was that?" Their faces were flushed, their eyes were bright or heavy-lidded, and they always looked up when a song ended and Mr. Entertainment rousingly exclaimed, "Let's hear it for—!"—whoever had just been caterwauling. They would clap languidly once or twice as though to prove that they were paying attention, then sink back into the medicated distraction of whatever dark thoughts or pain had brought them here to begin with.

Angie's Place had never had much of a problem with rowdy patrons. Those personalities inclined to guzzle booze and become aggressive somehow knew on walking into the place that here such nonsense wouldn't be tolerated. Perhaps it was on account of the "neighborhoody" feel of the place—the sense that everyone here knew everyone else, would look out for everyone else, and at the least hint of disturbance would do his part to suppress it. That wasn't true, but it was a serendipitous impression that usually kept the worst of the riffraff at bay. But in fact "things" did happen here, and tonight would be one of those times.

Earlier in the evening, a little after twelve o'clock, a man had entered the place and smilingly taken a seat at the bar, greeting the bartender with cheerful friendliness. He seemed to be the most likeable of fellows: just another nice guy. He was in his early thirties and a little overweight. He wore a cap and jacket, neither of which he took off. His first drink had been a pint of stout beer which he had put away in five minutes—apparently he had been very thirsty. In the next half hour he put away two more. Between them he had ordered shots of whiskey. With each drink he finished, with each pint glass or whiskey shot he consumed, he uttered an increasingly loud "Ah-hhhhh!" and, making a fist, lightly pounded the bar.

Like everyone else he had watched and listened to one singer after another, but the truculence that had been building up within him for the last forty minutes was reaching a breaking point. For alcohol always had the same effect on him. First it made him cheerful, gregarious, almost charming; then it made him more serious, contemplative, and critical to the point of argumentative; and finally it released his true, essential na-

ture, which was coarse and cruel. He watched as Mr. Entertainment announced the next singer—"Katie! C'mon up, Katie!"—
and his eyes were narrowed, his jaw working as though he were
talking to himself.

Katie was about thirty years old and everything about her
seemed limp, tepid, indifferent. She couldn't have stood out in a
crowd if she had wanted to; her most outrageous speech or
words wouldn't have drawn the least attention. She had mousy
brown hair and her blue eyes looked out at the world timidly
from behind her unfashionable glasses. She had no figure to
speak of and wore a single-piece, floral-patterned dress that ran
from shoulders to just beneath her knees with a line as straight
as a hanging drape. In every step she took to the microphone,
in every glance she gave or rather averted from the audience,
her shy insecurity was apparent. By nature she was severely in-
troverted and had to force every nerve of her being to get up
and sing, but she couldn't resist the temptation, the need for the
affirmation of applause, however brief or insincere.

When she reached Mr. Entertainment she leaned in toward
him and said something confidentially in his ear. He gave a few
quick nods as though to say, "Yes, yes, fine!" He looked about
him for a second, then reached down for another microphone
and handed it to her. She glanced up shyly at the people watching her as she held the microphone to her lips and explained:

"I always like to use a mic with a cord."

That was when the increasingly angry drunk at the bar, no
longer able to contain himself, shouted:

"Go hang yourself with it!"

People burst out laughing. They turned to him thinking he
had meant his shouted remark as a witticism, that perhaps he
had known it was crude but simply hadn't been able to resist
the opportunity to raise a laugh. But he wasn't smiling, wasn't
laughing, and his red, flushed face showed nothing but liquored-
up hostility. He really *had* wanted the poor woman to wrap the
cord around her neck and hang herself—perhaps from one of the
circulation fans turning slowly overhead. A few people, still
laughing or smiling, shook their heads at him as though he were
a naughty little boy and who had misbehaved.

Katie took the outburst in stride, at least apparently, for
she herself smiled and even seemed to be about to laugh. But

in fact she had been shaken to the core. She had heard the malevolence in the man's voice. She knew it came from an ugly impulse to insult and injure her. Far worse, her own insecurity terrorized her with the stark possibility that the veneer of her poise had been seen through, that not only he but everyone else clearly saw her faults and shortcomings. Her nerves buzzed with fear; her legs began to shake. She wanted to run away, yet she knew that doing so would only further humiliate her and that therefore must go through with her song, even if it killed her. Standing still as a statue, she began singing. She could hardly concentrate on the words as they flashed across the screen. She stammered, was off key, out of tempo; her voice wavered ridiculously. The larger, more active part of her brain was bursting with the withering thoughts: Why did that horrible man have to say that? Why had he shouted it out like that in front of everyone? Wanting to see her hang herself! Was it possible anyone could be so mean? And all she wanted to do was sing a song! She hated him for having made her a laughingstock.

When her song ended and light applause broke out, she hurried back to a table where she had been sitting with a few friends. They had all heard that she hadn't been up to par, and they all knew it was probably on account of the rude comment shouted at her. One of these friends, a young man, tried to tried to alleviate her upset by assuring her that she shouldn't take seriously anything people here said. "Don't you know these people are messed up?" he told her, patting, rubbing her back, leaning in to her with a comforting, reassuring smile and manner. "You can't take what anybody in here says seriously. They're all *drunks*, for God's sake! They're all plastered! What do *they* know? That guy's an ass. Just look at him!—you can see he's loaded up. He can't even stand at the bar without wobbling. You were good—really you were! Pick out another one, go ahead." And he pushed toward her one of the songbooks.

But she had lost the will to sing again; the sting of the humiliation still rankled in her heart, was still pumping its will-sapping poison into her soul. "No, no, I don't want to do any more," she said.

"What? Sure you do!" he insisted. "C'mon! What're'ya talkin' about? You can't do just one!"

"Oh ... I don't want to ... one was enough."

"Well, if you're not gonna put up a song for yourself, I will," he said, grabbing the songbook, flipping through its pages for a song he knew she did, and filling out one of the slips in her name. She saw what he was doing, protested against it, and tried to grab the pencil out of his hand, but he, with a laughing "Get outa here!" turned away from her and continued filling out the slip, then threw down the pencil and bolted out of his seat. She tried to stop him, she called out his name, "Gene!"—but it was too late, he was gone, was already making his way through the crowd, and in another moment was handing the slip to Mr. Entertainment, who dutifully and with a thankful nod took it and put it into the rotation cycle.

As it happened she would not have to worry again this evening about the drunk at the bar; at least, not that particular drunk. Having grown louder and more obnoxious by the minute, he had begun taunting everyone who got up to sing. For a while people found his antics rather funny since he would sometimes sing along in a gruff, roaring voice, or would, in mock encouragement, shout at the top of his lungs, "Sing it baby!" and clap with explosive loudness. Another time he called out to a singer to go stick the mic where the sun don't shine. But then he got off his chair and started dancing—or at least flailing his arms around, shaking his rear end, and barking out lyrics to a song not necessarily the one that was being sung. A few times he tripped over the legs of a chair and almost fell onto a table full of patrons.

The owner had had enough of him. It was in times like these that she wished she had a bouncer, but she wasn't afraid to confront anyone, especially when there was a crowd, since any drunk who dared to lay his hands on her would have brought down on himself every man in the place. Moreover she had an agreement with the bartender that if there was ever any "trouble" they would handle it "together"—which really meant that *he* would handle anything that became physical while she would call the police. And so now, at her request, the bartender followed her out from behind the bar and onto the floor. She stepped up behind the rowdy drunk, who was still shuffling his feet in dazed dance, and forthrightly and hard poked him in the back two times with loud, "Hey!"

The man spun around and fury flashed across his face. Perhaps he had been expecting to see another man and was eager to throw a fist. But when he saw it was a woman, the owner, he caught himself and even straightened up a bit as he stood unsteadily. He squinted a little as he tried to focus on her.

"That's enough!" she commanded, her eyes, her expression severe.

"Wha? Wha was enough? I was just dancin'!" he blurted out.

"This ain't a dance club. There's no dancin' in here. And you're gettin' rowdy."

"Wha ...?" He shifted his eyes up to the bartender who was standing just behind her, and knew he was there for reinforcement. "Wha's goin' on?"

"No dancing!" the owner said again. "And no more booze for you—you're cut off for the rest of the night."

"Wha ...?"

"You heard me. You're gettin' rowdy. If you can't sit down and act like a human being, I suggest you leave."

This "suggestion" offended the drunk and made his resentment surge. He wanted to fight, to show her, to show everyone, that he couldn't be talked to like that. Nor was he intimidated by the bartender, whom he knew he could take down with a single punch. But he wasn't so far out of his senses that he had lost all capacity for analysis; in his inebriated, dull-minded way he understood that all around him other men had been looking on, listening, regarding him with mounting, angry disapproval— clearly not on his side and therefore willing to unite against him if it came to a brawl; and while he might be able to take on two or even three of them, he knew he'd lose in a contest against fifteen. He stood there simmering in drunken frustration, his face red, his eyes bleary and glaring at the owner, the bartender, the people around him, aware of his ultimate powerlessness.

All this time the music had continued to play and someone was singing (oddly enough, as the holidays were months away) "It's Beginning to Look a Lot Like Christmas."

"Alright," the drunk said, seeming to have dismissed all his hostility at once. He straightened up a bit, pulled back his shoulders, and shoved his baseball cap lower down on his head so that the visor nearly hid his eyes. "Alright!" he said again, this with an air of offended honor. "I wasn't doin' nothing wrong, but if you want me to go, I'll go!"

He turned around and started to leave. The owner glanced at the bartender, who understood what she wanted him to do, and he stepped around her and followed the drunk through the crowd as though politely to escort him outside but really to make sure that he didn't destroy anything along the way. He followed him clear outside to the sidewalk and watched him walk off, his steps unsteady, wavering, and a few times almost tripping over himself. When the bartender came back inside a minute later he was clearly relieved. With a smile now, he shook his head and rolled his eyes as though to say good-humoredly, "See what I have to put up with?"

The incident had been handled with appropriate discretion; no more than a third of the patrons that evening even knew it had occurred.

Mr. Entertainment kept the night rolling forward. As soon as one singer finished he would at once turn on an upbeat, party-like number as background music while his wife queued up the next track. One after another he called up the singers, whose names were either real or assumed: Tara, Bobby, Eliot, Francis, Connie, Morgan, "Big C," "Sparkles," "Dynamite." There they were again, as they were week after week: the fat girls who sang their fat hearts out with sappy love songs; the tall, gaunt, awkward man-boys with thick glasses who squinted at the screen and missed half the words; the immigrant working man from Warsaw who sang classic Motown with a thick Polish accent; the one-armed, white-bearded Vietnam veteran who belted out protest songs from the late '60s; the "actors" who had never been nor would ever be more than an anonymous extras; the "singer/songwriter" who played badly and composed still worse; the Broadway belters who chose hackneyed show tunes and for whom a ballad became an exercise in lung capacity; the old man or woman of seventy or more who refused to believe they were too old to "go out" and "have fun" as they used to do thirty or forty years before, and who looked foolish and out of place; all, all were here, just as their counterparts might have been found in a dozen other karaoke bars throughout the city. They were

the lost souls of New York—the losers, the lonely, the
wannabes, the dreamers, the self-deceivers. Some of them had
no illusions about their inability to sing, but forced themselves
to get up in front of strangers, and face suppressed snickers, for
the sake of a round of applause, which, however brief and insincerely offered, at least gave an impression of appreciation, some
semblance of validation of their worthiness. They needed to believe that they were more than they were—more than just a few
atoms in the swarming, faceless, desperate commotion of the
city. They needed to believe that they had been born for something other than laboring at dead-end jobs, dating people they
couldn't love, sitting at home in thoughtless boredom, and always, always aware of the frightening swiftness of time, of how
in the blink of an eye it had left them at their time of life still
unanchored and insecure, still swaying in the winds of circumstances always beyond their control. They needed something,
anything, to help them believe they wouldn't be crushed in the
end.

In his many years of doing these shows Mr. Entertainment
and his wife had heard the best and worst of singers. They regarded it as a point of their professionalism that even when
someone took the microphone and howled like a catarrhal wolf,
they would give no hint of the pain it caused their ears but
would on the contrary either keep busy with the equipment or
even lend the poor deluded soul a little emotional support by
gazing on him with an air of pleased attention and then, when
he had finished, lead the applause. They knew of course that
most people who sang at their shows had but average voices,
and they always began an evening patiently prepared to have
their eardrums assaulted; but invariably the horrible sounds began to take a toll even on their inured nerves. In this regard
Mr. Entertainment's wife was less tolerant than her husband.
Even her good humor and sweetness of spirit couldn't overcome
the weakness of the flesh. If a stretch of four or five scratching,
screeching, scouring voices had come and gone, and there
seemed no end in sight of the auditory torture, she would step
over to her husband and say:

"Could you take over for a while? I need to go outside for a
little air."

He could always tell by the way she said "a little air" that the evening had begun to get on her nerves, that she "just couldn't take it anymore!"—as she would invariably explain herself when the evening was over. He understood. He smiled, sometimes laughed a little. "Sure, that's fine," he would say. "Take your time."

She would go outside to stand for a while in the grateful silence (or rather, the relative silence, since she could still hear the music coming from inside) and smoke a cigarette. Depending on her mood she would either hate the idea of having to go back inside or indifferently turn around and resume her duties. In any case her little break would have refreshed her spirits, and she would reenter the bar better able to endure another forty-five minutes of shrieks and wails.

She was always on the lookout for the "good" singers. She continually looked up to the crowd in search of them much as a sailor lost at sea might repeatedly look over the wastes of water for some sign of landfall. Should someone enter the bar whom she knew to have a pleasant voice, she would rush over to him with a songbook and plop it down in front of him with the command:

"Pick a song!"

"I just got here!" he would say.

"So what? Pick one! I'll put you up right now! You won't have to wait."

"But I didn't even have a drink yet."

"Oh! Alright. Drink! But then pick one! Pick two or three! Just ... just pick *something*—quick!"

—And off she would go, waddling away (she had the shifting, side-to-side walk of a heavy person, though her weight was normal), resuming her place by her husband and again keeping track of the singers to be called up.

She was not mistaken in her tastes. The people she thought sang well really were gifted. They had good natural voices—the kind that cannot be bought and whose engaging timbre no amount of training can bestow. They did not scream or shout. They did not strain. They did not engage in any of the fancy wavering and warbling that characterizes so much modern singing, and which coarse taste encourages with applause. Even when they were nervous they sang well, for even where talent is compromised it rises above the common run of things. Their voices sometimes blended so perfectly with the instrumental tracks it seemed as though they were merely moving their mouths to the recorded song. If they happened to be singing a ballad the effect was almost magical: throughout the room people would perk up their ears, and in the space of thirty or forty seconds the chatter and laughter would die down, the growing silence would, as it were, feed on itself till everyone had become quiet, and all would be turned in the direction of the artist, surprised that they should hear something so good in a place like this. They would congratulate the singer as she came away from the microphone, shaking their heads at her in awe, holding up their hands as they clapped and whistled. Should she happen to stop before her admirers and thank them for their enthusiasm she would listen for the two-hundredth time gushing praise for her talent and the suggestion, almost the demand, that she pursue music "professionally":

"You should be in a band.... You should go on auditions.... You should sing at nightclubs.... Why don't you try to get an agent? Why don't you try to get on TV? Why don't you try to speak to a producer or something?"

You should, you should, you should ... why don't you, why don't you, why don't you ...

For the two-hundredth time she would explain that she was already "trying" to break into "the business." She might mention the bands she had been in, the recordings she had made, and how she even had a web site they could go to in order to learn more about her. But if the singer was older she might explain how that kind of ambition was all in her past, that she had tried for years to make a name for herself in music and nothing had ever come of it; that now she only sang "for fun."

Generally it was only young people who seemed astonished to hear these extraordinary singers and learn that they had been unsuccessful in the pursuit of a musical career. Older people however never had this reaction. They knew better. They knew what life was. They knew that in small things as well as great the arbiter of success was often Chance, or, as some would have called it, Fate. The greatest talent on earth would always remain anonymous unless Luck came to meet it at least a little of the way. The youngest, most starry-eyed, and ambitious of these young, good singers would themselves one day come to understand this. One day they would look back on their lives, consider how hard they had tried, and tried and tried, and yet failed to make a career out of music even while living in the one place where the opportunities for doing so were greatest. Their consolation would be the knowledge that there was nothing else they could have "done" to have brought about a different result. The more thoughtful among them would even perceive how their fate had been decided by events to which, at the time, they hadn't given a second thought: a bus they had missed, an audition not gone to, a phone call not made, a party left too soon;— any one of a hundred things that however seemingly inconsequential at the time had in fact sealed their fate, pushing or pulling them to this anonymous point in time. In thinking this way they would make peace with their failures; could not feel bitter or cheated about it. They would have an insight into the infinite chain of events that is life and all existence, and how their own actions—for good or ill—had been but links in that chain, and necessarily therefore conditioned by those that had gone before and which had been beyond their control.

None of the singers at Angie's Place that night had chased fame more relentlessly than Johnny Soul—as he called himself. When people heard about him for the first time they were inclined to roll their eyes in snide amusement, wondering why anyone would invite ridicule by giving himself such a patently artificial and affected name. To his mind however it sounded suave and enticing; if anything, a help to further his "career."

He was a tall, bald, stick-thin black man of forty years old. Like so many tall, thin people he looked elegant. His gait was loping and leisurely. His hands were delicate with their long, tapering fingers, and when he took something up into them—a pencil, a wallet, a drink—he seemed to caress rather than hold it. Whenever he went out to sing he was always impeccably groomed and dressed in fashionable and somewhat formal attire. He was a charming conversationalist. Despite his outward flash he conducted himself with a quiet, cheerful, engaging humility so that people invariably liked him and were willing to overlook or ignore his ridiculous name. He had been singing since he was a boy and had been in various bands and vocal groups. Yet even in the days when record companies had been thriving and looking for people to promote, he had, either in a group or as a solo act, never penetrated beyond the outermost fringes of fame. He had "been around" for so long, and for so long had pushed himself into so many situations in the hope of recognition, that many of New York's musicians who played in small clubs or for recording sessions knew who he was. If they had been asked their opinion of his vocal ability they would have smiled and said only, "He's alright." And that was the problem: he was only "alright," only an offhand, shrugging, "good";—not exceptional, not exciting, not stirring. His falsetto voice came naturally to him and was pitch-perfect, but it was thin and lacked a certain heartfelt spontaneity. He was so focused on maintaining and cultivating a "soulful" sound that for him singing had become formulaic, and consequently the passion of the melody, the meaning and spirit of lyrics, were lost to him, and he would sing love ballads with the same easy, smooth, controlled blandness with which he occasionally attempted rock and roll. His stage presence was professional, however; a lifetime of public singing had made him comfortable before an audience. In the spotlight he had an easy, almost becalming demeanor, a quiet, inviting cheerfulness. He would turn his attention to first this and then that part of the room, careful to leave no one out, to invite all in. When reaching some tender phrase in a lyric he would, as though on cue, put out a hand and close his eyes. It was all very easy, very casual and ingratiating.

But ultimately Johnny Soul's one flaw was also the worst any singer could have: he lacked an artistic temperament. If he had had this, he would, in the first place, never have assumed his stage name; instinctively he would have known it was an embarrassment. He dressed well, and could modulate his voice to a vanishing point in a gossamer strain, and everything about his performance was polished, practiced, and planned to a tee; and yet for all that something essential and necessary was missing. For in art there is always less calculation than instinct—an immediate knowledge of the right way, and which not all the planning or forming after models can substitute for. Johnny Soul's problem was that he could not feel music in an immediate way; rather, he had a formula to follow, and he followed it rigidly. He could never quite convey the stirring joy or sweet wistfulness of a song because he himself did not feel it, or did not feel it enough. Had he been capable of doing so, the fame he had chased for a lifetime might have proven to be less elusive, though even then it would not have been guaranteed.

He occasionally dropped in on Mr. Entertainment's karaoke shows, just as he dropped in on a dozen other such shows throughout the city. He would sing till closing time. When he finished his first song that evening to light applause he held onto the microphone a moment longer to mention that he would be appearing at a certain jazz club in Manhattan. He gave the name and address of the place, and the nights he would be there, and added that he hoped everyone would come out and see him. To tell from the way everyone nodded and smiled with satisfaction it seemed that they were eager to see him perform there, though in fact a half hour later most of them had forgotten what he had said, and those who remembered would no more have paid to hear him sing than they would have paid to stick their heads in a microwave oven.

Of all those who would sing this evening, only one had yet to step up to the microphone, and now Mr. Entertainment called out her name:

"Dora! Where are you, Dora! Come on up!"

The announcement caught her almost unawares. She had been talking to Estelle, complaining of how the men tonight were all a little strange, none of them worth "going after," when, about to take another sip of her drink, she heard her name and swung around in her chair. Estelle gave a little patter of applause and said, "It's you!"

"Finally!" Dora said.

Despite her apparent impatience, she got up from the bar stool very slowly and then stood still for a moment as though preparing herself for her performance. In fact she was just making sure she was stable enough to walk. Three months before she had bounded off her seat not realizing how drunk she was and, after taking two steps, had tumbled to the floor, where she had lain for a few seconds sprawled out and flailing her arms and legs like an octopus yanked up from the ocean depths into the open air. Everyone around her had rushed to her assistance, some trying to help her up, others (those who had had more than a couple of drinks) yelling to leave her where she was—"Don't try to move her! She might have broken her neck!

Oh my God, you'll kill her!" She had been lucky that she hadn't broken a leg or a hip. She had been so humiliated that for two months she had stopped going out altogether, telling herself she really was too old for it. But after that period her pride had healed enough, and her lonesome, bored, empty life had again become so unendurable, that she had resumed her weekend carousing. Besides (she would tell herself), she wasn't going to meet anyone—by which she meant, anyone who might one day be her husband—by sitting alone in her living room.

The three songs that Dora always sang were "Fever," "My Heart Belongs to Daddy," and—the one she was about to do now—" Whatever Lola Wants." For nothing but the torchiest of torch songs befit this most *fatale* of *femmes fatale.*

She did all that a female singer could do to enhance sultry lyrics. Just as one wrings with all one's might the last lingering stubborn drop out of an old frayed wash rag, so did Dora wring out of herself whatever lingering sexual appeal remained in her spent, dry, withered fifty-nine-year-old person. She was off key, off tempo, and couldn't hold a note without gasping for breath thanks to thirty years of smoking, but none of that mattered because under the influence of three martinis she knew that whatever she lacked vocally would be made up for in her irresistible performance. Yes, she knew how to win men over! As she sang she hunched up her shoulders, puckered her lips, blew kisses, fluttered her eyelids, stuck out a leg as she raised— ever so modestly!—the hemline of her already low dress. She swayed, she twirled, she crouched, she rose and leaned back only to strand straight again and push out her chest with a curling, beckoning finger. She turned around, she looked over her shoulder, she closed her eyes, she interpolated a few pert "Ooo!"s between words. The laughter breaking out all around her, the astonished, unblinking eyes fastened on her, were to her mind proofs of what a great hit she was. Certainly her audience was fascinated—as what audience would not be? The young women looked at her with their mouths open. Coming to the end of the song, she planted her feet firmly apart and stuck her free hand straight up into the air as she finished off the last stanza in a sultry-slurring voice, singing how she always got what she aimed for, that your heart and soul was what she came for, that what Lola wanted, Lola got, that she was irresistible—so irresistible, you fool!—so you might as well give in ... give iiiiiiiiiiinnnnnn!

The music ended with a sudden, terminal crash of cymbals, in accordance to which Dora swung down her raised hand. Then she held her head high, put her shoulders well back so that her chest stuck out, and posed to receive the accolades she knew must come after her spellbinding performance.

And come they did—after a manner. The applause that broke out was vigorous and interpolated by whoops and hollers. The audience felt obliged to repay her energetic performance with some equally boisterous expression of approval. A large factor in their applause was also—pity: it was apparent to everyone that this poor, ageing woman was an emotional wreck, probably alcoholic, yet another lonesome inebriated soul trying to find her way through the darkness of her life.

"That's Dora, everybody!" Mr. Entertainment exclaimed into the microphone, watching her walk off and accept her kudos. "There she is, that's Dora!"

"Oh, God, you were great!" Estelle told her, when she had sat back down. "Just great!"

"Hah!" Dora said, pleased with the compliment, with herself, and too breathless to respond as she reached out for her drink, which she hastily and gratefully sipped as though it were a cup of water to soothe her hot, exhausted throat. As she sipped once, twice, three times quickly, she noticed at the far end of the bar a "young" man in his forties. She was almost unconscious of the way she fluttered her eyes at him. He smiled at her stiffly, uncomfortably, and turned away—a rejection. "Must be something wrong with him," she thought, at once dismissing him as not so much unavailable to herself as to every woman on earth.

"Alyosha? C'mon up ..."—Mr. Entertainment squinted at the name, scratched out as though with a palsied hand, on the slip of paper—"Alyosha?" He raised his head and looked out over the heads of patrons to see who this next, to him unknown singer might be.

There threaded through the crowd a slender young man with sandy hair and a narrow, drawn face. He wore baggy corduroy pants and a wrinkled white shirt open at the collar. Even in the dimness of the place he looked a little unhygienic. In fact

he had just gotten off a ten-hour shift at work and his disha-
bille, tousled hair, and the darkish rings beneath his eyes were
the results of his physical exhaustion.   Four hours earlier his
cologne had been overpowered by an earthier, animal odor.   He
lived only a few blocks away and Angie's Place was just another
one of the dozen businesses he passed each day on his walk to
and from the subway station.   For some weeks now he had seen
the sign in the window announcing karaoke night, and on those
Saturday nights had glimpsed through the window an unusually
large crowd and had heard music within.   Always he had been
too tired to go inside; he had just wanted to get home and rest.
On this night he had been no less tired, but this time, on a
whim, he swerved inside.   He was hoping to meet a girl but he
had been inside the place only five minutes when he realized he
could never be interested in any of the women here.   (He told
himself that he didn't ask for much, just a cute, a pleasant face,
and someone not too fat or too old.   Was that so much to ask
for?)   Nevertheless he decided to stay for a beer.   He had not
had a drink for a long time and when he got the beer it tasted
so good, was so refreshing, that he stayed for another.   After
two, he ordered one more, thinking that this would be his last
for the night.   After he had finished most of that one he considered that this wasn't such a bad place after all, was at least a
welcome break from his routine, and that he really did enjoy
hearing the singers and the music.   He also realized that he
wasn't as tired as usual; the alcohol had stimulated him.   A
songbook happened to be nearby.   He reached for it, opened it,
flipped through it; saw first a couple, then dozens of songs he
liked. Why not sing one? Yes, why not? He wasn't a "singer" of
course, but from what he had heard neither was anyone else
who got up there and sang, and he certainly couldn't do any
worse than they had.   And it did look like fun.   So why not?

Though he had never sung publicly before, when his name
was called he felt not the slightest nervousness or apprehension.
He had just finished his third beer and bounded happily toward
the microphone.

Alyosha was a Russian immigrant who had been in New
York for two years. He had only a basic understanding of English, and, what was worse, he had a speech impediment that
made him slur his words. In conversation people constantly in-

terrupt him with, "What was that?" or "Whatchya say?" If his speech impediment made his conversation hard to understand, it made his singing downright otherworldly: he sounded as though he were holding a half a pound of marbles in his mouth. His voice boomed over the loudspeakers as a rolling, roiling, growling *something* which no one could figure out. The voice was human; but what language was it? The closest thing it came to was the mumbling war-chant of antique American Indians as they spun and hopped around a campfire:

"Wha ... wee ... you too ... mmmm ... ooooo ... ah, ah, ha ... eeee, uuuuuu, eeee ... eeeoooeee ... sommer niiiighhhs, sommer niiighhhhs ... wah, wah ..."

—Entirely remarkable, entirely incomprehensible. Sixty pairs of red, glassy eyes turned in his direction (some of them seeing more than one Alyosha under the spotlight), and when these lolled away from him and back toward their tablemates they all asked the same silent question:

"What the hell *is* that?"

Nevertheless Alyosha was quite proud himself. He heard something very different from what everyone else heard. He even did a little dance, a kind of quick, shuffling two-step, out of sheer joy. He had never thought he could "sing," and he was delighted to discover that he was a brilliant vocalist. He could see that people were smiling at him—obviously, they were pleased by what they were hearing.

When he finished his audience applauded briefly; some people gave no more than one or two effete pats of the hands. One wise guy, in a drunken joke, held up his hand and tapped his thumb and forefinger together a few times. Others giggled. In his euphoria of success Alyosha didn't see half of these uncomplimentary reactions as he went back to his beer at the bar.

It wasn't unusual for people to walk out on singers—not because they wanted to be rude to them but simply because they were so tired or drunk that they wanted to go home and sleep. Other, more sensible people, always felt compelled to wait till a singer had finished his song, but even they would, in the meantime, move toward the door; and as soon as the last note of the music had died away, they would give a few insincere, perfunctory claps of applause and hurry off. Thus when Alyosha had finished several more people left the bar, bidding friends and acquaintances quick goodbyes, sometimes waving adieu to the proprietress or bartender or to Mr. Entertainment himself.

The time had flown by quickly. It was getting on to two o'clock in the morning. The crowd had thinned out. Depending on how busy the place remained, Mr. Entertainment would keep the show going, gratis to the owner, for another half hour. But on this evening he wouldn't have to worry about that. Every few minutes more people were leaving. Mr. Entertainment's wife began walking through the bar to gather up the spiral-bound song books, mentioning to people along the way that if they wanted to sing another song they had better submit it now because the show was ending soon. Very few bothered to submit another one. The bright-eyed, somewhat nervous eagerness with which they had come into the place had been replaced with a tired, jaded acceptance that the evening was winding down. Besides, by now no more than twenty persons remained in the bar, and even if a few of them wanted to sing again they were discouraged from doing so by a sense of how silly it would be to serenade so small an audience.

Hoping to squeeze out a few more tips out of the remaining patrons, the bartender left his station behind the bar, walked over to them one by one, and asked them if they wanted anything else. They all shook their heads, no, no, no. They had had enough; they were going to leave soon.

The two more people who did get up to sing received the kind of sparse, hopeless applause that comes from a mere ten pairs of idly clapping hands (for now only a dozen persons remained, and one of them was sitting at a corner table with his eyes closed and his head bowed over). Then the lights went up, indicating that the bar was closing. In the heightened illumination the faces of the remaining patrons looked worn and pale and yet, too, somehow satisfied as though whatever they had come here for they had received. Mr. Entertainment spoke into the microphone for the last time, thanking everyone for coming by and reminding them that he would be here again next week. With his extendable wand he plucked down the spotlight from the ceiling, turning it off. Flicking a few switches, he shut down his equipment and began packing it up: unplugging cords, closing CD boxes, taking down the loudspeakers, putting things back into their cushion-lined carrying cases. In all this his manner was serious, brisk, and efficient, and his expression was one of lugubrious focus and intent, so unlike the cheery mask he had worn all evening. In another few minutes he was standing at the bar beside the owner receiving a wad of twenty-dollar bills that made up his fee. She told him that it had been a good night and she looked forward to seeing him again next week.

To the very end a few people remained seated at the tables finishing off the last of their drinks. They watched Mr. Entertainment and his wife carry out the audio equipment. The bartender was no longer serving and was busy arranging clean glasses and taking stock of how much liquor had been used. He and the owner stood at the cash register—which in truth had been emptied twice during the evening—and went over whatever cash and receipts remained. Everything was very quiet.

At a quarter to three o'clock in the morning only one person remained: the man who had been snoozing. Now he opened his tired eyes. He had been sitting with several people at his table but apparently they had been strangers to him, for they were gone and the only evidence of their having been with him were the empty glasses they had left behind.

"Sir, we're closing," the owner called out to him.

He shook his head as though to say, "Yes ... I know ... I'm going."

He got up from the table, took his jacket from where it had been hanging on the back of the chair, and slowly, carefully put it on and zipped it up. He glanced out the window and noticed that it had started to rain: the street was shiny with moisture and reflected the red glow from a bright neon sign of an outlet store across the way. When he stepped out of Angie's Place and onto the sidewalk, he stood there a moment uncertainly, looking either way down the deserted street. He seemed to wonder at how empty and forlorn the city around him had become. Or was he thinking of something else?—something that surprised him, disappointed him? In fact there had occurred to him again the old truth ... that there are things that cannot be talked away, slept away, drunk away; that cannot be tamped down by involvement in a crowd, however large or lush, nor by music, though loud and varied: that there are things inside oneself that evade and survive these assaults by retreating into unconsciousness for a while, but which always emerge again as forthrightly as ever, undefeated and undefeatable.

He pulled up his collar around his neck and started off, keeping his head bowed against the drizzling raindrops.

VISITED

He damned whoever it was—damned them! Waking him up like this!

Oh! He would kill them! *Kill* them!

Rudely nudged out of a lovely dream, the super-intendent's heavy-lidded eyes opened to the darkness of the bedroom. The first thing he saw was the dully-lit face of the clock on the night table beside the bed telling the time at three o'clock in the morning; then he heard again the insistent, nagging, chiming bell of his front door. He mumbled another curse under his breath. To think that someone could be standing out in the hall ringing his bell at this time of the morning! If he had been more awake he would have been infuriated. He sat up a little and listened, hoping it had been an audile hallucination—some lingering, evanescent part of a dream—only to hear it again, the ting-ting-ting of the doorbell. And then there was a knocking!

Damn them!

He swung his feet out of bed and as he did so his wife, an amorphous form under the sheets in the darkness, stirred. In another moment she asked groggily, "What is it?"

"Someone's at the door," he said.

"Oh ..."—with a scratchy, breathy voice, too tired to have any more articulate reaction.

In the darkness he limped into the hallway. All of his adult life he had walked with this limp, the result of a shattered leg caused by a car crash he had been in when a teenager: his left leg was an inch shorter than his right, and even after all these years it sometimes gave him pain. He entered the living room, flicking a switch that turned on a single lamp at the far end of the room. When he reached the door he didn't open it immediately. One didn't just open one's door in New York City, especially when it was three in the morning. For all he knew someone had gotten into the building and was looking to rob an apartment. One of the great benefits of being a superintendent was that he got free rent, but the counterbalancing drawback was that his apartment was located on the ground floor and was consequently a more likely target for any robbers or criminals who happened to get through the front or back door.

"Who is it?" he asked, not without a purposeful, intimidating gruffness.

Through the door he heard the muffled woman's voice:

"Alex! It's me! Mrs. Slovitz!"

"Oh, God," he murmured, and to himself angrily, "What the hell could she want now!"

He unlocked his door and peered out of it, then opened it more widely. Standing there in the bright fluorescent light of the hallway was one of the tenants, Mrs. Slovitz. Alex had known the old lady for as long as he had been superintendent of the building—almost ten years—and had during that time helped her with any number of things; but especially after she had gotten sick she had begun to pester him with irritatingly petty requests, such as asking him to change a light bulb or to take out her trash, or she would complain about the heat not being on (when it was) or about a neighbor who was "making noise," though the only noises he made were the unwitting and unavoidable ones of daily life.

She was seventy-eight years old. She suffered the afflictions of unlucky old age: arthritis, scoliosis, high blood pressure, and worst of all an ailing heart. She never felt "good": always there was pain when she walked, a growing inability to digest food, a general, prostrating exhaustion that required an absolute effort of will to overcome. Over the last few years she had lost a lot of weight and looked skeletal. Her hands shook slightly, as did her head, and she walked with an uncertain, unsteady shuffle, as though she were but a misstep away from toppling over. Her white hair was so thin at the top that her pink scalp showed through it. Her eyes were small, sunken, and surrounded by skin that was somehow pink and tender-looking. When she was not wearing her false teeth, as now, her lips protruded outward and added touch of the hideous to her age-ravaged face. (She had taken down the mirror in her living room because it had shown her as she was, a small, frail, shriveled old woman—the very image that, in her younger years, she used to turn away from with revulsion.)

She was wearing a jacket over her pajamas and clutched its flaps together at her chest with her bony left hand. Now she was looking at the superintendent with wild urgency.

"Mrs. Slovitz what is it?" he asked.

"There's someone at my window!"

"What?"

"There was someone at my window!"

The superintendent's eyes narrowed on her. "What do you mean, at your window?"

"I was lying in bed," the old lady said, speaking so fast now that she gulped her air, "and when I looked at the window I saw him!"

"In your bedroom window?"

She nodded, yes, yes, yes, her old, reddened, somehow sunken eyes wider, more frightened than ever.

The superintendent was thinking how unlikely her claim was, for she lived on the sixth floor of a ten story apartment building, and there was no way anyone could be "at" her window. Even if there had been a burglar about, other tenants on other floors would have seen or heard something and called the police, who would have been there in a matter of minutes. He decided at once that she must have been dreaming. He was going to explain this to her, to tell her that she had to be mistaken, when she exclaimed:

"Please, Alex! Could you come up? *Please?*"

It was the last thing he wanted to do; he barely restrained himself from giving a short-tempered sigh; but as he stood before her he realized how much younger, stronger, taller he was than she—how much more robust a human being—and he suddenly felt sorry for her, for her age, her sickness, her fear as a little old lady who lived alone and would be the last person in the world capable of defending herself against a burglar, if one really tried to break into her apartment, which he highly doubted.

"Alright, Mrs. Slovitz. I'll come up and take a look. Just wait here ... let me get my shoes on ... "

The superintendent shut the door somewhat—not completely, but just to the point where it touched the jamb—and turned around and went back inside his darkened apartment.

He limped his way into his bedroom and went to the closet from which he took out a pair of shoes. He brought these back to the bed with him, sat at the edge of the mattress, and began putting them on. His wife had almost fallen back asleep in the few minutes since he had been gone, but she awoke again when she felt the bed sink as he sat on it, and she asked in a sleep-scratchy voice:

"What is it?"

"Oh ... Mrs. Slovitz ... from the sixth floor ... she said she saw something at her window."

"What?"

"I don't know. It's alright. Go back to sleep. I'm just gonna go up for a minute."

"Oh ..."—she let her head fall back into her pillow, and in another second added, "She's nuts, that old bat."

He didn't say anything in return. He agreed with her, but what was the point in mentioning it? He put on his left and then right shoe, tying the laces hastily, loosely, only so that he shouldn't trip over them, then stood up in the darkness and said, "I'll be back in a few minutes."

When he went back to the door of his apartment Mrs. Slovitz seemed to be somewhat calmer. She had taken a few steps back from his door. Undoubtedly she had realized how ringing someone's door at three in the morning was an outrageous imposition. Still clutching her jacket at her chest, she watched the superintendent as he stepped into the hall and turned around to lock his door, and as he did so she said in a pitiably apologetic tone of voice:

"I'm sorry, Alex. I didn't mean to bother you."

He turned to her and smiled tightly, artificially; but again her age and frailty aroused his pity, and he said kindly:

"It's alright, Mrs. Slovitz. No problem. Let's go."

Their footsteps echoed in the dead silence of the early morning hallway no longer polluted with the sounds of television sets, radios, and conversation seeping out from nearby apartments. They went to the elevators and took one up to the sixth floor. When they reached it he saw that the door to her apartment was ajar; in her haste to flee she had not bothered closing it. The superintendent rightly interpreted this as another proof of her terror. She would never have left her door open under any conceivable circumstance, for, as he knew, she had become rather paranoid over the last few years, suspicious of everyone and everything.

Once inside, she turned on each light she came to: the overhead light in the short hallway, the one in the kitchen, the lamps in the living room. Alex looked about him. He had been in this apartment any number of times and had always been a little oppressed by its smallness and the cheap furniture that hadn't been changed in thirty years. A kitchen table, too large for the tiny kitchen, stood in the living room; on it were a bowl containing a few apples and oranges, half a loaf of bread in a plastic bag, a carton of cookies, and a jar of instant coffee. A cup and saucer were already set up in anticipation of the morning's solitary breakfast. At the far end of the room two dressers bulked catty-cornered. A television was on one of them and on the other were framed photographs ranged in three rows. The largest of these pictures showed a voluptuous, pretty young woman in a one-piece bathing suit smiling widely and carefree as she stood hand on hip before a '58 Chevrolet. The superintendent had seen that picture before and once had asked Mrs. Slovitz about it, and had been surprised to learn that it was none other than herself. There she was, twenty-four years of age, when youth had been hers, and the joy of life and all the future spread out before her with a beckoning glow of adventure and high romance: when old age was so, so far away, so alien a thing, that it was something she could not even imagine. It made the superintendent sad.

"So where did you see this man?" he asked.

"It wasn't a man," she said.

"No? I thought you said you saw someone."

"Yes, but"—she shook her head—"I don't know if it was ... a man."

"You mean you saw a woman?"

She nervously shook her head, no, and averted her eyes from his as though in embarrassment.

"I'm not sure," she said.

"Well where did you see this ... person?"

"At my bedroom window," she said, nodding to the little alcove that served as a bedroom in this studio apartment. There, the bed was placed against the wall and took up a third of that small area and faced a single window with curtains that had been pulled apart and were pinned against the wall on either side. Nothing could be seen outside. The glass was black with the night and in its blackness reflected the image of the lit apartment within.

The superintendent went to the window, lifted it and the screen behind, and stuck out his head and looked about. Six floors below he saw, by the light of street lamps, the hedges that ran around the base of the building. Between them and the brick wall was a narrow space of some two feet, and all along that gutter there was nothing to be seen, no movement to be perceived. Then he twisted his whole body somewhat in order to be able to look straight up. Above him jutted the ledges of the windows of the apartments over this one, and beyond them the edge of the roof of the building, which formed a dark border against the night's sky. Not many of the stars could be seen on account of the ambient light of the street lamps but a half moon shone with bright serenity and shed its yellow light over the sleeping city. Outside everything was silent, still, in that almost magical way it is for only a few hours in the early morning. The superintendent knew that there was no way someone could have been standing on the ledge of this window unless he had rappelled down from the roof, and it was ridiculous to suppose that anyone would have taken the time, effort, and risk to do such a thing. Nor could this ledge have been reached by the fire escape, which abutted the living room window and was twelve feet away. He pulled himself back into the apartment, closing the screen and then closing and locking the window.

"There's nothing out there," he said, turning to the old lady.

"Well there *was!*"

"I don't see how there could be. There's no place for someone to get onto the ledge from."

"It wasn't a person," she said.

The superintendent tilted his head. "What do you mean?"

"It was ... like a person. But it wasn't."

He continued to watch her, curiously, expectantly.

"I only saw it for an instant," she said. "It was *like* a person, but ... smaller, like a ... child."

"A child?"—he leaned his head forward a little, his lips

faintly curving into a deprecating smile, for he was sure, now, that the old lady was out of her mind or had otherwise led him on a wild goose chase.

Mrs. Slovitz didn't take offense at his expression because she herself understood how crazy she must have sounded. A part of her had known he would not find anything—certainly that he wouldn't see what she had seen. She folded her arms against her chest as though she were cold, but really with a chilly sense of frustration, of not knowing what else to do or whom to turn to for help. If earnestness of expression and demeanor could have the power to convince, hers would have left no doubt in his mind about the veracity of her claim as she said:

"I swear to God, Alex, I saw something out there. It couldn't have been a full-grown person. It was too small. I thought it was a child. But it had large eyes and ... its face was different ... I don't know exactly how ... it was just standing out there on the ledge, bent over a little and looking in at me and—"—she stopped, for she saw the disapproving, even wondering way he was looking at her now. She knew too how absurd she was sounding. If someone had told her what she was telling him she would not have believed it. Maybe she *was* going crazy? She folded her arms more tightly against herself as though in defense both against him and against the memory of what she had seen.

"Mrs. Slovitz, you're on the sixth floor," the superintendent said. "No one could get up to this window. Even the fire escape isn't near this window, and if someone had been climbing on the fire escape other people would have heard it—they would have heard something."

"But it was there. I know what I saw."

"Mrs. Slovitz"—shaking his head, tiredly—"just think about it. How could anyone get onto that ledge? It's like ... four inches wide! Can't happen," he said, shaking his head. "You must have imagined it. Or maybe you dozed off and were dreaming and thought you saw something. That's all it was, Mrs. Slovitz— it was just a dream."

She shook her head decisively as though she knew that that was not true and she would never be convinced of it. But in fact now she was not so sure. Perhaps he was right. Or perhaps (she again thought) she was losing her mind.

"Believe me, it was a dream," he insisted. "Dreams can be very real. It's happened to me plenty of times that I'm dozing off and I think I hear or see something that's not there. It happens to everybody. It's not something to worry about. Okay? There's nothing there. I looked. Everything's fine."

It was pointless, she knew, to try to convince him he was wrong. He would have had to see it for himself. Gingerly, she glanced at the window and saw that it was as it should be, with nothing visible beyond it but the blackness of the night. But what if it came back? And what was she going to do if it *did* come back? Would she go down to the superintendent and ring his bell again? Would she call the police? Quite apart from her fear was the miserable knowledge that even if she didn't see anything at the window again she was so nervous that she would not be able to get to sleep. She went to the window and undid the pins holding aside the curtains, which dropped together.

The superintendent, once again assuring her that everything was alright, turned to leave. He was walking across the living room when she called out:

"Wait!"

He stopped, turned to her.

"Can't you just stay a few minutes?" she asked.

"Mrs. Slovitz, I'm *really* tired. I have to get back to sleep. I have to work tomorrow. *Don't worry!* There's nothing here. I checked. Okay?"

She said nothing and watched him depart with the sad resignation of one who knows that nothing she can do or say can change a dreaded outcome. She followed him to the door and when he had stepped out into the hall he turned to her and managed a reassuring smile and said:

"Lock your door—okay?"

She mustered enough politeness not to show her angry disappointment with him; it seemed to her that he could have stayed at least a while—even if it were only for five minutes. There were three locks on her door and one by one she locked each of them, then turned around to her apartment and looked out at it with an air of nervous anticipation. All the lights were on and it seemed impossible that anything freakish or frightening should happen in so brightly prosaic a setting; and yet, at the same time, it seemed inevitable. She shifted her eyes to the alcove that served as her bedroom and wondered if, already, it— that *thing*—was standing outside the window again. For a few minutes she remained where she was, afraid to go forward. But she couldn't just stand there all night. She bucked up her courage and ventured forth, peering into the alcove toward the window. Did she dare go up to it—pull aside the curtains and look? No, no; she couldn't. And yet ... she had to be sure; she *had* to be! As though something or someone were pushing her forward, she moved one step at a time to the alcove, then up to the window. There, she hesitated; she swallowed hard; she looked at the curtains themselves, moving her hand, inch by inch, toward them. She touched them, grasped them. Could she pull them aside? But she had to; she had to know! Holding her breath and with an expression of painful effort she quickly pulled the curtain aside—

There was nothing there. Outside the window was only the blackness of night.

"Thank God," she said to herself.

Still, she couldn't bring herself to sleep in her bed, in the alcove, so close to the window; not tonight. She gathered up her pillow and sheets and took them to the couch in the living room, deciding to sleep there.

The apartment was utterly quiet: not so much as a scraping footfall or a muffled voice from the neighbors living on all sides of her. She lay on the couch looking at the closed curtains over the living room window. She wished that the pale blue light of a new, breaking day were already visible; she, who for so long now thought that the days passed too quickly, longed for a new day to come. She wondered if what the superintendent had said could be true: that she had imagined what she had seen. But was it really possible that one's imagination could be *so* clear, *so* vivid? Could one really "imagine" something as clearly as one could see a table or a television set on the other side of the room? No—impossible! She knew what she knew. She knew what she had seen or hadn't seen. Before tonight she would never have "imagined" someone standing outside her window. But if she *had* seen something clearly that hadn't been there, then that could only mean she was losing her mind.

It had been hard enough on her to be sick in body, but the

thought that was also becoming sick in her head added another layer to her misery. If she went insane, what would happen to her? She'd be taken away to some horrible institution. For some time now the great fear in her life was that she would become too sick to take care of herself and be institutionalized— put into a "home." If she lost her mind that was bound to happen.

"Oh, God, please, not that," she thought.

As the silent minutes passed, and nothing out of the way was to be seen or heard, her anxiety subsided. But no sooner had it largely gone than the accustomed spectres of her life rose up to fill the vacuum and instill into her the worries and anxieties she had lived with for years. Again she wondered why and how she had come to this sad pass in life, old and sick and alone. She had never thought she would wind up like this. For her life had not been essentially different from the lives of other women. As a teenager she had indulged in all the silly, exciting, sometimes dangerous adventures of wayward youth; then she had her little flirtations and greater, exhilarating, painful love affairs; then she had settled down and married—twice— men whom she had fallen in love with, even if, some years later, she had come to loathe and divorce them. With her first husband she had had two children, a boy and a girl, Eli and Sarah. How cute, how sweet, they had been! In her mind's eye she often saw them as babies in a carriage, bundled-up in soft woolen blankets, their little faces, rosy and large-eyed, peering up at her wonderingly, trustfully, as she pushed them along. Yet for the last thirty years she had rarely heard from either one of them. She had grown grandchildren whom she had seen only in photographs. She knew why—because she had not been a good mother. It had taken her fifteen years of lonesome retrospection to see this grand fact about herself: that toward her children she had always been nervously impatient, always critical, scolding, even humiliating. She had tried to make up for all that. From out of the little money she received from her Social Security check she would send her son and daughter, now in their fifties, little packages of things for them and their children. She sent them birthday cards and letters in which she wrote how much she loved them. In return ... silence. The only times Eli had called her were when she had been in the hospital. Even then he had sounded distant and seemed eager to be off the phone. Sarah had not spoken a word to her in nearly twenty years. Yes, it had all been her fault: she had been a terrible mother. Why hadn't she been better? If only she had been better they would have come to visit her, she wouldn't have been so alone. If only ...

She felt her eyes watering, and then tears came. She wasn't sure if she was weeping for the loss of the love of her children or the loss of her health and her decline into lonesome misery. Perhaps she was weeping for both. One thing she knew for sure: nothing had gone the right way for her; everything had turned out as she had feared. Why did the last years of her life have to be so hard, so bitter as this? Ah, how she had hoped and prayed that things would go better with her! The days she had spent crying, the nights she had lain in her bed looking through the window praying, begging that these last years of her life be filled—not with happiness, for she didn't expect that much, but—at least with a little health so that she might enjoy her last years in freedom from pain and be able to enjoy the small pleasure of a walk in the sunlight. Had that been so much to ask for? Had she really been such a bad person that she didn't deserve even that little concession from God or Fate or whatever it was that determined one's destiny? But far from getting better she had gotten worse and worse, weaker and weaker, becoming a prisoner in her cramped little apartment, and always alone, all alone.

She raised her hands to her eyes, wiping away the tears, and a small, gurgling, choking sound erupted from her throat as she allowed herself the luxury of her grief.

Perhaps she would have cried more fully, more loudly, if just then she hadn't heard a scraping sound at the window in her sleeping alcove.

At the sound, in an instant, her tears stopped, and even her breathing ceased: and, still as a statue, she lay there, listening—listening.

She heard it again. This time she recognized it as a scraping against the outer screen.

With surprising power and nimbleness, given her age and ill health, the old woman sat up on the couch in a spasm of terror, clutching the sheets to her body. Could she have imagined that sound?   No—no; she knew she had heard it. There was something there! She had a sense of some terrible thing about to happen and thought, "I have to get Alex! I have to get out of here."

But before she could budge the curtains over the window in the sleeping alcove billowed out with a movement behind them, and then something—something large—plopped down onto the floor.

At first she thought it was an animal; then she thought it was a person, a child; then she realized it was neither.   Its arms and legs were too spindly, the torso of its body too slender, and its face, though having features correlative to those of a human being, was too keenly narrow, having a horribly knifelike quality: the nose jutting, curved, sharp, the lips small, narrow, tight, the chin protrusive and at the very end grotesquely curved upward. Its hands and feet were long and bony. It had no hair and a ridge ran atop its skull. Its enormous eyes were almond-shaped and a mursky misy blue-gray, but seemed to be without eyelids, without eyelashes, and no brows arched above them. Its smooth skin was of a dull, darkish yellow, with areas of brown specks, and had a sheen as though moist or oily. It seemed to be wearing some kind of body-fitting jumpsuit of nearly the same color as its skin so that it was hard to tell where one started and one left off. As soon as it had landed on the floor it had snapped its head in her direction as though it had known exactly where she was.   For a few seconds it watched her, several times dipping its head down and forward in a strange, inhuman gesture.

It is of course a cliché to say that someone is frozen with terror, but in this instance the cliché is strictly accurate. There is a fear so sudden and overwhelming that it bypasses thought and petrifies the body.   Mrs. Slovitz wanted to jump off the couch and flee but she could not: her limbs were immobilized. She tried to scream but all that came out of her mouth was a tiny, feeble, truncated sound, less a word than a mere exhalation of breath.   Only her eyes expressed the utter and urgent nature of her terror: they goggled unblinkingly at the unearthly creature that had entered her life like a nightmare.

Cautiously continuing to keep its eyes on her, the being got up from its crouching position. It was no more than three feet tall. It stepped forward, and with each step it held its hands up and a little outward as though to balance itself, for apparently it was not used to walking. It continually glanced about as though finding itself in a strange and potentially hostile environment. Balancing itself for a moment by placing one of its long-fingered hands on the edge of the bed, it stepped out of the alcove and just into the living room. There it stopped and peered at the old lady only ten feet away. Its large blue-green eyes blinked against the lights in the apartment.

The old woman, in her breathless, mute horror, shrank more deeply into the couch as though she were trying to bury herself into the protection of its fabric and stuffing. She heard herself emit a choking gasp. Her heart pounded furiously in her chest. She was sure that she was going to die. She kept telling herself, "I'm going to die ... I'm going to die ... If I don't get out of here, I'm going to die ..."

The creature tilted its head at her in a gesture that seemed an innocent attempt to understand who or what she was; then with a small, quick jerking back of its head it emitted a tiny yelp—first one, then several in a row; and seemed to wait for a response.

The old woman could barely breathe. It was as though something had compressed her chest and would not allow it to expand, had clamped around her throat, preventing her from uttering a peep.

The creature moved along the living room wall opposite her. With every step it took it would look about itself, regarding the most mundane articles in the apartment with an air of wonder or confusion, but never so involved in its review of these things as to be unaware of the human being a few feet away, for, often, it returned its eyes to her. Again, it emitted a little yelp.

The old woman told herself again that she was going to die if she didn't get out of here. She summoned up all her will to move her arms and hands, determined to break through the immobility of her terror. Yet when she finally found she could move her arms the first thing she did was grab the pillow from behind her and hurl it at the horrible thing.

In a blur of speed that defied organic physics the little being eluded the missile, darting toward the ceiling, ricocheting off of it, then coming down, in a graceful instant, on the table in the center of the room. It landed in a posture of readiness to jump again: its knees bent, its hands placed before it, its face turned up toward her, its huge, blue, slanted eyes unblinking, watching, waiting. Then it did something that struck yet more terror into the old lady: it lifted a hand, waved one of its long forefingers back and forth the way an adult might before a naughty child, and wheezed, "Uh—uh!"

That it had communicated to her, that she had understood what it was telling her, only horrified her the more.

Just then a sound penetrated the apartment: the muffled conversation of people who had just gotten out of the elevator down the hall and were walking to their apartment. The creature also heard these voices; it tilted its head and looked toward the door. The old woman thought that if she could only shout or scream for help those people out there, whoever they were, would come to her rescue; at the very least they would, hearing her distress, call the police. As though reading her thoughts, the creature again wagged its finger and shook its head, bidding her keep silent. But she could not have called for help no matter how hard she tried. Her throat was impossibly tight; her dread continued to paralyze her.

The voices in the hallway grew faint as the people there walked further away, and a closing of a door down the hall indicated they had entered their apartment.

The creature got down from the table in a quick leap and stood just behind it. It had something in its hand. Whether it had been carrying this object all the while or had produced it out of thin air the old woman could not have said, as she was hardly in a state of mind to be so observant. The only thing she knew, she saw, was that it placed the object on the table. Then it moved back to the wall and sidled along it to the sleeping alcove, then moved to the window, then leapt up behind the curtains, which once more billowed and roiled with its body; and it was gone.

Mrs. Slovitz couldn't see it but the creature had gained the outside ledge and stood on that narrow margin of brickwork with astonishing balance. It looked out over the neighborhood of two- and three-storied row houses whose roofs were visible as a checkerboard expanse of soft gray, dark blue, and black patches. It turned its face toward the moon, then looked at few stars visible amid the city lights, and emitted another little yelp. It bent its legs and, flinging its arms upward, leapt into the air. It flew up swiftly, spiraling corkscrew fashion, till it was lost in the darkness, had become invisible—on its way back to wherever it had come from, whether a part of this world or some other.

Inside the apartment the old woman remained where she was, still wrapped in her shielding blanket. She was sensible that her limbs were shaking of themselves. Though the creature—that horrible creature—was no longer to be seen and had apparently gone away she still could not move, and her heart was still beating fast. As the minutes passed, and she became more certain that *it* was gone, her fear subsided enough for her to regain control of her body. She could move her arms and legs now. She knew she could get up if she wanted to. She looked to the door of her apartment and it became the goal to be reached. She got off the couch, grateful to be standing, to be able to walk, and after taking a first tentative step rushed to the door with shuffling feet. With a surge of vitality she fumbled at the locks in her hurry to open them, and as soon as she opened the door she flung out of the apartment as fast as her unsteady legs would carry her, all the while whimpering, gasping for breath, as though only now she could allow herself the luxury of giving way to the excruciating fear that had consumed her.

She hurried to the elevators and took one down to the lobby. As she descended her hands and legs were shaking, and she gulped for breath. Only when she stepped out into the lobby did she feel somewhat safe. In that large, bright, public area with its tiled walls and floor, with its large windows giving out to the six-lane highway beyond, it seemed impossible for any but the most prosaic of things to occur. The lobby contained a gated area in which stood a small table and four wrought iron chairs. No one ever used this seating; it was only meant as decor. But now Mrs. Slovitz opened the waist-high gate to this area, went to one of the chairs, and sat down. She put a trembling hand to her mouth and looked about with the same fearful, lost, confused air of someone who has just escaped a collapsing house during an earthquake and is just now beginning to feel his shock. The thought of calling on the superintendent didn't occur to her. She was consumed with the thought that now she was safe ... safe ... safe ...

She sat there for the next two hours and during that time four persons emerged from the elevators and walked through the lobby. They all had that moist, fresh look of people who have just showered and put on clean clothes, and behind them trailed the scents of cologne or perfume. They were on their way to jobs that began early in the morning. The first three didn't recognize Mrs. Slovitz as their neighbor, as was entirely possible in a building with over a hundred apartments and with tenants who had such different lifestyles and schedules. As they passed the old woman on their way out they glanced at her with the curious yet disapproving expressions of New Yorkers irritated to find that the eccentricities they must put up with on the "outside" world have begun to infiltrate areas closer to home: for all they knew she was a crazy homeless person who had wandered in off the street. But one of the tenants leaving the building that morning knew who she was, for he had seen her several times before, though he didn't know her name. With fundamental human decency he stopped at the gate and asked:

"Are you alright?"

Mrs. Slovitz nodded, yes, her face drawn, pale, her eyes glazed over. She stared at him as though she didn't know who or what he was.

"Are you *sure?*" he asked.

She didn't respond; she continued looking at him uncertainly.

The young man thought for a moment that she might be suffering from some kind of dementia and wondered if he should call the police. Perhaps he would have done so if he hadn't been on his way to work. But he couldn't take the time just now. Besides (he reckoned) it was morning, there would be plenty of people about, and someone would find out what had happened to her.

That someone turned out to be the building's porter, Luca. He was a short, paunchy man in his fifties who lived with his wife in a tiny studio apartment on the first floor. He came from Hungary. In his five years of residence in the United States he had only managed to learn about a few hundred words of Eng-

lish. When he saw Mrs. Slovitz sitting in the lobby, and still in
her dressing gown, he knew something was amiss. He tried to
ask her what was wrong but his vocabulary was insufficient to
convey this concern, and Mrs. Slovitz was clearly in no condition
to make herself comprehensible to him. She only asked him one
thing:

"Where's Alex?"

"Alex?" the porter asked, latching onto the name. "Yes?
Alex?"

She nodded.

"You stay—you stay. I get for you!"

The superintendent had only just gotten up. He was still in
his pajamas, in his kitchen, making coffee. When his doorbell
rang he grumbled impatiently and at once thought it might be
Mrs. Slovitz again. He was a little relieved to see it was his
porter, only to find out that his first hunch had been right, for
the Hungarian handyman explained in his stumbling way that
there was indeed something wrong with Mrs. Slovitz, who was
sitting on one of the chairs in the lobby. "She ask for you," Luca
said.

"Oh ... that woman!" Alex muttered under his breath.
"What a pain in the ass!" To Luca, louder: "She's out of her
mind! She woke me up three o'clock this morning because she
thought there was a burglar at her window! She's a kook!"

Luca shook his head as though in sympathy with the trials
of being a superintendent but in fact he found this particular instance rather amusing. To think that Alex had to deal with
such difficult people—such people as he had never met till he
had come to New York City. He stood at the door managing to
suppress his urge to smile as he waited to be told what to do.

"Tell her I'll be out in a few minutes!" the superintendent
said.

Alex was determined not to let the old lady irritate him
twice in one morning. He was going to take his time. He drank
his coffee at the same leisurely pace he always did, maybe even
a little more slowly than usual, taking satisfaction in the
thought that he was putting *her* out by making her wait for
him. But before he had finished that first cup he felt guilty.
The poor old lady—how could he possibly wish her any ill-will?
As though she didn't have enough problems in her life! No mat-

ter how bad things were with him, he understood that they had
to be a lot worse for her, given her age and ill health. Besides,
maybe it was a lot more serious than he had thought: maybe
she really had gone crazy. In that case he would have to call
an ambulance and have her carted away. It was one of the disagreeable aspects of his job that he occasionally had to intervene in the sad last stages of life: in the last year alone two old
tenants had died in their apartments, and he had to go through
the depressing routine of notifying the police, informing the
landlord, and, sometimes, breaking the news to surviving relatives. There was also the added work of having to ready the
apartment for a new tenant. "Yes," he said to himself, sipping
his coffee, "life's not easy at the end." With this thought his resentment against Mrs. Slovitz relented, he put down his cup,
and left his apartment to go out into the lobby and find out
what was wrong with her this time.

She was still sitting in the gated area. Luca, under the
pretense of sweeping up, was nearby, keeping an eye on her.

When Mrs. Slovitz saw the superintendent she got up from
her chair and went over to him, shuffling over to the gate and
meeting him there. He had just asked her what was wrong
when she grabbed his arm—grabbed it impulsively, hard—and
spoke in a rushed, desperate whisper:

"It was in my apartment!"

"What was in your apartment?"

"That thing! That thing that I saw! Alex, it was some
kind of *thing!* I swear to God! I *swear* to God!"

She was working herself up into panic, her eyes starting
out of her head, tearing. Her grip on his arm grew even
tighter.

"Alright, alright ... calm down, dear." He patted her hand.
"Are you alright?"

She nodded. She sniffled as though she were about to
burst into tears.

"Someone came into your apartment?" he asked.

"No, it wasn't a person ... I swear to God it wasn't ... I don't
know what it was."

Yes, the old bat's finally flipped her lid, he thought. Either
that or she was having some kind of nervous breakdown, or perhaps she had taken too much of some kind of medication. He

wasn't sure whether he should try to calm her with a show of sympathy or to call an ambulance.

"It left something on my table," she said. "Alex, please, *please*—come up! See what it is! Take it away!"

She was crying.

"Sure, sure," he said, nodding, patting her hand comfortingly before gently prying it loose from his arm, then opening the gate for her. "Calm down, Mrs. Slovitz. Everything's alright now. C'mon, let's go back to your apartment. There's nothing to be afraid of. I'm going with you."

As he led her around the open gate and toward the elevators his manner was that of a caring son for a decrepit mother, for he put a hand gently on her back as she shuffled out onto the tile floor and seemed to guide her steps with, "Be careful now ... go slow ... that's it ... " He limped along beside her. A few times he grimaced for his leg was hurting him more than usual this morning.

In the elevator she told him how the thing had come into her apartment and scared her almost to death. She babbled out a description of its "horrible" face and arms and gestures; how it had jumped around, "like a devil"; how it had "threat-ened her life," and left something on her table, she didn't know what. Even as she spoke her breath came fast and she began crying with recalled terror. He listened to her in astonishment and began to believe that either she had gone nuts or that something out of the ordinary had indeed happened.

When they reached her apartment he saw that her door was open, that she had again fled without closing it. He went in first, stepping inside a little carefully but seeing at once that the place was empty, looking as desolate and forlorn as always, and so he entered it more confidently. Mrs. Slovitz followed him. First he went to the alcove window and found, as he had expected, that it was locked; then he went to the living room windows, and found they also were locked. "Yes, she's finally flipped her lid," he thought, as he turned around to her.

She was standing in the middle of the living room, a few feet away from the kitchen table that dominated that space. Her eyes were set on something there, and now she pointed at it, saying:

"Look!"

He did—he followed her line of vision to the object of her attention; but, unsure of what it was, he went over to it. He was just about to pick it up when she exclaimed:

"Don't!"

"What?"

"Don't touch it! It could be dangerous! You don't know what it is!"

"Mrs. Slovitz, I know what it is," he said; and before she could say another word he picked it up. He looked at it more closely, turning it around and around in his hands. "Sure, I know what this is. It's a stone—it's a piece of quartz, that's all. You never saw quartz before?"

He held it up, out to her. It filled his palm as a substantial, weighty thing. It was a large piece of quartz with several hexagonal, sharp-pointed spears growing out of a rough, dull, rocky matrix. The crystals were not especially remarkable; they seemed to be of inferior quality—milky-white and flecked with imperfections.

The old woman pulled back at the sight of it.

"Don't pick it up!" she said, shuffling away from him. "It could be dangerous."

"But it's *nothing*," the superintendent said. "Where'd you get it?"

She was shaking her head, no, no, no. It almost horrified her to see that he, that anyone, should handle something once held in the hands of that horrible thing.

"Well, wherever it came from, it's nothing to get so excited about. It's just a rock— "

His attention was diverted by a feeling of warmth in his hand. He looked at the crystal and noticed that its milky-whiteness had taken on a pink tinge, a rosy glow. At first he wasn't sure whether this was coming from within the crystal or was merely some refraction of the ambient light, but in the next few seconds, as the illumination intensified, there could be no question of its inherent nature. The color was comforting, beautiful; somehow it evoked a natural reaction to wrap one's hands around it more tightly, whereupon it became still brighter. Then it quickly grew warm, and this warmth, as though it was an actual, physical entity, suffused his hand and began moving up into his arm. The sensation was strange and yet so pleasurable that he had no inclination to release the crystal that had apparently caused it. Instead he looked down at his arm as though whatever it was he felt was a physical thing and he could watch its progress.

"What is it?" Mrs. Slovitz asked, seeing the way he looked at his arm.

He shook his head. "I don't know ... I feel something ..."

"Oh, I told you!" she broke out. "Didn't I tell you not to touch it! Didn't I tell you!"

"No, no ... it's alright," he said, in a low, calm voice. "It's nothing."

"Put it down!" she pleaded.

He heard her, and a part of him even thought it might be a good idea to do as she suggested, but another, surer part of him interpreted the sensation as benign. It worked its way into his shoulders, then down into his chest, filling it with warmth; then cascaded down, in subtle waves, into his abdomen, his hips, his groin; then worked its way still lower, into his legs, even to his feet, where it lingered. Soon enough it left his right foot but remained in his left, growing very warm there, almost hot, so that, for the first time apprehensive, he murmured, "Heyyyyy ..."

Mrs. Slovitz had noticed his sudden preoccupation with something going on inside him, and she feared for him.

"What? What?" the old woman asked, inclining her head toward him, her eyes wide as though something terrible was imminent.

"I just felt something ..."

"Put it down! Didn't I tell you! Didn't I tell you!"

—Just then, the warmth subsided even in his left foot. He opened his hand to examine the crystal and saw that the light had gone out of it: something vital in it had receded or (somehow he knew this too) been expended, and the stone was just that—a stone, no different from any other of its kind. He looked at Mrs. Slovitz uncertainly.

"Are you alright, Alex?" she asked.

He only shook his head, yes. But he was aware that something had happened to him, inside of him, though he wasn't sure what. He was about to place the stone back on her table when she almost shrieked:

"I don't want it! Take it away! Throw it out!"

The superintendent continued to hold it, then, and turned to go. With his first steps he noticed something—the easy glide to his gait. He stood still. He took a few more steps, more consciously; and there was no question about it: there was no lurch to his body as he set down his foot. His limp had not occurred. In the same instant he realized that he no longer felt any pain. He turned around to look questioningly at Mrs. Slovitz, who hadn't noticed the change in his gait and in whom the primary emotion was still fear.

"What is it?" she asked, her eyes wide with worry as though yet another new, terrible thing were occurring.

"My leg," he said, looking down at it.

Her eyes followed his, then she watched him as he paced back and forth before her, walking as easily and normally as anyone. "My leg ... my leg!"

Still, she didn't seem to understand. Her anxiety blinded her to the evidence of her own eyes; if anything, his pacing back and forth before her, and his growing euphoria, inclined her to think something bad was happening to him.

"I'm not limping," he said. "Look! ... See? ... I'm not limping! It doesn't hurt anymore!"—and he looked over to the crystal with an expression understanding and awed gratitude.

Then she understood. More than this: with a flash of insight everything seemed to fall into place. The countless hours, the countless lonely days, she had spent lying in her bed looking out the window praying for physical redemption had come in the form of that strange tiny being: the most ardent of her prayers had been answered. The object that it had left behind was the pledge of that fulfillment, a grand gift of the sort perhaps never before left to a human being, and meant for her. "Give that to me," she said, moving forward and reaching out her hand to the stone

Neither willingly nor unwillingly did the superintendent give it back to her. He was still unsure of what had happened to him, and the old lady's sudden and to him inexplicable change in behavior was but another confusing element of the moment.

Ms. Slovitz took the quartz into her withered hands with trembling anticipation. She held it fast and looked into it with hard, determined eyes. Her tight grasp became a frantic clench, and she shook the crystal as though she might squeeze or coax something out of it. But it remained cold, unresponsive; its hard, dead, milky-white translucence did not alter. Whatever healing or rejuvenating quality it had possessed had been of a finite quantity, once used, forever gone. In a few more seconds she understood this. She raised her eyes to the superintendent with a wondering, bitter disappointment.

"What is it?" he asked her.

She didn't answer. Her eyes became hard, angry, furious. She raised the stone in her hand and shook it before him. "You took it," she said, breathlessly; then, in a louder, more accusatory voice, "You took it!"

"Took what?"

"You took it!" she shouted. She threw back her head, her features contorting into a mask of pain and rage, her open, toothless mouth a wet, darkly pink maw out of which poured a wail of despair: "You took it, you took it, you took it! Why did you take it! Why did you take it from me? You're a thief! You're a thief—a thief—a thief !"

Before the barrage of these verbal assaults the superintendent fell back and away toward the door, opened it, stepped outside into the hallway, and, walking backward, but always with a strong and steady gait, saw and heard the old woman standing at her doorway, a pathetic, broken figure, madly wailing out at him curses and recriminations.

COUTURE

"If he's an actor, then I'm Queen Elizabeth."

Celeste told herself this as she stood before the young man whom she had just helped put on the coat she had made for him. He was twenty-two years old and made a living as a waiter in a burrito restaurant on First Avenue, but she knew him from a play she had worked on a year earlier and he had come by to pick up his coat. She still remembered how bad that play had been and how his acting hadn't been much better. He was tall and very handsome, with a classic, sculptured face, a shock of thick black hair that had a tendency to flop rakishly over his forehead, a slightly cleft chin, and a smile full of white, well-shaped teeth. No doubt a lifelong consciousness of his good looks, of his "presence" (as he would have called it), had convinced him that he was destined to be a movie star—the next Paul Newman or Robert Redford—for surely God had not created such a fine face and figure to languish away anonymously, or work much longer at "El Burro," where three days a week he held a tray over his head as he negotiated close-set tables and flashed his magnificent, tip-encouraging smile to customers as he asked, "Would you like yours spicy or mild?"

"Everything fit alright?" Celeste asked him.

He was standing in her foyer a few feet away from a full-length mirror leaning against a built-in bookcase. He gazed at himself with satisfaction, pleased at the way the cut of the coat complemented his broad shoulders and narrow hips. It also had a collar that he could lift up high—as he now did—for a touch of especial "coolness."

"I love it!" he exclaimed, turning around a little, looking to the side, then the back of him. "It's great! You're the best!"

She laughed, almost blushed at his enthusiasm, and was happy and grateful for his naive and therefore heartfelt outpouring of appreciation of her work. No, the poor boy couldn't act if his life depended on it, but at least he knew when something looked good on him. She watched him as he now unbuttoned the coat and reached into his back pocket for his wallet, from which he took out several bills he had previously folded and kept separate from the others—five hundred dollars, the final payment for the coat, which he handed her with a, "Here you go. Thank you!"

"You're very welcome," she said.

She took the money and, not even glancing at it, held it in her hand at her side.

As he prepared to leave he reminded her of the show he would be appearing in next month and said he would send her a couple of tickets. She told him that she looked forward to it, even though she doubted that she would go. She showed him to the door and was a little sorry to watch him walk out the door and down the hall. He might have been a bad actor but he was cheerful company. Only when he disappeared around the fourth-floor landing did she close the door.

She looked at the payment he had given her and counted it out—not because she doubted it was all there but because she was grateful at having finally been paid. The fact was that business had been pretty bad this year. It was already July yet all year she had only had eight clients, and had worked as the costume designer on two shows, which had paid very little. She had only made enough money to meet her most basic living expenses. She calculated how far this additional five hundred dollars would take her; and saw that it wouldn't take her far. She considered that to make ends meet she might have to dip into her savings account—those few thousand dollars she had managed to squirrel away over the last few, better years, and which she had saved for a rainy day.

If she didn't appear to be especially worried about all this; if she shrugged almost indifferently as she put the money into her pocketbook, intending to take it to the bank the next day; it was because she had been living in this precarious way for so many years that it had become the normal condition of her life. This is not to say that she had reconciled herself to it, but only that she knew from experience how the bad times pass and better ones come along. The only real worry was how long it would take them to come along. But there was nothing to be done about this either, and so she put it out of her mind as well as she could—as she always and wisely did to matters beyond her control.

Celeste Adams had been designing clothes since she was a little girl. As a child of seven she would dress up her dolls in little outfits of her own crude making. In her teenage years she had, like most girls, become conscious of fashion, but rather than follow the trend she had liked to set her own, wearing clothes she had made for herself and which had garnered her the pleased attention of fellow teenagers who of all people are eager for the novel. Even then her agemates had detected in her a talent for design.

By the time she was eighteen she knew, as everyone acquainted with her knew, that she would pursue a career in fashion. By then she had already designed a number of wonderful, complicated gowns and jackets and outfits. She accumulated a library of books by which she taught herself the history of clothing, their styles and manufacture, all of which she knew as well as historians know the names of famous statesmen and decisive battles. Despite her breadth of knowledge, she never directly copied any era; she had too many ideas of her own; or if she did borrow an element here or there it was so transformed in the alembic of her peculiar talent that it came out as something new and fresh. No one could say that she didn't have her own sense of style. People who once saw a shirt or jacket she had made would remember it so well that later if they happened to see someone wearing an article of her clothing they would ask, "Did Celeste Adams make that for you?"

She had been born and raised in Minnesota but had come to New York because that was the place to be if one had big dreams in the fashion industry. She had come when she was twenty-four years old intending to get a job with some big-name fashion house, gaining experience there, and then branching out into her own clothing line. In only a couple of years she realized how unfounded such a fantasy had been. She had had to settle for making money as a secretary in a real estate firm while trying to "establish" herself. She took courses at the Fashion Institute of Technology, which enabled her to meet people she otherwise wouldn't have known: not only other designers, but, through them, actors, singers, people aspiring to

careers in "show business." Slowly, surely, with great effort and
sacrifice, she had begun to make a reputation for herself as a
costume designer in the New York theater scene, having begun
by offering her services gratis to off-off-Broadway plays on the
Lower East Side. Since then she had designed or made costumes for dozens of off-Broadway plays. Most actors in New
York knew who she was or at least had heard her name. In one
sense it had been a boon to become part of that world, for it had
enabled her to build up a clientele, mostly of theater people and
their friends. On the other hand her initial fascination and interest in that crowd had long died away, for she had come to see
the futility of its characters, the silly and sometimes delusional
self-importance with which they posed and minced through a
city, a world, which knew them not, nor cared to know them.
She had lost count of the parties she had gone to and stood listening to self-styled actors, directors, or playwrights uttering
grand pronouncements on the arts as though they alone had
real insights into them, or parroting the political tripe fashionable among their set, and which they hadn't the courage to disagree with for fear of what others might think of them. Oh, the
knuckleheads and frauds she had come across since she had
been in New York! Except on rare occasions, and only for the
sake of getting or conducting business, Celeste no longer even
went to the many plays she was invited to see on a monthly basis, nor to the parties that her acquaintances now and then invited her to. She preferred to stay home and work, or, if she
didn't have work, then to read or watch television. Besides, it
was always cheaper to stay home and she had to follow a close
economy in order to meet her monthly expenses.

On this night however she did go to a small party at a
restaurant with the cast of the theater company whose latest
play she had designed the costumes for. As usual the director,
actors, and sound and lighting people drank too much, laughed
too loudly, and gossiped scandalously. They congratulated one
another on their brilliant work even though their play had been
running only a couple of weeks and was not—if current receipts
were any indication of the future—likely to survive the rest of
the month. Celeste couldn't deny however that it did her spirits
good to receive a joyful welcome from familiar faces and to feel
their undercurrents of admiration for her work.

She got home after two in the morning and she was very tired. She was a woman of regular habits and was not used to staying up so late. When she closed the door behind her she looked about with relief, glad to be back in her apartment. Her building, a brownstone built in 1898, was located between 1st Avenue and FDR Drive. Her apartment was on the fourth floor, and was in the long, narrow, "railroad" style, with two windows at the far end. Once those windows had had something of a view—the outlook, at least, of four blocks uptown. But a few years earlier the plot of land across the way had been bought up by a real estate development company that had built on it a high-rise luxury apartment building. Now all she could see was the back of this building: a plane of red brick interpolated with narrow windows which apparently belonged to bathrooms because when they were open one could, on a quiet night, hear toilets flushing. If she wanted to see anything outside now she had to look not outward so much as downward, to an area that the tenants on the first floor had denominated their "patio." This was nothing more than a patch of concrete on which a tiny table, a few potted plants, and an outdoor grill had been placed. A rusty fence surrounded it. In the summer these tenants would have their friends over for a "barbecue," and some twenty people would crowd into that tiny lot, chatting, holding drinks, smoking cigarettes, playing music, eating hotdogs and hamburgers, and acting for all the world as though they were VIP guests at some exclusive resort on the Riviera. Celeste had never glanced down at these events without a repulsed sense of how far some people in New York would go to suspend their dignity for the sake of trying to have a good time. But at least their music and merriment drowned out the sound of toilets flushing across the way.

Having come from Minnesota, having lived in a large house with a basement, five bedrooms, a huge living and dining room and kitchen, not to mention acres of land roundabout, she had told herself she would never get used to living in this little apartment. But ten years later, here she was.

She took off her clothes and slipped on an oversized t-shirt that dropped almost to her knees and went into the bathroom and brushed her teeth. Then she walked across the bare wooden floor to the other side of the apartment and got into the

bed against the window. She drew up to her chest a single light
sheet and closed her eyes.

It was a warm, late-July night in New York City. The window beside the bed was open and now and then a faint breeze
blew in from outside. She lay there with her eyes closed, feeling
the air waft over her face, and getting no especial refreshment
from it because it was so warm and humid. Though she had an
air conditioner she reserved its use for only the hottest days; in
this way keeping down her electric bill. As she lay there she
thought about the evening she had spent and the play for which
she had designed the costumes. By turns she was proud and
disappointed by her work. She went over in her mind a few of
the dresses and suits she had created; she could see them as
clearly, as precisely, as though the actors were standing in them
before her. She said to herself that this one was good, that that
one might have been better. Well, it hadn't been entirely her
fault if some of the costumes had been less than perfect. She
had been so rushed, after all. The original costume designer
had had a falling out with the director and Celeste had been
called, pleaded with actually, to take his place and help to make
the two dozen costumes for a show that would open in a single
month. One could only work so fast and hope to get things
right, and she had concentrated on the costumes of the five major characters. At any rate, it was too late now: the show had
started. She considered that she would tweak the rest of the
costumes if the show lasted more than a few weeks, but she
knew from experience that this wasn't likely. The little off-
Broadway productions she had been a part of almost never
lasted very long, and the producer or director (usually the same
person) was lucky if he made enough money to cover the next
month's expenses for the theater.

Was she happy here, now, after so long in New York City?
Such a question would not have occurred to her. She did not
measure her life in terms of happiness or unhappiness, but
rather in terms of success or lack of success, that is to say,
whether or not she was making a living by her art. In this regard she had come perilously close to failure. Once she hadn't
had a job in three whole months—and this with only another
two month's worth of living expenses in the bank. Homelessness had stared her in the face. A more common-sensical per-

son would at once have gone about trying to find a conventional job, no matter how hateful, in order to support herself, but Celeste only redoubled her efforts to find work as a designer, and succeeded. And somehow she had known she would. For unlike so many artists she had never doubted her talent. She was confident of its existence in the same way that an athlete, in the full flush of his prime, is confident in the strength of his muscles, the agility of his frame, the quickness of his reactions, knowing that the instant he is called upon to run or jump or swim his body will, almost of itself, perform flawlessly. With an objective, indeed self-critical eye she had always compared her own creations to those of even famous designers, and found their work often stale or preposterous in comparison. The very fact that she had known some success, that she had been able to make a living at her art, had bolstered her native self-confidence. On the other hand she was far from satisfied with merely making a living; her goal had always been grander. She knew she would never be genuinely fulfilled till her name was as well-known as the most famous designers of the day; till she had, in fact, achieved the status of a classic. She wasn't sure when this would happen, whether next week or twenty years hence, whether through dogged perseverance or through some spectacular freak of luck, but somehow she knew that her anonymity would give way to fame. Some day, some way, people would know who Celeste Adams was.

People who met her for the first time usually saw at once that there was something "different" about her. They might not know what it was, whether it were a good thing or a bad thing, but they would still be pleased by the excitement of curiosity she had aroused in them. No doubt part of this impression was owing to the clothes she wore—always of her own striking, sleek design, but it was also owing to a fresh simplicity about her person. Her features were pretty in a little girlish way, and the fairness of her complexion contrasted dramatically with her dark hair. She wore makeup lightly, and added a dash of eyeliner to the outer canthus of her lids, giving her blue eyes an exotic, somehow Egyptian air. Her hands were as simple as a child's; the nails were short, unpolished, unmanicured; and the ends of her fingers were sometimes reddened or chapped after working long hours on a garment. But to the tips of those fingers she was an artist in a way that ninety-nine percent of the so-called artists in New York City were not and could never be. For they had neither her sensitiveness nor her intuition nor her simple and instinctive sense of the beautiful. At a glance she knew what was lovely and right. She could not be taken in by sophistical "explanations" or "interpretations" of a work of art: when something was amateurish or the product of merely average abilities she saw it at once; and when it was a downright fraud (as so often it was among the endless "artists" she ran into in the city) she would merely raise a brow, or at most roll her eyes, and so express more eloquently than words could her indifference or contempt. And no doubt it was also this proud consciousness of her own talent that quietly invested her every movement and word with that ineffable "something" that people found so fascinating in her.

One day she received a phone call from a Mrs. Joanna Forster. Mrs. Forster said she had gotten Celeste's name through a friend of one of the directors whom Celeste had worked with on a play, and that she might be interested in having a dress made for her. She was planning a party at her home in several weeks and she wanted to wear something special. The more details Celeste learned, the more she realized she was dealing with a woman of means. For Mrs. Forster lived on Central Park West at 77th Street, and in referring to her "party" she mentioned that it was going to be catered, that she was expecting sixty guests, and that it was partly social and partly business for the sake of her husband who was an executive at CBS. She dropped the names of a few celebrities who had attended her previous affairs. She was looking, she said, for something new and unique, something formal yet not stuffy: she herself wasn't quite sure what, though she had a vague idea. Would it be possible for her to meet Celeste, perhaps see some of her work, and, if the "fit was right," discuss the matter? With enthusiastic politeness the young designer said that she would be happy to have such a meeting at any time. Mrs. Forster wondered if it were possible to meet the next day. Celeste immediately acceded. They made an appointment for one o'clock in the afternoon.

Celeste cleaned her little apartment as well as she could in anticipation of Mrs. Forster's visit. She swept the wooden floor, made her bed as neatly and inconspicuously as possible, and tidied up the miscellaneous items that during the course of a week had accumulated on the large sewing table spanning a third the length of one wall. She could not help having high hopes for securing this potential client. She remembered the names of the celebrities whom Mrs. Forster had mentioned. Who knew but that one of them, at her affair, would remark positively on her clothing and want to know where she had gotten it? Word of mouth among nonentities had enabled her to eke out a bare living; but among celebrities and the wealthy— she might do very well; indeed, so well as finally to make a start in her own designer name brand. At any rate, she could dream of such things.

Mrs. Forster was late: it was almost one thirty before she rang the buzzer. Celeste hurried to press the button that would open the door to the building, then stepped just outside her apartment to welcome her potential client. As she stood there she heard footsteps and the jingle of jewelry coming up the stairwell; then, in addition to those sounds, heavy breathing; and in another moment Mrs. Forster had stepped onto the fourth floor landing.

She seemed to be only a few years older than Celeste herself—in her late thirties. She was of medium height, thin and pretty insofar as prettiness is a matter of small and regular features. Her chestnut hair fell just a little past her shoulders. Her nails were long and polished and on her right wrist she wore a couple of gold bracelets. She was wearing designer clothes; they were casual but expensive. As she came up to Celeste she was smiling, still breathing heavily, and said, "Celeste?"

"Joanna? How are you! Nice to meet you!"

The two women shook hands. Celeste bade her come inside and shut the door.

"Oh my God, those steps!" Mrs. Forster said. "There's no elevator in this building?"

Celeste laughed a little and said, "No, but it's only four floors."

"I don't know how you do it!" Mrs. Forster returned.

That comment made Celeste laugh again; she was sure that her guest had spoken in a half-humorous vein. But in the

next few minutes she realized that Mrs. Forster had very definite opinions about the propriety of stairwells. She said that
she could never live in a place where you had to walk up more
than one short flight; after all, "I don't need to work just to
leave and come back home." Again, Celeste laughed a little and
assured her guest that though she herself had at first found it
inconvenient she now no longer gave it a second thought. "You
get used to it after a while," she said.

"Maybe," Mrs. Forster replied. She continued to look about
the apartment with a tight smile.

"Would you like some coffee or tea?" Celeste asked.

"Oh, no, thanks," she said. She fanned her face with her
hand. "I'm hot enough as it is!"

"Let me turn on the air conditioner for you!" Celeste said,
at once hurrying to the other end of the room and turning on
the unit, which hummed and blew into life.

"I can't stand the heat!" Mrs. Forster said, continuing to fan
her face.

"I don't like it myself. But it should get cooler in a few
minutes. Would you like some ice water?"

"Oh ... that's alright," she said, declining.

"It wasn't hard for you to find the building, was it?"

"No, not at all. I have to say that I didn't think there were
so many apartment buildings out this way—so far from everything. It's an old building, isn't it," she added, her eyes turning
critically to the ceiling.

"Yes, pretty old. That's why there's no elevator."

"I don't know how you do it."

"So I hear you're having a great party," Celeste said cheerfully, by way of cutting to the chase and finding out exactly
what Mrs. Forster was looking for and whether or not she, Celeste, would be able to give it to her.

In the next half hour, after Mrs. Forster had explained the
sort of formal evening she was planning, the two women sat
over two large portfolios of Celeste's best work. These included
large, crisp photographs of dresses and coats and jackets she
had made for people through the years. She also brought out
from her closet three rather extravagant costumes that she had
made for shows and which she had, with foresight, insisted on
keeping as examples of her work. They were among the best

things she had ever done. Each was enclosed and protected in a full-length plastic zippered bag. One of them was a long evening gown in green silk with white trimming and sequined neckline. Mrs. Forster, who all along had been growing more interested and enthusiastic in what she saw, was delighted by it. She took it into her hands and much to the young designer's satisfaction handled it with a happy appreciation for the fineness of its material and the meticulous workmanship, exclaiming under her breath, "Oh, very nice!" and "Beautiful!" Celeste explained that it had been used in a play, a period piece taking place in the 1920s—which accounted for the style. Only now when she was assured that Celeste had the talent and credentials to make her dress did Mrs. Forster open up a little more about what she had in mind for herself. Something in black, she said, something formal, very elegant, but of course nothing "over the top." She preferred simplicity of line to busyness, but she would, she said, like something that "flowed." She was very general about all these things; she might have been trying to describe any one of a dozen styles of formal attire. Celeste asked her if she had seen anything in particular that was similar to what she wanted, and Mrs. Forster said that in fact she had—and had it with her. From her pocketbook she took out a picture which she had cut out of a fashion magazine and handed it over to Celeste, saying, "Something like this would be nice, but something a little longer, a little less tight looking." It looked like an updated version of some classic Dior design from the '50s, only without the stringent wasp waist and with a V-shape whose point started beneath the left hip and whose extensions rose up to the right shoulder in front and in back. The model was wearing long, black gloves, which Mrs. Forster laughingly said could be dispensed with—that *would* be overdoing it! With her finger she pointed out the length, saying that she wanted something longer than this, something "freer" at the bottom, and ended by saying, "I am going to wear shoes similar to those, if that does you any good."

In truth, Celeste had only a very general idea of what Mrs. Forster wanted, but she was a creative woman and at once there rushed into her head a half a dozen variations she might create from such a style. She told Mrs. Forster that she would be happy to make several preliminary sketches—they would be rough but they would help them both firm up their ideas. Celeste asked if she could hold on to the picture for a couple of days. Mrs. Forster agreed. They parted amicably, indeed on far better terms than the first few minutes of their interview would have seemed to portend.

Two days later Celeste was standing in the lobby of a building on Central Park West beside a liveried doorman who announced her visit. As she stood waiting her eyes ran along the high ceiling of gilt-edged coffering, and in walking to the elevators she saw vases of fresh flowers set in alcoves along hallway and felt the sumptuous softness of new carpeting beneath her feet. The elevators themselves were paneled in dark, polished wood, with shiny brass accents. The Forsters lived on the 17th Floor. Beside the door to the apartment was a brass plaque inscribed in a script font with "Suite 17N". As soon as she stepped inside she was impressed with the vastness of the place. A marbled entranceway led down a short hall opening up to a sunken living room with great windows looking out over Central Park. Mrs. Forster and Celeste sat side-by-side on a couch in the living room and went over the designs she had worked up. They were very finished drawings, each one on good, heavy stock, which to Celeste's mind gave them an added degree of authority. Mrs. Forster took them into her hands one by one, always nodding, always approving, saying each time, "Oh, this is good!" or "Very nice!" or "I like this very much!" She was impressed with the ability of the designer to extract variations of design from an example provided. With each drawing Celeste explained what fabrics she might use to make the dress, the options for its trim, and the degree of formality it aimed at.

"Well, I think like this one best of all," Mrs. Forster said, finally, after laying out three favorite designs on her lap and spending some minutes considering them side-by-side. She had chosen the most formal of them: a long, sleeveless black gown with clean lines, a low back, and a strip of sequins running up from the hem on the left-hand side to the top of the right shoulder.

"I like that one too," Celeste said, partly because she really did, and partly to assure Mrs. Forster, who seemed not entirely certain of her choice, that she had selected wisely.

"How much would something like that cost?" Mrs. Forster

asked.

Celeste quoted a price. She uttered the amount with a slight hesitation as though only now she had considered it; but in fact she had been thinking a long time about what she would ask for her work. She had considered that as Mrs. Forster was a wealthy woman, she was not likely to wince or quibble at a quote that someone else might regard as outrageously high. Even so, it was a modest sum in comparison to what a similar dress might have cost if made by a well-known designer. After she had mentioned the price she coolly added that it included everything, labor and materials, as well as the time for several fittings. A deposit of $500 would also be necessary. Mrs. Forster was no more put off by the price than she would have been by a slight increase in the cost of a quart of milk. At once she agreed to it. With a little thrill of victory, Celeste took out of her pocketbook a small notebook, a pen, and a measuring tape, and asked her new client to stand up so that she might be measured. She proceeded to do this with a quiet, intense proficiency. When she left the building twenty minutes later, with Mrs. Forster's check for the deposit, she was exuberant. How good it was to have wealthy clients! What a relief! She would be making enough money on this one dress to pay her expenses for several months.

By nature Celeste was conscientious, but with Mrs. Forster's dress she was determined to be as careful, as meticulous as possible; to do the absolute best she could. She spent half a day in the fabric shops on 37th Street looking for the best material she could find; and found it—an expensive silk of Italian weave, and a shimmering gray satin and black sequins for the trim. These materials ate up most of the deposit money she had received from her client.

That week she immured herself in her apartment. She was capable of great discipline and could sit at her sewing table for five or six hours at a stretch, bent over patterns, cutting cloth, sewing. She took her time, determined that everything about the dress should be perfect. As she worked she often congratulated herself on having been bolder than usual in setting a high price for the dress. It was the kind of money, she told herself, that she should have been making all along. Why not? She was talented enough—her work was good enough. She de-

served it. If only, all these years, she had been charging more
for her work, she would never have fallen into the kind of strait-
ened circumstances that had lately so worried her. On the other
hand, she knew, that that wouldn't have been possible because
too many of her clients had been working-class people or poor
actors. Well, it didn't matter now. Her fortunes were changing.
She knew it, felt it in her bones. Good things were coming.
When Mrs. Forster's friends saw her in her dress they would
want something like it for themselves, and there was only one
person who could make it for them.

The dress required an enormous amount of hand stitching.
Especially the sequins (in their clear plastic containers they glittered like magical black sand) had to be carefully set upon the
gray satin trim running from the top of the right shoulder to the
bottom of the left-hand side of the hem. She worked on this trim
concurrently with other parts of the dress, allotting a portion of
each day to its creation, and never taking it up without a sense
of its importance to her life and career, and consequently with
the renewed determination to do it well. Under the bright light
of a lamp clamped to her sewing table she would hold the trim
material close to her slightly myopic eyes and slowly, surely,
steadily apply each glittery circlet; keeping her focus sharp and
steady on the needle's very point as she guided it through each
sequin's center, pushed it through the material behind, then
brought it up—with an exquisite sense of the minute proportions
involved—just beyond the circlet's edge, and so likewise attach
the next, overlapping sequin. It was slow, tedious, painstaking
work, so hard on the eyes that she often had to look away and
blink repeatedly. At any one moment it seemed as though the
trim would never get done, that it was simply impossible for
anyone, no matter how steadfast her industry, to make headway
in finishing its almost five feet of length. But as the hours
passed, what had started as a single line of sequins grew to be a
quarter of an inch, then an inch, and so forth; and as the tedious days passed inch was added to inch so that the trim got
done. At the end of each day her eyes would be sore from so
much close work; sometimes a stabbing pain pierced them and
she could not go on. She would set aside the dress that was
taking such wonderful shape beneath her hands, blink hard, and
look away—look, for instance, outside the window of her apart-

ment to the high-rise condominium across the way with its hundred bathroom windows. She would place the dress on her dress-maker's dummy, where it would remain till she took it up again the next day. Then she would make something for herself to eat, go outside for a short walk, and then come back home and watch the small television set upon a metal stand by her bed. She would fall asleep contentedly, with a sense of accomplishment for the progress she had made on the dress. Again she would think of the money she was going to get. And for just a few weeks' work! It was wonderful; like a dream. She wondered if she might not, when she got paid, splurge a little on herself. Yes, she could definitely use some new things: new blinds for the windows, perhaps a couch or an easy chair ... perhaps even a new television. There were so many things.

Her days were largely uninterrupted. She knew many people but she rarely received phone calls or visitors. In typical New York City fashion she was just another one of tens of thousands who lived isolated lives in the midst of millions. Of the friends she did have nearly all of them were involved in the arts, people she had met while working on shows or had been introduced to at parties. One day she received a call from one of them. Her name was Anne and she lived in the East Village. They had met while working on a low-budget movie several years before and for a stretch of several months thereafter had been rather close till separate interests and obligations had drawn them gradually apart; nevertheless, they had always kept in touch. "Why don't you come over for lunch or something?" Anne asked. "I haven't seen you for a while."

It was a welcome invitation to Celeste—it would be a grateful diversion from her labor—and so she happily accepted.

Anne was a filmmaker who who had made three movies, none of them being over forty-five minutes long. Several years earlier one of them had been shown on New York Public Television. If success for an artist is measured in the extent of the exposure of her work, then that night Anne had reached the pinnacle of her career, when tens of thousands of viewers had watched one of her movies. But ultimately it had meant nothing, for though at the time it generated what she called a few "leads," none of them had come to anything—none of them had led to other, paying work—and since then she had not made another movie. If someone had asked her why not, she would have said that she had never been able to raise enough money—which was true enough. But there was a reason even beyond this: namely, that she no longer had the will to work to so little effect. For a lot had changed in her life. Having, as she had told friends, "finally met a man she could live with," she was now married and, after two years, pregnant with her first child. As though by some sort of inertia she still talked about making movies and regarded herself as a productive artist, but she secretly knew that that part of her life was gone forever:—and good riddance to it! Years of struggle, of privation, of anxious hopes always dashed, and no one tiny success gained but at the expense of ten larger failures and disappointments, and all for the sake of making a movie hardly anyone would ever see—who needed that? It was no life. Certainly it couldn't hold a candle to the daily, indeed hourly satisfactions she found in the love of her husband and in the happy anticipation of having and raising her baby.

Celeste was surprised at how good Anne looked. She was not a pretty woman, but her pregnancy of four months had given her merely pleasant features a strange appeal, for her complexion was clear and healthfully ruddy, her eyes were bright, her lips were red and full. Despite her slightly protruding abdomen her figure looked better than it ever had, perhaps because a jaunty vitality had put a spring into her step and a certain quickness into her movements. She looked as though she were bursting with health, and in a sense she was: so healthy, so alive, that she could not contain it all herself and would soon be imparting it to another, a new and separate being.

"Look at you!" Celeste exclaimed, the moment she saw her and they kissed each other hello; and shifting her eyes down to Anne's protruding belly, "Look at you!" she said again.

"Isn't it something?" Anne said, looking down at herself. "Who would have thought it, right?"

They giggled together like two schoolgirls. Celeste was fully, naively happy for her friend. At the same time she was aware of feeling something—something uncomfortable, a sudden pang—that twitched within herself at the sight of her friend's pregnancy.

In one thing however Anne hadn't changed at all: she still lived in an odd and depressingly decorated place. The walls were painted a red so deep that it looked brown, and on them African tribal shields and grotesque painted masks vied for a place with the stuffed heads of an antelope, a wild boar, and a lioness, all looking into space with glassy-eyed indifference. Artificial tropical plants occupied every corner, their glossy plastic leaves spreading out several feet. A small stuffed crocodile peeped out from under the stand supporting the television, and another one lay beside a leg of the coffee table, its head adjusted upward toward the couch so that it seemed to be looking at anyone who might be sitting there. Two colorful birds stood taxidermically still and silent atop a bookcase beside the windows covered with bamboo shades. Celeste, as she sat on the couch in the cluttered living room, looked about for the first time with the understanding that however sweet and well-meaning Anne might have been, she had absolutely no taste, no sense of the beautiful, and perhaps—just perhaps—was afflicted with some mild mental disorder. What other reason could account for someone going out of her way to create and take pleasure in a claustrophobic and primeval environment of darkness, dead animals, and savage caricatures of the human countenance?

"I've ordered in some Indian food," Anne said, leading her friend inside. "It should be here any minute. It's from a place down the street—they make good stuff."

"Oh, that'll be great. What do I owe you?"

"Don't be silly! It's my treat! Come in, sit, I made some iced tea."

Anne disappeared into the kitchen for a minute and came back into the living room with a pitcher of iced tea and two glasses. "By the way," she said, ebulliently, "congratulations on your review! I saw it this morning."

"My review? What review?"

Anne's eyes widened and her mouth opened in disbelief. "You haven't seen it yet? I thought you must have!"

Celeste shook her head and watched her friend hurriedly disappear into the kitchen again and come back out holding the day's *Daily News.* She quickly flipped through the pages before finding what she was looking for and shoved the paper into Co leste's hands with a, "Look! They reviewed you!"

In the "Entertainment" section was a review of the play Celeste had worked on. The critic had been guardedly kind to the play itself, but he expressed outright appreciation for the talents of the stage and costume designers, mentioning them by name—both their names in a single sentence. Celeste felt a rush of pride and happiness at the sight of her name in print. There she was, in black and white, in a major newspaper, in an article that would be read by thousands, by tens of thousands of people. Her heart beat a little faster with joy.

"I wonder if Bobby knows about this?" Celeste asked, referring to the director of the play.

"I'm sure he does—he must."

"But he would have called me," Celeste mused aloud.

"Well, it just came out this morning. Maybe he doesn't know yet."

Celeste returned her eyes to the review, which she read over again. This glimmer of recognition was to her like a whiff of cold fresh air in a close warm room; a relief from the worry of work done in vain, a reassurance of better things to come. She had been in a good mood when she had gone to Anne's apartment but now she felt as though she were floating on air. Anne herself went a long way toward fostering this good feeling in her friend, for in so many direct and indirect ways she complimented Celeste on her talent, saying how sooner or later she was bound to do something "big." Celeste said that in a way she already had, and mentioned her new, wealthy client. "She's having some sort of party and I'm making a dress for her. With any luck my name'll get around among her friends, and I'll get a lot more work."

"Oh, that would be great! What's her name?"

"Joanna Forster."

Anne shrugged and gave a quick shake of the head: she had never heard of her.

"She seems very nice," Celeste said, and added, "At least I'll finally be making some real money!"—and she mentioned the thousands of dollars she was to be paid.

"Wow! That's fantastic! Congratulations!"

In the past whenever the two had gotten together Anne had talked shop almost exclusively: about her movies, about the movies of others, about the anonymous actors or directors she knew, about the world-famous ones whose movies were running in "limited engagements" at this or that movie house in the city. But a fundamental shift in her priorities had taken place. After the merest chit-chat about Celeste's or her own now dead career, she spent most of the time talking about her husband and baby. She announced that she had already chosen a name: Jareth, if it was a boy, and Cayenne, if a girl. ("Isn't that the name of a pepper?" Celeste asked, entirely politely. "Yes, but it's not just a pepper!" Anne insisted. "It's a place—it's very exotic-sounding, don't you think?") They had already begun "fixing up" the room that would belong to little Jareth or Cayenne. She showed it to Celeste. Formerly it had been the space where her husband had his office, but the desk, the computer, the printer, and everything else had been moved out, and now it was a bare room save for a fresh coat of pastel green paint and a dresser atop which was a colorful children's lamp in the shape of a hand holding three balloons—one red, one blue, one yellow, and each having a tiny light inside it. Even all this, Anne said, was but temporary, since she and her husband were seriously considering leaving the city and getting a place—a house—in New Jersey. When later the two women were sitting in the kitchen having their Indian food, Celeste could only wonder at how much her friend had changed, at how completely conventional she had become. All this was the more surprising because there was a time when Anne had prided herself on being as unconventional as possible. Celeste could not decide if this change in her friend's attitude toward life was a satisfying sign of maturity or the result of having resigned herself to the fact that she would never become the notable filmmaker she had hoped to be. Whichever it was, there was no question that Anne seemed happier, calmer, more at peace with herself than Celeste had ever seen her.

"By the way, me and Jeremy are going on a trip soon. We're going to Greece."

"Really?"

"You know how Jeremy loves history and all, especially ancient history. So he finally wanted to go to Greece at least once. He probably figured he'd never get the chance again once the baby came."

"Well, good for you! That should be fun."

"I'll show you where we're staying."

She brought to the table a couple of travel magazines that she and her husband had looked through while choosing destinations. One of these was large and heavy, full of glossy, color photographs of renowned or top-rated hotels around the world: splendid lobbies in England, palatial entrances in France, and sun-drenched rooms looking out over the Grand Canal of Venice. Fine dining was highlighted, and every few pages showed good-looking people sitting at dinner tables drinking wine while some trim, precise waiter served them gourmet foods from silver trays. Anni showed Celeste the place where she and her husband were going to be staying in Chios: a hotel built of white stone with a roof of brown tiles, its windows facing a pristine beach edging a sparkling, turquoise sea. Celeste flipped through the rest of the magazine, impressed with its photography. "Where'd you get this?"

"Jeremy bought it at a newsstand. You can have it if you want—we're finished with it."

"Oh, I don't need it."

"No, take it!" Anne insisted. "Otherwise I'm just gonna throw it out."

"Well ... remind me," Celeste said, gratefully. And sure enough when she took her leave Anne, reminded her to take the magazine, putting it into her hands and sending her off with a hug, a kiss on the cheek, and the promise to call her as soon as she got back from Greece.

During the few hours she had spent with Anne, Celeste had had to make a conscious effort not to think about, not to mention again, the review she had received in the newspaper. But all the while she had been thinking about it. Half the time that she had smiled or laughed over something Anne had told her had really been owing to an upsurge of happiness over the review. She could not help regarding it as another lucky break. She had had her share of good reviews in the past, but they had always been in small neighborhood publications, whereas this one was in a major newspaper. Who knew but that one of the thousands of people who saw her name might be a person who could further her career and contact her for some major project? With a secret, silent sense of contentment she imagined herself getting that phone call or letter requesting her services to work on some popular television show or projected Hollywood movie. Perhaps she would even have to move out to California ...

No sooner had Celeste gotten out onto the street than she headed for the first kiosk she saw and bought three copies of the *Daily News*. She intended to clip out the reviews and keep one for herself and send the other two to her parents back in Minnesota. How surprised they would be to see it!—they who had never quite shared her enthusiasm for her art, or her belief in her eventual success in it.

She got out of the subway station at Herald Square and set off for her East Side apartment. Along the way she passed a corner trash can and noticed that several copies of that day's *Daily News* had been flung into it.

When she got back home there were several messages on her answering machine. The first was from Robert, the director of the play. He was calling—too late now—to tell Celeste about the review. His voice was enthusiastic and proud for her sake, and he ended by saying, "When you get a chance, give me a call!" The second message was from her dentist's secretary who was making a "courtesy call" to inform her that her six month's cleaning was coming up and she ought to make an appointment. "No money for that," Celeste said to herself, pressing the button for the next call. It was Mrs. Forster. She had called to check up on the progress of the dress. Celeste immediately called her back. They chatted for several minutes, during which time the young designer not only assured her client that her dress was coming along nicely but also that she was ready to have her come over for a first fitting. Could she come in at the end of the week? They set the time for three o'clock on Friday afternoon.

It was hot and humid that day, and the air was still: the whole of Manhattan lay simmering under a blanket of thick, stagnant, stinking air. Remembering how much Mrs. Forster detested the heat, Celeste turned on her air conditioner full blast a half hour before the time of the appointment. Mrs. Forster didn't arrive till a quarter to four.

She came in wearing her usual casual but expensive designer clothes. If she wasn't overwhelmed with the heat it was only because she had gone from her air-conditioned apartment to an air-conditioned car. As usual, her makeup and hair and nails were impeccable. Apparently she never went out in public without looking her best, as though this were a part of the responsibility of being who she was.

Celeste did her fittings in the small entranceway to her apartment because the light from the overhead fixture there was bright. Mrs. Forster removed her shoes, pants, and blouse with a tinge of reluctance, and stood stiffly as Celeste helped her into the gown before the full-length mirror leaning against the bookcase. Mrs. Forster stood looking at her reflection while Celeste moved from this to that part of the dress, pinching here, tugging there, then standing back a little as she silently assessed and calculated.

"Do you like the material?" Celeste asked.

"Yes, it's very nice," Mrs. Forster said, looking at her reflection.

"Do you like the trim?"

"Oh, yes, very nice."

"Could you just turn around for me"—Celeste guided her around—"that's good!" She bent down to the hem.

"How long have you been living here?" Mrs. Forster said, now facing the small apartment.

"Oh, about ten years."

Mrs. Forster said nothing in return. Celeste did not look up and couldn't see her client's face, yet she felt emanating from her a vibration of amazement that anyone could live in such cramped and—compared to what she was used to—ugly quarters. Sure enough, in another moment Mrs. Forster remarked, "You could use some carpeting."

"Oh, I can't have carpeting," Celeste explained. "I work with pins, and I'm always dropping them, so I need to see them. Believe me, I've stepped on a few as it is!"

"Oh. I suppose that makes sense. It is small in here, though. Don't you think?"

"Yes, I'll agree with you there!" Celeste said cheerfully. She got up from her crouching position and turned Mrs. Forster back around toward the mirror, giving a little tug to the waistline as she looked over the older woman's shoulder. To her critical and practiced eyes, everything about the gown looked quite good— one of the best things she had ever done. She silently congratu-

lated herself on her design and execution in one of those moments, which artists sometimes have, of looking objectively on
their work and finding it good. Only minor adjustments needed
to be made at the waist and perhaps a little at the left shoulder; a few hours' work at most. In the mirror she glanced at
Mrs. Forster's face, certain to see there the same admiration she
herself felt, but saw instead a certain distant, critical, not-
wholly-pleased expression. "I do have to pull in the waistline
just a tiny bit," Celeste said, as though Mrs. Forster had also
seen there the need for a slight adjustment.

"I'm sure ... yes ... only ..." Mrs. Forster turned around,
and looked at herself, over her shoulder.

"What is it?" Celeste asked.

"I'm beginning to think about the length. It does look a little long to me."

"Well, of course, it is full length. That's how it was in the
sketch, remember?"

"Yessss," Mrs. Forster said slowly, shaking her head in acknowledgment. "But I was thinking"—her eyes shifting up and
down at her image, critically, not happily—"perhaps it would be
better if it weren't *quite* so long. I guess I didn't think it would
look this formal. It almost looks like a pageant dress or something."

"A 'pageant' dress?"

"It's just that it looks almost a bit ... *much*—you know?"

Celeste didn't know; but she said nothing; she smiled and
listened as her client continued:

"Do you think it would be possible to make it shorter? Perhaps somewhere just below the knee. What do you think?"

"That much shorter?"

"Sure, why not?" Mrs. Forster asked; and with her hands
she raised the hemline to her mid-calf. She looked at herself in
the mirror. "There. Yes. You know, I think that is better. I
really do. Much better!"

Celeste had to restrain herself from an astonished intake of
breath. The dress had been designed long; everything about its
other proportions and lines had been cut to that end. Moreover
she had worked hard to get it as it was, as good as it was, and
nearly perfect as it was becoming, and now it was to be changed
on what seemed a whim. On the other hand Celeste had heard

in Mrs. Forster's voice a determination to have it shorter. The designer was torn between pleasing a client by giving her exactly what she wanted or trying to convince her that what she wanted wasn't in her best interest. In a polite, even deferential voice, she said, "But I think it looks so nice long, the way it is. It looks wonderful on you. If we made it shorter, it would detract from the line of the trim—and that's what makes it look elegant."

Mrs. Forster seemed to consider this professional opinion. She looked again at her reflection in the mirror. Then she shook her head, slowly, negatively. "I don't know about that," she said. "I can just see that if it were shorter it would look a lot better. It would look so much ... freer. Do you know what I mean?"

"Freer," Celeste echoed.

"And it is summer. Something shorter and freer and cooler might be more appropriate."

"It would take more time, though, and I'd have to charge you more," Celeste said, thinking that if she could not convince Mrs. Forster not to meddle with the dress on stylistic grounds she might discourage her with the prospect of added labor and expense.

Mrs. Forster, however, never troubled her head about the expense of things. When she liked something, she bought it; when she wanted something changed, she made sure it was changed. She turned a pair of smiling eyes to Celeste. "Well, the party isn't for a month yet. How long could it possibly take to make the alteration? A day? Two? There's plenty of time. So ... yes! Let's do that, shall we? Let's shorten it."

Celeste nodded in agreement. She brought a tape measure over to Mrs. Forster, knelt down by the hem, and asked, "How much shorter would you like it?"

Mrs. Forster, after twice raising the hem uncertainly, finally decided on a length. Celeste measured the difference.

It broke Celeste's heart a little as, that night, she brought the dress over to her work table and began cutting into it. It was a terrible thing to have to tear into something on which one had nearly put the proud finishing touch. She worked silently and sullenly and a few times she shook her head and mumbled an exclamation against Mrs. Forster. Then she told herself that it was not right to have any animus against a client, someone whom, if anything, she ought to be grateful to for a commission. So what if Mrs. Forster had no taste and couldn't see a good thing when she was literally wrapped in it? Want of fashion sensibility wasn't a crime and in the end the only thing that mattered was whether or not she was happy with what she was paying a great deal for. The problem for Celeste was that she knew she was putting out an inferior product, which was not as likely to draw the interest of future clients.

Later that night, after she had grown tired of working on the dress and was lying in bed, she happened to pick up the travel magazine that her friend Anne had given her. She gazed with tired eyes on the pictures of the grand hotels in the beautiful places, at the sparkling entrances, the immaculate rooms, the perfectly set tables, the lusciously-photographed foods. She would have liked to visit such places but of course they were beyond her means, and she was too practical, too careful with her money for such things. When she reached the back of the magazine she came across pages of smaller advertisements for quaint inns, many of which were in the United States. They might be set amid the mountain scenery of Colorado, or on the pristine Carolina Coast, or in one of the Florida Keys. A few of them were in the northeastern states. One of them, in Maine, especially caught Celeste's eye. It was called the Freepointe Inn and was set on some sort of eminence overlooking an expansive rocky coastline with a charming fishing village in the near distance. A few of the rooms were pictured. They were spacious and bright, their walls painted a light blue with white trim around the windows and doors, and were appointed with stuffed armchairs, throw rugs, and four-posted beds. The main room, where guests could gather, had a more sedate, almost antique look, what with its stone fireplace, wood-paneled walls, and large oil paintings of landscapes in thick oak frames: the kind of subdued, comfortable place where people might relax after a long day, meeting and talking and having a drink. (Celeste never drank, but as she looked at that photograph she could just imagine herself sitting here with some kind of drink, and enjoying it to boot!). The accompanying text was as inviting as the photo-graphs:

Wake up each morning to a splendid view of the majestic Atlantic Ocean! Authentic French and English period antiques add splendor and beauty to each room. At the end of your day come home to relax in our Captain's Quarters for a nightcap (the first is always on the house!) and make new friends by a crackling fireplace. An experience you'll remember for the rest of your life!

There was a listing of the rates per night; expensive, as it seemed to Celeste—but not terribly so. It occurred to her that with the money she would get from Mrs. Forster's dress she could easily spend a week at such a place and still have plenty left over in order to cover her living expenses for a few months. But no sooner had this possibility crossed her mind than a warning voice—the voice of a conscience forged by a lifetime of practicality—warned her, "No, you really can't. Don't waste your money like that. You might need it."

Only minutes later the same voice piped up to protest against her Spartan restraint. It told her that she was wrong, even foolish, to deny herself a small vacation. "It's not as though you go on vacations all the time," it argued. "In fact, you've never gone on one. Why shouldn't you? You've worked hard for a long time, haven't you? You just can't scrimp and save all your life. You have to enjoy yourself too once in a while. The years go by fast. Now is the time to enjoy." The little voice added that even if she overspent and came up a little short one month—so what? She had a savings account that she could dip into, and whatever she took out she could make up for later, for other jobs were sure to come along. Just this once she shouldn't worry about money and do something she wanted to do.

She told herself that tomorrow she *would* book a week at the Freepointe Inn, and she had no sooner made that decision than she was proud of herself for having thrown caution to the wind. She felt as though she had been brave enough to trust to a better, freer, happier life. But when the next day came she didn't make the reservation. With the sober beginning of another new morning her usual practicality asserted itself in full force. Maybe one day she would take a vacation ... maybe when she had more clients, good clients like Mrs. Forster ... but not just now. She had to be careful. The future was too uncertain, and against its unforeseen but somehow inevitable treacheries the only possible buffer was cash in reserve.

To her second fitting Mrs. Forster was late as usual. Apparently she was one of those people who could never be relied on to be prompt. When Celeste opened the door for her she was again breathing hard, and this time without the smile or sense of humor with which previously she had made light of the climb. "Oh! Those stairs!" she said, shaking her head at Celeste with an air of reproach, as though the designer had taken her apartment for the express purpose of tormenting her clients with physical exertion.

Celeste smiled and said nothing. The remark, and more than this the manner in which it had been said, had somewhat irritated her, but she shrugged it off with the thought that after today she would probably never see Mrs. Forster again.

After a few minutes' small talk, Celeste bade her client try on the dress. As Mrs. Forster changed into it Celeste politely walked over to her long sewing table and turned her eyes down as she needlessly rearranged items. She heard the rustle of fabric, the subtle bustle of her client changing her clothes, and then heard her say, "Ah, that *does* look better!" Celeste looked up to see Mrs. Forster looking at herself from the side in the full-length mirror. She went over to her and pulled a little here, tugged a little there, patted down a crease, and guided her client to turn around.

"Perfect fit," Celeste said, both to reassure Mrs. Forster and in genuine appreciation for her own handiwork.

"Don't you think I was right about the length? Doesn't it look better?"

Celeste smiled and nodded. She couldn't bring herself to say "Yes" and lie outright. The dress was not as good as it had been, though owing to her talent it was still better than anything mass-produced and which might have been bought in a shop.

"It certainly fits you well," Celeste said. "It looks like we won't even have to make any adjustments."

"Mmmmm ... " the older woman murmured. She continued to turn around and around in the mirror, looking at herself from every angle. As she did so the satisfied smile began to waver, the admiring eyes assumed a more critical cast, and she puckered her lips a little, as though in curiosity, in ever-so-slight dissatisfaction. "I wonder ... " she said.

"Yes?"

"You know, I'm beginning to wonder ..." She put out her arms, looking from one to the other, then, keeping them held out, looked at her image. "My arms look so bare."

Celeste had to laugh a little. "It's a sleeveless dress," she said.

"Yes, I know. But you know ... it seems to me that ... oh, my arms look so *very* bare. I wonder ... do you think we could add sleeves."

"Sleeves?"

"Yes, you know ... something very sheer ... from the shoulder to the wrists. Just picture it!"

"Well, I don't think that would work," Celeste said, and despite herself her voice carried an irritated edge. Immediately however she tempered her attitude into one of kindly reassurance. "It's really meant to be sleeveless. You see, the trim gives it just enough interest—it kind of offsets the bare arms. It wouldn't look right with sleeves of any kind: it would be too busy, and I remember you're telling me that you didn't want anything that looked busy."

"But I don't think it would look busy at all," Mrs. Forster said, turning her eyes back to the mirror and again holding out her arms. "It's just that my arms are *so* bare that it ... doesn't look right. It looks like something's missing."

"I don't think the sleeves you're talking about would go very well with the bare back of the dress."

"Oh, why not?"

If at first Celeste didn't answer, it was because there were so many reasons that she didn't know where to start. The main reason was that it would just look a little odd, but how was she to say that without insulting her client's taste?

"Not at all, Celeste, not at all," Mrs. Forster continued. "Actually, I've always liked sheer sleeves. They always look so classy. Surely it wouldn't take much time to get the material and add them. Sheer sleeves ... a little pleated at the shoulder . .. a little snug at the wrists. That's how I see it. It would look wonderful. Could we do that? Could we add them?"

Celeste had to force herself to remain expressionless, to keep her lips closed, her eyes blinking calmly, regularly. At that moment she was surprised at how much she disliked Mrs. Forster. It wasn't because she had raised objections and insisted on alterations that had changed the design of the dress but rather because she couldn't see a good thing when it was right in front of her, and in that respect she represented to Celeste the kind of lack of taste that had made it so hard for her to distinguish herself in the fashion world. People too often only wanted what they knew, and when they wanted something that they didn't know it was invariably a step backward, not forward; and in this case it wasn't just a step but a giant leap. Nevertheless the designer felt it was important to maintain at least the illusion of amicability, reasonably telling herself again that she didn't "have" to like a customer or even what her customer wanted—she only had to be polite and provide the service for which she was being paid. Only business had brought her together with Mrs. Forster, and once that business was concluded they need never see each other again.

"If you want sleeves I could add them," Celeste said, looking over Mrs. Forster's shoulder into the mirror as she spoke. "Of course, it'll take a little longer."

"Oh, that's alright. We have time yet, and I don't mind coming back. I'm sure it's the right thing to do. How long do you think it would take?"

"Oh ... once I get the fabric, which I could get tomorrow—"

"Tomorrow? Not today?"

"Well, it's almost four thirty. The fabric shop I like to use closes at five. Even if I rushed I couldn't get there in time."

Mrs. Forster received this reasoning with the slightest air of disapproval, as though Celeste should at least have made the effort.

"I'll go first thing tomorrow, though," Celeste said. "I could have it for you by the end of the week."

"That would be fine," Mrs. Forster said.

Celeste bought the appropriate sheer fabric for the sleeves and spent the next two days making the alterations. She worked with her wonted application, but not with the same enthusiasm, for the dress, as it was now taking shape, was a corruption of her creation. It had been a grand, perfect thing in its lines and flow, but now it was to be butchered. This wasn't the first time one of her clients had made "suggestions," but it was the first time one of them had made them so contrary to the spirit of her design. Sheer sleeves—on a dress like this! It was ridiculous. But as though some guardian angel were looking over her best interests, a voice within her counseled that she mustn't lose sight of the forest for the trees. Artistic integrity had never paid her rent, and while the customer might not always be right, the customer always had the cash. Mrs. Forster was turning out to be difficult to work for, but Celeste reminded herself that she need never work for her again if she didn't want to. She could be very creative in coming up with excuses to decline a project.

A day later she received a visit from Robert, the director of the play for which her costumes had garnered a good review. He himself had once been an actor but had given up being in plays to directing them. He and Celeste had known each other for eight years. When she had first met him he had been thirty-five, and even then she had thought he was approaching an age when it was no longer seemly to be knocking about in little theaters and spending all his free time creating shows that never get an audience larger than forty or fifty persons on a given night. But now that he was forty-three he was definitely the odd man out. For one thing, he looked older than his years, for his frame had grown stout and his hair had thinned, and his age was never more apparent than when he was at the theater surrounded by the young, trim, good-looking actors whom he directed and tried to hobnob with. The struggling bohemian life may have something romantic about it in the young, who after all can legitimately regard their current hard times as temporary because they have many years in which to work toward success, but to continue in it after a certain age usually is nothing more than the foolish refusal to accept failure. Thus Celeste inly cringed a little as she listened to his glowing theater gossip. He filled her in on the recent doings of actors they both knew: who had gotten into a fight with this one, who was having an affair with that one, who kept forgetting his lines, who had stumbled on exiting the stage, who had almost been mugged on Eighth Avenue.... Then he dropped the bombshell: the play was ending soon.

"Already?" Celeste asked.

He smiled easily, but not so easily that his disappointment didn't show through. "I don't know ... I thought it would go at least through the summer, but the audience is already thinning out pretty bad. The other night we only sold twenty tickets."

Celeste pulled back her bottom lip in a gesture of surprise at, and sympathy over, such miserable box office.

"What about the review in the *News*? Didn't it help?"

"It did for a couple nights, then things just petered out again. You need more than one review in the *News* to get the momentum rolling. And it's not like we have big names in the cast or anything. Anyway," he said, throwing up his hands a little as though to toss aside his latest faltering production and everything to do with it, "I'm much more excited about the new project. It takes place in the '60s in New York. It's about rock and roll and hippies, and the Age of Aquarius and Free Love, and all that stuff. All the guys are gonna grow their hair long for it. We're gonna have music, dancing, and the dialogue is pretty funny. It's basically a rock musical, and it's gonna be very exciting; we're gonna have great lighting and sets." He went on and on about it. Though Celeste smiled, nodded, and seemed as interested as he was in these things, she felt uncomfortable, embarrassed, to listen to him, in much the same way one might feel on listening to a paunchy, flabby fellow of fifty, who had been a quarterback in his lean, mean, college years, suddenly get up and show off a few of his "moves"—now absurdly clunky and uncoordinated. She felt sorry for Robert, who clearly was going to be one of those poor souls who continue on to the sad, bitter end as an example and warning to the world of what not to do with one's life. "We're gonna be needing about a dozen costumes—all mod; and I remember your telling me once you liked mod styles. So I was thinking you'd be perfect for the job, if you're interested."

"Oh, Bob, I can't," she said, shaking her head. "I'm really busy right now."

"Are you sure? There would be money involved in it for you." And he threw out a sum that, given his shoestring budget, was very generous.

If he had come to her even a few weeks earlier she might have accepted his proposal, but now she was going to make ten times the amount of money he was offering without having to make a fraction of the commitment in time.   Besides, she was too wise to think that working on another obscure, off-Broadway play of the sort she had been doing for ten years was ever going to get her name recognized by the moneyed and influential people who could further her career.   She did not feel it appropriate to mention this consideration to Robert for fear he might think it selfishly ambitious; though he could hardly claim to be any different.   She repeated that she just didn't have the time. "Maybe on the next one I could work with you, but right now I'm working with a client and ... well, it's just going to take all my time for a while. Maybe after that ..."   Then she mentioned the names of a few other costume designers whom they both knew, and asked him if he might not contact one of them.

"They're not as good as you, and not as nice," he responded, with subdued, resigned cheerfulness at her having refused him. "I mean, if I have to go with one of them, I will, but I'd rather have you."

"I'm sorry. I just can't."

He shrugged. "Alright. I'll find someone else. It's a pity though. I think you would have liked working on it. I have a feeling it'll do really well." He looked around her apartment for a few seconds. It was very quiet just then, so quiet that there floated through the window, from the high-rise building in the near distance, the sound of a toilet flushing.

During his visit she had been seated at her sewing table, working on Mrs. Forster's dress. She carefully gathered up the dress in her arms and took it with her to the dummy, on which she carefully placed it. Robert watched her as she did this.

"That's pretty nice," he remarked.

Celeste laughed.

"What?"

"You think that's nice?"

He shrugged, suddenly not sure of himself, and looked at her with the uncertain expression of someone waiting to be told why he was right or—as he rather felt he was—wrong.

"Isn't it?" he asked.

"Let's put it this way: Don't give up directing to start designing clothes." They both laughed. "You should have seen it before—how really nice it was. Geez, I should have taken a picture of it when I had the chance! I wasn't thinking."

"You don't like it?" he asked.

"Oh, Bob, if you only knew.... This is really awful. Look at the back, and now look at the front, with those sleeves. And the length! It's a mishmash."

"So why don't you fix it?" he asked, naively.

"I can't 'fix' it. There is no fixing it. This is what the client wants."

"Well, if that's what the client wants, that's what the client gets—right?"

Celeste nodded.

"Is it finished?" he asked.

"Just about. Just some stitching has to be done at the bottom of the sleeves."

"Great! Then you'll be available to work with me!"—with a laugh and a hopeful leer.

"Sorry, Bob, I've got other things lined up," she said, lying easily because the alternative was an honesty that would have hurt his feelings.

He breathed deeply and shrugged, resigning himself to not having her. "By the way, after the show tonight we're all going out for drinks. Why don't you come?"

"Thanks, but I think I'll stay in tonight."

"Gettin' old, Celeste, gettin' old!" he said, in good-humored mockery.

The designer only smiled but had the distasteful image of him sitting amidst actors young enough to be his sons and daughters; joking, laughing, exchanging horseplay with them; never suspecting that their enthusiasm for his company was purely interested, arising from a desire to ingratiate themselves into his directorial favor—themselves unaware of the absurdity of wanting to become bigger fish in the smallest of ponds.

Later that afternoon she left her apartment to walk four blocks uptown to a grocery store and get something for dinner. The evening rush hour was in progress and even on this far side of Manhattan the sidewalks were busy with pedestrians. The streets were choked with slow-moving traffic, and the hot, humid air, loaded with the hundred poisons of pollution, was visible in the distance as a sickly brown haze.

She bought a can of crushed tomatoes, a box of pasta, and

the smallest jar she could find of grated Parmesan cheese. She liked putting artichokes in her sauce, and walked about for almost ten minutes before she found them, but when she took up the can and saw the price she put it back down.

At the checkout counter she stood behind a young man who had just gotten off work and was dressed in slacks and a shirt recently freed of its tie and open at the collar. He was a nice-looking fellow of about Celeste's age, but he looked the worse for wear: a little pale from exhaustion after eight hours of relentless paperwork, and still sweaty from the heat outside: spots of perspiration dotting the front and back of his shirt. At one point he turned half around and glanced at Celeste. She gave him a brief, tentative smile, and her heart fluttered a little to look directly into his eyes, which were an arresting blue. But he seemed to look through rather than at her and with an indifferent expression turned his head back toward the cashier. Celeste felt a little pang of rejection but in the next moment she understood that the poor fellow was just too tired to care about more than getting home after a hard day at work.

On her way back to her apartment she witnessed an ugly scene. Two cars had gotten into an accident at a traffic light. The damage was minor—on one side no more than a slightly bent fender, on the other only a shattered headlight—but the drivers had bounded out of their seats and were screaming at each other in a rage. One of them was an Indian with a turban and a beard, the other a short, pudgy Chinese wearing glasses and dressed in a business suit. Neither one of them spoke English very well, and as they stood only a few feet away flinging curses at each other their upraised and threatening fists rather than their words conveyed their sudden, furious hatred. It was hard to say who had thrown the first punch, or even if a punch had been thrown, but in the next moment the two men had fallen to the hot asphalt in a bear-hug of attempted mutual destruction. Barking out ugly expletives and murderous threats in their native languages, they rolled around on the asphalt beside their cars, desperately trying to kick, punch, scratch, and squeeze each other to death. The Indian's turban came off his head and the Chinese's glasses flew off his face. A few men who had been observing this from the sidewalk stepped forward to try to break up the fight, leaning over the men, gingerly trying to separate them with loud commands, "Stop it! Stop it! That's enough—enough!" All down the avenue hundreds of horns honked from backed-up cars, while those drivers nearest the scene and able to see what was going on either rolled down their windows or opened their doors and stood just beside their idling cars, shouting their various imprecations and agitated frustration:

"Get-duh hell oudah deh! If yah wanna fighd, go fighd on da sidewalk, yah stupid assholes!"

"C'mon, c'mon, we ain't got no time for dis bullshit!"

"Gedowda people's way, yah damn idiods! Yah damn id-iods! Yah blockin' dah street, yah damn idiods!"

Like so many other pedestrians who happened on this scene Celeste also stopped to look on. She couldn't help it: it was at once fascinating and horrible—the spectacle of two men, both well into middle age, conducting themselves not with the staid, calm dignity befitting maturity but rather wrestling around on the dirty street like two drunken youths, trying to bash each other's brains in. Now and then the onlookers glanced at one another with pursed lips and shocked, disapprov-ing expressions in which might be discerned their own embar-rassment at continuing to watch the conflict, as though to say, "Isn't this just terrible? We shouldn't really be watching this, should we? But it isn't our fault if they're fighting right in front of us, is it? Just terrible!" Celeste stood among the increas-ingly dense onlookers for only twenty seconds before she was sickened by what she saw, and on some deep level ashamed of herself for being part of the gawking congregation. She turned away and continued homeward, threading through the people around her. "Excuse me ... excuse me ... excuse me!"—impatient of their presence, of their close-packed, hot, clamorous bodies, of their outward, sanctimonious shock and disapproval, which dis-guised to themselves and others their secret pleasure in an in-terruption to the dull, mechanical, barely-tolerated routine of their lives. She wished she had the power to dispel them; that she might, with some magical wave of her hand, send them fly-ing to the four corners of the earth, away from her, away from the area, away from the city, and so have an unhindered, peace-ful path homeward, free of all humankind's pettiness and ugly, entrenched tribal violence.

When she got home she took a cool shower, and when she got out of the bathroom she could hear from the open window at the far end of the narrow apartment voices floating up from the downstairs. The people who lived on the first were sitting on their patio. Apparently they had a few guests over. After she had put on a t-shirt and underwear, Celeste went over to the window, stealthily pushed aside the shade, and looked below to see several people sitting on chairs. They were holding drinks and one of them was smoking a cigarette. Another, a young woman, was standing and spoke in a voice just loud enough for Celeste to hear her:

" ... *loved* it up there! I had the best time. They had a house overlooking Lake Champlain, on the *far* side of the lake, mind you, not the one near town: the far side's a *lot* less populated and a *lot* more exclusive. We went sailing in one of their boats in the afternoon, then they had a wonderful barbecue at the house. The house was gorgeous! *So* beautiful! Oh—you can't imagine. And the family was just great. Really, such class! Everyone looking like a Kennedy ..."

The telephone rang. Celeste pulled away from the window and went to the other side of her apartment and picked up the phone. It was Mrs. Forster who was calling to say that she was wondering if she could come by tomorrow morning for a fitting. She knew, she said, that she had an appointment for Friday; but so many things had come up—she was going to be so busy this week—that the only time she really had was tomorrow morning. Was it possible, at all possible, for her to come by then for the final fitting?

Celeste had wanted to take her time with the sleeves, but she reckoned that if she put in a few more hours tonight she could probably finish them. She told Mrs. Forster that it would fine if she came by in the morning, at, say, ten o'clock.

"I'll be there!" Mrs. Forster said. "Thanks *so* much!"

Celeste was disappointed at the thought of having to get back to the dress; she had looked forward to having dinner and lounging away the evening. But her work ethic reasserted itself. She reminded herself that she was engaged in the most profitable deal she had ever made, and that it behooved her to put aside all thought of rest or comfort till the project was done. Besides, hadn't she had enough leisure over the last six months while growing increasingly nervous because clients hadn't been forthcoming and she had been drawing on her dwindling bank account? What was that expression? "Get it while the gettin's good"? Absolutely right. Work now; play later—there would be plenty of time for play. And so after she had eaten her dinner she resumed her seat at the long, plain table, carefully laying out the dress before her and starting to work on the sleeves. She didn't get to sleep till two in the morning, but the sleeves got done. She set her alarm clock to go off an hour before Mrs. Forster's appointment. When it woke her she was still tired but dragged herself out of bed, made a cup of coffee, and prepared herself for her client's last visit. She turned on the air conditioner so that the apartment would be cool when Mrs. Forster arrived.

But she did not arrive at her appointed time of ten o'clock. Nor did she arrive at ten thirty. Nor at eleven. Celeste called her phone number but an answering machine picked up. It wasn't till a quarter to twelve that Mrs. Forster arrived. She huffed and puffed her way up the four stairwells, and as usual made a remark about the difficulty of getting to Celeste's apartment, saying, this time, just as she reached the fourth floor landing and putting a hand to her chest as she saw Celeste standing at her open door:

"Oh, Celeste, really! I don't know how many more times I can do this!"

She offered no apology or reason for her lateness. She acted as though she were right on time.

Celeste couldn't contain herself. As she showed her client into her apartment and shut the door, she overcame every polite restraint to say (though even then with a forced smile):

"I thought you said you would be coming by at ten?"

"Yes, yes, I know," Mrs. Forster said, breezily, offhandedly, "but things came up—I couldn't get out of them. I was *so* busy this morning you have no idea! I would have called you but I didn't even have a chance to *breathe* let alone make a phone call. But anyway—I'm here now! It's *so* good to see you!"

Mrs. Forster at once saw her dress on the dummy. "Ah, the sleeves look so nice!" she said. She went over to the dress and took the sleeves in hand, running her fingers along them gently, then more closely examining the stitching at the shoulders and the cuffs. She was smiling, shaking her head, evidently impressed. "You do great work, my dear," she said.

"Thanks."

"By the way, I bought a pair of new shoes to go with this. They're a dark gray suede. That should work—right?"

"I'm sure it will," Celeste said.

Mrs. Forster tried on the dress. She exclaimed her pleasure at the totality with which Celeste had realized her "vision," as she called it, of the sleeves. She kept raising her arms as she looked at herself in the mirror. Yes, the sleeves looked very nice! She turned slowly this way and that, all the while nodding with satisfaction. Celeste stood just behind her and looked over the garment for any, even the smallest thing, that might have to be adjusted, but not seeing anything, and wanting to reassure Mrs. Forster that the dress was finished, she said, "Looks great!"

"Yes, I really do like it." Mrs. Forster turned around a few more times, then stopped with her back toward the mirror and regarded herself over her shoulder. "Mmmm ... " she said.

"What?"

" ... the length."

"What about it?"

"Well ... it still seems just a tad too long."

"We measured the length the last time you were here," Celeste said, smiling tightly. "That's the length you wanted. You said it was fine."

"Did I? Did I really say that?"

"Well maybe you didn't actually say those words, but you said the dress looked good in the new length."

Mrs. Forster acted as though she didn't remember having any such reaction. "Well ... I don't know, maybe I did ... but now it does seem to be still a little too long. Just a tiny, tiny bit." She tittered out an artificial laugh, adding, "I mean really, Celeste, I don't want to look like a nun!"

With compressed lips and slightly flared nostrils, but in silence, Celeste continued standing behind Mrs. Forster, tugging a little here and there at the sleeves and acting as though she hadn't heard what her client had said. Didn't this woman understand that it wasn't magic? That the fabric was such that it would take time to unstitch everything properly and then raise the hemline again? And after she had already spent so much time on it! Within her the desire to excoriate Mrs. Forster for her stupid fickleness threatened to get the better of a politic and business-savvy willingness to put on a show of affable understanding and docility. But she could not bring herself to be, as she had been during every other fitting, spinelessly complaisant. Every time she looked at the dress now she didn't like it, and she despised Mrs. Forster for having made her dislike something she once had loved.

"Celeste?"

"Yes?"

"What do you think?"

"I think the length is fine," Celeste said in an even voice. "Actually, if you were to shorten the dress any more it would be too out of proportion. It wasn't designed as a short dress. I'll be honest and tell you that I didn't think you should have shortened it the first time."

"Oh?"

Celeste nodded, affirmatively, not without the feeling that she had ventured into dangerous waters by outrightly questioning her client's taste.

"Well, I thought it was a little too long, and I still think it is, unfortunately. I'm sure it could be shortened just a *tad* more. Look—look!" She lifted the skirt less than an inch. "Now, that looks *much* better! And there's one more thing," she said, moving her hands to her hips, setting them there. "The waist."

"What do you mean?"

"I'm thinking that if it had some kind of belt or band or something ..."—and she raised both hands to her waist, extending her hands around them so that, in the front, the forefingers of her hands met and gave the idea of a belt. "I think it would look very nice Could we do anything about that?"

"You want to wear a belt with it?"

"No, no, not *wear* a belt with it. I mean, have something sewn in—something added. I don't know, just something that would highlight the waist more. I was thinking ... maybe ... a satin sash or something."

"That would interrupt the line made by the band of sequins running down the front. That's what makes the dress."

"Oh, it wouldn't interrupt it at all!" Mrs. Forster objected, shaking her head. "In fact, I think it would *highlight* it. Yes, shorter, and with something to emphasize the waist—in satin, and dark gray. That would be absolutely perfect—very chic! And if there's anyone who can do it, it's you—those magic fingers of yours, Celeste! You sew like an angel. If only I had your talent!"

In a perfectly just world, Celeste would have responded by telling her client that she was a moron and that her condescension was obvious and disgusting; but of course the world is not perfect and among its many imperfections is the necessity of making a living, which in the upshot is a matter of those who don't have money deferring to, kowtowing to, and in short selling their dignity and souls to those who do, no matter how stupid they happen to be. In her mind's eye she saw the little envelope containing her rent bill which had been slid under the door that morning; and its image, a warning to pride, made her hold her peace. She forced herself to keep in mind that the fee for the dress would easily cover five times that amount, or four, if one included the cost of utilities and miscellaneous living expenses; and it would be the stupidest, most short-sighted thing in the world to lose at least four months of financial freedom because one gave way to a pet of irritation, however justified. And so, as always in the past, she maintained her easy demeanor, and she said, "Alright. I'll do what I can."

"Ah, you're such a doll!" Mrs. Forster said. For a moment it looked as though she would reach out and caress Celeste's face the way she might a charming little girl.

"Of course it's going to take more time," Celeste said, 'and I'm afraid I'll have to add that to the cost, since more work will be involved."

As usual, Mrs. Forster breezily accepted the warning, saying:

"Oh, I understand that."

"I should be able to finish in a few days."

"Oh, don't rush, Celeste, there's no reason to rush. In fact I won't even be in town next week." Mrs. Forster turned her back to Celeste so that she might unzip the dress. "I don't know about you," she continued, "but I just *cannot* stand this heat for another day! Usually my husband and I leave for the whole month of August, but wouldn't you know it, he's got to stay in town for business and we couldn't take off this year. It's just ridiculous."

"I can understand that," Celeste said. She had taken the dress and folded it over her arms. She brought it back to the sewing table on which she laid it down gently. She listened to the rustling sounds of Mrs. Forster getting back into her regular clothes.

"I would just die if I had to stay in New York all summer," Mrs. Forster said.

"Yes, it can be uncomfortable."

"It's horrible—just horrible! Makes you feel dirty; and I hate to feel dirty—don't you? I don't know how people do it."

She had slipped on her pants and was buttoning her blouse. She cleared her throat gently. "Do *you* stay in the city all summer?" she asked.

"Usually, yes," Celeste responded, but she couldn't have said why she used the word "usually," as though there were ever any exception to the rule.

Mrs. Forster shook her head in what seemed to be disapproving amazement.

"I don't know how you do it. You are something, Celeste!"

—It was so insincere, so condescending, that Celeste pursed her lips and looked away. "I'll go for the fabric tomorrow," she said.

"Good. I just know it's going to be a big improvement. When you finish that, just leave a message on my machine, and as soon I get back we can get this over with."

"That would be good," Celeste said. She saw Mrs. Forster out and had no sooner shut the door than she flicked off the lights in the tiny foyer, then walked to the opposite side of the apartment and shut off the air conditioner. She opened the windows, and in came the muggy August air. Her apartment quickly grew warm.

"What a pain in the ass she is," Celeste muttered.

That evening as Celeste tore into the dress for the third time, she shook her head with a frustrated sense of wasted effort. Already she had spent a third more time on the dress than was necessary. Granted, she was adding to her fee, she would be getting paid more, but her character was such that she disliked going over things that should have been—and in this instance had been—good to begin with. As she worked, undoing the stitching of the hem so that it might be cut and then restitching, she shook her head to think that in addition she would be adding a "sash" around the waist. "Ridiculous!" she murmured. "First shorter, then sleeves, and now a sash? God!" In pulling out a drawer for some pins the designer saw a box of her labels, which had her name in block letters and a "New York, New York" directly beneath it. She always sewed these labels into her finished garments in the same way that any other designer would as a mark of pride in her creation; but this time she would not be using one of them. This dress and her experience with Mrs. Forster had brought her neither pleasure nor pride; it had become just a tedious, irritating job, and the sooner she was done with it the better.

After several hours of work under the bright light of her table, with her eyes tired, she had a small meal and turned in for the night. Once again she took up the travel magazine Anne had given her and flipped through its pages. How she longed to visit those wonderful places! How open, spacious, free from care they all seemed! She came again to the ad for the Freepointe Inn, and in the four small pictures that were a part of it she could see how wonderfully rustic and isolated the place was. No poisoned air there. No desperately hot days. No millions of people scrambling over one another to make a living—in the process, turning into beasts of prey, truculent, nervous, ready to pounce and rip one another apart. No Mrs. Forster and complaints about the stairs; no idiotic criticisms and absurd suggestions. Only a crisp northern sky and the smell of the cool salt air coming off the Atlantic. Only open space for miles and miles around, and freedom ... freedom ...

She shifted her eyes away from the photographs and back to her apartment. To think that she had spent so many hours, so many years, here in this small place, sewing at that table! Suddenly it all struck her as paltry and hateful; indeed, she saw herself as some pitiful little drone of a creature who had stupidly labored long to little effect. It occurred to her with a suddenly strange forcefulness that she had done a disservice to herself by not more consciously chasing after pleasure, by not including pleasure as an aim of her existence.

She returned her eyes to advertisement for the Freepointe Inn and vowed that she *would* go there: she *would* leave her little apartment, her little laboring existence and the city with its hundred inconveniences and daily instances of petty meanness. Yes, she *would* do it even if she had to spend every dollar of what she was going to make on Mrs. Forster's dress! She felt that she had reached some kind of intolerable limit and that things had to change for her, that she had to be able to feel and breathe freely, if only for a single week. It was no longer a matter of self-indulgence: it was a matter of survival, of recruiting her soul so that she might continue on.

The strength and genuineness of her resolve was attested to by the fact that even the next morning she felt the same way. She even felt it more than she had the night before. After having her coffee, she took up the travel magazine and went to her telephone by the bed, where she sat and dialed the long distance number to the Freepointe Inn. After a few rings, someone answered: an older woman, and her voice was slow and comfortable and gentle.

Celeste inquired about booking a room for the last week of August, saying that she would like to stay for seven days. The woman on the other end asked her, first, if she had ever stayed at the inn, and when Celeste said that she hadn't—that she had only seen the advertisement in a travel magazine—the woman seemed even the more pleased to have gotten the call: it confirmed that advertising money hadn't been spent in vain. "Let me see what I have for you," she told Celeste, and came back on a moment later saying that, yes, she did have a room, in fact two, both of them equally good. One had a full size bed and one had a queen-sized. The former was only slightly smaller a room than the latter, and was a little less expensive. With a little thrill of doing something naughty, Celeste said she would take the larger room. The woman on the other end of the line said that a small deposit would be necessary, and Celeste hunted out her rarely-used credit card and finalized the reservation. She spent the next hour on the telephone arranging the details of her trip: calling airlines and getting the least expensive flight, then calling car rental agencies and reserving a car. (She hadn't been behind the wheel of a car for a couple of years, but she knew that after ten minutes of driving she'd be as comfort-

able as ever.) In the space of an hour—all the time it had taken
to make these arrangements— she felt a renewed energy and a
budding of joy within her, a fresh, exciting impatience of the
sort she used to feel when she was little and her birthday or
Christmas was only a few days or weeks away.

That afternoon she extracted from a closet a rarely-used
suitcase, laid it down at the foot of her bed, and flipped it open,
intending to start packing. She knew it was foolish to be packing so far in advance of the trip, but she didn't care—the very
act of doing so had something cathartic about it, as though with
each article she selected and packed some corresponding burden
lifted from her shoulders. The suitcase became half full with
undergarments, blouses, skirts, pants, socks, cosmetics, and
combs and brushes. She counseled herself to be selective about
what she would bring because it would be wise to travel light.
On the succeeding nights, after working on Mrs. Forster's dress
for several hours, she would luxuriate in the consideration of
what else she should bring on her trip. She would put things
into and take them out of her suitcase. Doing so gave her pleasure. She also started a list of things she might want to buy
and bring with her.

During this week whenever she spoke to friends or acquaintances she always mentioned her trip, starting off the revelation
in the same way: "Oh, by the way, I'm getting out of the city for
a bit ..."—and would go into the details about the place where
she would be staying. She gave them the specific dates when
she would be gone so that if she didn't return phone calls people
would know why. She always related this information with the
additional secret pleasure of thinking that now it was *she* who
was telling *them* of an intended vacation, and of hearing *them*
congratulate *her* on it.

The anticipation of her trip lifted and sweetened her spirit.
Not till now had she known how much she had needed a change
in her routine. She was conscious of how strange this was, for
by nature she was a homebody, liking nothing better than a stationary domesticity. But now she could even wonder if, after
she got back from Maine, she might not go somewhere else a
few months later. Who knew but that she would get referrals
from Mrs. Forster's party—get a whole stable of well-heeled
clients? She would be rolling in money, then; she would go on

as many vacations as she liked. The lush warmth and golden sunsets of South Pacific islands, the majestic architecture and museums of Europe, the exotic customs of the Far East—she wanted to see, to know them all. And surely the time to see them was now, when she was young and healthy, and had the strength to work and enjoy. As for one day regretting the cost of such things when, perhaps, bad times came again and she was even poorer than she was today—well, even then she wouldn't regret it. "I'll live on bread and water if I have to," she thought, laughing to herself a little. "And at least I'll have seen the world a little!"

Mrs. Forster called Celeste the day after she had returned to the city. When she showed up for her fitting she looked refreshed, reinvigorated. A healthy flush bloomed on her cheeks and her dark eyes sparkled. She had had her hair cut into a new style, shorter and younger-looking. Her voice was enthusiastic as she mentioned where she had stayed: a small hotel just outside Montreal; a delightful place where her room overlooked a lake on which "tons" of swans glided across the water day and night. And the weather? It had been delicious! During the day, entirely temperate, and at night just crisp enough that one had to wear a "little" sweater or "something"! Oh, how she missed the place already! Indeed, the moment she had landed at LaGuardia Airport and stepped off the plane she "could hardly breathe," the air had been so thick and humid. "If it's like this in September, I'm telling you now I'm going right back there!" she said, her eyes sparkling happily. "And my husband's coming with me even if I have to drag him along! And by the way," she said, "I brought something back for you."

"You did?" Celeste was surprised. She would not have imagined that Mrs. Forster could have been so thoughtful. In that moment she felt the little tinge of guilt we all feel when someone we have disliked is kind to us. It occurred to her that Mrs. Forster must have realized how difficult she had been and wanted to make up for it. Celeste watched her open her handbag, look through it briefly, and pull out something. A watch? A piece of jewelry? No: it was a small, plastic model of the Montreal skyline with the name "MONTREAL" running in large, blue, embossed letters across its ivory-colored base. It was the kind of thing one might pick up at an airport in a novelty shop catering to tourists.   Mrs. Forster handed it to Celeste, saying, "Isn't that cute?"

"That was very nice of you," Celeste said, looking down at it, turning it over and seeing the "Made in China" label glued to the bottom. She hated it—hated it. She wished she were alone so that could throw it to the floor and step on it.

"I just *knew* you would like something like that," Mrs. Forster said.

She had emphasized the word "knew" in a way that rang with scoffing condescension.

"You knew?" Celeste asked, unable, this time, to suppress her irritation. She smiled as she asked this, and acted for all the world as though she were grateful for the gift, but she held Mrs. Forster's eyes in a drilling, dire way. "How would you know that I would like something like this?"

"Well, I just thought you would," Mrs. Forster said easily, immediately, without forethought, without, even, apparently, the recognition that so silly and flimsy a "gift" might be inappropriate. "I just though it was so cute."

And it was precisely because she was so unconscious of the inappropriateness of the gift, and of the things she had said while giving it, that Celeste's sense of insulted pride subsided. The best that could be said about Mrs. Forster was that she had as little tact as she had taste.

She was eager to try on her dress. As Celeste helped her into it, she chattily mentioned all the last-minute arrangements she had made for her party, only three days away. She had had to finalize a few things with the caterer, contact a florist about the floral arrangements, and ensure the pianist she had hired from an entertainment agency was the same one she had hired a couple of years earlier, because he was so good and nonintrusive. Once in her dress she stood a little straighter before the mirror, looking at herself with a head that critically tilted this way and that. "I was definitely right about the sleeves and the waist, don't you think?" she asked, smiling at herself, evidently pleased with the addition.

It was hard for Celeste to bring herself to agree. She merely smiled in a non-committal way, then, feeling that this was not the substantiation Mrs. Forster was looking for, rendered the more definite approbation of a nod and a murmured,

"Yes, I think so."

"I knew it would look better this way." She turned to her side and curiously looked at herself in the mirror. All the while Celeste, behind her, gave a little tug here and there, thinking that she had never seen such a horrid dress and couldn't believe that she had made it.

"Thank God this is finished," Celeste said to herself.

"This trim ..." Mrs. Forster said. Her eyes, which had been going up and down her reflection, focused in on the sequined trim.

Celeste almost held her breath.

"I wonder about that trim, though," Mrs. Forster said.

Celeste said nothing. She was determined not to say anything. As though she might change the conversation, as though anything having to do with the making of this dress were a thing of the past, she said, "So how many people are coming to your party? Did you send out invitations or ... ?"

"Yes, yes, yes," Mrs. Forster said, quickly, dismissively, now looking at herself still more critically. She moved her hands over the sequined trim. She gently tried to move it, though she knew as well as Celeste that it was stitched into the garment. "This trim is a little wide isn't it?" she asked.

"Wide?"

"It looks a little wide."

"Not at all. It's just the right width." There was something dreadfully earnest in Celeste's voice as she said, "We don't want to do anything different with that. That's the best part of the dress."

"You think so?"

"Absolutely. Absolutely." Celeste could not have been more earnest if she were pleading for her innocence in a court of law. Her heart was beating fast and she was sensible of holding her breath again.

"Well, I guess it's alright ..."

Mrs. Forster made a few more turns in the mirror. As she did this, Celeste, again seeking to divert her client's hypercritical mind from finding any faults, reverted to the party. She asked what caterer was being used, what would be served, and so forth. Mrs. Forster answered idly and at one point a little impatiently.

"Well, let me help you out of the dress," Celeste said, and had just put her fingers on the zipper when Mrs. Forster said:

"Celeste?"

The designer looked over her client's shoulder at her in the mirror.

"This trim .. "—she ran her fingers along the sequined trim that ran slantwise along the front of the dress.

"Yes?"

"I agree with you. The width *is* fine. But somehow I don't think the black sequins are going to work here. I don't know ... isn't there something we can do about that?"

"Like what?" Celeste asked, the word "what" coming out with an irrepressible edge of impatience.

Mrs. Forster turned around to her and looked at her with some surprise, as though she couldn't imagine what could have provoked Celeste to speak with so uncharacteristic, so impetuous a tone of voice.

"Well, Celeste, I'm just saying that there's so much black on this dress—it's like I'm in mourning or something. I think we should at least add a little color to it. Do you know what I think? I know exactly what would work: a deep ruby red. Yes, instead of the *black* sequins we should use *red*."

"Red? You must be kidding. Do you know how much they would stand out against the black? It would be ... too much. Too flashy."

"Oh, but I don't think so. Not if it was a *deep* red. Yes, a deep, deep *ruby* red."

"The sequins are stitched in," Celeste said, as though that observation, that insistence, entirely obviated so much as the thought of changing anything about the trim.

"I understand that," Mrs. Forster said. "So they can be unstitched, can't they?"

"That would take a lot—a lot—of time. I don't know if I could do it in time. Your party is in three days."

"Yes, but surely it wouldn't take three whole days to make the change. You're so fast you could probably do it in a few hours. And believe me, I'll be more than happy to pay the additional cost. I don't expect you to do it for nothing. I mean," she said, returning her reflection in the mirror, "everything is just *so* dark on this dress, Celeste, that ... well, really, it looks like I'm going to a funeral or something. But the ruby red would brighten it up just right, and be so striking—it would be *so* elegant, *so* fabulous!"

It required all Celeste's will to restrain herself from angrily castigating Mrs. Forster's for her waffling and stupidity. Shortening the dress, adding the sleeves, then shortening the dress again and adding a waistband—for all the difficulties these alterations had entailed they had been relatively easy compared with changing a trim so meticulously constructed and applied, and which would have to be removed with painstaking care to ensure that the fine material was not damaged and leave telltale signs of tampering. It would also require at least a dozen hours more work on a project that by now had become hateful to the designer.

"I don't know what color you're talking about when you say 'ruby red,' " Celeste said. "That could be anything."

"Oh, but I know *exactly* what I want!" Mrs. Forster said. "I'll show you so there won't be any mistake about it."

She went into her pocketbook and pulled out a small change purse that was precisely the color she was talking about; it was even sequined. She emptied it of the few coins it contained and held it against her dress, looking into the mirror, her face beaming with satisfaction. "Yes, yes, yes, this is really *it!*" she said, enthusiastically. "This would look *fantastic!*" She handed the purse to Celeste. "There! That's *exactly* the color. Let's use that, or even something close to that, and we'll be fine."

Celeste took the purse in hand and looked down on it, trying to think of an excuse about why she wouldn't be able to fulfill this most outrageous of all requests. She was tempted to bluff her way out of it by saying that she was familiar with all the colors sequins came in, and that that particular red—indeed, red generally—was so little used, so much out of fashion, as to be almost impossible to find. But she knew that Mrs. Forster was good enough to find them herself. No, there was no way she could refuse. Again her only consolation was the money—the additional fee she would charge. And this time (she told herself) she was going to tack on a hefty additional fee that would make even Mrs. Forster wince!

"Alright," Celeste said, hating herself for saying so.

"Oh, you're a doll!" Mrs. Forster said breezily, not having for a moment thought that she was asking for something out of line.

"There's a lot of labor involved in that, though. I'm afraid I'd have to charge you again for the labor."

"Oh, I understand that."

"I might have to charge an additional—"—and she almost held her own breath as she uttered the very considerable sum.

It didn't faze Mrs. Forster one bit. She shrugged and dismissed Celeste's concerns with:

"Yes, yes, that's fine. I understand."

"It'll take time, too," Celeste said, as though she were determined to annoy her client. "I wouldn't be able to have it done before ... Thursday morning."

"What? *That* morning? That's the day of my party," Mrs. Forster said.

She clearly hadn't expected it to take that long. More to the point, even she understood that by then it would be impossible for her to suggest any other changes: there simply wouldn't be enough time for Celeste to make them.

"I don't think I could get it done any faster," Celeste said. "I have to be very careful when I undo the stitching. I have to remove the sequins one by one to make sure the material isn't stressed. And then they all have to be reapplied. And that's going to take time—hours and hours."

Mrs. Forster heaved a sigh and seemed to consider something, probably the fact that time had finally run out for her. As though she were resigned to this, she shrugged and looked a little defeated as she said, "Well, if you really can't do it any faster than that ..."

"I'm sorry. But I can't."

Mrs. Forster nodded her acquiescence begrudgingly. She took her leave with her wonted flighty, superficial cheerfulness, though this time it carried an element of strain.

The moment Celeste shut the door, she took up the plastic souvenir from Montreal and threw it in the trash. "I hate her!" she mumbled.

That night she had a strange dream. She dreamt that she was somewhere in Manhattan during a blackout. The city was sunk in a darkness so thick that she could barely see her hand when she put it before her face. Occasionally a car would go by and only in the passing, flashing burst of its headlights would she see her surroundings. She would see that she was far from home: somewhere (it seemed) on the Lower East Side. The streets were eerily deserted. Her spirit quailed at the prospect of having to make her way through a darkness that might hold a hundred dangers, and she considered that it might be better, safer, to remain in one place—to ensconce herself, say, in some nook of a building and wait there till dawn. But of course that would be a horrible ordeal, a torture of hours spent shrinking at every invisible sound around her. No, she had to get back to her apartment, however uncertain or dangerous the journey, and however long it might take. And so she began walking. She kept her eyes and ears peeled for any movements or sounds around her. Sometimes she heard voices. They did not seem threatening and perhaps belonged to people who, like herself, had been out and about when the blackout had occurred. Then again, perhaps they belonged to other, sinister characters—criminals taking advantage of the blackout in order to rob and injure. With a fast-beating heart and her breathing quick with anxiety, she passed one street after another; sometimes stopping and straining to see or hear whatever dangers might be lying ahead; afraid—afraid; but forcing herself to continue onward. She never seemed to make much progress. The blocks seemed terribly long. Even in all this time she had only crossed one. She told herself that they only seemed long on account of her anxiety, yet the better, more analytical part of herself understood that this was not so—that there was something wrong here, that the blocks, somehow, had become longer, impossibly longer. At this rate it would take her hours to reach home; and at the prospect of such a trek, her spirit quailed. She stood still, tired, paralyzed with a hammering sense of the futility of it all. No, she would never get home; not in this darkness; not with so much space to traverse; not with so many threats lying in wait for her.... And yet she could not just stand there. To stand there, to do nothing, was an invitation to be victimized, devoured. She *had* to keep trying; she *had* to keep going. And so she tamped down her doubts and fears and put one foot before the other, and forced herself to walk forward; to continue onward, for good or ill, into that evil ...

The next morning she remembered bits and pieces of her dream—the blind darkness, the anxious sense of being lost, the dread of lurking dangers. She remembered enough of it that she was able to interpret it to herself. "Do I really think things are that bad with me?" she asked herself. "It's so ridiculous! I don't feel lost at all. I feel perfectly fine— everything's just fine. Besides, at the end of the month I'm going on vacation—I'll be at that wonderful inn—and we'll see what kind of dreams I have then!"

As soon as she had breakfasted she went across town to the shop on East 44th Street where she bought accessories and found ruby red sequins matching those on Mrs. Forster's purse. Then remembering that she still needed things for her trip, she took a subway downtown to 14th Street and Union Square Park to visit the shops in that area that carried inexpensive electrical items. She wanted to buy a new hair dryer to take with her on her vacation. She found what she was looking for—a dryer conveniently light and small—as well as a tiny alarm clock (she didn't think she would need an alarm clock, but it was so tiny and inexpensive that she bought it anyway) and plastic containers in which to keep her toiletries. She also stopped into the Strand Bookstore and picked up a few used paperbacks. When she got home, she carefully packed these items in her suitcase, now bulging and heavy but complete with everything she needed. Then she settled down to work on the dress.

She had intended to hurry through with this final alteration, for she was no longer emotionally invested in the dress except to the extent that she was impatient to be done with it. But she found that she could not be less meticulous than she had always been. For it must be said again that she could not bring herself to do shoddy work. She might have despised the dress as a whole—disdained it as an example of Mrs. Forster's untrained foolish taste—yet in any one part of it she might still find something to be proud of, just as a painter may take pride in having achieved some fine blend of color in a painting he's otherwise critical of, or just as a composer may perceive one of his loveliest airs in an otherwise indifferent piece of music. She was enough of an artist to discern the good in the bad, and to value it for its own sake.

Replacing the sequins was the most difficult alteration she

could have been expected to make. Those tiny specks of glitter had to be removed individually, with patient exactitude, and each one would have to be replaced with no less care. Holding the material close to her eyes, and beginning at the left shoulder of the garment, she worked with a tiny scissors having needle-fine points, and one by one she gently lifted up and snipped the thread holding down each sequin. After every half inch or so she would pat down the material as though to soothe away whatever stress she had caused the delicate fabric from these little, repetitive traumas. She heaved long sighs as she went along. It was oppressively boring to her to have to do again what she had done before. She blinked hard and often every fifteen minutes or so, for the work strained her eyes. As she worked she put on music and hummed along to it. She constantly found herself wanting to get up, to do something else, but she recognized in these impulses the desire to flee from work that had to be done, and so forced herself to remain where she was and to continue. Now and then she would glance over to her suitcase. The sight of it would somehow reassure her of the better times to come. How happy she would be to go on her vacation! What a relief it would be from her usual drudging life! But first ... work! Work before pleasure—that was the ethic she had lived by.

And so she worked eight hours a day for two long, tedious, eye-straining days in a row, and the trim was finished, a deep ruby red against black, just as Mrs. Forster had requested; and so painstakingly done that even the closest inspection wouldn't have been able to tell that it was a replacement.

She put the dress on her dressmaker's dummy and stepped back to get a completer look at it. She complimented herself on completing the new trim, but on looking at the dress as a whole she almost wondered at its length, the sleeves, the waistband, the gaudy red sequins (as they looked against the black background). "God, that's awful," she told herself, almost laughing at the absurdity of the thing. Despite her relief at finally having done with the dress, she wished that she had been more insistent on maintaining the original design. Perhaps if she had done so it would still be the lovely original garment. Celeste wondered if she had not "sold herself out" for money, but she quieted her artist's wounded pride by telling herself yet again

that after all one had to make money to live, and that what
mattered was her client's satisfaction—everything else was pie
in the sky speculation.

And what, precisely, was she to charge Mrs. Forster? It
was odd that she had never seriously thought about the additional charges till this moment, but now she realized that she
had better take all her work, all her hours, into account, and
create a new, formal invoice. She sat at her sewing table with
pad and pencil and reckoned up the hours of labor, itemizing the
additional time it had taken to complete each step of each alteration. As it had taken her almost twice as long to make the alterations as to make the original dress itself, she might
reasonably have charged nearly twice the amount she had initially quoted her client. But she did not feel comfortable doing
this. It might have been strictly fair, but Mrs. Forster would
probably find it unacceptable to be charged twice the amount
she had agreed to. And so instead, and with a frustrated sense
of the necessity of the thing, Celeste increased the price by only
some forty percent.

Celeste was in good spirits as she awaited her client on
that Thursday morning. The darkness had lifted. The long
journey had come to an end. The work had been done; the reward was at hand.

As usual she had turned on her air-conditioner and cooled
down the apartment in expectation of Mrs. Forster's arrival. ("It
wouldn't surprise me if I get another thirty dollars added to my
electric bill this month," Celeste told herself when she turned
the unit on.) She also kept the light on in the entrance area as
though intending that her client should, the moment she
stepped into the apartment, see her dress in the best, brightest,
most revealing light possible. Celeste herself had laughed at it a
few times. How ridiculous it was!

Mrs. Forster arrived late as usual. She greeted Celeste in a
voice unusually energetic and cheerful. This time she didn't say
a thing about the four flights of stairs she had climbed; perhaps,
in her own way, she was getting used to them. On stepping
into the apartment she saw the completed dress, and said, "You
did it! You found the right color!"

"Yes," Celeste said. "The exact same color as the purse."

"Well! Amazing! Very *good*, Celeste!"

She laid down her pocketbook on the small table and chattily related how busy she had been over the last two days getting everything ready for her party tonight. Almost everyone she had invited was going to attend—there was going to be a big crowd! Only after she had been talking about herself and the party for five minutes did she ask, "And how have *you* been, dear?"

"Fine, thanks."

"You look good—you look happy. The world must be treating you well!"

They both laughed a little.

Celeste went over to her sewing table as her client tried on the dress for the last time. She picked up the itemized invoice she had created, intending to refer to it, to read off from it, when she mentioned the final price of the dress. She kept it in her hand, folded, as she went back to the foyer in order to assist her client, who, however, didn't need it: she had slipped on the dress quickly enough. As she had always done in the past, Mrs. Forster looked at herself in the mirror, turning this way and that, then turning around and looking over her shoulder. Celeste hurried to bring her a handheld mirror, which she accepted with a "Thanks!"

She held the mirror up and looked first over one shoulder, then over the other, smiling faintly, narrowing her eyes, going over, it seemed, every point of the dress and finding it satisfactory. She handed the mirror back to Celeste and faced herself in the mirror once more, running her hands down her thighs as though to flatten out the material. Her faint smile began to fade away. She pursed her lips. She looked down at herself, then back up at the mirror, murmuring a suspicious, "Mmmm," then held out her arms a little, tilting her head this way and that at her reflection. What had been a smile was now a frown; the eyes once pleased were critical and unimpressed. "Oh ... oh . .." she said, shaking her head, negatively.

Celeste paid her no mind; she shut out these reactions as simply, as automatically, as a child might pull the covers over its head in fear of a monster in its room. She knew as sure as she was standing there that once again Joanna Forster had found something she didn't like about the dress; and the very thought of it made her rigidly, determinedly indifferent. For it

didn't matter now. It didn't matter what Mrs. Forster liked or
didn't like: the dress was done—finished—for once and all.
There was no time to change anything. The party was tonight—
only hours away. With this in mind Celeste knew that she held
the trump card, and almost felt some satisfaction to think that
whatever her client regarded as wrong she would have to endure the discomfort of living with. There was only time for the
ultimate transactions of handing over the dress and being paid
for it. And so to Mrs. Forster's ominous murmur Celeste blurted
out in a bland and almost condescending voice, "It looks just
fine," and then she added, for good measure (she couldn't resist
the temptation), "It's just the way you wanted it."

Mrs. Forster glanced up at Celeste in the mirror and for a
moment she seemed unsure of how she ought to react to that
comment. She looked, and in fact she felt, as though she had
somehow been outwitted or checked. But this lasted only a moment. She stiffened, compressed her lips, and shifted her eyes
back to her own reflection, and once again she shook her head,
negatively, disapprovingly, in a way portending something Celeste had dared not even to imagine. And then she said, in a
quite simple, matter-of-fact voice, "I'm afraid this isn't going to
work, Celeste."

The designer only tilted her head; she wasn't sure what to
make of that remark, given the circumstances.

Mrs. Forster continued:

"There's still something about it that doesn't seem right. I
don't mean about the trim. You did a good job with that—it's
perfect, I couldn't have asked for anything better. I don't know
if it's the waist or the sleeves or what, but ... no, somehow it
looks worse than before. Oh, I know what it is: maybe the
length. Yes, definitely the length. With the new trim it just
looks too short."

"The length can't be made longer," Celeste said. "There's no
material to make it longer with. It was cut to be shorter. You
wanted it shorter."

"Well, yes, I did, but to tell you the truth, I didn't really
want it as short as you made it. I didn't say anything at the
time because I thought it would be alright, but now I can see
that you should have left it longer—much longer. Oh, Celeste,
Celeste," she said, shaking her head and flashing at Celeste a

disapproving, disappointed look, as though she had committed some stupid mistake which anyone with an ounce of sense would have known to avoid, "this isn't going to work out at all. Not at all."

"Well, there's nothing more I can do with this dress," Celeste said. And fearful that, even in that resigned statement, she had said something that her client might regard as impertinent and therefore have a reason to withhold money, she added, "Your party's tonight. There's no time to make any more changes."

"You're right about that—there isn't any time. Well, let me take it off," she said. Without another word, she proceeded to take off the dress. She got quickly back into her own clothes. During this process neither woman said a word, and both felt a tide of hostility flowing back and forth between them. For Celeste it was the first time in the whole of her career that she had ever had a client tell her she was dissatisfied with her work, and she was so conscientious by nature that she felt less insulted than inadequate, however much she told herself that it was Mrs. Forster who had insisted on making the unattractive changes. If only she had let the thing alone!

Celeste took the dress to her closet from which she took out a padded hanger and a long, zippered plastic enclosure in which the garment could be sealed for safe transportation. She came up to Mrs. Forster with the dress thus ready to be taken away. But the older woman only looked at her with an air of wonder. "Celeste, you don't think I'm taking it, do you?" she asked.

Not in a million years would Celeste have imagined this moment, these words. She didn't know what to say. She stood there dumbfounded; she really wasn't quite sure what Mrs. Forster meant. Still holding the dress elevated in her right hand, she could only say, "Excuse me?"

"I can't wear that dress. It's just ... just ... all wrong, you know? Maybe it would look good on someone else, but it's just not going to work out for me. And all the time I've spent here!" she added with an air of especial woe, glancing about herself as though every minute she had spent here had been itself a strain on her patience. "Oh, if I had only known! Well, I guess that's just the way things are. Some things work out and some things don't. Maybe some other time I'll have you make something else for me, something that doesn't have to be so perfect. And maybe," she added, looking at the dress Celeste still held up, "you'll be able to do something with that—sell it to someone else, I mean."

"What are you talking about?" Celeste asked. "I can't sell this to anyone else. It's custom-made for *you*."

"Oh ... well ... maybe you could just alter it for someone else. You're so good at altering things!"

She took up her pocketbook, and Celeste watched her intently, anticipating her taking out cash or a checkbook. Instead Mrs. Forster, with every indication of taking her leave, said in a breezily apologetic manner, "Well, I'm sorry again that it didn't work out. I might give you a call this winter, maybe then we can do something ..."

Celeste told herself, assured herself, that Mrs. Forster was going to pay her; surely she could not intend to leave without paying. It just wasn't possible that someone could think she didn't have to pay for something she had contracted to be made and which someone had spent so much time on. Celeste expected the older woman to catch herself, to say that she had almost forgotten something, and to hand over her payment. But Mrs. Forster did no such thing; instead, she turned to the door, reached out for the knob, and turned it.

Celeste felt a surge of panic as though she were trapped. By nature she was averse to confrontation, especially in the delicate matter of money, but the outraged sense of injustice toward herself forced her into speech and action. "Wait a minute!" she called out, just as Mrs. Forster turned the knob and opened the door.

Mrs. Forster stopped and turned around. "Yes?"

"You haven't paid me for the dress." Celeste's throat tightened with shame as she spoke the words, but they came out clearly, forcefully enough, and the anger in them was also audible.

"*Pay* you?" Mrs. Forster gave a little laugh, as though of incredulity. "But I told you, dear, I'm not going to be able to use it."

"You still have to pay me for it," Celeste said, breathing hard with the horrible embarrassment of forcing herself to be so forthright, but determined to stand up for herself.

"Why would I do that? Why would I pay for something I'm never going to use?"

"I made that dress for you," Celeste said, "just the way you wanted it—just the way you asked me to. Whether or not you use it is your business. But you still have to pay for it. Here— this is the invoice!" she said, raising it up in her hand, giving it a shake as though to prove to Mrs. Forster that her debt was a real, a substantial thing, a statement written down and item- ized in black and white, a thing to be acknowledged, honored, settled. In a hurried voice Celeste read off, or rather exclaimed, everything she had done on the dress, from its initial completion to the first, then second, then third, then fourth and longest al- teration. She quoted the final price, and looked up at Mrs. Forster with severe eyes and a face flushed with anger. "Here!" she said, holding out the invoice. "Look for yourself!"

"But Celeste that's ridiculous—"

"No it's not!"

—The response, the retort, the shout reverberated like a shockwave throughout the small apartment. Celeste herself heard it as though it had come from outside of herself. She could not believe she had been responsible for so loud, so vulgar, so ugly a sound; and when, in another few seconds, she realized she had indeed been responsible for it, she closed her mouth and looked about her, feeling the heat in her flushed face, feel- ing her arms and legs tense, her breathing swift; yet she was more determined than ever to have her way, to get what was hers and let no one—especially *this* woman—get the better of her.

"I put a lot of time into that dress—whole days and weeks," Celeste said, almost having to force the words out between clenched, angry teeth. "It wouldn't have taken me even half so long if you hadn't always been changing your mind, but you al- ways *did* change your mind: every time you came here it was something different. You were never happy, never satisfied. I did what you asked me to do because you were my client and I was working for you. I did everything you wanted. Whether or not you like it now is beside the point: the work is done—it was done for *you*—done the way *you* wanted it—and now you have to pay for it, for all my time and my work!"

Mrs. Forster looked at Celeste the way a schoolmarm

might look at a favorite student whom she had always thought delightfully docile and proper but who has just been caught in some shocking hooliganism: her eyes were wide, her mouth open a little, her air that of disapproving wonder. "Oh, Celeste, you can't be serious," she said.

At this Celeste let out a long silent breath and looked at Mrs. Forster as though she had suddenly come upon some strange new species of animal. All she could say was, "What is *wrong* with you?"

"What's wrong with *me*? There's nothing wrong with *me*," Mrs. Forster said, assuming again her wonted easy, condescending air, "but there's obviously something wrong with *you*. You must be tired or something. You *look* tired. You should rest, Celeste. Maybe you need to spend more time with your boyfriend. If you have one." She turned around, opened the door, and stepped outside.

A large, orange-handled pair of scissors lay on the bottom shelf of the book alcove just beside the full-length mirror. Celeste grabbed them up. "No, wait!" she shouted. She dashed out of the apartment and swiftly, like some elusive animal, leapt out in front of Mrs. Forster, holding the scissors out in front of her. "You stop!"

Mrs. Forster did, with a gasp, first looking down at the scissors held before her, then up at Celeste's flushed face, at her wide eyes, as frightened as they were furious. "Celeste!" she exclaimed. "Are you crazy?"

"You're going to pay me!" Celeste said loudly. "You have to pay me!" Her loud words reverberated throughout the stairwell and filled the halls. Celeste feared that her neighbors would come out and see her like this—she who had always been so retiring, who had always been so chattily friendly, who was the kind of person about whom they had always gossiped to one another, "She's such a nice girl ..."

"You're out of your mind—" Mrs. Forster began.

"You pay me now, or I swear to God—"

"You swear to God what? What are you going to do? Are you going to kill me? Is that what you're going to do?" Mrs. Forster's manner could not have been better calculated to disarm her would-be attacker, for it was both mocking and imperious, carrying the authority of the knowledge of the absurdity of this situation, namely, that no matter how furious Celeste might be, she could never be so mad as to harm someone physically. On the other hand Mrs. Forster was not entirely sure of this. Perhaps she really was dealing with a madwoman; in an instant, in her own mind, it all seemed to fit together, how this young woman, who certainly could have done better for herself even if she had just married a regular working fellow, was living alone here in this little bare-floored apartment at the back of some dreadful little building, spending her days and nights at a sewing machine. What normal person would do such a thing? And if she were mad, she could hardly be expected to act rationally. But Mrs. Forster reckoned—as those who think they are dealing with mad people often do—that she had a better chance of obviating injury to herself if she took control of the situation by appearing to be confident. In a cold, imperious, yet somehow witheringly reasonable tone of voice, she said, "Please get out of my way, Celeste, I don't have time for this. I'm late as it is."

"I'm not playing with you!" Celeste exclaimed, giving a shake to the scissors.

"And I'm not playing with you. Now, get out of my way."

Mrs. Forster stepped decisively forward, but Celeste didn't budge, though she unconsciously pulled back the scissors somewhat. With her free, left hand she shoved Mrs. Forster back with a resounding, "No!" This physical act made the older woman drop her pretensions to calm: suddenly invigorated, she loudly ordered Celeste to move away and raised her pocketbook as though to strike her. That she was still determined to leave without paying, that she could still think she was in the right, aroused in Celeste an uncontrollable fury. Her whole frame shook with nervous rage. The little angers and frustrations of a lifetime, and the still greater ones of the last few weeks, had burst open within her, flaming up irresistibly, consuming in one great heated flash her mind and soul so that she was no longer in control of her actions. The moment Mrs. Forster came near to her she thrust the scissors forward, hard and fast, shouting, "Stop it!" as though it were she who was trying to defend herself against attack. Through the handles of the scissors Celeste felt the blades puncture something soft yet pliable. She didn't know where she had struck; she only knew that she had. The nearness of Mrs. Forster to herself, the sensation of the scissors in her hands and the way they had met with and pierced some-thing gently resistant, as though they had entered into the yielding, spongy cheek of a plump pillow—all these things had an uncertain, a dreamlike quality about them.

With a grotesquely loud "Ugh!" Mrs. Forster jumped away, at the same time dropping her pocketbook. Almost falling, she stumbled back into the wall just beside the open apartment door, and here she stood, her mouth open and looking down at herself, at her blouse, the lower portion of which was already spotting with blood where the scissors had punctured the side of her abdomen. "Oh, no," she said, or rather whimpered, and looked up at Celeste with a piteous, helpless expression. It was the first time she had ever looked—as Celeste would have put it—"real": neither affecting pleasantness, nor curiosity, nor ex-citement, but rather looking and sounding just the way one might be expected to look in that circumstance. She placed her hand to her side, on the wound, from which there poured out so much blood that it made her palm wetly red. A few drops fell from her hand to the tiled floor.

In those first seconds, at the sight of the blood, Celeste was confused. She couldn't imagine what was happening, why Mrs. Forster was bleeding, and bleeding so much. Her heart, already beating hard, pounded with a kind of frenzied confusion to see her adversary's gory hand and the bloom of red on her blouse. In another second she realized that she had stabbed the woman and injured her in her some real, physical way, perhaps even mortally. She told herself that it hadn't been on purpose, that she couldn't be held responsible for it: it had been an accident—an accident! She would never really hurt anyone. She wasn't like that. She didn't have it in her. She approached Mrs. Forster with every intention of helping her; she intended to take her back inside the apartment, have her lie down, try to stop the bleeding, call a doctor, an ambulance, whatever was neces-sary. But Mrs. Forster interpreted Celeste's approach as a mad-woman's intention to deliver a coup de grace, and her panic and will to live cut through the paralyzing wonder at her injury. She glanced frantically about as though in search of an avenue of escape, then bounded off to one side—past Celeste—and ran down the stairwell, emitting breathless yelps of terror as with pattering footfalls and the jangle of her jewelry she flew down one flight after another. She ran out of the building screaming for help. As she fled down the block her screams became fainter and fainter.

Celeste looked about her in a daze. She couldn't believe what had just happened, what she had done. She wasn't a violent person; she hated, feared violence; she would never, never in a million years, attack, much less stab, anyone. Yet the drops of blood on the floor testified that someone had indeed been bleeding, and the scissors in her hand—the tips of the blades smeared with red—damned her as the attacker. She shifted her eyes to Mrs. Forster's pocketbook lying on the floor and bent down and picked it up, then turned around and went back into her apartment. She closed the door behind her and went to her sewing table, putting the scissors on it and falling into the chair there as though she were exhausted. For a full minute she just sat there, looking blankly at the wall in front of her; then, recollecting herself a bit, and noticing that she was holding the pocketbook, she clicked it open and looked inside it. She saw a wallet and lifted it out and opened it. It contained Joanna Forster's driver's license, several credit cards, and cash—ten twenty dollar bills and three fifties. She took the bills out and threw them on the table. "It's my money, after all," she told herself, though it did not amount to a fraction of what she was owed. It occurred to her that there might be something valuable in the pocketbook that she could sell, that would make up the difference, and so she rifled through it, pushing aside containers of makeup, a miniature brush, a small package of tissue paper, keys, a cell phone, a small black address book. She found a small change purse containing perhaps a little over a dollar in nickels, dimes, and pennies. She emptied them onto her sewing table and began counting them out with her fingertips—twenty-five cents, forty cents, sixty-cents— and as she did so she became sensible that something was wrong, that she didn't feel right. She felt hot and sick and her mouth was dry—so dry that it was hard for her to swallow. She had a headache that pounded in her temples. She got up from the chair and felt dizzy and unstable, and then noticed that her knees were shaking. Still holding the pocketbook, she went into the kitchen for a glass of water, but the moment she put it to her lips and took the first sip she felt sick to her stomach, so sick, so nauseated, that she was sure she would vomit. Indeed the astringent taste of stomach acid rose into her throat, into her mouth, and she felt the onset of a gagging reflex. Still holding onto Mrs. Forster's pocketbook, she hurried into the bathroom and fell to the floor and crouched down before the toilet bowl and began to retch into it. Her heaves were violent and loud; her body arched sharply as she placed her face deep into the bowl, the obnoxious receptacle only filling her with disgust and promoting another, yet more violent and painful spasm. This time a thick vile liquid sped up into her throat, reached her mouth, and dribbled past her lips. She heaved several more times, choking and coughing with the effort, then moaned in utter misery. She felt as though she were going to die. She wanted to die—if only so that she would no longer feel so sick and miserable. But her overwrought nerves having expended their tension, her stomach settled, her nausea subsided, and she sat back on her heels, breathing hard and evenly. She finally let go of Mrs. Forster's pocketbook and pushed the stainless steel handle of the toilet, flushing it, then staggered up to her feet. She remembered again that she had stabbed Mrs. Forster—perhaps killed her? No—no. It couldn't be. She had to be imagining it. She would never do anything like that—n-ever, never. Maybe she was dreaming. Wasn't that possible? Dreams were so real, after all. A dream ... yes, yes ... a dream ...

She washed her face with cold water again and again.

A loud rapping came from the front door. Celeste shut off the faucet and bolted upright, standing straight and stiff and looking into the bathroom mirror. Looking back at her was a pale, sick-looking woman with reddened, tragic eyes, an open mouth, and an expression of dreadful anticipation as though she knew that some terrible, inescapable judgment were about to befall her.

There was another, louder, harder rap at the door, and this time she heard a man's brusque voice calling out:

"Open up—Police!"

SOMNAMBULISM

Mrs. Ferguson inserted her diamond earrings—the ones she rarely wore but was happy to wear now—and thus put the final touch to her wardrobe. She sat back a little and looked at herself in the mirror of the dresser, and was content that she looked good. Then her eyes shifted to a long white cardboard box on the floor beside her, and her expression of blithe satisfaction changed to one of slight annoyance. The box contained her new personalized stationery, which, however, she was never going to use unless she could find the font she wanted to use with it. What this font was, she knew; she had seen it in an art and antiques magazine she subscribed to. She had torn out an example of it and given it to her daughter, Brittany, saying, "Honey, do you think you could find this for me?" But two weeks had passed and her daughter still hadn't found it. Really, why was it so difficult to find such a thing! In these days of the Internet, when you could look up anything, even the most obscure things in the world, one would think that finding a font would be easy enough! On the other hand (and as her daughter had told her) it wasn't as though she had the *name* of the font, but only had an example, an image of it: and that made the search considerably harder. If Mrs. Ferguson had lost some sleep over the matter (and she had) it was because she had vowed to herself never to use her new stationery unless she had that particular font— and she very much wanted to use her new stationery, for it was a pretty shade of pale blue, with gilt embossing on the top and elegant feathered edges.

"What's taking so long in there?"

—The voice, that of her husband, reached her in her bedroom. She called out:

"I'm coming now!"

She looked into the mirror a final time, patting into place her pearl necklace and adjusting her diamond earrings, then got up from the dresser. Her purse had been lying on the bed; she grabbed it up and then headed outside, to the living room.

Her husband was there waiting for her, looking impatient; no doubt he had been pacing the living room. At sixty-two years of age, Mr. Ferguson was twelve years older than his wife, two inches shorter than she was, and of a compact, sturdy build. He had a full head of graying hair and a completely gray mustache. There was something determined and energetic about his movements and expressions, and one could detect in him the serious, no-nonsense, brisk energy of the expensive Manhattan executive.

"Oh! Finally!" he said, when his wife came out to him.

—Yet he smiled at her with satisfaction. He appreciated the way she looked tonight, so elegant, so slender, so attractive—still. Six months ago she had turned fifty but she looked much younger. He had always been grateful to his wife for the way she had taken care of herself and for her sense of style; whenever she accompanied him to a social event he had reason to be proud of the way she looked. And so almost despite himself he said, "Very nice!" as he looked at her dress, which was mint green with tiny leaves embroidered in silver thread, low at the back, and clinging to her figure. Only a slender woman like her could have done the thing justice, and at that moment he was grateful for the fact that she was always watching her weight and had never over the last twenty-eight years of their marriage gained or lost more than five pounds.

"You like it?" she asked, looking down at herself.

"It's very nice."

She smiled widely. "Thanks. And you! Look at *you!*" She went up to him, and with an extravagant air of pride she unnecessarily began adjusting his bow tie, giving it little tugs this way and that as she intermittently, smilingly looked into his eyes. "Look how handsome you are!"

Her compliment was genuine but also strategic. She wanted him to feel good about himself, to be happy about accompanying her this evening. For initially he had not wanted to do so. When she had first asked him to go with her to tonight's event at the museum he had frowned and grunted and said, "No thanks—you go." But how would it have looked for her to go alone? And why on earth *should* she—she, a married woman? Other women were sure to have their husbands with them; it would have been humiliating for her not to have had hers. And so she had asked, then pleaded, then demanded that he go with her; saying that it was the only "right" thing to do; that she didn't want to go alone and shouldn't have to; that it was important for her to have him by her side. She asked so few things of him, she had said, that he could surely accommodate her in this one.

"Alright, I'll go," he had said, after a few moments' guilty consideration. "But I do *not* want to stay out late. I can't. I get tired. I want to get home early."

"We'll only stay a few hours," she had promised him. "We'll be back before eleven."

—And so he had agreed.

"Is the car ready?" she asked.

"It's downstairs."

"I wonder if it's still hot outside?" she asked, and glanced out of the window of their 31st floor apartment. From this vantage point during the day half the island of Manhattan could be seen spreading out beyond and a little below. But at night the view was more striking still, for then the towers of the city, with their thousands of lit windows rising tier upon tier, looked like so many stars that had fallen to earth, spangling the near atmosphere magically, serenely.

"Yes, it is, but we're getting right into the car."

It was not their car. In fact the Fergusons did not keep a car in the city, though they could easily enough have kept one in their building's garage. But at sixty-two years of age, Mr. Ferguson didn't have the patience to drive in Manhattan: he despised having to stop for a red light every few blocks and dealing with treacherous drivers who cut in front of you without any warning. Instead he relied on limousine services or, if he were out and about and needed a quick ride, on cabs. As he was wont to tell people who wondered at his indifference to having his own car, it wasn't as though he didn't own one, for he owned several—two luxury cars and a very expensive sports car; but they were all parked at his home in East Hampton. Out there, at least, he would say, driving was a pleasure. In the city it was just easier to pay someone "a few dollars" to take him where he needed to go. The only people who might have raised their eyebrows at the blithe easiness with which he regarded

this expense would have been those who didn't know how much
he was worth. Paying for a limousine service every day of the
week was for him no greater an expense than buying a morning
cup of coffee was for most people.

Though it was eight o'clock in the evening, it was still quite
hot and humid outside, for it was late August in New York, and
it had been another breathless day during which the city of steel
and concrete bakes under a merciless sun and soak in the heat
which is retained clear through till the next day, when the merciless baking begins all over again, even more intensely. Aside
from having gone to Bloomingdale's twice for about two hours at
a time, Mrs. Ferguson had stayed inside for three days in a row.
She had spent the time watching television, sipping cool drinks,
talking to friends on the telephone, and ordering in dinner for
herself or her husband. In fact it was unusual for her to be in
the city this time of year. She preferred to stay in their Hampton's home, where, as she would say, "one could breathe." That
she and her husband would be separated for almost two months
was never an issue for either of them. On the contrary they
rather looked forward to this private time, both secretly regarding it as good for their marriage; and they were right. But she
had missed him more than usual and had come into the city to
spend a week with him. There was also a particular reason
why she had to be in the city on this night: she and her husband had been invited to a special event at the Centre for Contemporary American Art, of which they had been benefactors for
some years. On this evening there was to be a preview of the
new Van Burgh Room, which was to feature works from newly-
discovered painters and sculptors. The room had been named
after the late Thomas Van Burgh, who had not only been the
CEO of Industry Credit Corporation but had also, after retiring
from that prestigious position, been one of the most assiduous
members on the Centre's Board of Trustees. In accordance with
his will, his widow, Cleo Van Burgh, had made a bequest to the
Centre of millions of dollars—precisely how many million, no
one was quite sure except those who had dealt directly with the
bequest. At any rate, a new space had been renovated in his
honor and tonight there would be a private showing of new
works of art to be exhibited there.

"Oouf!" Mrs. Ferguson said in disgust as soon as she

stepped out onto the sidewalk and into the city's hot, heavy August air.

It was not just the heat and humidity that she exclaimed against but also a rank odor—a stench of rottenness and decay. It came from halfway down the block where a small mountain of plastic garbage bags awaited carting away the next morning. They had been simmering in the broiling sun for a whole day, the organic substances within them putrefying and exuding a stench so revoltingly concentrated that even what little of it penetrated the plastic was sufficient to suffuse the air with its stink. She and her husband hurried to the limousine waiting for them only a few feet away. The driver was standing just beside the back door, and he opened it at the sight of his approaching passengers, greeting them with a smile, a nod, and a polite, "Good evening." Mrs. Ferguson got in and sat down, then moved over so that her husband could sit beside her. In another moment they were off.

"I'm still surprised that we weren't asked to make any recommendations this year," she said, after they had been riding a few minutes in silence.

She was referring to a conversation she had had with her husband only an hour earlier regarding their involvement with the Centre. They had been among the "Premiere Patrons" for five years, a position they shared with some thirty other influential New Yorkers who made large annual contributions to that institution. As such they had been invited to be part of the process of choosing works of art for exhibition. Mrs. Ferguson had enjoyed that responsibility; it had always been pleasant, even a little exciting to be conducted before a long row of canvases or sculptures by "up-and-coming artists" so that one might be struck by the work of some immensely talented but hitherto unrecognized person. The problem was that she had neither the interest nor the patience in assisting the Centre in other, more mundane matters such as voting on seasonal themes, assisting with advertising campaigns, or interacting with the Mayor's office. On receiving such requests in the mail she would simply and blithely disregard them—give them a toss into the wastepaper basket. In time they had no longer come, but neither had the invitations to review new artwork. That she and her husband nevertheless remained Premiere Patrons was obvi-

ous when, twice a year, they received, on beautiful stationery
and couched in the most deferential language, a request for a
donation. They unfailingly wrote out a check for a generous
amount. Mrs. Ferguson especially regarded it as a kind of sacrifice that had to be made in order to keep her and her husband
in good standing with the Centre, for as she often said to him—
and truly believed—an active participation in the arts *was* important, not only because art enriched your life but also because
it enabled you to move in the right circles, to meet and know
the "right" people. Tonight, for instance, she and her husband
were sure to be rubbing shoulders with prominent business leaders, television and radio personalities, and high-ranking members of city government; probably too with famous or soon-to-be
famous artists. Where else were you going to meet such people
if not at events given by an institution like the Centre? The answer was, you weren't. Instead you'd have to listen to *other* people—people to whom you were every bit as good, if not better—
crow about how *they* had been at this or that opening, and met
so-and-so, and been invited to this or that; and that would have
been intolerable.

"It would have been nice to have some say in what's going
to be displayed this fall," Mrs. Ferguson added, again referring
to the way she had been left out of the process.

"Well, it's no big deal," her husband said, easily. "Changes
every year anyway, doesn't it—what they show, I mean?"

"Not always. They have permanent displays."

"Oh. Well." He shrugged. The fact of the matter was that
he had never been half so interested in the Centre as his wife
had been.

"I'm sure Michelle Simpson wasn't left out of anything,"
Mrs. Ferguson continued, less to her husband than to herself.
She spoke with her eyes turned out the window, watching the
people on the streets as they drove down Lexington Avenue.
"And she has no taste whatsoever. She thinks she does, but she
doesn't. Those sculptures she wanted the Centre to exhibit last
year were awful—just awful."

Mr. Ferguson laughed lightly.

"Well, they were!" his wife said, herself smiling. "They
were the *worst*. People were laughing at them. They didn't
make sense."

"Doesn't have to make sense, does it?"

"Doesn't it?" she returned, with a challenging rise in her voice, turning to her husband and looking at him with an expression both severe and amused as though he had said something too absurd not to smile at it.

"Well, I don't know. Does it?"

"I would hope so! If we're just going to put anything in there, then why not just let *me* make something, and we'll put *that* there!"

Mr. Ferguson laughed lightly. "Maybe you should!" he said. But he didn't pursue the matter. The last thing he wanted to do was to get into any kind of animated conversation with his wife about art. The fact was that he didn't have any opinion about art. He didn't know enough about it and frankly didn't care about it. To him the paintings and sculptures he had seen over the last few years had all merged together into a fuzzy succession of colorful blotches and nondescript shapes. At this moment he tried to remember, to picture vividly in his mind, even one of the many things he had seen over the years either in the Centre or in any other museum, and for the life of him he couldn't do it. When he was standing right in front of something it might or might not make an impression on him; otherwise, it was as though it had never existed. He didn't understand people who, like his wife, took such things seriously, and he suspected that on a deeper level she herself really didn't. No one knew better than he did how practical she was. Her interest in museums, concerts, or the Centre was owing more to the influence of friends and acquaintances than to any native predilection. Nevertheless he looked forward to accompanying her to tonight's event. They hadn't "gone out" in a long time—months, in fact—and he felt it would do him some good to socialize, even if he had to be distracted now and then by paintings.

They had no sooner stopped at a traffic light on 31st Street than they heard loud voices coming from somewhere outside. They both turned their heads to the right and looked through the limousine's tinted windows in the direction of the disturbance. They saw a group of five young people, three men and two women, erratically walking and jumping and engaging in loud horseplay as they moved along the sidewalk. The men were

gangly, wore baggy clothes and caps, and one of them was holding something in a paper bag, evidently a bottle of liquor or perhaps a can of beer. The women were short, overweight, and
wearing skin-tight jeans above the waists of which their belly
fat bulged; they were just as loud and roughhousing as their
male counterparts. Each time they passed a pedestrian this
rowdy group would yell insults and threats at him, and then
laugh among themselves at the worried looks they had aroused.
And now one of the squat repulsive women went right up to a
man walking in the opposite direction, stopped right before him
so that he had no choice but to stop also, and pushed out her
hands and shoved him in the chest, shouting, "Hey, man, get
outa my way!" The man staggered back a few steps and then
looked at his attacker in astonishment. He seemed to realize he
had been assaulted, but he wasn't sure what he ought to do, and
in the next split-second his New York instincts kicked in and,
like a seasoned soldier on a battlefield who sums up his chances
of survival in the blink of an eye, he realized that there was no
way he could defend himself against a woman backed up by four
thuggish cohorts; and so he swerved aside—with a hop and a
skip moved out of her reach—and continued on his way at an
alarmed, fleeing clip. The thugs laughingly called out a few obscenities after him. Other pedestrians in the near distance, who
had seen this confrontation and the approach of this little mob,
discreetly and hurriedly crossed the street so as to avoid a similar encounter.

"What's going on out there?" Mr. Ferguson asked.

His wife didn't answer directly. She had been disgusted by
what she had seen. "Where are the police?" she asked aloud, and
wondered whether or not she should call them, for certainly
there was a crime in the making here. But at that moment the
light changed from red to green and the limousine drove off,
leaving the upsetting scene behind. She settled back into her
seat, shaking her head, both confounded and disturbed by the
little dose of reality she had just witnessed. Above all she was
grateful that she and her husband hadn't been out on the
streets but were in a car behind locked doors.

The Centre for Contemporary American Art was located in
the fashionable Soho area of Manhattan, right off Houston
Street. Like so many buildings in the city, the one in which it

was located had gone through many incarnations since its construction in 1900. Originally it had been a bank, then a bookstore of what then had been a major chain, then the offices of a food manufacturer, then a general office building, then it had been abandoned for several years on account of safety violations till it was rescued—at an attractively affordable price—by people in the community who foresaw in it a cultural establishment that would serve local artists. To this end contributions had been solicited from local businesses and wealthy artists or patrons of the arts. After ten years of existence it no longer required such patronage to maintain itself; it was now a well-established museum and it could have edged by as a business by what it collected in entrance fees by visitors, of which it had a usually steady stream during its weekday hours. But its charter had changed. The anonymous local artists whose work it had once eagerly promoted could now no more have had their paintings or sculptures shown there than they might have jumped to the moon. It wasn't that the Centre had a policy of only showing the works of the famous so much as that it had gradually come under the direction of the established, credentialed artistic world, which ever champions the already-recognized and suspects the anonymous and obscure, or whose favors are too often influenced by an agenda having nothing to do with art for its own sake. Its Managing Director, Mr. Roger L. Hodge, for instance, had been recruited from the Metropolitan Museum of Art, and several other senior officers had held similar positions with long-established museums and galleries in New York, Philadelphia, or Boston. It was still possible for a "new" artist to get his work shown here, but in this case the possible meant nothing more than the very rare exception.

A red carpet had been extended from the front door of the Centre across the sidewalk, and nearer the door itself hung red velvet ropes upheld by shiny brass posts. Two formally-dressed doormen stood there. To the pedestrians who passed by (always looking down uncertainly when they walked over the carpet), it was obvious that some sort of event was in progress here. Half of them didn't care what it was and hurried along with their lives, while the other half were curious enough to stop, look about, and crane their necks as they attempted to look inside the doorway

When the limousine stopped before the Centre, Mr. Ferguson said to his wife, "Stay here," and got out of the car, walked around it, and opened the door her. He even took her hand as though to help her out. Ordinarily he would never have been so gallant; he would have thought it was affected. But this was a special occasion and when his wife stepped out of the car with a smiling "Thank you" he even gave her his arm, saying, "Be careful, dear." He escorted her to the door where they were asked for their invitation. Mrs. Ferguson got it out of her pocketbook. As she did so, she saw, then felt something at her feet, or rather something that had stopped against her ankle. It was the wrapper of a hamburger from the fast-food restaurant on the next block. A light breeze had blown it against her. She gave her foot a little shake to dislodge the wrapper, but it wouldn't come off, and when she bent down to pull it away she saw that it left behind a little blotch of red—of ketchup—on her white shoe. She heaved a quick breath of irritation. "Imbecile!" she thought against whoever had thrown the wrapper in the street. Fortunately she carried a few tissues in her purse and wiped her shoe, but a trace of red remained. As she walked ahead of her husband and entered the lobby with him, she whispered angrily, "If people would only pick up their own trash!"

"It's nothing," he assured her.

Already some hundred guests, all in formal attire, had arrived and were gathered on the mezzanine, led up to from the entrance by a wide staircase. They held drinks and hors d'oeuvres offered them by young men and women—employees of a catering company—dressed in black and white. The atmosphere was that of a dinner party. The hum of conversation and the occasional tittering laughter reverberated in the marble-walled, high-ceilinged space. Many of the guests were already acquainted with one another, either in their personal or professional lives, or through previous art events. They belonged to the movers and shakers of the city: prominent business people, members of city government, the heads of major educational institutions or news media outlets. Most of them were Premiere Patrons, a category which the Centre reserved for those who donated generously to its operation. The Fergusons saw at once several familiar faces. Some of these people they liked and some of them they didn't, but of course they were too polite to be other than smiling and chatty to them all. The new Van Burgh Room was located down a corridor off to one side and which had a red velvet rope stretched across it.

A half hour later, an announcement was made by the Centre's Managing Director, Mr. Roger L. Hodge. He was a short, bald man with a bushy mustache and round eyeglasses. If one had gotten him out of his suit and dressed him in casual clothes he would have been the stereotypical image of an unattractive, stodgy college professor. Beside him stood his wife; or rather, she towered over him, for she was almost a foot taller than he was, and younger by fifteen years, and blonde and beautiful. On the other side of him stood a dour-looking old woman in a blue dress garnished with a corsage.

"Ladies and gentlemen, can I have your attention!" he called out.

The mezzanine became quiet as all of those gathered there turned in his direction.

"I want to welcome and thank you all for attending this evening's event. As most of you know, I'm the Director for the Centre, which I've been associated with—happily associated with!—for five years now. We are here this evening to commemorate the opening of the Thomas Van Burgh Room, which is to be dedicated to new American art. As most of you know, Thomas Van Burgh was a great and generous patron of the Centre. He was also one of the most important members of the Board of Trustees. We and the people of this city owe a great deal to him for his expert knowledge and leadership, which helped guide the Centre to what it is today. We're also very happy to have with us tonight his wife, Cleo," he said, turning to the old woman.

Those among the guests who weren't holding drinks applauded lightly; those who were, raised them slightly as a gesture of respect and appreciation.

For the first time the old widow's thin, tensed lips widened into a smile—somewhat.

"So please make yourselves at home," the Director summed up by saying, "and enjoy the new room. Inside you'll find brochures containing information about the items displayed. And by the way, after you've enjoyed yourself in the Van Burgh Room I hope to see you all on the rooftop garden for more cocktails and a little something to eat."

Light applause was offered up to the Director as he led the way, taking on one arm the hand of his wife, on the other that of the widow of Thomas Van Burgh, who, poor thing, walked so slowly that as the three of them made their way down the hall the crowd behind them swelled like the waters of a rushing stream building up behind a dam. Many were secretly annoyed that a stroll that should have taken twenty seconds was taking five minutes.

It was a large room, with maze-like partitions covered in a light beige cloth. Soft, indirect lighting provided the general illumination, but over the paintings themselves, which were hung some five to six feet off the floor on the partitions, tiny bright halogen lights shone. Soon little groups began gathering before the paintings, admiring them, commenting on them. Here and there were low wire stands containing narrow, glossy brochures of eighteen pages full of information about the works and their creators. Some of the guests, with these open brochures in hand, went from painting to painting; standing before one for several minutes, tilting their heads, sharing comments in subdued voices, nodding in appreciation before moving on to the next one.

If the works of Vittorio "Victor" Tocolini drew especial attention that evening it was because he himself was there. The Director, Mr. Roger L. Hodge, had not mentioned his presence and the Fergusons only found out about it while speaking to Mr. and Mrs. Dorman, who pointed him out as he had momentarily appeared in the near distance: a tall thin man of about thirty years old with black hair, dark eyes, and delicate features. To see him walk across one's ken had something eerie about it, for most of the men (and in one case, woman) whose works were being shown here tonight had not attended the event for the very good reason that they were dead. Those who were still alive were either very old or lived elsewhere—out of state, or in Europe, or heaven only knew where. Nevertheless the Fergusons didn't give Tocolini another thought until, accompanied by Mr. and Ms. Bender, they strolled around a particular partition and came face-to-face with his paintings. There were four of them, and they were largest in the room. One of them was seven feet wide by four feet high. They were remarkable for their vibrant colors and ability to convey a sense of dizzying motion. Bright reds and yellows, indigo blues, globes of orange, bars or triangles of purple;—all of them bouncing off or merging into one another, and every shape and color enhanced by glossy black lines, of varying widths and sharpness, stabbing through or among them;—they possessed an energy, one might almost have said a kind of *will*, that, if it did not raise them above the level of other paintings here tonight, unquestionably made them stand apart. Exclamations of "Oh, my!" or "Wow" or "Well, well!" erupted from the wide-eyed people who stood before these paintings as they sometimes leaned back a little as though beholding something exerting an actual force against their persons.

The Fergusons too were awed by them. Mrs. Ferguson commented that she had never heard of Tocolini before but that it was clear he was a talented man—he knew (she said) how to grab your attention! Mr. Bender had been carrying one of the brochures provided as a guide for this evening's exhibition and now flipped through its pages to find more information about the hitherto unheard of artist. "Minimalist-abstractionist school," he quoted, reading phrases here and there. "Influences are Picasso ... Lewis .... Cubism ... a key theme is man's spiritual quest in a highly technological age"—a phrase at which he stopped reading, puckered his lips, and looked back up to the paintings whose wild colors and motion had at first pleased him so much, though now he wasn't sure that they should.

Mrs. Ferguson leaned in to her husband and said a low, confidential, but hardly secretive voice, "You know, something like that might be interesting for our living room! Imagine it, right over the couch!"

"Kinda big and crazy, isn't it?"

"It's very modern," she responded. "I mean, you're right: those colors are a bit much—wouldn't go with the furniture. But maybe he's done other stuff ..."

"You ought to commission him to do something for you," Mr. Bender, interjected. "You know, let him know what you want, work it out with him."

"Do you think he would?" Mr. Ferguson asked.

"I don't see why not. You can always ask. You know, these people have to make a living too. I'm sure if you're willing to pay for it he'll do what you want. Besides, better to ask now when not too many people know about him than later when he becomes a big shot and charges you an arm and a leg."

—Advice Mrs. Ferguson considered very sensible.   She looked away from the painting and surveyed the area in search of Tocolini, intending to introduce herself to him and, discreetly and diplomatically of course, broach the prospect of commissioning him for a painting that would be suitable for her living room.   But at the moment he was nowhere to be found.

The works of some twenty-two other artists were to be seen, and the Fergusons and the other guests, drinks in hand, pleasantly strolled among them, invariably getting into conversations about whichever ones they might be standing in front of.   These conversations were characterized by humor, taste, and occasionally informed criticism or comment, for some of the guests were art lovers who had haunted galleries for a lifetime and knew what they were talking about.   It could not be said however that Mrs. Ferguson was one of these.   Thus while standing before the paintings of Eli Krauz she exclaimed to Mr. and Mrs. Torwalds, to whom she had very sociably introduced herself and her husband, "Well, that *is* lovely, isn't it?   There are so many beautiful paintings here tonight, but this one I really do like!   I wonder if the artist is here tonight?"—and she turned her eyes into the crowds as though she would recognize the artist at once if she saw him.

"I doubt it," Mr. Torwalds said, chuckling.

"He didn't come?" she asked.

"Don't think he can," Mr. Torwalds said.   "He's been dead for ten years."   And he chuckled again.

"Really?"

He nodded, lifting up the brochure in which he had read it (at the sight of it Mrs. Ferguson told herself she was going to pick one up the next chance she got), and said, "Suicide.   Shot himself in the head."

"Oh dear!"   She shook her head in disbelief and turned a pair of astonished eyes to her husband.

"Yep, it's all in here," Mr. Torwalds said, giving the brochure a little shake.   "He was despondent over something—it doesn't say what—and he just shot himself.   Says here he left behind over a hundred paintings."

Mrs. Ferguson, and in fact Mrs. Torwalds also, were both

shaking their heads, and the former could only say:

"You'd think that someone who could do *that* would think twice about killing himself ! Such a stupid thing to do! Such a waste!"

"Well, no one ever said artists were smart," Mr. Torwalds said. By the way, he was one of the aforementioned aficionados of the arts. In his younger days he had even dabbled in them— first as an actor, then as a writer. He had never succeeded in those pursuits and by the time he was thirty years old he had intelligently and logically concluded that while he still had his youth it behooved him to devote himself to something at which he might at least make a good living. He entered the financial world and by the time he was forty-three he had become one of the managing partners of a small but well-established and highly respected financial management firm. Whenever he looked back on his past he was always struck by the naiveté of his youthful ambition and the foolishness of the people he had associated with. In the honest light of mature retrospect he saw that nearly all of them had been big dopes, and he suspected that most of them hadn't come to a good end.

"He was probably sick," Mrs. Ferguson opined, and she turned to her husband, as though to ask, or at least see, what his sense of the matter might be. He only said:

"Ahhh, these guys ... !" —an expression of stern contempt toward those lacking the courage to face the difficulties of life.

They moved on with the Torwalds to the next few paintings, which belonged to an artist who was not nearly so unknown as the others; on the contrary, his star had been rising for the last several years and Mrs. Ferguson recognized his name, for she was an avid reader of the "Arts" section of the New York *Times* in which he and his work had several times been highlighted in full-page articles. Even before he had become known as a painter, Chad Andersen was acknowledged as the grandson of Theodore Samson Anderson, founder of the Andersen Tire Company, one of the world's largest producers of tires and rubber-based products for automobiles. At twenty-five years of age the "brilliant young man"—to quote a *Times* article—had graduated with an MBA and seemed on track to assume his birthright as a Captain of Industry; only to have an epiphany about himself and his place in the world, and to real-

ize (with what artist's heart-wrenching the abovementioned article had dramatically expatiated on) that tires, head gaskets, and
all things automobile were below his loftily creative nature; and
so had defected to Bohemia. No less remarkable than his provenance was the fact that in a world in which painters of genius
fall by the starving wayside every month or year, Chad Andersen had, after only two years of leaving Yale, exhibited his
paintings in some of the most prestigious art galleries in New
York City. Critics in the *Times* and other papers hailed his
work. "Deceptively simple," "fascinating studies in psychological
reduction," "an astonishing capacity to produce the macrocosm
in microcosm," were just a few of the phrases that interpreting
critics had used in describing his work. For Andersen was a
minimalist who had taken the notion that less is more to the ultimate logical conclusion that almost nothing must be nearly everything. From afar his paintings looked like merely stretched,
untouched, raw canvas, but on closer inspection one saw that
the "canvas" had been painted on, its austere desolation being
the artist's painstaking rendering of cloth that served as the
ground on which some black, purple, blue, or other-colored shape
had been minutely painted—so minutely that one was not likely
to see it from more than six inches away. Of several of his
paintings here tonight the largest and, evidently, most highly
acclaimed was called *Sunrise on a New World*. It had a dot, of
variegated orange, of about a quarter of an inch in diameter, set
smack in the middle of a plane of pure white.

"Fascinating!" Mrs. Ferguson said.

"It's very interesting how the dot just sits there," Mr. Torwalds said, tilting his head a little to the side with a jutting un-
derlip.

"Actually, it looks like something *on* the painting, not *in* it,"
Mrs. Torwalds said, momentarily looking away from the dot to
the rest of the large canvas—to the left, the right, up and down;
she breathed deeply, impressed with its size. "*Sunrise On a
New World,*" she said, repeating the name thoughtfully; and
shook her head, positively, before flashing a smile to the Fergusons and quipping, "Good name for it!" And she looked at it for
another moment before adding, "It does have a way of *hypnotiz-
ing* you."

"What do you think of it?" Mr. Torwalds asked Mr. Ferguson.

Mr. Ferguson shook his head. Before the admiration and approbation expressed all around him, he was beginning to doubt his gut reaction. To him it was just a dot.

"My husband is never sure if he likes paintings when he first sees them!" Mrs. Ferguson said, laughing, quick to divert attention away from him, to relieve him from the necessity of answering the question, which he might have done in an uncouth, embarrassing way.

"See anything you particularly liked tonight?" Mr. Torwalds asked. He had directed the question to Mr. Ferguson.

"We *loved* the Tocolini stuff," Mrs. Ferguson answered for him.

"Oh, we liked that too!" Mrs. Torwalds said, bending her thin, wrinkled neck forward as she nodded with what could only be called an intensity of agreement.

"Actually, my husband and I liked his work so much that we were thinking of commissioning him to do some work for us. If we could only find him!" she added, looking about as though to search him out again.

After the Fergusons had parted ways with the Torwalds they spotted Mr. and Mrs. Rohayne, with whom they were acquainted, and strolled over to say hello. A flurry of "How have you been?"s and "Good to see you again!"s marked their meeting.

"What on earth!" Mrs. Ferguson said, expressing wonderful uncertainty over the painting before which they all happened to find themselves.

"We were just trying to figure it out too!" Mr. Rohayne laughed.

Strange it certainly was: it had the look, or rather the feel, of something familiar, something alive, something sleekly fluid with the animus of writhing, biological life; circular it was also, and its patchwork of earth-toned coloration in places blended, in places stood out, from a background of mostly green. One might have mistaken it for some large, strange, essentially meaningless ring unless one had instantaneously and serendipitously seen what it was, or had the creative intelligence to cobble together from apparently disparate parts a meaningful whole. The title of the work, *Devoured*, was also a clue. Oddly enough

it was Mr. Ferguson who hit on the correct interpretation, announcing with a smile of triumph, "It's a snake!" The others narrowed their eyes on the painting, trying in those first few
seconds mostly in vain to see what he had seen, and only saw it
when he further explained, "It's a snake swallowing its tail—
see?" And one by one those around him did see, nodding, uttering little, "Oh, yes!"s and turning pairs of pleased, congratula-
tory eyes on him.

"By the way," Mr. Rohayne said to Mr. Ferguson, turning
away from the paradoxical symbol of self-consumption, "did you
hear what happened to Ian Hutton? You know him, don't you?"

"I've met him a few times, yes. What happened?"

"He was mugged."

"No!" Mr. Ferguson said.

Mrs. Ferguson's mouth opened a little.

"Just the other day," Mrs. Rohayne added. "Poor man!
They held him up at gunpoint and took everything from him,
and even after he gave it to them they beat him up. It's a wonder they didn't kill him!"

"Who told you this?" Mrs. Ferguson asked.

"He told us," Mr. Rohayne said. "We were just talking to
him."

"You mean he's *here?*" the Fergusons almost asked at once.

Mr. Rohayne nodded. "He and his wife, yes," he said. "We
were just talking to them."

"Didn't he go to the police?"

"He did, he did," Mr. Rohayne said, "he went all through
that."

"Where did this happen?" Mr. Ferguson asked, ready to
hear that Hutton had been somewhere where he shouldn't have
been: in the subway, say, after eight o'clock in the evening, or
perhaps somewhere in Brooklyn or the Bronx.

"I believe it was Central Park West, just a few blocks away
from his building on 71st Street."

Two Fergusonian jaws dropped.

"He's still got a black eye," Mr. Rohayne added. "Wait till
you see him!"

Mrs. Ferguson and her husband did see him, along with his
wife, not too many minutes after this conversation. Ian Hutton
was a naturalized American citizen originally from England.

Tall, handsome, still slender despite his fifty years, he had come to the United States at the age of thirty after having been for most of his youth infatuated with all things American. Back in those days, in England, the Americans, from what he had seen of them in movies and on television, had struck him as so much more vital and straightforward than his countrymen, and especially so much more interesting than his staid, landed, and aristocratic family. He had idealized Americans as honest cowboys, as mischievous but big-hearted gangsters, as romantic idealists fighting in a good cause against overwhelming odds. In growing up he had often expressed to his parents that he hoped one day to live in America, to which they had always responded in the same way: "For goodness' sake, why don't you just associate with the fourth class people here?" That was a snide answer, of course; meant to be humorous; meant much more to be serious and dissuasive. But twenty years ago he had made the move. Since then his life among Americans had chafed away his illusions about them, but had done nothing to undermine his idealism, which had, if anything, become more pronounced with age, as though he were determined to maintain it as a point of honor. To this end too he was involved in any number of causes meant to assist the downtrodden or underprivileged. One of these was "Hope House"—a halfway house on West 97th Street specializing in assisting felons who had recently been released from prison. It operated on the principle that if given the opportunity in the way of education and financial assistance even supposedly "hardened" criminals would gratefully take their place in society as productive, law-abiding citizens. He had been on his way there when he had been robbed and beaten up. The irony of that fact was not lost on him, and it was one of the details of the incident he always left out when relating what had happened to him.

So far this evening everyone had asked him about his eye, as well as the small bandage above his brow, and he had grown irritated at having to explain them over and over again and be the object of pity. Fortunately for him he did not have to explain it to the Fergusons, though he did have to bear their pity too, for they no sooner walked up to him and shook his hand than they said how sorry they were to have heard what had happened to him and that they hoped he was going to be alright.

"Oh, I'm going to be fine, fine!" he said, in the affable, off-hand manner which he had discovered was the best method of deflecting attention from himself. "It was just a little scuffle, that's all."

"*A little scuffle!*" exclaimed his wife who stood at his side. She was an American and he had been married to her for eighteen years. Her husband had irritated her several times this evening by having made light of his injuries. As she knew very well, the attack on him had been far worse than he was letting on. When she had seen him in the hospital—he had called her from there and she had rushed to his side—she found him sitting on the edge of an examination table, pressing an ice-pack against his eye, his hair tousled, his usually impeccably clean clothes streaked with the dirt of the gutter into which he had been pounded, his pink complexion white as a ghost, and his air and demeanor that of someone who wasn't even sure where he was or how he had gotten there. "They almost killed you, Ian!" she said.

"They did not almost 'kill' me," he said, discounting his wife's dramatic assessment. "It was just some stupid kids." He turned to the Fergusons, saying, "The problem with young people these days is that they don't have any guidance in their lives. That's the problem! The school system has let them down. There isn't enough money to teach them properly. If the city would only fund the schools properly ..."—and he left off, shaking his head negatively, as though he couldn't say enough about how lack of funds for public education had ultimately been responsible for his attack.

His black and blue eye still teared a lot and he continually applied one of his initialed handkerchiefs to it as he mentioned that he preferred not to talk about "it" anymore—it was in the past, it was over and done with, and he was here to enjoy the evening and take his mind off anything unpleasant. To that end he asked the Fergusons if they had been there long and which paintings had they seen. Were there any they had been especially taken with that he ought to take a look at? They mentioned a few. Mrs. Ferguson said he must, really must, see the paintings of Victor Tocolini, which were on the other side of the room and which would bowl him over with their size and colors and "energy." Mr. Hutton said that he would keep that in mind—would search them out—but that in the meantime he was quite taken with *these* paintings, the ones he had been examining for the last five minutes. They were the works of J.J. Sweete, a name which he mentioned with a laugh, saying, "What kind of name is that, anyway? That can't possibly be a real name!" His skepticism about the reality of that name arose in part from the fact that it belonged to an artist whose works were anything but bright and cheerful. He—or she—relied on a palette of mostly somber hues: dark grays, browns, dusky oranges, tenebrous purples, the deepest cinnabar reds. Moreover the subjects were ominous. In one of the paintings, *Undercurrent*, an impulsive, urgent stream of reddish-gray and deep orange swept across the canvas beneath bands of lighter colors into which they seemed to be eating and tearing away. In another one, entitled *Wave*, a threatening mountain of water rose up behind what appeared to be an island village—tiny edifices clustered along the edge of a bay, whose inhabitants (no more than stick figures) went about their business unaware of the imminent catastrophe about to overtake them. Perhaps the most disturbing of J.J. Sweete's works was *Sick*, which presented an abstract face corrugated and seamed with some kind of a consuming disease. Barnacle-like growths encrusted the eyes; a putrid rot had eaten away at the ears, now no more than cartilaginous stubs; the nose drooped as though made of wax and melting away, its ability to sniff out anything destroyed. The mouth too was afflicted with crevices and cracks, yet the lips were turned up at the edges into—a smile! That strange, grotesquely incongruent effect made one shudder. The head was tilted a little to the right in a posture of innocent, piteous wonder.

"I certainly wouldn't want anything like *that* hanging in my living room!" Mrs. Ferguson said.

"Horrible!" Mrs. Hutton added.

"But there is something interesting about it," Mr. Hutton offered. He had been as repulsed by the image as those around him, but he was sure that when it came to art—and to so many other things in life—his initial instincts were always wrong, the result of saturation in a circumscribed, narrow, somehow miscreated or illegitimate culture; and thus he was always determined to find the good in what had struck him at first as bad, the benign or even beneficial in what had seemed purely malign and malicious. And so now he leaned back in a manner bespeaking a conscious effort to get past his first impression and allowed his eyes to roam over the painting, examining its details in themselves and apart from the whole. After several seconds he announced that the "composition" was "masterly." Didn't everyone realize that those carbuncles around the eyes and the crevices of the forehead were composed of tiny distinct shapes? And the color! From any distance it *seemed* gloomy: but if you would only look into the thing more minutely, if you would only just step right up to it, a few inches away, so as to lose sight of the whole, you would see that within all that gray and dusky purple there were flecks of happy blue and cheerful yellow! In fact, the painting wasn't "sick" at all, but rather, in its essence, entirely healthy, hopeful, and uplifting! "You have to admit that the artist did a great job of blending those colors there, along the nose," he said, pointing to one of the more revolting instances of the portrayed suppurating putrescence.

"Well, I still wouldn't want anything like that in my home," Mrs. Ferguson insisted with a laugh.

The little group strolled along to the works of other artists. Their conversation deviated for a few minutes at a time to common acquaintances and general events, but on the whole they applied their attention to whatever painting they happened to stand before. Mr. Hutton always had an opinion to offer, and it usually differed from that of his companions. He never found anything to criticize negatively, and whenever anyone mentioned something he didn't like about a painting, he, Ian Hutton, would, not without some condescension, point out why the objection was mistaken or uninformed. As he spoke he repeatedly touched his tearing eye with his handkerchief. It seemed to be bothering him more by the minute. It was hard for the Fergusons not too look at it, at him, with concern, but each time they did so he followed the line of their line of vision to those particular few inches of his face. This made both him and them uncomfortably self-conscious. The Fergusons yearned for a tactful opportunity to excuse themselves and they found it in the person of someone who had just walked around one of the partitions and come into their ken.

"I think I see Beth Crawford over there," Mr. Ferguson said to his wife. "Yes, there she is. We should go over and say hello. Well, Ian, Betty, it was nice seeing you again. We'll talk later, okay? See you later, everyone!"—and off the Fergusons sailed, maintaining smiles that faded the moment they had turned around and taken a few steps.

Under his breath Mr. Ferguson murmured, "I don't know ... I don't know ..."

His wife didn't have to ask him what he didn't know: she understood it was an expression of his pity and wonder over what had befallen Ian Hutton. Even more than this was the dismaying sense that if something like that had happened to him, it could happen to anyone, even to them. Ah, life was so uncertain!

Beth Crawford was about fifty years old and had been a widow for seven years. Her husband had died in the crash of a private chartered jet, and from the lawsuit she had filed against the aircraft operator, which happened to be one of the largest in the country, she had added fifteen million dollars to her estate. Considering what that estate was worth—her husband had been the founder of Aspira Communications—the judgment had not substantially added to her wealth, and it had done nothing to assuage her grief. She had sued out of principle, and in this instance the principle had been upheld. She and her husband had been Premiere Patrons of the Centre. Undoubtedly if her husband had still been alive he would have been with her now, at her side. Instead, Courtney, the older of her two daughters, accompanied her.

It is often said, and truly, that if you want to know what a young woman will look like in twenty or thirty years, just take a look at her mother; the inference being that genes are a ruthlessly accurate predictor of one's future physicality. But in this case that formula would not have been pertinent, at least not insofar as it related to the influence of the maternal side. For the greater part of the Crawford girls' genetic makeup came from their father—which was unfortunate for them. Mr Crawford had been a charming, jovial, and intelligent man, but even his warmest admirers would have had to admit that he was plain-looking at best; and unfortunately for his daughters, they had inherited not only his name and money but also his looks.

They did not have their mother's pretty, wide-set eyes but rather their father's close-set, bulging ones. In them the maternal high cheekbones and graceful jaw line had been trumped by the heavy paternal jowls, so like those of a bulldog. Their mother had come from people who were tall, slender, and graceful; even now, in her middle age, she wore the same size clothes as she had done in her youth; but her husband had been chunky and thick-legged, his body square-shaped; and their offspring, in taking after him, had always been rather chubby as children, and now, as adults, were hopelessly bottom-heavy—that is to say (and to be colloquially frank) they had their father's huge ass.

Their plain looks and thick, wide-hipped skeletons had caused the Crawford girls no end of despair. As teenagers they had pored over New York magazines highlighting beautiful society debutantes whose features were pretty, whose hair was silky, whose legs were long, whose hips were slender as a boy's so that they could wear the slinkiest designer outfits and look like the semi-celebrities they were as they flitted from one trendy restaurant or nightclub to another on the arm of a handsome young man who was merely the latest in a long line of suitors. They knew that they would never look like that. Worst of all, they knew that they would never be the objects of intense attraction to the opposite sex; at least, not for their own sakes. Sometimes when walking down the street Courtney tried to catch the eyes of handsome young men: and while they might flash her a smile, or give a nod of recognition, they quickly looked away with the heartless honesty of mankind, who are always brutally swift in assessing the attractiveness of women. As for the men who did look at her, they were the gorillas of their sex, the dull-eyed, ignorant, hulking creatures, the very thought of intimacy with whom made her shudder. She might have been plain of face and inelegant of body, but she knew who she was and what she wanted; knew what would make her happy and what would not; and above all she was too proud of her qualities ever to dive into the muck of the bottom of the mating barrel for the sake of relieving her lonesomeness. If nothing else, she would always have the comfort of knowing that she hadn't lowered her standards, hadn't given in, hadn't been weak, hadn't defiled herself.

Fate having denied young Courtney Crawford the possibility of a dazzling social life and love, she had sought to distinguish herself in (as she would have put it) "more substantial" ways. She had excelled in school. She had applied to, and been accepted at, Harvard University, where she had majored in economics. She had already earned an M.B.A. and was now studying for her Ph.D., which she hoped to have by the end of next year. It was not she who disclosed this information—she was too modest to speak of these accomplishments—but rather her mother. For as soon as she had introduced her daughter to the Fergusons, and they had inquired into what she was studying in school, Mrs. Crawford blurted out enthusiastically:

"She's going to be a doctor!"

"Really?" Mrs. Ferguson asked, turning her surprised eyes to the daughter.

Courtney smiled modestly, cast a somewhat embarrassed but loving glance at her mother, and explained:

"Not a medical doctor. I'm going for my Ph.D. in Quantitative Analysis and Theory in economics."

"Well!" Mrs. Ferguson said, nevertheless impressed—mostly because she hadn't a clue what Quantitative Analysis might be and suspected it was complicated;—and *Harvard*, after all! Her husband, who had some dim inkling of the matter, was also impressed. He compressed his lips, opened his eyes wide with pleasure, as though it were refreshing for him to come upon a young lady engaged in such high-minded pursuits, and said:

"*Very* impressive!"

"My daughters are geniuses!" Mrs. Crawford said, laughing a little because she knew she was giving in to her pride. "My youngest daughter Vanessa made it into Yale this year," she added.

"Congratulations!" Mr. Ferguson said; and he repeated, "Very impressive! It must be very hard," he said, directing the comment to Courtney, who smiled and answered that yes, in some ways it was.

"You should see the things she's reading," Mrs. Crawford said. "I opened one of her books the other day just to see what it was about, and I was totally lost—totally! It was all figures and equations. Did you ever see those equations of Einstein? Well, that's what they looked like!"

"Ohhh, Maaa," Courtney cooed, blushing a little and shaking her head. "It's not quite the same thing."

"Oh, yes it is! Don't be so modest! It's easy for you because you're such a genius. But you'd be surprised: most people can't make heads or tails of that stuff."

"Your mother's right," Mr. Ferguson said. "It must take years of study to understand that sort of thing. When you get your Ph.D. do you have any special plans, or ...?"—and he left off with a shake of his head that invited a response. Yet he knew that neither Courtney nor her sister would ever have to worry about having a career if they didn't want one. Perhaps they were merely furthering their education for the sake of improving themselves; and of course that was the more admirable.

The young woman responded that she hoped to secure a position with an investment bank in the city. What she didn't mention was that her mother had already done half the work for her, having approached several friends in that industry. They had assured her that they would be happy to give her daughter an "opportunity" somewhere in their firms, starting her off in a position and at a salary that would befit her social and educational credentials. She would be plopped into a position toward which others had labored for a decade in the hope of being promoted to.

The introductory chat turned to the work of art before which they happened to be standing. The brochure described it as a "sculpture," but it certainly wasn't that in the conventional sense of the word. Resting on a pedestal, it looked, from a few feet away, like a window frame with dark glass. Getting closer, one saw that it consisted of two panes of glass several inches apart, the one at the back somewhat reflective, the one in the front darkly translucent, while between them hundreds of tiny, nondescript golden and silver things floated in a viscous suspension. Appropriately enough the work was called *Smoke and Glitter*. Courtney loved it. She exclaimed her delight as she held her face close to the glass and peered through it, tilting her head this way and that, the ever-moving objects within sparkling with new intensity each time she shifted her line of vision. Mrs. Crawford also stepped up to the artwork and squinted as she peered into that obscure interior and tried to unravel its glistening mysteries. "Just what *are* those things?"

she asked. But neither she nor her daughter nor the Fergusons could answer that question. They only knew that they emerged from out of the darkness, twirled or floated before one's fascinated eyes for a few sparkling seconds at a time, then fell back into the impenetrable gloom from which they had emerged—as though they had never existed.

"Must run by electricity somehow," Mrs. Crawford speculated.

"A battery, probably," analytical Courtney said. "There are no cords around."

"I wonder what *that* is?" Mrs. Ferguson said.

She was not referring to *Smoke and Glitter* but rather to something she had espied from the moment she had walked into the room, though now she was seeing it more closely. Evidently it was something very large, or at least very tall, for it rose up over the partitions on which the paintings were hung. The people standing around her followed her eyes to it, and Mrs. Crawford, who had already seen that object up close, said that it was a sculpture, "the most extraordinary thing," and that Mrs. Ferguson and her husband would do well to take a look at it. They agreed that they should do so and they took their leave, saying that they hoped to see the Crawfords later. As they walked off, and then rounded one of the partitions, Mr. Ferguson, without turning to his wife, said:

"Nice girl, that Courtney. Smart."

"Very smart," Mrs. Ferguson said. But she was thinking that her own daughter was smarter, though Brittany had never gone to Yale or Harvard, and indeed had only graduated with an Associates Degree in ... in ... well, at the moment she couldn't remember what it had been in, but she was sure it was something important.

That which had risen so high above all the partitions was a totem pole. When the Fergusons stepped up to it they added themselves to a small group of five persons who had already been standing before it. Among them was George W. Claire. He was a retired general who had served in Vietnam, and his friends and acquaintances referred to him as "the General." He hailed from an aristocratic military family in the south. Through one of those circuitous but by no means uncommon routes in life, by which people who seem destined to follow one path wind up taking another, he had met and married a woman from a wealthy New York family in the newspaper business, and on her insistence they had made their home and raised their children in the city. Especially in the early years of their marriage he had longed to return to his country roots, but even after his wife had died he remained in the city, partly because memories of his early family life here rooted him to it, and partly because his children still lived here.

The General himself had only come up to this exhibit, this sculpture, a few seconds before the Fergusons, whom he introduced himself to and then, with them, examined the object more closely.

It was a totem-like sculpture seven feet tall and carved by what must have been a blunt, imprecise instrument, perhaps a small hatchet or heavy knife, for it in no way nor in any part had a finished surface. It had the general outlines and appendages of a human being, but its features and limbs were either repugnantly coarse or hideously distorted. The top of the head was flat, and thick, bony, Neanderthalic brows beetled over huge, round, goggling eyeballs. The grotesquely wide nose spread halfway across the face and had fiendishly upraised and flaring nostrils. A mouth with fish-like lips gaped to show crowded, fang-like teeth. Down either cheek ran deep, zigzagging gashes (colored a dull red as though to mimic scarred flesh), and the ears had enormous lobes bored with huge holes. This grotesque head rested upon a disproportionately slender, corded neck which grew out of a chest bulging with asymmetrical, sagging breasts. On a protruding stomach rested two hands, their fingers intertwined and terminating in claw-like nails. Beneath the carved loincloth the thighs were thick, the musculature roughly chopped out, and the legs ended in taloned feet. The title of the piece was *Mumbo Jumbo*. One of the guests who was carrying the glossy guide to the exhibits read aloud to those around him that the artist of this piece hailed from a South Pacific island and his work "reflected the wisdom and rich heritage of his age-old island culture still untouched by the corrupting influences of modern man."

"Wisdom?" the General blurted out, his brows suddenly and almost angrily knit together as he turned to the man who had read from the guide. "Wisdom my foot!" There was a sudden stiffening of his body as though all the discipline of his glory days had come rushing back into his old frame, steeling it as though he were preparing to meet a threat. He looked back up to the sculpture and pronounced authoritatively: "It's horrible!"

"You don't like it?" Mrs. Abbot, one of the guests in the group, asked him.

"No I do not," he said. "In fact, I think it's degrading."

"Degrading?" Mr. Abbot asked, with a short laugh. "How so?"

"Because," the General answered, looking at the faces around him, "this is supposed to be a museum of art, and I think we would all agree that that word connotes something extraordinary—in a good way. But everything about this—this—*whatever* it is—is coarse, brutal, and backward. I would just like to ask you all, if the mind that hacked out this atrocity represents the kind of mind you would want for yourselves or—let's put it even more poignantly—hope for your children or grandchildren? Would you really be proud of it? Or wouldn't you rather cringe and want to sink into the ground and die? Of course the answer is the latter. And why? Because in your heart of hearts you all know that it represents a step *backward*, not forward, and the genius of species is to go forward—to evolve into something better and higher, not to revert into something more primitive. You know, really," he said, returning his gaze to the totem and shaking his head a little sadly at its horrid face, its bloodthirsty intensity, "when you consider how many artists there are creating beautiful things, elevating and inspiring things, you can't help but wonder who the numskull was who couldn't find anything other than this primitive piece of garbage to shove in our faces."

"I couldn't disagree more!"

—The voice, the protest, had erupted from none other than the still-bruised and near-cyclopean Ian Hutton, who, with demure American wife at his side, had come up behind the retired general just as he had pronounced the last few words of his opinion. "Primitive?" he asked, with a friendly, sociable smile which nevertheless carried a trace of a superior sneer. "Is what you just called it?"

"That and a lot of other things!" Mrs. Abbot said, bending back somewhat as she chuckled, then took a sip of her white wine, which he held in a napkin to protect her soft, delicate hands from the chilled glass.

"Well, I totally disagree with that!" Ian Hutton said. He was still carrying a handkerchief with which he dabbed at his tearing eye as, now, he looked up to the totem. "On the contrary, this is an extremely sophisticated expression of a very highly-developed intelligence."

"Oh really!" the General blurted, puffing out his cheeks, then looking at the Englishman more closely as though trying to detect whether he could possibly be serious; and seeing that he was, added sarcastically, "I suppose the man who hacked out this thing designed computer chips in his spare time."

Several of the onlookers, including Mr. Ferguson, chuckled, perhaps nervously because they detected in the General and Ian Hutton not only two opposite and irreconcilable points of view but also what appeared to be an immediate personal dislike.

Ian Hutton himself smiled, albeit with the touch of a sneer, and said:

"Actually, I'm sure he could have done that—if he had had the right training. The fact is that this magnificent sculpture exemplifies an extraordinarily advanced intelligence, which, however, lent itself to philosophical speculation rather than technological discovery and innovation. Take those bulging eyes, for instance," the Englishman said, raising his right hand and pointing with his index finger first to one eye then the other. "You think they're just crude attempts to replicate eyes. But that's not the case. Their size and disproportion are undoubtedly meant to convey man's astonishment at his minuscule proportions in the face of the greater universe; his strenuous attempt to fathom his experience as a conscious being in space and time, which he finds himself to be the center of. The enormousness of the nostrils bespeak a consciousness of the mysterious vastness of the aether, which extends into space, into the unknown universe, of its fundamental necessity not just for human but for all life. The neck, which is clearly intentionally disproportionate to the head, represents the wavering or unsteady foundation on which life depends—hints at fate or chance and the inevitable dissolution of our organic, animal selves. And yet the enormous breasts and protruding abdomen express the hope of creation, of regeneration, of the counterbalancing and appeasing knowledge that future generations will compensate for the mortality of the individual. Those claws on the hands? No doubt humanity's struggling grasp on its animal existence through human procreation."

"What about the scars on the face?" Mrs. Ferguson asked politely, leaning in a little, eager to learn. "And the ears? The big holes in them?"

"Well, apart from their sociological value in the artist's world-view, they both have tremendous aesthetic value. You may think that scarring one's face with thick gashes, or boring huge holes in your ears, is 'barbaric,' but I assure you, the only barbarism is to think so. In fact, it's quite attractive! But of course," he went on, dabbing his leaky, blurred eye again, "one has to have a certain level of sophistication to think outside of one's own culture, which is a very difficult thing to do since that's what one has been brought up with and all one knows. I daresay that even when there's a genuine effort to rise above that arbitrary standard most people fall short of success. But it's really the only way one can accurately judge an important piece of art like this. As for the title of the piece, *Mumbo Jumbo*—apparently you don't see the irony of it. It isn't 'mumbo jumbo' at all! On the contrary, it's a sophisticated statement of mankind's necessarily subjective and therefore restricted capacities to interpret and find meaning in the mysterious forces that shape his destiny and the history of the world. It is," Ian Hutton said, his voice rising somewhat with a more authoritative tone, "a *Critique of Pure Reason* in wood!"

And yet no matter how hard they tried, those who had heard out Ian Hutton still could not find the scars or the mutilated ears "attractive." They were still, in their heart of hearts, repulsed by it all. Why did they say nothing, then?— why were they passive?—why did they act as though they entirely agreed with what he had said? Because they doubted themselves. Ian Hutton had spoken so well, after all. Clearly, he was an educated man. Clearly, he had read a lot. He referred to things, to books, to ideas, none of them had ever considered or heard about. Who were they to contradict or question him? God forbid they should do so, be called out on it, and be mortified to have their ignorance exposed! They only knew what they felt— which of course was not good enough. No, no: better to be thought intelligent; better to seem on the higher, better, more sophisticated level! And so as they had listened to Ian Hutton, they nodded, yes, yes, yes, to everything he said, as though they perfectly understood how and why he had come to his conclusions, and to show that they themselves would—of course—have come to exactly the same ones.

"Yes, I can see what you mean, Ian," Mrs. Ferguson said, aware that her husband was rolling his eyes toward her. "There is a sort of strange energy about it, a kind of innocent wisdom."

"It *is* very striking," Mrs. Abbot said.

"It has enormous power," another said.

"Those eyes seem to look right through you!" said yet another.

At each of these comments Ian Hutton—his injured eye tearing away—smiled with a sense of proud victory and approbation.

As for the old general, he had stood listening to the Englishman with an air of polite but increasingly strained patience. He had hemmed a few times; tapped his left hand against his thigh; puckered, then compressed, his lips. When the *Critique of Pure Reason* had been mentioned (he had never read that difficult book, but he was aware of its major thesis) he had given a little stomp of his foot and his eyes had darted to Messrs. Ferguson, Abbot, and Kaiser as though he expected one or all of them to be as outraged as himself. That they were not only irritated him the more. In the subdued, almost shameful voice that he might have used in Vietnam to inform a superior about a failed combat mission, he took his leave, saying:

"Well, if you'll all excuse me ... "

Everyone bade him good evening, including Ian Hutton, whose manner was no less apparently polite. They all noticed that the old fellow walked off with his head held high, his chest out, his shoulders back; looking very military indeed.

Just then an announcement was made: the rooftop was now open for cocktails and "a little something to eat." Though one might have thought this invitation premature, as the guests had only entered the Van Burgh Room a little over an hour before, it was on the contrary perfectly timed, for the room was not so big, nor the works in it so plentiful, that one couldn't have seen everything there was to see well within that period. More than half of the seventy guests at once heeded the call and began leaving.

"Shall we go?" Mr. Ferguson asked his wife.

"If you'd like."

Mr. Ferguson turned to the others in the group around him, as though welcoming them to accompany him and his wife. The Abbots said they would be up in a minute. Ian Hutton responded that there were a few more things he wanted to see one more time, but that he and his wife would be up presently. The Kaisers agreed to go along. But on her way out Mrs. Ferguson espied in a corner of the room the figure she had been looking out for all evening. She put her hand on her husband's arm and said, "Wait a minute!" He and the Kaisers stopped, turned to her, then followed her line of vision to the figure standing in the corner and whose back was to them. To her husband she said:

"There's that artist we wanted to meet!"

Mr. Ferguson looked over to him, narrowed his eyes and asked, "Who? Oh, you mean that Tortellini guy?"

"Silly!" Mrs. Ferguson said, giving her husband a little slap-pat with her hand. "It's not *Tortellini*, it's *Tocolini*." She glanced at the Kaisers with a quick, somewhat embarrassed frown, as though to say it was just like her husband to get the name wrong and that they shouldn't think any less of him for it.

"Tortellini, Tocolini—whatever!" Mr. Ferguson said, shrugging. He was a little tired, and when he was tired he became more indifferent than usual. He had been on his feet for almost two hours and had had enough of paintings and talk about art for one evening, if not, indeed, for the rest of his life.

"Let's go say hello," Mrs. Ferguson said.

"Dear," he objected mildly, "why don't you go? I'd rather go upstairs and have a drink and relax."

"I'm with you," Mr. Kaiser said to Mr. Ferguson.

"Alright, listen," Mrs. Ferguson said to her husband and the Kaisers, "you all go up. I'll be there in a minute. I really do want to meet him."

Victor Tocolini was standing with his feet somewhat separated and his arms folded before him. As she neared him Mrs. Ferguson slowed her steps, for it occurred to her that she might have been mistaken about the identity of this man. A little cautiously therefore she came up beside him, all the while trying to get a look at his face, and only when she was sure that it was he did she venture to step right up beside him. She glanced at the object of his rapt attention—a small drawing of some kind. In a soft, polite tone of voice, as though she feared she was interrupting his thoughts or concentration, she said, "Mr. Tocolini?"

He turned and looked at her in surprise; apparently he had not seen or sensed anyone sidling up to him. He smiled in an innocent, polite, inviting kind of way, though in the next instant his demeanor stiffened somewhat as though in shyness before a stranger. Mrs. Ferguson introduced herself, saying she had seen his paintings this evening and wanted him to know what a great impression they had made on her. They were wonderful, she said: so colorful, with so much energy and motion and life! "I think they're the most exciting things here," she told him.

He smiled and said quietly, "That's very kind of you."

"Well, it's just true!" she said, somehow feeling that she had to reassure him on that point.

He turned his eyes away—down—and smiled a little tensely in what Mrs. Ferguson regarded as a charming exhibition of embarrassed modesty. She noted that he was an unusual-looking man, and not necessarily in an unpleasant way. He had a long, narrow face with close-set eyes, a very thin nose, and a small mouth. For some reason she could not help thinking that his face had an animal, perhaps a vulpine quality about it. His delicately arched eyebrows were very black, as was his hair, which waved over his forehead in an unruly cowlick and came down before his ears in wispy, tapered, false sideburns. In what was a purely nervous gesture he raised a hand to his suit jacket and felt the cloth along one of the lapels as though to smooth it down. She noticed that his hands, like everything else about him, were narrow, with long, delicate fingers ending in perfectly clean and tapered nails. "Nice-looking hands," she said to herself.

Mrs. Ferguson shifted her gaze to the picture he had been looking at so intently. It was a pencil sketch of a plant. The leaves and stems were no more than suggested by what seemed a few hurried lines. It was set in a flimsy-looking frame of unstained pine. Tocolini's own works were a dozen, a hundred times better—bigger, bolder, more complex and finished: the kinds of things whose worth jumped out at you from across a room and fairly knocked you over the head so that you couldn't ignore them even if you wanted to. To Mrs. Ferguson it was curious that he should be impressed or rather infatuated, as he seemed to be, with this little, half-done drawing, but in a flash the reason for his attitude occurred to her: eccentricity! Yes, of course, he was one of "those"—those eccentric artists. This did not especially surprise her.   In her time she had met and known many kinds of people, including   artists, and among these there were always a few who were ("I wonder why?" she asked herself) a little odd. In Tocolini's case it was obvious that while he had talent in producing original work he was bereft of judgment when it came to the works of others. It was all so obvious in this instance that Mrs. Ferguson couldn't help saying, "I wonder how *that* got in here!"

"What do you mean?" he asked.

She dared not insult the work directly, for to do so would in effect be to insult him, which was the last thing on her mind. She temporized, "It just seems so out of place here, doesn't it? It's so small and ... elementary."

"Elementary," Tocolini repeated, nodding, knitting his brows a bit. And as though she really had presented him with a word he himself had sought for in vain, he said, "Yes, that describes it very well. As to how it got here ... I requested it."

"*You* did?"

He nodded. "In fact, I more than requested it. I made the availability of my own works dependent on its acceptance here."

"Oh." Mrs. Ferguson turned back to the little sketch. She looked at it more critically. "Is it yours?"

Tocolini shook his head, no, and there was something regretful in that gesture. "No, it is not mine," he said. "It was done by someone else—someone I used to know."

"What's his name?" she asked, even as she took a step toward the drawing, in particular toward the little sign beside it that bore the artist's name and the title of the work. She read both these things to herself with indifference. She was about to say that she had never heard of him, but it occurred to her that neither had she heard of Tocolini before this evening, and so instead she asked, "Does he also paint?"

"He's no longer with us. But no, he didn't paint. He just drew—and even then, not very much, and only in pencil."

"That's all?" she asked.

He did not answer her; he returned his gaze to the drawing. Mrs. Ferguson wondered whether or not he had heard her question, but of course he must have heard it—she was standing right beside him and had spoken loudly enough. "Was he a friend of yours?" she ventured, thinking that his interest in the drawing arose from some intensely personal association.

"Unfortunately, no, " Tocolini said. "He was one of those people who are very hard to make friends with. We were just acquaintances."

"Are his works shown anywhere else?" she asked.

"No. There aren't more than thirty of his drawings that I know about, and half of those were merely started or left unfinished. This is one of the best of those he did finish."

Mrs. Ferguson thought: "If that's one of the *best* he did, I'd hate to see one of worst !"—but aloud she said only, "Oh."

She continued looking at the little drawing but in fact she was thinking of what else she might say to Tocolini in the way of light conversation. She wanted to continue chatting with him in a friendly manner the better to ingratiate herself into his favor. She wished that their personalities were such as to feel with each other an instantaneous camaraderie, but she was rather conscious of a slight strain between them, if only that of strangers who have met for the first time and don't quite know what to make of each other. But remembering his paintings, remembering above all the great blank wall in her living room, she began speaking again, this time saying, "Are your works being shown anywhere else? I would enjoy seeing more of them."

"No, they're not," he said, smiling; and he added, "It's nice of you ask, though."

"It's hard to believe, they're so good."

He smiled again, appreciating her compliments.

Now, she felt, was the time to ask. She did so as gently, as diplomatically as she knew how. "You know, I was wondering ... I like your work so much ... would it at all be possible for me to commission you to paint something for me? I mean, you *do* sell your paintings, don't you?"

"Yes, of course I do," he said, quietly; and turned his eyes away as he admitted it.

"Oh, I'm so glad," she said, truly relieved; and in a more comfortable voice, she continued: "I'd like to commission you to do something for me. I'd be honored. I love your work! Would there be any way to contact you? Or would you prefer to call me? We could discuss the details."

Tocolini offered Mrs. Ferguson a business card, which she took with a nonchalance that disguised her enthusiastic sense of victory. She was already planning to invite him into her home so that she could show him where she intended to put the painting and he could see her decor—which would surely help him choose his colors more appropriately.

"I was just on my way upstairs to the rooftop," Mrs. Ferguson said. "Would you like to join me?"

"Thank you, no. As a matter of fact, I'm going to be going soon."

"So early?"

"I have work to do," Tocolini said.

"Oh ... well ... it was a pleasure to meet you. Thank you for the card. I *will* call you!"

He smiled and bowed his head a little. "Thank you for your appreciation. I hope you have a good rest of the evening."

"What a nice man," Mrs. Ferguson thought, as she left him. She discreetly put the card into her purse once she was in the elevator.

She was pleasantly surprised at how pleasant it was up on the rooftop. It really was like a garden. Except for a few stone-bordered walkways, the roof had been covered in sod; the grass was rich, thick, freshly cut; and small trees and shrubs grew in giant wooden containers located throughout. The place had been especially accoutered for tonight's affair. Small electric lights formed charming illuminated festoons reaching from each of the larger potted trees to the other. Dozens of little tables had been set out; they had foldable but padded chairs around them, were covered with white tablecloths, and on each table flickered a candle in a little holder of clear glass. Soft classical music, coming from hidden loudspeakers, suffused the atmosphere otherwise filled with the low hum of conversation and the tinkling of glasses. A bar had been set up, and the catering staff was now standing behind a buffet table on which hot and cold food might be taken at one's pleasure. It was an atmosphere entirely relaxing, entirely pleasant, even a little dreamy.   As in the Van Burgh Room, so here little groups of people were talking or laughing among themselves, though this time most of them were sitting. Mrs. Ferguson found her husband nursing a cocktail as he sat by himself at one end of the roof, just beside the high ledge. She was glad that he was alone because she wanted to tell him the good news. She eased herself into the chair opposite him, smiling at him significantly.

"You talked to him?" Mr. Ferguson asked.

"I did," she said, triumphantly.

"And?"

"He's a very nice man," she said, and didn't mention that there was, however, *something* a little strange about him.

"And?" he asked.

"He said he'd be happy to do something for me."

"Well, well," Mr. Ferguson said, and raised his glass to her as though in congratulations on her enterprise and success; but then added, "Just make sure he doesn't soak you for a picture. Get that all worked out before he does any work."

"I'm sure he'll be reasonable," she said.

"He should be. *Very* reasonable. I never heard of the guy before tonight."

A waiter came by and asked them if they would like something. Mrs. Ferguson asked for a Cosmopolitan; her husband, who had been sipping a good scotch on the rocks, looked at his still half full glass (he had asked for a triple) and shook his head, no.

The waiter had no sooner brought Mrs. Ferguson her drink than the Director of the Centre, Mr. Roger L. Hodge, approached them. He was working on his second glass of wine and was in exceptionally good spirits. With his tall, young, beautiful, blonde wife on his arm, he had been making the rounds on the rooftop, strolling from one group of guests to the other, introducing himself and his wife to those he didn't know, exchanging banter and reaffirming ties with those he did. He always asked his guests what they thought of the Van Burgh Room, and they always complimented him on it, assuring him that it was a great success. He received these compliments with outward modesty but

with some inward gloating, for he had put a lot of time and effort into making it a reality. He had never met the Fergusons
and said he was happy to make their acquaintance. He extolled
their long association with the Centre—he admitted he had often seen their names as Premiere Patrons—and told them, as
he had told nearly everyone else, that tonight's affair couldn't
have been possible without their particular interest and assistance. He mentioned how the Centre had over the last few
years become a "true cultural icon" of the city, and how those
who had supported it "through their generosity" were the real
heroes of its success. But whatever that success had been was
only the beginning! Far bigger things were in the works! With
an air of proud confidentiality, as though he and the Fergusons
were comrades in some great and secret undertaking, he mentioned that negotiations were under way for purchasing the
building next door, in effect more than doubling the size of the
museum.

"I believe that in five or six years we'll be one of the most
important museums in the country," the Director continued,
consciously, strategically using the word "we," as he always did
when speaking to donors, in order to assure them that they really were a part of the organization and that their donations
were not taken for granted. Though his address was easy and
charming, he assumed a certain authoritarian tone of voice and
employed a certain official vocabulary, both of which came to
him automatically whenever he spoke of the Centre. He could
not help it: he had employed such a voice, such a vocabulary, in
so many letters and speeches that they had wormed their way
ineradicably into the center of his brain. "Let's face it," he went
on, "here in New York we have one of the most sophisticated
populations in the country, and that's what I want the Centre
to reflect. Sophistication—our *truly* expanded horizons—that is
what I believe it is key for us to present and promote. I've always personally believed that it is our responsibility and privilege to have a *tremendous* impact on the rest of the country, if
not on the rest of the world. Really, I don't think it's overstat-
ing the case to say that what transpires here today will be impactful tomorrow on places as far away and different as, say, St
Louis or Omaha—and if not tomorrow, then the day after, or
the day after that. Yes! That's the kind of influence we should

be proud of, and that's the kind I believe we can all work for through artistic institutions like our Centre!"

"That is so true!" Mrs. Ferguson said, taking another sip of her Cosmopolitan.

Mr. Ferguson nodded.

"People from all parts of the country," the Director continued, "from all parts of the world, come here to see the kinds of things that represent our eclecticism and dynamism. With the Van Burgh room we've certainly taken a big step in that direction, but it's hardly the last step. Far from it! When we purchase the new building we're going to have a lot more room to expand our aesthetic horizons in some really new and groundbreaking ways. I foresee exhibitions for the many kinds of art that are thriving in our city and create its unique character—for music, film, photography, crafts. For instance: ceramics. You'd be amazed at some of the things that potters are doing these days. Just the other day, in fact, I went to visit an artist in Long Island City who makes the most *amazing* tea pots."

"What was that?" Mr. Ferguson said. He had just come back to himself after his mind had momentarily wandered, for he had caught sight of Cleo Van Burgh, not too many feet away, sitting in a chair with her head bowed over, undoubtedly having fallen into a geriatric snooze but looking for all the world as though she had died.

"Teapots!" Mr. Hodge repeated. "There's an artist in Long Island City who makes the most amazing teapots. She decorates them with butterflies and hearts;—the detail is absolutely amazing. I'm determined to showcase her work. And street art. In my opinion it's always been underestimated. Have either of you ever heard of Big Wave D?"

"Big Wave who?" Mr. Ferguson asked, sitting up a little in his chair.

" 'D'—as in the letter. You might have seen his work on the street and don't even realize it. He creates these really interesting graffiti-influenced portraits and designs! Works totally with spray paint—acrylic—which is a difficult medium to master. Ever go over the Brooklyn Bridge? There are some things of his over there on the Brooklyn side, at the base. Anyway, we're in negotiations with him to do something on a mobile medium so that we can get it from Bed-Stuy, where he lives, to the Centre. We couldn't get his work into the van Burgh Room—just wasn't the right milieu—but eventually I'd like to see a whole new section of the museum dedicated to that kind of exciting street art. It's just *so* reflective of our city's rich diversity! That's what I mean when I say I'd like to see the Centre in the forefront of presenting new, fresh talents. We've even got some big corporate sponsors on board already! They've been very supportive of our intentions. It's just good business for them to show that they're in step with the spirit of the times. At any rate, we're going to have a museum that will help further expand people's horizons, and hopefully when our visitors go home—especially our less-fortunate friends from other parts of the country—they'll have been exposed to the progressive spirit of our—"

Several sharp pops interrupted his words; they were as loud as exploding firecrackers. They had come from somewhere below, from somewhere on the streets, in the near distance, perhaps a block or two away, and their the initial pop-pop-pop had echoed in the canyon formed by the city's tall buildings. Then more of them sounded, followed by a woman's scream, and then shouts. From the same direction car horns beeped frantically.

Mr. and Mrs. Ferguson, Mr. and Mrs. Hodge, and nearly all the people that evening on the garden rooftop of the Centre for Contemporary American Art stopped their various conversations and turned their heads in the general direction from where the sounds had come.

One of the guests walked over to the waist-high ledge and stood only a few feet away from the Fergusons. He could not help but overhear the somewhat irritated comment Mrs. Ferguson blurted out: "What's going on?"

"Gunshots," he said, turning to her. He was holding a drink and now he took a sip from it.

"Gunshots?"

"Sounds like it, yes. Something must be going on ..."

That something was indeed "going on" became apparent in the next few minutes when the distant sound of police sirens grew louder and louder as cruisers from within thirty blocks away came speeding toward the area. As they passed on the street just below the Centre, their sirens, deafeningly loud, drowned out the classical music on the rooftop, and the bursts of red and white from their stroboscopic lights bounced off the mirror-like windows of the tall buildings round about and slashed like photonic rapiers across the soft candlelight gracing the little tables. Many more guests had stepped up to the wall in order to look down and see where the police cars were going. They saw them converging on a place a few blocks away. Another series of pops, of gunfire, sounded; it was audible above the sirens. A few people could be seen running, fleeing, on the sidewalks directly below. People who had been standing near the ledge began urging one another to back away from it, realizing that somewhere nearby bullets were flying.

Though outwardly calm the Director panicked to think that this evening, which had been months in the planning, was about to be disastrously marred. He shuddered to think that by some freak accident one of his very important guests might be struck or, God forbid, killed by a stray bullet—for Premiere Patrons were not all that common. He therefore excused himself from the Fergusons and his wife and walked to an area where he was sure all the guests could hear him clearly, and there, in a loud voice, announced:

"Everyone, could I have your attention! Please! Everyone! There's obviously a police action in progress nearby, and until we find out what's going on I would suggest that we all go back downstairs for the rest of the evening. Please feel free to bring your cocktails with you! We will move everything else downstairs too! Please ... if you'll just start assembling at the elevator ... That's right ... Everyone to the elevator, please! Thank you ..."

The catering service that had been hired to provide the buffet and related paraphernalia were under the oversight of a man behind the bar who had the polished, whisking manner of the small-time entrepreneur eager that everything should be "perfect" in order the better to increase his chances of repeat business. The Director walked over to him and quietly requested that everything be moved indoors—set up on the mezzanine. The man nodded obediently, but was a little dismayed, for it had taken hours to set up everything here and now it all had to be dismantled and moved elsewhere. Nevertheless he hastened over to his employees, leaned into them and in a discreetly quiet voice instructed them that they were to begin taking apart the bar, carrying the tables and chairs downstairs ...

Fifteen minutes later most of the guests were once again assembled in the mezzanine or had wandered back into the Van Burgh Room. The police and now ambulance sirens that continued to blare outside were muffled to a whisper by the thick concrete walls of the Centre. The Director continued circulating among the guests, as easily, as charmingly as he had done up on the rooftop, but secretly he was irritated that the evening had not gone entirely according to plan. If there was going to be any kind of trouble, why did it have to happen on this of all nights! Murphy's Law ...

But the guests themselves were not much put out by the interruption or the request to return to the interior of the building. The nearby "police activity," as the Director had called it, dominated their various conversations for no more than a minute or two before they gave their attention over to other, more pleasant things. There was however one guest who for the rest of the evening brought up the matter to nearly everyone he spoke: he of the black and blue eye and cut forehead— the recently mugged Ian Hutton. That so many gathered here tonight had been, as it were, near eyewitnesses to another crime was for him the perfect starting point to descant on his favorite subject of how the ills of society all came down to societal unfairness. "If people had an equal opportunity," he said at least a half dozen times throughout the rest of the evening, "don't you think so-called criminals would be doing something constructive with their lives instead of committing crimes?—of course they would! They'd be in college developing their minds and contributing to society: they'd be teachers and surgeons and nuclear physicists! But instead they feel hopeless so of course they get guns and start shooting people! When are we going to learn that people need hope in their lives? You can't blame someone for punching you in the face or knocking you over the head when he realizes he doesn't stand a chance of getting into a good school and having a lucrative career. That's a natural reaction—anybody would do it. It's we, society, who are to blame! We should be funding more educational projects. We should be buying these kids books instead of guns, and taking care of them properly. Why, did you know that just this year there was a reduction in the school lunch program?"

The Fergusons meanwhile picked a little from the buffet that had been brought down from the rooftop to the mezzanine. For the next forty-five minutes they drank, munched, and talked. It was a little before eleven when Mr. Ferguson, looking at his watch, reminded his wife that he didn't want to stay out late. They said their goodbyes to those around them, called their car, and forty minutes later were back in their apartment.

The first thing Mrs. Ferguson noticed was the blinking light on the answering machine. She pressed the play button and her daughter's voice came through the speaker, saying she had found the font her mother had been looking for.

"Thank goodness!" Mrs. Ferguson murmured, feeling a genuine sense of relief, for, really, her new stationery just wouldn't have looked as good without that particular font.

After they had changed into their pajamas the Fergusons did not immediately go to bed. Though they usually went to sleep before twelve, they sat up in the living room. With the television on and its volume low, they sat talking about the evening they had just come home from. They agreed that it had been enjoyable. They briefly mentioned the several people they had met. Mrs. Ferguson told her husband which of the women were looking well, and which had aged terribly. He chuckled a few times at these commentaries. The fact was that without her makeup, her jewelry, her fine dress, and clad only in a cotton nightgown, she looked rather worn herself, yet her husband, looking over to her, said to himself contentedly, "Good old girl ..."

"What's on?" she asked.

"I don't know," he answered, looking back to the television set, taking up the remote control, and raising the volume. He clicked through the channels, never staying on any one of them for more than ten or fifteen seconds before moving on to the next. Then he came upon a movie from the '50s, a "classic" that was being shown for the fifth time this year. It was a love story, a romance, typical for its era: the man was tall, commanding, handsome, the woman beautiful, sweet, brave, ultimately yielding despite her initial reservations. They kissed to the soaring whir of violins whose strains expressed the ultimate satisfaction of their long-delayed love and their confidence of a grand future; and overhead there was a break in the cloudy skies and a beam of sunlight broke through; and once again good had won out over evil and all was well with the world.

"Ohhhh, we missed it," Mrs. Ferguson murmured. It was one of her favorite movies. She sounded disappointed, but she was not really, having seen it several times.

"News should be on," he said, holding out the remote control and clicking through the channels again till he reached one showing the news, which was already in progress.

A news reporter, holding a microphone with his network's logo, was speaking into the camera with an expression of intense concern. He was reporting on the economic stresses on the city's hospitals, so many of which had closed because their emergency rooms had filled with people who had no medical insurance and couldn't afford medical care. The camera panned over one such room: it was filled with poor, mostly third-world people, many of them mothers holding a sick child on their knees while one or two more of their children sat playing on the floor beside them. They were among the millions, the tens of millions, and tens of millions more on top of that, of the world's poor who had come into country by hook or by crook: just the tiniest fraction of the world's "huddled masses yearning to be free" …

"I'm so glad I met that Tocolini tonight," Mrs. Ferguson mentioned. "I'll call him tomorrow."

"If I were you I'd wait a few days," said her husband, shrewdly. "You don't want him to think you're too eager."

"Mmmm … you're probably right."

He was holding the remote control idly in his right hand and lifted it up a little as though he would change the channel, but he didn't and watched as now another reporter stood on the steps of large, classical-looking building in downtown Manhattan and explained how the latest government report indicated that Social Security system was going bankrupt and would no longer exist for Americans who were counting on it as a financial safety net in their old age. The reporter stated that a steady and increasing draw on entitlement programs was not keeping pace with revenues; the tax-paying middle-class was shrinking, a trend that had been going on for decades.

"By the way, Brittany called and told me she found the font."

"The what?" he asked.

"The *font*—the font for my stationery. Remember? The one I was looking for and couldn't find?"

"Ohhhhh, that. Yes. She found it?"

"Yes. Poor kid—she's been running around for weeks looking for it. She has to order it from some company overseas, of all places. Can you imagine?"

"Hm!" Mr. Ferguson muttered; then said, "She's something, that Brittany"—by which he meant, with admiration and pride, that if anyone could be counted on to find something obscure it was his daughter, who was tenacious if nothing else. Immediately afterwards another thought occurred to him—he wondered why it hadn't occurred to him before—and he asked, "Why'd you need that font anyway?"

As he asked this question he flipped quickly through a few more channels and stopped at another news program. On the screen flashed a surging crowd of thousands barely held back by policemen in riot gear.

"I needed it because it was the only one that would match the design on the top. You've seen my new stationery—haven't you? I thought I showed it to you."

Mr. Ferguson shrugged; he wasn't sure. He was looking at the television. The news report was coming out of Chicago where people were taking to the streets en masse to protest against the bad economy. Many of them had lost their jobs, their homes, their pensions, and their small savings. It wasn't just a shifting economic cycle that had brought them out into the streets like this but a new, alarming, and in the end unacceptable sense that the old paradigm had been replaced by a new one in which they were entirely expendable. As though suddenly shaken into wakefulness, they realized that all their emailing and telephone calls to their elected officials, and indeed voting itself, had done nothing to improve their lot; that they were as surely on the downward spiral as ever, and so were their children; and so finally—finally—they were furious.

"Didn't I show it to you?" Mrs. Ferguson asked, still on the subject of her stationery.

"I don't remember," he said.

"Yes, I *did*. You just don't remember. Boy oh boy, you don't remember *anything* anymore, do you? Anyway, I couldn't use a regular font: it would be too plain. I know—I could *see* it.

I need something that looked nicer."

On television, the protestors spewed threats and curses against their mayor, their senators, even the President. They were fed up with the promises and plans of politicians. They were sick and tired of theories and hypotheses, of "solutions" always ineffective or somehow undermined: they wanted, they demanded action! Nor would they be appeased by the assurance of action a few months or a year from now; no, no, they weren't buying it anymore; they wanted results tomorrow, now, yesterday.

"Did you use up the old stationery I got for you?" Mr. Ferguson asked.

"Hardly. I still have boxes of it."

"You didn't like it?"

"It was alright. But the new one's much nicer. It's important to have nice stationery."

A reporter on the scene of the protest said in a nervous voice that the atmosphere was "electric, that "anything might happen"—hinting at some great violence about to erupt. The hundreds of police wearing riot gear and lining the streets looked nervous before this angry, unstable human tide, for they knew that they would be overwhelmed if its mountainous fury was loosed. Elsewhere in the city violence had already broken out as scattered, smaller crowds ran down streets, smashing windows, overturning trash cans, hurling stones and bottles at policemen who tried to run them down or maintain order. Scenes of this were shown.

"Just *what* is going on out there!" Mrs. Ferguson asked, impatiently, as for the first time she gave her attention to the images on the television.

"Trouble," Mr. Ferguson said; and suddenly feeling tired he yawned. "It's in Chicago."

The news camera panned over the angry, shouting faces, zoomed into the bulging eyes, the open mouths, the raised fists.

"What are they so *angry* about?" Mrs. Ferguson asked in a tone of disapproving wonder.

"I guess they're out of work," Mr. Ferguson said.

"Well ... so? That's no reason to go *crazy*, for God's sake! Just find another job, that's all!"

"It's not so easy these days for a lot of people," he said,

aware of the turn the country had taken.

"Well, because they don't have skills," Mrs. Ferguson returned. "If they had *skills* they wouldn't be having this problem
... People need skills."

Mr. Ferguson nodded, agreeing to that extent.

"You know what it is?" she continued. "People don't go into
the right things. You have to be professional these days. Don't
people understand that? That's the only way you can get anywhere."

On television one of the demonstrators was being inter-
viewed, a microphone held up to his mouth as the camera
zoomed into his face. He was a man in his fifties, stocky, ill-
shaven, and missing a few teeth in his lower jaw. His speech
was quick and garbled;—the words tumbled out of his mouth
with a coarse, unlettered pronunciation bespeaking a mind no
more made for book learning than his body had been made for
pole vaulting. He explained who he was and why he was here,
but was so agitated that he shouted his words and sprinkled
them with so many obscenities that the network had to bleep
out much of what he said, making it difficult to follow him. Apparently he had been out of work for several months; had a
wife, three children, a mortgage; yet even while working had
been making less each year despite the cost of living constantly
rising; had been set upon, squeezed and squeezed, till he just
couldn't "take it no more." Blurting out that "som'm's gotta
give, here!" he poked at the air with a fat, dirty forefinger as
though driving home his point. Clearly he was a man at the
end of his tether: a man who had lost much and was therefore
ready for almost anything. He was like many of those around
him—the hundreds and hundreds, this tip of the iceberg of millions.

"People should go into medicine or law," Mrs. Ferguson continued. "Doctors and lawyers almost always do well. I'll tell
you one thing, if I were a young person I'd definitely go into
medicine. I'd be a big, big surgeon! A brain specialist. Something like that. I'd be working at the top hospitals and universities in the world. That's what *I* would do! What are you
smiling about?"

"Nothing!" Mr. Ferguson said. He hemmed a few times and
added, "You'd be a good surgeon."

"Damn right I would be. I'd be the best! And do you want to know why? Because when I do something I really *do* it— that's why!"

"But I thought you couldn't stand the sight of blood," Mr. Ferguson reminded her, and despite himself he was smiling.

"Well of course I don't *like* it. Who does? But if I *had* to do it, I'd do it. I'd get used to it, believe me. Or I'd become a lawyer or something. Or a scientist. I just don't understand why people just don't become doctors and lawyers and scientists!"

Mr. Ferguson gave the quite reasonable answer, "Well ... not everyone's interested in those things."

"Well, they *should* be," Mrs. Ferguson answered at once and testily. "After all, we all have to do things we don't like to do in this life. And anyway, without skills today you're nowhere. You have to do things that contribute to society. That's the thing. You have to do things that have *value*. It's a matter of economics. You have to produce things people *want*. That's what it is."

—Which simple generalization Mr. Ferguson was in no mood to question or gainsay. He only smiled a little at his wife's vehemence.

The news ended in a half hour, and when it did so Mrs. Ferguson, getting up from the couch, announced that she was tired and was going to sleep. She didn't go over to her husband to kiss him good night or otherwise show him any physical affection; rather she conveyed this through the tenderness of her voice as she took her leave, asking the question:

"You're staying up?"

"Oh ... just a little while. I'll be in soon."

He watched her walk off and disappear into a corridor leading to the bedroom.

He turned his face toward the high, clear, open windows that gave out to a view of the city whose thousand distant lights glowed like a veil of stars in the blackness of space. Then he turned his eyes to his hands, which rested on the padded arms of the chair and noted how heavily they were wrinkled and dotted with age spots. He let out a deep, sighing breath. It occurred to him again—as sometimes it did throughout the day— that he was sixty-two years old; an "old man";—there could no

longer be even a question about that. He shook his head and
smiled unhappily and let out a small astonished breath. Good
heavens, how life had flown by! It seemed that just yesterday
he had been fifty; and only a few days before that a young man
of twenty, a youth of fifteen, a child of seven! Good heavens—
good heavens—what a dream, what a mirage, this life of ours!
And yet he trusted that he would endure. He wasn't just anybody, after all. He had risen high in the hierarchy of life. He
was important. Why, he even had his name printed in half a
dozen Who's Who directories, which might be found in corporate
libraries all over the world.

"Andrew B. Wheatley," he thought.

Who was Andrew B. Wheatley, and why did Mr. Ferguson
happen to think of him now? He had been one of the founding
partners of Mr. Ferguson's company and his large, oil-painted
portrait, illuminated by a spotlight, hung in the waiting room to
the offices. It showed an imposing-looking man in his seventies,
dressed in a dark suit with a red tie and looking out on the
world with a ruddy face and white hair and bushy eyebrows: the
face of a man who knew he was somebody. His name was engraved in a large brass plate on the bottom of the ornate
wooden frame. Every employee or visitor who stepped into the
company's main office saw him. Mr. Ferguson wondered if he
might not have his own portrait painted and placed just as con-
spicuously. Why not? He was now the senior partner. Surely
he had as much a right to have his picture hanging there as Andrew B. Wheatley.

"I wonder if that Tortellini guy could paint it for me?" Mr.
Ferguson asked himself.

His attention was again diverted to the television when the
business report came on. It was this he had been waiting for.
It was a segment of only two minutes, a quick rundown of the
major stock indices. The newscaster reported another dip in the
stock market, and mentioned several probable causes: an increase in the price of oil, a war threatening in the Middle East,
a reduction in consumer confidence. Even after four years the
economy was still bad. Unemployment was still high; getting
worse, in fact, with each passing month. Still—as the newscaster mentioned—economists were "optimistic" and said that
"leading indicators" pointed to a recovery.

Mr. Ferguson half murmured, half huffed a doubtful, "Mmm!" Then he looked to one wall where, on a mantle over a faux fireplace, there stood an ornate, ceramic reproduction of a Louis XVI era clock. The minute hand was only a short distance away from meeting the hour hand: in a few more minutes it would be twelve o'clock—a new day.

He turned off the television, and, telling himself, "I'm tired," went to join his wife in the bedroom.

FLIGHT

With the quietly intense and serious mien typical of his profession, the doctor stood with his eyes steady on the blood pressure gauge as he pressed the diaphragm of his stethoscope into the inner arm of the man sitting on the edge of the paper-covered examination table. The man, Roman Kittie, had come in to the office on account of a rash he had developed—a band of red that ran across his neck. It had developed over the last few months and now it was quite obvious—a wide red band. If it had not been for this strange rash he would never have come in for the checkup, for he had been brought up in a lower middle-class family with its ethos of never spending an unnecessary dollar and thus never seeing expensive doctors unless one absolutely had to, that is to say, unless you were really "sick"— unless you were in pain. Granted, he had health insurance from his job, but it only paid a percentage of whatever bills accrued; and while he was not so poor as he had been as a child neither was he wealthy enough to afford the extortionate fees of American medicine. God forbid he should ever develop a "serious illness" illness—cancer, heart disease, kidney failure—for then the cavalcade of "deductibles" and his own share of the cost would leave him as broke as the most indigent person living on the street. As the blood pressure cuff began to loosen, he shifted his eyes, which had been trained on the wall opposite him, to the doctor standing at his side, awaiting the verdict.

"Your blood pressure is high," the doctor announced.

"It is?" Kittie was surprised, even startled.

The doctor nodded, gravely. "A lot."

"How much is a lot?"

"It's 155 over 95."

"That's a lot?"

The doctor nodded again, his expression inscrutable as to anything "more" he might know. He took the stethoscope out his ears and it dangled from his neck like a weird necklace. He stepped over to his desk atop which lay a red folder; it contained a questionnaire that Kittie had filled out on coming into the office. The doctor looked over it a second time, this time taking a silver ball point pen from his pocket and began writing, or rather checking things off and scribbling short notes here and there. Without looking up he asked:

"Do you smoke?"

"No, never."

"Drink?"

"Never."

"Are you married?"

Roman Kittie didn't see what that had to do with anything, but duly answered, "No."

"Were you ever?"

"No."

The doctor checked off a few more things, jotted down a few others, and then clicked the pen shut and slipped it back into his pocket. He looked up at his patient and said:

"If you want, we can start you on some medication to bring down that blood pressure."

Medication? At the word Roman Kittie grew a little stiff and felt himself become even more nervous than he had been while his blood pressure had been taken. Medication meant that it was "serious." Like most people who have been healthy all their lives, he was alarmed to think that he might have come down with a chronic illness.

"Is that absolutely necessary?"

"Well ..."—the doctor looked up and seemed about to say yes, but he detected in his patient's wide and almost imploring eyes a nervous personality whom it might not be a good idea to alarm—" ... it's a good idea. Of course you might try getting it down without the medication: losing a little weight, exercising."

"I do exercise."

"Oh? What do you do?"

"Well ... I walk a lot."

The doctor shook his head. "Walking isn't enough," he said, in an unemotional, clinical voice. "Losing weight, a cardio workout regimen, some resistance training to build up muscle mass—that would probably bring it down. Ever think of joining a gym?"

Kittie shook his head, no, and his spirit sank at the thought he might have to do what he hated: exercising. Walking was one thing; even walking at a clip he could tolerate; for after all one had to get from place to place. But the idea of lifting weights, running on treadmills, and building up a sweat was to him too repulsive even in thought. He hated to sweat. It made him feel dirty. "Maybe I will," he said, knowing very well that he was not likely to commit himself to it for more than a day or two.

"That would be a good idea. Alright, I'll tell you what. We don't have to put you on medication right now. Let's see what you can do for yourself in the next week or so, okay? If you can get that pressure down five or ten points, and maybe lose a few pounds—you'd be surprised what even five pounds can do—we can hold off on the medication. As for that rash you've got there ... I'm not sure. It could be a lot of things. Have you been eating anything unusual lately? It could be an allergy."

Kittie shook his head, no.

"Do you have rashes anywhere else on your body?"

Again, Kittie shook his head no.

"I'll prescribe you a lotion," the doctor said, pulling toward himself a prescription pad that was on his desk and scribbling something on it. "Just apply this at night before you go to sleep. Don't use it for more than four or five days, though." He tore the prescription off the pad and held it up for Kittie to take. "But I *do* want to see you next week—understand? I also want to have a blood work-up done on you. When's the last time you had some blood taken?"

"Blood? Oh ..."—Kittie left off just shaking his head. He had never had it looked at.

"Alright, let's take some now." The doctor leaned in to a box on his desk, pressed a button, and spoke in Russian to someone outside. In a few seconds the phlebotomist, a middle-aged, matronly woman in a white lab coat, poked her head into the room and listened to the doctor instruct her to take Kittie's blood. She put out a hand and quickly curled her joined fingers at Kittie, saying, "Come!"

She led him to a smaller room down a hall and, once he was seated, told him to role up his sleeve. She put on a pair of surgical gloves as though she were preparing for open-heart surgery. She applied a rubber tourniquet to his upper arm and told him to make a fist, then, with a forefinger, began taping his inner elbow, searching for a vein to pierce; going about the whole process with a disturbing gleam of anticipation in her eyes. After she had filled a vial with his blood she held it up before him and, batting her eyes somehow amorously, whispered with a Russian accent:

"Now I have your blood!"

Kittie smiled uncomfortably.

When he was finished he went outside to the waiting area to make his next appointment with the receptionist. She was one of two assistants to the doctor and happened to be on the phone speaking to someone in Russian. He idly stood before her and politely waited for her to finish. He saw that two other people were seated on the chairs in the waiting room. They were both old, in their seventies, and neither was an American—one could tell at a glance that they weren't. They had the shabby-refined look of poor Eastern European immigrants and were wearing sweaters as though it were a chilly fall day when in fact it was the middle of summer and it had been hot all week; indeed, the temperature outside was already pushing seventy-five degrees though it was only a little past ten o'clock in the morning. Roman Kittie shifted his eyes away from them and looked through the large window facing the street. The sun had been shining when he had stepped into the office forty-five minutes earlier, but since then an ominous darkness had settled over the city. Before leaving his apartment that morning he had heard on the radio a weather report saying that rain was on the way. It certainly looked like it was. He hoped it wouldn't start before he reached the subway. Glancing at the clock behind the receptionist, he quickly calculated that he could make it into work before eleven o'clock if he could get out of here in the next five or ten minutes.

"Yes, sir," the reception said, putting down the telephone and turning her attention to Kittie. She spoke English only moderately well and with a Russian accent. She had come from Moscow and had only been in the country for three months. She had gotten her job as a receptionist here because she was a friend of the doctor's wife. "You want to make appointment again, yes?"

"Yes, next week."

"Okaaaaay." She flipped through the pages of the appointment book on her desk and offered a few dates that were open,
and asked him which he wanted.

Actually he wanted none of them because they were all
weekdays and that meant he would have to take time off from
work again, just as he had done for today's visit. It was true
that he had never missed more than a few days at work in all
the years he had had his job, but he still was nervous at the
thought of it. A lifetime of conditioning had made him regard a
regular attendance at work as sacrosanct; the more so because
lateness was so frowned upon in his company. His department
boss, Mr. Coro, was very strict in this matter. Over the last
year a couple of new employees had been fired for having come
to work fifteen minutes late three or four times. —No, no, he
couldn't risk his job like that unless it was absolutely necessary.
He asked the receptionist:

"Are you open on the weekend? That would actually be
better for me."

The receptionist responded that the doctor didn't work on
the weekends, and that, moreover, now that it was summer, he
didn't work on Fridays, either. "I can to give you," she said,
looking at her appointment book, "next week on a Tuesday at
nine ... or maybe Wednesday after three ... or on Thursday we
have open some time at four ..."—and she looked up at him,
awaiting his decision. Kittie selected Tuesday morning and
watched her take up one of the doctor's business cards, write
down the date and time, and hand it to him. She also mentioned his deductible and asked him how much of today's visit
he would like to pay. He wrote out a check for the full amount.
He hated to have debts, the consciousness of which always irritated him with a faint but uncomfortable sense of burden.

When he left the doctor's office he stood for a moment on
the steps just outside the door. A small awning stretched out
above him; he noticed, in its corner, the gauzy whiteness of a
spider's web in which a fly had gotten caught and was vainly
trying to free itself. Then he shifted his eyes to the sky, and
what he saw misgave him, for it was darker and more menacing
than ever. The air was heavy with moisture and the smell of

wetness; it was still but also somehow waiting, biding its time. A storm was brewing and somehow the earth itself seemed stalled in anticipation of it. Then a few raindrops fell before him, hitting the cement with a plopping sound and forming dark, tendrilous spots. Thunder rumbled in the distance.

"Oh boy," Kittie thought. "Here it comes."

The subway station was five blocks away and he walked at a clip, just under a trot, in only a few seconds breathing hard, but telling himself, "It's good for me to walk this fast—good exercise!" He made it to the subway station just as the storm let loose.

The train going into Manhattan wasn't as crowded as it would have been during rush hour, and Kittie was able to find a seat. He and two hundred other passengers hurtled through a dark, dank, rat-infested tunnel while the clatter and shriek of the steel wheels beneath them filled their ears. A couple of times the lights in the car went out for a second as its contact with the powered third rail faltered, and in those few instants of darkness the light from some lamp in the tunnel itself would light up the passengers' faces with a ghastly flash. Everyone on that train sat in silence, some with their eyes closed and heads bowed, eager to grasp a few minutes sleep, others wearing impenetrably dark sunglasses which enabled them to see without being seen, still others looking up at the advertisements that ran along the length of the car just under the ceiling, and which tried to sell them everything from weight loss pills to rum to skin care ointments to travel packages to the paradisal beaches of some Caribbean isle. Still other passengers managed to look at no particular spot; their eyes turned toward the floor, or their handbag, or their hands set on their laps; or looking straight ahead, into inanity. Kittie too looked ahead of himself with vacant eyes, but he was thinking of what his doctor had told him, and was still unable to reconcile himself to the bad news.

"Imagine that!" he thought. "High blood pressure. Very high, he said. And now he's going to test my blood. He's sure to find something else wrong. Oh, yes, there's going to be things wrong. I just know it. Just what I need!"

His mind went back to his relative youth of only ten years earlier when he had been thirty-two. He had been just as stocky as he was today, but his body had been pretty solid, his arms muscular, the flesh under his chin concave, taut, his stomach flat;—well, relatively flat;—and all this without a minute of "exercise." But sitting at a desk all day, five days a week, had conspired with the passing years to turn him into a human marshmallow.

"Resistance training," he thought, despairingly.

Forty minutes later he stepped out of the train at the Union Square station and knew he was in trouble when he saw the people who had just come down from the street: they were bedraggled, a little breathless as though they had been running, and their umbrellas, as they shook or closed them, poured streams of water onto the tiled floor. When he climbed upstairs he saw that the city was engulfed in a driving rainstorm.

It was one of those late summer storms in New York City that build up for days, even for weeks, now and then teasing the metropolis with humid sprinkles, yet ever holding back, ever preparing for the great unleashing that will sweep away the hot putrid air in one great blast. Such blasts are sudden and violent and usually do not last long. Kittie and the others waited on the first landing of the subway station, looking up the steps to beyond the canopy that covered the station entrance. The sky was dark, the wind howled, the rain was coming down in a roar of profusion. They all expected and hoped that this wild weather would expend itself in a few minutes. But they were mistaken. This storm was not a fast-moving front but one of those slow, churning, enormous upheavals of atmosphere. The driving rain fell with unmitigated force; seemed at times to increase; and lightning occasionally flashed and thunder rumbled. As one train after another disembogued its human cargo, the landing became more crowded with people huddled together, squeezed against one another, looking out at the storm, impatiently waiting for it to let up even a little. Those who had appointments to keep and could no longer wait, or who realized that there was no guarantee this inclemency would soon relent, sidled through their fellow-commuters—"Excuse me, excuse me please!"—and climbed up to street level, hunching their shoulders as they opened umbrellas against the lashing rain. Within a second the nether part of their clothing was drenched—a warning to those remaining behind.

"Damn it!" Kittie exclaimed to himself, looking over the

heads of a few people as he too looked out at the gusting rain. "Damn it! Damn it!"

He had already taken time off from work for his doctor's appointment, and now it seemed he was to be further delayed by the storm. He wondered if he too might make a run for it, but his office was located six blocks away, one of them a long crosstown block, and he couldn't possibly make it there without getting drenched. He silently lambasted himself for not having brought an umbrella. He wondered if he went up to street level he might find one of those Nigerian street merchants who always seem to appear magically with carts full of cheap umbrellas the moment it begins to rain; but he knew that even they weren't likely to be standing about in this violent weather. Then from behind him he heard someone saying, "Excuse me ... excuse me ..." and he turned around to see a man, impatient of waiting, threading through the crowd till he had broken free of it and stood at the verge of the cement steps leading up to ground level. He had been holding a newspaper which he now opened and held over his head like a hat. He hesitated only a moment before he dashed upward and out of sight.

Kittie didn't have a newspaper but he knew there was a newsstand across the street. And it seemed to him that if *that* man could make do with a newspaper over his head, well ... Besides, he just couldn't wait any more.

He climbed the steps and adventured into the open. The driving rain lashed into his face, his clothes, but he forged ahead. He ran to the corner. The light just turned green as he reached it, and he ran across the street. At the newsstand there he took up a newspaper and plunked down a buck in payment. As soon as his change was laid down he swooped it up, put the newspaper over his head, and began walking fast uptown.

His office was located on Fifth Avenue, on Eighteenth Street. He made a beeline uptown on Union Square West. The rainstorm was coming from the north and the wind and rain lashed his face and body. Just as he turned left on Seventeenth Street a bolt of lightning flashed overhead, turning everything ghastly white, and a crack of thunder sounded so loudly that it seemed the earth had been split in two. The wind blew harder than ever and the rain, as though finally let loose from some skyey bladder, fell in sheets so that its rush and pressure reverberated throughout the canyons of a city like the shushing of a waterfall. Amid this deluge the sidewalks became deserted and traffic slowed down. Even the yellow cabs, usually recklessly zooming and weaving, advanced cautiously; their windshield wipers, even at high speed, struggling to clear away blurring cascades of water; their tires throwing up cloven waves the way the prow of a ship throws up on either side of it the yielding sea. The gutters became rivers which, overtopping the curb in some places, bubbled and frothed their way to the nearest sewer grating, falling into it with a loud, foaming, misted pour. The driven raindrops made a loud tattoo on the newspaper Kittie held over his head. The bottom of his pants were wet to his knees. It was all too much for even the boldest, most impatient pedestrians. Even Kittie realized he had to give up. He took shelter in the embrasure of a building along with several other people who were almost as wet as he was. They shook their heads at one another in silent sympathy for their common ordeal and stared out at the rain in defeated resignation. Most of them were holding umbrellas that had done them little good, and which, held downward, let fall streamlets of water.

The building in whose entrance he and others had taken shelter had been built by an airline company now long out of business. In the walls to either side were tall windows which, in the late '40s and '50s, had proudly displayed enlarged pictures of Douglas DC-7s and Boeing 707s beside schedules of flights to Philadelphia, Chicago, Los Angeles, or Miami. The pictures of those aircraft and their accompanying schedules had been successively replaced by advertisements for a dozen companies, each one entirely unrelated to the one that had gone before it. But there remained a vestige of the original intent of the building, for in the center of the vaulted ceiling was a large ceramic tile of a four-engine airliner. Kittie noticed it only by chance, only when he happened to run his hands through his wet hair and raise his head and eyes. He didn't know why it was there; so far as he knew it was purely decorative. The sight of it brought back a memory from his childhood. He smiled as he remembered the day he, a youth of fifteen, confided in his father—one of the few times he had confided anything in anyone—that he wanted to be a test pilot for the Air Force and fly the fastest planes in the world.

"A pilot, eh?" his father had said, good-humoredly and not looking at the boy as he read his paper, casually flipping the pages which he held up high, hiding his face.

It was a Saturday morning and they were sitting in the living room of their Bronx apartment. The father was sitting on the couch, his legs sprawled out before him, his demeanor somehow sagging, spent, the long hours of the work week having so exhausted him that he would spend the whole day lounging about, recuperating from it.

"Sure," young Roman had said. "I'm gonna fly jets! Fastest ones in the world! Experimental ones! The kind they drop from other planes, and they go up really really high and so fast, so fast ...!"—the boy clenched his teeth and almost shivered for sheer nervous eagerness at the prospect, the expectation of that magnificent, exciting future, and he saw himself in the cockpit of the latest, greatest jet airplane, wearing a silvered flight suit and a helmet with a mysteriously reflective visor, while his hands were steady at the complicated, multi-dialed controls of powerful engines that would zoom him up, up above the clouds, up to the top to the world, even to the fringes of space, where he alone would glimpse the wonder and the power and glory of the universe spreading out infinitely above him ...

"Oh, Roman," his father said, lowering the newspaper and peering out at his son with an indulgent and somehow weary smile, "don't be ridiculous—that's not a career."

And there had been something in the way his father had said those words—so simply, so quietly, with such complete, utter understanding of what was silly and what was not, of what could and could not be, that the boy's image of himself as a supersonic flier collapsed like a sand castle on a beach when an impulsive wave comes in and washes it away....

His father had been a stout bald man with thick, heavy glasses and an expression of stolid, quiet perseverance. It was a solid, serious face that made him look as though he were always about to say, "I know what's what, so don't try to tell me otherwise: I know what's got to be done, and I'm doing it!" He had been the second son of immigrant parents who had never properly learned their own language, let alone English, and who had eked out a bare living through manual labor. They had always reminded their son that they were "sacrificing" for his sake, so that he could go to college, get his "education," and have a bet-ter life than they had had. Accordingly he had graduated City College with a marketable degree in accounting. For the next forty-three years, five days a week, he had gotten up at seven in the morning and come home seven or eight in the evening too tired to do anything more than have his dinner, watch television for a few hours, and then go to sleep to start the routine over again the next day. Slowly, surely, inevitably his body grew pear-shaped from years of sitting at a desk and his eyes grew ever weaker so that each year his glasses got thicker; but even-tually he worked his way up the corporate ladder into a middle-manager's office in a skyscraper on Third Avenue and Fifty-first Street. Four months after his retirement he had a heart attack, and four months after that he suffered a stroke which left him paralyzed on his left side so that he had to be placed in a "reha-bilitation center," a term which was just coming into fashion in those days as the new euphemism for a nursing home. Quickly enough the assets he had accumulated after a lifetime of work were consumed in the expense of his care. He spent the last four years of his life strapped to a wheelchair, legally blind, and babbling incoherently.

The thought of his poor father flashed through Kittie's mind as he lightly bit his lower lip. "Poor man," Kittie said to himself. "What kind of life was that?"

"Excuse me," a man said, brushing by Kittie and threading his way through the little crowd.

The sky had begun to lighten, the rain had begun to relen-t—it was still profuse but no longer driving. People were ven-turing into the streets again, albeit with the hurried pace of chance-taking.

Kittie, glancing at his watch, seeing that he was forty-five minutes late—forty-five minutes on top of the hour he had said he would be late!—once again put his wet newspaper to his head and darted out onto the street. At times his hurrying legs skipped into a jog. He hurried along 17th Street, then turned right, heading uptown at Fifth Avenue. At the corner of 18th Street he had to stop to wait for traffic. He felt his heart beat-ing fast with exertion but told himself, "It's good exercise!" He stood impatiently at the curb, intending to dash across the street the moment traffic stopped. A cab roared by just inches

away from him, throwing a wave of gutter water onto him and
nullifying the effort he had made to keep himself at least a little
dry by holding a newspaper over his head. He looked as though
someone had flung a bucket of water onto him. He cursed aloud.
People who stood just behind him shook their heads in sympathy for his ruined clothes even as they thought (and Kittie just
knew they were thinking this) that it was partly his fault for
standing so close to the curb.

When the light turned green for him and other pedestrians,
he hurried up the block and again had to wait for traffic to pass
to cross the avenue, for his office building was just on the other
side. A huge, pond-like puddle of water had formed on the opposite corner because the sewer grate was stopped up. Some
were taking the long detour around it. Others, all men, were
jumping over it; barely making the curb. In the few steps before
he came to the obstacle Kittie decided he too would jump. He
took his leap—and fell short. His right foot landed in four
inches of street-dirty water, which splashed up into his pants
and instantaneously filled his shoe.

"God damn it! God *damn* it!"

But he didn't slow down; if anything he walked even faster
as though hurrying away from the humiliation of his failed leap.
By this time, too, the newspaper he held over his head was so
drenched that it was not so much a protection from the rain as
a dispenser of it over this or that part of his body—dribbling it
over his right shoulder or down his back, the small of which was
also dripping wet.

"Damn it!"

Walking hard and fast, and hearing his own labored breathing, he thought of how his blood pressure must be soaring, and
how dangerous that was. He told himself to slow down, that
none of this was worth getting a heart attack over. The image
of himself dropping dead then and there, a wet corpse on a wet
sidewalk, was at once absurd and horrifying.

Nevertheless he didn't slacken his pace; as quickly as ever
he headed to the building where the offices of Bartlett Berger
Investments were located. Once in the dry lobby, he deposited
the wet newspaper in a trash bin and stood for a few moments
catching his breath. His glasses were so beaded with water that
the world had turned into a blur, and he took them off, shook

them a few times, and wiped the lenses on the damp arm of his sleeve. His hair and face were dripping wet and he made the vain attempt of wiping them dry with his hands. The lower half of his pants were soaked so thoroughly that they were water-dark and dripping. The guards at the front desk watched him curiously as he passed and went to the elevator banks.

His goal was to get to the men's room to clean up. He was grateful that there was no one in the elevator with him; it would have been embarrassing to stand there dripping wet. When he got out of the elevator the first people he saw were the two young women who were receptionists at the front desk. They stopped what they were doing and looked at him with open mouths. "Roman—what happened to you?" one of them asked, actually standing up in surprise.

"Oh ... got caught in the rain ..." he said, hurrying by them.

"Is it raining that hard out there?" she asked, leaning forward a little to watch him escape down the hall.

"Yes—hard!" he called out.

He turned the corner and made for the men's room. He pushed open the door and was relieved when he found that no one was inside. For the next ten minutes he went through a stack of paper towels six inches high as he sopped the moisture out of his hair and clothes. In the mirror over the sink he saw that his face was flushed red with nervous impatience and effort. He noticed that even the rash around his neck was a little brighter than it had been earlier that morning. He glanced at his watch and saw that it was a quarter to twelve. Almost two hours late when he should have been less than one! He quickly combed his hair with his fingers and hurried out of the men's room.

The offices of Bartlett Berger Investments were laid out in such a way that the non-executive staff sat in the open at desks abutting one another and forming rows all across the floor. On the face of it, it seemed that such a layout couldn't provide any privacy, and strictly speaking this was true, but people have a way of psychologically adjusting themselves to such close situations. Just as happens in prisons, so here, the inmate-workers had psychologically designated the area immediately around them as theirs, as private and inviolable unless they had solicited someone's attention; consequently, everyone kept their eyes pretty much on their own work, in their own area. But when Kittie walked onto the floor, not only late but bedraggled, all heads raised, all eyes turned on him. A woman who sat in the first seat of his row and served as a secretary to several men on the floor, said in a loud, amused, concerned voice, "Hey, what happened to you!"

Oh, to have been able to tell her to shut up! To have had a nice thick piece of duct tape and slapped it over that big mouth of hers!

"Just got a little wet out there," Kittie said breezily.

He hurried to his desk, glad to reach it, to sit behind it, and so hide the wetness of his pants. He turned on his computer, opened the right-hand drawer of the desk and took out a stapler and a few pens, then went through a few requests that had been left on his desk by analysts who had stopped by earlier that morning while he had been gone. With relief he could see from the corners of his eyes that the people around him and in the room generally were turning away from him, returning to their work. Under the desk he slid off his shoes so that they and his socks might dry. He would have liked to take off his socks too—especially the right one, which was drenched from the puddle he had stepped in—but he would not have felt right sitting there barefooted. It would have been too embarrassing if someone noticed.

Kittie's job here at Bartlett Berger Investments was that of "Senior Research Administrator." As is so often the case in the business world, the august title was less an attempt to describe a position than to disguise its pettiness, for the only thing he really "administrated" was his keyboard, and his "research"—a word that conjured up patience combined with enlightened discretion—amounted to scrolling through a hundred database folders, and within these folders thousands of files, for information about nearly every company that had been in business over the last fifty years. This information was requested by the financial analysts whose job it was to use the data in composing reports for their superiors, who might be in the midst of putting together financial deals for large clients. One would have thought that after all this time Kittie would have known these databases inside out, but it happened that at least once a year everything was changed—the folders renamed, shifted about, their contents

deleted or moved elsewhere. He was told that this was the result of "maintenance" on the part of the technical staff. He had
complained about this every time it had happened, but no matter how many times he complained nothing had changed. He
was just a "Senior Research Administrator," after all, and he
was in no position to fire anyone for making his job more difficult. Thus he would spend the next two months having to re-
learn where everything was, and during that time he would
especially feel the pressure of meeting dozens of deadlines that
cropped up during the course of a day. No wonder that his
blood pressure had crept up over the years! "The next time
they do that to me," he thought, "I'm not going to give a damn!
If they tell me it's taking too long, well, to hell with them! It
can't be helped and that's that! I'm not a magician, for God's
sake! I'm not going to get a heart attack for them!"

"Roman!"

The voice was cheerful, sprightly, ringing; it came from
only a few feet away. Kittie turned to see walking toward him
at a bouncing clip one of the new analysts who had been hired
this year. His name was Michael Wright. He came from out of
state, as did so many of his newly-recruited colleagues. He was
a tall, lean, well-dressed fellow of twenty-six, and he was very
handsome, having a classically strong chin, straight nose, and
blue eyes that contrasted with his full shock of thick black hair.
Like many of his young colleagues, he had been hired in no
small part on account of his physical attractiveness, for the company hierarchy knew that some of these new recruits might
very well wind up as future executives in very visible positions,
and as much as possible wanted to obviate the embarrassing
possibility of the company being represented one day by fat,
bald, sloppy or otherwise unsightly creatures. And so there
Michael Wright stood, tall and well-built and handsome. He
had no sooner stepped up to Kittie than he said cheerfully,
"Hey, Roman, how are ya?"

Kittie almost shrank back from this assault of loud confidence, but held his place, forced himself to smile and mumbled,
"Good, good. Thanks."

"Hey, your shirt's all wet."

"Yes, I know. I got caught in the rain."

"Wow ... it's *really* wet!"

Kittie blinked.

"Don't you have another shirt or something?" young Wright asked.

"No ... where would I get that?"

"I don't know. Maybe you should go out and buy one?"

"It's alright," Kittie said, shaking his head.

"Oh ... well ... Hey, listen, I need a favor," the young man said, and held out a list of needed information. "Think you could print these out for me?"

"Sure," Kittie said, taking the list.

"Mind if I wait here?"

"No, that's fine," said the much-minding Kittie. He watched the analyst take a single step back to a row of low file cabinets against the wall, and half sit on, half stand against it, his legs a little apart and at a steep angle before him as he folded his arms and watched Kittie work.

Perhaps because he was self-conscious about looking over Kittie's shoulder, Michael Wright asked, "So what've you been up to? Do anything interesting over the weekend?"

"No."

"Just got some rest, huh?"

Kittie smiled and nodded. A little box came up on his screen, asking for a password, which he typed in; and in another second his display showed a partial listing of a hundred folders.

Then Wright said, "Hey, Roman, could I ask you something?"

Without turning around, Kittie said, "Sure."

"How old are you?"

"That's a strange question. Personal, isn't it?"

Wright laughed a little, "Oh, not really. I was just curious."

Kittie would have preferred not to answer but he said, "Forty-three."

"Forty-three.... Mmmmm."

Kittie wondered what was meant by the "Mmmmm." Somehow he could tell that Wright, standing just a few inches behind him, was looking at him, considering him.

"I had you pegged for a little older," Wright said.

"No, no," Kittie said, shaking his head and not taking his eyes off his screen, "forty-three."

"How long you been here?"

"Nine years."

"Woooooaaaa.   Nine years?"   Wright made a vague whistling sound. It irritated Kittie to no end. "I didn't know people lasted that long in this place. I've only been here six months and I've already seen two people get canned. Nine years ... well. I'll bet you've seen a lot of people come and go, eh?"

"A few," Kittie said, minimizing the dozens he had seen come and go over the years: sitting around him one day and gone the next.

"But you beat 'em all out, eh?"

"You could say that," Kittie responded.

"Well, I can't say I envy you," Wright said, and then he lowered his voice—it became confidential—as he added, "I don't see why anyone would stay here nine years, or even two. Let me tell you something, I can see where I'd be going in this place, namely, nowhere. They're *very* cheap here, Roman. You know? *Very cheap.* They take advantage of people. They work you to death, and what do they give you in return? Not much. They don't appreciate you. They don't take care of you. They just wear you down. That's not a place *I* want to stay in. No, a year at most, just for the experience, just for the resume, and that's it for me—I'm outa here." Wright gave a half-laughing, half-huffing sound, expressive of disgust or contempt, and wound up, "I may be dumb but I'm not stupid."

Kittie said nothing in return; he was tapping away on the keyboard. He was conscious that the young man, who stood just behind his right shoulder, was still looking at him, still considering him, and then heard him say:

"You know, Roman ... maybe you ought to get out of here."

At the remark Kittie felt his throat tighten a little, but he said easily enough, "And go where?"

"Anywhere. You have skills, experience. You could get something else. If you ask me, staying here for nine years is kinda crazy unless you're making a *lot* of money."

"It pays the bills."

"Yeah, but, c'mon ... *nine* years? I mean, really—you don't want to be here *all* your life, do you?"

Though outwardly calm, Kittie bristled, clenched his teeth a little, and poked at his keyboard harder. But he was only irritated because he knew that Wright had spoken the simple truth. For the last ten, fifteen, twenty years he had been sitting behind desks, no more than a harried clerk despite whatever "title" he happened to hold; with each passing year growing older, fatter, tireder; and having to show for it, after so many years— what? A dumpy apartment in Queens and high blood pressure! How was it that young Wright realized the value of his youth and vigor, and was not about to let anyone or anything dupe him into expending it to so little purpose? How was it that he was so wise, so clear-seeing, so early in his life? Kittie could not help regretting that he had not been the same way when he was that age.

He printed out the reports Wright had requested and handed them over to him. "Here you are."

"Great." The young man looked them over briefly, nodding every now and then to see exactly what he wanted. "Great," he said again. "Can you do me a favor and email them to me, too?"

"Sure."

"Thanks, Roman! See you later!"

Kittie was just beginning to attend to the other requests that had come in over the email system when the head of the department, Mr. Coro, came walking toward him. He was a robust, distinguished looking man of fifty years of age who had only last week gotten back from his vacation, a three-week romp through Switzerland and Italy. He had taken along his wife and two teenage children. Aside from his vacation he nearly lived in the office, routinely putting in sixty hours a week, and often coming in on weekends. He rarely came out onto the floor unless it was to make a general announcement about something affecting the department or company, or unless he wished to speak to someone in particular; and it was obvious that now he wanted to speak to Kittie, whom he was walking toward.

"Roman," he said, when he reached his underling, "how are you?" But the friendly greeting rang false; it was merely a preliminary to the real reason of his visit. "I need to speak to you a moment. Could you come into my office?"

"Sure," Kittie said, hurriedly slipping his feet into his shoes and standing.

"Your shirt's all wet," Mr. Coro said, apparently just noticing it.

"Yes, I know. I got caught in the rain this morning."

Mr. Coro said nothing more about it. The two men walked down the aisle of desks, the one tall, his gait gliding, sure, the other shorter, stouter, one of his shoes squeaking a little due to the moisture in its sole. Kittie had no idea what Mr. Coro wanted to speak to him about—unless it was about his lateness. Somehow he must have found out about it.

On reaching his office Mr. Coro opened the door for Kittie to walk in, and once they were both inside he said:

"Take a seat, Roman."

Kittie did so. He watched, a little apprehensively, as his boss walked around to his chair behind his desk and sat down. There were folders laid out before him. He opened one of them and took up a bound copy of one of the company's presentation documents, saying:

"Roman, this is a copy of an acquisition analysis put together for Dorman Tech Products. I believe you were working with Shelly Pang on this last week—weren't you?"

"Uh ..." Roman shook his head, uncertainly. He worked with so many people throughout the course of a week, and no sooner worked with them than forgot about them, that he couldn't be sure. He certainly knew who Shelly Pang was, a small, nervous, imperious Vietnamese woman who always emailed her requests with "URGENT!" in big red letters, and who, when she actually came to him, would wait beside him tapping her foot impatiently: an utterly unpleasant woman who in a perfect world would have been strangled in a dark alley a long time ago. He replied that he recalled working with her on something, but as to specifically what—

"Yes, you did, you were working with her on this," Mr. Coro said, interrupting him as he held up the document and gave it a little shake. "The problem is that a lot of the information you gave her was mistaken. It was wrong—old—no longer current. You were looking in the wrong place; you pulled up *last year's* report. That means that when she went into the meeting with the client, carrying this document, she didn't have the facts she needed, and all her work, not to mention the client's time, was wasted. I want you to take a look at this." He threw the document on the front of his desk where it landed with a slapping sound and slid a few inches toward Kittie, who duly reached out and took it up.

On nearly every other page Mr. Coro had circled the wrong things in red ink, and beside each of these circles would be two or three gashes of exclamation points, as though to scream out, "Here! Here! Here!" Kittie flipped through one page after another, apparently examining the errors but really just in order to gain some time to think of what to say in response. For there was no question that all these things that Mr. Coro had found and circled *were* errors, some of them even quite obvious, since clearly inappropriate dates were right beside them. Kittie couldn't imagine how he could have been so distracted as not to have noticed them. He thought about blaming the IT people for having shifted about and renamed directories, but that had happened six months ago, not last week, and, besides, previous upsets of the database couldn't excuse that kind of flagrant carelessness.

"Well?" Mr. Coro asked.

"Yes ... I see ..."—still looking down at the document, still flipping a page here and there. "I could have corrected these pretty quickly—"

"That's not the point. The point is that that's the information you gave to one of the analysts of the firm, and a very important analyst, I might add. Roman," he continued, shaking his head and now looking at Kittie with an air of warning, "this is not the first time you've made a mistake, though it's probably the biggest one. A few months ago you worked with Stan Bernstein down in Healthcare and told him the information he was looking for didn't exist when in fact it did, as he found out when he went looking for it himself. He was pretty upset about that, and needless to say I had to hear about it from his managing director. Before that you were assigned to help Emily Waring in International Mergers. She was new with the company and asked you to look over a final draft of her document to make sure nothing was out of standard, but there were a lot of things you didn't catch. I distinctly remember that one of the footnotes was in 10 point when it should have been in 9.5 point, and one of the index pages was out of margin by at least two tenths of an inch. Two tenths of an inch, Roman! I know—I measured it myself! Roman," he said, shaking his head, and looking at his underling now with grave eyes in which lurked the hint of a threat, "you've been with us long enough to know that success in our department depends on how much we're willing to strive for excellence. Excellence, Roman! That's the key to success in this department and in the company in general. We don't settle for second best here. We can't afford to. I have to know that I have the absolutely best people backing me up in this department—people who won't make big mistakes. Because I'm very busy myself, Roman: I can't be watching everybody every minute of the day to make sure they're doing their job properly; no, I have to be confident in their excellence also—understand? Now, I need to ask of you—to *demand* of you—that in the future you will be very, *very* careful with your work. I want you to check and recheck the information you're handing out. I realize that you get a lot of requests during the course of the day, and that sometimes you're under some pressure, but that's no excuse for getting sloppy. If you find that the end of the day's come and you need more time to finish your work, then I suggest that you just stay a little later and do it properly. It's worth staying another half hour to make sure things get done right. Well ... that's really all I wanted to say. I hope you understand how important all this is ..."

"Of course," Kittie answered, nodding.

During the course of Mr. Coro's speech—for it really had been a speech rather than part of a conversation—Kittie had felt wave after wave of heat pass over his face as, from one minute to the next, he flushed with embarrassment. He especially felt the rash around his neck grow a little warmer.

"Well, that's all Roman," Mr. Coro said, getting up from his chair.

"Yes, yes ... thanks," Kittie said, nodding, getting up, then leaving the room, hating himself for having uttered the word "thanks" as though he were grovelingly, servilely grateful for having been reprimanded.

When he returned to his desk, all his coworkers glanced at him, some more intently than others. They were all curious about why he had been called into the Department Supervisor's office. Half of them were sure it was for a negative reason while the other half thought it might be for something less ominous and more routine. Kittie could not bring himself to make eye contact with anyone around him, knowing that something in his expression or manner would give away the fact that he had been taken to task. For the next twenty minutes he had to make a conscious effort to calm his nerves, telling himself, "Alright, it's over, just calm down ... it's in the past, calm down ... it's not going to happen again ... calm down ... relax ... your blood pressure!"

But it was hard to relax when the day was, already, turning into its usual busy one. Already an ever-growing list of emails was awaiting him, and at least half of them had the words "ASAP" or "Urgent!" or "High Priority" in the subject line. Several of the senders had no sooner sent their messages than they called him on the phone to make sure that he had received them: a small red light on Kittie's telephone was blinking in notification of voice mail. He felt obliged to call back as soon as possible. "Yes, I'll get right on that," Kittie would tell this one. "Yes, I'm going to that one next," he would tell another. "That should be finished in just a few minutes," he would assure yet another. He worked as quickly as he could and always checked his work twice; sometimes, his ears still ringing with Mr. Coro's reprimand, he doubted himself and checked it three times. The last thing he needed was another excuse for Mr. Coro to call him into his office, and somehow he knew that if it did happen again it would be the last time, that he would be fired, and as much as he hated his job he hated still more the insecurity of joblessness and the intimidating, abasing, humiliating process of looking for work. Just the thought of it seemed to lay a leaden pall over his heart.

By three in the afternoon Kittie was already mentally tired. He had been looking up information like a demon, training all his concentration on folders and facts and figures, checking, then rechecking, the items he looked up and sent out. He wanted nothing better than to go into some dark, soundless room and sit there in absolute peace and quiet in order to recruit his mental vitality. In the past he had done just that: walked about the floor looking for an unused conference room and gone inside and closed the door behind him, sitting there with his head back, his eyes closed, allowing his mind to go blank, or to drift in healing reverie, then eating the lunch that he usually brought to the office with him—buying it in Manhattan was so expensive, after all. But on account of his doctor's visit that morning he hadn't had time to pack a lunch and so he decided to go out for it. Besides, it had turned into a nice day: from out of the windows on the side of the office he could see the mostly blue sky. He slipped on his shoes. They weren't completely dry and had a cool dampness to them, but they were wearable. Before leaving his desk he put a note on his computer monitor: "Be back in one hour"—followed by the time.

Outside a sea change in the weather had indeed taken place. It was hard to believe that had it been so darkly tumultuous several hours earlier for now the sky was bright and the air pleasantly cool. Fifth Avenue was crowded with people who were taking advantage of the suddenly fine weather.

Kittie went to a hole-in-the-wall deli on East 16th Street and bought the cheapest thing he could find: a bagel with cream cheese. He would have liked a hero sandwich, and perhaps even a container of soup, but he couldn't justify those prices to himself. "I could make five sandwiches and a whole pot of soup for that kind of money," quickly-calculating Kittie quietly quipped to himself.

"Want something to drink with that?" the man behind the counter asked, slipping the white-papered bagel into a bag.

"No, thanks," cost-conscious Kittie cooed.

He headed off to Broadway intending to eat his bagel in Union Square Park. A farmer's market was in full swing there. Small to mid-sized trucks of farmers from Pennsylvania, New Jersey, and upstate New York had parked along the northern and western edge of the park. Fresh produce was displayed in bushels on the ground or in great bunches on long tables, while baked goods, individually packaged in clear plastic wrap, rose in little piles on paper plates or in wicker baskets. Those who had driven these trucks, who had come to sell here, were clearly not from the city: they were plain, sturdy-looking folk, who wore simple, utilitarian clothing, usually jeans and buttoned-up shirts. The women especially stood out as rural characters on account of their lack of jewelry and makeup, which after all would be rather ludicrous in the business of picking squash or making cheese. Still holding his bag with the bagel, Kittie walked along the tables and looked at the items offered for sale and which often looked quite good. There were whole wheat breads, homemade pies and torts, muffins made with cranber-

ries and raisins, herb-flavored cheeses, and of course fruits and
vegetables, baskets of squash and corn, piles of watermelon and
cantaloupe, trays of strawberries, blueberries, raspberries.
Nearly everything had a handwritten label before it, proclaiming
it "All Natural" or "100% Organic" or "Homemade," along with a
price. The city-dwellers strolling through the market gathered
before these displays, their eyes goggling with excited pleasure;
and if they had come in twos or threes they oohed and aahed
and exchanged bubbling comments about how good, how fresh,
how delicious, how wonderful everything looked; acting for all
the world as though they had never before seen a radish or a
bran muffin.

        Kittie came upon an upstate farmer selling apples and
cider. Baskets of mackintosh and red and golden delicious apples were placed all around a table, which in turn had been set
up before the open back of his truck. Kittie would not have
given any of this a second glance were it not that he happened
to see the farmer himself—and was amazed at how much this
man resembled him, so much so that they might have been fra-
ternal twin brothers. He was just as short, just as balding, and
his round face was, point by point, similarly plain. The only significant difference was that his stocky frame was solid from
farm work, not, like Kittie's, flabby from years of sitting at a
desk. He was standing in the back of his truck, quickly and
easily taking down heavy bushels of apples that had been
stacked one atop the other. ("Cardio," Kittie said to himself.
"Resistance training. Low blood pressure.") He would place each
bushel on the lowered gate at the back of the truck, and his wife
would in turn put the bushel on the ground. She was about
forty years old, a little stout, and not especially attractive, but
there was something touching in the way she exerted herself to
help her husband. Just then she called out, "Hey, Teddy!" and in
another moment her son came walking around to her.

        "Help your father with these bushels," she told him.

        The boy was perhaps sixteen years of age, and in him the
mystery of genetics had worked unexpectedly positive results,
for unlike either of his parents he was tall, lithe, and attractive.
He leaped onto the back of the truck with the swift, liquid movement of some sleek young animal. His father instructed him to
continue taking down the bushels, giving him a loving pat on

the shoulders as he did so. The boy nodded and immediately started working. When the father jumped down from the truck to help his wife on street level he happened to see Kittie looking at him. Kittie felt as though he'd been caught doing something illicit, shameful; he was embarrassed, gave a brief, nonchalant smile, and hurried away. He headed into the interior of the park, intending to eat his bagel on a bench there.

He was feeling uneasy; then, he realized, what he felt was sad. It was because of that farmer who looked so much like himself and into whose life he had had a glimpse. No doubt it was a life harder than Kittie's own; but it was fuller, and even, despite the undoubtedly isolated rurality in which he and his family lived, more exciting. Just then he would have given anything to trade places with that man. He had a quick fantasy about leaving New York, abandoning his apartment, selling all his stuff, and running off to some opposite end of the world, to some ranch or farm and becoming a hand on it; working in the soil; planting, growing, building, harvesting; a fresh-aired, hard-working, outdoors life. But the fantasy collapsed when he considered that one had to be inured to that kind of exertion from one's earliest years. You didn't go from looking up financial reports one day to heaving bushels full of produce the next. And to do it *all* day?—him, at his age?

"Oh, Roman, don't be ridiculous," he told himself. "That's not a career."

On account of the downpour earlier in the day, the moist soil of the park gave off a fragrance of earth that was detectable even above the exhaust fumes of the ten thousand cars round about. Birds were singing in the trees. Most of the intermittent benches along the walkways were already occupied. Like Kittie, many people were taking advantage of the now fine weather to enjoy the outdoors. Often they were eating something, either as a break from their shopping or as a late lunch of the kind Kittie was having. The ubiquitous pigeons often strutted at a short distance from them, watching them, waiting for the kindness of a thrown scrap, which no sooner landed than they all darted toward it, the fastest among them plucking it up and swallowing it in a single gulp.

Kittie finally found a bench where he might sit down. Only one other person was on it: a young woman. She was eating a sandwich, half of which lay on a piece of white waxed paper spread over her lap. When he sat down on the opposite side of the bench she gave him the briefest of glances before turning her eyes back outward, to the park, as she chewed leisurely. She was very pretty, with red hair, a fine fair complexion, and the lightest of eyes—whether blue or green he hadn't been able to tell for sure. From what he could see out of the corner of his eye, her legs were lean and somewhat muscular, bespeaking a body equally well-proportioned and fit. Yes, she was very pretty.

He took his bagel and cream cheese out of the paper bag and began eating. He was however extremely conscious of the woman sitting beside him. He would have liked nothing better than to get to know who she was, to introduce himself to her and talk to her. He fantasized about their taking an immediate liking to each other and so beginning a romance. Yes, perhaps she was the love of his life just waiting to happen. Wasn't it possible? Kittie didn't disbelieve in fate. You could meet your future wife anywhere—at work, at the grocery store, sitting on a park bench. Of course the sticking point was how to make an overture without seeming crass. Perhaps he could comment on the weather? But what if she just nodded and smiled and turned away? It wouldn't be possible to follow up with anything equally casual. Then he wondered if he might ask her for the time and, as soon as she told him what it was, follow up by mentioning how unfortunate it was that he—she too perhaps?—couldn't remain out here long but had to get back to work. Surely that would get a conversation going and would be the perfect lead-in to the suggestion of a date. "Why don't we go for lunch together some afternoon?" he heard and saw himself suavely asking her in the rosily-lit theater of his mind. "That would be wonderful!" she said, her eyes, her smile, her manner sweet, and then she herself suggesting, "How about tomorrow?"

A pigeon landed in front of him. The animal strutted back and forth, ever turning its head in his direction, blinking, cooing, begging for a handout. Pitying Kittie took a little crust of his bagel and flung it to the creature, who plucked it up and swallowed it whole. From the corner of his eye he noticed that the girl at the other side of the bench had turned her head in his direction. She had watched him feed the bird. The thought that his kindness to animals was arousing her interest in him, or at least her admiration, prompted him to feed the pigeon another crust of bread. Two more pigeons gathered around, then another two. Kittie glanced at the woman and smiled, as though to say, "Aren't they nice?"—looking away when he saw that her expression was not especially pleased. He threw off yet another few crusts of his bread, this time talking to the pigeons, saying, "Here you go ..."

In the trees nearby some thirty more pigeons had been keenly focused on their luckier fellows who had happened upon a feeding, and at the sight of yet more edibles flying through the air they reckoned that they had better try to get some for themselves. They all took off together and dive-bombed toward Kittie's bench. By the dozens, in swiftly succeeding waves of gray and brown fluttering wings, they landed on the walkway before the bench and urgently strutted about looking for morsels of food. They drew close not only to Kittie but also to the other human being there—the woman sitting only a few feet away from him.

Nothing could have repulsed her more. To her mind pigeons were only somewhat less disgusting than subway rats. She sprang up from her seat with a loud, "Oh!" At her sudden movement and exclamation Kittie's first thought was that she had dropped something, and he was quite prepared to jump to her assistance and gallantly pick it up for her. Instead she was standing up and looking at him with her pretty features twisted into a mask of anger: the brows were knit, the eyes hard and accusatory.

"What's wrong with you!" she snapped. "Can't you see I'm eating! Damn it! Go somewhere else if you want to feed the damn pigeons!"—and she turned away and stomped off, leaving behind her, like a living presence, the dreadful air of her hateful contempt.

Kittie sat there as one overwhelmed, as one cowed by a catastrophe. What had been a delicious, warm glow his heart had gone dark and cold and painful. An initial impulse to apologize, to make amends, raised him to his feet, as though he would set off after her, but instead he stood there, choking on a stab of pain. He watched her fast-walking figure hurry away, grow smaller, mingle into the distant crowds, and then he looked about him guiltily, a little fearfully, as though there might have been witnesses to what had just happened; and he was relieved to see there weren't. He sat back down on the bench. He was still holding half of his bagel and cream cheese but he suddenly found himself without an appetite for it. The dozens of pigeons still milling about at his feet continued to gurgle and coo, to strut back and forth, watching him, watching him, waiting for him to throw more. Kittie almost hated them now. He had an urge to lash out at them, jump into them, kicking, stomping as he went, only to understand how unfair it would be, how it would solve nothing, make up for nothing, and only reduce his dignity further in his own eyes by taking out his anger on brute beasts.

He put the half-eaten bagel on the ground just beneath the bench and walked off. As he soon as he had taken a few steps away, the pigeons who had been milling about in the hope of a few crumbs found themselves offered a feast. They scrambled over one another in a dash toward it, converging on it as though they were sucked into a vortex, forming a grayish-purple hubbub of flittering wings, wildly bobbing heads, and talons that pushed and scratched. Perched in trees or on the ledges of buildings round about, other pigeons spotted this congress and wasted no time in joining it; they flew or dove landward at great speed, coming in by the dozens, by the score, landing sometimes headlong amid their brethren. In seconds a hundred of them vied with one another for the opportunity of a peck, and so dire was this competition—so determined and ravenous—that in only a minute there was nothing at all left of what the man had left them. The pigeons themselves seemed to wonder at how such a large chunk of food could have been consumed so quickly for they continued to strut about the area with a bewildered air, looking about intently, and at one another suspiciously, as though the rest of it had to be hidden away somewhere.

Kittie had gone out on his lunch break with at least the pleasant anticipation of time away from his desk, but now he returned to it in a much more somber and oppressed mood. A few people noticed this in him but did not inquire into it, thinking that whatever was bothering him was probably something minor and at any rate none of their business. He resumed his work as a "Research Analyst," though when he first sat down he just looked at his computer screen for a full minute without moving. He didn't speak except to answer the phone and even then his conversations were brief and without the polite good cheer that ordinarily would have characterized his tone of voice.

In the next row over from Kittie's sat a man in his mid- to late-twenties who rarely spoke to anyone except to say good morning at the beginning of the day or good night at the end of it. Several times Kittie had tried to engage him in conversation, if only for the sake of alleviating boredom, but trying to talk to him had been like pulling teeth. He was a social moron. While at work he had no time for anyone or anything but his work. He was clearly ambitious in the corporate sense of the word, putting in long hours—upwards of seventy a week. He knew that if he could stick to that grueling schedule long enough, if he could outperform everyone else in his row, in this room, indeed on the whole floor, his effort was bound to be recognized and he'd be promoted to a better, more lucrative group and perhaps even win a prestigious title of some kind. Now he was approached by one of his colleagues, a young woman of about the same age as himself. She was a frail, mousy-looking thing wearing a trim, conservative business suit which hid whatever curves her body had (it didn't have many) and made her look mannish. She had graduated cum laude from Ohio State University. One could just imagine how proud her parents were of her.

When she reached her colleague she didn't smile, didn't ask him how he was, didn't engage in the least whisper of friendly human interaction, saying, instead:

"Can I go over some number with you on the Borkland account?"

The young man nodded, yes.

"I just want to go over their latest financials with you—just to make sure we have the same things. I think there are some discrepancies in the European and Asian markets data."

Kittie did not watch them as they consulted together—at least, not outrightly; but he could not help occasionally glancing up at them, or seeing them through his peripheral vision, and certainly he heard their comments to each other, since they were only a few feet away.

"Is that a $455K in cell BB567 or is it 456?" the woman

asked as, squinting as she referred to the long printed spread-sheet she was holding. She referred back and forth from it to the monitor on her colleague's desk. Even with her glasses she was a little nearsighted and so had to squint hard

"No, it's definitely a *five*," he said.

"Oh ... good! Five!"—she marked it off on her sheet. "Alright ... now ... let's see ... go to cell DF533. 998,009.09. Is that what you have?"

She waited; she had to. It took time for her colleague to find the individual cell among ten thousand. He tapped on the keyboard and leaned in close to the monitor to see the results of his search, then, putting a forefinger on the screen, said:

"There it is! Yes! 998,009.09!"

"Great!"

—It went on for the next fifteen minutes: two human creatures in the full flush of their young maturity, both having all of life and its wondrous possibilities before them, putting the whole force of minds, for yet another day, into making sure that a five was not a six, a seven not a two, a two not a one. Their long and expensive education had enabled them to be thus meticulous not only for a few minutes at a time but for days, weeks, even months on end. Each time they found an error, or confirmed an accuracy, they looked and murmured at each other with the greatest sense of accomplishment. They couldn't have been prouder of themselves if they had been medical researchers who had discovered the cure for a disease....

But even they, for all their training, patience, and dedication, could not tackle the monstrous spreadsheet before them; it was simply too big and they realized they needed help. The woman straightened herself up from her stooping posture, heaved a sigh, and glanced about her. Her eyes alighted on Kittie, just opposite her.

"Are you busy?" she asked.

"Excuse me?" Kittie said, looking up.

"We need a little help here. Are you busy?"

"Well ... not at this very moment, no," naively honest Kittie replied.

"Great!"

She came over to him with her printout. It was four inches thick. She had gotten it printed out in the IT Department, since they still had a large, wide-carriage dot-matrix printer, which could accommodate many columns of the immense spreadsheet; even so the print was tiny and the rows so close together that one had to look hard to distinguish between them. She plunked the printout down on Kittie's desk, saying, proudly:

"You've never seen something like this before!"—and she laughed in a little mousy way as though she were about to reveal something wonderful to him.

She explained this was a printout of a decade's worth of transactions of Borkland Industries along with various analyses from several competing financial institutions. It was being used for a very important job, one that the CEO himself was involved in. Again with an air of pride she said that she and several other people had spent months accumulating this data. Yet despite their best and indefatigable efforts a few "inconsistencies" had crept into a certain large section of it. Heaven only knew how they had happened. "My machine crashed a few times— maybe that had something to do with it." Anyway, there were about three-hundred rows' worth of data that had to be checked against the original material, all of which was located in her directory, the location of which she proceeded to write down for Kittie. She stood over him as he opened it. There were hundreds of files, all of disparate format and degrees of legibility.

"Now," she said, opening the thick printout in the middle and flipping through the pages till she found the place she wanted, "these are the rows you need to get through. The company name is here, on the right. Sometimes it's abbreviated, so you'll have to kind of figure out what it is. So, you just have to check from here"—she made a checkmark beside the row—"to here"—and she flipped through page after page and after page, encompassing thousands of figures.

"All those?" Kittie asked.

"Well, it doesn't all have to be done today."

Kittie felt a little relieved.

"But I will need it by tomorrow afternoon."

"That's not much time," Kittie said, at once anxious again. "There's so much to do. And I have my own work to do—"

"Oh," she said, and looked at Kittie for a moment as though she were in a quandary. Then: "I'll go talk to Mr. Coro. Maybe he can get you to work with me on this project. It's pretty important."

"But if it's your project, isn't it your job?" Kittie wanted to ask.

Of course, he wanted to ask or comment on many things throughout the day, but again, as always, didn't.

Five minutes later his phone rang. It was Mr. Coro. Sure enough he told Kittie that his usual work had been temporarily transferred to someone else and that he was to work on the "Borkland Project," which, he emphasized, took "top priority"; indeed, he said it was "urgent." Kittie was on the point of objecting that there was so much to do that he was sure he couldn't finish it. He also wanted to impress on the manager how ill-suited he was for this kind of thing—he wasn't good with numbers. When there were so many of them they passed before his eyes in a blur of meaninglessness. But still conscious of the talking to Mr. Coro had given him earlier in the day, he knew his objection to working with numbers could only be regarded as lack of "excellence" in an industry dealing with facts and figures.

Poor Kittie! The moment he began working on the spreadsheet he knew that it was going to be a disaster, that he just couldn't do it. The numbers, in their tiny, multitudinous, progression across and up and down the page made his eyes glaze over; picking one out from the other was for him like trying to find the distinguishing features of a single ant in a jet-black, almost oily mass of writhing thousands. Nevertheless he set himself to the task. He told himself he had to try and do the best he could. It took him ten minutes just to find the first correct source file for the first row of numbers, and even more time to find the place from which the figures had come. It was clear that in each instance the data had been drawn from places not easily intuited. It was an hour before he had finished checking the first row (all the numbers were right). The tedium was enormous; he thought something inside him would burst. When he had finished that one row, and saw it was nearing five o'clock, he flipped through the succeeding forty large pages of printout with their hundreds of rows, their thousands of numbers ... impossible ... impossible ...

His phone rang again. It was Mr. Coro. He was just calling to find out how things were going, what progress Kittie was making. Again he impressed on his underling the importance of the job.   The Borkland Project was one of the biggest the firm now had; even the senior partners were "in" on this one.   "So Roman, please, just check your work.   We can't have any mistakes—not one!"

"Of course, of course," Kittie said.

His mouth was dry.   He looked up at the clock across the room: a quarter to five.   In the next fifteen minutes he wouldn't even be able to find the information for the next row of numbers, let alone check them.   He could stay late, of course; work all night; but even if he did so how much more could he really do?   Eight more rows?   Maybe ten?   Even assuming he gained some proficiency in the matter, it wasn't likely he could do more than a couple of pages.   Even then he'd have to stay here at his desk till two or three in the morning; and then how could he be expected to show up the next day?   He didn't have the energy for it.   He didn't have the will for it.   Just then he was so, so tired of trying and struggling....

He wondered if he should call Mr. Coro and frankly confess his unsuitability for the job.   Yes, he would use that word, "unsuitable"—it was so much more gentle, objective, clinical and therefore unanswerable than the forthright word "incapable," even if in the end it came down to the same thing.   He would explain that his character was unsuitable to this kind of work, that therefore he couldn't possibly finish it on time, and couldn't even guarantee that what he did finish would be accurate.

Oh, but it was impossible to say such a thing.   It would have been an admission of his incompetence, a substantiation of Mr. Coro's doubts about him as an employee in the firm, in a field, in a world that demanded "excellence."

His anxiety over the matter recalled to Kittie a similar sensation he had known earlier that day when the doctor had told about his high blood pressure.   Then his thoughts skipped to the farmer in the park, and the young woman whom he might have been in love with but who had yelled at him instead. Then he thought he about young Wright, whom he could almost hear again saying, "I can see where things are heading, namely, nowhere."   He remembered his father, the good, upstanding family man, the commonsensical, practical man, who had been so responsible and played by the rules and done everything right, and had left the world a doddering human wreck, leaving behind not even the legacy of one remarkable thing.

"I'm going to fly the fastest jets in the world!" Kittie heard himself saying from out of the past, remembering his exact words. "Do you know how fast they go now? Mach 3! I'm going to go at Mach 3!"

"Oh, Roman, don't be ridiculous. That's not a living."

—Ah, to have ever taken any kind of advice or guidance from such a man!

Kittie pursed his lips and nodded a few times as one does when some sudden illumination of retrospect enables him to have an insight into, or even explain completely, some long-standing question about his past. In this case however the revelation had less to do with the past than with the future. As though the gauzy or translucent curtains of a stage had finally been pulled apart, revealing a set which before that moment had been too indistinct to appreciate or pass judgment upon; or as though the morning sun had come up and revealed in sharp outline a landscape that till then had been uncertain, amorphous in the obfuscating gloom of night; so it was that Kittie, looking down at the thick printout and its hundreds of thousands of small-printed numbers, then looking at the rest of his desk, then shifting his gaze up to his coworkers at their desks, as some of them would be for hours yet, working overtime, silent, sedulous, sedentary, so dreadfully intent;—so it was that he seemed to see something in and beyond all of these things that brought a strange, an unwonted expression to his face; an expression that was quietly sure and self-satisfied, and the like of which might have been seen on the face of a man who has received, just in time, a liberating revelation.

He pushed away from his desk, leaned back in his chair, and let out a deep, relieved, resolved breath. He looked across the office through the windows to the still blue sky, and his lips trembled into a faint, knowing smile. He got up from his desk and left the floor as nonchalantly as he had left it thousands of times before. But this time it wasn't to leave for lunch or to go the to men's room or even to go home. To be sure, he went into the hallway and pressed one of the buttons for the elevator; but this time it was the button to go up, not down.

Fortunately for Kittie he had missed another visit by Mr. Coro, who, a few minutes later, was standing at his desk. He had come by to check on Kittie's progress with the Borkland Project, to impress upon him again the importance of accuracy. He had even prepared another little speech about excellence.

"Anyone seen Roman?" he asked, looking down the row of his employees, and watching as they all looked up and shook their heads, no.

"He was here just a minute ago," answered someone sitting at a nearby desk.

"Well, when he gets back, tell him to give me a call, will you?"

"Hey!"

—The exclamation came from someone at the other end of the floor, in the "Loans Department," which consisted of ten desks against the windows overlooking Fifth Avenue. He had had shouted out the word less perhaps in order to gain attention than to vent his own shock. It was clear that something had shaken him to the core: his eyes were wide open, unblinking, almost disbelieving as he stood looking out over the floor of his coworkers. "I just saw someone go down!" he said. "Someone jumped!"

Like a clarion call to arms, the employees on that side of the office scrambled up from their desks and hurried to the windows. They pressed themselves against glass and craned their necks as they tried to see what was happening on the sidewalk thirty floors below. At so great a height they could not see anything distinctly, but they could perceive the outline of a body on the sidewalk, its arms and legs spread-eagle. Dozens of pedestrians were running toward it; and a few of these no sooner reached it than they ran in the opposite direction, then ran back from where they had come, as though driven to insensible panic by the horrific sight they had beheld. They shouted out for someone, anyone, to call the police, to call for an ambulance, to get some help for a man who had apparently fallen out of a window. But there was no reason for them to have been so urgent about this, nor should any of them have been so upset as they were. For the fact was that Roman Kittie was at peace, having finally followed his heart and flown.

HAUNTED

I

Of all the places for an artist to live, New York City is one of the worst: its filth, its congestion, its crime, its putrid stinking summertime heat, above all its rush and scurry for money (a degrading mentality referred to as "career mindedness") eventually grinds down the coarsest spirit, and is absolutely lethal to any that happens to be of finer stuff. Even on the most basic, visual level it is depressing: it is all ugly asphalt, gray granite, dull red brick:—cement and glass and steel;—substances hard, inert, dead, and without life or hope of life. It cannot even provide a healthful breath of air because its atmosphere is laden with the poisons of a hundred thousand cars and trucks. Nor has it the quiet that settles the nerves, conduces to introspection, and assists creativity: on the contrary every hour, every minute of its day is fragmented and degraded with the honk of horns, the whir of engines, and the screams of sirens. Always there is movement, bustle, an interminable purpose and cross-purpose as millions of people hurry and scrape in order to make their livings; pushing themselves through another exhausting, alienating, demoralizing day in order to wring out of their urban life some shred of security; which is to say (for this is what it really amounts to) to pick the next fellow's pocket under the conscience-soothing rubric of "commerce." In time this kind of mule-headed existence quite undermines one's better humanity; obliterates any noble conception of achievement; leaves one incapable of judging life in any other than the mean-spirited terms of dollars and cents. Thus at the end of their lives so many here wallow in the regret that if only they had "worked harder," or had gotten a few "lucky breaks," they might have amounted to "more": might have had nicer cars, owned a home or perhaps several properties, and had the kind of "comfortable" retirement they had dreamed about, that is to say, the ability to spend a small fortune idling away a mindless leisure (perhaps traveling around the world in order to gawk at monuments and feed on strange dishes), or at least the ability to spend the last ten or twenty years of their lives comfortably watching television or otherwise staring into inanity. For some, on the other hand, this sudden realization of life nearly over acts like a tonic slap across the face, snapping them out of the decades-long enchantment of unquestioned values: enabling them to see— often with a start of bewilderment—how they sacrificed the best years of their lives to chase after a chimera, a mirage, a false ideal. In either case they are likely to see New York City as the cause or emblem of their disappointment. And yet who could deny that from afar the city looks magnificent? From a distance its towers, which rise so stately in the daytime, and its lights, which sparkle so enticingly at night, make it seem like a magic kingdom of the sort that dreams are made on. But like certain tropical plants or deep-sea creatures, whose brilliant colors or soothing patterns lure unsuspecting prey into a murderous clutch, so does this city, in its iconic skyline, in its myth, in its show of splendor, attract to itself a constant stream of dreamers, who think that so wondrous-looking a place must answer to a better, higher way of life, and who come here, and struggle and fail here, and add themselves to the human flotsam weltering on its hopeless tides of life.

I have sometimes wished that I had been a businessman;— the owner, say, of a cheese or a shoe store, with every fourth or fifth sale "off the books," the cash discreetly slipped into a tray under the counter;—my tax-free capital accruing by the day. Or perhaps a postal clerk or a public school teacher whose salary was guaranteed to increase with the cost of living, and part of a union that would spread out beneath me a safety net to catch me for the hard fall of old age. But no, I had to choose a different way, the harder, the really impossible path. —Or at least I would self-pityingly think till my common sense reasserted itself and it was clear to me again how it couldn't have been any other way—not for me, not in a million years. Heraclitus had it entirely right.

Resignation to one's fate has at least this to recommend it: your failures are incapable of too much disturbing your equanimity. When you believe things could not have been any other way, there's no point in getting upset about them. In my case this had come to mean an acceptance of my lifelong anonymity as a writer and consequently my chronic poverty. Twenty years of writing had resulted in several novels no one read, or rather (but for me this meant the same thing) which no mainstream publishers would publish. Thus I had come to accept the prospect of my latest effort meeting the same unrecognized and un-remunerated fate. Nevertheless I went through the usual motions of trying to have it published conventionally. As I had done for all my other books, I sent out query letters to three literary agents—only three. That number will probably strike my reader as unusually low, absurdly so if he happens to be another writer who knows that it isn't unusual to send out a dozen or twenty or forty or even more such queries before a book is accepted for representation. But I had never had the heart for that sort of thing—for that marathon of disappointment; besides, my fatalism had always assured me that if three attempts did not succeed, neither would three hundred, and that my only option would be to send my book out into the world with whatever small push I could give it. At any rate, and predictably enough, the first query came back, rejected. A few weeks later the second one did also. As I waited for the third I set about the time-consuming process of readying my novel for print as well as I could when ... the unexpected occurred: a letter with a request to see the whole manuscript. Six weeks later it was accepted for publication, and eight months later it became one of the best-selling novels of its time.

Perhaps it was only when the royalty checks arrived in my mailbox that I was completely convinced I wasn't imagining everything. I had never had so much money before. By the standards of the genuinely wealthy this new income was nothing to get excited about; the less so perhaps because it was likely to decrease rather than increase as time passed and public attention was diverted away from my book to the steady avalanche of new, better-advertised publications. But to me the money seemed a fantastic sum.

And I did what all sensible New Yorkers do the moment they no longer have to worry about keeping a job, the moment they have enough money to improve their lives: I fled the city.

I had always wanted to live in New England. It's a beauti-

ful part of the country, what with its rolling hills, pellucid lakes
and streams, and small towns nestled in soft valleys or cropping
up unexpectedly along winding roads. I was also drawn toward
it by its literary associations and crisp weather. For a whole
month I traveled through Vermont and New Hampshire, driving
and walking by day, staying at hotels and motels by night,
searching for a town in which I thought I might like to live. I
found them by the dozens. They had charmingly staunch An-
glo-Saxon names like Raleigh, Exeter, Chelsea, Fletcher, Fair-
fax, and they were often the picture-postcard epitomes of small-
town America, having shop-lined Main Streets, spired churches
whose bells tolled sleepily on Sunday mornings, and old men—
retired after a lifetime of farming—who sat on porches, smoking
pipes, reading newspapers, and discussing politics with gruff
common sense. There were also resort towns, slow and deserted
during the summer but populated to bursting in the coldest
parts of winter when legions of skiers descended on their nearby
slopes. I went from each to each, always liking the last one a
little more than the one before it, only for a day or two to pass
before bethinking myself that, after all, it wasn't quite right for
me, and so moving on again in search of something better. Finally I had to admit to myself that the problem wasn't without
but within, that though these places were pretty and peaceful,
they would never be *enough*. The beautiful scenery, the temperate summers, the fresh air and slow genteel life would delight
me for a few months, perhaps even a few years, but in time, inevitably, they would leave me unsatisfied. At first I couldn't put
my finger on why this was. Only on returning to New York did
I understand that those small, isolated towns all lacked what I
had grown too used to in the city, namely, the sense of possibility. It is the knowledge that there is always something to do,
somewhere to go, someone to see—even if that someone is only
a stranger. It is knowing that the latest fad or fashion origi-
nated in or quickly made its way there, and could be investigated for oneself rather than speculated about from afar. It is
knowing that even if it's two in the morning, and you're feeling
lonesome, you can always find a place where people are drinking and talking and laughing, and fling yourself into that woozy,
chatty communal mix, and forget your problems for a while.
But when you're out in the country—in the *real* country—you're

on your own and, what's worse, you *know* you're on your own. If you're feeling bad and the night is long, well, then the night is *very* long because you know there will be no distractions from your discomfort till morning, which impatient anticipation makes excruciatingly slow in coming. Though the odds were a hundred to one that I would ever again actually partake of the few good things New York City had to offer, I needed to know they were there, within reach. And yet it was equally true that I couldn't live in it any more. I had just turned forty-three and the diminished patience and energies of my time of life had made loathsome to me the city's dirty bustle and stupid competition. No, I couldn't live in it any more yet I couldn't live hundreds of miles away from it either. I seemed to be in a pickle. Then it occurred to me: What about thirty or forty miles away? —close enough to reach it under an hour by car or public transportation but far enough away that I never had to see it again if I didn't want to? Wouldn't that be the right balance?

"Just tell me when you see something you like."

The woman who said these words was slowly clicking the enter key on her keyboard, each depression bringing up on her monitor a picture of another property, another house, for sale. I pulled up my chair beside hers in the office of Brody Real Estate in Deer Park, Long Island. Her name was Sheila Greenbaum. She was in her early forties, quick-witted, intelligent, and always had about her a tinge of the artificial because she was always too obviously trying to be charming and "young." She had been in the real estate business for over a decade and had done pretty well for herself: she drove a luxury car and had a fulfilled penchant for diamond jewelry. I had come to her real estate agency after searching online for properties in Nassau County, and her company seemed to have a lot of the sort I had been looking for: single homes with a little land around them, yet close to the main highways and railroad stations with access to Manhattan. I had filled out an online form requesting information and it was she who had followed up the inquiry with a telephone call. In that initial interview I had told her what I was interested in and what I thought I could afford. She told me that the properties shown on the web site were not up to date, that she had many others she would be happy to show me, and invited me to go out to see her. And so there we were, sitting side-by-side.

Each time we came to a house I liked she would take her hand away from the keyboard and begin telling me about it. She was an encyclopedia of acreage, square footage, school districts, and community tax rates. She was equally voluble in expatiating on the kind of neighborhood that the house was located in. Unfortunately I always liked best the houses I couldn't afford: the ranch-style house set on four acres of treed land; the Victorian-accented house with its long U-shaped driveway leading up to a peaked and gabled facade; the contemporary home of sleekly curving lines and narrow windows, complete with a pool in the backyard. Mrs. Greenbaum never had to tell me what was out of my price range because I could see it for myself : the prices were always displayed beneath the pictures. Now and then she assured me that if I really wanted this or that property I could always get a larger mortgage because my credit rating was good. She knew that my money had come from writing a book, and undoubtedly had the mistaken notion that whenever I needed more money I could just scribble up another one. She didn't understand—as I did too well—that there might not be another book in me. For all I knew I'd be working behind the counter of a fast food restaurant in a couple of years. Thus I had to make sure that whatever I bought could be maintained on a poor man's salary. And so whenever she suggested that I extend myself financially and go for the better property, I answered, "No, let's see something else."

She had just clicked to the next photo, and it had no sooner come up on her screen than she clicked past it so that it had been no more than a passing blur.

"What was that?" I asked.

"What?"

"You went by one. I didn't see it."

"Oh ... I didn't think you'd be interested in that one."

"Well let's see it."

Something in what had been a natural smile tightened a little as she went back to the previous page. What came up was one of the most charming houses in her portfolio. It was two storied, yet small and compact. A gravel walkway led to the porch before the front door, and its white sashes and shutters stood quaintly out from the light blue of its walls. It had three bedrooms upstairs, a fireplace in the livingroom, and a large kitchen. The back yard, though somewhat narrow, was very long and ended at a stream bordering a bird preserve. But what especially caught my eye was the price: it was absurdly, almost unbelievably low. The property taxes were equally small. I asked Mrs. Greenbaum if there had been some kind of mistake: could that really be what the house was going for? She had been gazing on the screen with what was now a somber expression and only nodded, yes. I asked her if we might not go to see the property. She hesitated a little before saying:

"You know ... you might not be interested in this one."

"Why not?" And then it occurred to me that of course there had to be something wrong with it—that's why it was so cheap. Perhaps the plumbing had to be replaced; perhaps the basement flooded with even small amounts of rain, or the roof leaked, or some essential structural member had been found to be defective. A house that looked fine on the outside might very well be riddled with deficiencies, the repair of which would cause more headaches and cost more money than they were worth. But to my question Mrs. Greenbaum only responded by saying that it had "problems."

"What kind of problems?" I asked. "Maybe I could fix them."

My statement almost made her smile and she shook her head. "I don't think so."

"Well, what?"

It was remarkable how all her charm, all her chatty, enthusiastic pleasantness, faded away and a quiet, distressed, self-absorbed expression took its place. She glanced at her colleagues sitting at their desks throughout the room; she seemed to be grateful that they hadn't been listening to our conversation. Then, turning her eyes back to me, and speaking in a low voice she said:

"It's haunted."

I laughed rather loudly (only then did a few heads turn in our direction) for her statement struck me with the same comedic force as that of a punch line to a well set up joke. I had been waiting to hear he tell me about a flooded basement or the need for a new sewage system and here she was talking about ghosts! I looked at her for a moment critically, cynically, and almost proudly, as though to congratulate her in having pulled off a bit of humor.

But she wasn't smiling. Her somber expression never wavered. She even seemed a little resentful of my light attitude, as though I were mocking her.

"I'm not joking," she said, as deadpan as ever and with a little, emphasizing shake of her head. "The place is haunted."

"That's ridiculous," I returned, still smiling, though, already, coming to believe that she, at least, was serious.

"Two families have lived there in the last two years," she said. "They were both from the city, like you. They both moved out because of the things that went on there."

"Things like what?"

"Just ..."—she shook her head—"... crazy things. Sounds ... things moving ... you know, the usual."

"Mrs. Greenbaum, I don't believe in ghosts."

"They didn't either."

"Did they know about the house before they bought it?"

She nodded, yes. When her company had first acquired the house she had been notified of its "reputation," and had laughed it off. New York State had no law requiring her to disclose such information about "stigmatized properties," as they were called: houses in which terrible things—murders or suicides— had occurred, or which had reputations for "psycho-logical trauma." But her conscience had never allowed her to withhold such facts. From the first she had mentioned it to her clients. At that time she herself hadn't believed in the haunting, and had disclosed the information with a snide, cynical, dismissive air that made it clear she thought it was all nonsense. But the family to which she first sold the house were there only a few days when they reported to her that "things" were happening— reports to which she listened patiently and skeptically. Several times she went over to the place to see for herself what was going on; only to find nothing out of the way but scared faces, and to conclude that the owners suffered from some kind of shared hysteria. She had still doubted their mental health when they fled in the middle of the night. The next day they told her they wouldn't be going back and that she was to try to sell the place for them. It was only after the second owners, a young couple with "their heads on straight," abandoned the property that she came round to believing with a belief as strong as her skepticism had been. "You don't have people giving up their homes, that they've worked so hard for, unless there's something going on," she said. And it was then, when she no longer doubted, that she herself began to "feel" the house wasn't "right." She didn't know exactly what it was; certainly she had never seen anything out of the way; but to her there was something sinister about the place, something that seemed to "take you into it"— whatever that meant.

"Well, *did* something terrible happen in that house or not?" I asked. "*Was* somebody murdered there?"

She shook her head. "Not as far as I know."

"Well, then," I said, raising my brows and giving a shrug of my shoulders as though to say she had just unwittingly proven to herself the opposite of what she believed.

Now, here was the thing about me and ghosts: it wasn't that I didn't believe in them, but that I didn't believe in them in the common way. To my mind they were on par with UFOs: if they existed at all, they had to be very, very rare, and were more suitable as objects of physical and scientific than of philosophical or spiritual speculation. Even supposing that there were instances in which the life force (and how vague even that concept is!) of someone remained on earth after he had died, surely it could not act in the same way as it had done when substantiated in a body and controlled by a mind; rather, it had to be an unfocused, arbitrary, and faint energy incapable of interacting with, much less harming, the self-conscious and much more robust living. Supposing even that the remnant energy, the so-called ghost, *could* drive a puff of air against a door and close it, or make a knocking sound on a wall, or chill a circumference of space—so what? It wouldn't faze me any more than strange distant lights blinking in the night's sky. Besides, one doesn't live in New York City for any length of time without having come across things a hundred times more threatening than ghosts. Something really to be afraid of ? Try riding the E train through Queens at two o'clock in the morning!

"Just for the hell of it," I said, "maybe we can stop by and take a look—would that alright?"

That was exactly what we did, though not after first seeing other, "better" (as Mrs. Greenbaum assured me) houses. These supposedly preferable properties were all within my budget, or obtainable with a manageable mortgage. At each one of them the realtor animatedly talked up its advantages and attractions, encouraged me to "use my imagination" about how it would look once this or that were done to it, and generally tried hard to stoke my enthusiasm. But they were all disappointments to me, for they were either very small, or looked a little ramshackle, or were built so close to other homes that in one instance the walls of my living room were literally no more than eight inches away from the walls of someone else's. Still others were in themselves acceptable but located in bad neighborhoods—just one look around assured me that I would be living among folks who wouldn't think twice about knocking me over the head on a dark night.

"Have you thought about a townhouse?" Mrs. Greenbaum asked, as we drove, finally, to the house I wanted to see.

"No, I haven't. I don't consider townhouses real homes."

"Oh? Why not?"

"Because they're *attached*. I want a *real* house."

She blinked and let out a quick, exasperated breath, as though she had never heard such a thing in her life, but was not willing to argue the matter. Appropriately, she was entirely complaisant as a businesswoman and sought to cultivate the good graces of her clients.

We once again got onto the Long Island Expressway, rode eastward another twenty minutes, then turned off onto a service highway and rode for several miles down narrower but still main streets. We crossed over into Suffolk County. The landscape was typically Long Island in character: flat, uneventful, with wooden telephone poles lining the streets, their power and communication lines swooping from each to each; and houses, endless houses, one- and two-storied, their small front yards either messy or well-kept. Many of them exhibited the touchingly patriotic sight of an American flag sticking up at forty-five degree angle from some socket beside the front door. And there were innumerable places to eat: pizzerias, fast food joints, Italian and Chinese and Indian restaurants. The streets were fuller of expensive cars than one was wont to see in the city, which of course only made sense because here people could park them in the security of their own driveways or garages. We came to Fullbright Road and turned onto it. Along here the houses were fewer and farther between, separated by open spaces or patches of small woods. I had the sense that this was not so good an area as those around it; certainly it was further away from the "center" of the nearby town. Five minutes later we turned onto a narrow and ill-paved street. The car jiggled and shook over many small potholes. We were no sooner riding along a stretch of hedgerows than we made a right turn; and there we were, pulling into the driveway of the house.

It looked even more charming in person than it had in the pictures. It really was the sweetest place one could imagine. Once again I was struck with its toy-like quality: the way it just stood there, two-storied yet so compact and trim, the white outlines of its windows and front door so crisply visible against the blue-painted wall of its facade. Four small trees grew on the front yard and shaded the areas beneath them. Mrs. Greenbaum drove up the stone and pebble driveway leading to the house and parked only a few feet away from the front porch. This was, by the way, very narrow, only about five or six feet across, but when I stepped onto it I could well imagine putting on it a small table and a few chairs; it would be a great place to have breakfast and read of a given morning. Mrs. Greenbaum reached into her pocket-book and took out a large, round ring of keys, each one having a little paper label with the property number on it. Finding the one for this house, she opened the door and stepped aside for me to enter. She followed me inside, but had only just stepped across the threshold than she stopped and said, "Just help yourself and look around."

"Don't you want to show it to me?" I asked, smiling to think that she really wasn't going to do so, and for the obvious reason: that she took this ghost stuff seriously.

"I think I'd feel more comfortable right here. But please, help yourself!"

I raised my eyebrows and smiled and said nothing, then turned my attention to the room in which I found myself.

It was anything but gloomy. On the contrary it was the cheerfullest room one could imagine. The strong sunlight of a summer afternoon streamed through the front windows, showing a place wonderfully clean and empty. The walls were painted in a refreshing pastel mint green while the wooden trims around the doors and windows, as well as the ceilings, were a bright white. The oak floors were in excellent condition. They had recently been "done"—sanded and polyurethaned to a high gloss. And there was a fireplace! I happily went over to it and examined it, patting the wide ledge of the mantle and imagining how good a small sculpture or a series of knickknacks might be ornamentally set on it. The space above it would be a fine place to hang a picture—a painting, say, of a sailing ship, its full sails crowding forth on a wind-chopped sea. Then I bent down and examined the andirons. They were made of brass and each was topped with an orb four inches in diameter and needing only a polishing to gleam again. To sit before such a fireplace on a winter's evening, warmed by the flaming, crackling brands while one read a good book and sipped some wine—it was the very image of contentment.

The dining room was a bit smaller than the living room and the kitchen only a little smaller than the dining room. There was an oven but no refrigerator and the cabinets could have used refacing or a new paint job. I ambled back into the living room and the moment she saw me Mrs. Greenbaum asked:

"Have you seen enough?"

"I just started!"

She had never stepped entirely into the living room but rather remained just two or three feet away from the open front door—as though unwilling to give up her location to an easy escape route. Her eyes apprehensively darted from the floor to the ceiling and then to every wall as though she were expecting to see some terrible thing. She looked at me almost resentfully as though holding a grudge against me for having taken her here.

"It's a wonderful house," I said, cheerfully, putting out my arms, my hands, to the living room that was dazzling with the afternoon's cheerful brilliance. I turned happily toward the staircase, nodded toward it, and said, "Want to show me upstairs?" —But I knew she would decline; and sure enough, she shook her head no, barely managing a smile, and saying only:

"You go. I'll wait for you."

The stairs creaked a little under my steps but I hardly noticed this as my attention was focused on the beautiful oak handrail, along which I let my fingers trail despite its slight dustiness. Upstairs there was a single long hallway connecting the bathroom and three bedrooms, two of them large, one of them small. They were all bright and sunny. The small one struck me as perfect for an office and had a window overlooking the back yard, to which, incidentally, the photographs in the realtor's office had not done justice. For when I went down to see it for myself I saw—much to my leaping heart's content—that it was much larger than I had hoped. As the grass hadn't been cut all season, it covered the yard like some deep-green, luxurious, long-piled carpet. There were several trees here: a couple of maples, a weeping willow, and a slender birch, all spaced equidistantly apart. Off to one side and close to the house extended a patch of fenced-in earth some thirty feet long and which had once been a garden, though for lack of care weeds had invaded and overrun it. I could foresee myself spending contented hours digging in that soil and making good things grow. Strolling to the end of the yard, I came to the stream marking the end of the property. It was no more than four or five feet across, no deeper than eight or ten inches; its shallow waters flowed slowly, steadily, over the moss-covered stones of its bed. Rushes grew along its banks. Now and then a bubble wriggled up from its short depths or a ripple touched its surface—the telltale signs of insect or some other strange life. From the thirty acres of bird sanctuary on the other side of the stream came chirrups from the treetops.

I turned around and looked at the back of the house. Haunted? Yes, the place was haunted alright: it was haunted with everything I had been looking for.

When I went back inside I saw that Mrs. Greenbaum had backed out onto the porch. She was walking back and forth there, her arms still defensively folded. At the sound of my footsteps, she stopped and turned to me and watched me approach her. She looked at me in that blank yet expectant expression people assume when they expect to hear some bad news. No doubt she was waiting to hear me tell her that I had seen or sensed something out of the way. Instead I walked out onto the porch with a great, satisfied smile and proclaimed, "It's great!"

She smiled steadily, looking at me.

"It's even better than I thought it would be," I continued.

"Did you see the back yard? How big it is? That's a lot of land!"

She took out her large ring of keys and locked the door, and afterwards I followed her to her car and we drove away.

"How many people have looked at the place?" I asked her as we drove back to her office.

"A few. Five or six."

"And none of them liked it?"

"Not after what they learned about it."

"You mean after what you told them?"

She turned to me with displeasure as though I had insulted her. "Do you think I'm lying about it?"

"No, I don't."

"Why would I lie about a thing like that?"

"I'm sure you wouldn't."

Then a funny thought struck me and I laughed.

"What?" she asked.

"I was just wondering how many other haunted houses you have."

As soon as I said the words I regretted them, thinking that she would also take them as insulting. But on the contrary her mood lightened and she smiled and said, "It's the only one, thank God!"

"You really believe it's haunted? You really believe in that stuff?"

"I believe in what I see."

"But you said you never saw anything."

"I saw the people who left it, and saw how scared they were. I told you: people don't run out of their houses in the middle of the night because there isn't something going on."

"And that really happened?"

"Yes. I told you. To both families. One was there for a year, the other for only four months."

"But the house was built in the '40s. They couldn't have been the only families who lived there."

"You're right. Others have lived there."

"What about them?"

"I don't know about them. I only know about the last two families. That's when my company began representing the property." She drove for a few minutes in silence. She seemed thoughtful. Then she said, "Listen, take my advice, don't buy it. Even if you don't believe in ghosts—and who knows, maybe there really *aren't* any ghosts there—still, there must be *something* going on there, and so why even want to take that chance? Why, if there's even the smallest chance?"

"Well, that's easy to answer: because it's a nice place and I can afford it."

"I understand that. But in this case you have to have to go beyond thinking that way. If you buy the house, it's yours, with all its problems, and if there is something going on with it and you can't live there any more, what are you going to do? Nobody'll buy it from you. Nobody."

"That's not true. I'm buying it, ain't I?

"Yes, but you're cra—"—she stopped herself before she said the word.

"Go on, say it," I laughed. "Crazy. Right?"

She just looked at me with compressed lips, then turned her eyes away in embarrassment, and shook her head as though regretting what she had said.

"Don't worry about it," I said. "Everyone tells me that sooner or later. I've always been 'crazy.' But I'll tell you something: I'd rather be my kind of 'crazy' than sane in the way a lot of people are."

"I'm sorry. I didn't mean 'crazy' crazy. I meant ... reckless. You're making a big mistake."

"Listen, Sheila, you're a very nice woman—I like you a lot— and I can see you have my best interests in mind, which makes me like you all the more. But really I don't believe in ghosts. And do you want to know why? Really why?"

She glanced over to me as she drove.

"Because," I said, "all through history terrible things have happened to lots of people. Now, don't you think that if ghosts were real these poor people would always have come back to haunt and seek vengeance on their persecutors? Of course they would have. But they never did—they never do; and the reason they don't is because they can't. Once you're dead you're dead. You're like a stone, or a nail, or a puddle of water. See? Just another inert thing."

With her eyes on the road she shook her head vaguely and almost despite herself. She was too commonsensical a person to resist the logic of my argument, and yet something within her resisted my purely mundane interpretation of death. Like most people she wanted and perhaps needed to believe that one's ultimate value and condition as a human being in the universe must be of more consequence than that of a stone or a puddle of water, or even for that matter of any other animal; yet at the same time she was conscious that a belief in supernatural things impugned her intelligence and discredited her reputation as a "professional."   She considered what I had said and seemed to search for a suitable response, and finally took refuge in that cheap but effective method of argument that calls into question the limits of knowledge itself, saying, "Well, maybe that's true most of the time, but how do you know it's true all the time? No one can know for sure. Maybe there *are* exceptions. Maybe, somehow, some people *do* come back. And maybe most of them can't hurt people in this world, but then again maybe *some* of them can. Who knows?"

I could only shake my head and repeat that there was no real proof of a ghost in that house, or of ghosts anywhere else, except what people had told her—information she had gotten second hand.

"Although in a way it's a pity," I continued. "It would be kind of fun to believe in that stuff ; it would make life a lot more interesting. But then I'd have to believe in elves and goblins and fairy dust and heaven only knows what else—and I'm not prepared to go that far. But I'll tell you what I *do* believe in. I believe that whatever you bring to a house determines what's inside of it. A miserable, unhappy person will always bring misery and unhappiness to a place, but a happy person, or at least a relatively contented person, as I like to think I am, is bound to set a lighter tone. So you can be assured that when I'm living there the house will be as peaceful and happy as I am. It's going to be the *happiest* place on Long Island!"

Nevertheless I must have had some smidgeon of doubt about the house because in the next week I visited other real estate agents and looked at other properties; or perhaps it was nothing more than to assure myself that I really was getting the best deal possible. At any rate there was soon no question about this, for the additional houses shown me were by comparison pretty pathetic. It was always the same problem: those that were attractive, in good condition, and had a little land around them were the ones I couldn't afford, whereas the ones I could afford were too small or too shabby or located in dangerous neighborhoods. And so increasingly the house on Fullbright Road struck me as a gem of a place, a once-in-a-lifetime opportunity, a serendipity not to be passed up; and so I cancelled all my other appointments with other real estate agents, called Mrs. Greenbaum, and told her that I wanted to buy it.

"It's up to you," she said.

She helped me with the tremendous legalities involved in house-buying. She prepared the pertinent documents and presented them to me in neat little bundles which she fanned out across her desk, explaining to me what each one was and pointing out with her pen the lines on which I was to sign—"There ... there ... and there ..." At the end of one of them I couldn't help noticing a paragraph that wasn't part of the pre-printed form but which had been added. I read it over and looked at Mrs. Greenbaum in amused surprise. "Did you add this?" I asked, pointing to it. She nodded, yes. The added paragraph stated that I had been fully informed of the "stigmatized nature" of the property, and that I "whole-heartedly, without reserve, and in full understanding of the disclosure" nevertheless agreed to buy it, and "shall hold harmless both the agent and Brody Real Estate of any and all untoward or unwanted circumstances appertaining to the abovementioned disclosure." I wasn't sure what I found most amusing about this addition: either its turgid, convoluted legalese, or the immovable conviction in ghosts that had made Mrs. Greenbaum or her boss (and probably both of them) feel it to be necessary. But with a shake of my head, a frown, and a rather scornful roll of my eyes, I signed where I was supposed to. When the last document had been signed she pulled out of her top desk drawer and handed to me a large blue envelope to which a red and white mint had been taped. Inside was a greeting card in which the keys to the house had been taped, and she had written, "Congratulations and good luck! Sheila." I still have that card.

Six weeks later, on a very hot August afternoon, I moved in.

II

The moving company sent me a large van and two muscular fellows who got the job done—from door to door, from start
to finish—in four hours. I quickly arranged my few pieces of
furniture, but the general cleaning took a lot longer. Though
no one had lived in the house for eight months, and it had been
cleaned soon after its previous occupants had left it, a layer of
dust had accumulated on most of the surfaces. For hours I
mopped and wiped and polished till what had merely looked
clean became so in fact. By the time evening came around my
legs and arms were sore, and my hands were raw from deter-
gents. I told myself that I would have to get a pair of rubber
gloves to save my skin.

I furnished the house in what anyone would probably consider record time, mostly because I didn't have much to put into
it;—which was fine with me. I never understood people who fill
their houses with so much furniture that one can't walk from
one end of a room to another without having to weave around
an obstacle course of tables, chairs, planters, or whatever else
they can find to fill up an unoccupied space. Perhaps they want
to make the impression on others, or to reassure themselves,
that they own a great deal. But a home should be above all a
place of comforting freedom and peace and cleanliness; and
nothing better conveys these things than lovely light and becalming space. My few furnishings consisted of a futon couch,
my stereo equipment, a few tables and lamps, my bookcase and
books, a rug (on the large living room floor it looked way too
small), and several easy-to-care-for pothos plants on wire
stands, now set near the windows. My two framed posters were
hung on the living room walls. Upstairs my bed and an end table were the only things in my bedroom. These things had once
fully furnished my one-bedroom apartment, but in my house
they were spread so far apart as to seem barely existent. Later
that week I purchased a few other pieces of furniture at local
stores: a table and chairs for the dining room, two contempo-
rary-looking armchairs in lemon-colored fabric for the living
room, and another framed poster to hang over the fireplace—
and yes, it happened to be of a sailing ship.

I also turned the small bedroom upstairs into my office. I
bought a desk—cheap and flimsy but serviceable—and placed it

against the wall just beneath the window overlooking the back yard. I put my computer on it, as well as a flexible-necked lamp that could be turned this way or that.

I often took tours of my own house, going from room to room, looking in on each one with satisfaction. How proud I was of it all! How proud I was to feel that I had my own home! For my house was more than just a new residence: it was the tangible symbol of a new and better stage in my life, of a difficult past left finally behind. The financial difficulties that had always beset me had receded for a while. I had money in the bank and a "real asset," a house whose value was likely to grow as the years went by and which might be sold for cash in the case of an emergency. (Poverty has a way of making one always anticipate "emergencies.")

I also bought a car. It was a mid-sized coupe, two years old, silver in color, and got great gas mileage. I intended one day to take a long drive out to Montauk.

Even that first week in the house I didn't neglect my writing. My novel might have done well, but it hadn't done so well that I could go very long without writing another one. It would have done a lot better if the critics hadn't been so critical. My next one would be written with their suggestions taken to heart if only to gain better publicity and stronger sales. For one thing, it was going to be a lot more optimistic and accessible. The "heavy handed" (as one critic had put it) examination of motives and states of mind would be traded in for snappy plots and more "action," and my considered periods ("tedious and wordy"— snapped a journalist with the attention span of a snapping turtle) would be truncated and transformed into quick, declarative, and sometimes fragmentary sentences of the sort appropriate for an impatient reading public. It was also going to be funny—a comedy. Why not? Comedy had always been a part of my work; this time it would be the main part. All my creative powers would be focused on getting a laugh.

"But what about your artistic integrity?"

My friends, when you own a house and a car on Long Island, and have taxes and utilities to pay, and when your savings account, unless you can restock it, will be depleted in about a year, you begin to understand there is no conflict of interest between artistic integrity and popularity. Besides, one can be just as artistic in comedy as in any other genre. And ultimately comedy may be the most important genre of all, for one can chase after the secrets of life and the universe for a lifetime and come no closer to the answers than at first, whereas the ability to evoke even one bout of laughter is an immediate benefit to mankind.

Now, my being a writer has led me into some peculiar habits. For instance, my schedule. I write at night from about ten o'clock to two or three the next morning, a habit I fell into because my only free time was after I had gotten home from work. I would be too exhausted to write and instead would take a nap of a few hours, waking up at nine thirty or so, and only then, when my mind was rested, would I sit at my desk, usually with a cup of coffee, and have a few fresh hours for writing. This schedule had the added benefit of enabling me to write during the quietest part of the night. I have become so used to writing at night that when I have tried to write during the day the process feels unnatural, and the results—so they seem to me—below par.

The other thing about the process for me is that whenever I find myself struggling for the right word or phrase, or generally can't bring things together, I'm up and away from my keyboard and back to pen and paper. I have several very good fountain pens: my favorite being a huge instrument of swirling brown, orange, and black resins, tipped with a golden fine point: rather heavy in the hand, but instilling into one a sense of solidity and purpose. It has helped me coax along many a recalcitrant passage. Perhaps I was becoming impossibly severe with myself, but it seemed to me that in writing my new book the recalcitrance was turning up more frequently. There were some nights when all I did was write longhand. Afterwards I would look at the fifteen or twenty sheets of manuscript with a sense of relief at having gotten so much done, but also with impatience because now it all had to be typed over and undoubtedly in part rewritten.

When I had finished my work of an evening I would go outside to sit for a few minutes in the back yard. I had placed a small table and a folding metal chair there beside the drapery of the willow tree so that I might finish off my working "day" with a relaxing glass of wine while contemplating the night's sky. On every clear night the Milky Way put on the wondrous show of a million stars and all their worlds. One can't help but pity poor city-dwellers for whom the glare of street lamps obscures that celestial panorama: it's one of the reasons they have an inflated view of themselves and think their affairs so important: they are blinded to the greater yardstick by which they might accurately measure their small place in the general scheme of things.

It was wonderfully quiet at night. There was no muffled roar of cars and trucks on a nearby street, no distant sirens, no faint voices of people walking on the sidewalks just outside. The ceiling did not thump with the footsteps of neighbors upstairs, nor did the faint music from a television or radio filter through the walls. It was quiet—quiet. At first, it was too quiet. I wasn't used to such silence and it was sometimes hard for me to get to sleep. I had suddenly become conscious of the soft soughing sound my arms or legs made on the sheets when I moved, and sometimes I could even hear the beating of my own heart. It was also hot. I didn't yet have an air conditioner for the bedroom, nor even a fan. Through the open window came no relieving breeze but only the soft light of the moon and the singing of crickets.

Sometimes I told myself that I would take the Long Island Railroad into New York City for a day, that I'd get out at Penn Station, head over to Herald Square, stop in at the stores there, and buy something for the house or just walk about and get a taste again of all the bustle that was no longer a necessary part of my life. But the intention always fizzled away before the prospect of having to drive to the station, wait for a train, then spend time commuting back and forth. There was something about that—about that foremost reality of city life—that in the end always repulsed me into staying home. For I found that I could not do it, that I no longer had the heart, the will, to endure again even the small struggle of a dirty, public, city commute:—no, not even one more time. Besides, those were hours that would be better spent reading or thinking about my new book.

But one can only read or think about a single thing for so long. Sooner or later concentration exhausts the mind, which seeks relief in following its own unconscious impulses. For me those impulses increasingly directed my thoughts backward, to my past. Perhaps it was the quiet of the house, or the unprecedented if momentary freedom from financial worries, or the absence of the kinds of petty irritations accompanying life in the city;—however it was, I began to remember, sometimes with vivid intensity, people and events and feelings from thirty years before. Some of these memories delighted me in the same way that one happily stumbles on a favorite object one had lost and long forgotten. More often than not however they were the reverse of this, were somber, regrettable, and left me shaking my head in wonder as to how I had ever been able to forget them. My having forgotten these things was at least in part owing to the mind's grateful proclivity to suppress difficult memories. But now that they had floated up into consciousness, they proved to be, like zombies risen from the grave, impossible to re-inter. They recurred to me almost every day, and always in greater and greater detail. Sometimes I found myself coming back to the present after having sat staring into space and seeing and hearing and feeling—living all over again—some pleasant or (as was more often the case) unpleasant incident of my youth.

One afternoon, some five weeks after I had been living in my house, while I was in the kitchen nudging a new refrigerator into its alcove, the doorbell rang. I opened the door to a man and woman whose car was parked in my driveway—I hadn't heard it coming up to the house. They were both in their 30s and there was nothing particularly remarkable about them; they could have been any couple. The woman was standing just before her husband; it was she who had rung the doorbell. They introduced themselves as Jeff and Lisa Sutherland. From the moment she laid eyes on me she looked at me a little strangely—with concern, somehow—and her smile and attempt to be pleasant had a strained quality about it as she asked if I was the new owner of the house. When I told her that I was, she responded by saying that they, she and her husband, had lived here before me. She said she was sorry if she had disturbed me but had felt obliged to come by and see how I was "doing" with the place, and when I told her I was doing fine she pressed, "Do you mind if we speak to you for a few minutes?"

At once I knew this had something to do with the supposed

ghost. I remembered how the realtor had told me about the previous owners running out of it in the middle of the night, and in my mind's eye I saw the rather amusing spectacle of these two people scared out of their wits and frantically rushing out of the front door.

I invited them inside, an invitation which Mrs. Sutherland seemed at once eager and hesitant to accept in the way people will seem when curiosity urges them against their better judgment; but in another moment she nodded, smiled briefly, and stepped inside, followed by her husband. As they entered the living room they knew so well, they looked about them with overtly intense interest, their eyes playing among the walls, the ceiling, the floor, the dining room beyond, the staircase leading to the second floor; and only when they had made this initial, swift, and rather nervous surveillance—as though to assure themselves that there was nothing for them to be worried about—did they seem to relax. Probably only then did they notice how different the house looked in the way of appointments from when they had lived here. I invited them to take a seat on the couch, which could only comfortably accommodate two persons, while I sat on an ottoman a few feet away. Mrs. Sutherland was still looking about the place, now no longer with apprehension so much as with the wistful expression of someone who has misgivings about having given something up.

"You still have a lot of furnishing to do, I see," she began, turning her attention now wholly to me and smiling a bit more comfortably.

"Not much more. I kind of like the space."

"Yes." She nodded, looking down at the clean, polished, wooden floors—the floors she and her husband had paid so much money to have done. "The wood is great in this house. You don't find floors like this any more. It's not veneer—it's solid planks."

"Yes, they're very nice," I said only, smiling at her, waiting for her to get to the real point of her visit. However, this was something she was loath to do. For the next few minutes she recounted how enthusiastic she and her husband had also been about the house when they had first seen it, how happily they had moved into it and decorated it, what plans they had had for adding an extension to it. As she spoke her husband would

glance at her in a vaguely tense, impatient way in which I detected his silent urging for her to get to the point of their visit.
Perhaps she had thought better of it; perhaps it had come to
seem an impertinence or an unkindness in her to tell me things
that could only ruin my dream the way hers and her husband's
had been ruined. And yet all along I knew very well what she
wanted to talk about. If I didn't, in those first minutes, help
her along to it, it was because I didn't want to say anything
that might influence what she had to tell me. But after fifteen
minutes of small-talk, I grew a little impatient and ventured to
prod her along by asking why she and her husband, who had
apparently liked the house, had put it up for sale, and at so reasonable a price.

"Before I answer that," she returned, "could I ask you a
question? Were you told anything about the house before you
bought it?"

I came right out with it. "You mean about its being
haunted? Yes. It's not."

"They told you it isn't?"

"If you mean by 'they' the realtor who sold me the house,
no—she told me it *was*."

"Then why did you buy it?"

"Because I don't believe in that stuff."

"I didn't believe in it either," she said. She had leaned forward; she was looking at me hard. She had dropped all pretense at being the half-shy, hesitant visitor to a stranger; now
she was the woman who had been determinedly concerned not
to let happen to another what had happened to her. "I didn't believe it either—neither of us did—at first. But things began
happening. We saw things. It isn't a safe place. You're in danger here."

"What did you see?"

It turned out that they had heard more than they had
seen, though ultimately it was what they, or rather what she,
had seen that had driven them out of the place. Their habita-
tion had started tranquilly enough. For a whole month they
had happily exerted themselves in painting, redecorating, fixing,
planning. Everything had been coming along nicely; they could
scarcely believe their own good luck. Then they began to hear
"things." At night, as they lay in bed about to go to sleep, a

voice, a whisper, floated into their bedroom from the hallway outside. It was always faint and never lasted for more than a few seconds at a time; but it was audible and made them sit up in bed, listening, trying to figure out what it could be. The wind, they told each other—it's merely the wind; and it might very well have been the wind, had there been any; but the problem was that it occurred even on nights when the air outside was still. At other times they heard a scratching sound. Mrs. Sutherland, a light sleeper, would be wakened by it and lay in bed, in the darkness beside her lightly snoring husband, straining her ears to identify its cause. Yes, it sounded exactly like someone lightly running his nails against the wall. Lying there with eyes wide open, she would try to pinpoint in the darkness where the sound was coming from, hearing it first in the closet, then on the other side of the room, then on the ceiling overhead. She wakened her husband; and of course by then it had stopped; and the next morning he would attribute it to mice. But surely mice were not so heavy as to cause the sounds of footsteps that *he* heard one morning as he was preparing to work. He had just taken a shower and was standing, towel around his waist, shaving in front of the bathroom mirror. The door was open to the hallway and he heard footsteps coming toward him. He was sure it was his wife and expected to see her pass; but she did not pass and the footsteps continued. Curious, he stepped to the open door and looked outside at the very moment he heard another footfall, only to see—nothing. No one was there; the hall was empty, silent. His wife, he found, was still in bed sleeping. He confessed that the incident had shaken him up a little, especially in light of the strange things that had gone on before, and now even he had to admit that there might be "something going on."

They decided that they were willing to live with whatever that something was, for, after all, whether a sound was made by a ghost or the wind, a sound was only that, a sound, a vibration of the air, an ethereality without real substance—nothing that could really harm you. In an effort to assuage their fears over these phenomena they tried to convince each other that there was something a little romantic about having a ghost about: that it was probably the kindly spirit of a nice little old lady, or perhaps some jolly old gentleman—one of the original owners of the house, no doubt—who had found it impossible to let go of the place but who would also look over them like some guardian angel. They would accept it the way they had accepted the creaking steps, the damp basement, or any other peculiarity of the house.

"The thing was," Mrs. Sutherland explained, "we did love the place. I still do in some ways"—looking around the room. "But then other things happened. We couldn't ignore them any more. Doors would open by themselves. We both saw that," she said, turning to her husband, who, his eyes down, nodded once. "Then the faucet in the bathtub turned on a few times. Once it was running so fast!—both hot and cold water were turned all the way on! If we hadn't been home it would have flooded the place."

"And the lamps," Jeffrey Sutherland said.

"Oh, yes, the lamps," his wife echoed, remembering that detail. "We would be sitting here, in this room, watching television and one of the lamps would go out. The plug had been pulled out of the socket. It happened again and again."

Yet even these additional and now undeniable exhibitions of otherworldly presence didn't scare away the Sutherlands. They continued to try to put one another's fears at ease with assurances of the essentially benign nature of the presence or energy among them. Granted, there were noises; granted, things moved about; but not a hair on their heads had been touched. But now that they had been free of the place for some time they admitted to me, as they had admitted to each other, that they had remained here not out of steely indifference or bravery but simply because they couldn't afford to go anywhere else. They were middle-class folk who worked hard for what they had, and after what had been for them the immense expenses of a down payment, closing costs, initial mortgage payments, and renovations, they simply had not had the money to buy another home or even to rent an apartment. They were stuck; they had to make the best of it; they had *had* to make this their home, at least till they could get on their financial feet again.

"As the months went by, it only got worse," Mrs. Sutherland continued. "The doors would open and shut right in front of us. Things would fall off shelves—be *thrown* off shelves. And it was always worse at night. Oh, sometimes ...!" Sometimes the faint wooing became a distinct, loud cry, and little human yelps or barks of laughter erupted from downstairs in the living room. Mrs. Sutherland was always either awake or wakened when she heard such things, and they so frightened her that she would cling to her husband as tightly as a little girl clings to her daddy after having been scared by an imaginary monster. Of course, she woke the poor man up almost every night. He would have to pry her off himself. He would mildly upbraid her for her hysteria, saying that she couldn't keep waking him up like this because it interrupted his sleep, which he needed because he had to work the next day. He would tell her that whatever she had seen or heard was nothing, that she was overreacting, and that she ought to ignore it and go to sleep.

But in fact his nerves were not made of iron. His brave indifference or humorous dismissal of the strange phenomena was merely a psychological mechanism by which he sought to escape the humiliating sense of his inability to fulfill the husbandly role of protector.

Mrs. Sutherland tried to follow her husband's example and to be indifferent toward the increasingly odd goings-on in the house, but each day that went by, and especially each night, only further stretched her already excruciatingly taut nerves. On the other hand, sometimes a few days would go by during which nothing out of the ordinary would happen. These stretches of peaceful normality allowed her nervousness to subside and her good humor to return; she would begin to make up mundane excuses for what she had heard or seen, and to think everything would be alright. But then she would again hear the distant sounds, the whispers, the footfalls, and see objects move; and all more outrightly than before.

The great and decisive shock came not in the middle of the night but in the stark, sobering light of morning an hour after her husband had gone to work. She was mopping the bedroom floors when she heard a great clatter coming from downstairs. It sounded as though someone were going on a rampage below. Her heart fluttered in her breast—terror seized her—as she stood still and listened to the smash of pots and pans and the crash of glasses and plates. It went on for almost a minute, each second of which found her unable to move for sheer terror. Suddenly it stopped, and the silence seemed no less terrifying for the things it might be preparing. She felt trapped, afraid to go downstairs, and only when the silence continued and the worst of her nervous shock had subsided did she venture to do so, holding the wooden handle of the mop like a weapon as though she expected to find an intruder whom she would have to defend herself against. When she reached the kitchen she saw how all the cabinets had been flung open—every one—and their contents thrown onto the floor. Most of the glasses, most of the plates and cups, had shattered. But there was something far more distressing than even this: knives had been plunged into the counter beside the sink. They stood straight up, like some horrible threat and intimation of deadly violence. And then one of them rose up, turned slowly toward her, pointed at her, and began to tremble; and somehow she knew that in the next second it would be murderously flung at her.

"I don't think I even remember running out of the house," she said, not looking at me but rather into the air, into that horrific moment of her past, her face pale merely at the remembrance of it. "But I knew that that was that—I was never going back. Never. Not even for another minute."

We all sat there for a few moments looking at one another: the Sutherlands looking at me both hopefully and expectantly, as though, having enlightened me about the dangers of the place, I would start packing my bags at once; and I looking back at them with a mixture of sympathy and suspicion, for they struck me at once as sincere and impossible. Perhaps living a lifetime in the city had made me incapable of believing in disinterested concern for one's fellows, but I really couldn't accept that they had come to me out of purely altruistic motives. But of course in this it was I who was less than noble, not they.

In leaving, shortly afterwards, Mrs. Sutherland wished me "good luck" with everything, yet before stepping outside she hesitated at the door and turned to me with an earnest look. "You should leave, you know," she said. "You really should."

"Everything is fine here," I assured her. "But thanks for coming. I appreciate it."

She nodded, and glanced at her husband uncertainly, and they left.

As I shut the door I wished that I hadn't let her and her husband into my home. They had brought up—and brought up with disturbing clarity—an issue that I had all but forgotten about. I made a conscious decision to forget about them as quickly as possible.

Another month passed. August became September. From out of the north came cool air, chasing away the heat of summer. I had already written a whole draft of my next novel—the "follow-up" on which all my career as a novelist rested. It lay on my desk in my office, a thick manuscript three inches high. Not since I was a much younger man, and had youth's creative abandon untrammeled by critical discretion, had I been so prolific. A dozen ideas for other projects, other books, regularly crowded into my mind. But I couldn't give too much attention to any of them. With each week my once very popular book declined in sales; it was easy to foresee how soon enough its sales would be reduced to a trickle, steady, perhaps, but hardly able to support the expenses of my now modestly comfortable life. The new novel had to be finished and published as quickly as possible before the public forgot me and I could no longer bank on my "name."

My days passed as usual, reading or lounging in the morning and afternoon, writing at night, then relaxing for the rest of the early morning hours before heading off to bed. Every time the weather permitted I would sit outside in the back yard, sipping a glass or two of wine, perhaps smoking a cigarette, and enjoying the peacefulness of the moment as crickets sang to me and a million stars glittered overhead. On one such early morning I noticed that the lamp was still on in my office on the second floor. I thought I had turned it off but apparently I hadn't—I couldn't trust my bad memory to be definite about the matter. When I went back inside I turned it off and went to sleep.

I had grown accustomed to the usual small noises of the place, which were always of course more noticeable in the utter silence of night: a creak of a joist adjusting to the change in temperature, a rattle caused by a gust of wind, the patter of rain. But one night my ears had picked up something out of the way, and I awoke, opening my eyes to the darkness. I didn't know why I had awoken and at first I closed my eyes intending to go back to sleep. But then the sound that had penetrated into my unconscious mind, and registered there as unusual, perhaps dangerous, again occurred: footsteps. This time my eyes opened wide and I listened hard. The footfalls were intermittent but unmistakable. They were coming from out in the hallway. I looked toward the door. Between it and the floor was a space illuminated with the light coming from the bathroom down the hall; and across that strip of illumination moved the undulous shadow of legs or feet passing by.

Someone was in the house! My heart began pounding fast and hard with anxiety, and for the next few seconds I lay there completely still, terrified, not knowing what I should or could do. Then I realized that I could not just lie there and, perhaps, be discovered and killed. I had the presence of mind to be as quiet as possible—not to let the intruder know I was just behind the closed door. I got out of bed and picked up the lamp on the bedside table, intending to use it as a weapon. Holding it tightly and a little aloft, I slowly moved to the door and stood just beside it intending to smash over the head anyone who might open it. I'm not a brave man, and in retrospect I wonder at the panic that had transformed my native pusillanimity into courage. I kept my ears peeled and my eyes shifted down to the strip of illumination beneath the door in order to see by any shadow there when the intruder was on the other side. But apparently he had moved on. The question now was, Did I venture out and confront him? But how foolish it seemed to me, then, even to think about confronting him! What if he had a gun? What if he had an accomplice? Instead, I reached out to the knob and silently locked the door.

I went to the telephone on my night table and dialed 911. In a hushed, hurried whisper I gave my name and address and said that someone had broken into my house and requested the police.

In less than five minutes the distant wails of sirens penetrated the night. Outside the darkness was soon alive with flashes of red and white light from stroboscopes on the roofs of the police cruisers that had pulled into the driveway. The strict beams of flashlights sliced through the air as officers surrounded the house to ensure the burglar wouldn't escape. The hiss and scratch of their two-way radios mingled with the sound of their running footsteps. Loud knocking at the front door sounded through the house. For me there was still the dilemma of leaving my room and going downstairs to open the door, for the intruder might very well be just down the hall or in the living room, and he was bound to be the more dangerous now on account of his entrapment. But there was no choice: I had to get downstairs. I picked up my lamp again and, throwing caution to the wind, flung open the door (fully prepared to assault anyone on the other side of it), and flew down the hall, down the stairwell, across the living room, and lunged at the front door, dropping the lamp and frenziedly flipping open the locks.

Two policemen were standing on the porch, one behind the other. The one in front was older than the one behind him, and they both had their pistols drawn, ready to fire away. They both looked a little surprised to see me, and in another moment I realized I was wearing nothing but a t-shirt and a pair of boxer trunks. Only the extremity of the moment prevented me from feeling embarrassed.

"You called for the police?" the first officer said.

I nodded, and stepped aside, and they both walked in.

I told them how I had heard someone walking about upstairs and seen his shadow under the door. For all I knew he was still in the house. Pistols in hand, the officers went through the house looking for the intruder even as they spoke through their radios to their colleagues outside. I waited for them in the living room, nervously looking about me and wondering if it wouldn't be better, safer, to go outside, since at any minute bullets might start flying. But after a search that included every closet and every corner of the basement, the officers came back to me, shaking their heads, saying they had found no one. The older of the two told me he would fill out a report and extracted from his back pocket a rather long, narrow pad which he flipped open and prepared to write in. He asked me any number of questions: my name, age, how long I had lived here, what I did for a living, if I lived alone. He jotted down the answers. When he had finished he turned to his partner, who had been standing by during the interrogation, and dismissed him, saying he would be out in a few minutes. Once we were alone he dropped somewhat his air of distant professionalism and asked me if this was the first time I had noticed anything peculiar in the house. By the way he said the word "peculiar"—with a certain emphasis and accompanied by a hard, probing look—I knew that he was referring to the supposed haunting of the place, and I was surprised that he knew about it. Was its reputation really so widespread? I told him that nothing out of the ordinary had ever happened to me before.

"When you bought this house, did they tell you about it?"

"You mean about its being haunted?"

He nodded, yes.

"How do you know about that?" I asked.

"I only know that people have had some trouble here," he said.

"Trouble with *ghosts?*" I asked.

He was too conscious of his profession, of belonging to so staid and serious an organization as the police department, to admit that he might take such things seriously. Yet through his veneer of skepticism I could sense sympathy for my circumstances, and as though to prod him into frankness, into saying what he really thought, I said rather as a challenge:

"I don't believe in ghosts."

He raised a hand to his face and touched his brow, then lowered it to his lips as he glanced about the place.

"The other people who lived here," he said, "also used to call us because they thought someone had broken into the house. Did you know that?"

"No," I said. That was something Mrs. Sutherland had forgotten to mention.

"Same thing as with you ... they heard people walking around or ... making noises ... whatever. Every time we came we never found anyone. There was never any evidence of a break-in. A few times it was in winter and there was snow on the ground, so if anyone had broken there would have been footprints or something. There never were any."

"What does that have to do with me? I know what I saw and heard."

"So did they, sir. They even had evidence that someone had been here: broken dishes, furniture that had been moved, their kids who had seen things ..." He put away his report pad, shoving it into his rear pocket. "Hey, look, I don't know if there are such things as ghosts or not, I'm just telling you what I know from having been called out here over the last few years. We've been out there dozens of times—dozens—and in the end we never find anything."

"So what are you saying, that I shouldn't call you if I think someone's broken in?"

"Not at all. If you think someone's broken in, call us. That's our job, to check it out. I'm just saying that"—he raised a hand, as though in uncertainty—"maybe there are things going on here that we can't help you with."

"Ghosts," I said, in such a way, with such an air of impending mockery, that it made this man, who was as old as myself and tougher tenfold, shrink back within himself at the thought that he might seem ridiculous.

"Whatever," he said, suddenly putting back up a rather gruff front in order to save his dignity.

After he and the other policemen had gone, there I was again, alone in my quiet, my isolated, and now—could it really be possible?—haunted house. I didn't and couldn't go back to sleep. In order to occupy myself, to take my mind off what had happened, I turned on the television and tried to become interested in whatever program happened to be on. I stayed in the living room till a quarter to six in the morning, by which time the light of dawn began gratefully to seep through the windows. Only then did I go back upstairs, get into bed, and get some sleep.

Our capacity for getting used to things must have been programmed into us by a prescient Nature that foresaw we would often find ourselves in difficult and inextricable situations to which our only option would be adaptation. I told myself that even if this were a genuine haunting, it amounted to nothing but the sound of footsteps and passing shadows, and was something I could live with. In the full light of day I could even find it amusing to think that I was living in a haunted house. But was I, like the Sutherlands before me, playing psychological tricks with myself for the sake of enduring or overlooking a horrible truth?

In the end I couldn't bring myself really to believe that the footsteps I had heard, the shadows I had seen, had been caused by anything supernatural. The notion seemed more and more ridiculous with each passing hour. Even though the police and afterwards I myself went through the house and checked every window and door to make sure it was locked, I still told myself that somehow someone had gotten in. Who knew but that there were professional thieves who could enter and leave a house without a trace of intrusion? If they were skillful enough to pick a lock open, they could surely on their way out pick it closed. And yes, there was a part of me that knew how in thinking this way I was grasping at straws to make sense of what had happened. Of one thing I was certain: if by any chance there had been a burglar, I was never going to feel so terrified and helpless again. If he or anyone else entered my home in the middle of the night, he was going to get a lot more than he bargained for, namely, a bullet between the eyes. I decided to buy a gun.

Why not, after all? Why does anyone call the police when he feels physically threatened but because they have the power to protect and defend, and wherein does this power reside if not in their guns? I needed to have that same power.

I bought a shotgun. It was twenty gauge with a pump mechanism and fell on the low end of the Remington line. The man who sold it to me in the sports and hunting supplies store explained to me that it was perfect for shooting skeets and small game. There was a small shooting range behind the shop where I was able to "test" it. After shooting it a dozen times I felt comfortable with it. With a box of ammunition and tax, it set me back $435—a lot of money that would have to be made up for by stinting myself a few things in an already Spartan life. But the moment I walked out of the shop with it, my sense of relief was immense. At the very least I would never have to feel again the embarrassment of a police officer standing over me in the middle of the night, intimating, by his shaking head, that I might become a nuisance.

And then, on the same day, I got a big dog.

When I had gotten up that morning getting a dog had been the furthest thing from my mind, but on my way back from the gun shop I happened across an animal shelter and out of curiosity, and also perhaps as a delay to getting home, I pulled into the graveled driveway of the low, light-blue, flat-topped building and went inside.

The first, main room was large and lined with caged dogs who were either barking, silently wagging their tails, or lying on their stomachs with heads reclined on outstretched forepaws.

There were about fifteen people inside; most of them were parents who had come with their children to adopt a pet. In one corner stood a giant of a dog, a powerful, heavy, hulking animal who probably weighed as much as I did. Unlike the other dogs he wasn't in a cage—the shelter didn't have one big enough for him. Rather he was tied with a steel chain to a radiator in an area surrounded by a low wire fence. He stood looking at me as though he had been expecting me. I shuddered at the sight of him: What a monster it was!—how big! And what an expense such a creature would be to maintain! It would probably cost more to feed a dog like that than it would cost to feed myself. His tail wagged crazily at my approach and he tried to get my attention with pathetic yelps as I purposefully kept my eyes averted from his and walked past him.

The employees of the shelter were local high school or college kids who worked there part-time, making either minimum wage or nothing at all—doing the job gratis, out of their love of animals. They all wore blue shirts blazoned with the shelter's logo. Most of them were girls. There were four of them scattered about the room, talking to the families who had come to adopt, talking up this or that dog. One of them hurried over to me with a bright, "Hello there!" She wanted to know what kind of dog I was looking for, taking it for granted that I was. As she must have heard a hundred times a day I told here I was "only looking," and she, not skipping a beat, said:

"Well let me show you around!"—and without waiting for an answer or acquiescence she led the way.

Of the thirty-one dogs on display that day a few were purebred but most were mongrels. Most were young but a few were old. The poor things all shared a kind of quiet, hopeful desperation to get out there. They looked up at you with pleading eyes, knowing very well that they were being judged. If towards the end of the day it seemed to be a bit of an effort for them to be sociable—if they remained lying down, only languidly shifting their eyes to you, and giving but a begrudging wag of the tail— it was because for hours they had done their best to be liked and chosen, to show themselves chipper and loveable, only for all that effort to come to naught, only to be rejected again and again and sap them of their will. As I knelt down before their cages one by one, and the girl working for the shelter gave me their histories and glowing reports on their personalities (no doubt exaggerating in some instances so as to incline me to adopt), one big bark kept interrupting her discourse and filled the place with its deep, loud, insistent volume: the huge dog chained up by the radiator. He only fell silent when I turned to look at him. Then our eyes would meet; his agitation ceased; he would stand still, narrowing his gaze on me, licking his chops and impatiently pattering the floor with his forepaws.

"Look at that, he's looking right at you!" the girl said, smiling widely, apparently surprised. "He must like you! Wanna take a look at him?"

"No thanks. Way too big for me."

"Oh, but he's a pushover!" she insisted, and rather impertinently pulled me by the shirt and insisted that we *had* to "say hello" to Buddy. Just as she reached the wire fence around the dog she called out, "Buddy, somebody wants to see you!"

The dog barked, he yelped, he wagged his tail frantically; he pulled at his chain, rose rampant and frantically pawed the air. He had a very long tongue and it flopped about almost shamelessly.

At two years old he was fully grown; a dog larger than usual for his large breed—of which, in truth, I wasn't sure, and so asked, "What is he?"

"Well," the girl said, "we think he's a Great Dane mix."

"Mixed with what?—a horse?"

The girl laughed; noddingly admitted that he *was* a "big one"; but hurried to add that he was one of the sweetest dogs they had ever had, and that if I brought him home he would just want to play with me all day.

The dog's attentive brown eyes watched every least change and shade of expression on my face, followed every least movement of my eyes, my hands.

"Wow, I've never seen him act like that toward anyone," the girl said. "He's really crazy about you!"

She explained that he had been in the shelter for two weeks and was regarded as a "hard placement" on account of his size. ("No kidding," said I.) She grabbed one of the three leashes dangling from her belt and attached it to his collar as she led him out from his fenced-in area. The first thing he did was to jump on me, almost knocking me over, his tongue flying about crazily as he tried to get in a few licks. My escort suggested that we take him outside, where there was more room. Just behind the building was a small plot of land where the dogs were regularly walked and where a potential adopter could spend a little private time with a potential adoptee. Once outside Buddy repeatedly tried to jump up on me and lick me, and the one time I allowed him to do so he was so heavy that I was barely able to sustain his weight. With his paws on my shoulders and his big watermelon head only inches away from my own he swiped his washrag of a tongue over my face a few quick times.

"Oh, my God!" I exclaimed.

"Hey, this dog *loves* you!" the staffer said.

He was so happy to be out of his cage and with me that his energetic glee was divided between prancing in place and trying to jump on me. When he had calmed down a little he was still wagging his tail frantically and looking at me with a great smile. For dogs *can* smile—they have a way of pulling up their gums at the outer edges into an unmistakable expression of joy. "So, you like me, do you?" I silently asked him, as he watched me and seemed to be reading my thoughts. "That's very flattering. And you know that on some deep level I like you too. Who knows?—maybe we really are two of a kind, just made for each other. But the thing is, Buddy, you're huge, and I was really counting on something more manageable. How could I possibly keep you? I wanted a dog that would stay in the house with me; and you—in the house? I might as well keep a horse in my living room. And you'd eat me out of house and home. I can barely take care of myself, let alone you too. I'm sorry, you're a very nice dog and I'm sure you'll find an owner that can appreciate you, but I don't think I'm the one. It's just not possible ... believe me, it's for your own good ..."

Much to her disappointment, I told the girl that I didn't think this dog was appropriate for me. She tried to convince me otherwise but finally yielded in the face of my polite but adamant refusal to consider him further. Together we walked him back toward the shelter. But as though he knew what was happening, Buddy balked; he planted his hand-sized feet firmly on the ground and wouldn't budge. He had had his little taste of freedom, had sensed the possibility of a new master, and the

prospect of returning to his forlorn, chained-up existence beside
a radiator repulsed him to the bottom of his dog's soul. "C'mon,
you, c'mon!" the girl said, trying to pull him to no avail. She
asked me to get behind him and push while she continued to
pull and cajole. Buddy paid no mind to her and continually
turned his head around to look at me with eyes pleading to remain outdoors and in my company. Eventually he stood up,
moved forward with begrudging, halting steps, and followed the
tug of his leash. At the threshold of the shelter he balked
again, and there was more pushing, tugging, cajoling, scolding.
It was another five minutes before we finally got him back to
his corner in the main room. Just when I stepped away from
him, grateful that it was all over, he began to howl. He raised
his head and, with his eyes set upon me, let out a series of
howls so long, sad, and despairing—so obviously the expression
of an injured, longing spirit—that a human being would have
had to be utterly and degradedly heartless not to have recognized them for what they were.

"Ohhhh, looook!" the young woman said, perhaps purposefully giving the knife in my heart another turn. "He doesn't
want you to leave him! He loves you. Look at him!"

I didn't want to look at him. I knew myself too well. It
would be giving in—it would be surrender. But I did look at
him. Buddy at once stopped howling; just breathed hard, with a
kind of wheeze on the verge of a whine, and locked his eyes on
mine with the most hopeful, pleading expression a dog can assume. He even raised a paw and began raking the air as though
motioning for me to come back.

"Oh ... Alright!" I said. "I'll *try* him. But I can't guarantee
that I'll keep him!"

She was delighted. She assured me that if was really un-
manageable he could be returned; adding in the same breath
that she was sure I had made the right decision. "You'll see!
He'll be no trouble at all! Buddy just wants to be loved."

Needless to say, Buddy was ecstatic.

He wasn't housebroken and his first "mistake" terrified me
more than any burglar could: for there it was, only a couple of
hours after he had come home: a pond of urine spreading out on
the polished wood of the living room. He stood beside it looking
at me with a wagging tail, evidently proud of his accomplish-

ment. He only realized that he might have done something wrong in the face of my loud scolds. I hurried into the kitchen and came back with a roll of paper towels and set about the disgusting work of cleaning up. At that moment I vowed to get rid of him. Back to the shelter, tomorrow! I was not about to let his huge calls of nature turn the inside of my house into a cesspool. But my outburst and anger toward Buddy weren't entirely owing to his mistake; he had merely and unwittingly dropped the last straw onto a composure that had been stressed to the breaking point by a week of fear and frustration. And as he followed me back and forth to the kitchen, often wagging his tail and wanting to play, I couldn't deny that it was a comfort to have his faithful company.

"I'm giving you one more chance," I told him. "Just one!"

But in fact he would have more than a dozen chances before he got things right.

I intended for him to live in the house and sleep in my room beside the bed—my guardian. I laid down on the floor for him a triple-folded comforter which any normal dog would have been happy to spend the rest of his life on. Not Buddy. When the girl at the shelter had told me that he just wanted to be comfortable, she had been speaking literally. That creature refused to sleep on the floor. He reckoned that if a mattress was good enough for me then it had to be good enough for him. Every time I got into bed at night and told him that he must lie on the floor, and pushed down his bottom with a "Stay there!" he would just as soon get up onto his forelegs and sit staring at me, impatiently licking his chops as he watched for permission to hop aboard. When this wasn't forthcoming, he slowly, tentatively made his move, putting first one, then another paw on the bed, and inching forward as though he might achieve his objective by stealth. The first few nights I did my best to make him understand he wasn't welcome in my bed. I always shoved him back down to the floor with a commanding, "No!" But good heavens!—what a stubborn, single-minded dog! He wore me out. After unsuccessfully trying to make him stay down ten times in a row, I was too frustrated and tired to object when he finally crawled onto the bed and gingerly, almost delicately stepped over me and onto the free side of the mattress, where he plunked down all of his one hundred and forty-two pounds.

What was worse, he was determined to have his head close to mine and share my pillow. Of course it was ridiculous, but no matter how many times I pushed away his head, it always found its way back next to mine.   As though that weren't enough, fifteen minutes later he would throw an arm—I mean a leg—over me, and in that relaxed, comfortable, warm posture his breathing became even and he would fall asleep.

Over the next few days I made a point of spending time in the back yard with Buddy and my shotgun. It had occurred to me that if someone was surveilling me as a target for robbery or worse, he could only do this from the wooded bird sanctuary behind my house. Therefore I wanted him to get a good look at what he would be up against if he tried any more shenanigans. Apparently this strategy paid off : over the next two weeks nothing out of the ordinary happened. The house and my life reverted to their accustomed, grateful peace, quiet, and sense of security. My nerves settled and I returned to my writing.   I was very proud of myself. It seemed to me that I had taken matters into my own stern hands and had carried the day.   I was also relieved to think that my investment in my house was safe after all, that I could continue to live there happily.

Buddy proved to be the best of companions. He never left my side and he was an attentive guard dog.   Whenever he heard anything unusual his head and ears would perk up, his jaws would tighten in anticipation of aggression toward a stranger, and, should the noise continue, he would be up and off in order to investigate, filling the house with his loud, deep, threatening barks. Of course he had certain drawbacks, some of which had been foreseen, some not. For instance he ate a great deal, and to my chagrin I found that dog food wasn't all that cheap. He was also very needy. He hated to be left alone. I could scarcely drive the single mile to a grocery store but he wanted to come with me. Sometimes I just wasn't in the mood to take him and told him to stay put, that I'd be right back. He always understood what I was telling him and his reaction was always the same: he went to the door, sat before it, and moped, his sad, hopeful eyes silently pleading with me to take him along; and half the time I did so. But worst of all was his snoring.   During the course of the night he would wind up on his back—his legs spread-eagle—and begin snoring so loudly that it woke me up. I would have to shake him awake with a "Hey, cut it out!"—upon which he would roll over onto his side, raise his head a little, look at me bleary-eyed and wondering what was the matter, then let his head drop and lick his chops a few times as he went back to sleep.

One night after work, while sitting in the back yard and watching Buddy, at the river's edge, sniffing out frogs, I noticed that again the light was on in my office. Now, this time I recalled very well that I had shut it off. I wondered how it could have gotten on again. A faulty switch, perhaps? But then behind the gauzy curtains a shadow moved from left to right; and not just any shadow, but that of a person. The outline of a head, shoulders, and torso had been unmistakable. Someone was up there!

Unfortunately I didn't have my shotgun with me; it was in my bedroom. The thought occurred to me that if he—whoever that intruder was—got into my bedroom before I did, and found the gun, he would undoubtedly use it against me. I had to get to it first, and I vowed that the moment I had it in my hands I would blow his head off.

I called Buddy over to me in an intense whisper and made toward the house. In an instant the dog was at my heels, then ran in front of me. He sensed that something was wrong. When I opened the back door he dashed into the house, zooming into the dining room, then into the living room, where he hurriedly sniffed about; then, seeing that I was making for the stairs, he again rushed past me to the second floor, his heavy paws thumping on the steps. When I reached the hallway I saw him standing before the office, looking at it with a tilting head, growling: he knew someone was in there. I went to my bedroom, took up the shotgun, undid the safety, and holding the weapon and ready to fire went out to the hallway and stood before the office door. For a second I wondered if I really had it in me to blow away someone who might be in that room. I knew that I did—that I wouldn't think twice about it. This wasn't one of those improbable movies where the good guy holds the gun out before his ruthless enemy but inexplicably holds his fire and is consequently overtaken and killed.

I waited for a few minutes behind Buddy, expecting the doorknob to turn and the door to open. When after several minutes it didn't, I took the initiative and flung open the door. Buddy dashed in and I stood at the threshold and very nearly pulled the trigger, but in that split second I saw that there was no one inside.

It took me a minute just to calm down and catch my breath. When Buddy too had calmed down, and stepped over to me inquiringly as though to ask what we should do now, I stepped into the room more fully and looked about. Things had been disturbed on my desk. The keyboard had been moved to the side and my pens were not lined up in their accustomed array. Most disturbing of all, my manuscript had been tampered with. It no longer lay in a neat pile but was rather disheveled, and a few dozen of its top, most recent pages had been flung to the floor. Then I heard something behind me, a breath, a whispered sigh, and I turned in its direction; my eyes scanning the area, the corner of the room, from where it had seemed to come; and I saw something—I wasn't sure what. There was a darkness, a shadow there. At first it was hard to tell whether it was really a distinct entity amid the general gloom in which it stood, but on concentrating a little, on looking at it harder, I saw that it was different, was darker than its surroundings and even had a vaguely human outline. As though it abhorred discovery, it whisked away, a swift, dark blur; but its evasion was not so quick that my eyes had not been able to follow its general direction, and in the next few seconds I found it again, in the opposite corner of the room, where it was still more visible.

Fantastic!—that was my first reaction. A ghost—a real ghost! What was it made of? How could it exist? Did it see? Could it hear? What did it feel and what did it think? And just as I considered whether or not I should approach it, it dashed away, out of the room, out of the open door.

In another second a great racket came up from somewhere in the house below. I went downstairs, Buddy at my heels. The enormous clamor was coming from the kitchen. What I saw there I will never forget; it made me hold my breath in sublime wonder. Every cabinet door was swiftly opening and banging shut in a kind of mass flutter of mayhem. The wire dish rack by the side of the sink trembled and jumped, the plates and flatware in it clanking and chinking. The light in the middle of the ceiling fluttered on and off as though with an unsteady electrical current; elsewhere in the house lights dimmed or blinked. A subtle, prickly, ticklish, somehow ominous electrical tingle crawled on my skin. Buddy was barking at all this as he stood beside me. He would back up a few steps, then jump forward in a kind of half-hearted pounce, only to back up again; wanting, yet not daring, to venture forward. The animal sensed that this disturbance was caused by something outside of natural experience and, frightened, he eventually took a few whimpering steps behind my legs from around which he peered nervously.

After the initial shock wore off I even became somewhat objective about the nature of the phenomenon that was causing this disturbance: trying to figure out where it might be coming from, what it was made of, how it was able to move physical things. I stepped inside the kitchen so as to be the more fully among it. I pressed the barrel of the shotgun against one of the cabinet doors to ensure it remained closed; which it did for a moment; only to swing back out hard and forcefully. And then—everything stopped. The movement, the noise, the dreadful sense of otherworldly energy or anger dropped away. But this was not the end of it. One other remarkable thing occurred. A quick current of air passed by my ear. It was not the sensation that a breeze might give, or a fan, but rather that of an object—a *hand*—which swiftly passes by and just misses your head. I spun halfway around with the sense that someone had tried to touch or perhaps assault me.

Of course I didn't get much sleep that night. I was emotionally shell-shocked from what I had experienced. I went into the living room and sat there expecting at any moment another harrowing incident. But nothing else happened; the house remained still, quiet, its old peaceful self. Buddy sat beside me and for a while he too looked about in expectation, though eventually he lay down, closed his eyes, and began snoring in blissful sleep. I sat there for hours thinking, thinking of when I had first seen the house, of how I had loved it, of how I had insisted on buying it; and of how the realtor, Mrs. Greenbaum, had warned me against it. I silently railed against my stupid stubbornness, and asked myself what I was going to do. My first thought was to sell the house, but the obvious sticking point was that no one was going to buy it. Like every other person who had owned it I began to experience the oppressive sense of being "stuck" here. And like those other people I began to rationalize my situation and tried to convince myself that having a ghost about wasn't the catastrophe it seemed to be. "Let's say it does show up again," I told myself; "so what? It's just some pots and pans rattling, and lights blinking. It's just footsteps out in the hall or knocking on the walls. Nothing really threatening ... right?"

"Right," one part of myself assured me.

"Wrong," another part countered, more cogently.

For I couldn't know that whatever was causing these things wasn't a danger. If this ghost, or whatever it was, had the power to move things, then it could very well move them against me. I remembered what Mrs. Sutherland had said about the knives stuck in the kitchen counter and how one of them had been poised to fly at her...

Looking down at the shotgun, at Buddy, I shook my head to think to what lengths I had gone to defend myself against something that (as was now clear to me) couldn't be defended against by conventional means. There *was* a ghost in this house as surely as I was in it. What could I possibly do about it? And yet I *had* to do something. I had to have peace in my own home. I had to feel secure in it. I had to be able to sleep at night. Above all, I had to be able to work. The first draft of a new novel had been finished in a blaze of content-induced inspiration, but the haunting had obliterated my ability to continue to create, that is to say, to edit creatively, and I was spending my days in static frustration, unable to do anything other than anticipate terrible things, and *that* was something I couldn't afford to afflict me.

III

If I wound up turning to religion for help, it wasn't because I was "religious" but because it seemed I had no other resource. There was also a certain logic in supposing that people and institutions that for millennia had been concerned with the spirit, both before and after death, would have insights into hauntings and be able to dispel them. I called the nearest man of the cloth I could find, who happened to be a certain Rabbi Hersch (not his real name of course) of the conservative Temple Beth

Shalom. I described my problem to him, telling him all about the history of the house and what I myself had experienced, but after hearing me out, and hemming a few temporizing times, he replied that he didn't think he'd be able to help me.

"Why not?" I asked.

"Well, we don't believe in ghosts," he said, simply.

"Oh, really? Then you need to spend a few nights in my house."

"Are you sure it isn't a neighbor? Maybe some neighborhood kids are playing a prank on you."

"I don't have any neighbors."

"Well ... uh ... excuse me for asking, but ... are you on any *medication?*"

"No, rabbi, I am *not*," I said.

He must have heard the edge in my voice, for he didn't immediately say anything, and I continued:

"I am telling you that my house is haunted. I've seen the ghost myself !"

"You *have?*"

"I have."

A pause. "Hmmm ... well ...."

Still, he would not seriously entertain the notion. He said that while he was "conservative" in religious matters, and knew that God's wonders were illimitable and beyond the scope of man's knowing, he nevertheless was also a "modern" man who looked at curious matters with a "scientific" eye—and assured me that what are normally taken for ghosts are really phenomena that have very ordinary explanations: he mentioned three or four things that had nothing to do with anything outside one's head. Our conversation grew increasingly strained and in the end he all but called me a kook.

With a priest I had better luck, perhaps because I made my appeal in person.

If you took Fullbright Road south for about a mile, then turned right onto a street named Millay, and traveled down that for about a quarter of a mile, you would come to a small grocery store at which I had sometimes stopped to buy overpriced bread and half-and-half. About two hundred feet away from this store, on the other side of the street, was the First Holy Trinity Church, a small, white, wooden building with a louvered steeple.

The steeple held no real bell but rather a loudspeaker that peeled bell sounds on Sunday mornings and, during the Christmas season, played ringing carols.

That Sunday I sat at the back of the church during services and must have cut, apart and alone as I was in the last pew, a conspicuous figure. Most of the congregation consisted of older women, mothers and their young children, and men who struck me as somehow awkward. All morning the priest kept looking in my direction. Perhaps my exhaustion was evident to him despite the distance between us. Earlier that morning I had looked into the bathroom mirror and seen dark rings under my eyes: the unsightly consequence of not having slept more than thirteen or fourteen hours over the previous three nights. For something had always awoken me: some loud sound in my bedroom; some clangor of pots or dishes in the kitchen; some calling of my name—yes, an actual voice, calling my name! At these sounds Buddy had reacted even more dramatically than I: he had sat up, spluttered threatening growls, then hopped off the bed and dashed downstairs to run about the house for the next fifteen minutes, shattering the early morning with his huge and frenzied barks. It had gotten so bad that the previous night I had slept in my car; or rather, had tried to do so. But it had been impossible to get any real sleep there either, despite the blankets I had brought, and despite my fatigue, for the night was cold and the back seat was too short and lumpy. Buddy had had no choice but to lie on the floor beside me, and every position he could assume there was awkward and uncomfortable, so that he too remained largely awake.

The priest, then, noticed me from the first, as he was bound to notice anyone new in his small congregation, and all morning kept glancing at me.

Father Dominic Potz was in his sixties, of medium height, stout, and had thinning hair. He wore wire-framed glasses that magnified his light gray eyes. Throughout the service he smiled, winked, and nodded to his flock as though they were all personal friends who had happened to stop by his home on a social call. He exuded charm and goodwill. He was the ultimate showman: he had an instinct for comporting himself in a likeable way. He delivered a sermon of his own composition, which was discreetly musical and filled with fine phrases: obviously

the man had a literary bent. His congregation listened atten-
tively and appreciatively, at the right moments nodding in
agreement, tittering politely at his attempts at humor, and falling into a glum, almost repentant mood whenever he reminded
them to have a care for the short-comings common to all men.
In the end, he asked for God's blessing on everyone.

As every good priest should do, at the end of the service he
stood on the steps of the church and said goodbye to his depart-
ing congregation. They formed an orderly line to shake hands
with him and exchange a few polite or affectionate words. I
took my place at the end of the line. When he saw me only a
few persons away, he glanced at me a few times—always smiling—and was clearly pleased and expectant about meeting
someone new. We shook hands and I introduced myself, mentioning that I had bought a house on Fullbright Road.

"A nice area!" Father Potz said, giving a quick, approving
shake of his head. "How do you like it?" he asked, shifting his
eyes to the cars, station wagons, and pickup trucks by which all
his flock were leaving, the overwhelming majority of whom he
wouldn't see again till next weekend.

"The area's fine, Father. Unfortunately, the house I bought
has a bit of problem. I thought you might help me with it."

"Oh? How so?" he asked, still entirely jovial.

"My house is haunted."

His smile faded and he looked at me curiously, as though
trying to figure out whether I were serious or not. Seeing that I
was, he assumed a more deliberate, less trusting air, and asked:

"Why do you say that?"

"I say that because it's true. I hear footsteps when there's
no one there, and voices, and things move. I need help."

He could see I wasn't lying—he believed me—but that
didn't mean he acceded to my request. He proceeded to hold
forth on why what I thought was a ghost probably wasn't.
Surely, he said, I wouldn't think very much of him if he just accepted such claims at face value. He acted as though he had a
reputation to protect, and part of protecting it was convincing
me that whatever I had experienced could be logically explained.
Was I claiming—he asked—a case of demonic possession? If so,
well, there were "certain procedures" the Church had for authen-
ticating such things before any such extreme rite could be ad-

ministered.

"Father, do I look possessed?"

"You look ... tired."

"I am. I've barely slept in almost three days. I'm telling you there's a ghost in my house. I've heard and seen it. I don't know how it got there but I'm telling you it's there. Now there must be something you can do. Can't you at least come over, take a look or say a prayer or ... *something?*"

My request had in it enough despair to appeal to his humanitarianism, if not to his religion.

"Alright. If you'd like."

I convinced the good Father that there was no time like the present and fifteen minutes later he was following me to my home in his car. He brought with him a fancy, leather-bound New Testament and a large golden crucifix. He walked just behind me as we entered the house. At the sound of our entrance Buddy, who had been upstairs, probably lying in bed amid the comfort of crumpled sheets, came running down the stairs and bounding toward us. Before this enormous charge Father Potz stepped back and exclaimed, "Woa!" but I assured him that Buddy was friendly and only wanted to say hello. Still, he wasn't a fan of dogs and for about a minute he stood apprehensively rigid as he was sniffingly investigated. He had probably also been apprehensive about what he would find within the house, but when he saw before him clean, spacious rooms flooded with light, he became easy on this point also. Gingerly maneuvering around Buddy, the priest stepped into the living room, stood there looking about with approbatory nods, and said, "Nice place you got here!"

"Thanks."

"Yes, very nice.... *Love* the chairs. Where'd you get them?"

I told him the name of the store.

"Really? I've never been in there. I'll have to check it out. I could use a few new chairs. So!" he said, turning to me, cheerfully, "where does this, uh, *ghost* hang out?"

"No particular place. I've seen it upstairs in my office, and a few nights ago it was opening and closing the cabinets in the kitchen."

"You *saw* it?"

"I saw ... something, yes. It was just a shadow."

The terse specificity of these incidents seemed to surprise him; suddenly, he looked at me with the bank stare of someone who realizes he might have gotten into something he hadn't counted on. Then he cleared his throat a little and said, "Well, how about if I just give the house a general blessing? That should take care of it!"

For the next twenty minutes he himself haunted the house, going into every room, walking through every hallway, standing before every closet, and venturing down into the basement; holding up the crucifix before him in his left hand while in his right he held a brown vial of holy water, which he flicked here, flicked there, at specific moments during a mumbled Latin exhortation to the offending spirit to be gone forevermore. When he had finished he came to back to me and Buddy, who were waiting for him in the living room, and with a great, satisfied smile asked me if there were anything else he could do for me. I responded that there wasn't and thanked him for coming, even as I was suspicious of the swift ease of his ministrations.

"Well, then, I'm glad I could help out. And"—lifting an exhortatory finger—"don't forget about us, will you? Come to church now and then. Why not? It can't hurt and it might do you some good."

I told him that I would take him up on the offer—that he was sure to see me now and then—and as I led him to the door I pressed on him a small donation for his church, which he accepted only after repeated importunities.

I watched him get into his car and drive off, then I shut the door and turned back inside the house. The complete and heavy silence obtained once more. I stood there listening— watching— waiting; wondering if it was possible that Father Potz had done the job. More than anything I wanted to believe that he had done so. At my side Buddy looked up at me, watching me, curious about my listening, waiting immobility. I gave him a few idle pats on the head and murmured, "Well, my friend, it looks as though we've finally got the place to ourselves"—at which he tilted his head and wagged his tail a little in sympathy with my satisfaction.

Of course when something seems to be too good to be true it usually is, which is why it strikes me in retrospect as ridiculous that Father Potz or anyone else could have exorcized with a

few pro-forma incantations, a few perfunctory sprinklings of water, the ghost of the place. Besides, I now see that this was not
your "average" ghost. Whatever human impulse or essence had
given rise to it had long ago transmogrified into something else,
something so far apart and alien from the general nature of
mankind as to be unaffected by its ultimately bogus rituals.
Very likely it had indifferently followed Father Potz about the
house as he had gone from room to room dispensing his blessings and compelling it be gone.

Two days and nights passed uneventfully. I slept well
those two nights. On the third day, my body and mind fully
rested, my ambition returned to read and write. I read most of
the day and by six o'clock I was at my desk and working on my
book. What a relief it was to sit down to it again! How much
time I had wasted! I wanted and intended to make up for it.
When I went upstairs to my office (Buddy of course following
me, then lying on the floor beside me) I picked up the most recent few pages of the manuscript, read them, and tried to get
into the same spirit that had created them, and which would be
necessary to continue where they left off. I pulled up the file on
my computer and began typing.

One always hopes it will be easy to write—that an access of
inspiration will let the words and ideas flow freely, and sense
and sentiment will be one with the words even as they appear.
Practice helps to ensure this ease, which, however, for me, has
always been a very fragile thing: compromised by but a few
days' hiatus from work. And so at first I did struggle a little
with carrying on the book till an hour had elapsed and something of the old confidence and ease returned, making me the
more eager to continue. I remember telling myself that I might
very well write all night in a rare marathon of creativity.

By ten o'clock I had gotten some fifteen pages done and
printed them out. I took the pages into my hands and proudly
neatened the edges by tapping each side of the little pile against
the desktop, then I laid it down square before me with the intention of reading it over. I had only read the first line when ...
a couple of clicks sounded.

Keys on the keyboard had been pressed. There, on the
monitor, was the proof of it: the number 13.

I wondered if I had done it, only at once to realize that my hands hadn't been anywhere near the keyboard.

Then it happened again, and this time I saw it with my own eyes: another key—an A—clicked down.

Silence.

I stood up at my chair and looked about me. Buddy, lying on the floor, raised his head.

I knew something was going to happen, something strange; and it did. With a fury and a flurry the keyboard clicked away madly as though hands were pounding it indiscriminately. On the screen garbage verbiage swept across the screen where the last sentence of my own writing had left off. I stood silently watching this, less afraid than astonished as though some new phenomenon of nature were revealing itself to me. The ghost typing continued for some thirty seconds, and then stopped.

From behind me came a faint, tittering laugh. I turned around to see a movement of darkness sweep out the door, and the door itself slammed shut so hard and loudly that Buddy jumped up and I myself started out of what had been a stationary, static wonder. Both my dog and I stood listening to the slamming of other doors downstairs, one after another, again and again, for nearly a minute. And then that racket also stopped ...

In the ensuing silence I could hear my own heart beating hard as astonishment gave way to fear—but fear of a strangely immobilizing kind. Usually when we are afraid of something we have a definite idea of what it is; experience, or at least logical deduction based on experience, enables us to understand its nature, and directs a specific and not unreasonable defensive reaction. But before a threat entirely unknown?—before something that even our wildest imagination cannot conceive? Then we stand in static amazement, our minds, overloaded with the effort to make sense of what we see, having little or no capacity left over with which to direct us to some definite reaction. And so I just stood there; watching, listening; aware that I *should* do something—but completely at a loss as to what could be done. When I finally left my office and stepped carefully into the hallway, I stopped, listened, and, only after hearing nothing for some minutes, ventured on. With every step I anticipated some sudden frightening thing popping up in front of me. But nothing did. I went from room to room, and all was silent, still, the

way it should be. But of course by now I knew very well that in
this house things were never less normal than when they
seemed to be so.

A few hours later I was still awake, sitting in the living
room, on the couch, with Buddy, who was lying beside me with
increasingly tired, closing eyes. Whenever he nodded off I
would nudge him awake, saying, "Hey!" He would open his eyes
and look at me expectantly for a minute as he tried to figure
out what I wanted. Poor thing, to be the vassal of such a master, in such a situation! But if he was irritated with me he
never was so for more than a few seconds. Invariably he once
again lowered his head onto his extended forepaws, looked to
the left and right a few times under raised brows, and, after
licking his lips once or twice, would close his eyes. Really, I
never thought I would envy a dog, but I envied him just then: to
be able to sleep—to forget one's problems—to live only in the
very present.

But there could be no sleeping for me in the house that
night. I got off the couch (Buddy suddenly wide awake and following me) and went upstairs to gather up some blankets and
pillows, and headed outside to try to sleep in the car again.
And this time, in order to help me along, I brought a bottle of
whiskey.

The night was already chilly and before morning it would
get very cold. Buddy's body somewhat warmed up the air in
the car but despite his presence and the blanket covering me I
felt cold in the back seat. Eventually only the whiskey took the
chill out of the air and the edge off my despair. I offered a swig
to the dog but he just sniffed the bottle once and quickly turned
away from it. And so covered with a blanket, and sipping Ken-
tucky bourbon, and wanting more than anything else for the
night to pass and morning to come, I sat staring through the
windshield at the house that seemed so peaceful under the blue
light of the stars but which represented a major debacle in my
life. For the first time, too, I saw it the way Mrs. Greenbaum
had seen it. Only now could I relate to her silent, morose, resistant attitude when we first drove up to the house in the full
light of day. What had then struck me as its charm now
seemed to me a wilful deception by which to hide its true, sinister nature, and the better to entrap the naive and unsuspecting.

A quarter of a bottle of whiskey later I fell asleep, but in a few hours I woke up shivering with cold and afraid to move my head because of a stiff neck. I was exhausted and very thirsty on account of the alcohol. Buddy too hadn't slept well and now that I was awake he stood up on his forelegs, yawned, and looked at me expectantly, almost with an air of tired accusation, as though to ask, "What the hell are we doing out here?"

"Impossible," I told him, "it's impossible to live like this."

The next day I went to see Father Potz again, and when I rang the bell at the rectory he opened the door. At the sight of me he uttered a surprised, automatic, "Oh! Hello there!" and then fell silent as he saw in my face the pale expression of some trauma undergone.

"You look terrible," he said.

"I had to sleep in my car last night."

He suspected why. He invited me inside and listened to me tell him what had happened with an uncharacteristic serious-ness of expression bespeaking his now confirmed belief in the truth of what I was saying; for he hadn't really believed in the ghost before, not even as he had gone through the house with every appearance of taking it seriously and, as a man of God, blessing it away. But now that he did believe it—believe at least that something was there—he was at a loss as to how he might help me. He put his hand up thoughtfully to his mouth and looked about a little distractedly—thinking, thinking what to do. He paced the room, stopping a few times as though he would say something, only to stand silently and then continue pacing. His behavior made it clearer to me than ever that the subject of ghosts disturbed and even repulsed him; he acted as though it challenged his ecumenical standing and belief. And since that time I have noticed the same reaction among other "religious" people. They relegate the subject of ghosts to the dangerously diabolical or the pathetically psychological—as something either arising from the menacing pit of hell or the sad clinicalities of mental derangement. They will readily admit the influence of angels and saints because a scripture or some long-dead authority of their church says so, but dismiss as pre-posterous any living, first-hand account of, say, the spirit of one's recently deceased grandfather or uncle floating in the liv-ing room. It seems to me a grossly arbitrary prejudice. But so was it with Father Potz who seemed determined not to get involved in the matter.

"I know!" he said, suddenly, brightly. "It just occurred to me! There's this place out here .... oh ... what's it called ... para ... psycho ... something.... Wait!" He hurried over to a bookcase from the bottom shelf of which he took out a Suffolk County Yellow Pages and began flipping through it, quickly finding the entry he had been searching for and putting a finger on it. He looked up to me cheerily and said, "This is what you need, my friend"—and with his finger still on the entry he came over to me to show me his discovery: The Suffolk County Paranormal Society.

"What is that?" I asked.

"Just what it says. They do all that paranormal stuff. You know—ghosts, ESP, stuff like that. Probably UFOs and aliens too, for all I know."

"Father, this isn't a joke," I said, wearily.

"I'm not saying it's a joke!" He leaned away from me a little and regarding me with the surprised and somewhat offended air, as though I had insulted him. "I'm trying to help you," he said, innocently.

I nodded in acknowledgment and apology, and watched him go over to his telephone and dial the phone number for the organization. When his call was answered he identified himself in a matter-of-fact tone of voice, mentioning that one of his parishioners—as he referred to me—had a "problem" and was not sure how he ought to go about solving it. Apparently in answer to several questions he said, "Yes ... yes ... well, I don't know ... I don't think so ... I'm not sure ..."—until, finally, he said, "Well, he's right here. Why don't you speak to him?"—and handed me the phone.

The woman on the other end of the line asked me all sorts of questions: when the haunting had begun, how it manifested itself, whether I had been physically assaulted in any way, and so forth. She asked me about the history of the house and I told her all I knew. She asked me if I had ever had any similar experiences. She received my answers with the distant aplomb of a doctor hearing patient describe his symptoms. She took my phone number and told me that she would pass the information along to her "Director"—I am afraid I rolled my eyes at the word, and Father Potz, seeing this, questioningly tilted his head at me. She told me that I should be hearing from someone soon, probably no later than this evening. I handed the phone back to the priest.

"Well?" he asked.

"They're going to call me back."

"Good! Now we're getting somewhere!" Clearly he was relieved at having thrown the uncomfortable ball into someone else's court.

Though some glimmer of hope seemed finally to be visible (no more than a glimmer, however, since I had no idea what a "paranormal society" could do for me), the fact remained that in practical terms my situation was at the moment as bad as ever. For I still had to spend the night in my house, and the very thought of this terrified me. Standing in the dark, close, yet somehow snug living room of the rectory, it struck me that this was the one place I really wanted to be, for its numerous religious portraits and symbols seemed to indemnify it against the diabolical intrusion of ghosts. Several times I was on the verge of asking Father Potz if I might spend the night here; only in the next moment to hold my peace, aware of how presumptuous such a request would be. We hardly knew each other, after all. But as each second brought me closer to leave-taking, to going back to my house, my nervousness, my dread took greater hold of me, I became distracted, heaved deep sighs, looked appealingly to the cleric before me. At times Father Potz spoke to me and I didn't even hear what he said. He asked:

"Are you sure you're alright?"

"Yes," I said; but then, more honestly, "No."

He tilted his head, looked at me as though to say, "What is it?"

—Oh, but I had to ask him! I knew it was wrong of me, that it was an imposition on his good nature and, as such, rude; but I felt that I had no choice. Prefacing my request with an apology for making it, I explained to the priest that I didn't want to go home, for obvious reasons, but that unfortunately I didn't know anyone I could stay with "in the meantime." Would it be alright—did he think it was at all possible?—that I might spend the night with him, in the rectory? I hastened to add that I would be perfectly happy sleeping on the couch, and that

I would leave as early as possible the next day.

As I knew would happen, he didn't respond at once and was perhaps even a little resentful that I had asked the favor. He raised his brows and seemed about to explain why he couldn't, unfortunately, accommodate me, then looked to me and clearly felt bad for my predicament. No doubt he also felt impelled by his station in life to be a comfort and help when he could. In the end, the same essential goodness of the man, which had drawn him to his faith, influenced him now despite himself. I could see and hear that he had granted my request by the way he asked, tentatively:

"Well ... are you really sure you don't have anywhere else to go?"

"I suppose I could sleep in my car again. And I wouldn't mind it so much if were summer. But it was really cold last night."

"Well ..."—looking about a little helplessly—"... I suppose it would be alright. There are three bedrooms here. I suppose you could stay in one."

My relief was immense. I felt as though a terrible burden had been lifted from me—a reprieve. I thanked him profusely and made a silent vow to myself to make another generous contribution to his church. Father Potz seemed confirmed in the rightness of having conceded to my request, for he smiled confidently.

"And Father, I hate to ask you this, but would it be alright if I brought Buddy with me?"

"Buddy?"

"My dog."

"Oh ..."—he looked worried. "That big thing?" —It was as close as to a refusal as he could come.

"I know he's big, Father, but he won't be any trouble at all. He's very sweet. He wouldn't hurt a fly. And I just can't leave him alone all night." And when it seemed he still vacillated on this point I added the nudge: "One of God's creatures, Father ..."

He relented.

I shook his hand and said I'd be back that evening.

Later that afternoon I received a call from one Lucy McKenna, the "Director" of the Paranormal Society. She pretty much asked me the same questions the previous woman had asked me. For fifteen minutes she heard me detail the bizarre goings on in the house, especially of what had happened the day and night before, and how I had gone to Father Potz and he had recommended her organization for me. She sounded excited to hear all this and said she would like to "investigate the phenomenon" as soon as possible. I told her the sooner the better, and suggested the next day, but she told me that earliest she could "set something up" would be next week—a whole four days away. She had, after all, she said, to make arrangements with the "medium" she worked with—at the very mention of which I felt a despairing, almost sickening sense of my predicament: that I should ever feel I had no choice but to throw in my lot with a group of possible quacks and shysters.

I decided too that I wouldn't go back home during this time. There was no point in remaining in a place the very sight of which had come to disturb me. Nor did I intend to remain with Father Potz: I couldn't bring myself to impose on him for so long a time. I told him that I would find another place to stay, would look up a motel and move in there for a while. He said nothing, only nodding, apparently agreeing to that. We spent the evening talking and he began to feel more comfortable with me so that, the next day, he made the suggestion that I remain with him till I "got things cleared up"—an offer for which I was very grateful.

The woman I had spoken to on the phone, Lucy McKenna, came with her "medium" four days later, in the afternoon.

Now, there are expressions and words from sometimes the briefest encounters, the most indifferent-seeming moments of our lives, that we never forget. At the time we think nothing of them; they seem as trivial as any other incident of the day. Then a week or a month or a year later we recall them, and thereafter they stick in our memories and grow in significance. This happens because they come to epitomize a whole time of our lives or some period in which we changed in some fundamental way. And so I will never forget the words:

"Oh, it's definitely a child!"

—Thus the medium, who had only just stepped over the threshold and shaken my hand. She had but taken the briefest look about before making the pronouncement. Then, asking, "Do you mind if I look around?" she proceeded to walk further into the living room in the center of which she stopped and stood for a whole five minutes, her eyes closed, her head slightly held back; listening, waiting, sensing; absorbing whatever it was that she alone could absorb.

Her name was Trudy and she was not what I had expected to see in a "medium," but then again the only thing I had expected was someone strange, and though already she rather fit that bill, she didn't *look* the part. If anything she looked overwhelmingly ordinary, the kind of woman one could find any day of the week in a supermarket pushing a cart down the frozen food aisle. In her early forties, of medium height, she had bleach-blonde hair and was overweight by about thirty pounds. She wore jeans that were too tight and a sweater that was too large even for her buxom torso. Her roundish face, with its slight double chin, was comfortably mild and unassuming; she had probably been fairly attractive in her younger, slimmer years. She lived in Levittown with her husband, an electrician, and three children, all under the age of ten. On account of the youth of her children, and the need to mother them properly, she was picky about which "assignments" she agreed to take on (apparently there were a lot more haunted houses on Long Island than one would think) and she always insisted on seeing for herself the venue she was asked to investigate. She worked for free, having always regarded her "gift" as something bestowed on her by God for the benefit of her distraught fellows. I never found out what religion she was, and I don't think she had one. She wore a tiny, gold-capped crystal around her neck, but it was uncertain whether that was an emblem of her spiritual belief or merely a piece of jewelry.

"Yes, it's definitely a child," she said again, this time turning to Lucy and me with an air of pride in having quickly identified the nature of the spirit.

"Are you sure?" I asked.

"Absolutely," she said. "A young boy. Probably thirteen or fourteen ... no older than that."

"Well, tell the little bastard to get lost!"

She smiled at what to her was an amusingly naive demand.

"I'm sure he's heard you say that a hundred times," she said. She turned back to the room, directing her gaze to the staircase, and added, "But he won't leave. Not like that. Do you mind if I go upstairs?"

She went up to the second floor with a kind of hesitant respect, a studied carefulness, letting her hand glide along the handrail as she ascended, her face, her eyes lifted upward to the landing, watching and listening, it seemed, for the thing she knew to be there.

In a low, confidential voice Lucy said to me, "This is very, very good!"

"Why?"

"She's never been so definite before. That means there's something here."

"I could have told her that," I said.

Trudy was upstairs less than two minutes when we who were downstairs heard her voice—it was no more than an inarticulate cry of surprise—and a few seconds later she came hurrying down to the living room in that awkward, panting way overweight people have when they try to descend steps quickly. She looked flushed, worried; her eyes were wide and tense. Something had scared her. When she reached us she announced, "It's terrible!"

"What is?" Lucy asked.

"Just ... whatever happened!"

"What happened?" I asked.

She only shook her head; she herself couldn't say exactly. She had been walking down the hall when a horrible commingling of dark sensations had struck her in the pit of the stomach and suffused her whole being: anger, resentment, despair, and uttermost hopelessness. As she spoke she put her hands to her stomach as though she could still feel these things churning, eating away within her. She breathed deeply and said she would like to go outside for a while, and Lucy and I followed her out onto the porch, where she stood in silence, continuing to hold her stomach, swallowing frequently but slowly coming round to her old, calmer self. A few times she looked to the front door as though to see into the interior of the house; always, again, thoughtfully. Then she turned to Lucy and me with an air of decision.

"I think we might need to hold a séance," she said.

Oh, this was getting rich! A little, impertinent laugh

burped out of me. Fortunately for me, it was so small and quick that neither of the women around me recognized it for what it was: an expression of scoffing incredulity.

Lucy herself seemed to hear the suggestion with reserve or mild disagreement, regarding her medium a little critically. Apparently "séances" were not things that the Suffolk County Paranormal Society usually did, or (as was in fact the case) had ever done. She asked her colleague, "Are you sure?"

Trudy nodded, yes. "It would be best, in this case. The thing is ... I *need* to make contact. There's so much anger and sadness there." And shifting her eyes to me, she said, "You *do* want to get rid of him, don't you?"

"Of course."

"But you should know something: there's no guarantee I *can* get rid of him ... not something like this."

"Why not?"

"Because"—she looked back to the house, and gave an uncertain shake of her head—"I think this one's more complicated."

"That doesn't tell me very much," I observed.

"It's in everything about the place," she said, turning her eyes up to the ceiling of the porch, then floor, then to the open door and the interior. "It's in every brick and stick of it. It's saturated with it, through and through. It *is* so nice on the outside ... it all so pleasant, happy, sure of itself ... but in the inside it's all ..."—and she left off with a shake of the head as though at a loss for words to describe the completeness of the malign manifestation. She turned to Lucy and said, "We can come back tomorrow night and do it. I think we should take Mike and Adam with us too."

Lucy explained that they were two fellows who worked with the Society and who were responsible for recording important investigations. She asked for and received my permission for them to come to the house and set up their equipment. She was also forthright in telling me that the Society would have full and exclusive rights to whatever recordings they made of any paranormal activity. At first I balked at this—it seemed to me that she was a little too quick to make money at my expense—till she explained that it was one of the few ways that Society had for making money and remaining a solvent entity.

On that consideration I relented: after all, their organization, like any other, had to have the means to stay in business, and, besides, they weren't asking me to pay for anything.

Later that night as I sat in Father Potz's rectory, both of us holding hot cups of tea, he shook his head doubtfully about the séance to be held in my house. If he had felt put off by the notion of a ghost he was definitely hostile to that of a séance. He tried to talk me out of it, using, first, the secular arguments that it might very well be a setup, a vehicle for fraud, and then switching over to his dogmatic conviction that spirits were either forever and gratefully enfolded in the delights of heaven or were eager to escape from the fiery chambers of hell—in which latter case a séance only abetted their release and its dangerous consequences. Then he surprised me by asking:

"Are you *so* sure that there is a ghost there?"

—Yes, surprised me; as though even now he couldn't believe in the truth of the thing.

"Do you believe I'm making it all up?" I asked him.

"No," he said, after a reflective moment. "I know you've told me the truth. I know you have—I can see it. It's not that. But this thing ... this ghost ... isn't possible, isn't it conceivable, that there's something more to it? Isn't it possible that it's there for a reason?"

"I don't care what the reason is. I can't live there as long as it's there."

"It hasn't harmed you, though."

"Yes it has. It's done the worst kind of harm to me: it's made it impossible for me to work."

"Oh, my," he said, shaking his head and looking at me now as though with disapproval for an unhealthy obsession. "You sure are keen on your work."

"It's all I've got," I said. "It's all I am."

"Oh, please. You're much more than that."

"No. I'm nothing but that. In everything else I'm a total failure, but in my work I succeed—at least a little. That's why it means so much to me. I bought that house so that I could work. And I *was* getting a lot done till this ... this *thing* happened and stopped everything. I won't be able to work again till I get rid of it."

Father Potz considered my words for a few seconds,

shrugged a little as though accepting them at face value, and then asked, "Well ... what will you do if your séance doesn't work and you can't get rid of it?"

"I don't know. I guess I'll have to find another place to stay. Don't worry," I said, laughing a little to see a shadow of alarm pass over his face, "not here."

"Where?"

I just shook my head and forced an indifferent smile. The fact was that I had nowhere else to go. I had never considered the possibility of losing my home. Ironic that the spectre of homelessness loomed greater for me then than in all the years in which I had never owned a home and had struggled with paying rent!

The next evening, at six o'clock, Lucy and Trudy came with the two men, Michael and Adam, who were also associated with the Paranormal Society. Michael was thirty years old and came from a Connecticut family whose wealth had saved him from the tedium of working for a living and left him time to pursue his otherworldly interests. He talked as though chasing ghosts was the most exciting and interesting thing a man could do in life. Adam seemed to agree with him, but he was not so financially lucky, for he came from poorer stock and could only assist the Society on those days when he didn't have to work. They carried several plastic and nylon cases containing video cameras, electromagnetic sensors, digital sound recorders—all meant to record whatever activity the séance summoned up. They placed a camera pointing down the hall upstairs, another one in a corner of the dining room, so as to include a full view of it and the kitchen, and one more in the living room, intended to record the séance itself. They had brought a small, round table with foldable steel legs. The chairs I provided, using all four from the dining room table and going out into the back yard to fetch the lawn chair to complete the seating for five.

Trudy insisted that we hold off on having the séance till after sundown. She said there were practical, "scientifically-based" reasons for doing so; namely, that at night there were fewer sources of interference scrambling through the atmosphere—no rays from the sun, less cell phone radiation, and so forth; all of which interfered with ghosts' ability to come forward, and which accounted for their invariably haunting places in the dead of night. "We'll have to leave Buddy outside too," she said. "Animals can see and sense things that we can't, and he might disturb us."

Poor dog, he didn't like being banished from company, which excited and pleased him. I led him outside to the back yard and told him he had to stay out there a while. He stood on the back steps looking quizzically up at me, not understanding what was going on, and as soon as I turned away and closed the door on him he began barking and scratching at the door to be let in. Several times I had to go back to him and tell him to be quiet—that this was only a temporary situation—before he settled down.

It was just after dark, at seven o'clock, when we took our seats around the table, in the center of which a candle had been placed and was now lit. Trudy asked me to shut off all the lights, which I did with the misgiving recollection of Father Potz belittling the séance as the vehicle for a hoax. I remember looking carefully at the table they had brought to see if it had any secret or sliding compartments, and noting that it couldn't possibly have them since it was of the simplest, flimsiest sort. Michael sat on one side of me and Lucy on the other. In the flickering, dim orange light we all gave one another brief, encouraging smiles and for the first few minutes most of us felt like kids playing a spooky game. Trudy told us to join hands, and then counseled us that she herself wasn't sure what to expect. She would, she said, try to make contact with the ghost of the place through the intercession of her "spirit guide"—a phrase which raised my suspicion for its hackneyed flavor. She added, "No matter what you see or hear, don't break the circle and stay in your seats."

The medium closed her eyes and lowered her head. For the next ten minutes we sat in a silence interrupted only by the sound of our breathing or the fidgeting movements we made in our chairs. We all intermittently felt a little uncomfortable holding one another's hands. When we were not watching Trudy, expecting her at any minute to give some sign that she had detected or was otherwise influenced by a spirit, we cast anticipatory glances at one another. I confess that as the minutes went by and nothing happened I began to castigate my gullibility in expecting succor from people who made, if not a livelihood, then certainly a hobby, out of chasing ghosts. My sitting among them holding their hands at a candle-lit table struck me suddenly as ludicrous. If there was something going on in the house, a spirit or a force or an entity of some kind, it seemed to me that this couldn't be the way to get rid of it.

Trudy looked as though she had fallen asleep. Now and then her lips moved ever so slightly as she sent up some silent incantation or appeal. The candle burned steadily. To my right, Michael sat patiently, now and then quietly clearing his throat; to my left, Lucy kept her eyes on the tabletop just in front of her. Adam, the youngest among us, sat with his mouth a little open, expectant as he glanced at each of us in turn. How much longer were we to wait before our medium opened her eyes and informed us that she wasn't "getting" anything, that this wasn't going to work? The irony of the ghost's failure to come forward wasn't lost on me. It would be just my luck that it stayed away when I had four persons to witness it.

Another five minutes passed and even Lucy was getting impatient and seemed to be on the verge of speaking up. But then something did happen, though it was so subtle and faint that none of us could definitely have said its cause was supernatural. The flame of the candle, which had been burning with a soft and steady glow, guttered as though someone had lightly breathed against it; its small light wavered and wobbled and threatened to go out. We all sat up a little straighter. Lucy tightened her grip on my hand, and Michael and Adam, whose postures had sagged with either relaxation or boredom, became more alert and glanced around the table. Trudy heaved an audible breath.

Then a couple of things happened that struck me at the time, and even more so now, as bizarrely out of place. First, a horn sounded—a short, sharp toot. It came from above us, just over our heads. It was the last thing any of us expected to hear, and we all, except Trudy, jumped a little in our seats and turned our heads up toward the darkened ceiling. Then the next weird thing: something fell onto the table: a stemless rose. It had to come out of nowhere. There was no way it had been hanging or otherwise put above us. It had materialized in an instant and dropped onto the table. One's mind raced to think what connection there could be between it and the tooting of the horn a second earlier. We were all astonished before the power that could produce these things, and felt a chill bafflement at the intelligence which had so incomprehensibly paired them.

As for the possibility of fraud—the idea did cross my mind. But when I looked to Michael, then to Adam, then to Lucy— looked hard and perhaps a little angrily at them, as though to challenge them against trying to hoodwink me—the only thing visible in their faces was an astonishment no less innocent than my own. Besides, their hands had all the while been on the table for anyone to see.

Something moved in the darkness of the dining room— there was a sound of an object scraping across the floor. We looked in that direction but could see nothing clearly.

Trudy had had her eyes closed, but now she opened them, looked at us, and reminded us again in a whisper, "Don't break the circle—stay in your seats." Had she heard the horn? Seen the rose? Apparently yes; they were par for her strange course. She closed her eyes again and murmured something, speaking to someone, to a "you" whom she asked for assistance, saying that she wanted to make contact with the spirit in the house. From the darkness of the dining room came a low, barely-audible gurgle as of a person struggling to form words...

Something about Trudy was changing. She sat up more rigidly as though steeling herself against some obnoxious change occurring within her. Her lips were clenched increasingly hard; she seemed to be struggling. Her arms no longer rested on the table but stretched straight out and stiffened. Her hands clasped hard those of Adam and Michael. Then one side of her hair blew outward as though someone had mussed it up; she jerked her head away from that direction as though repulsed by that invisible hand. Her lips became still more compressed with determination and she shook her head negatively as though in renewed resistance against something. For a few seconds she almost relaxed, and then opened her eyes.

There was a change in them. Ordinarily they were hazel and light but now they had darkened and there was a gloomy and somehow masculine intensity about them. Everyone could see that she wasn't herself. Her demeanor, her aura, as it were, had changed. Her cheerful, helpful personality had been over- whelmed and pushed aside by one that was angry and pugnacious. She looked first to Michael and Lucy on either side of her as though she didn't know who they were, then shifted her eyes to me, whereupon her eyes narrowed with hostile recognition. She swallowed hard a few times and with little shakes of her head, which were the only outward signs of some internal resistance, and she murmured, "No ... no ... no ..." She wasn't speaking to me; she was speaking to *it*. For whatever influence had compromised her personality had not been able to command it completely. There was a part of her that remained safely aloof from it, and which ensured the continuation of her own will and objectivity. It was just this ability to segregate her personality from otherworldly energies that constituted her talent as a medium. No matter how forcefully or malevolently spiritual forces entered into her, she had the ability to maintain the core of her being and conscience, and so remain an objective and accurate relay between the worlds of the seen and unseen. Now she was clearly engaged in that internal grapple with a force that would have overtaken and controlled a less able person. Though *its* eyes were on me, *she* not only kept it in check but silently, internally interrogated and probed it, trying to learn its origins and intentions, perhaps too any weaknesses by which it might be undermined. Her hands constantly tightened their grip on her tablemates to either side of her; at times it seemed she was holding onto them for life itself. Then Trudy's mouth became a rictus of pain or anger and her eyes rolled back into her head as she made a strange gurgling sound. The candle guttered as though someone had breathed on it.

From upstairs came a bang: a door slammed. A few moments later a hundred pieces of paper billowed down the stairwell as though driven by a whisking wind. I recognized them as the pages of my manuscript. They scattered on the stairs and flew some distance into the living room, where, once they had settled, they were whirled around again, blown up toward the ceiling, against our faces, onto the table.

I am not someone who is easy to anger but the sight of those pages, of the labor of hundreds of hours, of the hope of the years to come, thrown indifferently and hatefully about like that, raised my gorge. "Bastard!" I said, and glared back at the entity looking out at me through Trudy's strangely unfocused eyes. Though she had instructed us not to touch or speak with her during the séance, she was the only conduit through which I might vent my rage against the thing that was wreaking havoc in my life, and so I spewed my curses and vituperation at her— at it.   Lucy, Michael, and Adam kept shushing me, reminding me that I had to be quiet, but the floodgates of my anger had been opened, and I continued to assail the ghost with every vile name that gutter English could summon up. And *it* heard me.

It heard me, and it saw me, and, more than anything else, it knew that in me it had come face-to-face with a will no less inflexible and, yes, even more cruelly determined than its own. And it lashed out in frustration.

Trudy lunged back in her chair, both the chair and herself sliding back for the space of two feet.   The force that had pushed her back was so strong that Lucy and Adam would have been pulled out of their chairs had they not let go of her hands. The last thing anyone saw before the candle went out was that Adam had stood up and was making toward her, apparently on the way to rendering her assistance.   In the darkness the rest of us also stood up, not sure of what was happening or what we ought to do.   We all felt a cold rush of air that had come out of nowhere and which swept up the manuscript sheets on the floor, tossing them up again so that they fluttered around us. The dining room table slid across the floor and slammed hard into a wall.   In the darkness other things moved, fell, or were flung and hit the walls with loud, shattering impacts.   Apparently Trudy had fallen: in the darkness I could see that Adam and Lucy were helping her to her feet, asking her in subdued, hurried voices if she was alright.   A beam of light cut through the darkness: Michael had taken out a tiny flashlight attached to his key chain.   A rumble, a shudder, vibrated the floor, the house, so that the windows clattered in their sashes. That something unseen could be so powerful as to shake a house at its foundations appalled even my worst apprehensions. The medium sensed a calamity in the making.   She announced that we had to get out of the house—now!   By the light of Michael's little flashlight, we all headed for the door.   Even as we did so the pictures slatted on the walls and the chairs we had been sitting on in the living room slid before us as though to block our passage. "Go go go!" Trudy commanded. We bundled out of the house close on one another's heels, and only when we had gone some distance into the front yard did we stop, breathless, excited, grateful to be out of the cauldron.

The racket within the house died down; only occasionally a muffled crash or bang sounded as something was thrown or pushed over, but in a few minutes even these sounds stopped, and the house just stood there, silent, dark, apparently benign. The ghost had won out: he had ejected the human intruders, and could be still.

I looked to Trudy for some indication of what we were supposed to do next. She saw the question in my face and answered wordlessly with a shake of her head: she didn't know. That gesture betrayed her own shocked surprise at what had happened. She had never come across the kind of malevolence we were experiencing. She had been used to spirits wanting to make contact with the living in some yearning, guiding way;— the deceased restless to convey their love or bid a final farewell to those they had left behind. Or she had made contact with earthbound entities eager to be helped on their way to a more peaceful state of eternal existence. But on this night she confronted something essentially restless, in pained turmoil, a kind of wounded wolf, and she found herself lacking any intuition about what it was or how to deal with it.

I asked Michael for his flashlight. I had to go back and get something: my manuscript: not the hard copy, which was scattered throughout the house and which I wasn't about to begin gathering up, but rather the electronic file, which was backed up on a flash drive. It didn't contain the latest additions to my book—about thirty pages—but the bulk of it was there, and it had to be saved because the prospect of trying to rewrite it would have made me give it up altogether. Trudy warned me about going back inside. The spirit, she said, was "unpredictable," and intimated by the tone of her voice and dire expression that its enormous hostilities were directed particularly at me. Without thinking of my words I answered that I could be more hostile and unpredictable than it—an indication of how, just then, my will to achieve my goal had taken possession of me. The ghost might take my house from me, but he wasn't going to get my work if I could help it.

I went back to the house and dashed inside. I almost slipped a few times on sheets of manuscript littering the stairs.

When I reached the hallway on the second floor, "things" began to happen: just behind me, as though following me, there was the pounding of fists against the walls. I paid them no attention. I hurried to my office to find the lamp on the desk there flickering uncertainly and a certain electrical sensation filling the air. I opened the right-hand drawer and felt about for the flash drive, and no sooner found it, and closed my fingers around it, than the drawer slammed shut hard against my wrist. I shouted with surprise and pain, but I pulled up my hand with the drive securely clenched, and turned around to leave. Then the door of the room slammed shut—so hard, with such a bang, that my heart skipped a beat. And I saw in the gloom that there was something there. *It* was there. At first it looked only like some dark amorphous mass, a shadow darker than the darkness around it, and having the outlines of a head and shoulders and torso. The form was not definite; it was blurred and wavered the way waves of heat waver in rising from a street on a hot summer's day. It was smaller than myself; no more than four feet tall. Just as Trudy had known it was a child, so I too, then, knew, felt, the same thing. Yes, a child; a boy; but why was it in this house? And what did it want from me?

Panic urged me to fly toward the door and escape, and I had been about to do so when it, the entity, attacked me.

It could have attacked me physically. It could have hurled any object in the room at me, fast and hard, causing me bodily injury. But it chose instead the more hurtful option of attacking me in a way peculiar to its capabilities: it assailed me psychically. It rushed at me—swept into me—and invaded my soul, filling me with its own dark, painful essence, its own rank, roiling, debilitating emotions. Till then I hadn't supposed, or perhaps I should say recalled, that it could be possible to feel so bad about the world or oneself. A despairing sense of entrapment, an enraged sense of powerlessness, an abysmal lonesomeness without hope of relenting—such were the pernicious states of being that tore at my soul. *They* were the stuff the ghost was made of. *They* were the motive force behind its continued existence in the world of the living. Against negative influences so overwhelming my own will seemed to faint away. I felt weak and my legs trembled and I thought I would fall. But the sensation of the flash drive still in my hand recollected to me the book it contained, of the work that had gone into it, of the work too that was to be done; and *this* rallied my spirit, bucked up my courage, steeled my determination. I *would* not be bowed this thing that had entered me. Let it do its worst, it *could* not be allowed to prevail. I would fight it to the bitterest end of the world. And even if I should be mistaken in my powers of resistance, and perish in the attempt, well, then, fine; fine; for even in losing I would win on some high plane of principle for having nobly persevered in the uneven battle.

The ghost of the place hadn't expected that kind of reaction. It had sought to destroy me, but on finding it could not do so it left me even more angrily than it had entered into me. As it did so I felt weaker than ever. The room seemed to spin around me. Meanwhile the entity dashed over to my desk and there exerted itself in a kind of last ditch, frantic effort to do me ill. It swept aside my pens and took up the remaining part of my manuscript and threw it into the air. The drawers of the desk were flung open, pulled out entirely, and clattered on the floor. The electric sensation of the air increased greatly, and my sense was that a new, yet greater danger would befall me unless I could get out of there at once; and so the will to self-preservation rallied, and I fled. I ran down the hallway, and down the stairs. I ran through the living room and through the front door and onto the porch from which a flying leap transported me over the steps to the front yard.

Trudy and the others, who had been waiting for me to come out, were terrified at the sight of me running toward them. They fluttered around me, quickly, nervously, fearfully asking me what had happened. They saw the way I was holding my right wrist and knew I had been injured. I spluttered out how the ghost had attacked me.

"You are not going back into that house!" Trudy said.

As though she had to tell me so! That was the last thought in my mind; at least, it was at that second.

"There's nothing we can do here," Trudy said. "We have to get out of here."

She was scared—scared. They all were. Lucy, Michael, and Adam nodded: yes, yes. They were eager to leave, to flee. While I had been in the house their nerves had calmed down somewhat, but the sight of me flying out of the place had again filled them with fresh sense of danger.

Lucy looked to me in anxious sympathy. Just then she must have realized that for me this evening meant nothing less than the loss of my home, and that I might not have anywhere else to go. She seemed about to say something, to offer something, only in the second to hold her peace with an air of disappointment in the way people will when their good nature urges them to extend a kindness that, on second thought, they realize would inconvenience them too much. But her better nature gave way and she said:

"You can stay at my place tonight."

I neither accepted nor declined. I held my throbbing wrist and turned back to the house whose windows were dark and which was sitting there as quietly as ever. I stood there with a desolate sense that everything was lost—everything worked for, gone; everything hoped for, in vain. The bright new beginning had been in the end—illusory. There was to be for me no new beginnings; only another extension, another variation of the past. You cannot go forward, fate, or whatever it is that rules men's lives, seemed to be saying: you cannot go forward but only stay where you are, or even go backward. For you there will be no bright little corner of the world; no peaceful back yard; no animal preserves with chirping birds; no peace and quiet; no security; no chance to work in contentment; only worry of some kind, struggle of some kind, insecurity of some kind. Got it? Do you finally—finally—understand?

Oh, yes. Got it. Finally, I understand!

"C'mon, let's go," Lucy said.

She turned away—they all, Michael and Adam and Lucy—turned away. They started toward the van they had come in.

I didn't follow them.

"It's *my* house," I mumbled.

"Well, you can't stay here tonight," Trudy said.

Later, Trudy would remind me of how strangely peaceful my voice sounded as I said:

"I'm not going to let this happen."

"But you can't *stay* here," she said. "Let's go. We can come back tomorrow. In the morning. During the day. Maybe then we can do something."

—But I shook my head. I knew better. I was too old to be taken in by promises and possibilities. I took things for what they were. Despite what silly people think and write, the world has a way of naively presenting itself: a lot of the times things really *are* what they seem.

I looked to Adam, to Michael, and said:

"I need a lighter! Do you have a lighter or matches or something?"

Adam said that there was a lighter in the van, in the glove compartment. He brought it to me and I flicked it a few times to make sure it worked. Its flame was bright and strong in the night.

"What are you going to do?" Lucy asked.

"No one gets my house but me."

She looked down at the lighter in my hand, then raised her eyes to me. She understood, and asked, "Are you crazy?"

Now, many years before, while attending one of the three colleges I eventually flunked out of, I had a school chum who happened to be the son of a neurosurgeon. He was a bright, chatty, effervescent boy and a brilliant student (that is to say, he was docilely industrious) who was right on track for following in the lucrative footsteps of his well-respected father. One day I admitted to him that I was failing all my classes but that none of it mattered to me because the only thing I wanted to do was write. He looked at me peculiarly as though seeing me for the first time, smiled, and said forthrightly: "You're crazy!" In all the years since that day a lot of other people have told me the same thing. The comment, the observation, always slips out of them somewhere along the line; it never fails. Of course when one or two or three people tell you something unflattering about yourself, you can always attribute the criticism to some idiosyncracy on their part, whether it's a thoughtless way of speaking or some strange, unfounded personal grudge against you. But when dozens and then hundreds of people throughout the course of your life all tell you the same thing, and pretty much in the same words—if you keep hearing that you don't know how to dress, or that your hairstyle is old-fashioned, or that you're "crazy"—well, then, it's more than likely that they see something in you that you don't, and you had better start taking the criticism to heart. Then again, when it comes to craziness, perhaps a man doesn't see it in himself because the moment he tries to do so, to analyze himself, he has put himself into a different, analytical, and therefore uncharacter-istically logical state of mind;—has become, in effect, a different person, who is no longer crazy;—and in this brief moment of sanity concludes that those who would make him out to be "crazy" don't know what they're talking about. What a convoluted, self-serving psychology! Yet for all that the fatal streak subsists; lurks under the surface of the calm or cheerful normalcy; needing only the right combination of circumstances for it to burst forth.

Does a ghost understand madness? In all likelihood, not.

I went back to the house. I went inside, went directly to the couch, and put the lighter to it.

Madness? No, it's not something a ghost understands or is prepared for. A ghost understands fear, and plays upon it; it understands religion, and plays with it; but it hasn't a clue about how to react to madness, which is so unpredictable.

The couch caught fire easily; the flames, feeding on its rich fuel of cloth and cotton batting, sent up enormous quantities of smoke and heat. I pushed it against one of the walls. I laughed and sneered as the flames mounted, I spat and cursed, I put out a hand, a defiant middle finger, and held this out and turned around a few times to give a good view of it to the ghost, wherever it might be, and said aloud that my patience was not to be tried, not to be tested, not ever, not by anyone, not by any*thing*, certainly not by   *it*....

I stepped back and away from the quickly gaining fire and all that heat. I left the house, closing the door behind me. From within came the sounds of objects moved about and angrily flung. Something large and heavy slammed into the door itself—perhaps the burning couch. The windows began to glow with a flickering orange light from the growing fires within.

When I had reached her, Lucy, still staring at me, asked in a shocked whisper, "What are you doing? Why did you do that?"

"As you said—I'm crazy."

No one asked me anything else, and none of us spoke to one another for a long time. We stood watching the house burn. The light within grew brighter, the fires hotter, and in a few minutes more the first tongues of flame poked out of the tops of the window sashes and licked at the eaves. Thick smoke spread

out along the underside of the porch roof, curdling, billowing upwards at all sides of it. When the fire had punctured holes in
the wall and ceiling, and could feed on the open air, it burned
more fiercely. We who stood watching on the front yard kept
stepping back from the tremendous waves of heat that came
from the conflagration. We all expected to see or hear some
dramatic indication that the ghost of the place had been finally
expelled or destroyed—some sounding cry or at least some definitive burst of flame that would indicate the spirit's termination.
But nothing like that happened. The fire burned steadily and
the house, mostly made of wood, was quickly consumed. The
only additional dramatic event was the collapse of the roof,
which sent into the night sky a great uprush of sparks and ash.
It was then, too, that we heard the first distant sounds of sirens
as fire engines rushed toward the area. Perhaps a passing mo-
torist had called the fire department. But by the time the two
red trucks came careening around the hedges along Fullbright
Road with all the loud drama of ear-splitting sirens and flashing
lights, the house had been largely consumed. The firemen
jumped off their trucks and set about pulling hoses and dousing
the flames. Their captain hurried over to us and asked us if we
were alright, if anyone else was in the house, and—only after he
was satisfied on these points—what had happened. The others,
who knew what I had done, said nothing; they watched me,
wondering perhaps whether or not I would lie. But I didn't. I
told the man that I had burnt the house down. And when he
asked me why, I only shook my head and didn't answer. Really,
what would have been the point in trying to explain?

Two weeks later I sat before an agent of the company that
had provided the insurance for my house. I didn't deny the information that the fire department had provided him, namely,
that the cause of fire had been arson by my own hand. Considering those circumstances, he told me, there could be no reim-
bursement, and of course that didn't come as a shock to me.
After going through the formalities of the case, he looked at me
as one man to another and asked outright why I had done it.
Again, there was no point in trying to explain, and I answered
by saying I'd rather not say.

There were three things still in my possession: my car, my
nearly-completed manuscript (or so I thought at the time), and

my dog. Good old Buddy! He had been completely safe during the fire. In the back yard he had stayed at a safe distance from the flames. On the night of the fire his barking had cut through the loud commotion of the firemen and their hoses and their trucks just as they were putting out the last of the fire, and no sooner had I heard them than I took a circuitous path to the back yard and was reunited with him.

The last of my savings was spent in boarding at a motel near Ronkonkoma. The rooms were cheap and small and rather unclean. The clientele was mostly made up of young people checking in for a night of intimacy, or older, seedier characters with certain addictions and questionable business dealings. I could have sworn that one night I heard the crack of a gunshot.

My next great shock came when I discovered that the flash drive I had rescued from my desk was—blank. The book that I had spent months working on was gone. Though I spent hours trying to retrieve whatever files or parts of files the drive might still contain, it was all to no purpose; it had been wiped clean. Yes, I was shocked but, after a quickly passing phase of despondency, not especially angry. Maybe it was that strain of madness in me manifesting itself again: the unexpectedly wild or inappropriate reaction: but for some reason the big disasters in my life don't bother me half so much as the petty irritations. Or maybe it was something else, something better and saner: that recognition, again, of how little we really control in our lives.

My house might have burnt down but the land on which it had stood was still mine, and I learned that there was no regulation about what sort of structure I could put there. Of course I could hardly afford to build another house. What little money I was able to scrounge together, through credit cards and the cashing in of certain retirement plans accumulated during my corporate years, enabled me to buy a cheap but serviceable shelter. It was, or rather is, a third-hand Airstream trailer. It is cunningly constructed, everything in it being of a miniature, exactly-fitted kind so that kitchen, living room, bedroom, and "dining area" are all crammed within a space of twenty-eight feet. I am writing this at a little fold-down table in the "kitchen," with Buddy over there, lying on the padded bench that pulls out into a bed. He has just stopped licking one of his paws and is watching me watch him. His large presence doesn't make living here any more comfortable, especially at night because the bed is narrow and he takes up the whole thing and absolutely refuses to budge even when I poke him in the ribs and tell him to move over.

As for the lost manuscript, I tried to rewrite it. I spent a whole month pulling up from the depths of memory what I had written—managing only to salvage corrupted bits and pieces amounting to some fifty pages. Sometimes I wrote passages superior to any of those in the original book. But there is a uniqueness and naturalness of first composition that can never be recaptured, and I soon saw that the reconstructed book would only be a poor shadow of its original. One night I gathered up that second, unsatisfying partial manuscript and burned it outside the trailer.

For now I have put off the notion of writing a comedy. Understandably, I'm in no funny mood. Besides, there are other things to be written: things that have over the last few months bloomed up unexpectedly within me and demand expression; things about the past; things that have, one might say, haunted me.

TRANSPLANT

The woman, four months pregnant, sat in a waiting room at Mt. Sinai Medical Center, one of her hands resting on her distended abdomen. She was staring down at the floor, her eyes not looking at anything in particular unless it were some internal vision of things that had been or were to come. Her name was Alice Keene and she was sitting here with her mother and her mother- and father-in-law, who also had the hangdog look of people who find themselves in a terrible situation and are hoping against hope. Now and then each would look at the other with a reassuring expression, but it was a kind of brief, assumed expression that is easily seen through as false, as forced, for in fact they all had a foreboding sense of the future. They were waiting for the outcome of Andrew's operation. He was Alice's husband of four years and he was undergoing heart transplant surgery. Five years earlier he had exhibited symptoms of what had been a congenital heart defect, and over the last year especially the ailment had steadily degenerated to the point where his life had hung in the balance. The last few months had been very difficult for him. He had spent whole days in weak lassitude, unable to take more than a few steps at a time, and whole nights he had lain awake, grappling with shortness of breath and painful edematic swellings. It had been only a matter of months before he died unless a heart could be found for him. "As soon as we have a suitable donor we can schedule him right away," the doctors had told Alice, but the suitable donor seemed not to be forthcoming, and week by week, day by day, Andrew grew sicker and weaker, and it seemed he would die at the tragically early age of thirty-five. Then the call had come: a donor had been found—a young man who had been killed in a traffic accident. By this time Andrew was so weak that there was only a fifty-fifty chance he would survive the operation. Now, as she sat in the waiting room, Alice tried not to think of these terrible odds. She forced herself to believe that everything

441

would be alright, that there was some justice in the world for Andrew and for her and her family. Within her the new life kicked, and she pressed her hand a little harder against her abdomen. She told herself that her husband *must* live—that everything *must* turn out alright. Their first child could not be allowed to grow up without a father.

Long before the operation the doctors had told both her and Andrew about the statistics involved in such transplants. If it was successful, Andrew was almost sure to live for another five years, and more likely than not at least ten. It was possible that he would even live another twenty years, and with luck as many as twenty-five. From the moment Alice learned of these odds the future had for her taken on the aspect of a numbers game: a matter of calculation based on actuarial tables as to how long she could count on any happiness in life. Five years— that pitiably small stretch of time was almost guaranteed to her. But that was not enough; that would not be fair. Ten years—that was much better, of course, but still, objectively speaking, too little. She sat there thinking that only if he lived out the longest possible time, say another thirty years, would there be real justice in his and her case. For then he would be sixty-five years old, which was not really "old," to be sure, but neither was it young, and he would have lived the greater share of life available to any man. They would have built a life together, and raised to adulthood the several children they had always planned on having. "But," she thought, moving her hand away from her swollen abdomen and licking her lips that were nervously dry, "I would do anything if he could live even for one more year—anything." For she loved her husband more than all the world. She could not lose him.

A week later was one of the happiest days of her life when she wheeled her husband out of the hospital and toward the van that would take him home. Well, perhaps "happy" is not the right word to use; perhaps the word "relieved" would be better. The surgeon who had operated on Andrew reported that he was healing well and, barring any unforeseen complications, would make a good recovery so long as he adhered to his drug regimen, ate properly, and rested. There seemed to be no reason, the doctor said, why he should not have many years of a good, productive life ahead of him.

"Whatever you want, whatever you need, you just tell me!" Alice told her husband, as she and one of the paramedics who had taken him home and placed him carefully in bed. He lay looking tired but already better than he had looked for the last year that he had lived with a failing heart. And indeed she could hardly do enough for him. She was his selfless servant, making him food, or ordering food that he liked; washing him, shaving him, dressing him, combing his hair. In the afternoons she read to him from magazines and newspapers; and while he slept she sat by his bed watching over him, praying for him. She prayed even though logic told her that it made no sense to do so, since the God whose help she sought was the same God who had made the need of help necessary. Day by day her husband got better. A month passed and he regained a great deal of his strength and began doing most things for himself. After the second month one would never have known that he had undergone major surgery except perhaps for the telltale sign that he had lost a little weight; but even this sign would doubtless disappear as he continued to satisfy an appetite that had reasserted itself.

Of course one couldn't expect a person who had undergone so physically traumatizing an operation as a heart transplant to be in all ways as he had been previous to it. Alice intuitively understood this; she expected it. And so it was that after several months she noticed subtle changes in him. For instance, he no longer poked loving fun at her. His formerly rambunctious sense of humor had subsided into something more reserved and subtle and sharply cutting. He became a little more critical of himself as well as of others. She did not mind these changes in him; they were slight and infrequently exhibited; but they were there. "You know, you never used to say things like that before," she once remarked when, one night as they had been watching television, Andrew made an emotional outburst at a newscaster's report.

"Oh?" he asked. He shrugged as though it was something he hadn't noticed and didn't think was important.

There were other changes and not all of them were bad; some of them were surprisingly, unexpectedly, good. He was more openly affectionate with her. When they walked down the street he would always reach out for her hand to hold it. Unexpectedly he might lean in toward her and kiss her.

"What was that for!" she exclaimed, the first time it happened.

"For nothing!" he said, smiling happily, proudly.

She was as pleased as could be, even as she shook her head and thought how odd it was.

From the moment she had told him she was pregnant, he had doted on her, and he continued to do so. For instance, she gained a great deal of weight—more than she ever thought she could: at only five feet six inches tall she had come to weigh a hundred and seventy pounds! She lamented this fact; she disconsolately shook her head over it and expressed the worried opinion that this was the "end," that she would never lose it, never go back to the way she was. "You look *fine*," Andrew would tell her, in one instance placing both his hands on her bulging belly and smilingly, reassuringly, looking into her eyes. "Don't worry about it! You're *supposed* to be this way! Don't you know that? You'll see—you'll lose it after the baby's born. It just takes time. Give yourself a break!" At this kindness she took his hands off her belly and raised them to her lips and kissed them. She had always loved him because she knew that he was, despite gruff or impatient moments, essentially kind; but it seemed that he had developed a new and deeper level of understanding and compassion.

Alice gave birth to a healthy girl. When she had first learned she was pregnant they had discussed what they ought to name the baby. They had agreed that if they had a boy they would name him Sam and if they had a girl they would name her Emma. Now that she had the girl, however, Alice wanted to name her Grace, out of deference to their good fortune in being able to resume their lives. Grace was indeed adorable. She looked like both her parents. It was hard to tell which part of her took after the mother and which after the father. Andrew delighted in her. He never tired of holding her, tickling her, talking to her, keeping his eyes on her even when she was lying safely in her playpen. After a few bungled first attempts, he became an expert changer of diapers, and never went about that unpleasant business without making baby coo and smile. "What a wonderful father he turned out to be," Alice often told herself as she watched him.

But to the degree that Andrew had become a good confidant and father, he was becoming in some respects less attentive as a husband. Toward the end of her pregnancy and several weeks after having the child Alice had not felt amorous toward him, and with some guilt she had almost been relieved to think that he, still recuperating, would not be nettled with unsatisfied desire. That indeed seemed to be the case. But as she became more of her usual self, and her desire for him increased, she found in him no corresponding impulse. It wasn't that he was no longer interested in her; only that he was not nearly so aggressive as he used to be. She told herself that the poor man just didn't have the energy he used to have, that he had to be helped along even in this. Having one's heart torn out and another put in its place, after all—wouldn't that knock the hell out of anyone? And so now it was always she who initiated love-making. She assumed her new role with good-humor and an apparent naughty satisfaction, always looking at him with a sly leer and almost conspiratorial grin as she would draw close to him, kiss him, touch him, and carefully lead him into intimacy. She always felt she had to walk the fine line of arousing his interest yet not forcing him into something he might not be in the mood for. On this evening for instance, as they lay in bed, she turned over to him, raising herself on one arm and wrapping the other around him. She brought her face close to his, her eyes suggestive and her voice soft, inviting. "Hey there," she said.

"Hey there," he said.

"Baby's asleep," she said. "Finally."

"Yeah. It's about time."

"And how's *my* daddy," she said, pressing herself still more closely against him. In a single, smooth gesture she put her hand on his belly, then ran her fingers along it, up and down. He murmured with pleasure and wrapped an arm around her, but said, "Tired."

"Really?"

He nodded. "A little."

She watched his eyes, trying to gauge how tired he really was. It had been nearly a year since the operation. He had regained all his lost weight, and his complexion was as fresh and healthy as ever; to look at him one would never have known how close he had come to death. He had long gone back to his job as an insurance adjuster. But at the back of her mind, always, was the thought that he might never entirely be the way he used to be, and that she must not force him into an exertion he didn't want to engage in. Moreover he regularly took medications, and surely these had debilitating side effects. True, there had been nights when he had been as passionate as ever, but they were the exceptions to the rule; what had been irrepressible, goading, pawing eagerness had subsided into a soft complaisance. She wondered sometimes if this state of affairs would be permanent. If so, she knew that she would accept it, for one had to weigh the good against the bad, and nothing would have been worse than losing him altogether.

One late afternoon she called him at the office as she always did. They chatted about Gracie for a few minutes, and then Alice told him what she was making for dinner. He mentioned that he would be a little late coming home that night because he was going to stop by Macy's after work. It had occurred to him, he said, that he hadn't bought any new clothes in a while and he was hoping to find a sale going on. His announcement surprised her, for usually it was she who bought his clothes, and he had never gone shopping with her in the past without a great deal of resistance. "I thought you hated going shopping," she said.

"I do, usually," he said, laughing a little as he leaned back in his chair and looked about the office, half deserted now that it was almost six o'clock. "I don't know ... I just feel like going tonight. I haven't been there for years. And I could use some new stuff."

He waited for her to say something, but she didn't, and he asked, "You need anything while I'm there?"

"Oh, I don't know .... we could use some new towels."

"Towels?"

"Bath towels. We could use some new ones. But don't get any crazy colors!" she warned jokingly, for she knew that like some men he had a poor sense of choosing appropriate colors for certain things.

"Keep dinner warm for me," he said. "And you eat, if you're hungry. Don't wait."

"No, it's okay," she said. "I'll wait."

He had a novel feeling of eager anticipation to get to the

store and he walked downtown from his office on 41st Street, just off Sixth Avenue.

He had not been to Macy's in so many years that he had forgotten the layout of the store. When he pushed through the revolving doors at the Broadway entrance he asked the first clerk he saw about the location for towels. She directed him to the sixth floor. When he got there he found that there was a sale going on and the department was crowded. Most of the buyers were women who had come from work, and who, despite their general air of fatigue, were nonetheless energetic in rifling through the shelves and bins, often reaching out over one another to grab an item that caught their eye. Just the thought of competing with them daunted his intention but he bucked himself up to the task and found a stack of towels that seemed tastefully restrained in color—they were off-white with light gray stripes—and he bought half a dozen of them. Afterwards, carrying his purchase in a brown paper bag, he made his way downstairs on the escalators. On the ground level he noticed the store directory indicating that the men's department was on this floor.

In the men's department, he lingered at the tables of shirts and ties. He would search for his size, pick up the packages, and slip his fingers under the plastic wrapping in order to feel the material. Whether this was fine or cheap he could tell at once, and he was rather surprised at his ability to do this, for he didn't remember ever having been so astute in this matter. Frequently, too, he would look up and around him, looking for ... what? He wasn't sure. Jackets? Pants? Shoes?

After he had paid for his shirts he had no intention of buying anything else and he started to leave. The logical thing to do would have been to head back to the Broadway entrance, since it was closer to the subway station he needed to use; but instead he walked to the exit at the opposite end of the store. Once more he passed the tables of shirts and ties and assorted men's accessories. He passed a couple of counters where watches were sold, then moved on to yet other counters full of cologne. He noticed an employee of the store standing just off to the side of the aisle and holding up a bottle of cologne, his forefinger on the atomizer, ready to spray. He was one of the sales clerks promoting a new scent, for he accosted patrons and asked them if they wanted to try it. Invariably they smiled politely and shook their heads, no, as they hurried on. Andrew felt a slight but real sense of annoyance to think that he too would be accosted, and for the same reason that everyone feels this way: because he didn't want the product and knew he would feel guilty about refusing it. And yet he certainly had a better excuse than most people, namely, that he didn't wear cologne. He never had. Something about it irritated his nose and gave him a headache. As he approached the sales clerk he turned his head away from him and assumed the self-absorbed air of someone who was not expecting and perhaps would resent the interruption of being accosted. But this attitude was no discouragement to an employee whose salary came mostly from commissions on sales, and who today hadn't sold very much. When Andrew passed by him—when the two men were but a couple of inches away—the clerk held up the green bottle he had been holding and asked in a forthright and pleasant voice, "Sir, would you like to try a new scent by Michaud?"

Andrew couldn't have said why he stopped; he had not intended to do so. Perhaps he had just felt too guilty to pass by with a mere shake of the head the way everyone else did; after all, the poor fellow was just trying to make a living. And so he stopped. "Alright," he said, putting out his left hand in order to receive a brief spray of the cologne. He noticed that the clerk was about the same age as himself and seemed to be about the same weight and height. He had an open, cheerful, well-scrubbed face, though his hairstyle—combed straight back and close to the head—gave him a somewhat severe appearance. Like the other sales staff here he was wearing a full business suit, for in this department especially the store wished to project an image of professional formality. And yet his black tie did not match his blue jacket—Andrew noticed this, and thought it odd. There was something else that Andrew noticed, or rather that he felt. He felt that he knew this man. He didn't know where he knew him from, but he was sure that he did—that they had met sometime, somewhere before. He put his sprayed hand to his nose and smelled the cologne.

"It's just a little strong at first," the clerk explained, "but in a few minutes it settles down and it's very subtle." He watched Andrew hopefully.

Andrew nodded with approval. In fact, he was surprised at just how much he liked it. "How much is it?" he asked.

There were two prices, one for the two-ounce bottle and one for the four. "But if you get the four-ounce bottle it comes with a free grooming kit," the clerk added in a tone of voice that made it sound as though no one in his right mind would pass up the offer.

Andrew again put his hand close to his nose and smelled the cologne. It was already subtler, finer, its crisp, clean scent coming through more clearly. He told himself that if this cologne had been out "before" he certainly would have worn it. "Alright," he said. "I'll take the four-ounce bottle."

"Terrific!" the clerk said, genuinely pleased at the first sale he had made in half an hour though he must have fumigated at least a hundred hands. He stepped behind his counter, on which several brands of cologne, all of them in boxes of rather elegant, minimalist design, were ranged in low rows. He leaned over, slid a glass door to the right, and reached in to the display case and brought out one of the large bottles of the cologne. Then he turned around and pulled out a bin from which he took a small vinyl bag containing the free grooming kit. He placed both items on the counter beside the cash register and punched in the sale, saying, "Will this be cash or charge, sir?"

"Charge," Andrew said, taking out his wallet and handing over a credit card. As did so he was surer than ever that he knew this sales clerk from somewhere. But where, when? Had they been old school chums? Had they been colleagues in a former job? Where *did* he know him from? Ordinarily he never gave more than a moment's notice to people whom he thought he recognized from somewhere but there was something more urgent about this instance, and so he couldn't help saying, "You know, you look familiar to me. Have we met before?"

For the first time the clerk looked at Andrew with something other than distant politeness; he knit his brows together somewhat as, for a few seconds, he looked searchingly at this stranger and made an attempt to place him. But finding him not at all familiar, he merely shook his head, no, and said in a vaguely regretful voice, "No sir, I don't think so."

"Are you sure? I could have sworn I know you from somewhere."

With a brief, polite smile and a shake of the head the clerk said, "No, I don't think so." He slipped the credit card through the reader and rang up the sale. Before returning the card, however, he looked at it, at Andrew's name, as though willing to make another attempt to remember this stranger. He spoke out the last name. "Is that how you say it? No, sir"—shaking his head again—"doesn't ring a bell. I probably just remind you of someone. It happens to me a lot."

"I guess so," Andrew said, taking back his card and putting it into his wallet.

The clerk put the cologne and grooming kit into a glossy bag which he handed to Andrew with a formal, "Thank you, sir."

When Andrew got home that evening at seven thirty his wife was waiting for him. Two place settings were on the table in the small dining area beside the kitchen, which was separated by a low ledge from the living room. Little Gracie was in her playpen, surprisingly quiet as she lay on her back, her little legs and arms shivering with new life as she stared up in dumb fascination at a toy mobile of yellow, red, and blue plastic rings gently rotating above her. The first thing Andrew did was to go to his daughter; he lifted her up, kissed her, and called her his baby; and still holding her in his arms he went to his wife and greeted her with a kiss.

"Hey, are you wearing cologne?" she asked, smiling, as she pulled away a little from him.

"Oh, yeah, you smell it? I bought some," he said.

"Well *that's* a first!" she said.

"I don't know. I kind of felt bad for the guy who was selling it. But it's pretty good, don't you think?"

Hours later when he and his wife lay in bed, comfortable and warm beneath the sheets, she moved toward him, put an arm around him, and drew close to him. She had missed him a lot that day. She slipped her hand over his chest, her fingertips moving up and down it in the gentlest, most tender of massages. She wanted to be close to him, to be embraced by him, to be loved by him. "Tired?" she asked.

"A little," he said.

There it was again, that "a little." But she needed him more than usual now.

"Are you sure?" She pressed her body against his and the hand that had been on his stomach she discreetly slipped just beneath the elastic band of the boxer trunks he wore to sleep.

"Yeah, actually I am."

"Well ... "—slowly, she drew her hand away. But she took up his own hand and brought it to her lips and kissed it, and held it against her cheek, almost as though this could be a substitute for the kind of intimacy she longed for. In kissing his hand she smelled again the cologne that had been sprayed on it and which lingered, however faintly, even after he had taken a shower. "That is a nice cologne," she whispered. "What's it called?"

"Oh ... some stupid name. 'Always.' "

"I don't think it's stupid," she murmured. "I like it."

She kissed his neck two, three times. Close to his body, to his warmth, she snuggled up against him, her arms and legs and stomach against his body, grateful that in the end he was there with her and she with him. In the end, she told herself, that was all that mattered. Then she lowered herself a little and rested her head against his chest, and listened—listened—to the beating of his heart.

TEETH

When I first met Nicole I didn't like her. In fact I despised her because I thought she was one of those mean-spirited persons who delight in pointing out the errors or shortcomings of others in order to make herself look better. I had taken a temporary job at an advertising agency in the Lipstick building on Third Avenue and she came in the second day I was there, entering the office with the subtlety of a typhoon, the reticence of a megalomaniacal queen of the world—announcing in a loud yet lilting voice "Helloooo, everybodyyyy, I'm baaaack!" as she flung about her long dyed-blonde hair as though to make her already substantial person yet more obvious. She was thirty years old, a tad overweight, and her face rayed out eagerness, enthusiasm, and a disagreeable because too-bounding self-confidence. Her over-whelming presence seemed to dare anyone to get in its way or divert attention from itself. She had just come back from her vacation, but as though she were still on St. Croix she wore an outrageously bright-colored outfit with a glaring tropical print. She began loudly, extravagantly telling everyone about the good time she had had. Oh, it had been so wonderful! she announced. Everything had been so lovely! The beaches! The hotels! The dinners! She had gone sailing! She had gone snorkeling! She had seen sharks! Big ones! She had lain on the beach for days at a time, soaking in the glorious sun, and at night she had gone to dinners and parties, drinking huge Tropical Sunrises and dancing the Limbo! It went on and on for about fifteen minutes. Then, giving me the merest glance, which nevertheless dripped with hauteur, she complained, "You know, you go away for a week and everything changes in this place!" But it was only when she sat at her desk that the fireworks began. It was one whining, fault-finding exclamation after another about how "someone" had tampered with the settings on her computer, had moved things on her desk, had taken stuff from her drawer, and so forth, all the while glancing at me with the malice of a grand inquisitor. Everyone else in the office either laughed at her outbursts or tried to soothe her irritation in mock-sympathetic voices, but her exhibition only filled me with disgust and I turned my head away from her as I would from an unsightly pile of garbage. I despised the woman and couldn't see how I was going to work in the same place with her.

Less than a week later we were the best of friends. I had been entirely wrong about her. Her loud, whining complaints had been made, as I soon came to see, in a seriocomic way: less for the sake of placing blame and reducing others than for drawing attention to herself. For Nicole thrived on attention. She had to be the center of it at all times. No matter what group she happened to be a part of, she naturally strove to be its ringleader, setting the subject and tone of its conversation, directing the moment others might chime in, always ensuring that her voice, her opinions, her influence was the main one and left the final impression. She thrived on holding court. She was a great lover of going out for drinks after work. She knew where the best happy hours were. Even if you didn't drink or weren't interested in going out she managed to coax you into her entourage through her peculiarly effective method of persuasion, which consisted of a mixture of good-humored insult and guilt-inducing entreaty. "Oh, c'mon, it's only for an hour!" she would say; or, "You're not going to do anything at home anyway!" or "What's wrong with you?—you can't spend a little time with your friends?"—and so one went along. Refreshingly forthright in speaking her mind, she loudly, floridly blurted out things that others laughed at under their breaths as shockingly uncouth but which they themselves secretly thought. When one got to know her still better, one saw that her flamboyant extroversion, her love and need of attention, and her quickness to indulge in alcohol arose from a dozen insecurities, but these she herself freely admitted to, and her confidence in this regard only the more completely won you over because it added to her already engaging personality a note of fragility, making you want to protect her as well.

One would never have known it to hear her talk, what with her thick Queens accent peppered with "ain't"s and generally freewheeling indifference to grammar, that she had a background in English literature. She had studied it for four years at New York University and had graduated with a degree. She had been working at the agency for two years and, like so many of us in those days, she was there only to "make a living" till she could do what she really wanted to do, namely, work for a magazine, preferably as an editor, and preferably for a tabloid because temperamentally she was a gossip and loved popular culture. She was always talking to my yawns and wandering attention about movie stars, television personalities, and the tawdry goings on of celebrities. I could never help thinking that while she was a remarkable woman, she might have been ten times more so had the energy that she used for finding out all the minutiae of such forgettable persons had been dedicated to weightier matters.

"Why don't you work for a newspaper?" I asked her once. "Or be a teacher?"

"Please!" she said, only, with a frown. She had no interest in those things.

For a whole year we worked together, often had lunch together, and chatted regularly on the phone. She became one of the few friends I had. She was always telling me about how she had sent her resume out to this or that magazine. Now and then she had offers to become an editorial assistant but the pay was so low that she said she couldn't be so impractical as to accept it. "This is New York, after all," she would say; "I got rent to pay."

The years passed. I moved on to better things, or at least to different things, going through a new job every other year. As for Nicole, she finally landed a position as an editor that paid her a liveable salary. Her bosses loved her, the way everyone did. She did her job well, with enthusiasm, even with a passion; she worked hard and many hours a week; she got promotions. I wasn't surprised when I learned that the parent company of her magazine was launching a new fashion tabloid to be called *Vivacity* and she was going to be made its Editor-in-Chief. Fortunately for her, the magazine proved to be a great success. It was renowned especially for its candid pictures of celebrities at their worst—drunken, disheveled, distressed, or black-eyed from a brawl. Every image was accompanied with a sensational, alliterative caption of the sort which staid literati

sneer at in public and secretly devour, such as, "Hollywood Hot-
tie Hitches Up Her Hooters!" or "Box Office Biggie Goes
Berserk!" or "Superhero Star Sinks in the Stews!" Nicole, as
Editor-in-Chief, was responsible for the layout as well as for
some of the copy in the magazine. Most of the best headlines
and captions were also hers. And as the reputation, or at least
the sales, of *Vivacity* increased, and became something of a wonder in the cutthroat and competitive world of tabloids, so did
Nicole's reputation as an editor. She gained entree into places
that she couldn't have imagined when she was just another
clerk working with me. However questionable its subject matter
and intentions, the magazine, on account of its growing popularity, took on a patina of authority; and in keeping with the bro-
mide that no publicity is bad publicity, the very people in the
entertainment world who had once reviled it now tried to have
their names mentioned in its pages.

The years passed, the wheel of life turned, and she married
Jake, a photographer who worked at her publication and who
made a name for himself by snapping the now famous picture of
the thirty-five year old heiress Mona Stanhurst sprawled out
drunk in a gutter on the Lower East Side. (Nicole's caption to
that picture, "Mona's Martinis Make a Mega-Mess!" surely ranks
as one of her better ones.) They had two children, two little
girls who were the cutest things one could imagine, all red hair
and freckles. Every few months she would invite me over to her
home in Glendale, which wasn't too far from where I lived.
Then one day she told me she was moving to Long Island. She
and Jake had for a long time been house-hunting and had finally found something they liked in Nassau County. "You'll
come out often," she told me; "this doesn't mean we don't see
each other!" "Of course not," I said. But I knew better. It was
one thing to live within ten-minute bus ride of someone; quite
another when you were separated by thirty miles. Still, we did
manage to see one another, though not nearly so frequently, and
nearly always at some place in Manhattan, a bar or a restaurant, where we would have dinner, drink, and catch up on each
other's lives. But even these get-togethers became rarer, and
before long we had settled into a pattern of calling each other on
the telephone no more than three or four times a year.

It was during one such call that Nicole seemed especially

wistful about our friendship and announced that we "had" to see each other again. And the perfect opportunity, she said, was coming up. *Vivacity* was giving itself a party to celebrate its fifth year in successful existence. Management was going to rent a restaurant and for six hours, from 8:00 PM to 1:00 AM, senior staff, journalists, and invited guests would enjoy an evening of free food and drink. It was, she assured me, going to be an "event" covered by the New York media, even if only in passing. "Important" people would be there—and she rattled off the names of five or six persons whom I had never heard of before and have never heard of since. She told me that as the latest edition of *Vivacity* concentrated on the modeling industry, "guests"—models—from several of New York's top agencies would be attending to add glamor to the event and provide eye-candy to photographers covering it. "Who knows?" she said, laughing. "You might even pick one up!"

Now, I had come to a point in my life in New York where nothing was more disagreeable to me than having to travel into Manhattan. Over the last twenty years I had had to go into it at least three times a week in order to make a living, and just as constant exposure to a noxious agent can sensitize one's system to its toxicity, so had constant contact with the heart of the city made me the more disgusted by its rushing multitudes and filth and poisoned air. Once the flexibility of youth had enabled me to overlook or endure these things in anticipation of the entertainments offered by the city. But I was older now, my tastes had matured, my standards for a decent life had risen. It no longer seemed a fair exchange to tolerate a dozen degradations a day for the sake of a blaze of dissipation on a Friday or Saturday night. I longed for a comfortable, constant, imperturbable gentility, which each trip into Manhattan only thwarted and checked. Therefore when Nicole invited me to her magazine's affair, I politely declined, saying that I didn't think I would be "up" for something like that.

"What is that supposed to mean?" she asked, her tone of voice expressing more wonder than curiosity. For she *did* know me: she knew when I was beating around the bush and trying to avoid saying what I meant.

"Nicole, really ... it's just so much of a hassle to get into the city."

"It only takes you twenty minutes!"

"More than that. And it's going to be at night. And you know how the trains are at night—you have to wait for them. And you know the kinds of characters riding the subways at that time. And it's hot. I don't want to wait on a hot platform for a train—get all sweated up. It's just too much for me ..."

"Oh, my God!" she exclaimed, exasperated at what she regarded as my ridiculous fussiness.

She spent the next five minutes trying to dispel my objections. She made it sound as though waiting for a New York City subway train in the summer was pleasant as a stroll through some New England park on a crisp autumn day. There was a moment when, as she painted this rosy picture, and obliquely impugned my intolerance of such things, that a growing irritation tempted me to fire back by asking her why, if getting about the city were such a lark, she had not herself remained in it rather than escaping into the Long Island suburbs; but I held my peace. I merely repeated, and this with a self-deprecating laugh, that the commute was just too miserable and would defeat the whole purpose of going out to have a good time.

She breathed impatiently, but said nothing. Perhaps she was thinking up other arguments to entice me into going to the event; only to dismiss them one by one because she knew that nothing else she said was going to change my mind.

"Alright, listen," she said, with some exasperation, "how about if I could get you a ride into the city?"

"What do you mean? Send a cab for me?"

"No, *not* send a cab for you," she said, as though she might have wanted me to attend the affair, but was not about to shell out any of her own cash for me to do so. "I mean get you a ride in. A friend of mine lives around you and he's coming, so how about if he could pick you up and take you back? Alright? Then you won't have to take the trains." Before I could object to this (I had been about to say that I didn't want to put anyone out), she said she was going to call this friend of hers right now and that I was to stay by the phone because she would call me right back. She did so ten minutes later. Her friend Tom, who lived only a few blocks away from me, had happily agreed to stop by my place and pick me up. He had assured her that he would be happy to do her the favor.

Tom Grauer turned out to be a young man of twenty-seven years old, stylishly tall and trim, with light brown hair and a narrow and handsome face. His personality was cheerful and engaging. When we met he shook my hand warmly and made me feel as though he had been looking forward to meeting me. He had a 2009 Mustang, and he drove it fast along the Long Island Expressway, repeatedly veering right to pass cars on the leftmost, fastest lane because they were going too slow for him. He told me he had known Nicole for several years, having worked with her at one of his previous jobs. Like myself, he had come to appreciate her brash, engaging personality, and a friendship had developed between them. He hadn't seen her in more than six months, he said, though, again like myself, he kept in touch with her by telephone. He was glad to have been invited to "the party" (as he called it), not only because he would get to see Nicole again but also because it was a Friday night that he would otherwise have spent at The Shamrock Cottage, a neighborhood Irish pub to which, he told me, he had been going way too often, meeting the same hopeless and boring crowd, and which had pretty much turned into—to use his colorful phrase—"a sausage bar."

"Hogarth's" was the name of the restaurant where Vivacity was giving itself a party. It was located on Park Avenue South at the corner of 35th Street. On this evening the large windows facing the street were covered from behind with long drapes so that no one passing could see what was going on within. Two business-suited doormen of the bulky, bald-headed, gorilla variety stood before the doors. One of the men held a clipboard with a list of invited guests and after he had checked to make sure that our names were on it he held the door open for us and we entered. Inside, about forty small tables ranged throughout a spacious interior and were mostly occupied by groups of people talking and drinking. Thumping dance music was playing—though not too loudly. A long bar extended along one side of the place, and here too people sat and drank. Beyond the bar, at the back of the establishment, in a large, open area, a buffet had been set up: two rows of gleaming stainless steel receptacles between which rose colorful floral arrangements and burning candles. Here groups of people stood holding their drinks and small plates. A projection screen extended across the back wall, and an overhead projector flashed onto it images of models strutting down catwalks, and well-known fashion designers putting last-minute touches on their latest designs, and assorted well-dressed men and women—the movers and shakers of the fashion industry—meeting one another or giving interviews. The tenor of the evening was casual-formal, for nearly all the men wore jackets, and all the women were dressed well and wore jewelry. These guests seemed to comport themselves with that breezy, comfortable, yet proudly self-conscious air of people who know they occupy positions of some influence, or at least think they do.

Tom and I walked into the place as comrades in uncertainty. After all, the only person we knew was Nicole, and she was nowhere to be seen. "Well, we might as well get ourselves a drink," Tom said, nodding toward the bar, to which we both headed as to a refuge. I ordered vodka and orange juice. The drink was strong and cold and good. Tom had a beer, and as he lifted it up to take his first sip he said, "Remind me, no more than two of these! I have to drive back tonight."

It was then, as we stood there, that we both noticed something remarkable. A good percentage of the women around us were extraordinarily beautiful. Every thirty seconds there passed before us some tall, slender, expensively dressed creature whose features were wonderfully perfect and who walked with a natural grace. In passing they sometimes cast a polite smile in our direction, but even that vague upcurling of their lips had a way of lighting up their faces and tugging at your heart. Every other minute Tom gave me a nudge with his elbow and nodded in the direction to which he had spotted yet another beauty. "They must be models!" he said to me, stating the obvious, and not looking at me but rather shifting his wondering eyes from one part of the restaurant to the other, from one model to the next. He couldn't have been happier if he had been a child who had been locked by himself in a toy store.

My reaction wasn't different from his, though it was more discreet. These beautiful women amazed and delighted me also. I know there are those who say that human beauty is illusory or deceptive because it is transitory or because even in its most perfect manifestation it may be combined with an empty head;

and for all I know some of those women might have been dunces. But that is no reason to think less of a beautiful face or figure, these being their own reward—gifts to the world as surely as any beautiful sky or landscape might be. Moreover there is something mean-spirited, even perverse, about a quickness to denigrate beautiful people simply because they are beautiful: as though one were handed some fine thing to treasure and, rather than beholding it with joy, turning it over and over in search of a flaw, and then, when no flaw can be found, breaking it apart—and thus willfully denying oneself the pleasure of a perfect possession. It was therefore with a sense of amused confidence in Tom's good if naive spirit that I watched him turn his head every few minutes to look with goggling eyes after some tall, enticingly-dressed, elegant woman whose slinky walk and coy glance hinted at a hundred romantic possibilities.

We had been at the bar for fifteen minutes before we saw Nicole. Actually it was she who had seen us first and came toward us. At first we didn't recognize her, for she had changed a great deal. She had lost weight and lightened her hair. She was wearing fine, stylish clothes; she also was taller because she was wearing high heels. She was accompanied by her husband. She hugged and kissed us both and bade us follow her to the buffet, where we filled our plates from among a dozen delicious foods and then found a table where we all four sat with several of her colleagues from the magazine. Tom sat beside her and often leaned in to say something confidential in her ear, and immediately afterwards she would look up, catch sight of someone—of one of the models about whom he had apparently asked—and turn back to him and murmur an answer.

But it wasn't till *she* arrived that Tom's enthusiasm, no doubt aided by his second beer, reached a pitch almost of indiscretion, for from the moment he caught sight of her his eyes never left her. She was accompanied by three other models as tall and as beautiful, but not quite so beautiful, as herself. For hers was a sultry beauty. Dark, wavy, abundant hair fell to her exposed, fair shoulders. Her brows arched high and finely over her large, dark, liquid eyes, the lids of which hung heavily and suggestively. Her mouth was wide and the lower lip full, and when she smiled her teeth were bracingly white and finely-shaped. The line of her jaw was chiseled and perhaps somewhat masculine, but this only added to her beauty a touch of stateliness. Expensive-looking people—executives from the parent company of *Vivacity* and its sister publications—often approached her, greeted her with cocktail kisses, talked to her. A photographer who had been hired for the evening almost at once started taking pictures of her and these people as they conversed.

"Who is that?" Tom asked.

"Oh, that's Marcella Castiglione," Nicole said. "She's a new model from Italy. She's becoming very popular very fast."

Tom continued to stare at her. "Does she speak English?"

"Sure. With an accent, of course. She's very sweet."

"You *know* her?"

"I've met her."

"It won't be long before she's on *Vogue*," one of the women at our table announced. She was a journalist who worked for one of the umbrella company's publications and had written about Marcella, who, she went on to say, must have just gotten back to the United States from London, where she had done a fashion show.

Apparently to be successful in modeling, as in so many other vocations, one has to be in the right place at the right time—come along at the right moment for one's career to take off at a clip. Marcella Castiglione had come along when the marketplace for models was lacking her type of beauty, which was of the classic Italian kind. She had come from a small town outside Naples and had been "discovered" by a photographer who worked for a fashion magazine based in Rome. He had promised her that she would be a star on the runways of Milan and Paris and New York, and the promise was being fulfilled. In only two years she had gone from being the anonymous child of a poor family to having her picture splashed in print and electronic media all over the world, and to having the kind of wealth that she had not been able to imagine. She had the world on a string.

She also had Tom on a string. He watched her the way a crouching lion watches its unsuspecting prey, with, however, this difference: that she wasn't so unsuspecting as all that. No matter whom she was speaking to, she managed to glance about as though to see who was present but really, one felt, to see who might be watching her. For while she might have started out as a shy but pretty Italian girl of peasant origin she had in the space of only a few years come to feel comfortable with her high place in the world. She knew that more people wanted to know and meet her than she wanted to know and meet. The balance of power in her relationship with the world, or at least her world, was all in her favor. She was beautiful, wealthy, and, after a manner, famous.

At any other place or time she and Tom would never have been able to meet each other, for she would have been occupied with and protected by an entourage, and he, however taken with her looks and ordinarily confident, would have had been discouraged from approaching her by the thought that he was out of her league. But this was one of those circumstances in which a lot of people knew a lot of others, and through that network otherwise impossible introductions could be made. For instance, the journalist at our table who had happened to interview Marcella about her latest show in London. Marcella recognized her and, with a nod and a raising of the hand, came walking toward her and our table. Soon the introductions had been made all around.

Marcella saw Tom's intense interest in her. She was probably amused by it, as she was by so much of the panting attention she aroused in men. And yet there was attraction on her part too; she did not ignore him the way women ignore men in whom they have no interest. She flashed one of her great, dazzling smiles at him, and he smiled back, tense with a rising hope—the hope that he would meet her more fully, talk to her, have some time alone with her. This was an opportunity she offered, for she asked her friend the journalist if she might join the table, at which all of us exclaimed our eager acceptance.

Marcella and Tom sat opposite each other so it was not easy for them to converse. But they didn't have to. Their eyes did all the talking. I saw with amusement how tensely attentive Tom was to her. Before she had come to the table he had been as comfortably talkative as anyone else; now he seemed to be silently on his guard, watching her, sitting up straighter and with great attention whenever she looked in his direction and made a general comment. I glanced at Nicole to see if she noticed this; by the way she smiled at me knowingly I could tell she did. Then Marcella asked Tom a direct question: Did *he* work at *Vivacity* too? He told that he didn't; that he was only here because he knew Nicole. Marcella nodded, rather appreciatively, as though she were glad that he wasn't associated with that or any other business that had a connection to her own. Then she asked him if he lived in New York, and when he said that he did—that he lived in Queens (she nodded again, but of course she didn't know Queens from a hole in the wall)—she exclaimed that she loved New York—loved it—and was hoping one day to make it her permanent home. She was, she said, renting an apartment on the Upper West Side, on 65th Street just off Columbus Avenue—such a nice area, she was friends with all her neighbors. If only her parents, she said, would agree to move to the United States! That would be the deciding factor for her in actually buying a place, a big place, a real home here. But they didn't want to leave their little Italian village—they were getting older and were set in their ways; and in actually buying a home here she would feel as though she were cutting herself off from them in some fundamental way—they, certainly, would feel as though she were abandoning them;—and she couldn't do that, could she? Did Tom know what she meant?

There was a nervous splutter in his answer as, nodding, smiling, he told her he knew exactly what she meant and that her attitude about the matter was exactly right. She told him, in that open-hearted way Europeans sometimes have, that she could tell he would understand such things because he had a kind face. This compliment emboldened him to make some gesture by which to show his interest in her. "Can I get you something to drink?" he asked, getting up even as he asked the question. She seemed to consider for a moment, then herself got up and said she wasn't sure what she wanted and would go with him. They both asked everyone at the table if they wanted anything else to drink, but everyone shook their heads, no, and we watched them walk off together.

None of us made more about it at the time than what it seemed to be: two guests going to the bar and who would return to their table within a few minutes. Only, they didn't come back immediately. Now and then one of us would look up to see what had happened to them and see that they were still at the bar, talking to each other, by turns laughing and listening and oblivious to everything but each other. At one point they disappeared altogether. When they eventually did return to our table they remained for no more than a minute before Marcella told Tom that she wanted to introduce him to a few of her friends and they were both off once again. They remained together the rest of the evening, at one point taking a table by themselves, sitting close together, and talking to each other confidentially, having eyes only for each other, and this to such an obvious degree that people who might otherwise have come over to Marcella to say hello or chat with her could see she was "involved" with a young man and might not wish to be interrupted.

After more than three hours—it was midnight—I had had enough of the evening and was ready to go home, and I would have suggested to Tom that we go, but he was having such a grand time with Marcella that I felt guilty about asking him to leave. He was a single young man and this might very well wind up being some long-term relationship for him; perhaps even his future wife. So I didn't want to interrupt. But when an hour later everything began winding down, and most of the guests had gone, and the music had stopped, and the staff who worked in the place were beginning to clean off the tables, I had to assert myself a little. I went over to him and Marcella and told them that the place was closing down and that I would wait for him outside. I walked outside with Nicole and her husband and a few other people who had straggled at our table. Her husband shook hands goodby with me and walked off to a parking lot a few blocks away to get his car, and in a few minutes the others also left, either getting into cabs or walking back to nearby apartments. When Nicole and I were alone I said to her:

"Well, it looks like Tom got pretty lucky tonight."

Nicole nodded, agreeing with me, but there was a certain reserve in her manner, a certain sly irony in her tone of voice, as she remarked, "Yes, that is something, isn't it?"

"Marcella's a beauty, that's for sure."

Nicole flashed me a brief smile and responded in a skeptical tone of voice, "Oh, sure."

"What? You don't think so?"

"Marcella's a nice girl," Nicole said, "and she's beautiful. But ... she has issues."

"What do you mean, 'issues.'?"

Unwilling at first to be more specific, she only repeated, "She has issues."

I laughed. "Everyone has 'issues'! It's only a matter of degree. From what I can see hers can't be any big deal. Unless of course," I added, piscatorially, "she's addicted to drugs or booze. I hope it isn't that."

"Oh, no, nothing like that. She wouldn't even take a glass of wine. Didn't you notice? She doesn't drink alcohol. She's a good Italian girl: she would never do anything like that. No, it's something else. I guess you didn't notice it. No one ever does."

"Notice what?"

Rather than answer me, she looked away and commented to herself bewilderingly, "I don't know ... really ... I shouldn't even tell you."

"Tell me *what?*"

She turned back to me with an air of resignation, as though she were being forced to admit something she had sworn never to disclose. "Marcella Castiglione? Poor thing ... she has no teeth!"

"What do you mean, she has no teeth?"

—For, really, Nicole's pitiful and matter-of-fact statement had been so unexpected, so, somehow disconnected from the subject and the whole rest of the evening, that I wasn't sure what she meant.

"Marcella has no teeth. She wears dentures."

How could I not have laughed a little at that? I was sure that it was one of Nicole's wry jokes. She had been drinking all evening and her eyes, ultra-visible now under the glaring nearby street lamps, were tired and a little red. It would have been just like her to pull my leg for a moment's entertainment. But in her voice and expression and manner ran an undercurrent of earnestness; and then she added, in an almost threatening way, "Listen, don't you dare say anything to Tom!"

"About what?"

"About what I just told you!"

"Oh, c'mon, Nicole, you're not serious!"

"I'm telling you the woman has no teeth!" she said, looking at me with hard, serious eyes.

"How is that possible?"

"What do you mean, 'How is that possible'? It just is. She lost her teeth when she was a kid."

"How would you know that?"

"Because I know. There are some people who know, and I'm one of them. Connections, baby. Things get around if you're in the right circles."

It was just so hard to believe that I shook my head and, smiling, peered expectantly at Nicole as though at any minute she would burst out laughing at having put one over on me. But she didn't laugh; on the contrary, she suddenly looked apprehensive, and said, "I shouldn't have even told you. But now that you know, I'm warning you"—putting up a finger to my face—"don't you say anything to anybody! Don't ever tell *anyone*. Swear to me."

But before I could swear to anything the door of the restaurant opened and Tom and Marcella came walking out, she by his side and with a hand placed on his arm. At the sight of them, Nicole dropped the threatening demeanor toward myself and assumed a cheerful sociableness. Tom was beaming. So was Marcella. We all exchanged a few words about what a great time we had had. I looked at Marcella as she spoke to me and was conscious of her teeth. They were so white, so evenly proportioned, the gums so evenly pink, that it began to dawn on me that Nicole must have been right, that they *had* to be false. Nature didn't create such perfect teeth; only dental laboratories did. I made a point of not looking at Marcella, not trusting myself with lowering my eyes to her mouth and thereby giving her to understand that I knew her secret.

Nicole's husband pulled up to the curb in his car. Nicole hurriedly kissed me on the cheek; did the same to Tom, to Marcella; and with a little wave of her hand bade us all goodbye and told me and Tom she'd give us a call soon. Tom and Marcella and I watched her and her husband drive off.

In parting Tom and Marcella gave each other only the slightest peck on the cheeks, with Tom saying, "I'll call you—we'll do something!" But we had no sooner turned the corner and were walking back to York Avenue where he had parked his car than he jumped—actually jumped, as though he had stepped on a nail—and, brimming with excitement, exclaimed to me half under his breath, "Can you *believe* it? God, what a knockout that woman is! *Marcella—Marcella!*" he said, saying her name with a thick, Italian "ch" sound and bunching up a few of the fingers of his right hand. *"Marcella Castiglione!* God, what a name! It's like the name of a Champagne, or an ocean liner, or ... or a movie star! We're going out with each other to-morrow night!"

"Congratulations."

"I got her number! Didn't even have to ask twice. I'm telling you, she really likes me. She does! Can you imagine?"

"Why shouldn't she?" I asked.

"Why? Because look at her! I mean, this girl is just *outrageous!*"

I said nothing, only smiling, shaking my head, amused and touched by his enthusiasm, which arose from the understanding that women who looked as good as Marcella usually did not go out with men like him, knowing they could "do a lot better" than a working guy from Queens.

Even all the way back home he continued to rave about her, telling me how much fun she had been to be with, what a great personality she had; as much perhaps to convince himself as to convince me that his attraction to her was not entirely based on her looks. As I thought about what Nicole had told me about Marcella's false teeth (it had been hard for me to accept the truth of it, but now I *did* accept it), Tom's happy exclamations about having met her began to make me feel uneasy. I knew very well that he would not have looked at her twice if she had been a plain woman; that however much he harped on her "personality," it wasn't her personality that had for him been the main attraction. He had been attracted to her because she was beautiful in the same way a little boy is attracted to a big yellow ball rather than to a little gray one. He was excited about her because this beautiful woman, who seemed able to choose any man in the world, had chosen him. His male pride had bloomed; he felt good about himself in a way he had never felt before.

It wasn't my place to disclose Marcella's secret to him. I was the less inclined to do so because so far as I was concerned I was never going to see him again. But when he had stopped his car before my apartment building and I was just getting out, thanking him for the ride, he said, "Hold up a minute!" He leaned toward the glove compartment and took out a pen and a stray piece of paper, and jotted down his phone number. "I only live a few blocks away from here," he said. "We ought to go out for a drink or something. It'll be fun."

"Sure," I said, and gave him my number in return.

"Maybe during this week," he proposed. "We'll stop in at The Shamrock. It's just two blocks over. You know where that is, right?"

"Sure. That would be fine."

I didn't expect to hear from him again and, to be honest, I was hoping that I wouldn't. It wasn't that I didn't like the fellow. I liked him well enough. But then again, I like a lot of people well enough, but that doesn't mean I look forward to the interruption of my routines in order to satisfy what is usually their eagerness to escape boredom. Besides, he was fifteen years my junior and shared none of my interests, and I was too realistic about the nature of friendship to think that any meaningful version of it might develop between men of such divergent ages and characters. Nevertheless he did call me on a Wednesday night and invited me out for a drink. I accepted because he happened to catch me in an indolent and indifferent mood. He was already sitting at the long, oval bar before a half-empty pint of Guinness when I arrived at the pub. He bought me my first round. For two hours we sat there drinking and talking, glancing up now and then at a television perched on a shelf behind the bartender and on which a sports event was being shown. During that whole time he spoke almost exclusively about Marcella. Yes, they had gone out on their date, and not only had he had a good time, but he had had the best time of his life. He was surprised at what he was feeling for her. He had never felt anything like it in his life, he said, looking away from me as though embarrassed to admit the intensity of his feelings to another man. The strength of his emotions bewildered him, made him uneasy. How could he feel so much so fast? It was "scary"—because it seemed logical to conclude it would grow still greater and lead to a "commitment," to the marriage and children which no other woman had ever made him want, and which he had thought himself incapable of wanting. In fact he was actually thinking about marriage—yes, he, thinking about marriage! He alluded to himself as a husband and father with a house in the suburbs and who made the daily commute to and from the city. It was all so unlike him, these thoughts, he said; and yet he couldn't help it—they seemed more and more attractive to him. With a contentedly resigned shrug and a rather dreamy look in his eye he said that there were some things you couldn't say for sure you would never do; there were "things" that just "happened."

Obviously he didn't yet know about Marcella's teeth. As he spoke glowingly about her, about his feelings for her, I sat there forcing myself to smile, to seem pleased for his good fortune, even as my stomach began to churn with the sickening sense that here was a man whose happiness was based on a lie which sooner or later he had to discover. I thought about Nicole and how insistent she had been on my not revealing Marcella's secret him. At the time I had thought it an understandable and even noble desire on the part of a woman to protect another woman's chances for romance; but where did that leave *him?* Why was *he* so easily, so conveniently, thrown under the bus? A part of me wanted to tell him about Marcella because I hated to see him made a dupe of, but another part of me saw that he might regard my disclosure as an attempt to throw a little muck into his happiness. In the end I decided it was none of my business. This was something he would have to find out for himself.

I can only speculate on what was going through Marcella's mind during this time, but it's the kind of speculation that seems to me rather obvious. She was afraid of telling him. She was afraid that once he knew he would no longer be interested in her. Despite her beauty, her growing fame, and her wealth (for as a coveted model her fees had become enormous), she was terrified at the thought that her secret should be known. Perhaps at other times a fierce pride asserted itself in her breast, and she told herself that she didn't care what Tom or anyone else might think about her for having false teeth. Perhaps she told herself, "If he cares about me, it won't make a difference to him; and if it does make a difference to him, then he obviously doesn't care about me and he's not worth my time!" Isn't something like that what all proud people say to themselves when considering how a potential lover will regard their flaws? But this kind of bravery is usually as fleeting as it is forced: working well in theory, hardly ever in practice; for while we have our pride, we also have our needs, which have a way of clawing down the most dignified resolves. Marcella was a good-hearted and essentially simple woman who yearned to be loved. Several times she must have decided that she would tell him about herself. And yet the moment she talked to him or saw him her resolve failed, and she held her peace.

How do I know this? Why do I think it? Because over the next two months Tom himself unwittingly gave me the clues whenever we would meet and he would tell me about the "good times" he was having with Marcella. He had a good memory for details about what she had said and how she had said it, and which only went to prove how infatuated he was with her, how he hung on to her every word and gesture and expression. He was especially amused by the "strange" things she said and the worried expressions that always accompanied them. Her mind, he said proudly, worked a thousand miles a minute—you could see she was just thinking, thinking, thinking away, the self-absorption glittering in her eyes. And then she would come out with it—the wonderful, charming, absurd thing she had evidently been considering so hard and so foolishly. For instance, at one point while they were having dinner she had idly looked down at her plate and then raised her head to him and asked:

"What do you like best about me? Is it the way I look?"

"Well, I certainly like the way you look!" he had responded.

"But that's not the only reason why you like me, I hope."

"Of course it's not, don't be silly. I like everything about you."

"But what if I didn't look the way I do?"

"As long as you don't look like Frankenstein, I think we'll be fine!" And he laughed.

She smiled at his joke. She lowered her eyes and tapped her food with her fork. She looked up to him with a new and disarming kind of intensity, as though she had resolved on something (oh, Tom!), only to shake her head subtly, to back off her determination of a second earlier, and to ask instead:

"Well ... would you still like me if I gained weight?"

"Oh, please—you? Let me tell you something, you could stand to put on a few pounds. You're so thin!"

["You know," Tom had told me on another occasion, "Marcella's got a great body—she's got longer legs than I do!—but she really *is* a little too thin. She could use another ten pounds, easy. I think she'd even look better, if that's possible."]

"But what if I gained *a lot* of weight?" she pressed.

He shrugged again, smiling. "There would just be more of you to love."

"What if ... something else happened, Tom. Something worse. What if ... my hair fell out."

Tom laughed. "And you went bald?"

She laughed too a little; it was so ridiculous. "But what if it *did?*" she pressed

"Well, then," he said, leaning back in his chair and assuming an expansive, thoughtful demeanor, as though giving himself up to a serious consideration of the preposterous hypothesis, "I guess I'd have to buy you a wig! Yes, that's what I'd do: I'd get you a wig. A great big fuzzy one, all yellow and blue. Now *that* I'd like to see!" And he laughed at the absurd image of her that he had conjured up.

"But honestly, Tom, what would you do?"

"Oh, Marcella, who knows!" he said, throwing up his hands a little, and wondering at what seemed to him a new, strange, but amusing side to her personality. "That's such an odd question. Why would you go bald?"

"I wouldn't *want* to go bald," she said; "I'm just wondering what you would do if it happened."

"Well, it's not *going* to happen, so don't worry about it."

"It's just that ... you know ... looks aren't everything."

"Who said they were?"

["Poor thing," he said, by way of an aside, "I didn't realize till then that she probably was sick and tired of guys just running after her because of the way she looked. I guess that does get to be a drag after a while. I don't blame her." —Oh, Tom!]

He leaned in toward her; put out his hand, taking hers. His words were all affectionate reassurance. "You're silly. But you're you—that's what I like about you!"

His words gratified her and must have emboldened her to make her revelation then and there. For about fifteen seconds she stared hard at the table at which they were sitting, she opened her mouth again, she took a deep breath in preparation for the grand announcement, and ... did not make it.

As their relationship progressed and Tom began to spend evenings with her, Marcella must have ensured that he would find no telltale signs that she wore dentures. She must have hidden away all the cleaning powders and adhesives which she used for them.

Even after two months he continued to suspect nothing. At most he had a sense that there was yet a lot to learn about this woman who had graced him with her beauty and her love.

He found out the truth in the most dramatic way. It was the kind of thing that one couldn't make up—the kind of thing that was stranger than fiction. They had gone to an amusement park in New Jersey and gotten on a ride called—forbiddingly enough—"Super Spinner": one of those monstrous, powerful contraptions designed to whizz you about till you're dizzy or half dead, laughing all the way. Marcella laughed too; but unfortunately for her at the most inopportune moment: for she opened her mouth widest just as the car, into which she and Tom were tightly strapped, jerked upward at an incredible rate of speed. Her teeth dropped out in the opposite direction.

I sit here writing this and shake my head over it. I can't imagine what must have gone through that poor girl's head when she, flying up, up, up, saw her teeth falling down, down, and down. "Embarrassment," "shame," even "mortification" are words that simply can't begin to express the dreadful terror that must have gripped her, wrapped itself around her heart with claws of ice, ripped through her like a sharp blade. Perhaps in those first seconds she wasn't sure what the object was that had dropped away in a flash of pink and white, only to close her mouth and feel upper and lower jaw meet to a degree they shouldn't have—to feel the hard yet spongy flesh of her upper gum touch that of her lower, and her lips bulge out horribly; and all this as the person she wanted most always to impress, always to make proud of her—the person she loved—sat beside her. Surely her scream at that moment had nothing to do with the excitement of the ride.

She kept her head averted from Tom, and as soon as the mighty contraption lowered their car to ground level she popped out of it as though the seat in which she had been sitting lay atop a compressed spring just sprung. With head still averted from him, she said, she shouted out, that she had to go, and walked off at a clip, and then broke into a run. After an initial moment of stunned wonder, Tom set off after her. He trailed just behind her, asking her what had happened. He tried to walk by her side, but she would not look at him, turned away from him, demanded that he let her alone—that she wanted to be let alone! He put out a hand to take hold of her arm or shoulder, pleading with her to tell him what was wrong (the poor man thought it was something he had said or done), but she jerked away from him and, refusing to face him, commanded him to get away from her in a voice so loud, so urgent, so dreadfully imperious—with a spirit so forcefully agitated, so growlingly determined—that it leapt out at him with the ferocious energy of an enraged animal, overwhelming him and stopping him in his tracks. She continued away from him and he stood there, still and speechless and watching her hurry off into the crowds as though everything about him were hateful to her.

Her behavior left him in a solitary daze.

He called her at home that very evening. There was no answer and he had to leave a message on her answering machine. He left her several messages the day after also, and several more the day after; and still she did not call him back. He was sure that her behavior was owing to something he had done, perhaps something he had said. He racked his brains to think of what it might have been. Always he came up with nothing. He did not hear from her for a whole week because that's how long it took her to get another set of dentures. Ordinarily it would have taken a lot longer than that, but she demanded of her dentist that he provide her with a new set at once, and he in turn imparted the same sense of urgency to the laboratory making the prosthesis. But all this rushing took its toll on quality. The new set was not quite so good, not quite so natural-looking, as the old one. The teeth seemed a little too large, especially the two front ones so that they had a vaguely rodential quality. Marcella herself must have noticed this as soon as she put them into her mouth, but she was so desperate to have them that she was willing to use them till better ones could be made. All that week, while waiting for her new teeth, she had immured herself in her apartment, had hidden away from the world, burning with shame and anger and disgust, and undoubtedly aware of the horrible responsibility, no longer to be evaded or avoided, of explaining herself to Tom.

Yet even when they finally talked over the telephone, she was not honest with him. To his inquiries about what had happened that day in the amusement park, about why she had not returned his phone calls, she gave the cryptic response that she had "had her reasons"; and when he insisted on knowing what those reasons were, she would only say, quietly, "I'll explain it to you when I see you."

She told him that she loved him. He assured her that he loved her.

Tom would later tell me that he noticed at once the difference in her teeth. During their first face-to-face interview after almost two weeks of separation, he could not help staring at her mouth. With what must have been a hopeless, sinking, heartbreaking sense of resignation, Marcella saw how his eyes kept turning to the lower part of her face. Now she knew that he knew and that only politeness restrained him from mentioning it. And yet even then—even when she knew it was a matter of minutes before he understood completely—she did not come right out and tell him that she had no teeth but rather, as her eyes filled with tears, she sat him down and talked to him about her past. She told him how she had grown up in a poor family that lived in the Italian countryside. Her parents were good and kind people but they came from peasant stock, were uneducated, and did not know what it was to "take care of themselves." It hadn't been as it was in America where parents regularly take their children to a dentist for checkups and cleanings. At that time, in that place, dentists were resorted to only when there was too much pain to bear; by which time it was nearly always too late and the only affordable cure was extraction. Moreover her teeth had been especially bad—"soft" and prone to cavities. Her parents too had lost their teeth early. What had made the situation all the worse was that as a child she had craved sweets. All children, of course, love sweets, but she had craved them with a positive, incessant craving. She regularly engorged herself on them. She would sneak them out of the kitchen at night while her parents slept, taking them back to her room, lying in bed and eating them, sucking on them, consuming them with a little girl's perfect contentment: sugared almonds, toffee caramels, sprinkles-coated struffoli, anise-flavored pizzelles, and cannoli filled with chocolate cream. She had been especially fond of Torrone, that sugar-and-honey, nougat-filled candy that when dry was hard as a brick, but which, with eating, became gooey and sticky. She would nibble on a chunk of it for an hour at a time, often at night just before going to sleep; and as she slept with a belly full of it, the dense sugars that lay impacted in the pits and grooves of her teeth silently invigorated the germs there, enabling them to eat away at the enamel with sinister efficiency. By the time she was fourteen years old most of her molars had been yanked out of her head. By the time she was eighteen she had only five carious teeth left, so that when she smiled her otherwise very pretty face became hideous, and so she had had those yanked out too, and had gotten dentures. She was ashamed of them: Oh!—if Tom only knew how ashamed of them she was! But there was nothing she could do about it. It wasn't her fault; it was just her bad luck. And if she had, up to this moment, never told Tom about them—if she had withheld the truth—even if she had lied—it was only because she was ashamed of herself, and because she didn't want him to leave her. She knew she had fallen in love with him after they had been together only a few times, and she had been afraid that if he found out she had no teeth he would no longer want her. Couldn't he understand that? Couldn't he forgive her? She hoped he would—she felt he would. He had always been so good to her; he was such a good man; he was her best, her only friend, whom she would give her life for;—surely, surely it wouldn't matter to him.

Tom listened in silence, and sympathetically. He felt sorry for her. At one point he had taken her hand as she had spoken, as though to give her strength and support. He understood how hard it must have been for her, who put so much stock in her looks and much of whose life, indeed, was based on them, to have kept such a secret. He managed a comforting smile and assured her, first, that she shouldn't feel bad about herself for wearing dentures, and that, second, it was of no consequence to him—absolutely none. "Marcella," he said, feeling strangely disconnected from the words he spoke, "did you really think that was going to make a difference to me? You should know better than that. It doesn't matter: it's nothing—nothing!"

But in fact from that moment his love for her began to die.

It wasn't that his avowal of continued devotion had been insincere; he had meant every word of it at the time. But he himself didn't understand how much his love for her, and then his wariness of her, was based on something over which he had no control. The moment he had left her after her disclosure—he had embraced her reassuringly and kissed her (a brief kiss)—he began to obsess over her toothlessness. As many times as he told himself that it didn't matter, the insistence with which it obtruded into his consciousness proved otherwise. He had never been an imaginative man, but now suddenly in his mind's eye he kept seeing her without her dentures: the fine, thin, bow-like lips rising into a smile—only to expose uneven gums above and below, the hideous gateway to a disgusting dark maw. Her beauty somehow made it worse, for it acted as the bright foil in contrast to which the defect was the more flagrant. Above all was the conviction that there was something "wrong" with her in a physiological, that is to say, a fundamental and genetic way. Surely it wasn't natural for anyone to lose her teeth as a teenager; not to lose them all, the way she had. He remembered how she had told him that her parents had also lost their teeth early on, and he deduced that it was a family trait which had been passed on to her. Something deep in his being whispered to him that it would be obscenely wrong in him to ignore this fact and blithely continue his relationship with her to its usual conclusion of marriage and children; that doing so would make him complicit in promoting and continuing a genetic flaw, and thus to betray his own children from the start. Yes, the little girls or boys he and Marcella might have together would undoubtedly be pretty little things, their faces sweet, their features fine, their eyes as large and sparkling as their mother's; but they would also carry the defective gene. He couldn't allow that to happen—not to *his* children! It was remarkable that he, who had never especially wanted to be a father—who had reckoned that it was just as well that he had never had kids, since he wasn't likely to give them the kind of attention and dedication they deserved—that here he was making decisions on his life based exclusively on theoretical progeny!

During this time he called me and asked if he might stop by my place because he "really needed to talk about something."

The moment he appeared at my door his distraction was obvious. We drank some scotch together and after his second one he opened up to me about what he had discovered about Marcella, and the discussion they had had and which I've related above. As he spoke his movements were jerky, nervous; his legs, his feet fidgeted; he kept his eyes mostly averted from mine and when he did venture to meet them he smiled in a painful, hopeless way. He gropingly and touchingly tried to explain the complicated, instinctive, bizarre-and-yet-not-bizarre reasons he had for feeling as he did. When he had finished speaking, he braved a look at me and asked, "Can you believe all this?"

I said only, "I'm sure you're not lying."

"Can you believe it!" he said, this time to himself and shaking his head. He looked about the living room, thinking, holding an empty scotch glass in his hands. I refilled it for him and he took another long sip. "So!" he said, turning to me, "what do you think I should do?"

"What do you mean?" I asked, feigning innocence.

"I can't help thinking about them—her teeth, I mean. What am I supposed to do with her now?" he asked.

"Tom, you make it sound as though you bought a pen and it's run out of ink. What do you mean, what do you 'do' with her now?"

"But I don't know that I can go out with her any more," he said, with a note of desperate pleading, as though he were being pressured into doing something against his wishes.

I shrugged and shook my head and looked as though his attitude bewildered me, though by this time—and especially after witnessing his worry with its undercurrent of loathing—the young woman's toothlessness began to strike me also as incongruous with any notion of high romance. Tom's problem was that he was basically a decent guy, and therefore affection, honor, and pity urged him in the direction of accepting Marcella's physical shortcoming, only for each emotional step he took in that direction to increase a disillusioning repugnance. He was caught in a storm of equally strong but opposing forces, and in that maelstrom he twisted and twirled and was worn ragged.

As the older, the "mature" man, and the one he had come to for guidance or at least an objective opinion, I could not in good conscience tell him that he was making a big deal about nothing, for if that had been the case Marcella's condition could never have occupied even my thoughts as it had.   There *was* something bizarre about so great a beauty being—well, *not* beautiful.   The best I could do was to assure Tom that he might not want to resist his more generous sentiments and inclinations.

"You know," I said, evenly, soberly, "teeth are just teeth."

He looked at me in an unsure, probing, way, wanting, expecting, needing to hear me say more, and so putting me under some pressure to expatiate on the matter, which I did rather gropingly:

"Who says you have to have perfect teeth? Very few people do have perfect teeth.   If you look around, you'll find that most people have pretty bad teeth.   Even people with really good teeth—if you look closely enough, they're not as good as you thought: some of them are always a little crooked, or a little stained; there's always something going on in there.   Plaque and stuff.   As a general rule, people don't floss, and they're almost never thorough when they do. That's just the way it is— that's the way people are.   For instance, my teeth.   They look alright in the front, but do you know how many fillings I have? I must have at least a dozen.   You know why? Because I didn't go to a dentist until I was nineteen years old.   My parents never took me.   They couldn't afford it—you know what thieves dentists are.   They're thieves of the worst kind: they don't hesitate to practice ruthless extortion even on the poor.   Anyway, when I finally went my mouth was a mess.   You should have seen the doctor after he examined me.   He shook his head and frowned and told me how bad it was. He actually had to write out a contract telling me how many teeth had to be drilled and filled, and how much the project—he actually called it a 'project'!—would cost.   Let me tell you something, my friend, it was three months of intermittent pain.   If silver amalgam ever reaches the price of gold I might actually be worth something. In fact I've got so much metal in my mouth that I'm a walking antenna.   It's true! Sometimes I hear this ultra-high frequency in my head—especially in the middle of the night, when everything's quiet, and I'm lying there, in my bed, listening hard: it's a faint, thin, high-pitched sound.   I'm sure it's my teeth picking up radio waves or something.   And all that's not to mention the several root canals I've had, and you have no idea how expensive all *that* was! Anyway ... the point is ... the point is, Tom ... everyone, really, has bad teeth to some degree. And as for dentures, well, just try to look on the good side of it. Because there really is a good side to them. For instance, brushing your teeth. When you wear dentures you don't have to stick a toothbrush in your mouth and swallow half a tube of toothpaste; you just pull your teeth out and hold them in your hands and brush them—get them super clean. And you never have to worry about cavities—at least, I don't think so. And if they crack or something, it can't hurt you because they're not really a part of your body, and you can just go out and have them repaired, or even do it yourself with Crazy Glue or something. Know what I mean?"

He sat there, leaning forward a little, holding his glass in two hands, and staring at me with an open mouth. He was looking at me hard as though not sure what to make of what I had said. And in fact I myself, after I had finished speaking, was aware of how earnestly but ineffectively I had been striving to say something he might take comfort in.

He finished off the scotch, put the empty glass on the coffee table, and stood up, looking at me more hopelessly than ever. He went to the window and for a minute stood there looking out of it. He sighed a few times. He returned to the couch and sat down, shaking his head as his distressed eyes stared at the floor. Then he raised them to me and said in a voice full of hopeless distress:

"But I *can't* keep going out with her! It's ... it's starting to affect me. I can't sleep."

"How is that?"

He told me. He had been having a recurrent troubling dream. In this dream it was late afternoon and he was leaving the workplace. He walked out of the building to the parking lot and when he reached his car he was shocked to see that the door on the driver's side had been removed. He was only slightly relieved to find that nothing inside the vehicle had been stolen or damaged. He stood there anxiously wondering what he was going to do now—how he was going to get home; and decided he had no choice but to drive without a door. The noise of the roadway was loud, the sight of it frightening, as it slipped away just inches beneath him at sixty miles per hour. Other

drivers who came alongside him gawked to see him sitting
there, seat-belted behind the wheel and totally exposed. He kept
his eyes on the road, refusing to look at them. He could only
hope that he didn't pass a policeman who was sure to stop him
and give him some kind of ticket. When he reached his home,
which was not an apartment but a proper house in the suburbs
with a white picket fence and a little dog barking in the front
yard, he pulled into the driveway with a sense of relief; but his
anxiety surged afresh when he saw that the door of his house
was missing: there was nothing there but a stark, open jamb,
dark with the dimness within. He gingerly stepped inside and
noticed that every other door was similarly missing; every room,
every closet, every cabinet was wide open and exposed. Then he
heard voices of children, of little girls, calling out happily,
"Daddy's home!"—and he knew he was their father and was impatient to see them. He heard the patter of hurrying little feet
and in another moment three little girls came rushing toward
him, their arms stretched forward, shouting ecstatically,
"Daddy!" They were the prettiest little girls one could imagine,
with long, curling black hair, fresh cheeks, and large dark eyes.
He crouched down to receive their eager embraces, and just as
they reached him he saw that none of them had teeth; that
their gaping mouths showed only ridges of gums. They piled on
top of him, struggling with one another to get at him, to cover
him with gummy, slobbering kisses. He tried to push them
away gently, then more vigorously, and finally began to panic
and with a strong arm pushed them off him, sending them flying, only for them to land a few feet away and pop right back
up and resume the assault on him; crowding round him, fighting with one another to get him, to shove their faces into his, to
kiss him with their toothless mouths; disgusting him, horrifying
him, suffocating him;—so that he woke up, his heart beating
fast.

"I've had that dream nearly every night this week," he said.
"So you see ... this thing is affecting me. I ... I just can't do it!"

He said that so forthrightly and surely that it sounded as
though he had finally come to a decision; yet once again an element of uncertainty entered his voice as he continued:

"You understand, don't you? I like her a lot ... I think I
was in love with her .... but I just can't do it ... I just *can't*."

He shifted his eyes away from mine and his lips worked in silent consideration and thoughtfulness for a few seconds before he broke out with:

"She has no teeth, for God's sake!"

—And with that he slumped down a little, as though the struggle to utter these words had exacted from him his last ounce of strength. He miserably stared at the wall opposite him and ran his fingers through his hair a few distraught times. I wanted to say something comforting but couldn't think of anything appropriate. Then he started speaking again:

"I watch her eat dinner, and I know they're false. And when she laughs or smiles, and they flash out—so big and white—I know they're false. And the worst, the absolute worst part? I don't even know if I can tell you. The worst part is when I kiss her. I know, I can feel, they're false—like plastic or plaster or something. Oh, it's just so horrible! And maybe even that's not the worst of it. There are some nights when I wake up and lie there beside her, and she hasn't taken them out because she can't bear for me to see her without them, and I hear them—clacking! Do you know what that's like, to hear someone's false teeth clacking in your ears at night? And let's say I *did* keep seeing her, let's say we got still more involved. There's bound to come a point when she'd feel so comfortable around me that she wouldn't care if I saw her without her teeth—and then what? Oh, God." He stared into space as though entranced by that unsettling prospect. He lowered his head and ran his hands through his hair again, the very picture of misery. "And then if we had kids," he continued, in a low, less dramatic and more thoughtful voice. "Can you imagine? What would happen to them? I know what would happen to them. I know, already: they'd all lose their teeth. I can't let that happen ... not to my kids ... it wouldn't be fair ..."

The problem really was this: Tom was a better man than most. He had a good, living heart in his breast; was kind and wished to hurt no one, least of all Marcella. But he had glimpsed something beyond his and her small, brief, circumscribed lives. The fount of his ineradicable revulsion toward Marcella's condition really arose from an unconscious knowledge that he was obligated toward those who came after him; that he was a mere link in the long chain of generations. In her own way Marcella acted out of a similar impulse, for as a woman she wanted children more than anything in life. This yearning enabled her to rationalize away the likelihood of transmitting to her children the very traits that had made much of her own life unhappy. She had undoubtedly convinced herself that her children would never lose their teeth; she would make sure of it by lavishing on them all the best dental care money could buy. In retrospect I can't help thinking that Tom's attitude and actions, though at the time they seemed to me horribly superficial, were actually noble: for what did they amount to but a fundamental concern for his progeny and, by way of extension (though he never thought about the matter so deeply), for the welfare of humanity itself?

At the time I only saw, as he himself did, the reprehensible aspect of his behavior. I also saw that there was only one thing for him to do.

"You need to stop seeing her," I said.

"How?"

"Just tell her you're not interested any more. Tell her you don't feel the way you used to."

"Oh, that's impossible! How can I tell her that when we were just together last night!"

"I'm not saying to tell her today. You have to do it gradually. You have to start to distance yourself from her. Don't see her every day or every other day: begin to see her twice a week, then once a week, then less than that. Believe me, she'll get the message."

"But she'll know! She'll know why I'm doing it!"

"Well, if she ever raises the issue outright like that, then just deny it; say it has nothing to do with it. No reason to hurt her feelings. Lie. Make an excuse. Everybody does it. Say you met someone else."

But he shook his head, no, knowing that that kind of excuse would never do. She would know the real reason for the separation, and it would devastate her. Already he was suffering at the thought of causing her that kind of pain.

"Look," I said, "what matters is that you're not happy. Just look at you! There's no law that says you have to stay with someone when you're not happy with them—for whatever the reason."

"But she's such a *nice* girl," he responded. "And she really is beautiful—the most beautiful girl I ever went out with. If it only weren't for her teeth."

"Oh, Tom, please!" I said, irritably, "you have to make up your mind! If you can't stand the thought that she has no teeth, then there's no point in staying with her, no matter how nice or how beautiful she is! She doesn't need pity. She needs a man who wants to be with her. So do yourselves both a favor and make up your mind. If you're really unhappy with her the way she is, and you are, then there's no point in going on with it. Life is too short to be miserable. End it, already!"

He took my advice, or rather gave way to what was inevitable. He gave me a call every other day to tell me what was going on, not so much because he was eager to have me involved in his personal life as because he wanted confirmation that he was doing the right thing. He no longer saw her every day or every other day, and when they did go out he made sure that his shows of affection were brief and infrequent. As they walked along he would release his hand from hers under the pretext of pointing out something along the way. His kisses were mere pecks on her lips. He began to make excuses about why he couldn't spend the night with her: because he was tired, because he didn't feel well, because he had to get up early for work the next morning. He knew that she knew the reason for this change in his behavior, just as he knew he was breaking her heart, for he could see it in her face, hear it in her voice, sense it in the way she mustered her pride and answered him with an indifferent-seeming, "No problem" or "I'll see you tomorrow, then." He would come away from her hating himself for the way he had acted. In flashes of objectivity he saw himself as repaying the purest, most unselfish devotion with an obscene hardness of heart. Yet never once did he seriously consider turning around, going back to her, and apologizing for how he had behaved. He could not help it. He knew the way he ought to be, but the way he ought to be was a theory that did not square with the hard reality before him.

Each time he left her during that difficult period she, who understood why he was acting as he did, must have vowed in a surge of prideful anger never to call him again—to let him be, to let him go. She must have reasoned that he wasn't worth so

much as a second of her time if he could really be so superficial
as to be put off by the fact that she wore dentures. But when it
comes to resolves, the mind is often more pliable and obedient
than the heart, and despite her determination to forget about
him, even to despise him, she found that she missed him horribly. After a week during which she heard nothing from him she
could bear it no longer: she broke down, she abased herself in
her own eyes and called him. She called as though there were
nothing wrong between them, as though it were just another
call between lovers who missed each other; and he himself, in
those first few seconds when he heard her cheerful, "Hi, how are
you?" betrayed his pleasure at hearing from her again with his
own enthusiastic greeting. She never asked him why he hadn't
called, but the question hung sensibly between them and could
not be ignored, and he eventually addressed it, inventing yet another excuse for his absence from her, saying that he had been
extremely busy lately, had been so tired from work that he just
wanted to sleep, that, in short, he had been in no mood or condition to see anyone. He knew she knew these were lies, and
he feared she would call him out on them. But she didn't because she was just grateful to hear his voice again—to reestab-
lish some connection with him, even if it were the tenuous,
impalpable, essentially empty one provided by phantom electronic signals whizzing back and forth on a telephone wire.
With each word they spoke they came closer to making another
date; the whole impulse and inner nature of their conversation
tending in that direction; and Tom felt increasingly uncomfortable, as though he were being pushed into something he wanted
no part of. And yet he could not bring himself to refuse her request to see him again. He clenched his jaw with resolve, he
scowled, he hated the words that came out of his mouth: "Sure,
when?" After they had made that date he hung up the phone
and cursed aloud his own weak inability to resist being pulled
back into a hurtful, hopeless vortex of a relationship with her,
for what was the point of it when the unbearable problem remained, and she still had no teeth—when the great beauty still
had the grisly flaw?

Their last meeting was a disaster because Tom, as he admitted to me, treated her wretchedly. He didn't mean to, he
said, but he saw clearly in retrospect that he had. When they

met he embraced her with such cold quickness that one might have thought someone was holding a gun to his head and forcing him to touch a monster. Thereafter he was nervously impatient, smiled insincerely, and constantly averted his eyes from her. In everything he did or said he made it clear that he would have preferred to be anywhere else but in her company. Nothing she could do—short of growing a new set of teeth, that is—could change the situation. Marcella realized how hopeless their relationship was. She didn't hint or suggest that they spend the night together. They parted with a brief, insincere kiss and the promise to speak to each other "soon." They never saw each other again.

Marcella went on to have a great career. Not more than a handful of people know about her secret, and they have always remained honorably close-lipped. (Obviously, "Marcella Castiglione" isn't her real name—the last thing I need is a lawsuit on my hands.) Her fabulous face and figure have graced the covers of the most prestigious fashion magazines in the world. She looks as beautiful, in fact more beautiful than ever. In one of those not uncommon twists of fate, she is famous for her smile full of the whitest, most perfect teeth one could imagine— believably so, as it happens, since she has had the sense to make sure that they aren't perfect in every respect. She's also made her first foray into films, where she's bound to have another and still more lucrative career. Now and then one sees her on a nationally syndicated talk show, and invariably the hosts ask her about her personal life and whether or not she is "seeing anyone special." "No, no, not yet," she answers in that shy, enticing way that is so special to her. And every man in the audience, entranced by what he sees, wishes that he could be the one to be with her.

Tom's future was not quite so rosy. As might be expected, he and I quickly drifted apart after his affair with Marcella had ended. What I learned about him came to me through Nicole. His penchant for speed on the highway got him into a nasty automobile accident that so badly mangled his left arm there was a chance it would have to be amputated. Luckily for him, the surgeons at Long Island Jewish worked a miracle and he was able to keep it; still, it was never afterwards the same: it became stiff, hard to move without pain, and permanently crooked at the elbow. Doubtless on account of this semi-disability he began rethinking the relationship he had had with Marcella. Firsthand now he knew what it was to have a physical problem that one had no control over and which was to be indulged with sympathy. A lot of his old guilt returned. He wrote her a note telling her what had happened to him over the last few years—filling her in on the accident and its consequences—and posing the possibility that they "see" each other again, if only for a cup of coffee or a drink. He never heard back from her.

CONTEMPT

After Jeannette Lambert died at the age of eighty-seven it was generally agreed in the family that she had had a "hard" life, the hardest part of which had been poverty. She had never had other than the poorest-paying jobs because she was an illiterate who could barely scratch out the letters of her name. She had retired at sixty-two years of age—the moment she was able to collect a Social Security check—but she had not entered a nursing home till she was eighty-four. And how did she spend those intervening twenty-two years, while she still had her health and each day was her own? Watching television. She watched it for eight hours, sometimes for as many as twelve or fourteen hours a day. It filled her head with images of people winning fabulous sums of money on game shows, of celebrity millionaires jetting to exotic locations, of movie stars dressed in chic clothes and wearing dazzling jewels, smiling as they walked up red carpets and into glittering theaters to receive awards. All of this convinced her that she had missed out on the main point of life—namely, to be wealthy; and she always bemoaned this by saying that she had had "no luck." When she was not watching television she had ample time to look back on her past and grow increasingly bitter about her (as she took it to be) misfortune; and it so poisoned her mind that she could find pleasure in nothing. The hundred common, free or inexpensive things in which a healthy mind might have taken joy, such as a walk in the park on a lovely day, the luminous color of roadside wild flowers, the sight and sound of children playing and laughing, or even a good meal—none of them touched her with joy or could make her smile. How could you smile when you didn't have a mansion and servants and jewels and fine clothes and the ability to travel in high style wherever you wanted to go? Thus long before she got sick and had to be institutionalized she was one of the most miserable persons on earth; and this, in the end, because she was one of the most empty-headed.

She had had her first heart attack when she was seventy-eight. In the following three months she aged ten years. Her face became drawn, her hair took on a coarse, frizzled texture, and she developed a stoop. She withdrew into herself and she always looked worried. She became further embittered by the betrayal of her body, as though serious illness were something that ought never to have happened to her—something that was only supposed to afflict other people. She had never considered her own mortality but as something hazy, unreal, hypothetical, a kind of boogeyman people had sadistically made up to frighten her, and which it was not worth her time to think about. Now the reality of her own eventual death had risen up before her and refused to be ignored. She was incapable of coming to terms with it. She grew depressed. Her family tried to give her encouragement and hope, telling her that she had no reason to be so gloomy about her future. They told her that she had "only" had a heart attack, which people had every day and not only recuperated from but went on to live full, energetic lives. "It's not like it was in the old days when people died of this stuff!" they told her with an assured, knowing air, as though they had devoted hours of study to the matter and she would be foolish to question their assertions. "Nowadays they just treat these things and you're as good as new! But of course you have to take care of yourself! You have to make an effort and change your bad habits! You can't do the things you used to do—oh, no, no! You have to watch what you eat! No more fat! No more fried foods! Watch your salt! Try to exercise! You never did walk enough, you know, and the body needs to move! Walk, eat right, go for your checkups! You'll see—you'll be fine, just fine!" Of course none of this was true, at least not in her case, and those who said it with so much conviction were themselves medical ignoramuses, their non-knowledge in this field having derived entirely from movies and television shows in which some patient invariably hovers for a half hour at death's door before being brought back to vibrant health and happiness by the almost magical ministrations of a brilliant doctor. Such interviews, where the blind led the blind, would have made the misanthrope laugh.

Month by month, year by year, Jeannette became a little

more drawn, a little weaker, a little sicker as her diseased heart increasingly failed. The friends and relatives who had once assured her she'd be get better saw for themselves that she was spiraling into the grave. They nevertheless continued to encourage her—what else could they do? And though she seemed to heed them as intently, as hopefully as ever, she heard within herself the whispers of intuition telling her that she was coming to the End, and nothing that anyone said or did was going to make a difference. A few more heart attacks struck—small ones, to be sure, but which, in her condition, were catastrophic. After each one she hung on to life by a thread, surviving only because she had made it to an emergency room on time and received the ministrations of modern medicine, and because yet again an overwhelming fear of death marshaled her will to cling to life. She received from the State a nursing aid who stayed with her eight hours a day, who cooked and cleaned for her, and kept her company; a jolly, good-humored Romanian woman who spoke broken English and was long-suffering in the face of Jeannette's nervous sick-bed demands and insults. She accompanied her charge to the doctor once a week, made sure she swallowed her dozen medications every day, and saw her off to the hospital when she had to have a "procedure" done—several angioplasties and, eventually, a pacemaker, which stuck out as a horrible bulge beneath the wrinkled, translucent, old skin of her withered, indrawn chest. But these were merely temporary obstacles for Nature, which continued to take Jeannette's life inches at a time where it could not do so in one fell swoop. She would lie in bed for days on end, too weak to do more than watch television and nibble on the meals for which she had no appetite. She became as thin as a scarecrow. Then one morning when she tried to get up, her legs wobbled and buckled beneath her. She no longer had the strength to stand or walk. That was the end of what little independence she had been able to cling to; she could no longer live alone after that—no longer get herself a glass of water or walk to the bathroom. She spent the rest of her days in a nursing home. In the last six months of her life she had been reduced to a ghostly bent-over figure in a wheelchair, a living skeleton, sleeping half the time, the other half not quite sure where or who she was, and always pumped up with a dozen drugs—sedatives to calm her nerves, anticoagulants to prevent blood clots, orexegenics to stimulate her appetite, diuretics to make her urinate, laxatives to move her bowels, in short, a host of pharmaceuticals precisely chosen and carefully administered in order to wring out of her failing flesh every smallest iota of life, and thus ensure that she suffered to the very last second possible.

She had had one child, a daughter, Georgette, who all her adult life had lived in Paris and had seldom come to visit her mother in America. Indeed Georgette had rarely even called her. There had been tensions between them through the years. When her mother had gotten sick Georgette had made one of her rare phone calls, less out of loving concern than out of guilt. Only when her mother was committed to a nursing home did she make the effort of actually getting on a plane and flying to New York to visit her. She had been unnerved by what she had seen; indeed, it had taken her several minutes even to recognize her mother in the pitiful, skeletal creature hunched over in a wheelchair. Until that moment Georgette would never have believed that someone could be so frail and wasted and yet continue to live. After that visit she announced that she would not be coming back to the United States, as though her mother had already died and the reason for such a return had been removed. That had been two years earlier. But now she was coming back in a last trip across the Atlantic, to New York City, to pay her last respects to her mother's grave.

"She's coming next week," Aunt Carrie said. "She asked if she could stay with me, and of course I said yes. The poor girl wants to see where her mother is buried. She asked about you, by the way. She wanted to know how you were and what you've been doing. It would be nice if you could invite her to stay at your place for a few days. I'm afraid she'll be awfully bored in my house. And you know how she always liked you, always thought so highly of you ..."

These words were directed toward Samantha, a thirty-three-year-old woman who, though not attractive in a conventional sense, had even features and bright gray eyes in which by turns glittered an engaging contentment and a cynical skepticism. She had been on her way to the library to return a few books when she met up with her Aunt Carrie—an "aunt" through marriage and now a widow. They often met in this way because they lived just a few blocks away from each other. These chance meetings were always characterized by the cheerful conversation of people who like each other, and Aunt Carrie never failed to invite her niece over for visits or dinner. Invariably Samantha politely refused, in part because she didn't want to impose, but also because she didn't want to detract from her writing time. For Samantha was a poet. She had been writing since she was a teenager and even now, after all these years, she continued to dream of making a name for herself in literature—of becoming famous and, if not wealthy, at least making enough money to give up forever the silly office work by which she made a bare living. All this of course proves that she was also fatuous, for nothing could be more ridiculous than hoping to make a living from poetry in an age in which even prose writers starve; but at the same time nothing could have better attested to her talent: for how can one be a poet—a real poet—and *not* be fatuous? Practical people do not give up huge chunks of their lives to dream artfully in meter and rhyme.

The news Aunt Carrie had just imparted was received indifferently by Samantha, who said only, "Well, when she comes just call me. If she wants to stay at my place for a night or two, that's fine."

"I'm going to pick her up at JFK. Why don't you come with me."

"Oh ... I don't think I could. I might have stuff to do that day ..."

"I haven't even said what day it is!"

They both laughed, a little uncomfortably.

"What day is it?" Samantha asked.

"Tuesday, the tenth."

"Yes ... really ... I don't think I could. Work—you know."

But Aunt Carrie knew when she was hearing an excuse. She knew that her niece was only working part-time and had most of the week off. "C'mon, Sammi," she said, looking at her knowingly, "it won't take that long. I don't want to have drive all the way out there by myself. Why not?"

"Well ... I'll see. I'll see. If I don't have anything to do that day— "

"You won't. I'll call you!"

Samantha had been the less inclined to accompany her

aunt to the airport because she was not especially fond of Georgette.   They hadn't been in each other's company too many
times in their lives, but those times had always been to Samantha indifferent at best.   Besides, seeing Georgette would only
be remindful of her mother, Aunt Jeannette, on whom Samantha never looked back but with bad memories. For the old lady,
though illiterate and dumb as a rock, had consistently impugned Samantha's literary ambition.   "I don't see why you
spend so much time doing *that,*" Jeannette used to say, and
would utter these snide, vaguely or outrightly insulting comments before family or strangers alike. "Where is *that* going to
get you? Poems! Really!" And on other occasions, just as publicly: "If you paid half as much attention to dressing nice as you
do to those books you've always got your nose in, you might look
a little better!" And on still other occasions: "You're not getting
any younger, you know! Don't you think it's about time you
start looking for a husband? Don't you want to get married?
What's wrong with you? Go out there—find a rich man! That's
what you *should* be doing! That other stuff you're interested in
ain't gonna get you nowhere! Just wasting your life, my dear—
just wasting your life!"

It wasn't till she had come into the full flush of maturity
that Samantha understood how consanguinity never confers a
right to belittle; makes it in fact the more malevolent and intolerable. Inevitably she became less and less patient with her old
aunt's sniping remarks till one day the pot boiled over—years of
silently absorbed insults, which had been fermenting and roiling
within her, erupted into a counterattack as unexpected as it
was stunning. It happened that they were seated at the same
Thanksgiving dinner table and the conversation had turned to
matters related to the economy and work, which somehow led
into the subject of Samantha's job and then of her life generally.
Aunt Jeannette, as she nibbled on a piece of Jeannette breast,
complacently burbled her hope that Samantha had finally
"wised up" and wasn't spending so much time reading and writing, that she had "grown out of it," that now she "knew better,"
and was concentrating on getting some kind of "real" career.
The poet clenched her jaw, stiffened, and glanced about as a
surge of anger shot up into her gullet, almost choking her, consuming her, taking possession of her. She leaned forward and

pressed herself into the table so hard that it seemed she would overturn it. She glared at her aunt as though she were about to leap up and kill her. "Why you little, miserable, illiterate moron," she said, so loudly, so full of vibrating fury, that her voice was hoarse, almost otherworldly, in its inhuman energy, "why don't you shut your mouth instead of commenting on things you know nothing about? I don't expect you to understand what I do because you're stupid—you've got the dull brains of a cow! You were *born* stupid—do you understand? A seven-year-old child can at least read and write *something*, but you're so stupid that you can barely write your name! And on top of it all you were a rotten mother, which is why your own daughter got as far away from you as she could, and doesn't even call you because she can't stand the sound of your voice. You're a piece of garbage, Jeannette—a piece of stinking, stupid garbage. Not I but *you* are the biggest failure this family has ever had—you, you! So if you want to start criticizing somebody you had better start with yourself!"

—The outburst had been so unexpected, so loud, so terrible in the fullness of its malevolence and intent to destroy, that everyone at the table sat in utter silence, with open mouths, their hands frozen on forks they had been eating with or the cups they had been about to lift as they turned their wondering gazes at Samantha, at Jeannette, at one another. The outburst was the more astonishing because it seemed to have come from out of the blue, without any provocation, and from a woman who, if anything, had always been so sweetly reticent. The silent shock persisted for almost a minute, and when it had subsided enough for people to come to themselves someone was heard to whisper, in a tone of utter confusion and vague disapproval, "Oh, Sammi." Samantha never knew or cared who had said it. Her sense of outrage was still running high. Her heart was still beating fast with the adrenaline of someone on the attack, and her eyes were still set with cutthroat determination on the foeman, her aunt, as though daring her to utter one single peep of defense.

Jeannette sat in silence, absolutely still, looking down at her plate; then she made a smacking sound with her lips and rolled her tongue over her teeth before shaking her head slowly a few times. With each passing second she realized how fully she had been called to account, exposed, humiliated before the family. A lump rose into her throat and she felt like crying. She wished she could flee. Above all else she knew that any attempt she made to defend herself or counterattack would bring down upon her another round of thunderous and devastating insult of the sort she had never thought her niece capable of. Just then she thought Samantha shockingly cruel: it did not occur to her that she had been ten times crueler. She only murmured, "Tsuh, tsuh, tsuh ..." as though her only option was to make light of her niece's attack, to put it into the light of a child's groundless tantrum. "Tsuh, tsuh, tsuh," she said again. But for the rest of the evening she did not say a word, and did not look again at Samantha; who, for her part, became especially loud, chatty, and eager to laugh, knowing that her every word and exaggerated guffaw gave another turn of the knife in her aunt's heart. She could not help it: she wanted to inflict as much pain as she could on someone who had caused her so much of it.

For years thereafter Samantha and Jeannette did not speak to each other. So far as Samantha was concerned she would have been happy never to see or hear from her old aunt again. But then Jeannette had had her heart attack, and reports of her miserable debilitation softened the poet's heart so that she had gone to visit her. The sick old woman's outpouring of gratitude on that first visit made Samantha feel a little guilty for having stayed away so long. But later visits only confirmed the adage of the leopard never changing its spots, for Jeannette, when she learned that Samantha was still writing poetry, once again began making belittling remarks about it.

But this time, somehow, such remarks no longer carried much of a sting for the poet.

"She's old and sick and unhappy," Samantha would tell herself, holding her tongue and saying nothing in the way of self-defense. "And she's *such* a stupid creature ... as dumb as a rock ... how can anyone take her seriously? Poor, poor thing: to be *so* stupid! To think that I had ever gotten upset by anything *she* could say! It's just ridiculous. Just ignore her ... She doesn't know any better. Just ... try to help her a little."

And so the poet had often gone to visit the old lady, getting her things she needed at the grocery store, spending time with her to keep her company a few hours a week, reassuring her that she shouldn't worry because everything would be alright.

Samantha thought about these things on the morning when she accompanied her Aunt Carrie to pick up her cousin at JFK International Airport. Halfway there, she sat with increasing uneasiness to hear her aunt talk of what a fine person Georgette was—of how well she treated everyone, how she always had the family in mind, how sweet, how innocent, how thoughtful a "girl" she was.

"You know," Samantha interrupted, "Aunt Jeannette was sick for years before she died. Georgette never came to see her more than two or three times."

"Well, Sammi, she couldn't," Aunt Carrie said. "It's not cheap to fly overseas, and she doesn't have a lot of money. She had a family to take care of, too, you know."

"Alright. I can understand that—sort of. But it doesn't cost much to make a phone call. She never called her, either. I know. I was there."

There was nothing to be said to that. Aunt Carrie pursed her lips and silently kept driving. After a few minutes Samantha asked:

"Are you going to take her to the cemetery?"

"Yes. Tomorrow, if the weather's alright."

"Do you know how to get there?"

"I have the directions, and a map. I'm good at following maps."

"Why did they have to bury her so far away?" Samantha asked, referring to the obscure cemetery in Nassau County, Long Island.

"They buried her where they could," came the answer, the "they" referring to the State, which had covered the final expenses of a woman who, only two years after retirement as a sales clerk, had gone through her paltry savings and thereafter had lived solely on Social Security and welfare benefits. "If you'd like to come with us—"

"Oh, no," Samantha quickly said, putting up a hand as though mere verbal negation would not be convincing enough. "No, no. I can't go. I'm too busy."

"Well ... it's up to you."

Despite the somber reason for the visit, Georgette in no

way looked depressed or gloomy as she came off the airplane, pulling behind her a large wheeled suitcase. The moment she saw her relatives waiting for her beyond the deplaning area, she came toward them in little hurried trotting steps and gave a little shriek of joy as she embraced them. She hugged them enthusiastically, kissing them often, exclaiming her pleasure at seeing them both and saying how much she had missed them, how she had thought about them all the time! And how wonderful they looked! Oh, Aunt Carrie looked better than ever! Hadn't changed *at all!* And Samantha—why, Samantha was just *gorgeous!* "Look at you!" she kept saying, standing back a little from her cousin with a great, appreciative, incredulous smile. "Just *look* at you!"

Georgette Arnaud was fifty years old and the divorced mother of two grown boys. Her features were small and even. She had been very pretty in her youth. Beauty of course is always its own reward, but its fortunate possessor must pay for the privilege by one day having to witness its dissolution, which was something Georgette had not been prepared for. In the last several years she had never looked into a mirror without the sinking sensation that her best days were behind her, and that they were going to fall behind a lot faster and further if she didn't "take care of herself"—watch her weight, make sure her hair was dyed and styled, and wear the best clothes she could afford. She had always been a great lover of jewelry. In her youth she had loved it because she had not been wealthy and yet it had made her feel rich; now her proclivity for trinkets had a more practical basis: she trusted to the dazzle of diamonds and the lustre of gold to make up in some measure for what additional wrinkles around her eyes and mouth had taken away. As she sat in the passenger seat beside Aunt Carrie on the way back into Queens, she reached into her handbag for a compact, flipped it open, and examined her face in its little round mirror. She puckered her lips a little. She snapped the compact shut and put it back into her bag.

Only after they had been driving for a while, and Georgette had finished asking after Aunt Carrie's affairs and relating a few of her own, did Georgette raise the subject of her mother's death. "I hope she wasn't in any pain, that's all," she said, and turned around to Samantha in the back seat, appealing to her for information on this point.

"No, she wasn't," Samantha said.

"Thank God for that!"

But Samantha hadn't told the entire truth. Physical pain the old lady certainly hadn't suffered—at least, not much. But every day she had wrestled with loneliness, regret, and the anxious fear of death. As her mind degenerated she had been reduced to a frail, sad, broken, immobile creature who in moments of lucidity carped and caviled, or shed tears of self-pity, or was silently conscious of her dependence on strangers to get her a glass of water, to take her to the bathroom, to clothe her, to get her up in the morning, to put her to bed at night;—a miserable end to a miserable life.

"Sammi, I really, really want to thank you for all you did," Georgette said, turning around still more in her seat, the gold necklaces around her neck jangling a little as she did so. "I know you used to go and see Mom all the time. I really appreciate that. Oh! If only I lived here in New York! I would have had her move in with me! I wouldn't have left her alone like that! Poor woman ..."

"Well, she always appreciated your visits," Samantha said; and couldn't resist adding, "And always looked forward to your phone calls."

"Well, I came as much as I could," Georgette said easily; and seemed not to have heard the remark about her phone calls. "Believe me, it's not easy for me to travel like this. It's *so* expensive! And things are a little hard for me now financially. But ... well, I just *had* to do it this time. I just had to see her, I mean, to see where she was buried. Poor Mom," she said, shaking her head and suddenly, for a few seconds, genuinely, unquestionably sad.

Aunt Carrie changed the subject and said how she was planning a fine dinner for Georgette. "I know just what you like," she said, and proceeded to name the dishes she had already cooked and which only needed heating up. The subject of food led them to the subject of "affairs" at which the family had gathered—birthdays, weddings, anniversaries, some of which had happened fifteen, twenty, or more years before when Samantha was much younger or only a child. Many of these events had been formal and meticulously-planned, held in expensive, glittering catering halls. The poet sat in the back seat looking out the window and listening to the names of people she had known or had heard of—people who were either still alive but very old, or who had died years before: uncles, aunts, distant cousins, relatives through marriage: people who, in her earliest youth, had seemed a natural and permanent part of her life, but who now survived only in memory, and there but indistinctly: a smile across a table, a profile turned upward while blowing upward a thin stream of cigarette smoke, a portly body—a little inebriated—getting up onto a dance floor and adding to the raucous joy of the celebration. Oh! So many people, from so many years ago, and so many of them gone ... gone ...

Georgette turned around to her cousin again and asked with a great smile:

"And so what are *you* up to these days, Sammi?"

Samantha mentioned the name of the company she worked for in Manhattan. She did not mention that she worked there only part-time.

"Like it?" Georgette asked.

Samantha shrugged. "It's alright. Pays the bills."

"Are you still doing that other stuff?" Georgette asked, her smile and overt enthusiasm continuing unabated.

Samantha gave a little shake of her head as though to ask, "What stuff?"

"You know—that writing stuff."

... *that writing stuff.* Samantha wasn't sure what to make of the phrase. She looked at her cousin and tried to figure out if the whiff of condescension that accompanied the words had been intentional or owing to some unintended inflexion of voice. But what she saw left no question about the matter, and even astonished her, for it was as though the dead had come back to life: there, on Georgette's face, was the very same expression her mother had assumed in a hundred denigrating remarks about Samantha's poetry. The same contemptuous eyes, the same sneering curve to the smile, the same air of stupid self-assurance—it was all there in perfectly realized atavism. Automatically, reflexively, an upwelling of anger urged Samantha to utter a withering retort; but she was objective enough to consider that it would have been out of all proportion to the question that had been asked of her. Nevertheless she was curt in her deceptive response:

"Not really."

"Oh, well, *that's* good," Georgette said, almost breathing a sigh of relief. She glanced at Aunt Carrie with an air of satisfaction before turning back to her cousin, saying, "You were doing that for so long, weren't you? What a waste of time! Well, I guess you finally saw that it wasn't getting you anywhere and you wised up. I always say, 'Try everything, but when something doesn't work out, you have to cut your losses and go on to something else.' That's what Mom used to tell me and she was right. I guess you must regret it now, right? I mean, by now you probably could've been married, with kids of your own. Of course, you're still young enough! Don't get me wrong about *that!* How old are you, anyway? Thirty-five, isn't it?"

"Thirty-*three,*" Aunt Carrie said.

"Oh, thirty-three," Georgette echoed, nodding. "Well, that's *nothing* these days—and you *do* look a lot younger. I hope you're going out. New York must be full of single guys. You have to go to the right clubs, though—I know that much from when I used to live here. I mean, you can't go out to any places here, in *Queens*—you'll just meet schmucks. You have to go into Manhattan, to nice places. You want to meet someone *nice.* Someone who's established. Who has something to offer. Are you seeing anyone these days?"

Samantha said nothing; she regarded her cousin with a feeble, forced smile as silently steady as it was disarming in its rank insincerity.

"Georgette, how are the kids?" Aunt Carrie asked. She had glanced in the rear-view mirror and seen, and much more sensed, Samantha's irritation, though she had misinterpreted the reason for it, and she wanted to avoid the potential for an unpleasant exchange between cousins.

"Oh, the kids are great," Georgette said, turning back around in her seat so that she was again facing forward. "They're certainly not kids any more! Jacques is twenty-four, now. Hard to believe, isn't it? Time flies. He's in business for himself, now. Shoes. He's doing very well. He started out with just one store, and now he has three! He deals directly with the factories in China. He even won an award! He sold the most shoes in Paris for the manufacturer in a six-month period. I'll show you the picture when we get home! As for Emile, he's still in school—he has another year before he graduates. He's getting his degree in business management. I'm so glad he finally decided to take that. You can't go wrong with business courses—employers like to see that. They know you're serious about your future."

"Your mother would have been proud of them," Samantha said.

"Oh, it's such a pity they never got to see their grandmother more than once!" Georgette said, the sarcasm of Samantha's comment having been lost on her. "They only saw her when they were kids and she came to Paris for a week. I wanted to come with them to visit her so many times, but ... well ... you know how it is ... the expense of it ... and then something always came up ... school or work or something. It's just a shame ..."

When they had gotten back into Queens, Aunt Carrie invited Samantha to come back to her home and have dinner with her cousin.

"Yes, Sammi, come back with us!" Georgette exclaimed happily, turning around in her seat to face her cousin.

"No, thanks. I have some things to do later."

"Oh, Sammi, what could you be doing that's so important?" Georgette asked, innocently enough.

Samantha regarded her cousin with eyes so hard and cold that they might have been blocks of ice, in which however an unmistakable light of hostility flashed. "I told you," she said, her voice deadpan with a dreadful surety of purpose, "I'm busy."

"Oh ... well ... it's up to you," Georgette said, turning back around, her smile fading fast, confounded by the incomprehensibly sudden negative attitude toward her. She became certain of this when Aunt Carrie stopped before Samantha's apartment building to let her off, for Samantha got out of the car and directed a goodbye to her aunt, and when Georgette chimed in, "I'll call you later—maybe we can spend a day together or something!" she received not so much as a glance in return, as though she didn't exist. The moment Aunt Carrie drove away Georgette asked in bewilderment:

"What *on earth* is wrong with her?"

"What do you mean?" Aunt Carrie asked. But her question was disingenuous. She too had had seen Samantha's icy demeanor toward her cousin.

"I'm not sure. She looked like she was mad at me or something."

"Why should she be?"

"How should *I* know! She didn't even say goodbye to me. She didn't even look at me. Did I say something wrong or something? I don't know ..."

"Oh, I'm sure it's nothing. You know how Sammi is. She can be temperamental sometimes."

"I'll say!"

"I'm sure it's nothing. Her head was just somewhere else. She's always ... thinking of things."

—But in fact Aunt Carrie had never known Samantha to be "temperamental," and had offered her explanation as a palliative to family relations.

Samantha had no sooner left the car than she wished to forget everything about Georgette. They had nothing in common. More to the point, Georgette was too much a replica of her mother, looking like her, speaking like her, regarding the world in much the same way; in short, a dolt whose personality was fundamentally antagonistic to Samantha's own. The poet vowed she would not see her cousin again except to say goodbye to her before she went back to Paris, and with any luck even that might be avoided.

As usual she sat that evening at her kitchen table and worked on her poetry. For nearly a year she had been composing her longest poem ever; already it was a hundred pages long. It was cast in a free verse which relied heavily on rhythm and on infrequent, tantalizing near-rhymes. She knew that its length, manner, and subject matter of freewheeling existentialism made it preposterously "unpublishable" (to use a word popular among mainstream publishers who are never prouder of themselves than when publishing books they wouldn't have looked at fifty years earlier) but she was also sure that it was her best work, embodying her maturest thought and skill. There were lines in it that made her jump for joy and which she could scarcely believe sometimes that she had written. She often allowed herself to think that this was the work that would lead to her eventual success, even if "eventual" meant a time after her death, and "success" meant recognition by that small minority whose good opinion is alone worth having. In the meantime poetry was for her an end in itself, the one real passion in her life, the thing that gave her joy and comfort. It was, to her, what religion was to the zealously pious.

Time passed unawares as she added line after line to her work, as the words formed off the pinpoint nib of her pen and she sometimes mouthed them, pronouncing them in a whisper to herself, listening to their sound, considering their sense, her mind racing ahead to the next ten, twenty words in a process not so much a matter of calculation as of intuition, of somehow knowing or sensing when things were right or wrong—when the sound, the phrase, conformed as exactly as possible to the inner impulse. When it fell short of this it had to be reworked, and throughout the evening she would get up from her seat and consider variations. On this night she wrote with an easy prolificity. She wondered if she were entering some new, better, higher phase of her ability. More often than not she wrote a line once or twice and knew it could not be done better, and she would say to herself, "There!"—her satisfaction great.

She wrote for almost three hours before her eyes grew tired and her back a little sore and she decided to take a break. She got up from her chair and walked about her apartment to stretch her legs. It was just after midnight and very quiet: the only sounds were those of an occasional car or truck going by on the street outside. She ambled over to the living room window and pulled aside the blinds and looked out. The sidewalk was deserted. The only signs of life came from a gas station across the street where a few motorists filled up their tanks under bright lights. She let the blinds fall back into place and stretched and looked about her. She felt a pang of lonesomeness. She caught herself thinking that it would be good for her to be in a relationship, perhaps to get married; to have someone else around. She thought of the men she had had in her life. They had all been attractive, indeed beautiful. She had never understood those women who said (and who had sometimes said to her, in confidence) that they didn't care what a man looked like so long as he was "nice," had a good sense of humor, perhaps too (this was always a great recommendation) had money.

But Samantha, as she looked to the couch now, recalled the lovers with whom she had sat or lain there, and felt proud to think that all of them had been beautiful. Bill, Ben, Thomas, Michael, Roy, Steven. —Steven! Of them all, he had been the most magnificent—so tall, so slender, so blond, his eyes as brightly blue as some fine morning's sky; why, even his hands and feet had been perfect as though a sculptor had taken pains to ensure the littlest of his bones adhered to an ideal type. It was true that he had also been a little slow upstairs, poor fellow; that he hadn't known who Yeats was, and had sat unmoved, uncertain, when she had, in an access of enthusiasm, read to him "Of All the Souls That Stand Create";—but when you looked as good as he did, when you were your own perfect creation and delight to the world, was that really so much of a shortcoming?

And then she thought of the others. There was Sherry, Lisa, Alana, Courtney—the latter being a kind of female, brunette version of Steven, so strikingly beautiful had she been that people turned their heads when she passed.

Oh! What would Georgette have thought about all *that!* She would have been scandalized, horrified, stupefied with wonder. Her expression on hearing about it? Wide eyes, an open mouth, a certain pallor about the forehead and cheeks prefatory to a fainting fit or at least the need to sit down. Samantha chuckled at the image she conjured up of her cousin's discomfiture. What a silly, scatterbrained creature Georgette was! For a passing second Samantha thought of pulling her cousin aside and confessing them all, all these relationships and encounters, and so taking a naughty delight in what was sure to be a dramatic reaction. For, of course, Georgette wouldn't have understood.

" ... as though I do," Samantha said aloud.

No, she really didn't understand it. She couldn't have said why she had fallen in love with Steven any more than why she had been equally mad about Courtney. Quite apart from the difference of sex they had also been totally opposite personalities. The only thing they had had in common was that they had both been beautiful human beings. The poet told herself that surely she wasn't so shallow as to lose her head over merely a pretty face and figure. In that case she would have been no more sophisticated than a child or even an animal who is drawn to a shiny trinket. "No, it wasn't just because of that," she told herself. "There was more to it than that. They were both nice people. Steven was fun to be with and Courtney was smart ... and ... " —and yet for all that she suspected that she was not being honest with herself. She knew very well that on any day she might meet a dozen people who were nice and smart, but that didn't mean she was attracted to them and it certainly didn't mean she was going to fall in love with them. No. Her lovers had been beautiful, and those who had been most beautiful she had loved the most. She admitted it to herself. She felt embarrassed about it. She wished it had been otherwise; she wished she were different; for it all seemed to her very shallow. On the other hand she knew she hadn't been able to help it, and still couldn't. A beautiful face was like a light chasing away the darkness in her soul, just as an unattractive one deepened the gloom and even made her shudder.

"Well, it doesn't matter anyway," she thought. "None of them worked out. None of them ever do."

And so here she was again, alone and working. She looked about the apartment. She asked herself how long she had been here. Eleven years, came the answer. How quickly they had passed—as though in the blink of an eye! She remembered the day she had moved into the place, so happily, so grateful for having found an apartment she could afford, and how that joy had for the space of a year resulted in her writing more than a hundred poems. Nearly every week in those days she had sent out two or three examples of her work to magazines or book publishers or literary agents. But the exuberance of her genius had not gained her any financial remuneration. Of all those poems not more than a dozen had been published by two small literary magazines, and in each case the "payment" had been a copy of the publication. She no longer had any of those copies; she had thrown them out a few years later because she had decided that the poems weren't good after all and that there was no point in holding on to embarrassing reminders of one's early limitations. She wondered if having had her work appear in these obscure and now largely non-existent publications had been her dance in the sun—the pitiable most she was ever to achieve in the way of recognition as a poet. That this might be the case made her smile despite herself: it was laughably absurd to think that out of a lifetime of work only a handful of short lyrics should have been no sooner printed than forgotten. And yet as tragically ridiculous as that scenario sounded it was not, she knew, impossible. How many poets acclaimed in their own day had fallen by the wayside, time having proven their works, once widely read and spoken of with admiration, as indifferent after all, and had therefore sunk into oblivion? How could she possibly think that her work, which had never found a public during her lifetime, would survive after her? What sense did it make then to put so much effort into it? Why *not* do something else, something that would redound in some tangible reward to herself? She was still young—she might still choose a different, practical profession, which she was bound to succeed in if she dedicated to it even a fraction of the time and energy she devoted to poetry. Yes, why not?

Unfortunately there was this one, all-important rub: nothing but poetry could arouse in her a similar love and consequently a similar willingness to sacrifice. That was the thing that those who had tried to dissuade her from writing had never understood, and which she herself at times forgot: that for her poetry wasn't a whim or a hobby indulged in at the expense of more "important" matters but rather a way of life dictated by her character. She wasn't a poet because she wanted to be; she was a poet because that's what she *was*—because her character compelled her to find in that vocation and way of life its natural fulfillment. That it was a difficult life to lead was beside the point, since, ultimately, she had no choice in the matter.

On the other hand she knew there was something hopeless, maybe even tragic in continuing to devote herself to something which the world paid little attention to. Who read poetry any more, after all? There was so small a market for it that even the most "popular" and prolific poet was not likely to make much of a living by it. And Samantha's poetry, though cunningly crafted, was often dark and pessimistic, saying things that people didn't want to hear or think about. It seemed to her sometimes a trick of nature or of fate that she should have become consumed by an art whose profit could only be that of personal gratification. On the other hand she knew there was something to be said even for that. For it was no small thing, no small bit of luck, to have a purpose in one's life. Had she not, time and again, seen the essential unhappiness of those who didn't have that?—who, without the lighthouse of a goal to guide them, drifted from day to day, from year to year, from one desire or enthusiasm to the next, each one leaving them as dissatisfied, as lost, as achingly empty as ever? If only for the anchor-like stability of her passion she knew she ought to be grateful: it would always be the one sure thing amid the welter of life's doubts and disappointments.

"Well, it is what it is," she told herself, resignedly, referring both to her life and her poetry.

She returned to the kitchen table and took up from where she had left off. Another hour passed. When she had reached that point at which further effort was futile—when her concentration flagged and the words no longer came well—she put aside her writing and went to sleep.

The next morning while still in bed she heard—or thought she heard—the telephone in the living room ring several times. Later, after she had gotten up, she discovered that indeed it had; there were several messages on her answering machine. They were all from Georgette who had called to say that she and Aunt Carrie wouldn't be going to the cemetery today because it was raining and had decided instead to go into Manhattan for a few hours. She hadn't been there for years and wanted to go to a few stores "just to look around." Wouldn't Sammi go with them? They would have such a nice time. Lunch, she said, would be on her. "Give me a call back as soon as you can!"

"That'll be the day," Samantha said, erasing all three of the messages.

It rained most of the morning and well into the afternoon. When the rain stopped it was still cloudy and gloomy outside. Except for a five-minute run across the street to get a loaf of bread, Samantha spent the day indoors. She cooked, read, listened to music, or turned on the television for ten minutes at a time to watch snatches of programs. Most people would have thought she spent her days in wasteful idling. At one time Samantha herself would have thought the same thing and castigated herself for it. But no longer. Now she knew better. She knew that it was her leisure, and even her solitude, that fueled her creativity, that enabled her to have and develop her own thoughts and dream her own dreams, all of which prompted and invigorated her poetry. She knew that if she had had, like most people, a full-time job, the concentration required to fulfill the repetitive, intricate, and invariably mindless duties of that kind of mundane employment would have robbed her of the energy or will to write each day. Of course she would have had a lot more money; she would have been able to afford more of the things she had been led to believe she ought to have. But that would also have amounted to a betrayal of herself, of the great good thing that she felt to be in her, and she could not and would not allow that.

Late that afternoon she received another telephone call. The answering machine picked up, and a voice said:

"Hey, Sammi, it's me, Georgette. Listen, why don't you come over Aunt Carrie's for dinner? Are you home? Call me and come over!"

Forty minutes later:

"Hey, Sammi, it's me again. Where are you? You must be out or something. Anyway, we're having dinner here at Aunt Carrie's. If you get in and get this come on over! I want to see you! Bye!"

And the third phone call, an hour after the first:

"Sammi? Helloooooo .... Sammiiiiii ... are you there? Where are you? It's me, honey, your cousin. Where did you go all day? Listen, honey, tomorrow me and Aunt Carrie are going to the cemetery. I thought you might want to come. I'd love to have you come with us. Call me! I'll wait to hear from you!"

"You've got a long wait," Samantha muttered, and went over to the answering machine and erased that and every other message her cousin had left.

On account of the proximity of her apartment building to Aunt Carrie's house, Samantha considered that the best way of avoiding her cousin was to remain at home. It would be just her bad luck to run into Georgette on the street. On the other hand her pride recoiled at having to put herself out on account of someone she thought so little of. No, she decided, she was not going to make herself a prisoner for so much as a single minute on account of an imbecile relative! And so she went about her business as usual. That evening she went grocery shopping. The next morning she went for a walk in the park, then stopped by the library to see if a book she had reserved had been received. She considered that her concern about meeting up with Georgette had been baseless. New York City was a big place; even in her quiet neighborhood the sidewalks shifted daily with hundreds of people, all indifferent to one another, all unknown to one another, going their own, disparate ways. The odds were a thousand to one of running into the very person one was hoping to avoid.

But it is the irony of chance that things happen just when they're least wanted or expected.

Samantha was just leaving her building a few minutes after noon when she reached the front door, pulled it open, and was shocked to see Georgette step into the entrance. Georgette's joyful surprise was immediate and intense as she nearly walked into her cousin and exclaimed, "Sammi!" Samantha scarcely had time to catch her breath at her bad luck before her cousin's arms were wrapped around her in a bear hug of affection.

"I was *hoping* you'd be home!" Georgette said, still hugging her, and finally pulling away with, "Oh my God! I told Aunt Carrie, let's just stop by to see if you're here, and here you are! I called you so many times! Why didn't you call me back?"

"Why? Uh ... I wasn't at home ... I had to work ... I got home so late all the time ..."

"Oh, it doesn't matter! I'm just so glad to see you! Listen, I want you to come with us—with me. We're just on our way now to the cemetery. Aunt Carrie's parked just outside. Sammi, come with us!"

"Georgette ... really, I ... don't think I can. I'm kind of busy—"

"Oh, Sammi, *please.* I don't want to go there by myself."

"But you're not going by yourself, you're going with Aunt Carrie."

"Oh, but Aunt Carrie ... it's not the same as going with you. You and I have so much more in common. [Samantha blinked.] And Mom loved you so much. I know—I just know—she would want you to be there too. It may be the only time we'll ever get to say goodbye like this."

"You know, I ... I wasn't planning ..."

"Oh, I know you probably don't want to go," Georgette said, and now she pulled away from her cousin a little, and looked at her with an air of embarrassed regret as though she knew she were imposing. "I know you probably think I'm a pest, don't you? But I don't mean to be a pest. I don't mean to bother anybody—least of all you. I think the world of you, Sammi—whether you believe it or not, I really do."

Samantha wouldn't have been a poet if her heart, and consequently her resolve, hadn't been softened by those words. "I'm sure you do," she said quietly, shaking her head as though that were never an issue with her.

"The thing is that I really don't want to go just with Aunt Carrie. It wasn't Aunt Carrie who took such good care of my mother. *You* did. Maybe you think I don't realize how much I owe you for all that, but I really do. I want to do so much for you this week—I don't know, just, somehow, to show you my appreciation for all you did. I just think I should make it up to you somehow ... I don't know how ... maybe pay you or something—"

"Georgette, that's ridiculous," Samantha blurted out, blushng for embarrassment.

"—but the thing is, that I want you to know, *really* to know, what I think about you, because I don't think you do. I know we haven't seen each other often, but I do love you. I was so happy to see you again. You're part of my family, after all. That's how I really feel, Sammi. Even if you don't feel that way about me, that's okay, but that's how *I* feel about *you*. And that's why I want you to come with me. It would just make it so much easier for me if I had someone there who really knew Mom and cared for her the way you did. And we won't be there long: just a few minutes, that's all. Won't you come—just for me?" And she inclined her head forward, and leaned in a little with a mouth ever so slightly open while her eyes glittered with teary hopefulness; her whole person exuding a pitiful neediness that was as irresistibly and heartbreakingly pathetic as the whimpering pleas of a small child.

Hating herself for her lack of resolve, the poet nodded and said quietly, "Alright, Georgette. I'll go."

"Oh, you *are* a darling!" Georgette said, and planted a kiss on Samantha's cheek, then took her hand and, holding it tight, led her out the door.

When Aunt Carrie saw the two cousins walking out of the building—and hand-in-hand to boot—she sat up a little behind the wheel of the car and her eyes opened in wonder. She couldn't imagine how that kind of reconciliation (as it seemed to her) had occurred. She turned around in her seat to watch Samantha get into the back seat, and the moment they exchanged glances she realized that Samantha was present under some kind of duress. Georgette got back into the passenger's seat in front and exclaimed her joy at having been able to "catch Sammi" just as she had been leaving. "Another few seconds and we would have missed each other!" she crowed. At that remark Aunt Carrie looked into the rearview mirror to see her niece looking back at her with the solemn, dour expression of defeat.

Samantha found herself sitting next to a floral arrangement that Georgette had bought to place on her mother's grave. It consisted of white and yellow chrysanthemums inserted into a heart-shaped Styrofoam backing, and at the center of it a rather large, red plastic heart with the word "Mom" embossed in golden lettering. The poet was not sure whether it was touching or as absurd as a child's Valentine's Day card. The flowers filled the car with their strong perfume.

The cemetery was located in the middle of Nassau County. It took just under an hour to reach it. It was called the "Nassau Gardens Memorial Park"—a name that was a sop to a society that preferred happy prevarications to gloomy realities, for there was nothing garden-like about it, nor by any stretch of the imagination could it be thought of as a park. It had no clusters of shade-giving trees, nor bowers of flowers, nor paved walkways, nor so much as a single pleasant prospect. It was instead some forty acres of flat Long Island earth, fenced in all around to keep out vandals and zoned comfortably apart from all wealthy and middle-class communities. The planners of the "Memorial Park" had been men of solid municipal sense and thus it was laid according to a severely utilitarian method of a grid, making it easy to place, find, and—when necessary— recycle grave space. The thousands of graves lay close together in strict, long rows, which began, in official documentation, at AA1 and ended—to date—at UU57. One could find a particular grave by applying to the caretaker who had an office in a small red brick building located just inside the entrance gate.

On this mid-afternoon Aunt Clarissa, Georgette, and Samantha found him sitting at his desk before an obsolete, ten-year-old computer resting on a gray metal desk. He was a short, overweight, shabby-looking fellow of about fifty years of age, and a lifelong government employee. He was scrapingly eager to be of assistance to his visitors—he didn't receive many, after all, and helping them filled him with a warm sense of usefulness. He asked them for the name and approximate death of the deceased, and with this information he applied himself to his computer. In twenty seconds he found the location of the grave and with a stub of a pencil he scratched out the information on a slip of paper. Then he rose to his feet and took a few steps toward a wall on which was spread out a map of the cemetery. It showed the terrain in outline against a numbered grid, within each one of which were numbered rows.

"There it is!" he said, placing his finger on a specific point "UT78—Section U, Row T, Plot 78 ... yes, it's right there. If we go outside I can show you where to go."

Once outside, he pointed to an area in the far distance and explained that if they drove in that direction they would find "Section U." He advised them to pay attention to the markers which were at each of the four corners of every section; they would see for themselves how the letters accumulated, and of course the number of the grave related to its distance from the gravel road.

"You can't miss it," he assured them, and handed Aunt Carrie the slip of paper on which he had written the location.

Aunt Carrie was careful to note each section that they approached or passed, calling them out aloud, "There's UM ... there's UN ... UO ... UP ...."

On either side of them the low headstones were regimented in severely straight rows. They extended for acres and in the far distance narrowed through perspective just as the veins of a spread fan narrow to their point of juncture. So many graves! So many reminders of the transitoriness of life! So many who had been born, lived, loved, perhaps had had children, perhaps not;—who had been regular folks working for a living, or who had always lived from hand to mouth;—who had been content or unfulfilled, ordinary or extraordinary, cheerful or morose, kind or wicked;—whose hearts had been sustained by beautiful dreams and high hopes, or had been devoured by hatred or rotted by petty envy;—so many players on the stage of life that had made their entrances, acted out their little parts, then exited, never to be seen or heard of again; and all of whom, however different their lives had been, however much or little they had achieved, had died so poor and alone that the only place willing to receive their earthly remains had been *this* place:— this hopeless, hidden, unlovely place, the modern-day equivalent of a potter's field.

As they drove along and the gravel of the road crunched beneath the tires, Georgette sat in a silence more remarkable for her former chattiness. She craned her neck now and then as though to get a better look at the rows of gravestones all around her.

Then Aunt Carrie said: "There it is—U-T!"

She pulled the car over to the side of the gravel roadway and stopped. The three women got out of the car.

"Sammi, can you hand me those flowers?" Georgette asked, leaning into the car through the open door she had just stepped out of, her manner solemn.

Samantha lifted the heart-shaped arrangement and guided it over the lowered front seat into her cousin's hands.

"Thanks," Georgette said.

For a few seconds they all stood at the edge of the grassy section of the cemetery not sure which direction to walk in. Aunt Carrie, glancing down at the slip of paper the caretaker had given her, led the way. She walked along the path running along the foot of the graves with her head turned toward them, but even from that short distance it was sometimes hard to see the names on the headstones, so small were they—granite slabs no more than five inches high and superficially engraved; the last benefits of a cost-conscious State. Though the plots were numbered in official documentation, no such tag or designation was physically attached to them.

They passed some forty graves before Aunt Carrie said, "Oh, there it is."

Anyone could see that the plot was newer than those around it. The outlines of the rectangular burial hole could still be made out because even after a year the grass with which it had been covered had not grown in so fully as to blend in totally with the older, more established growth roundabout. The headstone was inscribed with Aunt Jeannette's full name and, beneath it, the dates of her birth and death.

When she found the grave, Aunt Carrie stopped at the foot of it and looked on it in silence. Georgette came up behind her and stood at her side. Together their gaze rested sadly on the plot and the little headstone.

Samantha was impatient for Georgette to lay down her flowers, stand a few dutiful minutes over the site, and leave.

Then something could be heard—a sniffling sound. Georgette shuddered, and then her shoulders heaved as she let out an irrepressible cry of grief. In the next few moments she was bawling freely, saying aloud through her tears what a good, dear, wonderful mother she had had, how much she had loved her, how much she missed her, how she had been the best, yes, simply the best of human beings! Why had God taken her away so suddenly? Why couldn't He have allowed her to live just a little longer—just so that she might have seen her one more time? Georgette sniffled and wiped at her eyes. How it was possible for her to feel so much grief over the death of someone she had never bothered to see while alive was questionable to Samantha, inclining her to think that her cousin's reaction was hysterical in nature. Aunt Carrie also seemed surprised by this sudden show of emotion, but she placed a hand on Georgette's back, patting it gently, consolingly, and saying in a low, soothing voice, "I know ... I know ..."

Her frame still shaking as she cried freely and loudly, Georgette stepped up to the little headstone, then lowered herself on her haunches and laid down the heart-shaped flowers she had been holding. She remained in that position for fifteen seconds, whimpering softly, then falling silent as though her grief had spent itself or she had commanded it. But this was only seeming, for she suddenly let out a loud, long wail of grief. She got onto her knees, her shoulders sank inward, and she balled convulsively, dramatically, her whole body shaking with tremors in heaving, irresistible anguish. Aunt Carrie glanced at Samantha in alarm; for a split second she seemed uncertain of what had just happened; then she stepped over to Georgette, bent over her and again began patting her on the back, cooing out comforts, telling her it was alright, that everything was alright, yes, yes, it was alright, she shouldn't cry, "Shhhh .... shhhh ... darling ..." Georgette, not looking at her, took her aunt's hand and with a subtle pull guided the older woman down beside her, so that they were both kneeling before the headstone in the way that worshipers in a temple might kneel before an image of their god. Then Georgette turned around to Samantha, and put out her hand—reached out to her—in a gesture both pathetic and desperate. "Sammi," she said, or rather tried to say through her continuing, gulping, convulsive tears, "Sammi, come here!"

Samantha went toward her, almost despite herself, for she was disgusted at what she saw. She was disgusted first by the show of emotion whose suddenness was so inconsistent with authenticity, but she was even more disgusted because it was expended over the memory of a woman undeserving of the homage. It was one thing, and a very proper thing, to mourn for the good and wise; quite another to do so for the bad and foolish. Even the fact that Aunt Jeannette had been Georgette's mother could not account for or excuse her behavior, for the two of them had never been close, indeed had been for most of their lives estranged. Why such grief, then? The poet sensed that ultimately her cousin was crying for herself, for this glimpse into her own mortality—perhaps the first real glimpse of it that she had ever had. For once her mind had been abstracted from clothes, jewelry, looking good, and the success of her son in the shoe business, and she had come face to face with the prospect of being planted in the dirt. But whether she was crying for herself or another, her grief, insofar as it was real, could not be denied. This too was something that the poet felt. The thread of sympathy between her and her cousin was of the slenderest kind, yet in these circumstances it was sturdy enough to pull her forward—to draw her in, step by unwilling step—till she was standing beside the kneeling figures of her cousin and aunt.

Samantha took her cousin's hand and gave it a gentle, consolatory squeeze. But Georgette was not satisfied with this. As she had done with Aunt Carrie, so now with Samantha, she began pulling downward and giving her cousin to understand that she was to kneel down beside her, as though any sympathy or consolation not expressing itself in prostration was inadequate to the moment.

"It's alright ... it's alright ..." Samantha said gently, consolingly, but not deigning to kneel—holding back, not allowing herself to be pulled down to her cousin's level. She wanted to shake her hand free of her cousin's grasp. She glanced to the headstone incised with Aunt Jeannette's name, and that name repulsed her. She hated being here. She hated being put into this position. Why had she allowed herself to come? Why hadn't she been stronger and resisted pity getting in the way of her better judgment? She felt another tug at her hand.

Aunt Carrie looked up at Samantha with an expression that was at once knowing and pleading, as though she knew Samantha didn't want to comply yet would have asked her to do so, if only to help allay Georgette's extravagant grief.

"Oh, Sammi, please!" Georgette begged, pulling her cousin's hand rather hard now. "Please ... pray with me ... just one prayer!"

As though she had gotten first her fingers, then her hand, then her arm caught in some machine with powerful turning rollers drawing her irresistibly inward, Samantha, even as she leaned back away from her cousin, took a step forward, bent her legs a little at the knees, then bent them more fully, and finally—hating herself for giving in like this, hating Georgette for making her do this—got down on the ground, on the grass, beside her cousin, kneeling there before the headstone, before that name, and the memory of that person, who represented everything she despised as antagonistic to her ideals. In silent anger she watched from the corner of her eye as Georgette clasped her hands together and began mumbling a prayer as though her mother could hear every word she said. She told her what a good, dear, sweet mother she had been, and how much she missed her, how much she thought about her every day. Georgette wanted her mother to know that her grandsons were fine. She wanted her to know that Aunt Carrie and cousin Samantha were also here, and loved her too. She thanked her for everything she had ever done, especially all that she had ever taught her. She sniffled as she added, "Oh, Mommie ... everything I am I owe to you."

Those particular words, uttered at such a time, by that particular person, struck Samantha as bizarrely, outlandishly comi-

cal; indeed she could not see how they could have been meant
otherwise. She felt a laugh rise into her throat but managed to
contain it as she glanced to Georgette in order to find in her
some indication that she hadn't been serious;—some twist of the
mouth or gleam in the eye that confessed her understanding of
the inappropriateness of such words in relation to the deceased.
But on the contrary Georgette had never looked more serious or
wistful. Her dolorous intensity of sentiment became for Samantha the engine that catapulted the moment into the exquisitely
because so ridiculously funny. She put a hand to her mouth to
hold back, force back, her laughter; she tried with all her might
to suppress it; but it would not be held back, and came out as a
sudden, single, breathy laugh.

Georgette looked at her.

Samantha called on all her willpower to delay, to tamp
down, to quash the hilarity that now overwhelmed her. She
knew that she couldn't, she mustn't, give way to it; not here—
not now! Mustn't, mustn't, mustn't! Her face contorted with
the effort to maintain a respectfully quiet attitude. Her eyes almost squeezed shut and her mouth moved uncertainly as
though she were grinding her teeth. Her effort was so intense
that she looked as though she were in pain. And maybe she
would have succeeded if she hadn't just then glanced at her
cousin. But Georgette's tears had streaked her mascara, and
her lipstick had smudged, and somehow she looked too much
like a clown, the clown that she was, the fool of empty head and
jangling baubles, whose breast heaved with pride over a son
who sold shoes, and who had gotten on her knees, and expected
others to get on theirs, as she expressed thanks to someone
even more foolish than herself. It was just too much, too
exquisitely backward and ironic to bear! The poet turned away
from her cousin and clamped both hands against her mouth in
an attempt to hold back the laughter she felt rise into her
throat, telling herself, commanding herself, "This is not funny!
This can't be funny! This is so sad ... graves are so sad ... death
is so sad ... sad, sad, sad! ... don't, don't!" But with the ineduca-
bility of fate the door gave way, the floodgates opened, the dam
cracked: a bout of laughter—loud, propulsive in its intensity—
burst out of her. It came in a fast, steady, yet ever more impulsive flow: staccato, moderato, vivace, molto presto; it grew

louder, even more raucous; it seemed to feed on itself, to over-whelm her completely; making her gag, making her cough; then making her lose her balance so that she toppled over onto her side, holding her hands against her abdomen as her legs pumped the air as though she were running in place. Her face had become a strange, strained, empurpled mask of hilarity so complete and urgent that it seemed to be hurting her. She saw her cousin and aunt sitting up straight, looking at her with blank, open-mouthed faces of alarmed bewilderment;—a sight that only provoked her into more choking, squirming, crying laughter. It went on like this for almost a minute.

When the worst of the hysterical paroxysm had ended, Samantha righted herself, sniffling and wiping the tears away from her eyes. She began shaking her head with the first un-derstanding of the obscene inappropriateness of her behavior. She could hardly believe what she had done. What had been hi-larity changed into a deep sense of shame. From the corner of her eyes she could see that her cousin and aunt were still turned toward her. She dared not face them. She knew they were staring at her with horrified disbelief. Nor was there any explaining her behavior, which was suddenly inexplicable even to herself. "What have I done?" she asked herself as the last of her hysterical glee dribbled away into a disgusted sense of the inappropriateness of her behavior. She knew that nothing could excuse what she had done—nothing. Just as a few minutes be-fore she had been unable to stop the wave of hilarity overcoming her, so now she felt a dark, massive, damning sense of guilt en-gulfing her soul. The unthinkable, the unforgivable things she had just thought and felt and done! She turned to her cousin with an expression in which a sad, sick sense of self-revulsion mingled with an urgent plea for forgiveness.

Georgette got up from her kneeling position and turned and walked off, toward the car, the door of which could be heard shutting when she got into it. Aunt Carrie and Samantha also got to their feet. The two women looked at each other. Aunt Carrie was shaking her head, her brows knit, looking hard at her niece as though for the first time seeing in her something she could not have imagined and did not understand. "Why did you do that?" the older woman seemed to be saying, accusingly. Samantha looked as though she would say something, perhaps try to explain herself, but in the end she said nothing and kept her eyes down in shame. Still shaking her head, Aunt Carrie turned away and headed for the car. Samantha followed her.

No words were spoken by any of them as they drove back home. Georgette sat still and silent in the front seat, her head turned out the window, looking at the passing scenery. Now and then she cleared her throat. Perhaps she was suppressing tears, or anger.

Aunt Carrie drove without looking once into the rearview mirror at Samantha, who sat most of the time with her head bowed and a grim expression as more and more, with each mile traversed, she regretted her actions. When Aunt Carrie dropped her off at home she did not immediately get out of her car, but sat there a few seconds, looking at the back of Georgette's head, before saying quietly:

"I'm sorry about what happened at the cemetery, Georgette. I didn't mean it. I don't know why it happened. I guess ... I was just nervous or something. I'm sorry."

Georgette did not turn around or move; she looked straight ahead, out of the windshield, at the wide boulevard on which they were parked, watching the endless strings of traffic coming and going.

Samantha got out of the car, closed the door behind her, and began walking the fifty or so feet to her apartment building, hearing Aunt Carrie drive off as she did so.

Once again that evening she sat at her kitchen table before her unfinished poem, but she could not continue with it. The concentration so usual with her while composing had been replaced by something different—something sorrowful and even a little disgusted. All day she had replayed in her mind the scene that had occurred at the cemetery, and the more she thought about it the more she despised herself. For there was this one inescapable fact about the matter: Georgette, however ignorant or foolish, was at least decent enough that she would never do to someone what Samantha had done to her.

A mirror hung on the wall opposite the kitchen. Over the years Samantha had glanced up to see herself reflected in it ten thousand times as she wrote at the kitchen table. But this time as she beheld the eyes looking back at her she saw in them something other than fatigue or the quiet joy of a phrase well turned: for the first time she saw—a streak of cruelty, which, she knew, of all human faults and frailties was the worst and most unforgivable. She lay down her pen and looked over the poem that had occupied to some degree her every waking moment for the last year. How could the same fatal flaw not be in it too?

SCREAM

Outside in the cold March night the rain fell hard, driven by a wind from out of the cutthroat north. It had been raining hard like this for hours. The wind whistled through the bare-boughed trees and moaned as it whipped around buildings. It knocked over trash cans and scooped up litter—pages of newspapers or miscellaneous food wrappers—and scudded them down the street. It was the kind of raw night that makes people glad to have a warm home and fills them with a rarely-felt or renewed pity for those who are homeless and live outdoors. But by eleven o'clock in the evening the winds had died down to intermittent gusts, and the rain fell less heavily. Those who watched the late evening news broadcasts heard weathermen assure them that the winds and rain would taper off by morning. Tomorrow, they said, it would still be gloomy, the skies would still be overcast, perhaps there would be a shower or two, but it would be nothing like what they had seen today.

For many in this Bronx neighborhood the late news was the last television broadcast they watched before turning in to sleep. And so one by one, in hundreds of apartments or homes, windows once illuminated went dark as people turned off television sets and lamps and went to bed. In the next couple of hours there was hardly a lighted window to be seen, and most of these only because the residents within left a light on in the living room or bathroom as a matter of course.

It was a middle-class neighborhood, though not without its wealthy doctors, lawyers, and high-paid civil servants. The young people who lived here were wont to complain that it was "too slow," that there was never anything "to do," or even that there were too many old people about, and indeed many of the residents were over sixty and retired. On the other hand all these factors contributed to the quality of life here. It was quiet and relatively clean. Crime was very low. Now and then one heard of a burglary, or a brawl that had broken out in one of the two local pubs; but such events were rare, and the police were usually on the scene in minutes to stop the crime or quell the disturbance. Insofar as New York City neighborhoods went, it was one of the better ones.

By two in the morning it was as quiet and still here as it would ever become throughout the course of twenty-four hours. The streets were deserted except for the occasional car prowling slowly along in search of a parking space, which was never easy to find here, for the residents were generally affluent enough to afford cars yet unable or unwilling to pay the considerable expense of a private space in a garage. And yet persistence usually paid off. If one drove around this block, and then that, and then another, one was sure to find some inviting gap along what at first sight had seemed an unbroken line of cars. The objective of course was to park as closely as possible to one's home, but in the end if one had to walk a block or two or three—well, sometimes one just had to do it.

It seemed that this would be the case this early morning for the young woman who had fifteen minutes before gotten off work from her job as a bartender. She was twenty-six years old, had short black hair, a pretty if somewhat stern face, and for the last year had worked at the Billiard Bar—so named for the three pool tables at the back of the establishment. She didn't like her job; it was hard on the feet, hard on the muscles of the face to keep smiling for hours at a time. And it was oh so tiresome to have to ignore the ogling and fend off the leering, leading questions of men who had been drinking and tried to pick her up. For them she always had a stock answer: "I don't think my boyfriend would approve!"—followed by a good-humored laugh. It was the perfect rebuff: short, sweet, to the point, letting them know she wasn't available yet at the same time sparing their feelings—and thus ensuring her tips. Now, as she approached her neighborhood, she smiled a little to think of all those inebriated men who would talk to her throughout an evening, who in some instances had known her for years, and who never suspected that she wasn't interested in men at all. They would have been shocked at what her real life was like. She wondered at how people took it for granted that everyone was the same as themselves.

She turned her car onto the street where her apartment building was located and so became one of the drivers who slowly searched for a place to park. No doubt on account of the bad weather most people had stayed home and the cars on either side of the street were set bumper to bumper. She drove to the next street over, sitting up close to the steering wheel as she squinted through the rain-bespattered windshield for some break in the cars, just one lucky break that wasn't before a driveway or a fire hydrant. She noticed that she wasn't alone in her search, for another driver was just behind her, driving just as slowly and carefully. She told herself to keep a keen lookout because if she passed a space, though it were only by a car's length, the driver behind her was sure to slip into it. People in New York had no sense of politeness, of deference to others when it came to parking their cars.

She drove four blocks away from where she lived to an area where there were no apartment buildings but only homes, and whose lower population density translated into a greater likelihood of finding a parking space. She soon found one. As she parallel parked, the driver behind her waited patiently, then slowly passed by, continuing his search. He too got lucky: a hundred feet ahead, he too found a spot.

With the engine still running, the wipers still squeaking back and forth, the young woman turned on the dome light of her car and, leaning forward, felt about under her seat. "Where the heck is it?" she asked aloud, blindly feeling on the floor for the umbrella she knew to be there. She found it under the passenger's side. She opened it as she got out of the car and, continuing to hold it somewhat awkwardly with her left hand, she locked the car door with her right. The rain was falling evenly. She was glad she always kept an umbrella in the car.

The driver who had parked further up ahead also got out of his car. He was wearing only a light jacket, which seemed insufficient against the raw weather; nor did he have an umbrella; but the things going through his mind with mounting intensity made him impervious to the inclemency. He put on a baseball cap, which he pulled down low on his forehead, hiding nearly the whole top part of his face.

He had been following the young woman from the moment she had left the Billiard Bar. He followed her now in the darkness and with each step closed the space between them. As he walked with ever-increasing determination he held something in his pocket, gripping it tightly. If it hadn't still been a little windy and raining—if there had been no light splatter of the raindrops on the sidewalk and streets—the young woman might have heard his approaching footsteps. But she did not. She had only walked one block when the man caught up with her. With the pounce of a predatory animal, he leapt toward her, threw his left arm around her neck, jerked her back toward him, and plunged a knife into her back. She dropped her umbrella, her pocketbook, her keys, and even as she felt the painful, jabbing intrusion into her flesh she instinctively struggled to free herself from the strong, murderous man-arm pinning her back. She kicked from behind, shoving her heel keep into his upper thigh, and turning around somewhat she dug her nails into his face and scratched hard and deep. The frenetic power of her resistance so surprised him that he momentarily loosened his grip on her, and she, in the same instant dropping down somewhat and kicking him again, managed to get away. As she ran off she screamed so loudly and shrilly that it seemed her voice would carry for miles. She ran down the block, screaming as she went. The man, still holding the bloodstained knife, set off after her in the rain and the dark, her screams no deterrent to him whose mad and manic determination had surged in his frantic brain and blocked out every other consideration but one: to catch her, to finish what he had started.

Here and there a light went on in the houses on the street along which she ran. In one such house Jed and Norma Thompkins, both light sleepers, simultaneously awoke to the screams, though these had already begun to grow faint with distance. In the dimness of their bedroom, in the low blue glow that managed to filter in from the night outside through a curtained window, they looked at each other.

"What the hell is going on?" Jed asked.

Norma said nothing, only shook her head and moaned with tiredness. They both listened intensely. Faintly now, yet still distinctly, they heard the screams.

"Something's going on," Jed said. In his boxer underwear and a t-shirt he left the warmth of his bed to brave the rather chilly air of the bedroom and shuffle over to the window. He pulled aside the curtain, separated the louvers of the Venetian blinds behind, and peered out. Through the droplet bespattered pane of glass he saw the dark tranquil scene of the short lawn before his house, the rose bushes there which had been pruned to basic, thick branches, and, beyond them, the street which in its wetness reflected the light of the street lamps.... And again he heard a distant scream.

"I don't see anything," he said, his voice low, almost whispering. "But we should call the police."

"No," she said, at once and quickly. She was herself surprised a little by the swiftness of her response, and added, in a voice more considered, "Don't get involved."

He went to the night table on her side of the bed and turned on the lamp. Both he and she blinked against the new brilliance. There was a telephone on this table and Jed picked it up. He began dialing but had only punched in the first numbers when Norma rose up on one arm, reached out with the other, and pushed down the receiver switch.

"Jed, *no,*" she said.

"Someone might be in trouble!"

"No! ... listen ... it stopped."

They listened. There was silence, or rather the light pattering of the rain against the window and the occasional gust of wind; but she was right, there was no screaming.

"I think we should call the police," he said. He had a bad feeling that if the screaming had stopped it was for no good reason.

Faintly, he heard the screaming again.

"Listen!" he said.

Norma heard it too. That it was still going on, after all these minutes, in the dead of early morning, convinced her that it was a crime in the making—that something terrible was occurring—but at the same time she didn't want to know about it, to be a part of it, a part of something so ugly and horrible. She had lived in New York all her life and every time in the past she had heard about a violent crime she had shaken her head and secretly given thanks that it hadn't happened to her or anyone she knew, that it had been something only read about, only exposed to through the safe intermediary of a television or a newspaper. She didn't want to know about such things; she couldn't, she told herself, "take" them. All she knew now, all she wanted to know, was that she was safe; that the heavy front door and all the windows of her house were locked; that she was protected from any ugly violence of the outside world. And because this was all she knew and all she wanted to know, her mind raced for some benign alternative to account for what she and her husband had heard, and she found it, saying:

"It's Saturday night. It's just some kids who are drunk."

"It was a woman screaming."

"Why?—girls don't get drunk? The girls these days are worse than the boys. Just forget about it."

"I don't know"—shaking his head, the phone still in his hand, as he listened, listened amid the sounds of the wind and rain.

"Jed, put the phone down. Just go back to bed. It was nothing."

He glanced at the dim, greenly illuminated face of the clock on the night table on his side of the bed. It was a little after two-thirty. He was just putting the phone down when for a moment outside the wind ceased to blow, the rain to fall, and in that relative silence he heard it again—faint, far away, yet somehow more desperate than ever: screams.

"You hear?" he asked, in a whisper, holding the phone, looking down at his wife.

"Just go to bed! It's nothing."

She reached out and took the phone from his hand and hung it up; then she reached out to the lamp and shut it off. Outside the wind picked up a little more and the rain resumed.

"Go to sleep," she said; and added, with a tad more irritation, "What's wrong with you? You don't have enough problems, you're looking for more? Just go to sleep."

The husband shuffled in the darkness to his side of the bed and once more got under the covers. The sheets had already grown cold and he was impatient for them to warm up. He lay on his back, looking up into the darkness, listening. His wife lay on her side, her back to him. He thought she was already going back to sleep but in fact she was, like him, staring into the gloom. She was hoping, almost praying, that she would hear no more screams, no more of anything other than the wind, the rain, the occasional passing of a car or truck. Her husband was hoping the same thing, and he thought:

"She's right. It's probably nothing. And even if it *is* something ... she's right, I don't need more problems."

—For of course he had his own. On a recent visit to his
doctor he had complained that "sometimes" he didn't see as well
as he used to, and after a quick examination the doctor had said
he might have cataracts and recommended him to an ophthal-
mologist who confirmed the diagnosis. He had them in both
eyes and would eventually have to have them removed. Jed
hadn't made an appointment for the operation; he was putting
it off because he had a lifelong fear of doctors and hospitals,
though everyone he spoke to assured him that the procedure
was "nothing." —And this wasn't even to mention his back and
feet, which were also beginning to give him problems. They
were starting to hurt if he took more than his usual, daily forty-
five minute walk. As for Norma, well, physically she was alright, but with her there was always an issue, always some distracting, irritating thing going on. Most recently she was
engaged in a fight with a building contractor who hadn't laid
down the kitchen tiles to her exact liking. She spent half the
day complaining to her husband about what she was going to do
to that "damn thief"—how she was going to take him to court,
get her money back, get more than her money back, sue him for
damages, smear his reputation, make sure he never worked
again ...

Yes, they had their own problems. Why invite more into
their lives, especially now when they were both "older" and really shouldn't have to endure anything unpleasant? Hadn't they
had enough unpleasantness in their lives; or at least, hadn't he?
Jed had only been retired for three years. Before that, for forty
years, he had had to engage in the dreary rat-race of making a
living in New York City: five days a week commuting to and
from Manhattan on a filthy, demoralizing subway train, climbing steps up and down, weaving and hurrying through streets
choked with the rush and scurry of hordes of people competing
with one another to get to work on time, to go to lunch on time,
to get home on time;—the faceless, hurrying masses of which he
had been a part for so long, and which had ground him down,
worn him out, leaving him, at the end of each day, utterly exhausted, and at the end of his life (or rather, he thought, not at

the end of his life—no, no, his life was hardly at an end!—but rather just before his retirement) haggard and even a little bent. Yes, he had done his time; he had worked and endured enough; he had done what he was supposed to do and was reaping the reward he was supposed to reap: a small pension and his and his wife's Social Security income, which enabled them to keep their house, to keep their car, and insured them against want for the rest of their lives. So maybe Norma was right. Why invite problems? Now was not the time to have so much as a single unnecessary one. He just wanted to be let alone in peace and quiet.

Faintly, in the cold distance, above the wind gusts and the patter of rain, Norma and Jed heard more screams.

The young woman was running for her life, screaming as she ran. With every scream she knew that she deprived herself of breath and consequently the vigor that might have hastened her flight but intuitively she understood that she could not outrun her attacker and that her best hope for survival was to attract attention and get help. Her screams were so loud that many heard them; were awakened by them, as Jed and Norma had been, or, already awake, started at them and went to their windows to peep out carefully. The screams were of such a frantic, impulsive nature that even the stolidest, stupidest person heard in them a dreadful life-or-death situation. As such, they made people shudder in the center of their souls. They knew that whatever was going on out there was the horrible, ugly, dangerous side of life in the city, and they cringed at the thought of it, wanted no part of it, were determined to distance themselves from it; so determined that they made excuses for what they heard, telling themselves or one another, just as Norma had told Jed, "Oh, it's probably nothing ... it's just people being rowdy ... forget about it!" And if they couldn't convince themselves to forget about it, they told themselves that someone else would do something; that there were plenty of other people who had heard the screams and some of them were bound to call the police; people who "could" do it—people who weren't as old or as sick or as tired as they were, people who (this thought with especial self-pity) "had the strength" to deal with whatever dark, traumatic consequence might be incurred from getting involved in such things. But they themselves? No, they couldn't do it. They had their own problems. They couldn't get involved in anything so horrible as people hurting or possibly killing each other. Oh, God, no; that would be too much for them—much too much! They just wanted to be let alone.

As Jed lay in bed with his eyes closed, trying to sleep even as he listened to the wind and rain outside, he realized that he was—hungry. He had eaten less than usual for dinner, and afterwards there had not been the usual snack of cookies he munched while watching television; so now he felt an uncomfortable emptiness in his stomach. He knew he wouldn't be able to get back to sleep unless he ate something. For the second time in five minutes he flung the covers off himself and got out of bed.

"Where are you going now?" his wife asked in tired irritation.

"Kitchen. I'll be right back."

He shuffled out of the bedroom, careful of his steps in the darkness in which furniture loomed as black amorphous entities and open doorways bloomed blackly out of the soft deep gray.

When he reached the entrance to the kitchen he blindly put out a hand and felt for the light switch; and flicked it on. He squinted against the light.

He walked to the refrigerator and opened its door. As usual, it was stuffed and yet there wasn't a single thing he could just eat; everything had to be cooked or otherwise prepared. He told himself to remind his wife that the next time she went shopping she should buy things he could eat quickly: yogurt or cold cuts or ice cream. His eyes shifted to a box of corn flakes on top of the refrigerator and he resignedly reached out to it, taking it, along with a half-gallon container of milk, to the table.

It was deathly quiet in the kitchen at this time of morning. Only the soft tick-tick-tick of the wall clock could be heard. His spoon clinked against the ceramic bowl as he lifted the corn flakes to his mouth and slurpingly ate. At one point he lowered the spoon and held it still, held his breath, and listened ... listened ... and he thought he heard screams again above the whisper of the wind; but he couldn't be sure.

"It's your imagination," he told himself.

It was not his imagination; only, this time the distance between him and the screams were so great that he could hardly have heard them even if the wind had not been blowing or the rain falling.

For the woman was still running for her life. Two dozen blocks away she continued to flee her would-be killer. She was exhausted, injured, in pain, terrified, and didn't scream now only because she knew that every time she did so she was robbing herself of a breath needed to continue her flight, to keep ahead of her pursuer, to survive. She veered into an alley between a bakery and a hair salon. Twenty feet into it she slammed into several dark plastic trash cans, toppling them over, hurting and bruising herself. These fallen trash cans inhibited her attacker's pursuit for a few seconds as he crashed into them and nearly fell over. But he never really fell; he only stumbled and quickly regained his balance. Even if he had fallen and had needed a minute to get up and compose himself, it would hardly have mattered, not now, not in this situation: for she had run into a dead end. Sixty feet further on there was nothing before her but three steep brick walls. When she realized where she was, and that the only exit was the way she had come in, and saw moreover her attacker coming toward her, she knew that her only hope of survival was someone coming to her rescue; and so she screamed again; or rather tried to scream with the breath and might that was left to her. But one of her lungs had been punctured and when she took a deep breath it pained her as much as the knife-stab that had torn into her; and the sound she produced was muted, breathy, wheezing, ineffective; and she tasted a wet saltiness in her mouth—disgusting, alarming blood. Even so she managed to scream somewhat. In the upper floors of a nearby apartment building lights went on in windows as people awoke and wondered what was going on "out there."

She had been stabbed three times, twice in the lower, once in the upper back; both times deeply, painfully, but non-fatally. She could also feel the warm blood running down her skin. Only fear and adrenaline had enabled her to run as she had; and the same adrenaline now surged within her as she saw the knife-wielding man coming at her. When he reached her she fought for her life. She put out her hands to block his assault. She tried to punch and scratch and kick him. She managed to grab his hand, the one with the knife, and held it away from her, and with all her might tried to turn it against himself. But she was no match for his male power and murderous rage, and she was the weaker on account of exhaustion from running and from loss of blood. The man caught one of her kicking legs, pulling it hard and fast so that she fell, landing on the cement floor with a hard thump. He pounced on her. He plunged the knife into her side, into her chest, into her abdomen; again and again, again and again. Each time she felt the strange painfulness of the sharp blade cutting into her body. These sensations filled her with new bursts of panic; she tried to fight back even more frantically; but somehow her arms, her hands, would not respond—her body would not perform her will. He stabbed her in the heart: she became still at once. She lay on the wet alley floor as lifelessly and inertly as a doll that has fallen from a child's hands.

The killer stabbed the dead body another seven times, each time hard and panting with mad vengeance. When he got to his feet he looked down at the shadowy corpse with a sense of angry victory. Only now did he think of himself—of the crime he had committed and the possibility of getting caught and punished. While chasing his victim down the sidewalks he had seen the lights in nearby houses going on as people awoke to her screaming. It occurred to him now that the police must have been called many times over. Undoubtedly they were on their way, closing in on him from all sides. He turned around and ran out of the alley, then slackened his pace so as to be less conspicuous, all the while intending to make a dash for his car if he heard approaching sirens—but hearing none.

In his kitchen, Jed was relieved that he heard no more screaming, no matter how hard he listened. He had finished his cereal and felt the better for it; his stomach was no longer growling. But he hadn't really enjoyed it and he could still have gone for something else, something better, something sweeter or more substantial. Again he told himself that he would remind Norma the next time she went shopping to buy some snacks, cookies or cupcakes or maybe cheese crackers; something he could eat quickly, something nice and tasty.

CLOSURE

The defendant was a young man in his late twenties and everything about him bespoke a brutal nature: the prognathic lower part of the face, the full, edacious, thick lips which he continually smacked, the low and sloping forehead above protuberant brows, above all perhaps the small, close-set, lusterless eyes, which looked out on the world with an air of absolute indifference as though he would just as soon destroy all things as let them be. He heard the verdict without emotion, but then again he had sat through the entire trial with the most stolid expression and demeanor. Even when the prosecuting attorney had detailed the heinous nature of his crime, how he had kidnapped and tortured and killed a little girl of twelve years old, and had shown enlarged photographs of the gruesome crime scene to a stunned and sickened courtroom, he had sat there without expression, only blinking casually and even looking a little bored. His only real reaction had come when the father of the murdered child had gone berserk with heartbreak and tried to attack him. For two weeks this father had sat beside his wife, whose face was pale with grief, and had often whispered becalming words to her, but when he saw the large photographs of the blood-drenched crime scene something happened to him: he fidgeted for a moment—his lips trembled—his wife later would mention how she heard him breathing quickly, as though he couldn't catch his breath—and the next thing anyone knew a cry of rage filled the courtroom and he had leapt over three rows of benches separating him from the defendant with the intention of ripping him to shreds. Only then did the killer show any emotion, only then did any surprise or fear come over his thick, thuggish features, for at the sight of the enraged man coming toward him he got up off his chair and stepped back, putting up his shackled hands as though to defend himself against the attack. But before he ever had to do so, the bailiff, both lawyers, and two police detectives sitting in the front row (witnesses for the prosecution) blocked and restrained the father, swarming over him, pulling him down to the floor, subduing him as he kicked and screamed and pleaded to be let go, saying that he had to get at that bastard, at the murderer, so that he could tear him apart limb from limb. By that time everyone in the courtroom was standing, his wife also, crying out her husband's name. The father was led out of the courtroom and the judge ordered an hour's adjournment before continuing.

Two days later, during the closing arguments of the case, the prosecution had proven the defendant's guilt beyond a reasonable doubt. The defense attorney, who had started the case insisting on his client's complete innocence, had no alternative but to change his strategy from getting his client off scot-free to appealing to the jury for leniency on account of his client's youth and "troubled past": a boy born into an indigent family, who grew up without a father, who dropped out of high school, who had a low IQ—"mentally impaired and not entirely aware of his actions."

The jury forewoman, a corporate secretary in her early thirties, stood up and rendered the verdict on behalf of the jury. Her manner was reserved and nervous, for she was filled with a sense of her weighty role in the matter of rendering Justice. Like the rest of the jury she came from New York's middle- and lower-middle classes; like them she worked to exhaustion every day for a mere living, watched the news at night and believed what she heard, and the dream of her existence—aside from finding a well-heeled husband—was to win the lottery and retire in luxury. Like the other jurors she had been impressed by the expensive accoutrements and severe ritual of the American legal system. The well-groomed attorneys in their tailored suits, the berobed judge sitting augustly elevated on the bench, the unhurried process by which every element of the trial was assembled and followed through—it had all filled her with an intimidating sense of the power and authority of the State. She could not help feeling it one of the most important moments of her life when the judge called upon her to read the verdict. Her legs shook a little as she stood, and her voice wavered as she pronounced: guilty as charged of first degree murder. The judge thanked her and the jury for their consideration. The forewoman smiled beatifically at his compliment and sat down with an immense sense of importance and accomplishment.

The defense attorney was not surprised by the jury's verdict; he himself knew that the hardship story he had peddled before them was a last-ditch effort. The best that could be hoped for, in the way of sentencing, was that the judge would take into consideration the extenuating circumstances of his client's past. In this he was not to be disappointed. The judge, His Honor Sidney Steiglitz, read his decision: twenty-five years in prison. The mother of the slain little girl cried out that twenty-five years was not enough: that he had murdered her baby and deserved nothing less than the death penalty. Her husband shouted the same thing, raising his fist to the bench, his face red and furious, his speech spluttering envenomed saliva. Both parents knew very well that there was no death penalty in New York State, but they had not been able to restrain themselves from calling out for it in the same way that one cannot help yearning for a breath of air while drowning, or for a sip of water while dying of thirst. Their outburst was not something they had to think about: it was simply and immediately human.

His Honor banged his gavel with restrained impatience and called the parents to order. When they continued to assail him, indeed to insult him, to call him a fraud and his decision a travesty of justice, he calmly nodded to his bailiff who went up to the distraught couple and ushered them out of the courtroom. The dignified order of The Law was restored. His Honor pronounced the sentence again. The defense attorney stood by his client with an air of satisfaction at what had turned out to be, given the irrefutable evidence against him, another successful pleading before the court. The defendant stood with his wonted bored expression as though the prospect of spending the next twenty-five years in prison was a matter of little concern to him. With a bang of his gavel, His Honor closed the case. All rose as he left the bench and glided out of the courtroom into his adjoining office.

Judge Sidney Bernard Steiglitz had been on the bench for almost thirty years. Before becoming a judge he had been a defense attorney. As a youth still in college, then a young law student, he had had an overweening concern for the poor and

disadvantaged, for he had taken to heart the good values instilled into him by his parents, and above all the one that en-
joined those blessed with means and a good life to help those
whom fate had cast into less fortunate circumstances.   But
somewhere along the way this noble ideal underwent a peculiar
transformation by which poverty and ignorance not only explained unsocial behavior but to a large degree excused it. According to this credo, people who grew up in difficult
circumstances were in some measure—and often in great measure—unable to distinguish between good and bad, between
right and wrong, and consequently the bad, wrong, or criminal
choices they made couldn't be held entirely against them. He
was convinced that a man's character was not his fate, at least
not in any such simplistic way, but rather that the character
was a malleable substance and could be molded into a predeter-
mined course so that someone who, say, becomes a notorious
murderer could just as easily have become a living saint, all
kindness, altruism, and good works. It all had to do with one's
childhood, on how one was raised, the "opportunities" one had
had. The only thing that separated the coarse bullying boy who
set fire to cats and sneered with pleasure over the creatures'
screaming agony, from the shy, gentle lad who read poetry,
loved music, and spent his isolated hours daydreaming of storied places, was a pair of loving parents, adequate family income, and a good school.

The colleagues he had befriended pretty much shared this
view of his—which is precisely why he and they had found one
another companionable Like him, they had graduated with law
degrees from universities of good repute; there was therefore no
question in any of their minds about their own intellectual brilliance. Whenever they got together socially there was always
an undercurrent of pride in their academic history and credentials, and they would discuss the universities they had gone to,
the professors they had sat under, and the fellow classmates
who had gone on to this or that notable position in business or
government with an air of satisfaction at having been a part of
it all. His Honor and his colleagues shared a sense that they
were not only servants and enforcers of the law but also the enlightened agents of a much-needed change by which a brighter,
more equitable society might be forged.

In the thirty years that he had been on the bench His Honor had been true to these earliest ideals of his. His sympathies had always lain with the oppressed offender—but only if he really *had* been oppressed, that is to say, if he had been poor, come from a "bad" family, or had otherwise had some obvious disadvantage in his life; otherwise—woe to him! For if he had come from easy circumstances, if he had money and good education and a thriving career, and in spite of all that had broken the law, then he was sure to meet in His Honor a kind of avenging angel determined to visit a swift and harsh justice.

Among the perquisites of His Honor's long tenure on the bench was month-long hiatus of rest and relaxation, which he usually took at the same time each year—spring, and in particular around Easter. The wet, snowy, lowering New York winter would by that time have added its own burden of gloom to his duties at the court, from which he would long for a break. Over the years he and Muriel, his wife of thirty-two years, had taken advantage of this time to travel, and they had pretty much been all over the world: they had visited the major cities of Europe, the Middle East, and had even gone to Cambodia—which they had both, much to their surprise, liked a great deal. In more recent years however they had stayed closer to home, in part because they couldn't think of any place to which they wanted to go badly enough as to endure the bustle, stress, and expense of getting there, and in greater part because they had become grandparents. Their only daughter Erica had given them two beautiful grandchildren—Louis and Emily, six and four years old respectively—and their thoughts now were to spend as much time as they could with "their" babies. Unfortunately for them their daughter, soon after giving birth to Emily, had announced that she and her stockbroker husband were moving out of Brooklyn. They had brought a house, a beautiful, four-bedroom house, in Scarsdale. On first hearing this news His Honor and his wife felt sad and somehow betrayed, but also understood that the move would be better for their grandchildren, who would have a huge back yard to play in, go to good schools, and not be exposed to the nasty life of the city streets.

"Besides, when you come to visit, you'll both stay for a week!" Erica had announced. "We've got a lovely room for you."

And that had become the routine. In addition to their occasional visits throughout the year, the grandparents remained a week—or rather, four days (His Honor wisely insisted on the shorter stay)—to be with their daughter and give as well as receive the joys of family life. With every visit they were sure to bring something for their grandchildren— toys or goodies of some sort. Aside from birthday or Hanukkah presents, Erica always asked them not to buy anything for the kids, saying that they would only come to expect it and that they had to learn they "couldn't always get everything they wanted." His Honor would smile at that stern morality, knowing it was based on his and his wife's own impecunious background, and which they had instilled into their daughter as a child. But they also knew that it no longer applied to them or their daughter or grandchildren. Besides, what good was money if you couldn't spend it, and what better thing to spend it on than making children happy? —Thus the Steiglitzes, the most typical of indulgent grandparents. Thus also the fact that once again His Honor, while driving north on the New England Thruway, turned off on an exit several miles before the one which led to his daughter's house but which (as his wife very well knew) was the way to a chain toy store.

"Sid, what are you doing now?" his wife asked, tiredly, impatiently, knowing very well what he was doing.

"I just want to pick up a few things," he said, not looking at her.

"Oh, Sid ... the kids don't need anything else."

"Well ..."—shaking his head, as though that was hardly a reason to go empty-handed—"... I just want to get one thing."

She didn't make any further objection; she herself wanted to make her little darlings happy. She did not however accompany him into the store and fifteen minutes later watched him come out with two big bags full of carton-enclosed toys. She watched him put them in the back seat and smiled as he got back behind the wheel. To her question about what he had got the kids, he said he had bought Louis a model airplane to build, and for Emily a coloring set; not mentioning several other toys and candy.

Their daughter's house had no immediate neighbors; the closest house was about three hundred feet away. Erica had always said that she liked the privacy. It was a two-storied, four–

bedroom house with, on one side, a garage up to which led the wide, smooth, asphalted driveway. His Honor and his wife pulled into the driveway and parked just behind their son-in-law's Audi. "Looks like Alex is home," he said, wondering why his son-in-law would be home during a work day, then flattering himself by supposing that the young man wanted to be there to greet and spend time with his in-laws.

When they got out of the car His Honor grabbed up the bags of toys from the back seat, and with his wife they walked to the front door and rang the bell.

They waited for almost a minute but no one came to the door. They rang the bell again, waited again, and still it did not open. They looked at each other and His Honor's wife remarked, "They must be home. They knew we were coming. I wonder if they're out back." She started off to the side of the house where a narrow concrete walkway led to the back yard. His Honor remained at the front door and rang the bell again, and this time—for no conscious reason—he put his hand on the doorknob and turned it. Unlocked and, in fact, not entirely closed, the door gave way at his slightest push inward, and with a mixture of surprise and gratitude he stepped inside, into a short entranceway of no more than five feet that gave a full view of the living room and, beyond it, the kitchen.

No one was to be seen, nor anything heard: it was entirely quiet and still. He called out for his daughter:

"Erica? Erica, you here?"

And then he called out for his son-in-law:

"Alex? Helloooo? Anybody home?"

The living room was clean and neat as usual, though a few brightly-colored plastic pieces of a dismantled toy might be seen on the couch. His Honor set down the bags he was carrying. He walked through the room to the bright, modern kitchen and saw through its window that his wife was in the back yard and, having found no one there, was coming back toward the house.

"Huh," he said aloud, and backtracked into the living room.

He called out again for his daughter and her husband, and then climbed the stairs to their bedrooms on the second floor.

Days, weeks, months, and years later he would tell himself that he knew something was wrong when he had reached the second floor landing and saw how all the doors of the rooms stood ajar to precisely the same degree. Yet at the time he seemed not to notice this and walked forthrightly forward, passing first his son-in-law's office, peering into it and finding it empty, then going on to the next door to the master bedroom.

"Erica?" he said, knocking lightly and then gently pushing the door open.

It would have been hard for someone who saw his face just then, as he stood on that threshold, to know what his first impression was of the scene before him. Except for his slightly open mouth, his expression was blank. In another few seconds his mouth opened a little wider, as did his eyes; his complexion paled; and something urgent invested his demeanor. He stepped forward carefully as though into some unknown, dangerous region, and with each step an aching horror swept through his spirit and seemed to suck out the breath of his being. The bodies of his daughter and her husband lay on the bed. They looked as though they had been sitting on the edge of it and had just fallen over. The sheets were moist with the blood that had seeped out of the bullet holes in their heads. Their eyes were open, glassy, unseeing. His Honor stood over them in frozen silence and told himself, "No," as though refusing to believe what he saw. Then the remembrance of others, of his grandchildren, peremptorily brought him to himself; an actionable panic surged through him; he turned around, hurried out of the room and ran down the hallways to the bedroom where his grandson and granddaughter slept. The little girl was in her bed, the boy on the floor, both of them lying in disturbingly awkward angles. His Honor hurried to his grandson, bent down by his side, and turned him over. The child was dead. They both were dead. The front of their pajamas were red and still moist with blood.

"Oh, my God," His Honor whispered to himself.

He got up but he felt his legs weak beneath him. He stared down at the children.

"Sid, are you up there?"

He heard his wife calling him from downstairs. In the ten seconds it took him to back out of the children's bedroom and reach the hallway he knew that he could not allow his wife to see what he had just seen; that he had to keep her away. He had to come to himself, to control himself, to command his desperate horror in order to do what was necessary to make sure she was not destroyed. He knew that if she saw what he had just seen she would be destroyed forever.

She was just standing at the foot of the stairwell—had just put her foot on the first step and was about to ascend—when she saw her husband come into view above her. As soon as she saw his face she knew that something was wrong. She had never seen him look like that. Little did His Honor realize how ineffectual, how transparent, was the mask of calm authority he tried to assume. His wan complexion and the desperation in his eyes gave away the tumult in his soul. She saw the shakiness of his steps and the way his hand gripped hard the handrail as he descended, as though to steady himself. Though he bent the whole force of his will to project an air of self-possession, the impression he in fact made filled his wife with alarm. Almost in a whisper she asked, "Sid, what is it?" In response, His Honor uttered an uncertain syllable and, when he reached her, put both his hands on her shoulders and turned her around, saying, "Go into the living room." His words came out as a hoarse, cracking whisper.

"What's going on?" she asked, or rather exclaimed, and as her eyes looked past him up to the second floor. And something terrible gripped her heart and she asked impulsively, "Where are the kids?"

He took her hand; he held it tightly; he pulled her along with him into the living room and said that they had to call the police. She followed him for only a few steps before stopping, yanking back hard from his grasp.

"What is it!" she exclaimed. "Where are the kids!"

She turned around as though to go upstairs but he hastily got in front of her and blocked her way.

"No, stay here," he said. "We have to call the police. Just *stay here!*"

The worry that had been building up in her over the last twenty seconds became panic and burst up within her like a geyser. The thought that "something" had happened to her daughter and her grandchildren made her react thoughtlessly, instinctively, almost violently. In that moment she was not thinking nor could be restrained; hers was the immediate, indomitable instinct of motherhood. Violently she pushed past her

husband and ran up the stairs. He called out to her, commanded her to stop, to come back down, but she paid him no
heed and continued; and in another few seconds her animal
shrieks of horror filled the house and—like a kick in his pants—
jolted him out of his temporary inaction. He went upstairs and
found his wife in the master bedroom half inclined over the
body of her dead daughter, repeatedly screaming out Erica's
name as she tried to raise the death-heavy corpse whose lifeless
head hung hideously down. His Honor had to use considerable
force to make her let go and drag her away. "We have to call
the police, we have to call the police," he repeated to her, guiding her away, out of the room and down the stairs. Halfway
down she collapsed. She fell into a semi-conscious, rambling,
shivering swoon. His Honor was not such a young man that he
could easily lift and carry his wife, but the extremity of the situation gave him the strength and determination to do so, and
once he had gotten her downstairs he laid her down on the
couch in the living room. "Stay here, stay here," he told her,
commanding her, pleading with her. And he called the police.

The investigation into the murders took three months, and
ended without discovering who had committed them. The investigators were however able to conclude the probable series of
events as they had happened. The motive had evidently been
robbery. There was no evidence of a forced entry into the house
so it was likely that he, or they (for there was not even enough
evidence to indicate whether it had been more than one person),
had gained entrance simply by knocking on the front door, then
pushing his way in when it had opened. He had shot first the
husband, then the wife, then the children. Afterwards he had
gone through each room looking for anything valuable. The husband's wallet had been emptied of cash, as had been the wife's
pocketbook. Before he had handled anything, the murderer had
put on a pair of gloves to ensure that he left no fingerprints behind, which in itself probably meant that he was a former con-
vict who might have been identified through them. No one in
the surrounding area had seen or heard anything of the murders, which had taken place late on the evening before the visit
of His Honor and his wife.

It was one of those cases, the seasoned investigators knew,
that would never be solved without a "lucky break"—a witness

coming forward with new information or a confession. But they did not admit this to His Honor and his wife, in part because they hoped that yet another inspection of the crime scene might yield a new clue or bit of evidence, and in part because they understood that such news would only be another blow to the bereaved parents.

During the course of their lives His Honor and his wife had either singly or together expressed condolences to people who had lost their children but now that they were on the receiving end of this situation they experienced firsthand how every well-meant expression of sympathy does little to alleviate grief and may even refresh the memory that causes it.

His Honor took a leave of absence from the court. For the next three months he suffered in silence. His wife, having no male inhibitions about expressing her grief, cried off and on for a month after the murders; afterwards, though she did not weep, she sat for hours in immobile, dolorous contemplation, the rings beneath her eyes growing deeper and darker with each passing week. She ate little and began to look old and frail as though some insidious parasite were eating away at her from within. His Honor knew what she was going through, for the same horrible vacuum had opened up within himself: the unendurable sense that everything in their past had been pointless, and before them lay a wasteland of unrelieved decay. Behind this lay the instinctive understanding, as old as mankind itself, that one's children, and then theirs, were a pledge against the sad, brief existence of one's single life. Only in them did one go forward and did one's speck of humanity keep at bay a coldly indifferent universe which would as soon crush out one's existence as it would that of a bug. But now that comfort and pride had been ravaged away from them. They saw themselves as they were: two ageing persons in a marriage which was—it was so clear to them now!—based only on the comfort of long acquaintance and without the love that shores up and sustains in the face of a storm. They lived together and apart at the same time. In their separate solitudes they groped to find meaning in their lives. His Honor tried to find it in his career. He would reflect on his years of public service, on the esteem of his colleagues, on the way people generally regarded him with unspoken admiration or awe;—things in which he had always found satisfaction and which had enabled him to walk through the world proudly. But now these things seemed to him utterly empty and meaningless.

In the months after the murders His Honor often bitterly reflected on the irony of his having fallen victim to violent crime—he who had (as he considered it) dedicated his life to making society safer. He had always known of course that no one is immune to crime, but his years as an attorney and then as a judge, of first representing and then passing judgment on criminals who had stood before him captive, humbled, and, as it were, emasculated before the unyielding fact of the Law which he embodied—this had instilled into him on some level a sense that he was shielded against barbarous forces to which the rest of the world was liable. In this regard he now saw how deluded he had been: a man who, because he dressed in a robe, sat elevated behind a bench, and received the scraping deference of Lilliputians, thought himself apart and above the sometimes degraded life of the world at large. He knew now, for sure and keenly, how entirely he too was exposed to it, a part of it all.

In a thousand silent, hopeless, tearful, lonesome moments, His Honor sat in his office at home looking at the picture of his daughter and grandchildren, contrasting their framed, shining, joyous faces with the abattoir scene in which he had last seen them. He had never been an imaginative man, yet his mind richly churned out scenarios in which the murders had occurred. He could almost see the way his son-in-law had tried to protect his family, how his daughter had pleaded for her life and the safety of her children, and how the little ones had shaken and cried with fear. As these scenes played out in the theater of his mind he would put a hand to his pale lips and shake his head, his eyes open, unblinking, staring into space for several minutes at a time; entranced by the horror of it all.

He began to know what it meant to live in the past. For the future had become only a blight, a wasteland without hope or life, only the past containing light and laughter. He often remembered his daughter when she had been a child, daddy's little girl, her face so bright, cheerful, looking up at him with some sweet question as she played with her dollies or ate an ice cream cone; or how, as a teenager, she dressed up in some fad fashion and trinkets and went out with girlfriends; or how, as a young woman, she brought home her dates, so hopeful of her parents' approval—and so often frowning, disappointed, when she saw that her father, though polite, disapproved. "Dear sweet girl," he murmured to himself, shaking his head, remembering everything about her life.

In the months after the murders he would call the detectives working on the case at least once a week in the hope of hearing they had made some progress in it. Always he received the same answer that there was nothing new to report. "Sir, believe me, if we learn anything new, anything at all, I'll call you," the lead detective would assure him. But of this too His Honor quickly despaired. He had dealt with criminal cases long enough to know that there was a window of a few days or weeks or, at most, months, when any evidence that was going to be of use in the case would be found. He also knew that some cases were never solved. It didn't take any especial intelligence or cunning on the part of a criminal, especially one that struck in the middle of the night and without witnesses, to leave no significant clues behind. Every year there was a certain percentage of murders that were never solved. In this case, the only evidence that had been found were the bullets in the bodies of the dead. They had come from a .38 caliber pistol.

After a year His Honor returned to the bench. Everyone who worked with him or knew him at the courthouse welcomed him back with friendly handshakes and good cheer. No word was spoken to him about his loss, as everyone wanted to make his return an occasion of relief and joy to him. He himself looked forward to resuming his duties. If nothing else, he still had his work to look forward to.

But he had returned to the courthouse a changed man and a different kind of judge. He was aware of the transformation in himself when he looked over the docket for the first case he was to try since his return: a robbery of a convenience store in which the robber had slashed the owner with a knife, and who had been caught only because he had been identified in the recording by a surveillance camera. He was a twenty-seven year old man whose criminal record stretched back to his sixteenth year, and who over the last five years had been involved in three other robberies. In the past His Honor would have looked over the defendant's history and thought: "I wonder what he went through to turn him into that kind of person?" Now he looked it over and asked himself with grim determination: "How much longer do we tolerate someone like this before he kills someone?"

The atmosphere set by His Honor in the court during that trial became a precedent for all the succeeding cases he presided over. He would come into the courtroom, take his seat at the bench, and glance up at the defendant with a quick solemn expression in which his contracted brows and hard, piercing eyes conveyed a warning of what was to come. During the trial he consistently overruled the objections of the defense even as he allowed every kind of evidence and testimony for the prosecution. In years gone by he had coolly pronounced the sentence, called the case to an end, and left the bench; now he gave a tongue-lashing to the defendant, reviling him as a scoundrel, a degenerate, a monster who ideally ought to be eliminated for the good of society; and he spoke with such a snarl, his voice so dripping with contempt, that it seemed he would like nothing better than to come down from bench and himself wring the defendant's neck. He was so often and so entirely sympathized with and advanced the cause of the prosecuting attorneys that they would often look over to their opposing colleagues with an air of surprise and apology.

It wasn't long before rumors and rumblings were heard that His Honor was acting erratically, and not too much longer after this the defense attorneys who had been sneered at, insulted, or otherwise given short shrift in His Honor's courtroom reported him to the New York State Commission on Judicial Conduct to which they submitted a Formal Written Complaint stating that he had abused the power of his office, and exhibited a "consistent and baseless bias against the defense." The Complaint itemized instances of this. When His Honor read over the Complaint his reaction was one of surprise and anger—surprise that his colleagues should, as it were, transgress the unspoken law of respect and indulgence for a fellow professional of the legal system, and anger because he believed he had, if anything, meted out the strictest justice. "Idiotic pipsqueaks!" he muttered, reading the names of the attorneys who had submitted the complaint.

He expressed his anger to one of his colleagues, Judge

Michael Cohn. The two men had known each other for many years and had sometimes consulted on cases. They were about the same age, were both New Yorkers, indeed had grown up in the same neighborhood and known each other as children. His Honor showed the Complaint to Judge Cohn, saying, "Can you believe this crap?"

In fact Judge Cohn could, for as he read over the Complaint he found in it confirmation of the rumors he had been hearing for some time about His Honor's one-sided behavior in the courtroom. Indeed, once, out of curiosity, Judge Cohn had sat in for an hour on one of His Honor's trials and had seen for himself His Honor's immediate and unrelenting hostility toward defendants.

"And of all the judges in Brooklyn, why do you think they would file this complaint against you?" Judge Cohn asked, hoping to make his friend come to see for himself the error of his ways.

"Why? Because they're out of their minds!"

"Even if they were out of their minds," Cohn said, "they didn't have to bring this particular complaint against you. You don't think," he continued, the tone of his voice politely venturing, "there's anything—anything at all—to it?"

His Honor looked to his old friend with a new and distant deliberation, the way a man will when he begins to suspect that the person he thought to be on his side might not be. "No."

"So it just came out of the blue, then," Judge Cohn returned, smiling with a mock innocence that seemed to point out the more acutely the incredibility of His Honor's response.

His Honor was nettled and said with some irritation, "I've sat on thousands of cases in my time. I think if there was something wrong here these charges would have been brought up a long time ago—don't you?"

"Depends," Cohn said, shrugging with an air of uncertainty. "Apparently they cited cases—"

"Twelve cases," His Honor said. "They cited twelve. Out of thousands and thousands!"

"Well ... maybe ... " Judge Cohn said, now looking as though he genuinely thought His Honor had a case to make in his defense. But then he went on: "On the other hand, unless I'm mistaken, those twelve cases weren't so intermittent. All kind

of recent, aren't they? And similar? They show a pattern.
They're all harsh sentences—very unlike you. Totally out of
keeping with your record."

"So what? There's no law that says I have to rule the same
way all the time."

"No, but there is a law, an unwritten law, that says when a
man who has been consistent for many years suddenly isn't,
that something's not right with him. You know ..."—Judge
Cohn hesitated. He had been about to mention forthrightly
what to him was obvious: that His Honor's experience with
crime had made incapable of genuine impartiality. He sought
for the gentlest phrases he could. "Maybe it's just hard for you
to be objective, Sid, after what you've gone through; and that's
understandable. But I have to be honest with you: I've seen
how harsh you can be. You're impossible with defense attorneys
now. You insult them, you shout at them, you dismiss their
most reasonable objections, even as you let the prosecution get
away with flagrant indiscretions. You're on a mission to slap
every criminal behind bars. I daresay that if there was still a
death penalty you'd be frying people every other day. But
you're not appointed to be an executioner, my friend: you were
appointed to the bench to judge objectively and to give people
justice."

"Justice!" His Honor exclaimed, his eyes narrowing and his
lips twisting into a simper almost of disgust. "You must think
you're talking to a first-year law student!"

"I don't know what you mean by that."

"I mean that I'm too old to be taken in my fine phrases,"
His Honor said; and seeing that his auditor was still acting as
though he didn't understand, or was still making a show of noble naiveté, he continued, "Stop it. Just stop it. You know
what goes on. You know as well as I do the judicial system in
this country, and certainly in this city, isn't about justice: it's
about lawyers trying to win cases. Whether they're on the right
side or the wrong side is immaterial to them: if there's a buck
or a reputation to be made, they're there. And you want to
know what's the most obscene thing about all that? That I
bought into it—that I let it go on year after year; that we all
did in one way or another. But I don't want to hear again in
my courtroom some snot-nosed attorney pleading that his client

should be somehow excused for robbing an old lady or shooting a police officer because he didn't get the opportunity to go to college. That stuff don't fly with me no more—get it? I see what's going on. I finally *see* it. It took a lot to make me see it, and maybe I saw it a little late, but at least I eventually *did* see it—and I'm not tolerating it any more. Don't tell me about 'justice,' my friend. The fact is that for the first time in my life I'm finally giving it to people to the best of my ability."

Judge Cohn hadn't expected to be barraged by a manifesto so considered and passionate. The warmth of its delivery had an eloquence which rather cowed him, for it made any cooler response seem in comparison pale and unconvincing. He couldn't deny His Honor's accusations against the judicial system; he knew firsthand the kinds of shenanigans that went on in it. In his own courtroom, for instance, he had often prevented the introduction of incriminating evidence because of legal technicalities which his gut told him were antithetical to justice. He had sat patiently as defense and prosecuting attorneys raised petty objections with each other's strategies or tried to nullify the credibility of witnesses by bringing up unpleasant facts about their past or personal lives, though these had had nothing to do with their testimony. Of course there were problems with the legal system, but Judge Cohn believed and wanted to believe that for all its faults it was the best that could be had. He felt sure at any rate about one thing: that a judge's office was limited, and that His Honor had overstepped those bounds. He said:

"Maybe you've forgotten that your job is to referee the case and apply the law—not to be the jury."

"That's not fair. I've never usurped the power of the jury."

"According to the Complaint, you repeatedly guided jurors in the way they were to accept or interpret the testimony in your courtroom. You led them in the direction you wanted by skewing what they could or couldn't accept as testimony."

"Only when it was obvious the defense was acting inappropriately."

"But that's the whole point, Sid! What you think is 'inappropriate' may not be—in fact, isn't. You're not there to judge the evidence; you're there to ensure it's presented in an orderly and appropriate fashion; and it's up to the jury to decide whether they accept or reject what's presented to them."

"So I'm supposed to let the defense mislead them?"

"You're supposed to let the jury be the jury."

"The jury!" His Honor exclaimed, with more disdain than ever. *"What* jury? The juries in *this* city? Do you—really— respect the juries we have these days?"

Judge Cohn was about to answer at once that yes, he did; but he held back, because he didn't.

"Of course you don't!" His Honor said. "How could you? The voir dire's become nothing more than a weeding out of anyone who's got an ounce intelligence or principles. It's become attorneys trying to seat the stupidest people they can find—people who aren't critical, who accept what they're told, who are easy to persuade and think that because a lawyer's wearing an expensive suit and struts back and forth like a big shot that he must know what he's talking about. And God forbid anyone should be a victim of a crime! We don't want *them* on the jury, do we? They might have had an epiphany about life, about the reality of the world:—they might see things too clearly! They'd make a criminal trial a matter of a couple of days rather than a couple of weeks or months! Maybe they'd even show us that we're not so necessary after all—that a lot of what's really justice in this world comes down to having a little common sense. No, no, no," His Honor said, shaking his head, "we want the formalities, the procedures, the twistings and the turnings for things that could and should be straight and honest and true, otherwise a lot of us might see what a bunch of frauds we are! And in the end, when we've gotten it all wrong, as we often do, and the cretins of the world are given a slap on the wrist and wind up back on the street again hurting innocent people who expected us to do right by them;—what do we say about it?— how do we explain it to ourselves? We tell ourselves 'We couldn't have known' or 'That's our system.' Which is bullshit. We *knew*—we knew very well. We just didn't have the courage to admit we were part of a flawed system and that therefore we ourselves might be frauds. We were cowards. We didn't do our duty. Me? I'm just trying to do my duty, finally."

Judge Cohn adjusted his glasses and looked away from His Honor, shaking his head regretfully because everything he had just heard only convinced him that his colleague was no longer able to be an impartial judge. "Even if everything you say is true," he said, "the fact remains that you have to work within the system as it is, and not subvert it to coincide with your opinions and views. If you don't like the system the way it is, Sid, then I suggest you run for office and pass legislation. That's the way it's done in this country."

"That's not practical and you know it."

Judge Cohn lifted a hand a little as though to say, "Nevertheless, that's the way it is," and aloud he said, "I don't know Sid ... I don't know what else to tell you ..."

The preliminary investigation by the Commission into His Honor's conduct found that he had indeed "acted improperly" and without exception in his most recent decisions. For this he was censured, but allowed to remain on the bench. Any other judge would have taken the censure for what it was worth— namely, a serious warning that if the offending practices didn't cease he would be removed from office. And His Honor did take the warning for what it was worth. During the next several months he managed to check himself whenever he felt the sudden, angry impulse to intervene during a cross-examination or presentation on the part of the defense. But this was New York City, and the sheer number of criminals and thugs who were paraded before him wore down his most conscientious attempts not to become emotionally involved in their cases, especially when they had long and violent records.

It was not long before another Complaint was filed against His Honor. Though he once again defended himself against it, the court transcripts, for a second time, belied his heterodox conduct. There was no question but that he had repeatedly given the prosecution every advantage even as he had put obstacles in the way of the defense.

Like members of any other guild, jurists are disinclined to prosecute their own, first out of that sympathy toward members of their own profession, and second (and more importantly) out of an unspoken and semi-conscious understanding that in strictly holding their fellows to high standards they set similar expectations for themselves. But in this case the judges who sat on the Commission could no longer excuse His Honor's behavior without an obvious dereliction of duty, and voted to remove him from his seat in the Criminal Court. His Honor's initial reaction to this decision was to take it to the Court of Appeals, but knowing how that institution usually upheld the Commission's decisions, he decided not to do so. He accepted his reassignment to Civil Court in Manhattan. He was there only three months when presiding over cases of contract disputes, broken relationships, and negligence filled him with a sense of the pettiness of what his career had devolved into; and after considering that he was sixty-one years old and perhaps would do well to start enjoying his life more, he resigned his position and retired.

"And what are you going to do with the rest of your life?" his wife had asked him, when she heard his decision.

"Oh, I don't know ... maybe do a little more traveling, see the world a little more. There are a lot of places we haven't been to, you know."

His wife received this prospect of his, of their, future with a quiet, sad smile, and looked at him with doubtful, even hopeless eyes. She knew that any traveling they did would be less for the sake of seeing new places than to escape the inescapable at home, inside themselves. But she only asked, "And *then* what, Sid?"

"What do you mean?"

"I mean ... I don't think I have the energy any more for all that. But even if I did ... what's the point? I've seen enough places. I don't need to see any more." And, after pausing a few seconds, she added, "It wouldn't change anything."

"Well," he began, but he didn't follow through on what had seemed to be a counter argument. He knew that she was right. No matter where they went, no matter how interesting or glorious the place, *It* would always be with them, that weight on their spirits, that darkness behind every apparent bright enjoyment.

The first six months of his retirement were difficult for His Honor. He always had the sense that he ought to be doing something. He was often bored. He was an intelligent man but his intelligence was of the secondary rank, which must always be occupied in some visible process and cannot find satisfaction in its own quiet, internal exercise. A few times he found himself pacing back and forth in his living room.

"For God's sake, Sid, do something with yourself!" said his

wife, who, used to mindless leisure, was content to do nothing or watch television for hours at a stretch. "Why don't you go back to school—take classes or something? Or learn to do something? You like music. Why don't you learn an instrument?"

At first he scoffed at the idea; then it struck him as good. He had always liked music, the piano especially, and now he had plenty of time to learn it. He bought an expensive keyboard and found a teacher in his neighborhood—a young man of twenty-five with long hair, a scraggly beard, and ever-cheerful temper who was a rock musician and gave lessons. But after three months of struggling even with exercises His Honor lost interest and was, perhaps rightly, sure that he had no aptitude as a musician; and there seemed to him no point in enduring so much frustration for the sake of becoming less than mediocre. The keyboard was neatly put back into its box and stored away in the corner of a hallway closet.

The years passed and he grew used to retirement; eventually he came round to learning that there was a magic in waking up in the morning and having nothing to do—in knowing the day ahead was entirely his own. He read a great deal; not law, but novels, historical works, and even a smattering of poetry. He fell into a routine of sitting before his computer in the morning with his cup of coffee and looking over the latest news. If the weather was fine he would go out a little before noon to walk for an hour. If he grew tired and would take a seat on one of the benches across from a neighborhood playground and watch the children as they chased one another with shrill screams of delight, bounced up and down on seesaws, or begged their young mothers or fathers for another, stronger push on swings. Should an ice-cream truck come down the street with its storybook jingle the children would bound off the swings or slides or ladders and rush to their parents to clamor for money with which to buy an ice cream cone. His Honor, delighted by the scene, would laugh aloud. But a few times his laughter would catch in his throat and a shadow would pass over his face as he remembered a little girl he used to take to parks like this and push on swings and buy ice cream for; and he would sit there, a sword through his heart.

Several times a week he made a point of eating out at one of the many restaurants in his Brooklyn neighborhood. Usually his wife accompanied him, but when she didn't he had no qualms about dining by himself. His new favorite place was a small delicatessen restaurant with seating for no more than twenty persons; he always had to get there before five if he wished to be seated at a table. The food was simple and abundant, brought on large plates or deep bowls, and always accompanied by several included "extras." He suspected that some of this food might not be exactly healthful, for it had a smacking tastiness belying its high fat and salt content, but he enjoyed it so much that he found it hard to resist, and rationalized eating it with the thought that by the time it took any physiological toll on him he'd probably be so old that he wouldn't have much longer to live anyway. He was sixty-five now, but he looked and felt much older.

One late afternoon while he was sitting in this restaurant munching on his usual order while looking down, to the side of his plate, at the magazine he had bought from a local newsstand, he saw from the corner of his eye someone coming toward him and stopping a few feet away; and then he heard a voice exclaim, "Well, look who it is!"

His Honor looked up from his plate to see standing before him none other than his old colleague, Judge Cohn. They had not seen each other in four years and His Honor was surprised at how much older his former colleague looked. He had lost much of his hair, and what remained was white. He was much thinner, had developed a stoop at the shoulders, and the first indicators of great age—brown spots on the skin—marred his forehead. He had become an old man.

"Mike," His Honor said, smiling.

"Well, look at you!" Cohn said, taking a step forward and putting out his hand to shake His Honor's. "My goodness—*Sid Steiglitz!* Look at you! How the hell have you been!"

For the next two minutes they expressed mutual surprise and pleasure at seeing each other after such a long time, and each assured the other that he hadn't changed much, though each also knew the other was thinking that he had.

Cohn accepted His Honor's invitation to sit at the table with him.

"I thought you left the city or something," Cohn continued. "None of us ever heard from you again."

"No, no," His Honor said, quietly, shaking his head, smiling, "I'm still here, right where I always was." And he added: "I suppose I should have kept in touch but ... well ... "

"Ah—don't apologize. I understand. You look good, Sid, you look good. Put on a few pounds, I think—eh?"

"A few," His Honor said.

They both chuckled.

"I can see you don't have that problem," His Honor said.

"Oh, but I've had others! Right knee's not what it used to be—hurts like hell. Arthritis, they tell me. And a few other things," he added, hinting at unfortunate medical issues he preferred not to discuss.

As they ate they talked about old times at the courthouse, of the people they had known and worked with. His Honor learned of how a few had died (some of them much younger than himself), of others who had been promoted, of still others who had moved away. His Honor learned that a lot had changed in Cohn's life. Two years ago he had stopped presiding at the Criminal Court and been appointed to the Parole Board. He freely admitted that it had taken a little "canvassing" on his part, not the least part of which was urging "a friend" to say a few good words about his career and availability to the Governor. Still, as he had never been a man with many "connections," he had been surprised by the offer, and had jumped at it.

"I couldn't be happier," he said, as he set about devouring his meal: an egg salad on rye with a side order of coleslaw and a cup of coffee. "Let me tell you something, I should've gotten out of the courtroom years ago. Listening to all those shyster lawyers jabbering away at you all day eventually gets on anybody's nerves—as *you* know." He took a great bite of his sandwich and chewed away with a happy smile.

"How is it treating you?"

"Oh, it's alright. The hours are decent. Of course you don't make the decisions by yourself and sometimes we have disagreements, but on the whole we get along pretty well. It's kind of ironic that I met up with you, actually. A case came up the other day that I think you decided. Mario Trent. Ring a bell?"

His Honor shook his head, no.

"Ah, well. It *was* a long time ago. Twenty years, at least."

"So why is he up for parole now?"

"Oh, you know how it goes," Cohn said, chewing heavily from the last big bite of egg salad sandwich, then holding up a finger as though to excuse himself, to ask His Honor to be patient while he chewed thoroughly and swallowed. He took a sip of coffee, gulped hard, put down the cup, and continued, "Good behavior. Model prisoner—that sort of thing. Seems he turned himself all the way around. Became educated—became a minister of all things. Church of ... mmm ... something or other. Don't remember. Anyway, it's amazing what prison does to some people."

"Mario Trent ... Trent ..." His Honor spoke the name a few more times as he looked off into the distance, trying hard to recall the man, but unable to do so. Twenty years was such a long time. Except for a few truly exceptional cases, he couldn't remember most of those he had presided over. "What did I put him in for?"

At the question, Cohn, who had popped the last of his sandwich into his mouth, hesitated in his chewing. Only then did he realize he had raised the taboo subject of violent crime to someone who had suffered directly from it. Wishing to avoid causing pain to his old acquaintance, he quickly tried to think of something less touchy to talk about, though at the same time he understood that a sudden or ungraceful change in topics would only highlight the one he had broached. Therefore he replied with a cool albeit distracted forthrightness, "Oh, I think it was a homicide case. Anyway, don't get much of those cases. Usually it's just small-time stuff. And I don't think I'll be doing it much longer. I think I'll be retiring next year. Probably get out of New York. It's a wonder *you* didn't leave, Sid. How come?"

But His Honor, rather than answer the question, was looking into mid-air thoughtfully and said in an abstracted tone of voice, "Trent ... Trent ... Don't remember him." He turned his eyes back to Judge Cohn. "So he got out after doing twenty."

Cohn gave no reaction, nor made any gesture, that would indicate he had heard His Honor's remark. He took more of his coffee and asked, "So tell me, what have you been up all this time? Enjoying your retirement?"

"It's alright."

"Done any traveling or anything special?"

His Honor shook his head.

"And how's your wife?"

"She's good."

"Give her my regards when you see her. She probably won't remember me. I only met her a few times."

"Yes," His Honor said, indifferently, his eyes looking down thoughtfully, as he clearly was thinking about something; and then asked, "What was his sentence?"

"What?"

"That fellow Trent ... you said I was the one who sentenced him?"

"Well, yes, I *think* you were," Judge Cohn said, with the slightest trace of impatience in his voice, having tried, unsuccessfully, to get away from that subject. "I'm not a hundred percent sure. I only just got the case the other day and really didn't read it through carefully yet. I'd have to check it out." — All of which was a lie. Judge Cohn remembered every detail of the case, having studied it at some length, and having two days earlier made his decision with regard to it: parole on good behavior.

"What did I sentence him for?"

"He was sentenced to twenty-five to life."

Twenty-five to life. His Honor recalled himself handing down that sentence time and time again, and somehow he knew that he had given the sentence in this case also.

"What were the details of the case?" His Honor asked.

"Sid, I really don't know. As I say, I haven't had a chance to look over the case yet. Let me tell you something, my memory's not so good these days: I read something and I forget it two minutes later. But then again everything's falling apart on me. I had a physical two months ago and my doctor did some sort of test on the arteries and told me they have obstructions. I'm probably minutes away from a stroke or heart attack."

"I'm sorry to hear it. What are you doing to take care of that?"

"Oh, he gave me a few things to take, which I'm taking. By the way, my wife and I might go down to Florida. Found a little place down there." He was going to add another reason for his moving to Florida, namely, to be close to his two sons who lived there, but this time he caught himself in time and did not mention his children.

"Sure you'll know what to do with yourself all day?" His Honor asked, finally becoming casual again. "Retirement's not all it's cracked up to be unless you have something to do."

"Oh, believe me, I know *exactly* what I'll be doing: sitting on the beach or going fishing."

His honor smiled quietly and nodded, then he watched as his old colleague looked at his watch, and assumed the impatient air of a man who realizes he's running late. He called over the waiter and asked for his check, which was handed to him. He took out his money and placed it on the table along with a tip, then pushed back his chair, saying, "Well, I got to go. Sid, it was *really* good seeing you again!"

"Can I ask you something?"

"Sure—what?"

"This Tent guy you're going to review ... where is he now?"

"Rikers. Why?"

"Just curious. When do you think you'll be deciding the case?"

"Ohhh ... a few weeks."

"Gonna let him out?"

"Listen, Sid," Cohn said, only now deciding to drop somewhat his facade of casuality, "I know how you must feel about these things ... but this man turned his life around. From everything I know about the case, he's not the same man you sentenced."

"You think people change that much?"

"Maybe not. But maybe sometimes—in rare cases—yes."

"And he's the 'rare' case?"

"Maybe."

"But then ... maybe not. Right?"

Cohn only shook his head and smiled in a way that was both amused and regretful of His Honor's tenacity, and said:

"Once a lawyer always a lawyer, eh Sid?"

His Honor smiled and shook his head. He watched his old colleague leave the restaurant. He knew he would never see him again. He smiled to himself to think that they hadn't even bothered to tell each other they would keep in touch. They were too old, had lived too long, knew life too well to bother speaking such empty words.

His Honor had come to spend hours on his computer reading the news or looking up archived legal cases that piqued his interest. He had discovered a New York State site providing resources for investigating ongoing and past cases. It enabled him to look up pending parole cases and the decisions made about them; and, what had become most important of all for him, the release dates.

One day several weeks after his having run into his old colleague at the deli, His Honor, who was naturally a late sleeper, got up an hour before dawn. It was a cold October morning and he had no sooner dressed than he put on one of his long dark overcoats, tied a scarf around his neck, and headed out the door.

The city bus that takes visitors to Rikers Island is the Q101R. From Queensboro Plaza it works its way north through Queens. Many of the women passengers it picks up are on their way to the prison to visit boyfriends, husbands, or sons incarcerated there. Those who are visiting boyfriends have put some effort into looking "good" for their men. Their notion of looking good has in many cases meant squeezing into jeans too small for their fat bellies and posteriors, or wearing abundant gold-plated jewelry (including grotesque nose piercings), or styling their hair into stiff curls as though they've been epoxied into place. On the whole they are an unpretty sight; their features thick, coarse, unpleasant; their dull eyes reflecting yet duller minds. Their speech is slurred with inarticulateness. It is as loud as it is vapid; rudimentary in vocabulary; peppered with obscenities as though four-letter words were a matter of course. They are, these women, the daughters of New York City's vast underclass, and the mothers who will ensure its continuation. They are the repulsive-bewildering end result of sixty years of coddling, excuse-making, and political whoredom, which for the sake of looking fashionably philanthropic, or the sake of a few more votes, winked hard at Tartarean stupidity, saying, in effect (if not in verbatim actuality), "Nothing at all wrong with your mule-headed benightedness, my friends, nothing at all! It's just another way—just as good, just as legitimate, just as beautiful as any other! Never let anyone tell you otherwise!"—and so was left to follow its own downward course, reaching this lowest, most abysmal level, beyond which it cannot go and remain sociable and *outside* a prison.

His Honor sat on the bus the odd, old man out. He sat there solitary and silent. He was both fascinated and disgusted by what he saw and heard. Here was a New York he had heard about but never seen for himself. He realized how isolated his life had been. He had lived it in his doorman-protected building, or in his high-rent Brooklyn neighborhood, or at his vacation home upstate, or at the courthouse where he donned an impressive robe and was "Yessirred" and "Nosirred" and made way for and kowtowed to as an important, powerful functionary of the State. He had gone from one nice, protected place to another. But here! Here was the real thing, the real city; the bowels of it, the down and dirty of it; which knew nothing of proper procedures and imposing robes—and was, if anything, inclined to scoff at them!

His Honor sat just behind the driver and watched as this underclass of New York fill the bus at every stop. Some of them went right by the driver without paying the fare, and when he tried to stop them, calling out to them, "Hey, you have to pay!" they would return, "I'll pay you when I get off!"—in a gruff, angry, shouting voice, and with expressions of deadly threat as though they were quite prepared to punch him in the face if he continued to pester them. Of course they had no intention of paying. Nor did the driver press the issue, though it was part of his job to make sure riders paid the fare. But he had long ago learned his lesson about too dutifully looking out for the profits of the MTA: knives, and once a gun, had been pulled on him. His employers were well aware of the danger he and other drivers were exposed to because they had posted a large sign by his seat warning that "assaulting a bus operator is a felony punishable by up to 7 years in prison." But what are words to brutish minds? Nothing more than the most effete and ineffectual intimidation. And so the driver had learned to hold his peace. The only thing he cared about was going home at the end of the day to his family. It was not worth getting shot or stabbed over a $2.25 fare—as he would have told his boss if he were ever called to account for his misfeasance.

The bus worked its way to the northernmost part of Queens, finally reaching an area where a sewage treatment plant could be seen to the left and, to the right, the expansive flatness and terminals of LaGuardia Airport. Airliners taking off or coming in for landings filled the air with the thunder of their engines. The bus rolled forward onto the Rikers Island Bridge, and when it had reached a point some halfway across one could see clearly enough the island ahead: the starkly flat terrain with clusters of squat white buildings surrounded by high fencing.

The bus stopped before the Visitors Center. The bus driver opened doors and the passengers began piling out. As most of them had been here before—some had been coming here for months or years—they knew the routine well enough: their bags and persons would be searched for drugs or weapons, then they would have to leave their belongings in lockers, and the only jewelry they would be allowed to wear would be engagement or wedding rings, perhaps a necklace—and of course a nose ring, if they had one. Afterwards they would be divided into two lines so that a drug-sniffing dog could be guided along their persons, pushing his snout here and there among their legs or arms, eagerly wagging his tail in the hope of gaining the least whiff of marijuana or cocaine. One of the officers in charge of this procedure always started it the same way, holding the dog's leash wrapped twice around his hand and announcing in a half-humorous voice: "Okay, listen up, people! The dog's name is Max and he works here with the rest of us, and he's going to find out if you're hiding anything you shouldn't be bringing in here. If you are, it's not your lucky day! We've got plenty of vacancies here at Rikers!" Only when the visitors were cleared of this suspicion would they enter a Corrections Department bus that would take them to one of the island's ten jail facilities where they might have to wait hours more before seeing the person they had come to visit.

But His Honor did not have to endure any of these inconveniences. When he got off the bus he didn't, like the others, wend his way along the fenced-in walkway leading to the Visitors Center; instead, he remained outside, on the sidewalk abutting the road where the bus stopped.

If it had been later in the morning there would have been people already waiting to board the bus for its return trip back to the city, but this had been the first bus of the day and was scheduled to remain here an extra measure of time to take the first passengers from the island. The driver shut down the en-

gine and produced a copy of the *Post*, which he spread out before him on his steering wheel. He idly turned a few pages,
now and then leaning into them to read something or look at a
picture when he noticed that someone—His Honor—hadn't gone
into the Visitors Center but was still on the curb, idly striding
back and forth there, his hands thrust deep into the pockets of
his coat. He opened the doors of the bus and said in accented
English:

"I don't leave for half hour!"

His Honor nodded. "Okay," he said.

The driver looked at him curiously, then shrugged and
closed the doors to keep out the chilly air, thinking, "Some people are strange."

Among the first passengers back into the city every day on
the returning bus were those who had worked the night shift at
the prison. Among these were the guards: big, robust men in
uniform. They came walking toward the bus with the big man's
hard-stepping waddle. Others were janitors or cooks or trades-
men who had worked through the night in one of the buildings.
His Honor would watch them approach and sometimes give a
nod of hello and a slight smile as they passed him. The bus
had been sitting silent for twenty minutes, but now the driver
turned on the engine, which revved into life and settled down to
a deep purr.

From the Visitors Center emerged one of the guards in full
uniform along with a civilian wearing a brown jacket, a wool
cap, and carrying a knapsack. The guard walked beside him,
escorting him out, as he did so pointing to the bus beyond the
fence, then turning around and going back inside the facility.
The man carrying the knapsack made his way through the
fenced walkway toward the waiting bus.

His Honor had a hunch. He went up to meet the man.

"Excuse me, are you Mario Trent?"

"Yeah," the man said. "Who're you?"

"My name's Sidney Steiglitz. I was the judge who tried
your case."

"Uh, huh," the man said, with an indifferent nod, for the
information almost didn't mean anything to him: his trial had
been so long ago—from such a different time in his life—that he
barely remembered it. He watched the old man in front of him

raise one side of his coat, his hand still in his pocket, and in the same instant that he recognized a pistol barrel beneath the coat's fabric the first shot rang out.

It was followed by two more.

Mario Trent dropped his knapsack and staggered back a few feet exclaiming, "Hey, hey, hey!" He fell to the ground, squirming, clawing at the cold cement with desperate fingers, shocked by the pain in his chest, trying to raise himself up but unable to do so because suddenly weak. He gasped for breath; the panic of incipient death seized him. Wide- and wild-eyed he watched the old man—this crazy old man whom he didn't know from Adam—come over to him, stand over him, and forthrightly point a pistol at his head. His Honor pulled the trigger three more times. Each bullet tore apart the face and skull and brains of the just-released murderer, whose body jumped at the first and second shot, and which received the third as indifferently as a sack of dirt.

Everyone in the nearby waiting bus looked out the windows in the direction of the gunfire. The off-duty guards were the first to react, though gingerly at first, since they didn't know whom or what they were dealing with. Only when they saw that the old man had dropped his gun—was immobile and somehow spent as he stood over the body at his feet—did they rush toward him, converge on him, tackle him to the ground.

They threw His Honor down to the concrete hard, without regard to the fragility of his age. All of them were shouting, "On the ground—on the ground!"—though he already was on the ground. His Honor moaned and grunted with the pain of several bulky knees pressed into his back to keep him pinned down, though he had no intention of resisting. He said nothing. These big, strong, young men who were holding him down, crushing him, slapping handcuffs on his wrists: what was the point of explaining anything to them? They had no idea what they had just seen. They didn't understand. Even when, one day, they learned all the details, they *still* would not, really, understand. And so the old man lay there prostrate and subdued, one side of his face pressed against the grating concrete, he a mere nothing, mere putty, in the forceful hands of the big strong men who had overcome him.

In that posture, his eyes open, staring straight ahead at the sideways world, he thought of his wife. What a shock it would be when she learned what he had done! He knew as surely as he was lying there that he had, in the short term at least, added to the burden of pain she carried through life. But in the long term and ultimately he had given her a reason to be proud and in some measure comforted. In the long term, and in a way that seemed to him suddenly the pinnacle of his career, he had served Justice. As yet more correctional officers came running out of the surrounding buildings and crowded round him, and he lay on the concrete, he was aware that his heart was suddenly, wonderfully light, joyous as it had not been in years. He thought of his daughter and grandchildren. His lips formed the words, "For you ..."

SEPTEMBER

Miguel Herrera's journey had taken him from a dusty village fifty miles outside Mexico City across a dirty, shallow stretch of the Rio Grande River and into Texas; then eastward across the green, hot, humid southeastern United States; then upward and yet more eastward through the rolling Carolinas and into Virginia; and from there up into the flatlands of Maryland and the rich, farm-checkered state of Pennsylvania; after which he had been transported, via throughways and turnpikes, across northern New Jersey to a great blue bridge, the mighty Verrazano, and then, finally, to his destination, New York City. Through the nearly two weeks of that journey he had walked for miles and had ridden in vans with darkened windows or in the backs of pickup trucks covered over with tarpaulins. There had always been the worried anticipation of the police stopping the vehicle in which he was being transported and finding him out. But luck had been on his side; he had reached his destination, the lower middle-class neighborhood of Jackson Heights, Queens. All he had to his name were the clothes he was wearing, a flimsy wallet containing thirty dollars, and a scrap of paper with the telephone number, address, and name of the man who was supposed to help him. He found the address soon enough, climbed the dark stairwells to the third floor, and knocked at the door. He found himself standing face-to-face with a gaunt, ill-shaven Mexican to whom he announced the name of the person he had come to see, only to learn that he had moved out three weeks earlier and had left no forwarding address. On hearing this the blood went out of Miguel's face. He felt like crying. He was tired and hungry and dirty, and since the day he had left home he had lived in a haze of uncertainty, and now it seemed to him that just when he had thought his troubles were largely over they had begun all over again. He didn't know what he was going to do or where to go. He

couldn't survive on the streets—not *these* streets, about which
he knew nothing, and which, as he had already seen, seethed
with fierce indifference to any one atom of a human creature.
He pleaded with the man before him for assistance. Could he
just stay here for a night or two? He had nowhere else to go.
He had no other contacts and didn't know anyone. He promised
that he would be no trouble; none at all. And he would pay—
not now, of course, because he only had thirty dollars left, but
the minute he started working and had some money, any
money, he would gladly pay it!

Fortunately for Miguel the man before him was old enough
to see the boy for the immature, clueless, and perhaps pathetic
dupe he had been, and after satisfying himself through a few
brief questions that Miguel really didn't have any other options,
he rubbed his rough, bony hands across his face and said, "Wait
here a minute." He closed the door on the boy, who leaned his
head forward and heard voices from within. One of them was
the "old" man who had opened the door for him, the others were
also men. From the other side of the door he caught a few
stray words and phrases, in tone some of them considerate or
pleading while others were more animated, negative, protesting:

"One night ... Pedro's friend ... nowhere else to go ... rent ...
no room! ... where? ... He's just a kid ... could sleep on the floor .
.. not here! ... nowhere else to go ... too many of us as it is! ...
it's just for a few nights ... then *you* do it! ... I don't want it ..."

Then there was silence for several seconds, and the door
opened once again to the old man who said:

"Alright. We can help you out. But just for a night or two!
Understand?"

Miguel nodded and gratefully, uncertainly stepped inside.

Four men already lived here in this small one-bedroom
apartment. Three of them happened to be there at this moment. One was only a few years older than Miguel himself,
while the other two were both, as Miguel thought, "old"—in
their thirties. The first thing the boy noticed in the place was
the faint, unpleasant, commingled odor of cigarette smoke and
something that had been fried; then he looked around at the
general sloppiness of the place. Jackets and shirts hung from
doorknobs, pants and sweaters draped over chairs, and the two
end tables on either side of a black, flimsy metal-framed futon

couch were littered with crunched-up food wrappers and butt-littered ashtrays. The apartment had parquet wood floors, but they hadn't been cared for and were scuffed everywhere. A rug covering the central part of the living room was smudged and stained from dirty shoes and food and drink that had been spilled on it over the years. On the walls hung a few cheap, framed pictures, the most prominent of which, above the well-worn couch, was a picture of Jesus, his aureole iridescently metallic-colored and his holographic eyes closing and opening if you changed your angle of view.

Two of the men ordinarily slept in the living room, on the futon that was flattened into a bed, while another two had the bedroom. The man who had opened the door to the boy brought out for him a worn quilt and a pillow and said he could stay in the living room, in the corner. Miguel watched the man lay out those things for him, and was grateful.

Later, after he had showered and been given something to eat—cold rice and beans, bread and butter, and a cup of coffee—he told the men about himself, where he had come from, how and in what company he had traveled to New York City, and of his intention of finding work. He assured them that he would do anything—anything at all, no matter how hard or how little it paid; and he assured them that as soon as he made even a few dollars, he would be happy to pay them. And because the boy's poverty and enterprise in coming alone to the United States was so much a reflection of their own histories, the men relented in their initial disinclination to help him, though his presence would be another inconvenience in their lives.

"You want to work in a vegetable market?" one of the men asked him.

"Sure!" the boy said, eagerly; and he repeated that he would work anywhere, for almost any wage, because he was eager to establish himself.

"I'll see what I can do," the man told him. "But you'll be working for Russians, or Koreans. You never worked for them before. It's not easy—they're pretty tough."

"I'm tougher," the boy answered, with a confidence that was rare with him, and which he assumed only because he felt he had to make an impression of worldly-wisdom on his older, jaded hosts. Besides, he couldn't conceive of not holding out at a job at least for a while, no matter how unpleasant it was.

These men filled him in on how it was to work in this country. They told him that he mustn't expect to get a decent job anywhere without a Social Security number, and when the boy asked what that was they shook their heads and glanced at one another with eyes that seemed to say, "This one really *does* come from the sticks!" They explained to him that it was a number all Americans had so that their government could know exactly where they were, what they were doing, and how much money they made. And you needed it for everything legitimate: from getting a job to renting an apartment to buying a car. There were a few ways to get around having one but they were always only temporary. You could just make one up—just invent the numbers off the top of your head—and hope the prospective employer didn't ask to see any substantiating "card." A lot of times they didn't bother to ask for it; they knew very well you were here illegally and were willing to take a chance on hiring you because the lure of cheap labor, of making more money for themselves, was greater than the fear of government reprisal. And even if the government discovered what they were doing, they always had the excuse that they didn't know you had lied—though of course they had known it from the first—and the extent of prosecution would be a manageable fine.

The other way was to obtain a false Social Security card.

"There's someone who makes them down the street," one of the men told Miguel, laughing a little. "He's Chinese. He makes them for twenty bucks. Prints them up in the back of his store, I guess. You wanna see?" And without waiting for the boy's response he reached into his back pocket, took out his wallet, and slipped out his false Social Security card. It looked legitimate enough, having the man's name, an official United States seal, and perfectly laminated. "I suggest you get one as soon as you can."

That evening he listened to the men relate the experiences they had had in this crowded, dirty, strange, ever-bustling city. They made it sound like a lawless place full of crazy people, and sometimes dangerous. They warned him about taking the subway trains late at night. "Make sure you're in a car with other people." It would be better, they told him, if he could find work in Queens so that he wouldn't have to go into Manhattan or

Brooklyn, since that only took more time. As for finding a place to live, it would be impossible for him to find a place of his own on any salary he could expect to make; besides, all the landlords of the nice places, the good buildings, would expect him to have credentials such as a stable work history and a good credit rating. "What's that?" the boy asked; and heard the explanation with a sinking sense of the obstacles before him. His only hope, the men told him, was to find a group of guys he could become roommates with. If he looked in the Spanish paper he would probably find ads in the back in which people were looking for roommates; or he could ask around, once he made acquaintances. But even then he mustn't expect much—at most a bedroom of his own, which would probably take up a sizeable portion of his pay. "Maybe you could get something out by Jamaica," one of the men told him; and he laughed, showing a gap where one of his incisors had rotted away.

The boy didn't see the humor in the suggestion till he was informed that it was a part of Queens that he most certainly wouldn't want to live in, since it wasn't safe.

A few days later he was working at a greengrocer on 82nd Street in Jackson Heights. The Korean owners of the store had already hired one illegal Mexican. His name was Antonio and he came from Chihuahua. He had been in the United States for almost a year and knew a lot of people and promised to help Miguel get a place to live. In the morning they would unload trucks bearing crates and cartons of refrigerated produce, which would have to be unpacked, cleaned, and laid out in bins running around the outside wall of the store under a green awning that read, "Lucky Fruit Farm." They had to refill the plastic bag dispensers, clean the sidewalks, and pick up after the steady stream of customers who rudely made a mess by dropping fruit or vegetables and not bothering to pick them up. Especially notorious in this regard were the old ladies, who would sort through piles of apples and oranges and onions in a foolish search for some perfect piece. There was never a minute when Antonio and Miguel weren't busy with something, and the latter wondered how the former had managed to keep up the place so long by himself. At the end of the day the boy was so tired that he only wanted to eat and go to sleep. On his one day off, Sunday, he would look for a place to live.

He found his new accommodations in a house whose Chinese owner had converted it into a kind of hotel. The house was located in a run-down residential neighborhood on a street a few blocks away from the Van Wyck Expressway, and ironically enough not all that far away from Jamaica. Abandoned lots bordered either side of the house, and a tall wooden fence, painted green, surrounded it. Inside, partitions reaching not quite to the ceiling sectioned off the living, dining, and two bedrooms, each section able to accommodate a narrow cot and a night table. Including Miguel, fifteen men lived there, five of them Mexican, four of them Chinese, two Pakistani; all of them illegal; each group pretty much keeping to itself and barely tolerating the others. They all had to share the kitchen and bathroom, and both those spaces were notoriously dirty. Most of the arguments that broke out among the men were about how this or that one was a pig who wouldn't clean up after himself, or was cooking food that was stinking up the whole place. Even so the rent was $250 a month—but where else could you live in New York City for that kind of money? Each of the men had the same idea: putting up with the crowded dirtiness till he had saved enough money to move into better quarters.

"Just hope they don't raid the place," one of Miguel's housemates, José, told him. He was twenty-five years old, came from a dirt-poor town on the Mexican side of the Texas border, and had been in New York for three years, and here in the house for six months. "It's illegal, you know, what this guy is doing," he explained to the boy, referring to the man who owned the house and was charging them all rent. "He only gets away with it because there aren't any neighbors around. I was living at another place like this where the neighbors called the cops and they closed it down and we got chased out. But this place is in the middle of nowhere—at least, for New York. And there's a fence. That's probably why he put it up—so people can't see what's going on. I'll bet he's got a few places like this." José stopped as though to consider the meaning of his own observation, then shook his head a little and whistled with an air of amazement before saying, "You got to hand it to him: he must be *raking* in the cash!"

Miguel listened and shook his head in wonder, impressed at the enterprise (even if it was illegal) by which people in this country found ways to make a lot of money. He wondered that anyone could be so brazen. He did not understand that in a city where an apple might cost a dollar it was easy even for decent men to become obsessed with money-making.

One day at the end of Miguel's shift at "Lucky Fruit Farm" the owner called him aside and said he had some "bad news." He explained that he couldn't "keep" him any more owing to "expenses," and with an air of blithely feigned regret said that Miguel needn't come back tomorrow. He handed the boy cash for the few days he had worked that week, and wished him good luck.

Miguel had never thought that "Lucky Fruit Farm" would be the last place he would work, but he had hoped to be there long enough to accumulate a comfortable savings. So far he had only been able to save two hundred dollars. Fortunately he had recently paid his month's rent, but he knew he would be short for the next month when it came and therefore he had to scramble for another job. He asked his housemates if they knew a place where he might work. None of them did. He wasted no time in trying to find work for himself. He stopped in to every fruit stand, restaurant, and bodega he could discover to ask for a job. His enterprise paid off. He became a busboy at a Mexican restaurant called "Aztec Fiesta." With the exception of the owner and one of the cooks, everyone else on the staff was illegal. Miguel almost felt at home here among all his countrymen; at least he could spend the whole day at work and not have to speak a word of English, that impossible language the very sound of which intimidated him.

In the next eight months the boy did two things to help ensure his success in the United States: he obtained a false Social Security card, and made a conscious effort to learn English. His attempts to teach himself the language cost hours of solitary frustration every night as he tried to absorb words and phrases from a paperback Spanish-English dictionary; writing them out in a notebook; always keeping his eyes and ears open for new words, and looking them up. But oh!—the words! They seemed never to end! What, were there millions of them? When he heard Americans speak it seemed to him that the words they gabbled were just the ones he hadn't learned. Several times out of sheer disgust with his lack of progress he gave up learning altogether and resigned himself to eternal but blissful ignorance of this impossibly complicated language. But a day would pass, and he would find that he really did understand some things, and both pride in himself and resolve to improve would once again take hold of him, and he would return to his nightly studies.

He also found another place to live, this time a basement apartment in Elmhurst, which he shared with just one other man, a legal immigrant from Panama. The half of the rent he paid consumed most of his money, but it was such a pleasure to come home to privacy, to quiet, to a real, full living room and a clean bathroom and kitchen, that he accepted the compromise; and despite this expense his close economy enabled him still to put a little money aside. He calculated that if he could stick it out at his job for a couple of years or so he could build up a respectable nest egg and be relatively secure. But once again it seemed that his plans were to be undermined by circumstances beyond his control. Citing a drop in business, the owner of the restaurant announced that he had to reduce his staff, and Miguel was again laid off.

One of the waiters, Louis, with whom Miguel had always been on good terms, called him over when he learned about this. "Listen," he said, "I might be able to get something for you. It's a restaurant in the city—you know, Manhattan; a really *nice* place," he said, emphasizing the word to the degree that his eyes widened, rolled a little, and he almost frowned as though human speech could not do justice to the grandness of what he was alluding to. "I heard through a friend they're looking for a few busboys, so I'll see what I can do for you. You'll need a resume, though. Do you have one?"

Miguel didn't even know what a resume was.

The waiter laughed a little. "Don't worry, I can do that for you," he said. "What about a Social Security number? Do you have that?" he asked, and in such a way—with a half-curious, half-expectant smile—that made it clear he wasn't necessarily referring to something legal.

Miguel nodded, smiling, understanding, and rather proud of himself for having spent the money on the card.

"Okay," the waiter said. "I'll call my friend to see if the job is still open."

It was, to the boy's grateful relief, and an interview for him was scheduled. Louis interrogated him for ten minutes to get information for the resume, writing things down on a sheet of paper, often shaking his head negatively, disapprovingly, and murmuring to himself as he scratched away, "No, no, you don't want to say that ... we'll say this!"—evidently making things up as he went along. When he had finished he had expanded Miguel's work history by five years and had articulated each job into more "duties" and "responsibilities" than the boy had in fact done. Louis explained to him that in America you had to make yourself look good on paper, even if you had to "stretch" the truth a little. "That's just the way they do it here."

"But what if they ask me about it?"

"They will ask you about it. So you just tell them what's on your resume."

"You mean lie about it?"

Louis looked at the boy in a way that would have been disdainful if it hadn't been equally sympathetic.

"Miguel, listen to me. This is New York. If you don't lie when you go for a job, you don't get the job. Remember that."

"But what if they check?"

"If they check, you don't get it, that's all. But at least you give yourself a chance. Otherwise, you have *no* chance. Understand? There's nothing wrong with trying to help yourself get ahead a little."

The boy nodded, accepting the reasoning of this older fellow who seemed to know about the way things worked in this city.

The next day Miguel received his resume from Louis, who handed him a manila envelope, saying, "I made ten copies for you." Miguel pulled them out. He was at once impressed at how well his resume had been laid out and printed. It seemed to him a weighty, official, impressive document.

Louis went on to give him a last piece of advice. "Wear your best clothes for the interview. Buy new clothes if you have to. Make sure you look your best. It's a high-class place—one of the best in New York. If you can get in there, you'll have it made—at least for a while," he added, referring, as the boy knew, to the issue of his illegality.

Miguel took the waiter's advice about his wardrobe. He had a fairly new pair of pants but he bought a new shirt and tie. He polished his shoes to a high gloss.

When he arrived the next day for his interview, he got off the appropriate stop on the subway, walked along the long platform, then negotiated his way through an underground mall to take one of several side-by-side escalators to street level. He stepped outside and crossed the street to a plaza with cement benches ranged around a water fountain in the midst of which rose the bronze sculpture of an abstract sphere glinting in the sunlight. And just beyond it rose the great buildings: the two gigantic skyscrapers that dwarfed him and everyone and everything else around them. Astonishing! He gulped hard in the face of things so sublimely huge, and continued on.

Thirty feet away from the revolving doors he stopped again, astonished, intimidated, by the size of the tower he was about to enter. He bent his head back, and looked upward. How huge this building was! Its immensity blotted out the world around him. Its exterior grillwork of strict straight lines narrowed in perspective as it rose in one sheer thrust to the high undersurface of the sky itself. Even what seemed to be top of the building was not really so; was rather an illusion owing to his vantage point close to the base. In fact the uppermost floors of this structure rose up still further—wonder-fully, breathtakingly further—to a region where only eagles or airplanes soared.

Miguel watched as a stream of people who were mostly young (very few were in their fifties or sixties) entered through those doors on their way to work. He marveled at how well-dressed most of them were: the men in jackets and ties, the women in knee-length skirts or pants suits; the tenor of their clothing tending toward the formal, the conscientiously-prepared, the "serious." They entered the building with an indifferent, sometimes morning-tired air that was itself intimidating, for it showed how this was all routine for them, a marvelousness they had known so long, experienced so often, that it no longer made any impression on them. But to him it was all new, and it astonished and amazed and pleased him immensely. He recalled his village with its dusty streets, ramshackle homes, and dilapidated shops. Could anyone there have any inkling of *this?* Could they even *imagine* it? No—no. And of them all, of all those hundreds who lived there, including the town braggarts who liked to think they knew and had done so much;—of them all only *he* was really here! Just then he was proud of himself for having come to the United States. And how much prouder he would be if he was able to work in such a place!

Well, he would go through with it; he would try to get the job. Bucking up his courage he continued on, pushing through the revolving doors and entering the lobby. Even this was grand. It was spacious and bright and clean, its floor and walls lined with a bright, polished marble, and surrounded, one story above, with a mezzanine just beneath which hung colorful flags. With some trepidation the boy walked up to the front desk and, pulling out a piece of paper, read the name of the restaurant and the person he had come to see.

But the boy only realized how accurately he had been told about the classiness of this restaurant when he got off the elevator and entered it. He had no sooner passed through the glass door—under an emblem of a yellow sun shooting golden rays against blue background—than he entered a space characterized by exquisite cleanliness, fine newness, and expansive sumptuosity. And yet it was also intimate, what with the many linen-covered tables either lined singly against the windows or generously spaced out among the floor. His first thought was: "This is for rich people."

He inquired for the manager whom he was supposed to meet and was escorted to an office. The door was open and the manager had been sitting at his desk, at a computer, going over something. "Come in, please," he said, and nodding to the chair before him: "Take a seat."

It seemed to the boy that the manager also was a rich man. He was dressed impeccably. The fabric of his suit shimmered in fine-spun smoothness and against his white shirt a silk red tie was held in place with a diamond-studded gold clip. His face was ruddy, fresh and smooth, his hair severely combed back, and he smelled of fine cologne. Everything about him bespoke polished authority and an acquaintance with the best things in life. "He's so, so rich," the boy thought, as he noticed the gold watch peeping out from under the man's left sleeve. He thought to himself that if he had a watch like that back in Mexico he would have been the wonder and envy of his town. The thought that this American was rich made the boy respect him the more even as it plunged him into deeper doubt about his own appearance. Remembering that his shoes, though polished, were old, he tucked his feet far back under his chair, to hide them.

"Did you bring a resume, by the way?" the manager asked.

"Yes," the boy said, and reached into his shirt pocket and brought out the paper, which he had folded into quarters.

The manager smiled a little tightly and at once Miguel knew he had done something wrong—but he wasn't sure what. He watched the American unfold the paper and look over the experience detailed there. And as, anxiously and hopefully, he watched, the boy wondered why such things were necessary at all. Why was it necessary to go through the trouble of writing things down and printing them in such a specific way when he could speak it all out in a single minute? Why all this fuss and formality about being hired? It wasn't as though he were applying for an important or complicated job; he just wanted to be a busboy; and anyone could see that he could do the work. Why did everything in the United States have to be so regimented, so strict, have so many ridiculous rules and customs, about the most basic and commonsensical of things?

"From Mexico?" the manager asked, looking up from the resume.

"Yes, sir," Miguel said.

"Where?"

"Galeana."

The manager smiled and shook his head a little; he didn't know where that was. "How long have you been here?" he asked.

"Six years," Miguel lied. He didn't like telling the lie; he knew it was wrong; he felt guilty about it; but Louis had told him to say it, and so he had said it. He wondered if the American believed him.

"And you live"—turning his eyes back to the resume—"in Queens?"

Miguel nodded.

"You were a busboy at Aztec Fiesta? You were there for three years?"

"Yes, sir," Miguel lied.

"What was your salary at the last place?"

"What?" he asked, not sure of the English words.

"How much did they pay you where you worked."

"Oh. Five dollars."

"Five dollars an hour ... ?"—the American, almost despite himself, let out a disdainful breath, then looked at the boy for the first time with some indulgence before murmuring in a good-natured voice, "You should've asked for a raise."

Miguel smiled—not at the remark, which he wasn't sure he understood, but in response to the man's manner, which seemed suddenly kindly, and for which he was grateful.

The manager considered. He kept looking at the boy's sparse resume a little despairingly but also with a faint smile of amused indulgence. He felt himself confronted by a moral dilemma, for he suspected that the boy was illegal. This wasn't the first time an illegal immigrant had appealed to him for work, and in the past, in order to ensure he wasn't being duped, he had insisted on proper documentation: not only a Social Security card (the fakes were hard to spot these days) but also birth and academic certificates. Invariably the applicants never came back. He was sure the boy was illegal and was on the verge of interrogating him more fully about his provenance when, looking up into the boy's waiting, eager, innocent face, he felt a sudden surge of pity. The manager wasn't an especially imaginative man, but he was always sensible of his good fortune in life and of how others were not so lucky. In hiring the boy he would be breaking the law but in turning him away he would be only making what was undoubtedly an already tough life a little tougher. He thought too of how the poor kid had been working for five dollars an hour—five lousy bucks for breaking his back and jumping at the least word of the cheap bastard who hadn't blinked an eye at taking advantage of him—and his pity increased along with a sense of his moral dilemma. He let out a silent, resigned breath as he glanced up at the boy, and despite his better judgment he said to himself, "Ah, to hell with it! If it's a phony number I'm not the one who'll get in trouble." Aloud he said:

"Alright, Miguel. I think we could use you. Do you think you could start on Monday?"

"Oh, yes! Yes!" the boy said, himself sitting bolt upright, the joy flashing in his eyes.

"We'll put you on the second shift. Would that be alright?"

The boy nodded; overjoyed.

"It's from two to ten—ten at night, understand?"

Miguel nodded, eagerly.

"Yes, understand!" he said, smiling widely, shaking his head. "Thank you, sir! Thank you!"

The manager smiled and leaned back a little with the air of a man who's hoping he's made the right choice. He noticed the boy was watching him keenly, waiting for him to get up or otherwise give some indication that the interview was over.

"Don't you want to know how much you're going to get paid?" the American asked.

Miguel, not sure of the question, shook his head and inclined it forward a little in an attitude that seemed to request a clarifying repetition of the statement; by way of response, he only shook his head a little uncertainly.

"I'll start you off at $12 an hour. Understand?"

"Yes, sir"—he replied, automatically. But in the next instant he became sensible of just how much more money he was going to be making. Quickly he did the math: $12 an hour x eight hours a day x five days a week ... why, that was over $400 a week! It was outrageous!—a fortune! And in a month it added up to ... $1,600? ... less? ... no, wait ... it was more! It would be almost $2,000! Miguel sat there suddenly rigid, almost afraid to move, to speak, as though some stray movement or word of his might break the spell, might reverse his incredible good luck.

"Alright, come with me," the manager said, getting up from behind his desk, "I'll show you around the restaurant and introduce you to a few people."

For the next fifteen minutes Miguel followed the American as a disciple follows his revered master, quietly, intently, heeding his every word, eager to please, to do the great one's bidding, to be worthy of having been selected. He was given a tour of the general layout of the restaurant. The boy marveled at its vastness, its elegance, how the tables were richly dressed with fine linen tablecloths, shimmering plates, glasses so clean they sparkled, and precisely-laid flatware immaculate with a mirror-like shine. As he was led about, the boy often glanced to the narrow, ceiling-high windows that gave out to breathless views of the city below and the countryside beyond. He marveled at the sight. It was like being atop a mountain; it was like flying close to the clouds. He wished he could have shown all this to his family and friends back home. He told himself he would buy a camera and send them pictures of it all.

The manager took the boy into the kitchen, and this was no less impressive than the restaurant itself. It was a vast space filled with sometimes huge appliances and counters of stainless steel so clean that it seemed downright antiseptic. Chefs and sous-chefs, wearing white aprons and high chef hats, stood behind their various counters prepping for the day: chopping vegetables, mixing batters, cracking eggs, slicing, coating, creating individual servings in small porcelain dishes. Now and then amid these sounds of scraping and cutting they called out to each other in good-humored, casual conversation. The manager walked Miguel through the kitchen and as he did so he greeted each member of the staff with quick but familiar "Hello, how are you!" or "How are you doing today!" He knew them all, was friendly with them all. With Miguel trailing behind him, he would mention to his employees how he wanted to introduce them to a new busboy. The chefs and sous-chefs would nod, smile, or perhaps raise a flour-whitened hand in a more expressive gesture of greeting, all welcoming him, telling him they were pleased to meet him.

Toward the back of the kitchen they came upon the pastry chef and to him also the manager introduced the new busboy.

"Eh, howahhya!" the pastry chef said, his Whitestone accent thick.

Miguel was amused to see that he was an enormous man, not only fat, which he certainly was, but also tall and strongly built. His face, round as the moon, had two chins beneath it, and his barrel chest bulged outward and became one with a protruding abdomen, no doubt the result of partaking too often of his flaky, creamy, sugary creations. But he seemed a likeable fellow, and of them all he was the only one who, after saying hello, gave the boy a further word of welcome by saying:

"Glad yah comin' abawd, Miguel. We needya back heah!"

"Help show him the ropes, okay, Phil?" the manager said.

"Shueh. No prawblem." And to Miguel: "Ya gonna do good, doan' worry!"

Miguel nodded and smiled and was immensely grateful for this encouragement.

The first day of work was full of hectic uncertainties, and if it hadn't been for several of the other busboys, who also spoke Spanish, Miguel would have been harried to desperation. Even as it was, he felt an intense pressure throughout the day to remember the layout of the restaurant and which tables were where, since waiters were continually calling out to him the numbers of those which needed to be cleared. He would hurry out to them carrying a collection tub into which the used articles were placed, and then reset the table with fresh linen, washed dishes and flatware, and generally make sure everything looked pristine for the next guests. He was also at the beck and call of the chefs and sous-chefs who would ask him to fetch them things in the huge, walk-in refrigerator at the back of the kitchen. Some of them, sometimes, when they were under pressure, seemed to think he was a personal resource and insisted that he help them. This did not irritate him because to his mind he was here for eight hours a day and whether he worked for this or that person would not add another minute to his time. This equanimity and easy complaisance made him instantly popular with the staff. He seemed to hit it off especially well with the pastry chef, Phil, who, no matter what he was in the middle of, found time to answer the boy's questions or show him where something was, often taking him there himself.

For all of the first day on the job Miguel often looked to the windows, to the grand views stretching for miles in all directions; always marveling at being up so high, as though perched in some mythical aerie overlooking the world. During his first few days he was sometimes uneasy to consider how high up he was, but soon he no longer gave the matter a second thought because he was busy with his work and also because everything about this environment inspired a sense of pleasant security. The floor beneath one's feet felt as solid as the earth itself ; the decor was bright, clean, restful to the eye; the people who worked here, and the guests who lunched or dined here, went about their duties or pleasures with an easy, indifferent confidence. One might *know* that one was a thousand feet in the air but it did not *feel* that way. Indeed one felt even more comfortable and secure here, where everything was ordered, refined, "professional" than on the loud, bustling, chanceful and therefore uncertain world of the city streets below.

The quickness with which the boy grew accustomed to working here made him feel proud. He felt like just another New Yorker who took for granted living out a large part of his life in the stratosphere of a tall skyscraper. A few times he fantasized about one of his brothers or sisters coming to New York and visiting him here. They were sure to be just as naively impressed as he had been. To their whispered exclamations of awe, he imagined himself telling them with an offhand, sophisticated shrug:

"Yes, it's a big building. The views are pretty good. So ... let me show you something else ..."

The first week flew by, and by the end of it he was comfortable that he knew everything there was to know: all the names of the people he worked with, the numbers and locations of the tables, the storage places of everything needed throughout the day, the personal preferences of the chefs and sous-chefs in the kitchen.

For some mysterious accounting reason the first check for new employees always took four weeks to come through. The first one he received would recompense him for two weeks, since employees were paid bimonthly. Miguel knew exactly how much his gross income would be, and the figure consistently astonished and delighted him. In the margins of the notebooks he used to learn English he would add and subtract numbers as he calculated and recalculated his income—smiling and sometimes licking his lips in that quiet, immensely satisfying game of plotting his future with a mathematically sumptuous accuracy. He knew exactly what he would do with that first big lump sum; he had it already apportioned out. First, of course, he would pay his share of the rent and utilities—he certainly wanted no problems on that front! Then he would send a goodly chunk of the money back home, perhaps as much as fifty or sixty dollars. Then he would buy a pair of new shoes, and perhaps another pair of pants. The rest he would save as the start of what would be in a year a comfortable nest egg.

He remembered how his mother had once told him that sometimes what seemed to be setbacks in life were actually blessings in disguise. He had never understood that observation till now. He reflected that if he hadn't gotten laid off from his last few jobs he never would have been led by a series of events (in retrospect they seemed to him inevitable) by which he had come into his present lucrative position.

When he considered how things had turned out for him he was so seized by a sense of joy and gratitude that he gave thanks to God.

One Monday as he came in for his shift he was approached by another busboy. His name was Hector and he came from Ecuador. He was twenty-six years old and was married and had a four-year-old daughter. He worked here full-time on the morning shift. A few times his and Miguel's shifts had overlapped and they had talked briefly and developed a casual friendship. Now Hector stopped him as they passed and said:

"Hey, Miguel, I need to ask you something. What are you doing tomorrow? I mean, what's your schedule?"

The boy shrugged and said, "Same as usual—two to ten."

"Wanted to ask you something. Would you be interested in working my shift tomorrow? I can't be here, my wife's making me go with her to see her family"—an expression of distaste passing over his features as he spoke, as though someone had shoved a piece of smelly cheese under his nose.

"Well, I don't know," Miguel said. "What's your shift?"

"Six to two," Hector said.

A part of Miguel quailed at the thought of working two shifts. He was often tired at the end of his own, and doing two, one after the other, would stretch even his endurance. But the thought of the extra income (again, he quickly calculated: Fifteen hours x $12 an hour ... $180!) decided him. He just couldn't pass up that much money. Besides, it was unlikely that he would ever be asked to do someone else's shift again, and so wasn't likely to have another opportunity to make so much money in one day. He agreed to do it, but expressed his doubt about whether he would be allowed to do so.

"Oh, don't worry about that," Hector said, clearly relieved at having found his replacement. "I'll talk to the boss. She'll approve it."

And so she did. And Miguel was as pleased to think he'd be working a long next day as Louis was disappointed to think he'd have to spend it with his wife's family.

Ordinarily Hector might have gotten the time off merely by asking for it, but no one could be spared on that particular day because the restaurant was hosting a "big" conference for a client who was expecting two hundred guests. Hector suggested to Miguel that he get in a half hour earlier than usual. The boy nodded and assured Hector he would do so. "Another six dollars," he said to himself, since he worked by the hour and used a punch clock to track his time.

The next day, a Tuesday, broke with the kind of cool, clean, autumn weather that in New York always seems so much more brilliant and invigorating than anywhere else, coming, as it does, after a summer of oppressively humid heat. The effect that this annual change has on the New Yorker is immediate and visceral. It transforms him into another, better, more vigorous creature. The cold clean air turns his face ruddy, glowing, less unlovely. It energizes his animal being: a spring enters into his step, which had merely trudged over endless sidewalks, and a hardier beat quickens his pulse. He raises his eyes to the sky scrubbed clean by northern winds, and, amid all that new, fresh, cool brightness, thinks that perhaps New York is not such a bad place after all. He may even feel—as he has not felt for a year—that there are grand things in store for him: the fulfillment of some long-held ambition, or even the magic of a new romance. But as is usually the case with euphoric states of mind, this one too is temporary. It may last for a few hours or a few days, but eventually it will subside, and even magnificent days such as this one will be taken for granted—lost, unseen, unheeded beneath the oppressive, daily inconveniences and irritations of city life.

To Miguel the gorgeous day reflected and added to his soaring spirits. As he made his way toward the revolving doors of the great building in which he worked, he gave a final glance at the perfect sky and almost wished that he didn't have to go inside. It would have been wonderful to have the morning to himself and enjoy this weather. He might finally have gone to see some of the places he had heard so much about: Central Park, the Brooklyn Bridge, maybe even the Statue of Liberty if the cost of the ferry wasn't too steep. He promised himself that the next time he had some time off and wasn't too tired he would go to those places, and reminded himself that he must get a camera so that he could take pictures to send back home.

The restaurant's employees were especially busy that morning as they prepared for the big conference. It was going to be held in the "ballroom"—a large room located on the floor beneath the restaurant proper, and which was used to host everything from wedding receptions to birthdays to bar mitzvahs. The Wall Street firm sponsoring the event had sent out invitations for two hundred persons, and though it wasn't likely that all of them would attend, the restaurant had been contracted to provide enough food for that number. Miguel and two other busboys would be working this morning. They were overseen by one of the assistant managers, a young woman in her early thirties. She instructed them where to set up the long, curving buffet tables as well as the smaller tables at which guests would sit.

Present also were sixteen employees of the company sponsoring the event. Most of them were women. Miguel wondered at them. Like so many of the businesswomen he saw in New York they were snappily dressed in conservative business attire and went about their duties with the same single-mindedness of their male counterparts; or rather they seemed somehow even more brisk or determined as they animatedly chatted with this or that one, or comported themselves with a perky attentiveness that, given the early hour, was surely contrived. Some of them were nice-looking. A couple of them were middle-aged, and whenever the boy glanced at these he experienced a half-amused, half-disturbed feeling of the sort one might have at the sight of an adult abandoning the dignity of her years in order to exchange meaningless babble with the inchoate understanding of a toddler.

The assistant manager repeatedly went over to two of the men who worked for the company sponsoring the event and would complaisantly, almost fawningly ask them how everything was going and if she could do anything for them; for it was her job to ensure that her guests were provided for. They assured her they were satisfied with everything. They had come early to set up promotional displays for their company's products and services: pamphlets, fact sheets, vertically-standing cardboard cutouts faced with glossy photographs. These men were not more than thirty years old—not much older than Miguel himself. And yet how different from him they seemed! Meticulously groomed and wearing trim suits, they went about their business with a focus and confidence that seemed to epitomize what he had come to understand as the New York "professional." He despaired a little to think that he would never be like them: dressing as a matter of course in fine clothes, going about this city with air of sophisticated ease and command. He wondered how people like that came to be, and dimly perceived that at least a part of the answer had to be good luck: to have been born an American, to have been brought up in its ways, to know as a matter of second nature how to take advantage of its opportunities. Between them and himself, who came from such a different place and culture, there seemed an unbridgeable divide. He felt this the more keenly when, now and then, one of those Americans glanced up at him and looked at him blankly, smilelessly, almost as though they were looking at a piece of inanimate furniture, and which in any case was wholly different from the instantaneous warmth they exhibited toward any of their fellow important business people.

By the official start of the breakfast at eight o'clock, Miguel and another busboy had laid out all the food on the buffet tables. There were stainless steel chafing trays full of fluffy scrambled eggs, and trays of bacon and sausages. There were platters laden with cream cheese squares and sliced salmon, and wicker baskets, lined with fancy white paper, containing all kinds of bagels and muffins. There were bowls of fresh fruit salad, and still larger bowls in which single-serving cartons of milk or juice or flavored yogurt lay chilling in ice cubes. And of course there was coffee, supplied by four large steel urns, with, beside them, cups, saucers, creamers, and packets of sweeteners.

The guests began arriving at eight o'clock. The cool clean weather had had its invigorating effect on them: they all seemed fresh-faced, eager to begin their day. They were all well-dressed and well-groomed. On entering the ballroom they politely introduced themselves to one another, shaking hands, smiling, chatting about what companies they were with and what their jobs were. It occurred to Miguel that they all must have gotten up very early in the morning—in some instances, perhaps even earlier than he had—in order to be here. It always amazed the boy how American business people started so early in the morning and stopped so late at night. If they worked such long hours, what possible time could they be spending with their families?

Or maybe they didn't have families so that they could work so
much? Or maybe they loved their jobs so much that for them it
wasn't work at all, but just the way they lived, confidently and
happily, day after day? He wondered what the truth of the
matter was.

Within minutes of entering the room the guests would discreetly make their way to the buffet table. Knowing breakfast
was to be served many of them hadn't eaten at home before
coming here. By ones or twos or threes they picked up fresh
plates and helped themselves to what they wanted, sometimes
hesitating between two equally appetizing offerings before making a difficult choice, or taking a little of each, then taking a
seat at one of the tables, invariably with people they knew or
had just met. They always politely put a napkin over their lap
before eating. They seemed very cheerful as they enjoyed the
buffet and talked business. Often they looked out of the windows and commented on the fineness of the weather and the
great view. Miguel happened to pass one of the tables at which
a man and woman were sitting near a window and overheard
him saying:

"What a day, huh?"

"Absolutely gorgeous!" she replied.

"It doesn't get any better than this."

"So beautiful!"

The breakfast was only to last an hour. Afterwards the
guests were to go across the hallway to a suite where a "presentation" (Miguel wasn't quite sure what that meant) was to be
given about "risk management"—another mysterious, important-
sounding term.

Even by eight thirty however most of the anticipated attendees had not yet arrived. The persons who had shown up—
there were but a little over fifty of them—represented a small
fraction of those who had been invited. The men who worked
for the company sponsoring the event had not of course expected
everyone to come, but one could see by the way a few of them
looked up and checked their watches that they were less than
impressed by the turnout so far.

Miguel of course did not know this, which was why he wondered at what seemed a scandalous opulence of the buffet table.
There was so much food that even if everyone present ate his

fill there would still be a lot left over. Since working here he had been bewildered at the great quantities food thrown away. He had never forgotten the time when, as he had been smuggled into the United States, he had sat in the back of a hot van for fourteen hours without food or drink. What he wouldn't have given, back then, for a half-eaten bagel or a half-empty carton of juice! He couldn't help thinking that if there was a lot of food left over from this breakfast he might be able to take some of it home. The large tray of cream cheese and the bin of bagels, which was sure to be thrown out, could be his breakfast for a week—maybe for two. In the past he had never, out of shyness, asked permission to take any food back home, but he told himself that before he left for the day he would find out if he could do so. Why not? Food was expensive, and he knew what it was not to have it, and every time he saw it thrown away his heart broke.

A half hour into the breakfast Miguel took up a plastic bin, ventured out into the ballroom, and began clearing tables of used plates. He worked as self-effacingly as possible, silently, deftly, and with an air of immense complaisance taking up whatever items had been used and were no longer wanted: plates smeared with butter, cups sometimes half full of coffee, torn or empty sugar packets, partially-eaten rolls or pastries. He was always a little grateful to those guests who, when he took away their plates, leaned back a little as though to defer to him and murmured a smiling, "Thanks!" But most of the people did not give him a second glance. They took it for granted that restaurants had busboys and busboys cleaned tables. When Miguel hesitantly, almost daintily reached in front of them to take away their plates they maintained their posture and, if they had been talking, kept chattering over his arms as though he weren't there.

It was nearly a quarter to nine and some of the guests had already gone into the conference room; several of the tables, at which people had been sitting, were empty. As he cleaned up one of these tables Miguel noticed a woman put on her jacket and take up her pocketbook as she prepared to leave; evidently, she wasn't staying for the presentation. She bade goodbye to the man she had been talking to, shaking his hand and saying in a hurried voice, "I'll definitely follow up with you on that!"

Apparently she had another appointment that morning and was afraid of running late; she hurried off. No sooner had she pushed through the glass doors of the restaurant than she saw an elevator down the hall about to close and called out, "Could you hold that please!" At the sound of her voice a hand shot forth to hold the doors open for her. She hurried to the elevator in quick trotting steps and slipped inside—just in time.

Miguel headed back to the deployment area with a plastic tub full of things he had picked up from tables throughout the ballroom. There was a dish-washing station here where the plates were wiped of larger remnants of food and quickly rinsed, then stacked on carts to be taken upstairs for a thorough washing. The fellow who did this came from Trinidad and stood over a stainless steel sink holding a spray-nozzle from which he directed the hot water over the plates before piling them up beside him. He gave a quick smile and offered a "Thanks" when Miguel brought him yet another tub of used cups and saucers and plates.

"What a nice guy," Miguel told himself.

It occurred to him that everyone was nice here. No question about it, here there was a better, finer class of people than in any of the places he had worked before. Here there was no nuisance of a "boss" looking over his shoulder to make sure he was always busy. Here there was no one always ready to castigate or blame him for doing something wrong. Even after a few days on the job at this important, "prestigious" restaurant, the boy had begun to perceive something fundamental not only about New Yorkers but about people generally: namely, that good people, people with real class, always tried to make your life easier, not harder; went out of their way to be kind, not cruel; and gave you the benefit of the doubt, even when they might have a reason to suspect otherwise. He did the job that was required of him, and so long as he did it no one bothered him, no one questioned him, no one, even, after a few days, guided him unless he asked for guidance. To the degree that he was given this autonomy and trust he was grateful, and gratitude made him conscientious and loyal to his new employer. But that did not mean that everything was perfect here. The boy noticed that the waiters, who on a busy day or night could make a lot of money in tips, were for the most part Americans, while the kitchen staff and busboys (strictly salaried, making less) were immigrants. Such a state of affairs could only have come about through a conscious decision on the part of management. The boy shrugged his shoulders even at this discrimination. He knew better than to be disappointed because something wasn't perfect. He was too satisfied just to be working and making the kind of money he was making. And who knew? Perhaps if he worked here long enough, and learned English well enough, he might be promoted to a waiter and make more money than he could imagine.

"Yes, I really lucked out with this place," he told himself, exiting the area to which he had taken the latest tub of used plates. "At least here there's a future—"

He had no sooner pushed through the swinging doors and stepped back into the ballroom than he heard a loud whirring sound. In the next fraction of a second he realized it was coming from outside and he looked to the narrow windows giving out to the bright blue sky, and then—

A huge bang sounded, and something massive, powerful, shook the building.

The floor swayed backward, carrying Miguel, carrying everyone and everything, with it. Then it moved forward. Then it moved back again. The fluidity of the sensation was weird and appalling. It was a shockwave that traveled down the length of the building.

The boy skipped and hopped in a little dance of balance-keeping.

From the room behind him came the sharp, ringing clatter of plates and flatware falling onto the tiled floor. Another one of the busboys there shouted out something—a curse—at the otherworldly swaying of the building.

The people gathered in the ballroom gave truncated, gasping shouts of surprise.

All who had been standing wobbled, shuffled, struggled to keep their balance; they put out their hands on either side of them as though to break their impending fall.

One of them, a middle-aged man with a thick red neck bulging above a tight collar, reached out to the edge of a table to steady himself but missed it and tumbled hard.

The lights flickered; then went out. The clean, bright, fluorescent lighting gave way to dusk as the only light came through the windows, outside of which, indeed, was no longer the bright September sky but an ever-changing darkness of curdling smoke. Despite all that smoke Miguel's first thought was: earthquake! He had experienced one as a youngster, and this was similar: the way the building shook, the sudden, startling fluidity beneath one's feet; only, this was worse—far more intense. He thought about the tallness of the building, of its relatively slender vertical proportions, and of how it could not possibly remain steady but must topple over onto the streets. At such a prospect his heart raced.

No sooner had most people regained their balance than the swaying stopped and the great building stabilized. In that regained stillness everyone in the room reacted in the same way: with an instinctive immobility—a succession of five or six seconds in which they stopped breathing, their bodies froze, and their eyes darted about as the whole force of their intellect tried to understand what had just happened. None of them could have imagined that an airliner had just crashed into the building a mere eight floors below their own. At the sight of the billowing smoke outside one of the women screamed:

"Oh my God!"

Dozens of people rushed to the windows. They placed their hands on the jambs that were but twenty-two inches apart and placed their faces close to the glass and looked downward in order to see what had happened. But their vision was obstructed by the thick, dark, curdling smoke that engulfed the whole top part of the great building and swept upward with such velocity that it seemed as though it were being sucked into heaven itself. Amidst this smoke countless white flakes fluttered and spun: thousands, tens of thousands of sheets of paper that had been blown out of offices. They were the memoranda, letters, bills, contracts, and reports that were the stuff of office work. In their production people had racked their brains, and spent sleepless nights, and fussed and argued and even gotten sick over. Many a young man and woman had denied himself many a pleasure in order to compose and complete them. And now here they were, overtaken and commanded by a force none of their weary-eyed, sedentary, success-minded compositors could have imagined;—here they were, these "important" papers, flying, fluttering in mid-air and mingling with other paper debris of far lower pedigree: the menus of local eateries, the printed emails containing gossip or jokes, lavatory paper towels and toilet paper;—all, all of them having been blasted out into the world with a furious indifference.

"We got to get outa here, got to get out—go, go!" shouted a man who had been one of the first to go to the windows, who had looked out on the immense darkness of the smoke, and who had understood at once the massive explosion that must have caused it.

Everyone had the same idea and impulse: to get out of the building as fast as possible. Few were inclined to wait for "instructions" from someone "in authority," for the experience of most of these New Yorkers had proven to them time and again that people "in authority" often didn't know what they were talking about, least of all in an emergency. They hastened out of the ballroom and headed for the elevators or the stairs with the single-minded idea of evacuation. But like all those above the fire line they had no sooner stepped into the hallway than into thick, acrid smoke, which the force of the explosion had sent hurtling through elevator shafts and stairwells. Those who, coughing violently as they went, reached the elevators, pushed the call buttons which no longer worked, while from the bottom, top, sides, and middle of the closed steel doors smoke poured forth with hot ferocity and volume. Everyone who had ventured into the hallway soon came staggering back, coughing violently, pale, terrified.

Smoke had rushed through every space and passage between floors, especially though that which was most extensive and open: the ventilation system. Already in the ballroom smoke was curling out of the vents, spreading over the ceiling, coalescing and accumulating there into a haze. It smelled not only of things burning but also of some kind of petroleum fuel. A few of the men recognized the odor as that of kerosene.

The assistant manager who had helped set up the ballroom for this morning's conference had been in her office when the building rocked. Like everyone else her first reaction had been to freeze and look unblinkingly into space as the floor shuddered and the building swayed. Then the billows of smoke funneling upward just outside her office window had struck her with be-

numbing wonder. In the next few seconds she regained some
self-possession, and her first thought was of her responsibility
for the safety of the guests and staff, for she was also the fire
warden for her company on this floor. She hurried through
dark corridors to the ballroom where she saw people standing in
clusters as though drawn to one another for advice or protection, looking agitated, their voices anxious and sometimes loud
as they speculated about what had happened or on how they
might get out of the building. She announced that they were to
follow her into the hall where they would go to a stairwell down
which they would "evacuate in an orderly fashion"—using a
phrase that she had always heard during her fire warden "training" sessions. Those who had already entered the hallways told
her that they were impassable for the smoke. But this objection
did not fit into the training she had received, and she insisted
on leading everyone out of the ballroom. If those who knew better from their own, firsthand experience nevertheless heeded
her instructions, it was owing to their panic, which looked to
leadership from any quarter.

No sooner had the guests followed her into the hallways
than they began coughing violently. She hurriedly led them to
the appropriate stairwell, but as soon as its door was opened,
smoke, heavier and denser than that in the hallway, billowed
out of it. The door was closed at once. The remaining two
stairwells were also tried and found to be equally impassible.
Coughing and gagging—and alarmed at the way others were
heaving and choking—the assistant manager told everyone to
return to the ballroom. They would wait for help there, she
said.

Once she and everyone else had gone back there she went
to a phone on the wall with the intention of dialing a number
for building services in order to find out what had happened
and what she should do. But when she lifted the receiver, she
found it was dead—there was no dial tone. She tried another
phone on a nearby wall. It too was dead. In fact most of the
phone and electrical lines to the upper floors of the building had
been destroyed.

Smoke was filling the place fast. What had started out as
wisps of gray gracefully emerging from the vents became a
steadier, darker stream. Were it not for the largeness of the

space the atmosphere here would have already been thick with smoke. Those who had been coughing only lightly or intermittently started coughing more loudly and continuously. Many held their hands against their mouths or noses as though to prevent the noxious air from infiltrating their lungs; some of the women grimaced against the malodorous chemical smell of the smoke with what seemed—given the enormous urgency of the moment—a misplaced fussiness. But no matter how thick or evil-smelling the smoke, one could not but breathe it in, and in the ensuing minutes the people trapped here understood that it, rather than any fire (which no one had directly seen), was the real threat to their lives.

As bad as the smoke was on the 106th floor, it was still worse on the floor above, where the restaurant proper was located. The assistant manager on duty there had also followed her fire warden training and had led her staff and guests into the hallway to a designated stairwell, but it had been too smoky to negotiate; they had struggled down only one flight when she had exhorted them to get off on the 106th floor, thus increasing the crowd there to some 170 persons. The arrival of these newcomers had at first a positive psychological effect on those in the ballroom, first because it momentarily diverted their attention from their own situation and secondly because it promoted the relieving sense that an increase in the number of people needing rescue would be a spur to those charged with carrying it out. But what little comfort this initial and (as it might have been called) selfishly satisfying thought provided soon gave way to the succeeding, objective understanding that the smoke—in its continuing accumulation—could not long be held out against. There was too much of it. Already it was hard to breathe.

As soon as the two assistant managers saw each other they came together and told each other about the conditions on their respective floors. After the briefest speculation on what might have caused the explosion, and on the extent and location of the fire, they consulted with each other about what they ought to do. Each saw in the eyes and heard in the voices of the others a repressed, panicking sense of their impossible situation, of being confronted by something that nothing in their professional training, indeed nothing in their lives, had prepared them for. They also wondered at the lack of any general announcement.

So often in the past the intercom had blared into life with an introductory, attention-getting beep or wail followed by a booming male voice informing everyone of a test being conducted: yet now, when the real emergency had arisen, the system was silent, dead.

People repeatedly came up to either of the restaurant managers to ask, "What's going on?" or "Where do we go?" or "Where is the fire?" or "When will the Fire Department get here?"—impulsive, clamorous, sometimes angrily demanding questions to which neither woman could possibly have the answer, yet each of whom felt compelled to respond to in some hopeful and pacifying way, as though it would have been unforgivably remiss in her not to have some better, fuller knowledge of the situation. She would say that while she didn't know exactly what was going on she was sure that every effort was being made to put out the fire; that the Fire Department and other emergency services were undoubtedly "on their way," and perhaps only minutes from arrival; that it was just a matter of being patient, of holding on, of remaining calm till rescue came.

—Which did not seem implausible to those who had gone to the windows, looked down, and seen, between the billows of rising smoke, an ever-growing congress of fire trucks and police cars on the street below. Whole blocks of the city around the building were flashing with the strobe lights of hundreds of emergency vehicles, which in turn translated to thousands of emergency personnel who must have swarmed into the building. True, the elevators did not seem to be working, but, as everyone knew, elevators had special modes of operation used exclusively by fire departments in case of emergency and which overrode the usual controls. What they did not know was that an airliner had crashed into their building, penetrating so deeply into it as to cut through elevator shafts and their cabling. Only as the minutes passed without rescue, and the thick, billowing smoke outside the windows continued rushing up with unabated fury, and the ballroom grew darker, smokier, warmer;—only as the conditions around them quickly degenerated did people understand that the firemen might be confronted by circumstances that not all their skill and equipment could overcome.

And yet as conscious as everyone was of the smoke and its dangerousness, the thing that gave impetus to this fear—the essence of its terror—was the knowledge of the height at which they were trapped. If only they had been on the tenth floor, or even on the twentieth, they might have thrown caution to the wind and attempted to hurry down smoke-filled stairwells to the ground floor. Then, too, the fire department might have been able to engineer some kind of rescue through the windows. But they were a quarter of a mile above the ground; they were so high up that attempting the stairwells would end in certain asphyxiation. The little internal voice that had always whispered its warning to them when they had entered a high floor of a skyscraper now came back to reprimand them with sickening loudness and clarity. They should have known, they should have known, they should have known! Yes; they should have known, and now they did know, but now it was too late, the worst had happened, and here they were, trapped.

Someone suggested that they put wet napkins over their noses and mouths to filter out the smoke. But the napkins on the buffet tables were made of paper and were unsuitable to the purpose. Tablecloths were therefore cut with knives and ragged-edged pieces of cloth handed round. They were dipped into the reservoirs of melted ice at the bottom of containers used to chill food. Miguel held a piece of the damp cloth against his nose and mouth but found, like everyone else, that it was a poor makeshift filter. Whatever benefits it offered in the way of reducing particulates was offset by the way it obstructed the drawing of breath. It was a nuisance that antagonized one's fear.

Those who had cell phones—and nearly all the business-people did—had from the first been trying to place calls. Many were trying to get in touch with husbands and wives, mothers and fathers, sisters and brothers. They were usually unsuccessful because in that part of Manhattan the cell phone networks had become almost instantaneously overloaded as tens of thousands of people tried calling friends and relatives, or were being called by them, to find out where they were, if they had seen or knew what had happened, if they were alright. The first guest in the ballroom to learn what had really happened was a young man in his late twenties who had managed to get through to his wife. She had been home watching television and had seen the news flash of an airplane having crashed into One World Trade

Center. She was watching the tower burn even as she spoke to her husband who was trapped inside of it. As soon as she told him what had happened he announced it to everyone:

"It was an airplane! An airplane hit the building!"

There were exclamations of surprise, of incredulity. How was that possible? How could any pilot have been so incompetent as to run into a building so huge as this one? That the impact had been purposeful—an act of terrorism—did cross some people's minds, and they expressed this possibility; but at this point most thought it had been a freak accident. Still others learned that it wasn't just any airplane that had hit the building but an airliner, and that entire floors of the building were destroyed and on fire. This information went a long way toward escalating the general level of dread, for it made clearer the enormous and perhaps inescapable scale of the catastrophe.

Others had frantically been dialing 911. Those who reached an emergency operator hurriedly explained who they were, where they were located, and that they needed help. They blurted out that there was a lot of smoke. They would have to endure listening to some civil servant who, safe in her cubicle perhaps miles away, adhered to a standard operating procedure even in this unique and most excruciating circumstance, asking them to spell their names or to try to elaborate on the conditions they were in or who might be with them;—as though any of that mattered! In their nervous impatience the callers wanted to shout reprimands and insults, yet they were conscious of the uselessness of anger against bureaucracy, which always demands a moronic adherence to protocol; and only when this was satisfied could the caller relate the information that alone mattered, namely, that he and others were trapped on the 106th floor, that there was a lot of smoke, that it was hard to breathe, and that someone had to come to rescue them—now!

—But even then the civil servants were not about to be "unprofessional," and in a calm voice replied:

"Yes, we know what's going on. We're getting help to you as soon as possible. Try to stay calm. Don't panic. Help will be there soon. How do you spell your last name again?"

The assistant manager for the floor announced that she was going to try to call "for instructions" from the phone in her office. Miguel and everyone else watched her disappear into the hazy air as she made her way out of the ballroom.

On her own, away from the guests of the restaurant for whom she felt responsible, she felt her fear increase. She told herself that she must remain calm, that she could only be effective if she remained calm. It was very dark in the corridors along which she walked; if she had not walked them so many times she would not have known her way. The sudden, great quantity of smoke indicated an immense fire somewhere, and she could also, now, feel a rise in temperature. When she reached her office, illuminated by the subdued, smoke-filtered light coming from outside, she picked up her phone and found that it too was dead. She reached for her pocketbook on a file cabinet, opened it, and took out her cell phone; then she went through the Rolodex on her desk for the emergency number of the police command post in the lobby. She called it and the line was busy. She stood there pressing the redial button again and again. "C'mon!" she thought, holding the phone tightly, impatiently against her ear. "C'mon—c'mon!" When she got through on the tenth redial a man's voice answered not with his name but with a harried, "Command Post!"

She told him her name, the company she was with, and what floor she was on. "We're having a smoke condition," she said, using the phrase she had heard in her fire warden training sessions, and which now sounded ludicrously inadequate to describe the thick, acrid smoke that had accumulated with frightening speed. "We have most people here on the 106th floor, the 107th is way too smoky. We need direction as to where we can lead our guests and employees, as soon as possible"

In fact the officer who answered the phone was sure of nothing except what he saw around him in the lobby, and what he saw was pandemonium. People were shouting different, conflicting things. Some called out that the explosion had been caused by an airplane crash; others that there had been a bomb. Already firemen from every fire station in lower Manhattan were gathered around their chiefs who barked out orders to go here or there or to begin climbing up the stairwells to the fires. On the second story mezzanine people were hurrying, stumbling over themselves to reach the ground floor. The concussive force of the explosion had swept down the whole length of the building to damage even the lobby itself. Marble tiles had been shaken loose from the walls and had crashed to the floor; several of the tall windows looking out to the plaza had shattered, while others had been damaged and were lightninged through with cracks. A woman rushed out of an elevator, screaming and charred and smoking, having either been caught in a fire on an upper floor or fire having somehow penetrated her car. Outside things were falling to the ground with sharp crashes and loud pounding thuds. Every time one of them sounded he and others looked up, looked outside, wondering what it was.

—And so now, at this call from the restaurant on the top floor, which was one of dozens he had already fielded, he could not in good conscience give definite information or instruction. He could only give assurances that her condition was noted and would be attended to as soon as possible. "Okay," he said. "We're doing our best. We've got the Fire Department, everybody ... we're trying to get up to you, dear. Alright, call back in about two or three minutes, and I'll find out what direction you should try to get down."

"Because our floor is really smoky!"

"Are the stairways, A, B, and C blocked off and smoky?"

She told him that they were, and added that the electricity and emergency phones were also out.

"Oh, yeah, they're all ... all the lines are blown out right now. But everybody is on their way, the Fire Department ..."

"The condition up on 106 is getting worse," she said, as much to herself as to him.

"Okay, dear. Alright, we are doing our best to get up to you right now. Alright, dear?"

Suddenly she realized that he hadn't given her any real instructions. "But where ... where do you want us to go here? Can you at least direct us to a certain place on our floor or in the building?"

He couldn't possibly know that, and hesitated, "Uh ...."

"Like what tower," she said, and suddenly realizing that the word "tower" didn't make sense, revised herself and said, "like what area ... where can we go where there's not so much smoke?"

How could he possibly know that? How could he know what was going on over a hundred floors above him? He fumbled:

"Unless we find out exactly what area is the smoke ... where most ... most of the smoke is coming up here, and we can kind of direct that. As I, uh ..."—just then he thought that he might ask someone, an engineer, say, for the kind of specific information this woman was asking of him, and said more authoritatively: "Call back in about two minutes, dear."

"Call back in two minutes. Great."

She took the phone away from her ear and ended the call. No sooner had she done so than regretted having agreed to wait. Even two minutes seemed to her an unnecessarily long time. Surely if he had known what to do he would have told her; he was just trying to stall, to hide his ignorance, his incompetence! Just then she hated him, hated all men, hated their stupidity and thick-headed lies, but in the next second she thought that he probably *did* need a few minutes to check something—to go over floor plans, say, or to speak to someone who could give him the information he needed. Yes—yes, that was it! He was doing his job; he wanted to be sure; he was checking for her, and when she called him back he would have an answer. And so she waited, standing at her desk, coughing lightly, thinking, "Everyone's waiting for me, I have to tell them something." She tamped down again the horrible anxiety that from the first had been creeping up within her and which only a sense of her responsibilities had enabled her to suppress. As she waited she glanced about her at the office in which she had spent so many hours of her life. It had always been so bright and cheerful: the white walls, the framed art posters, the pictures of smiling relatives on her desk, the potted plants strategically placed on the window sills. And that view outside her windows, which on a clear day could stretch for fifty miles, and of which she had always been quietly proud as though it were the visible, tangible proof of the heights she had reached in her profession;—now it had turned into an ugly, threatening canvas of thick, curdling smoke, which not the worst of her nightmares could have pictured.

She waited. She waited. She coughed often. She realized she was breathing very hard. She looked outside to the smoke rushing upward in curdles of black and soft gray, by turns entirely obscuring or letting through the light of the sunny September day. She was conscious of how only a few inches of

glass separated her from that turmoil. She was also aware of
the rise in temperature. That it was getting hot so quickly could
only mean that the fires must be nearby—perhaps on the very
floor beneath her own. The thought of this increased her panic.
If fire should break out on this floor there would be nowhere to
go, since any other place, any other floor, would be impossible to
get to, what with all the smoke in the hallways and stairwells.
She kept glancing at her watch. The minute hand seemed to
move forward with the tiniest of increments, with an agonizing
slowness. She saw that only a single minute had *just* passed.
In the next twenty seconds she checked her watch three times.
Panic prompted her to call back now, at once, but something
else, something stronger, held the impulse in check, and forced
her to wait, to follow, as it were, the rules—just as she had always followed the rules. And so she waited. As soon as two
minutes were up she made the call. It took her a dozen times
to get through. When it rang, the man who picked up was not
the same one she had talked to earlier.

Again she gave her name and the company she was with.
"We are still waiting for direction," she said, either not understanding that she was talking to someone new, or taking it for
granted that this person, whoever he was, had been informed
about and had followed through on her previous call. "We have
guests up here."

'How many people do you have up there, approximately?"
he asked

She told him. He repeated her answer, and asked, "And
you're up on 106 or 107?"

"One—O—Six!" she spelled out, impatiently. "107's impossible. The smoke condition on 107 is—"

He interrupted her words as he spoke to someone beside
him. But then he gave her to understand that he had not been
ignoring her, that he understood why she was calling and what
she wanted to know, saying, "We're sending officers and fire personnel up there at this time. We're evacuating as soon as possible."

"But we ... right now we need to find a safe haven on 106,
where the smoke condition isn't bad. Can you direct us to a certain quadrant?"

"Alright," he said; but was again distracted by the goings

on around him; then returned to her, saying, "We are sending somebody up there as soon as possible. If anybody can get to the staircase, that's fine. We are sending up there—"—again, he stopped mid-sentence, distracted by a static-laden voice coming through loud on his handheld radio.

She was angered as though at an insult at his having mentioned the stairwell. As though anyone with common sense would not have tried that first! "You can't!" she answered sharply. "The staircase is—"

"Alright, we're sending ... we're sending people up there as soon as possible."

"What's your ETA?" she asked, almost demanded. She wanted to pin him down to a definite answer, a definite time, something he could not easily wiggle out of.

"I ... ma'am, I have to get on the radio. As soon as possible. As soon as it's humanly possible."

She was about to say something else when she heard a loud bang, saw a flash of light from outside her window, and felt a shudder in the building. Her heart skipped a beat. Through the smoke outside she saw waves of smoke of a different, newer, lighter color, and amid this, just as there had been earlier, the confetti-like turning and twisting of thousands of pieces of paper, some sheets of which lightly tapped at her office window in passing, and one or two of which momentarily—and in a way that was ghastly—pressed against the glass before flying off. There had been another explosion. She thought it had occurred in this building.

With a renewed sense of panic she left her office and made her way back through the smoky corridors that led to the ballroom. Maybe someone there knew what had happened. Certainly everyone had felt the building shudder again, as she had. But in the next second she wondered what she was going to tell the people waiting for her. She had told them that she was going to find out what they should do, and now the only thing she could tell them was that they had to wait. Wait! That was the *last* thing any of them would want to hear; and she knew that it was the last thing any of them—including herself—could afford to do. But it was all she had to offer.

Holding her cell phone in one hand, she reached out with the other to the wall in order to guide herself in the darkness.

As she stepped carefully along she went over in her head the
fruitless conversation she had had with the man in the lobby.
She recalled asking for directions to a safe "quadrant." She had
used that word twice. Why had she used it? She never used
that word. It was so stiff, so formal, in these dire circumstances
somehow so inappropriate ...

In the ballroom people moved in the smoke like dark spirits
haunting a mist; from any few feet away only their vague outlines might be seen, or their coughs heard. Some were pacing
frantically, aimlessly, out of barely-tamped-down panic. Most
were still holding pieces of dampened cloth against their noses
and mouths. They often brought their hands up to their eyes,
which teared against the irritation of the thickening smoke.
Some held cell phones, poking at keypads, trying to make calls.
The assistant manager entered among them and announced
that she had called "downstairs" and that help was on the way.
As though this information was no longer of any value or interest, several people asked her instead about "the explosion." Had
she felt it, had she seen it? Did she know what had caused it?
They had seen it clear as day: the bright flash of light outside,
and then the way the smoke out there had thickened, and all
those papers filling the air. She could only respond that she
had felt and seen the same things they had, but didn't know
what had happened—whether there had been another explosion
somewhere in the building or somewhere nearby. She could
only tell them that she had spoken to an officer in the lobby and
that help was on the way. She was aware of how ineffective
she sounded, and was impelled to add the same words the policeman had told her, and which she herself had been so offended at:

"As soon as possible."

One of the men, an IT manager who lived on Long Island,
had finally managed to reach his wife with his cell phone. She
had been watching news of the attack on television. She knew
that her husband was supposed to be in one of the towers, but
she didn't know which one, or on what floor. She had tried to
call him but her calls, like those of thousands of others, had not
gone through on account of overloaded circuits. When the second plane hit the other tower her heart had jumped in her
chest, and hope of her husband's safety shifted to the only two

possibilities left: either he had been on a floor beneath the impact zones and managed to escape, or he had not gone to his appointment. When her phone rang, when she grabbed it up and heard her husband's voice, she exclaimed, "Thank God!"— and without waiting for him to respond she assailed him with the question that had been tormenting her for twenty minutes: Where was he? And when he told her that he was in the struck tower, she asked, "What floor?"

"106th"—and he coughed violently.

He knew, he said, what had happened: a plane had hit the building. "There's been another explosion," he said.

She told him that the explosion had been another plane hitting the other building.

For a few moments he said nothing and she could hear in the background other voices, and coughing. Then she heard him announce to the others:

"Another plane hit the other building! It was another plane!"

Everyone who heard this looked toward him, toward what for many was a mere voice in the smoke. Few had believed that the airplane crashing into their building had been an act of terrorism; now there could be no doubt about it. Some of the men cursed aloud. They cursed the people who had done this to them. They cursed them to hell and destruction.

For Miguel it was strange to hear about "terrorism" in this way. He knew what it meant, but it seemed too weighty a notion to have anything to do with the small anonymity of his life. He didn't know or care much about politics. He didn't dislike anyone and couldn't see why anyone should dislike him. He had always wanted the best for everyone. Why should anyone try to harm him? All he had ever wanted to do was to make his way through the world in some peace and comfort. These people around him, these big businessmen and businesswomen, who knew so much more about the world than he did, and had so much more influence in it than he ever would—it was they whom such things as terrorism, politics, wars, and the relations among countries ought to have affected; not he. He had just wanted to make some money so that he wouldn't be so poor.

The boy watched as the assistant managers again drew close together and consulted with each other. The befogging smoke hid their expressions, and their words were inaudible above the surrounding commotion of people coughing, milling about nervously, or talking in loud voices into unresponsive cell phones. Again employees and guests kept coming up to them, asking or demanding of them that something be done—that someone be called—that a way out be found to get off the floor; —to which they responded, not without exasperation, that they would all just have to wait.

Some would not wait.

It logically occurred to some not only on this floor but on others above the fire line that the most likely avenue of escape was the rooftop. At least there one would be out in the open and be able to breathe, and a rescue by helicopter might be possible. Driven by a panicking will to live, guiding themselves by handrails up dark, smoky stairwells, coughing violently as they went, they climbed toward the doors that had become to them the very gates of life, only to reach them and find them—locked. With all their frantic might they tried to pull open the handles; kicked, pushed, and then rammed into the doors in an attempt to force them open; but they were steel-solid, unyielding, an immovable obstruction to the outside world and air and potential safety. Once again the formalities and inconveniences of city life with its inhuman rules and regulations had arisen, this time to mortal effect. For these doors were kept locked out of "safety concerns"—which was really to say that building management did not want thrill-seekers or suicides gaining access to the roof and creating the liability of an expensive lawsuit. Yet even if the doors had been unlocked, and people had made their way onto the roof, it was unlikely that helicopters could have landed because of the thick, blinding smoke and the strong updraft of the fire-heated air. Rescue by helicopter is always a delicate affair, requiring special equipment, specially-trained pilots, and the right circumstances; and here and now none of those factors existed.

Still others, in an attempt to find better air, wandered along dark corridors and pushed through doors to offices, conference rooms, store rooms, and restrooms. In most cases their efforts were in vain, for the interconnected ventilation system ensured that the smoke was distributed fairly evenly throughout the floor. After a while these desperate souls realized that they

were wasting their time.   In some instances, in the darkness
and the disorienting smoke, they panicked at a loss of sense of
direction; and the fear of death that had prompted them to venture out of the ballroom would be overwhelmed by the greater
fear of dying alone, and they would, with an equal or greater effort, make their way back to the others.   But there were a few
for whom a desperate enterprise had paid off—at least somewhat and temporarily. A few fumbled and bumbled their way to
offices on the western side of the building, which were a little
less smoky because that morning a faint breeze blew out of the
northwest, nudging the smoke in the opposite direction.   But
even in these places it had become hard to breathe, and the
heat was increasing fast.

"We're trapped!" a woman screamed, her voice cutting
shrilly through the commotion in the ballroom.   "We're gonna
die here! We're trapped—there's no way out!"

Everyone who heard this scream regarded it as the expression of his own terror. Miguel saw who it was: a woman, or
rather the figure of a woman standing in the smoky haze, her
outline limned against the dim light coming through the windows. He could not have known that she was the mother of two
small children and that her cry was less for herself than for her
babies, whom she feared she would not see again, not live to
raise and protect.

No sooner had she screamed than the people who had been
closest to her tried to calm her down in voices which reached
Miguel as quickly-spoken and therefore not-wholly-comprehensi-
ble English. They were assuring her that she was mistaken.
They told her that help was coming and that she mustn't let
herself "go"—that she had to be calm, had to save her breath,
that everything would be alright. They told her these things despite their own fears and doubts.

The manager and assistant manager likewise were engaged
in trying to comfort those who were becoming sick from the
smoke, or to becalm those who teetered on the verge of uncontrollable panic. But each of them, as she went about doing this,
on some level resented her duty toward the restaurant's "guests"
as a distraction from concentrating on her own, personal plight.
For who was there to help *her*, after all?—she who needed it as
much as anyone else? On the other hand each also understood

that it behooved her to direct outward, toward a specific goal or objective, the nervous energy which would otherwise have become self-destructively internalized in a way that she saw all around her: in the way people paced back and forth, or moaned or cried, or futilely applied themselves to cell phones.

But one man had reached the limit of his patience and obedience. "We have to break the windows!" he shouted. "We need air!"

The assistant manager from the floor hurried over to him and began trying to persuade him that that was the one thing he must not do. She argued this in part because she believed that rescue was imminent and it was her duty to prevent damage to the restaurant, and in part because, as everyone knew, opening a window when there was a fire only fed the flames and made the situation worse. With this latter argument she persuaded him to hold back, adding that he—that all of them—had to wait till the Fire Department reached them.

"We'll be dead by then!" the man gasped—his voice disintegrating in a loud, violent fit of coughing.

She could see that he or one of the other men would sooner or later break the windows for air. The smoke was too thick and hot. Assurances meant nothing when you couldn't breathe.

"I'll call downstairs again!" the assistant manager said.

—It seemed the only thing she could offer in the way of calming the people around her.

As though for the sake of privacy, and to fulfill her intention the more certainly, she stepped away from the others into a deserted area. There, in full view of the ballroom and the people coughing and milling about in panic, she opened her cell phone and again called the command station a hundred floors below. Again it took her a dozen times to get through. She reached the same man she had spoken to earlier. Just as before, she announced who she was. Without letting her go on, and as though to assure her that he knew who she was and why she was calling, the officer on the other end of the line blurted out with a tinge of harried impatience:

"Okay, uh, ma'am, as soon as is possible. I've notified everybody to be notified, to get up there."

She wanted to say something else, to impress on him again the urgency of her situation, of the situation of everyone on the floor, of how absolutely impossible their circumstances had become and the necessity of immediate rescue. But she had heard in his voice the irritation of having to bear another, redundant explanation, and this checked her. Frustrated, angry, she ended the call, thinking, "Idiot! What the hell is wrong with him! So I've called before! Where the hell are they, then?"

She stood there angry, frightened, and very hot. She started coughing hard again. It was a violent, hacking fit that lasted for some twenty seconds and left her somewhat nauseated. When it was over spittle wet the hands she had raised to her mouth and she felt miserably light-headed. She had a sudden, dreadful presentiment of death. Something inside her told her that she was going to die. She heard herself muttering, praying, "Oh God ... oh God ..." She felt tears coming to her eyes out of sheer nervous pity for herself. But in the next moment she bucked up her courage. An enormous effort of will enabled her to tamp down the horrid presentiment. If there was a chance, even the slightest chance, that she would survive, she knew that it might depend on maintaining some composure, on forcing herself to think and calculate clearly so as to be able to seize the life-saving opportunity when it arose. She had to keep her head, had to keep trying! "You'll be alright," she told herself, commanded herself. "You'll be alright! Just ... just ..."— she wasn't even sure what.

She looked out into the smoke to her fellow employees and the restaurant's guests: over a hundred people to whom she had announced, for a second time, that she was going to find out what they should do or when they would be rescued. She felt miserably inadequate to think that she had nothing new or encouraging to tell them. Suddenly it seemed to her that she hadn't been aggressive enough with the man who had taken her call. He hadn't understood what was happening up here—all this smoke and heat, and her and everyone else's inability to breathe. He hadn't understood how bad it was! If he had known, if he had *really* known, he wouldn't have been so short with her, so cavalier, so pro forma. Well, she would make him understand! She would make sure that he sent people up to rescue her and everyone else! She wasn't going to accept anything less than his instantaneous action! Once more she pressed the redial button on her cell phone, and, coughing,

coughing, coughing, held it to her ear. Almost as she expected the line was busy and she couldn't get through but this time she was more determined than ever, and hit the redial button five, six, seven, eight, nine, ten, eleven, twelve, thirteen, fourteen, fifteen times in a row till the call went through. The same man picked up in the same way, blurting out his last name and location.

She announced who she was and what company she was with, but this time in a strong, almost angry voice, and added at once, "The situation on 106 is getting rapidly worse!"

The officer didn't immediately respond to her. Instead he spoke to people around him, though she could hear him well enough: "We got another call here from the restaurant on the top floor and she says it's rapidly getting worse."

Loudly, as though to get back his attention, she spoke into the telephone: "The fresh air is going down fast! I'm not exaggerating!"

"Ma'am, I know you're not exaggerating. We're getting a lot of these calls. We are sending the Fire Department up as soon as possible." And as though to assure her, finally and for all time, that he knew of her situation, that he knew how dire it was, that he had indeed heard everything she had told him, he repeated her name, said she had called four times, that there were—as she had told him—75 to 100 people on her floor, the 106th.

She listened and coughed hard a few times. "What are we going to do for air?" she gasped.

"Ma'am, the Fire Department—"

"Can we break a window?"

"You can do whatever you have to get to, uh, the air."

—It was the confirmation she needed, the spur to follow her common sense. The man in the ballroom who had wanted to break the windows, whom she had dissuaded from doing so— he had been right after all. Yes, they *had* to break the windows to get air. The smoke was too thick and it was too hot. If they couldn't breathe, nothing else mattered; they would be dead before rescue came.

She heard a banging noise. Through the smoke she saw that one of the men had gotten onto a buffet table and was hitting a sprinkler head with his shoe, unreasonably supposing that somehow it had gotten stuck, and that if he could only get it working it and all the other sprinklers would go on and shower the floor with a spray of refreshing, cooling water. She ignored him, however. She announced that she had spoken again with the command station downstairs, that the Fire Department was on its way, and that they could break the windows for air.

Several men grabbed up chairs and headed toward the windows. Loud, sharp bangs sounded as they started to break the glass. They acted with such sudden, impulsive, forceful male energy that the women who had been standing next to them shied away as though in fear of getting hurt. But the thick, hardened panes did not give way easily; they had to be struck several times before they broke clean through, and yet more effort was required to remove the sharp edges embedded in the jambs.

People in the room, including Miguel, went toward the open windows, lured by the hope of cool, pure air.

Those who had broken the windows realized their efforts had been mostly in vain unless they were willing to stand at the very face of the building. The man who had broken the first window did this, forced to it by the heat and smoke at his back, steadying himself by placing his hands on the jambs on either side of him. His spirit cringed at the sight below him:—a far mortal drop that instinct urged him to pull away from. But the possibility of fresh air was an irresistible lure, and so he thrust his face and body forward. Even so he was miserably disappointed, for smoke enshrouded the whole top of the building as in a suffocating jacket. For a few seconds at a time he caught a whiff of purer air but he also caught the full brunt of the heat rising in simmering waves from the burning floors beneath his own. Through shifting smoke he saw, over a thousand feet below, the crosshatch of streets, the ant-like movement of people there, and the red and white flashes of lights on police cars and fire engines.

Someone called out the suggestion that a tablecloth be waved out the window as a distress signal. There was still the thought among many here that their situation was not known about, or the direness of it insufficiently understood, else why would the firemen have not come already? A tablecloth was yanked off a table and hurriedly brought to one of the men at the windows with, "Take this! Wave this!"

It was not the only object competing for the attention of the crowds below. From other broken windows on other floors people waved objects in a bid for notice and rescue. On the streets people pointed to them, exclaiming to one another, "Look! Look, look!" And all would look, many with their hands held against their mouths in horror as the most elemental of all human sympathies enabled them to have a sense of the dread of those far above them. And as they looked they saw still more horrible things.

The intact floor directly above the impact zone had within minutes become impossibly hot as the flames below it licked at its concrete bottom, making it as hot as the surface of an oven. On that floor the very adhesive beneath the carpeting began to smoulder and burn; then the carpeting itself, its polyester filaments, began to melt. In panicking desperation people at once broke windows for relief. Often they were piled up four or five high—men and women climbing, scrambling over one another in an effort to feel and take a breath of fresh air. But the air wasn't fresh; it was full of fire and smoke; the world was nothing but fire and smoke. For these people there could be no enduring. There were only two options: a horrible death by burning, or a quicker death by jumping. And so many did what they had to do: they stood at the precipice, with unbearable heat at their backs, with lethal smoke all around them, with patient fires below them; and rather than suffer intensely any longer, and in the uttermost despair of which the human spirit is capable, they jumped. They jumped by ones, they jumped by twos; they jumped, in some cases, holding hands—two people who had, in one horrible instantaneous recognition of their fate, reached out to each other for the comfort and courage necessary to endure it. Their bodies, small and insect-like against the stolid lined face of the skyscraper, fell with a dreamlike steadiness or tumbled with a slow, horrifying grace. In the few seconds of life remaining to them they were able to take a few breaths of pure air, and to feel again the crisp September day against their skins, even as their one thought was, "Now I die!"—no sooner thought and feared than ended, expunged, obliterated when they hit the ground: people once so full of the potential for good and joy and love reduced in an instant to heaps of broken flesh and smudges of blood smeared across the debris-strewn plaza.

In the ballroom Miguel, like many others, watched those at the windows, in particular the man who was balancing himself with one hand against a jamb while with the other he frantically waved a tablecloth. And, watching him, the boy knew for sure that there was no way out of this and that he was going to die. There could not be so much smoke and heat and not consume and kill him—not kill them all. That man at the window was wasting his time. The very fact that he had had to break the glass and stood so dangerously at the edge of the building proved how impossible the situation was—how surely he and everyone else were doomed.

A memory occurred to Miguel. He recalled the first time he had thought of coming to the United States. A man from his village who had come to this country a few years earlier had returned to visit his family, and was cutting an impressive figure. Everyone was talking about him, about how he had changed, how good he looked, how well he had done for himself, what with his new clothes and the gold jewelry flashing on his wrists and hands. The sight of him had inspired Miguel to do and be the same. How stupid he had been for that! It had been the fatal first step toward death. If he only had stayed home! He would have given anything to find himself magically transported back to those days when he had had nothing and yet everything; when he had been poor as dirt but had had the greatest of all blessings—life. He offered up a prayer, a promise, that if he got out of this he would go back home. Yes, he would go back tomorrow, taking what little money he had saved or even none of it, if somehow his return rested on that condition. For there would always be something he could do back home to make some money—to survive. He could work on a farm. He could do odd jobs. He could do *something* to make enough to get by on, to live on: and just getting by, just living, *would* be enough. How could he have been so stupid as not to see that?

For the next ten minutes it was his own foolishness that obsessed him as he stood there in the smoke, coughing and hot and miserable and afraid. It seemed to him that he had no one to blame for what was happening to him but himself. He loathed himself for the bad judgment that had led him to this place. Of all the places in the United States he might have gone to, why did he have to come to New York! And why, of all the places in New York in which he might have worked, had he chosen to work here, in this tall building! How stupid he had been not to listen to that little voice inside him that had warned him of the danger of working so high up. He almost began to weep for his own stupidity. There flitted through his mind the idea that he shouldn't be so hard on himself because, after all, there had been things in his life over which he had had no control, things which had formed his personality and influenced his decisions. But the excruciating nature of his circumstance prevented him from pursuing this notion further, thus depriving him of whatever comfort the downtrodden or beleaguered may derive from the incontrovertible logic of determinism.

For Miguel and most of the other people trapped on the floor the makeshift filters they had made out of dampened cloth had by now dried out and were less effective than ever. Many had dropped them as useless. Most were coughing continuously, violently. But even more dangerous than the smoke's irritation to lung tissue was its conveyance of a hundred poisons into the bloodstream. These poisons accumulated to the point where the liver and other organs could no longer metabolize and neutralize them, resulting in increasing stages of sickness: first a slight light-headedness; then dizziness; then headache, which became severe and in some cases pounding; then nausea; and finally a general, debilitating misery as though whatever was "wrong" was wrong with oneself as a whole and down to the marrow of one's bones. Combined with the heat and the smoke and the sense of entrapment, this sickness heightened the suffering that only minutes previously had seemed incapable of increase.

But in time one became so sick as to be beyond mere misery: the poisons inhaled became so concentrated in the blood as to have a downright destructive effect on the body. Thus what had started out as dizziness or nausea gave way to physical debility. People in the ballroom began to grow unsteady on their feet and felt compelled to sit down either on chairs or on the floor, especially the women whose constitutions were less robust than those of the men.

Miguel too became sick, first with headache and then with

nausea. He held one of his hands against his aching abdomen. Feeling so dizzy that he feared he would fall, he stepped away from the broken windows that had brought him little relief and walked aimlessly about in his misery, winding up at the other end of the ballroom where he leaned against a wall. There was no one around him and he was grateful for this. He coughed almost continuously and, when he didn't cough, he heard his panting breaths and felt the heated atmosphere reaching into his throat. Though he still felt panic, still wrestled with the fear of what seemed imminent death, his mind was more consumed with his actual, physical sickness. He dry retched several times. He felt so felt so weak that he could no longer stand. He slid down to the floor and sat with his legs sprawled out before him. He retched again and coughed so violently that he toppled over and lay in a fetal position. The first additional sensation he had was of the intense heat of the floor. It was so hot that he couldn't continue lying on it. At the same time he was so sick and weak that he couldn't get up—not just now. He lay there with his face turned downward, his nose nearly touching the hot, stinking carpeting.

But then against his nose, and in his nostrils, he felt, he smelled, cooler, better air. He lay perfectly still. Yes (he realized in another moment) there *was* air!

It happened that he had fallen in just the right way for his face, or rather his nose and mouth, to be within a current of a better air invisibly wafting across the floor. The chances were a thousand to one that it should be present—that it should have entered the building from, say, some broken window in another place and then wound its way in a relatively unadulterated channel around walls or along corridors to pass just here, where his head lay;—but so it was. It was not, this air, pristine by any means; it was still smoky; but it was purer than the air around it and could keep him alive. And so he lay there absolutely still, and consciously, carefully breathed. He kept his tearing eyes closed against the thick, stinging smoke.

But the heat of the floor! It was so hot that he wanted to get up from it. But he dared not. This stream of air he was breathing was so unexpected, so unlikely, so precious that he could not risk losing it. He had to bear the heat; it was the lesser of two evils. He tried to force his attention to other things, to, for instance, what he could hear, since hearing was now the only sense by which he could be aware of the goings on around him. There was a lot less coughing, he realized. There was no longer the bustle of people walking aimlessly about. He wondered if people had left the ballroom. Perhaps they had found a place where there was more air; or had they (he asked himself this question as though it were the most likely possibility) died? He listened still harder. In the near distance there was an occasional voice, more bouts of coughing. Now and then he heard a fluttering sound and recognized this as coming from the people standing at the open windows and waving things— jackets or shirts or tablecloths—in an attempt to be noticed, to be rescued. But gone was the sound of many feet shuffling to and fro, of the many voices in desperate consultation, and the muttered curses of people frustrated by cell phone calls that weren't going through. Had he been able to see through the smoke he would have seen people sitting with torsos slumped over and heads bowed as though in sleep but who had really fallen unconscious—who had taken the first long leap toward death.

On the other hand the boy did not have to see this to know that it was so. No one could survive long in this thick smoke and intense heat. Reason told him that he too must eventually succumb. Yet he no sooner thought such a thing than a part of him refused to admit it, to believe it. Death is so antagonistic to life that so long as life endures the prospect of dying remains essentially repulsive and something one cannot, on the deepest level, accept. Thus he could not help thinking that even if everyone else died he would not. He clung to faith in an imminent rescue. He kept anticipating the commotion of firemen barging into the room. In his mind's eye he saw them breaking down the door, holding axes, water hoses, bringing oxygen masks; pulling him up from the floor, leading him to safety. There were a few times when he could have sworn that he heard their voices. He listened for them hard. And certainly he was hearing *something:* odd, sharp, thudding sounds.

In trying to analyze what these sounds were his unclear mind drifted and fell into semi-consciousness. In that seductive, nebulous state of being his hopes somewhat manufactured his reality. For minutes at a time he thought he heard the arrival of firemen, and felt joy to think that he would be saved. But when he came to himself again he would open his eyes to darkness and stinging smoke, and realize that he had just been "sleeping." It seemed to him that he could not have drifted off for more than two or three minutes, though in fact it had been closer to fifteen. Again he felt the hot floor, and again bent the whole force of his will against the urge to get up lest he lose the flow of better, cooler air still wafting across his nose and mouth. Nevertheless he shifted his body, moving his legs and arms and torso as though trying to find a more comfortable position. "Just stay where you are," he cautioned himself. "Just keep breathing. As long as you can breathe you'll be alright. The heat, the heat—don't think about the heat. Just breathe. One breath after another. One breath ... another breath ... another.... That's the only way. The firemen will come. It can't take them much longer. You have to hold on ... "

His mouth was as dry as cotton and he was intensely thirsty. He thought of the small cartons of juice and milk that had been chilling in the large, ice-cube-filled plastic bowls on the buffet tables. By now of course the ice had to be melted. Indeed there was probably not even any water in them, for he recalled how people had dipped parts of torn tablecloth into them in order to make moistened filters to press against their mouths. But the cartons of juice and milk must still be there; he hadn't seen anyone drinking anything. Even if they were warm, even if they were hot, he would guzzle them down, so thirsty was he. But how could he get up, negotiate his way through the smoke, and then possibly hope to find again this exact place, this tiniest and only spot where life was possible? In his mind's eye he saw himself searching for it frantically as he coughed wildly and heaved for breath. No, he would never find it; he would die in the smoke. Perhaps he would choke to death even before he reached the buffet tables. It was better to remain where he was, to remain thirsty but alive. And so just as he had done with the excruciating sensation of the heat, so now he did with his dry mouth and thirst, telling himself to ignore them, to refuse to let them torment him, to think of something else, of anything else but them.

Time passed but he could not have said how much. A few times he opened his eyes and realized that he was again coming to himself after having passed out. Each time this happened he would again listen hard to try to understand what was happening around him.

He felt the floor rumble, and through his right ear, which was nearly pressed against the carpet, he heard a low, growling roar. He realized that the whole building was subtly shaking. He tried to analyze this sensation. Was it caused by something in the building, or by something further away—outside? To his mind it lasted no more than three or four seconds, though in fact it lasted almost ten; and in the end he had no idea what had caused it. Only those people half hanging out the windows had a better, though in the end equally inaccurate, sense of what was going on. Through the hot smoke rising over their faces they saw, below, great, whitish clouds of dust rushing out over the city streets like some horizontal, earthbound nuclear cloud. They could only assume that some huge explosion had occurred nearby.

They could not have imagined that the skyscraper beside their own—corresponding to their own in all proportions and strength—had tumbled down. If someone had told them this they either would not have believed it or would not have been able fully to comprehend it. For buildings as huge as these did not just "fall down." And if they did they would surely destroy whole city blocks. That they could fall, with an almost fussy neatness, into their own footprint seemed an impossibility. But the difficulty in conceiving of this arose out of a misconception of the particular construction of these skyscrapers, which were not, like others, built from cages of steel but rather of an inner core and an outer frame between which stretched acres of flooring. These buildings were strong enough to hold fast in the face of hurricane-force winds, and even to absorb and remain standing after the impact of a jet liner, yet for all that their immense substance was only seeming: they were made up mostly of insubstantial air.

The voices that Miguel again heard in the near distance were those of a few men and women standing at the windows who had seen and exclaimed their surprise at the "explosion." In anticipation of another and perhaps larger explosion, which would affect them or at least the building they were in, a few of these people had pulled back from the windows and retreated somewhat into the ballroom; no sooner doing so than deciding in an instant that it would be better to perish out there, on the ledge, where at least now and then they could catch a whiff of good air.

Now the nature of physical pain is so self-involved, so bends consciousness to itself, that it prevents all outside, alien, diluting distractions. When in pain we have little or no patience for anything else. Planetary destruction itself may be imminent—but what is that to us, who are doubled over with the sword-stabs of an inflamed kidney, or retching on account of poisons in our blood, or nearly crying for heat so great that it feels like red-hot irons pressing into our skin? When we cannot take a single breath without pain, then the fate of the world, of the universe, means nothing to us. In such dire circumstances every second seems to last for a minute, and each minute seems to drag out for an hour. But even as the whole force of our souls is concentrated on the apparently immovable moment, even as we tell ourselves or others, "I can't stand this any more!"—time passes, the seconds become minutes, the minutes quarters of an hour; and we endure what seemed unendurable. We endure it because we cannot help clinging to the hope that the ordeal will end and we will survive it; and even should we lose consciousness and the capacity for hope, our organism continues the struggle for life in its own silent, organic, animal way.

For Miguel and those who were still alive and conscious above the impact zone, the state of mind was a flux of intense fear, poisoned wooziness, hope of rescue, and moments in which memories from safer, happier days abstracted attention away from the dreadful present. These intermittent, self-involved scenes of safer, better times in the past bubbled up in the mind like dreams, and they served the same purpose: to pacify and mollify. But they could never do so for more than a few seconds or minutes at a time. The moment one came back to oneself one was aware of intense heat and smoke—one was flung back into the painful, mortal reality.

Just as the survival of those trapped in the floors above the impact zone depended on how long they could endure the ever-increasing heat and smoke, so the existence of the building itself depended on how long the integrity of its structural steel could withstand the fires burning within it. They had been burning now for over an hour. They were not hot enough to melt the steel: but they were hot enough to weaken it, and this at its weakest point, namely, where the airliner had plowed into the building at more than four hundred miles per hour, destroying or damaging the central core of main support beams. There, where the impact had been immediate and most destructive, and a fireball fed by 10,000 gallons of jet fuel had burst, and the fires had burned hottest, girders once entirely solid and stiff had begun to falter. They bent with anguished moans, and trusses broke away from perimeter brackets with sharp bangs, and rivets that had been immovably tight for thirty years gave way with pops that sounded like distant fireworks. With each structural element that failed, more pressure and weight was placed on those that remained but which had themselves been compromised and were the less able to bear any additional load. There came the point at which these cumulative failures could no longer be compensated for by adjacent, intact structures;— when these too, weakened by the heat, gave way;—and the sudden, inevitable collapse occurred.

Those who were still conscious in the ballroom—and there were not many besides Miguel—heard a roar, felt a shudder, and felt themselves falling as the world dropped away beneath them.

Somewhere a man shouted "Oh my God—!"—an exclamation cut short.

The top ten floors of the building, and all their thousands of tons of weight, fell onto the subordinate floors. These, unable to sustain the tremendous impact, in turn collapsed one atop the other, each one adding to the irresistible force and weight of the dropping mass.

Miguel felt something huge fall onto his head and back; his body gave way to something fast and heavy with the easiness of a leaf tossed by a gusting wind. He tumbled downward over and over ...

—Once, when he was very young, he had been at the beach, in the ocean, and a wave had caught him up just as it broke—right there in the crux of its most violent and driven waters; and had enfolded him, flung him down, pushed him forth crazily; his body no longer under his control, a mere plaything of gargantuan powers. Over and over he had tumbled ... over and over ... as now.

Things blunt, sharp, impulsive, tore into his body, into his legs and arms and back.

The sudden killing wounds are not felt as pain; they are felt as pressures. An arm is torn away, a leg is sliced in two, an aluminum brace crashes through the breastbone with a heavy crunch. It is sudden, swift, immensely indefinable.

And so the boy felt a heavy, crunching sensation at his neck, and the next thing he knew————

The forces involved in the collapse of the skyscrapers were enormous beyond reckoning. Steel girders and concrete flooring smashed together with all the destructive force of falling tons. They ripped into and tore apart all materials of lesser strength and density. Thus glass windows, gypsum drywall, and the marble or tile slabs of an elegant lobby's flooring;—thus desks and chairs, and computers and telephones, and printers and lamps, and everything from the largest of duplication machines to the smallest framed picture of a child on a proud father's desk;—all came together, smashed together, became part of the enormous abrasive roiling that tore apart and ground once solid objects into particles of dust. And compared with steel and concrete, with heavy wood and tough plastics, how much more fragile was poor human flesh? Thus it most easily of all became part of the monstrous cloud of dust that billowed up and outward from the falling skyscraper, that swept through thoroughfares and insinuated itself into every old, winding, cobbled street of historic downtown Manhattan, covering those who had tried to outrun it but who, finding they could not, had fallen into gutters or taken refuge behind parked cars, holding their arms protectively over their heads, shutting their eyes tight, trying not to breathe the noxious stuff, the sinister dust, which nevertheless worked its way into their mouths and nostrils, into their lungs and blood, and so became forever a part of them, of every beat of their hearts.

By the time the dust-cloud began to settle, that whole lower part of the city, once so vibrant with commerce, with the impatient noise and movement of traffic and pedestrians, was quiet, deserted, stilled except for the shifting, dust-misted air and pieces of paper curling or scuttling along the whitened ground. Above this blanched desolation the surrounding buildings stood like tombstones visible above an eerie fog.

Throughout the city and the country, throughout the world, the attacks and the destruction were broadcast live. And people the world over looked on mutely, with shaking heads, with hands pressed against mouths, entranced by the sublime horror of it all; and as though language were incapable of expressing the full enormity of what was happening, those who saw it could only think, could only say:

"Oh my God!"

"Oh my God!"—as the planes hit.

"Oh my God!"—as the fires raged.

"Oh my God!"—as trapped people hung out of windows a hundred stories up, gasping for air, terrified, waving their arms to be noticed, crying out for rescue.

"Oh my God!"—to think of those trapped there, suffocating there, dying there.

"Oh my God!"—to see or learn that some were flinging themselves out of windows, preferring a fall to their deaths rather than to be burned alive.

"Oh my God!"—as the towers collapsed.

"Oh my God!"—as sinew and steel, and plastic and brains, and wire and blood commingled into the rushing death-cloud that covered lower Manhattan.

Again and again, all over the country, all over the world:

"Oh my God!"

Two months later in a little village in Mexico a woman was hanging her laundry on a line strung between the corner of her ramshackle house and a tree in a dusty plot of earth thirty feet away. Though she was in her late forties, she looked well on into her fifties, for her hair was largely gray and her brown and somewhat pockmarked face was heavily seamed. She was not and had never been attractive. Her life had been the hard one of a poor mother of five, though, thank God, only the little ones remained at home and the oldest three—again, thank God, all boys, who after all could take care of themselves—had gone off to make their ways in the world. She blessed them all as she thought of them.

As she hung out the underwear of her twelve-year-old daughter she saw the postman coming down the dirt road. His rounds were like clockwork; she always saw him at this time of day. As usual he carried his postal bag over his left shoulder, half resting on his flank, half on his stomach. He held several envelopes in his hand, sorting them as he prepared to leave them under the doors or in the post boxes of the next houses along his route. His name was Enrique, a quietly jovial man with a gray mustache who had been delivering the mail for thirty years. He had to be at least sixty years old now, the woman thought, and said to herself, "Poor man, how much longer can he keep doing that job?—walking around all day like that? Especially in the summer, when it's so hot. He has grown children—don't they help him?" But when he had reached her she called out gaily:

"Enrique, how are you?"

The old man's face, which had been serious and intent on looking at addresses on the envelopes, bloomed into a smile showing gaps of missing teeth.

"Good, good! How are you! More laundry, eh?"

"It never ends!"

They shared a quick laugh as he held out an envelope for her, saying, "Here you go!"

"Thank you!"

He nodded.

"Enrique?" she asked, before he had a chance to move on.

He looked at her.

"You want anything to drink? Some water or coffee or ... something?"

He gave a quick negative shake of his head as though he wondered why she would ask him such a question, only to smile with an expression of gratitude for her little kindness and say:

"No, I'm fine, thanks. I'll have some coffee when I get back to the post office."

He went on his way.

The woman didn't recognize the writing on the envelope. The name of the sender was obviously Spanish, but it wasn't familiar to her. Then she saw that it was from the United States—from New York—and she knew it had to be from or

about her son, Miguel. She smiled and her heart beat a little
faster with joy. She hadn't heard from him in so long! She had
prayed for him every day, often several times a day. She was
eager to learn how well he was doing. She tore open the envelope.

The damp laundry, hanging on the line, swayed a little in
the breeze as she started to read.

INNOCENT

The arctic landscape was white, scintillant, magical; it was clean, fresh, and pure. The sky was clear and blue, and its light was half absorbed and half reflected by the snow-covered ground and the crags of ice that rose like gigantic uncut diamonds beside the sea. There, where the pure cold waves of the North Atlantic met the white, snow-covered terrain, thousands of harp seals were congregated. They were cows who had come here some two weeks earlier to give birth. Their small pups had started out white as the snow on which they lay, and some of them still were, though by this time most had shed that coat for one of a darker, maturer hue. They had only just been suckled; some were suckling still. In a few days or weeks more they would waddle to the edge of the ice-bound shore and dive into the surf to start their lives in the sea. They filled the air with their short quick yelps, the audible expressions of their hunger or discomfort, or of the sheer nervous energy of vigorous new life. Their mothers, the cows, who paid their little ones a little less heed than formerly, basked in the sun. Sometimes they pulled themselves up onto their foreflippers and looked about, but they could not see far clearly, for the mucosal drip that continually washed over their eyes and protected them from the salt sea made their sight blurry on land. Only a few of them, and only those on eminences, detected something strange at the edge of the world—there, on the sea in the distance. It was the superstructure of a ship making its way toward land. Eventually it anchored several hundred feet from shore, and there was a flurry of movement on its decks as men climbed down into half a dozen smaller boats and headed to shore.

The men were Canadian sealers, for the annual seal hunt had begun. As their motorboats came closer to shore they gazed landward in great anticipation. A lookout on the ship had spotted the herd of harp seals toward which they were moving.

They were dressed for the climate as well as for the acts they were about to commit. They wore woolen coats over several shirts and sweaters, woolen caps, and high rubberized boots. Each of them carried a hakapik, a kind of long club outfitted with a blunt hammerhead that tapered off into a curved, sharp-pointed hook. Some had even made their own hakapik by bending long nails into a hook and affixing it to the end of a baseball bat. When their boats had landed, they spread out on the shore and began trudging landward.

The seals became agitated as the men approached. The cows began braying nervously, as though in warning to one another, and a sense of panic spread throughout the herd. Where possible they dove into breaks in the ice; but most were not near such routes of escape and instead began retreating inward, landward, away from the oncoming figures. But while graceful and swift in the water, these creatures were ponderous and obtuse on land.

The men no sooner reached the seals than they scanned the herd for the pups. When the men came still closer, the adult, female seals reared up, showed their teeth, and brayed threateningly. The men paid them no mind. They calmly and methodically walked up to the pups and, raising their spiked clubs, smashed them into the heads of the young animals. Usually the little body at once fell flat in death; or sometimes it gave a little jump and shivered before it expired; or it might be only injured, in which case it twitched—till another bash into its head ended its life.

Minutes after the slaughter had started the air which had been filled with muzzling moans and whimpers of new life was filled with the howls of hundreds of adult seals at a pitch of hysteria; for while these animals could not understand why their offspring were being attacked and injured, they saw and knew that this was happening, and it aroused a panicking maternal instinct to try to protect their young, or to express the frustration at their inability to do so.

As they killed again and again, as they snuffed out one life after another, as their boots and the bottom of their pants became spotted and then soaked with blood, the men felt no pity, no remorse, no pang of guilt. They did not think twice about what they were doing. For weeks they had prepared themselves for this event; indeed, they had looked forward to it with a sense of delicious anticipation. For they would make money from it— not as much money as in the past, perhaps, but still something. The fur of the young seals still had a market. It would be sold to clothing manufacturers and form, say, the elegant trim of a sophisticated lady's winter coat. Or it would be sold to some Chinese toy manufacturer to be used as the external "lifelike" fur of some stuffed animal. If anyone had suggested to these men that they were committing a cruelty they would have responded—if they had deigned to respond at all—that they were just making a living; and if someone had insisted that their manner of making a living involved the suffering of another creature, those among them who were not articulate would have sneered or spat, while those who were might have repeated what they had been taught as children, namely, that these seals were just animals, and animals were made by God to be "used" as men saw fit. Indeed some of these men regarded themselves as religious. Beneath their jackets and shirts and insulated undergarments hung gold or silver chains at the end of which dangled the image of their Lord and Savior, Jesus Christ. Sustained by their faith, and paying no mind to the cows who howled in distress as their pups were assaulted before their eyes or dragged away from their sides, the men worked with cool, business-minded efficiency.

When they relented in their clubbing, the hunters turned their attention to the piles of the dead or dying bodies they had accumulated. With the air still filled with the braying of cows hysterical over the attack and destruction of their young, the human beings began skinning the carcases. There was a particular way to do this. First one plunged the blade into the soft underbelly, then, with a sawing motion, brought it up to the rib cage, then still further up to the neck, around which one made a circumcision, then made a similar cut around the fins till one could tear away the whole pelt. During this process blood accumulated in pools around the men's feet, and flowed as little streams for a space before freezing into water-diluted ribbons of pink ice. Each time a furred skin was removed, the rest of the body was tossed aside like a piece of garbage: and in truth it didn't look like much: merely some amorphous, moistly-red, fleshy thing. Certainly it did not look like the creature that had once felt hunger, yearned for warmth and coddling, and looked out on the world with wondering, infant curiosity.

The slaughter of the young animals went on for hours. The men responsible for it would gladly have butchered all of them, but, in the first place, that would have taken them all day, and, in the second, they could not take more than their state-imposed quota without the risk of prosecution. They had to be satisfied with the hundreds they had killed—at least, on this day.

And over this carnage the sky shone as brightly, as cloudlessly, as serenely as ever—as though the Universe were indifferent to it all.

*

In another, much warmer part of the world, in Seville, Spain, a noisy, celebratory crowd filled the bleachers of a stadium and sent up a great cheer as the famous matador, Pedro Barra, walked forth. He walked somehow shyly, humbly, as though he would have preferred not to be the center of so much attention. But then, as though it would have been ungracious not to accept or at least acknowledge these vociferous kudos, he looked up and about and raised a hand in a quick wave—a gesture that engendered another roar of cheering. Certainly it was easy to see why the women in the audience were so enthusiastic about him. He was tall, lean, and handsome, his profile perfect in the jutting straightness of its lines. His figure was accentuated by his tight-fitting *traje de luces*—his glinting, silver- and gold-threaded outfit—and his *capote de paseo*, a dress cape of blue satin, gave him a romantic panache. By the time he had stopped in the center of the arena the cheering died down and was succeeded by a hushed expectation. All eyes were on him as he crossed himself, lowered his head with closed eyes, and clasped his hands together in prayer. Though the crowds could not hear what he murmured ("Jesus, my Savior, protect me, and let me be victorious!") they knew that he was praying and were the more enamored of him on account of it:—for was it not refreshing, was it not inspiring, to see a man so famous, so adulated by the masses, so refulgent with skill and bravery, nevertheless humble before God? Indeed, a large part of his popularity arose from his reputation as a religious man, for the onlookers could not but be disposed toward someone who shared their deep faith.

After he had stood a moment in the center of the arena, and the applause and cheering had subsided, the matador looked off to one side and gave a subtle nod. From out of the darkness of a chute at the far side of the stadium a bull came charging out into the open.

Cheers erupted from the crowd at the sight of the animal running into the light so fast and hard that it seemed the devil himself were at his heels. He was a fine, big, powerful animal, the result of generations of human effort by which his kind was bred for the spectacle of which he was now a part. The program gave his name as Bright Eyes, and while it was hardly possible for most of the spectators in the stadium to see how well deserving he was of this name, they could all see his energy and speed as he dashed a quarter of the way around the stadium, kicking up his back hooves as though in conscious pleasure of his own vitality. When he finally slowed his pace and then stopped, he saw the lone man standing in the center of the great space, and watched him suspiciously.

The spectators jeered Bright Eyes for his caution. From hundreds of seats throughout the stadium, human beings impatient for the show to begin whistled and called out insults to him, laughing as they did so. Bright Eyes heard this great, strange, impulsive accumulation of human voices but did not understand it, any more than, over the last few days, he had understood a number of things that had happened to him. He had been taken from the pasture in which he had grazed peacefully all his life, then shoved into a crate barely large enough to move about in, men conveying him, poking him forward into one strange place after another—this the strangest place of all! A dim remembrance of his pasture, of its green and spacious peacefulness, flashed through his mind.

Onto the arena came a man on horseback. He carried a long lance and his horse was draped on either side with thick, mattress-like padding. He was one of the *picadores*—the spear-bearers, whose job it was to injure and tire the bull. His horse was blindfolded so that it should not see the danger toward which it was being led. The picador rode up to Bright Eyes, who snorted and stamped his feet in growing suspicion. The picador continued to ride up to him and, just as he reached him, he turned the blindfolded, docile horse to one side, so that the bull was to the rider's right. Bright Eyes lowered his head, his horns, and lunged inward and upward into the horse's belly, but the horns were incapable of penetrating the thick padding there, and the only effect of his effort was to make the heavy horse wobble somewhat and take a few clumsy steps sideways. The picador leaned over toward the bull and struck. He pushed the lance into the base of the bull's neck, piercing the hide, slicing into the powerful muscles there.

Bright Eyes bucked away at the painful injury.

"Olé!" shouted the multitude, the men and women, the fathers and sons, the wives and mothers.

"Olé!" they cried, happily, as the picador again rode up to the bull, came close to him, and again cut into his neck.

"Olé!" tens of thousands of Spaniards shouted, more excited than ever, for they now perceived the first glint of red—the first flow of blood.

Bright Eyes, who had been vainly trying to gore his attacker—for to his mind the man and horse were one, equally hostile—shuddered with pain, backed off, and ran for a space.

The picador rode up to the bull two more times, and each time the bull tried to gore the belly of the horse, but always his efforts were ineffective against the thick padding. It was almost a pity that he hadn't been born in an earlier age when the horses of the picadors were not protected. In those days a bull would rip open the belly of the horse whose guts would go splattering about as it whinnied and neighed and was pressed onward, ever onward by the man riding on its back.

Meanwhile the picador stabbed Bright Eyes repeatedly with his spear. From the wounds blood bubbled up and streamed down the bull's shoulders in a crimson so bright and red that it was easily seen from the farthest seats in the stadium.

"Olé!"

And yet again the bull backed off in frustration at his inability to repel his attacker. He was out of breath from his exertions, and the sharp pain in his neck and shoulders from the lancings made him hang his head. On seeing this the picador knew that he had done his job of weakening the animal. He pulled back his horse, turned it around, and galloped away, raising his bloodied lance as though in victory. He was a very proud man and the Spanish public looking on acclaimed him with great cheering.

Now it was the matador's turn to exhibit once again what it was that set him apart from other men: why he had achieved fame above all others, and women's breasts heaved to look upon him, and he stood out to the world as a shining credit to his nation and culture.

Unlike other matadors, the great Barra did not rely on *banderilleros*, the men who specialized in injuring and riling up the bull further by implanting into its neck and shoulders the *banderillas*—long, barbed, beribboned darts. No, *he himself* carried out this office—and so more fully courted danger.

A horseman came riding out to him with these implements of torment, which the custom the great nation had made colorful and cheerful: in this instance, the *banderillas* were silver, with bright green, purple, and red ribbons attached to the ends. The matador took one in each hand and with long, slow motions of his arms waved them over his head so that their ribbons streamed around him. It was a wildly extravagant and entertaining gesture but there was more to it even than that: it was the equivalent of shouting into each onlooker's ear: "I rely on none but myself, and I am afraid of nothing!"

The crowd ate up the showy braggadocio. The men whistled and whooped and shouted their approval, for the matador seemed to them at that moment an incarnation of their notion of manly ideal. As for the women, especially those in the first rows who could see him clearly, they gazed on his svelte figure and etched profile, and their imaginations took them and him to places more private than a bullring. They grew a little warmer, and fanned themselves briskly.

In the meantime Bright Eyes was standing alone, blood dripping from his lanced neck over his shoulders and down his forelegs. He had been breathing hard from his recent exertions against the picador and his horse, and his mind was somewhat befuddled from the pain of his wounds. He did not understand why he was here or how he had been injured; the events of the last few minutes, in their detail and consequence, already seemed to fade a little in his mind, leaving behind only the urgent sense of danger and threat. He watched as the matador

stepped toward him holding before him things long and gleaming and having streaming tails. He had no idea what they
were, though instinct made him nervously wary. Thus Bright
Eyes lowered his head, focused in on the approaching man, and
stamped his forefeet as a rising impulse to charge took hold of
him.

He charged of a sudden. He kept his head low, his horns
thrust forward, his eyes turned upward; kicking up sand, he
headed toward his target with killing intent; but when predator
and prey were no more than six feet from each other—when
only a second remained before contact—the matador jumped up,
jumped away, eluded the horns that would otherwise have im-
paled him, and even as they swept by beneath him he descended and plunged the barbed darts into the animal with all
the weight of his falling body—implanting them deep, deep into
the shoulders, where they anchored inextricably.

Bolts of pain shot through the bull.

"Olé!" humanity cheered.

Bright Eyes stopped short, bucking with agony. He felt the
weight of the *banderillas* on his hide and identified them with
the pain lancing into his chest and lungs. He tried to shake
them off, but his exertions only instigated sharper waves of
pain. He was dazed. He could not understand what was happening to him, or why. He remained still, snorting hard, blood
dripping down his back. He turned around and saw the human
being approaching him, holding another set of *banderillas* that a
horseman had delivered to him. The ribbons on these were
even brighter and more cheerful than those on the previous
ones: gold, yellow, orange—the most festive of colors.

The spectators watched the matador approach Bright Eyes
again one careful, inevitable step at a time. He held out the
banderillas with outstretched arms, their barbed, razor-sharp
tips pointing downward and inward. Just watching him made
one grow tense. The stadium fell to a hush. Magnificent, the
artistry with which Matador Barra held the attention of ten
thousand! And it seemed that he was able, through some sympathetic power in his gaze, to enchant the bull to a benign stillness, for Bright Eyes stood motionless. In fact the injured
animal was silently enduring his pain, and his lack of movement was owing to the rising sense of approaching danger. He

knew the man was going to injure him again and he was gathering up his powers to strike and destroy his tormentor. Sure enough he pounded the ground with his forefeet and charged with all his might. Again, in the nick of time, the matador leapt up and away from the oncoming horns, and in coming down again implanted the barbed spears deep into the creature's flesh.

The crowds went wild.

"Olé! Olé! Olé!"

The calls rang out from every seat, from every tier, from every throat, for all saw the bull stumble, saw his weakness, the new lag and languor of his demeanor, and the new rills of blood that poured down his flank, making half of it red as though someone had poured a can of red paint over him: they saw it clearly, this first peep of his death, and they could not contain themselves:

"Olé! Olé! Olé"

They were mailmen and civil engineers, secretaries and housewives, bread makers and bankers, bus drivers and plumbers, pensioners and entrepreneurs; they represented the whole gamut of their society from top to bottom; all come together in this grand stadium to gaze upon, to enjoy, to delight in the matador's skill and the studied, paced, procedural destruction of another seeing, feeling, hearing, thinking creature.

Having lost much blood and feeling himself weak, Bright Eyes, after turning back around toward the human being who had assaulted him twice, stood there snorting hard, catching his breath, in pain.

A horseman rode out to the matador and handed him his sword over which was draped the *muleta*—the short red cape by which the acclaimed man would do his close dance of death with the weakened but still dangerous animal. Even in taking the *muleta* the famous Barra knew how to excite another round of admiration from the onlookers. Holding the cape first to one side of himself, then to another, and always with a flourish, he stepped a wide circuit around Bright Eyes. It was an arrant, almost arrogant peacock show, a thing at which purists of the matadorial tradition had frowned. But the people loved it and cheered.

In order to keep his sights on the man, Bright Eyes first turned his head, then shuffled in a stationary circle. Of one thing he was instinctively certain: that the man was the menace to be reckoned with, the enemy to be destroyed. And now he saw the man had stopped circling him and was walking toward him, holding the cloth close to one side of his body in a gesture of dare and defiance and mockery. Bright Eyes lowered his head, stamped his feet, and drew upon his flagging energy and charged. His back hooves kicked up the dirt of the arena as he built up speed and rushed his target, who, however, once again, eluded the points of his horns, which glided beneath the waving cloth. And Bright Eyes heard thunderously around him:

"*Olé!*"

The bull charged again; and again; and again. Each time he did so, the man seemed to disappear in a dazzle of sparkles from his sequined suit and a crimson blur from the cloth he waved.

"*Olé!*"

Bright Eyes stopped short, spun around, and this time hesitated, confused about why he could not put an end to his tormentor; but the dreadful sense of danger, of threat standing there before him, impelled him to charge again, and yet again, and yet again. Each time he did so he missed his mark, and each of his misses evoked the roar of ten thousand human voices. Loss of blood, confusion, panic, fear, pain, frustrated exertion—all conspired in draining might from the animal's once-powerful limbs, in making the once-alert eyes grow uncertain and dull. He stood languorously, his head bowed, blood flowing freely from the wounds in his neck and shoulders, watching the human being who now approached him and then, when only a few feet away—drop to his knees!

What arrogance! What bravado! What other matador would have done such a thing?

The crowds cheered wildly.

But the gesture was not so brave as it seemed. The man could see that the animal before him was exhausted with wasted effort and loss of blood, which reddened the arena sand all around.

The bull mustered enough strength to charge again—even if the charge was nothing but a plodding trot. This time the horns came so close to the matador that many in the stadium thought he had been gored; here and there, in the stands, some jumped up, horrified to think the great Barra had finally met his doom. But no! He had not been injured. Once again, he had been too quick for the bull. Once again, he proved himself to be a man among men!

"*Olé!*"

Several times the matador got down on his knees and provoked the tired animal. Each time, Bright Eyes mustered his will to attack. During the sixth such pass, the bull's legs buckled; he stumbled, fell onto the earth, scrambled up heavily; and stood snorting and breathing hard, bleeding hard, staring dully at the human being.

The matador could see the animal had been driven to his uttermost limits of endurance.

And now came the final, supreme act of showmanship; the pièce de résistance in this brave and great man's routine; the thing which set him so far apart and above others, and for which he was especially esteemed and famous. There in the arena with tens of thousands of eyes upon him, and with hardly a glance to the bull not many feet away, Barra took off his jacket and threw it aside, then unbuttoned his shirt, and threw that aside too, and stood there bare-chested and exposed, as though willing to stake his life on his own, unadorned, brave humanity—or on his trust in God.

The crowd roared its approval. The men clapped and shouted encouragement while the women, at the sight of his smooth, toned, slim-hipped body, fanned themselves a little more quickly, and even middle-aged matrons shifted in their seats with hot imaginations.

From the folds of the *muleta* the matador withdrew his sword.

It was not just any sword. It was *his* sword, his special sword, which had been made for him many years before and by which he had built his magnificent reputation. It bore on its shaft, just above the cross-guard, a short prayer to His Lord and Savior, asking for bravery and safety. Taking it in hand, he held it aloft as though to show it off to his applauding admirers. It flashed in the sunlight like a column of fire. The crowd sent out another wave of applause. When he lowered the sword he held it out before him with a stiff arm and sighted the bull along its blade as though he were calculating a trajectory.

Bright Eyes saw the gleaming instrument and did not know what it was, but he sensed a new threat in the way the man drew himself up and moved toward him with the wavering cloth. When they were ten feet away, the animal charged. The man eluded the horns by a fraction of an inch. Even as Bright Eyes flew by he felt a horrible, crunching sensation at the base of his neck as the matador plunged the sword into him, slicing into the body between the shoulder blades and past the top of his ribs, just missing the aorta in which blood was pumping fast with fear and pain and anger.

All around the air reverberated with an immense *"Olé!"*

The bull's legs buckled beneath him. The inertia of his bulk and charge carried him forward several feet till he landed hard and painfully in the bloodied sand of the arena. With forelegs crumpled up beneath him, with back legs rather comically sprawled out behind, he lay upright on his stomach, dazed. He felt a sudden salt wetness in his throat, and in the next moment blood filled his hot, dry, mouth, then bubbled out of it and dripped from his hairy chin like a red liquid beard. He groaned and grunted at the constricting, suffocating sensation of blood filling his lungs. He lowered his head and stertorously gasped for breath as he saw the man approaching him. Death panic seized him. He tried to get up: but he could not. Somehow the will to move had been severed from the body itself. Nature had diverted his remaining vitality to maintain the most fundamental processes of life itself, namely, the beating of the heart and the expansion and contraction of the lungs.

It was not the clean kill the matador had wanted or that the crowds had hoped to see. The dramatically instantaneous snuffing out of life had been denied them. But it was clear that Bright Eyes was almost dead—that he would not be rising again. It was only a matter of delivering the coup de grace. From even this less-than-optimal circumstance the great Barra knew how to extract another ounce of crowd-pleading drama. He came near to the prostrate, hard-snorting bull and walked around him a few times, then stopped just at his side and placed a foot on his back in a gesture of domination and victory. The animal saw the terrible nearness of the man, and felt the pressure of his foot, yet these had lost their power to infuriate him to action as he struggled for life. He could only lie there groaning, bleeding, struggling to breathe; he could only watch and wait. The matador raised his sword and threw back his head, looking off to the highest tiers of the stadium as though to ask, "Well? And what do you think of me? Tell me the truth! Am I not the greatest matador of all?"

The crowd roared. Many of the men shouted ecstatic implorations for him to deliver the killing sword-thrust, their faces turning red with joyous anticipation of the death-blow. Even some of the women, caught up in the intense enthusiasm of the moment, forgot to be demure and shrieked out for the kill.

Barra turned his attention to the bull, and carefully, almost delicately lowered his sword and placed it against the animal's heaving chest. With his left arm held up as though to balance himself, he hesitated—just a moment—and then, with a spasm of power, a burst of joyful determination, he pushed the sharp blade inward, using every muscle and pound of his body to guide the blade unerringly into the dying animal's heart.

Bright Eyes gave a low, blood-spluttered bellow, shivered, and fell over, dead.

"*Olé!*"—the cheering was immense.

"*Olé!*"—the pride of Spain rose to its feet.

"*Olé!*"—yes, men and women of all ages, from the lowliest street hawkers to the finest lawyers to the devoutest altar boys, all, all rose to their feet, and clapped and cheered.

The matador pulled out his sword from the carcase; he held it high; he turned to all quarters of the stadium to receive the accolades that continued to shower down on him. He walked away from the dead animal a lone figure: the pride of his nation. Festive music blared through loudspeakers.

And overlooking it all was a sky that shone as brightly, as cloudlessly, as serenely as ever, as though the Universe were indifferent to such things.

*

In yet another part of the world the farmer Dong-sun Sung drove his battered pickup truck over a pitted dirt road, bouncing and shaking with the vehicle as it crossed the rural South Korean landscape, and finally came home. It was not much of a home, merely a one-storied, ramshackle structure with somehow uneven walls, as though its builders had been amateurs and not professionals—which was the fact of the matter. It had been painted a pale yellow, but the paint was chipping and peeling everywhere, adding to its distressed appearance. For some months now his wife had been after Dong-sun to repaint it, but so far he hadn't complied with her demand, in part because he hadn't had the time, but also because it was an expense he did not want to have to pay out. He was a poor man who just eked out a living for them both on his forty acres of land. True, last year had been a better year than most—his crops had brought in more money than usual—but he knew that one had to prepare for the inevitable rainy day, and it was more important to put money away than waste it on the unnecessary expense of paint. The house, he told himself, could wait another few years before it absolutely had to be repainted. Of course, when his wife found out about the dog she would probably reprimand him for his extravagance. Buying a dog instead of paint for the house!

"Let her yell at me," he thought, defiantly. "I need what I need."

Dong-sun had not been feeling himself lately. Over the last year or two he had been having pain in his feet and knees after a long day in the fields. In the mornings he no longer rose out of bed especially invigorated and he could tell that he wasn't as strong as he used to be because it was harder than ever for him to lift or pull heavy things. He also grew tired more quickly, so much so that after a morning's work he would come home and take a nap. At forty-eight years of age ("only" forty-eight, as he told himself) he felt as though he were sixty; certainly it seemed to him that while other men his age were as vigorous as ever he himself had begun to decline. He had raised these doubts with his wife. "Well, what did you expect?" she had told him, shrugging. "You're not a kid any more. Just take better care of yourself and try to get more rest, that's all." That was hardly an answer—neither practical advice nor helpmately comfort. He himself was sure that at least part of the problem was owing to a years-long indifference to his health, of which he had never thought twice—as most people don't, so long as they have it. It had occurred to him that he had to start eating more healthfully. He must get into his system something that would recruit his diminishing strength. Of course as he and many men in his country knew, there was nothing more likely to do that than a hearty meal of dog meat.

Dong-sun had indulged in eating dog meat only a few times in his life, many years before. In part this was because there was no one in his area who raised dogs for eating, and in part because such meat, in the distant markets in which it was available, was prohibitively expensive. But surely one's health was not something about which one should economize. He had reconciled himself to the expense of the animal just as one does to an expensive but necessary drug.

No sooner had he shut off the engine of the truck and gotten out of it than his wife, who had been in the kitchen and seen his arrival through the window, came outside. She was a short, thin woman who had never been attractive but had always been sensible. Her hair was half gray though she was only a year older than her husband. She saw the crate in the back of the truck and walked a few steps toward it to get a better look at what it contained. It was not a total surprise for her to see that a dog was in it. For some few weeks now her husband had mentioned buying one, saying that dog meat would be just the thing to make him feel better. If she didn't reprimand him now it was only because she was objective enough to know that Dong-sun rarely bought anything for himself and that it wouldn't have been fair in her to fault him for this purchase, which after all he deemed a necessity.

Dong-sun assumed the somewhat nervous, uncertain demeanor of a husband who knows he's done something that might incur his wife's anger.

"So, you bought the dog," she said, frowning, looking at him with disapproval.

He nodded. He avoided her eyes.

"What did you have to get a live one for? Why not get one already killed and cleaned."

"They didn't have that," he said.

She shook her head disapprovingly and looked again at the animal. With his snout sticking through a gap between the rough slats of the crate, the dog had set his eyes on her and was wagging his tail with a tap-tap-tap as it struck the enclosure on either side. He was dusky yellow in color, with a dark snout, crumpled ears, and black eyes beneath dark slender streaks of fur that looked like eyebrows. Of no particular breed one might nevertheless have seen in him hints of a St. Bernard or Labrador ancestor.

"Where are you going to kill it?" she asked.

"Behind the shed—in the ditch."

She looked again at the dog. The dog looked back at her. Something—she couldn't say what—stirred within her, uncomfortably. She turned around and went into the house, her arms still folded, still shaking her head. "Money on a dog!" she told herself, walking off. "And I know it was probably a lot! I know they're not cheap! We could have spent that money on other things we need!"

Dong-sun took up the dog cage and carried it a short space to the front of a nearby shed and set it down there. He went to the shed and pushed open its door, shoving it hard; it gave way with a metallic screech as the rollers beneath it turned resistantly over a rusted rail. For a few minutes he disappeared into the gloomy interior and when he came out he was holding a length of steel pipe, a knife, and a skein of hempen cord. He tucked these items under one arm and took up the crated dog, which he brought around to the back of the shed. Here the earth declined away from the back wall for the space of thirty feet before it leveled off to a fallow field. Just where the declivity became level, a ditch dimpled the earth. At one time it had been deep enough that a man might have stood in it and his head would have barely been at ground level. Dong-sun had dug it eight years earlier as a receptacle into which household refuse was dumped and burned. Years of usage, combined with run-off soil from hundreds of rainfalls, had long filled it up. Now it was a gentle depression overgrown with grass and weeds. Beside it the farmer set down the cage and opened its door.

There was already a collar, of sorts, on the dog—a length of rope tied around its neck. "Come on," Dong-sun said, pulling the animal out.

The dog wasn't hesitant to leave the cage; on the contrary, he was eager both for freedom from the cramped enclosure as well as to be closer to the human being. Ten thousand years of breeding had made amenable to him the look, sound, movement, odor, and aura of mankind. On the farm where he had been raised, he and his litter-mates had scurried and fallen over one another to receive from men's hands some pat on the head or stroke on the back, some scrap of affection thrown them with their food. Despite the somewhat harsh way the man had pulled him out of the cage, he stood wagging his tail, albeit uncertainly. He looked about him. He glanced at the man once, twice, then looked away, keeping his head bowed in submission. He licked his lips and sniffed first the air and then the leg of the man whose hands lowered to him, bearing something—a length of cord.

Dong-sun wrapped the cord around the dog's snout several times, each time a little more snugly than the last, though not so tightly that the animal couldn't breathe. The dog backed up as though to escape these strictures, then shook his head and with first his left, then his right forepaw tried to wipe them off himself. Swiftly, the man wrapped another length of cord around the animal's hind legs, tying them tightly. Unable to balance himself, the dog fell over, and the man quickly wrapped another length of cord around the forefeet. The dog squirmed, paddling his hind- and forefeet in the air as he tried to free himself from their bindings. For some minutes he did this, then, recognizing how vain the effort was, or anticipating the man would release him from this strange process, he lay still and waited.

If Dong-sun had wanted to kill the dog outright he could have done so with one or two hard bashes to its head; but that was not the point. The point was to make it suffer before it died; and the more it suffered, the better. For as Dong-sun had learned from his father and other men in his country, when a dog suffered its organs released into its blood certain compounds that imparted an invigorating quality to its flesh. Thus even as he stepped a little to one side and raised the steel pipe for the first blow, the man used all his intuitive intelligence to consider where and how hard he could strike so as to cause the most painful damage without actually killing the animal.

Dong-sun lifted his pipe with both hands over his head and brought it down swiftly and hard on the dog's hind legs. The femur of the uppermost leg broke clean through beneath the blow. The dog jumped and screeched and its forelegs frantically pawed at the air. Its screech became a loud whimpering as it squirmed and its eyes opened so wide that what were normally warm brown irises became bulging orbs of mostly white. It raised its head as it struggled to get up, to flee, but with each movement its broken leg caused it excruciating pain, and it yelped and whimpered anew.

Dong-sun aimed his pipe again, this time at the forelegs, strategically thinking that when those were broken it would be impossible for the dog to get away even if it managed to slip out of its bindings. At the swift, hard impact another leg cracked. The dog jumped as though something beneath it had catapulted it upward. Screeching and yelping, it squirmed so violently that it turned itself over onto its other side, its head rising and falling with each whimper and moan. It pawed the dirt with its broken legs only to bark-yelp continually in agony.

The farmer then smashed the pipe into the dog's chest. Ribs shattered. The animal let out a long yelp which changed into a staccato, high-pitched squeal quite loud considering that the snout was still tied nearly shut. Its tongue poked out between its black lips. Rolling back its wide-open, uppermost eye, the dog tried to see the man who stood above and a little behind him as though trying to anticipate what he would do next; trying also perhaps to understand why he was doing it.

Dong-sun again smashed the pipe into the animal's chest—cracking more ribs—then applied himself again to the dog's legs. With each impact of the steel pipe, with each bone broken or piece of flesh torn into, the animal jumped up a little as its body contracted hard with shock and pain. It screeched, yelped, whimpered, though these sounds now came in shorter, almost staccato bursts.

The Korean farmer stepped over to the front of the dog. The animal's uppermost eye watched him in terror. Dong-sun swung the pipe hard across the dog's snout, obliterating the flap of skin over the gums, knocking out teeth, and pulverizing that section of the jaw. The animal shivered and shook, whimpered and wheezed: bloodied saliva frothed around its broken gums. It squirmed no longer with a conscious effort to flee but merely out of an abundance of pain coursing through its body.

And now Dong-sun held back. He stepped a little away and patiently watched the broken beast for some minutes; seeing how its chest expanded and contracted quickly as its punctured lungs labored for breath, how its legs flailed feebly, how it raised its head a little from the pool of blood that formed around its shattered jaw; satisfied that it was in immense pain, that agony was coursing through every fiber of its body.

"Let him stay like that for a while," the man told himself. "Better for the meat."

In between short, choking snorts the dog emitted soft high-pitched whimpers.

"Sounds like a pig," the man thought.

The Korean again began beating the dog, bringing the pipe down on the legs, the chest, the hips. Though he hit just as hard as previously, the dog's whimpers subsided as its consciousness grew numb and was nearly blotted out with a suffering beyond suffering. Soon Dong-sun was hitting the dog and couldn't tell whether the animal were moving as a reaction to the beating or merely from the pipe hitting his body. Now and then the man relented in his pounding and looked carefully at the dog to see if it was still alive. He saw the telltale signs that it was: the flicking of a paw, a slide of the tail, a blink of the eye. Dong-sun was astonished at how the creature clung to the last remaining bit of its life, or rather how persistently life clung to it. He also knew it was not possible to make the animal suffer any more since it had fallen into a semi-conscious state. All that was wanting was the coup de grace. Dong-sun positioned himself to the side of the dog's head, lifted the pipe, and brought it down with all his might. The skull cracked. The dog's body jumped a little—a final jump marking the exit of life. A few minutes earlier its wide-open eye had been frantic with panicking life; now it was a mere circle of blue-black-red pus in a broken, bleeding skull.

The Korean gave the dog's body a kick with his foot. Unresponsive. Inert. Dead. He lay down the pipe and untied the ropes around the dog's legs. He took up the long, curving knife he had taken out of the barn and began skinning the carcase, turning it over this way and that. In pulling away the furry skin he exposed the flesh beneath: it was bright red—proof, he was sure, of its saturation with those strange, wonderful, life-enhancing compounds so ironically the by-products of agony and which would increase his strength and virility. He eviscerated the guts and began cutting up the animal into portable pieces.

As he did this he put his lips together and whistled lightly, just as he often did when he was repairing a fence or was out in the fields hoeing weeds. He was considering the many ways his wife might prepare the meat, and he told himself to remind her that she must not cook it overmuch: that it should be rare—very rare—with all the bright, red, rich blood left in as pristine, as nutritious a state as possible.

At one point he flipped the dog onto its other side, turning upward the undamaged side of its head. Its eye on that side was wide open and reflected a sky that shone as brightly, as cloudlessly, as serenely as ever, as though the Universe looked on such things with utter indifference.

*

It was just such a sky that not too many days later, on the other side of the world, looked down on New York City.

The day before an impetuous rain had fallen, washing away somewhat the thousand poisons that pollute and haze over the city's air, leaving it cleaner, brighter than usual. On West End Avenue at 76th Street, two men stood on the sidewalk just beside a large, dark, maw-like gap between two squat buildings—the ever-open entrance and exit to an underground garage of a livery car company. One of the men was smoking a cigarette, taking impulsive, angry puffs and shaking his head negatively, angrily, while the other stood much more casually, his hands in his pockets as he leaned against a wall. They were both drivers for the same company. A few minutes earlier they had heard from their boss the unpleasant announcement of a reduction in their salary. The rate of reduction was small, merely a few percentage points, but it rankled nevertheless.

"It's not fair," said Alejandro, the man with the cigarette, taking yet another puff and expelling the smoke in a quick, irritated stream. "He should be giving us a pay *increase*, not a *decrease!* The cost of living is going up, not down! My rent goes up every year—doesn't he understand that, the bum!"

"Well," returned the other man, whose name was Sandesh, "like he said, there were a lot of accidents this year and his insurance rates went up for the company, so he has to adjust the pay scale to make up for it."

"But that should be *his* problem, not *ours!* It's *his* company, ain't it? That's what they call the cost of doing business. And since when am I responsible for other people's mistakes? If a driver gets into too many accidents, he should be fired."

"He did fire a few," Sandesh remarked.

"Well, fire more! We shouldn't be blamed for other people's stupidity."

Sandesh pursed his lips and blew out a long breath. It was hard to disagree with Alejandro's frustration. On the face of it no one could argue with the unfairness of taking a pay cut for something for which one wasn't responsible. But Sandesh was one of those rare men who try to look at things from his opponent's point of view, and he mentioned to Alejandro, "Well, we do all work for the same company."

"Bullshit," Alejandro said, and blew out a stream of smoke.

Sandesh held back from saying anything else, not wanting to antagonize his coworker into still greater flights of resentment. Instead he shook his head as though in sympathy with Alejandro's anger, and, looking at his watch, said, "Well, things'll work out. I got to go in." He turned around and disappeared into the gloom of the garage. Fifteen minutes later he was driving out of it behind the wheel of the Lincoln Town Car that he had had to buy to become a driver with the company.

Sandesh spent so many hours behind the wheel that he sometimes was not so sure he had made the right decision in coming to the United States. Back in India, in Mumbai, a man did not have to work this hard and long to make a living—at least, he had never done so. It was true that there a man like himself would not have had a nice car to drive, a nice house to live in, and a constant variety of foods and clothing, but this abundance came at a price, namely, that of time. Time to spend with one's wife and children; time to relax, time to dream, time to enjoy. Even after all these years in the United States there was a part of him that could not accept without balking the American construct that one lived to work rather than worked to live, as it was in practice. But he too had fallen into that pattern, especially after marrying and having children. Now and then he fantasized that he was single again, responsible only for himself, working only enough to afford his simple needs, and having the prospect of time—gorgeous time—spreading out be-

fore him like some opulently appointed buffet table, to be partaken of when and how he pleased. What a life that would
have been! But on further consideration this fantasy would lose
its enticing glow and darken to a vision of bleak lonesomeness.
He was not the kind of man to live a solitary life. He did not
like to be alone. He only felt comfortable when he knew that
other people were around him, living in the same general space
he occupied, and that he could walk into this or that room and
find someone whom he might talk to, listen to, feel some human
connection with. Despite the responsibilities of family life, he
understood that it had given him more than it had taken from
him. When he imagined what his life would have been without
his wife and sons, he cringed before a sense of unbearable
emptiness. To have had "time" to himself on those terms would
have been no blessing. And so he would resign himself to the innumerable hours spent behind the wheel, knowing that at least
when the day was done he had three beloved faces to come
home to.

As he drove he kept in his ear an earpiece connected to his
cell phone, which throughout the day would sing with incoming
calls from his wife or one of his sons. Of all he had, of all he
had ever done in his life, he was proudest of his two boys, Kirat and Anram, twelve and sixteen, respectively. They were the
apples of his eye. There had been some contention between him
and his wife in naming the boys, for he had wanted to give
them English names. After all, he had told his wife, they were
living in America now, and it was appropriate for their first
names to reflect their new home and language. "William," for
instance, he thought, sounded grand, being the name of kings,
and he had also liked "Arthur," which had rung in his ears as
both stately and romantic. But his wife would have none of it.
"We're Indian, not English," she had told him.

"But we're not living in India," he had countered.

"I don't care. I don't *want* English names. I don't *like*
them. We're giving them *Indian* names, and that's that!"

There was no arguing against that kind of vehemence, just
as there was never any arguing with Orpita once she was determined to do something. Sandesh often shook his head over the
frustratingly unforeseen development of her character, which
had been so sweet and yielding during their courtship, and had

become so overbearing and demanding in marriage, and never more so than in matters relating to the children. He had met her during his first and only year of college in Mumbai, and they had fallen in love—or at least had fallen into enough like that he had decided she would make a good wife. He had come to the United States and had been here for two years before sending for her. Against the wishes of her family she came to join him. America was not what she had thought it would be. After the initial wonder of the towers and rush of New York City had worn off, she had begun to see beneath its wondrous shimmer the sad reality: the abhorrent violence, the bland, cardboard-tasting food, the mad freedom given to children, the single-minded, rather desperate lunge for money that turned men and women into exhausted, nervous, entirely selfish beasts. But she also quickly got used to its fast pace, the variety of its excitements, and the abundance of fine things to be had if only one could afford them. Twice since their marriage she had gone back to India to see her family, and each time she had returned with relief, saying how glad she was to be back "home." Sandesh knew that she could never again live in India any more than he could. They had grown used to this different and in many respects better Western world.

And yet India wasn't so far away as it seemed. In their neighborhood of Jackson Heights, Queens, there was a stretch of eight or nine blocks that were as Indian as any in the world. Indian markets lined the main streets and sold everything from saris to Hindi music to highly filigreed, Indian-style jewelry. On weekends one might walk down nearby 74th Street and Broadway and find oneself amid crowds in which there wasn't even one American in sight.

Their single-family, two-storied house was located on a street along which all the houses had been built in the same two-year period in the early 1950s. Their original owners had mostly either long since died or moved away from a neighborhood that had changed too much for their comfort. The houses here were of only two styles—one with a wide, two-windowed dormer rising on the roof, and one without. Each house had its own tiny front yard, a small yard in the back, and a narrow driveway separating it from the next property over. Naturally Sandesh and Orpita had come to know their neighbors who lived on either side of them and would, on seeing them, say hello or chat for a few minutes. It happened that one Saturday morning as Sandesh brought in a bag of groceries from the trunk of his car—his wife had just come back from the weekly shopping—he saw his next door neighbor, Mr. Jeffries, leaving his house. He was a hale fellow in his late fifties with a rosy complexion and a protruding stomach.

"Hey, Sandesh!" Mr. Jeffries called out.

"Hey, how are you, my friend," Sandesh returned.

"Good, good. How are you doing?"

"Good, thanks."

Sandesh noticed the long, brown, canvas case that Mr. Jeffries had slung over his shoulder. He knew what it contained: a rifle.

"Taking off for the weekend?" Sandesh asked.

"Yup," Mr. Jeffries replied, happily. Nearly every week in the autumn he went "upstate," where he had, as he called it, a "cabin" and where he indulged his love of hunting. He would always rave about what a great time he had "up there"—amid the rolling hills, the fresh air and rippling streams, the magnificent foliage. He prided himself on the number of deer he shot; somehow he always managed to kill half a dozen with each outing; not to mention rabbits, squirrels, birds, and whatever other creeping, crawling, climbing, or flying creature happened into the sights of his trusty 12 gauge. And yet he never brought his kills back home with him. Once Sandesh had asked him about this, and he had just shrugged and said, "Oh, I can't be bringing back deer to this place! No, no, I only shoot for *sport!*" On still other occasions he had asked Sandesh if he would like to accompany him, assuring him that he would get a great "kick" out of it, that there was nothing in the world like stalking through the woods with a shotgun in your hand, breathing in that fresh clean air, stopping often, listening, listening in the silence for the slight crackle of leaves or the sudden soughing of nearby brush that indicated something was out there, unconscious of your presence, and then, as quietly, as stealthily as can be, raising the gun to your shoulder, putting your finger on the trigger, waiting, waiting, preparing for the moment when the animal would amble into your sights, and then—bang!—the perfect shot: the sudden keeling over: that indescribable, exciting sense of power and victory.

And in fact it did sound at least somewhat interesting to Sandesh, who had never gone hunting in his life and had never even thought about it till he had come to know Mr. Jeffries. But he worked so many hours during the week that the only time he had to spend with his family was during the weekends, and he would not have wanted to give up any of that family time. "Maybe one day when the kids are a little older," he would tell himself. "Maybe then I can get away and do something like that ..."

When he went back inside, his wife was in the kitchen and his youngest son, Kirat, was seated at the table. The boy had his mother's large, liquid, black eyes, and his straight black hair was cut straight across the forehead, ending just above his delicate brows.

"Hey, kiddo, what do you have there?" Sandesh asked, and walked over to the table to see that his son was already eating some of the cereal his mother had bought that morning.

"Circle-O's!" the boy said through his laborious, happy chewing, and picked up the box and proudly showed it to his father. It was the latest cereal targeted at children and which the boy had seen advertised on Saturday morning television between cartoons. The artificial coloring of its round, "fruit-flavored" bits had already leeched into the milk, turning it a pale red.

Sandesh looked to his wife. "Why is he eating this? Why don't you make him some lunch."

"He doesn't want it," Orpita said, with a defensive sing-song to her voice, as though she were a little insulted that her husband could really think she had not tried to make him eat something more healthful. "He wants that."

"Oh, Kirat, that's not a good lunch," Sandesh told his son.

"I like it!" the boy insisted, and as though to prove it, or to discourage his father from taking it away from him, he greedily shoveled into his mouth another spoonful of the round-shaped cereal.

"Of course you do—it's full of sugar."

The boy just shook his head and continued eating. The moment he had opened the cereal he had reached his hand deep within its crunchy, sugar-powdered contents and fished about for the "prize"—a cheap plastic toy. It was a kind of pinball game in which a thumb-operated flipper propelled a small steel pellet up into the rounded top of the case, causing it to fall back down and negotiate a tabbed, zigzagging path in the course of which it might or might not land in any one of several numbered indentations, thus producing some kind of score. It was an inane toy but the boy took great pleasure in it, taking it up between spoonfuls of cereal. "Look at this," he said, holding it up for his father's admiration.

"What is that?" his father asked.

"Pinball. Wanna play it?"

Sandesh smiled and shook his head, no, saying only, "You should eat good food."

There was a sound of footsteps hurrying down the stairs a few feet outside the kitchen and in another moment Sandesh's older son, Anram, came into view. He was sixteen years old, youthfully gangly, already as tall as his mother and catching up to his father. Like Kirat he too had large, dark eyes, though the elongated structure of his face more closely favored that of his father. He was dressed in jeans and a light blue jacket, and he was carrying a football which he would toss up a little, caress in his hands, then toss up again. Without saying a word to his parents he headed across the kitchen to the door.

Kirat put down his spoon, sat up a little straighter, and impulsively asked his brother, "Hey, where you goin'?"

The older boy didn't even bother to look at the younger as he walked by. "Out!" he said only, and was out the door.

Kirat looked after him, longingly. He would have liked nothing better than to tag along with Anram. But it was the regrettable and perhaps inevitable fact of his relationship with his older brother that the latter was at an age when he frantically wants to be regarded as "grown up," as a man, and is therefore determined to distance himself from anything or anyone linking him to childhood: thus, nothing could have been more humiliating to Anram than to be seen cavorting about with his "little" brother. Countless times Kirat had pleaded with Anram to be allowed to go with him, only for the older boy to respond with a curt "No" or "Can't" or "Not this time." At these rebuffs Kirat would feel as though he were a cipher, a nothing, an entity unworthy of a second's consideration, and he would mope and be miserable. In time he had stopped asking and pleading with his brother to be allowed to go with him—he had become conditioned to rejection.   As he watched Anram leave the house he felt again a small urge to call out and ask if he could go along, but he held his peace.

He turned back to his cereal and continued eating, though without the eagerness and pleasure of a few seconds before.

"Can we go to the park today?" Kirat asked his father, looking up from his bowl of cereal.   Probably he hadn't even been thinking about going to the park until his older brother had mentioned it.

"Uh ...."—Sandesh really didn't want to have to do anything on his day off.   He wanted to lounge about, watch television, eat. On the other hand he had a sense of fatherly duty and guilt prevented him from immediately denying the boy.   Before he was forced to answer, however, his wife said:

"Sandesh, you have to cut the grass this weekend, and take in the grill.   You said you were gonna do it last weekend and you didn't."

The father tilted his head to his son, as though to apologize already for not having the time, then suggesting, almost apologetically, "Why don't we go tomorrow?"

"I want to go today."

"Your father has stuff to do, Kirat," Orpita said; and looking to her husband said again, "The grass and the grill.   This weekend."

It was almost always like this: Sandesh's weekends were a mixture of trying to cram in some relaxation amid domestic duties.

"And by the way," Orpita said, going to the refrigerator and picking up something from the top of it, "we got this in the mail yesterday.   Wanna go pick it up?"

"What is it?" her husband asked, taking the slip of paper from her.

It was a notice from the Post Office notifying them of a package that was being held for them.   Sandesh noticed the sender, and said, "It's from your parents.   What'd'they send you?"

Orpita shrugged, shook her head.   "I have no idea.   Get it and see."

"Can I go with you?" Kirat asked his father.

"Sure, sweetie. Wipe your mouth," Sandesh said, seeing how is boy's mouth was red from the dye of the cereal.

Twenty minutes later father and son got to the local post office only ten blocks away and found themselves standing at the back of a long, slow-moving line, for it was Saturday and busy with people who didn't have time to come here during the week. Moreover as this government agency had a monopoly on the mail service, it had in practice no qualms about keeping customers waiting forever, and thus throwing yet one more inconvenience into the lives of people whose urban existence was harried by them. It took a half hour to reach the thick Plexiglass window behind which a bored, resentful-looking clerk expressionlessly took Sandesh's notice and disappeared with it into a back room. He stayed there for almost ten minutes—surely he was taking a little break. When he finally came out he was holding a box whose large size surprised its recipient. Sandesh couldn't imagine what his parents-in-law had sent. He signed for the item and walked out of the post office with it, giving the rather heavy box a little shake as he went.

"What is it?" Kirat asked.

"I don't know."

"Can I open it?"

"No, Kirat, it's not for us. Grandmom and Grandpop sent it to your mother. See? It's got her name on it. We'll let her open it."

Orpita herself was surprised at the package. She had not been expecting anything from her parents; they so rarely sent her anything in the mail, and a box this size would have cost a lot to send. When she took the box into her hands and felt how heavy it was, how substantial the thing inside must be, her curiosity was piqued the more. She took a knife from the kitchen and carefully cut through the packing tape with an even, slow pace, as though fearful of damaging the contents. As she did this her husband and young son stood at her side with curious anticipation, watching her open and push aside the flaps of the box, then take out wads of crunched-up newspaper that had been used as padding. Orpita emitted a surprised, pleased, "Ah-hhh!" as she reached into the box, grabbed the item within, and lifted it out.

It was a statue of the god Vishnu, sixteen inches high, of

fired ceramic, painted in rich enamel coloring and in places
gleaming with gilt. Standing on a coiled snake, the god was
blue-skinned, intimating his sky-infinite, world-dominating presence. He wore a yellow dhoti of draping folds and a dark green
robe with yellow and red embroideries. A long necklace of white
blossoms, like a long lei, hung from his neck, and a golden,
crested helmet topped his head. He looked out on the world
with a serene expression; his mouth was set in a faint yet somehow imperturbable smile as though he were aware of how he
had always been and would always be. Two of his hands were
raised and two were lowered, and each of them held an object: a
white conch shell, bespeaking the primeval source and sound of
creation; a lotus flower, whose opening petals symbolized spiritual consciousness and liberation; the warlike mace, smasher of
materialistic tendencies; and finally, around the index finger of
his upraised right hand, a hollow, circular, sharp-edged ring—
the chakra, the spinning weapon that was flung with terrible destructive power against the enemies of the god.

"Wowwww," Kirat intoned, his eyes wide, his mouth open.

"Oh, how nice!" Orpita said, turning it over this way and
that, admiringly.

Sandesh, though he smiled, was not nearly so impressed.
It seemed to him that if her parents had wanted to send a gift
they might at least have sent something useful—like some cash.
Moreover the statue only reminded him of his wife's mother,
with whom he had always had a strained relationship—which
was, Sandesh would have said, all her fault. And he would
have been right. She had never been enthusiastic about having
him as a son-in-law, in part because she believed her daughter
could have done better, and in part because she was a devout
Hindu who decried Sandesh's indifference to the faith. (Back in
Mumbai, they had several times almost gotten into arguments
about religion, she always complaining about his heathenish
impiety, while he had all but told her that anyone who believed
in such things had to be either gullible, stupid, or both.) To
Sandesh the statue seemed to be his mother-in-law's rude attempt to intrude herself and her beliefs into his household. If it
had been up to him he would have thrown the thing out, or—
better yet—auctioned it off online: at least the few bucks he
might get for it would make up for the effort of having gone to

pick it up.

"Don't you think it's a little gaudy?" he asked, with a sneer in his voice, hoping to make his wife think that liking the statue bespoke a vitiated aesthetic sensibility, and that she ought to be embarrassed by it.

But she looked at it with unwavering admiration. She had grown up with a similar statue in her mother's home. "Gaudy?" she asked. "Not at all! I think it's gorgeous!"

"Uh!" he said, despite himself; and caught himself from uttering a yet more vigorous expression of disgust. He was thinking: Oh, that mother of hers! That woman! Why doesn't she mind her own business! Sending us junk!

But at least the boy liked it. For Kirat the statue had all the fantastic charm and fascination of a dinosaur or dragon. It appealed to his child's sense of fantasy. He fired off questions to his mother about why the god stood on a snake, or was wearing this or that, or was holding those objects in his hands. She explained everything to him, and as she spoke the boy, in rapt attention, shifted his wondering, supremely interested eyes from her to the god.

"Just atrocious!" Sandesh said to himself. "I hope she doesn't plan on putting that out in the open where I have to look at it all day."

His worry couldn't have been more self-fulfilling, for Orpita, saying "I know just the place for it!" planted it in what was the most obvious place in the house: atop the bureau in the hallway outside the living room. That location ordinarily hosted a few framed pictures, two candelabra, and a cut crystal bowl filled with artificial fruit, but now these items were removed or repositioned to make room for the imposing statue. One would have to walk by it when coming into or leaving the house, and if one sat in the living room watching television one always saw it in the corner of one's eye—some gangly, four-armed thing looming there, insistently, everlastingly. Sandesh told himself that he would never get used to it and began revolving in his mind arguments or plots by which he might prevail on his wife to remove it out of sight.

But people can get used to almost anything if they see it often enough, and after a few days Sandesh didn't pay the statue a second thought. It became part of the house, a part of the expected decor, no more remarkable than the clock on the kitchen wall or the gauzy drapes over the living room windows. He even got into the habit of putting it to utilitarian use by slipping his car keys over the statue's uplifted, chakra-sustaining forefinger—much to the annoyance of his wife.

"Don't do that!" she reprimanded him.

"Why not?" he asked.

"It's not made for that!" she answered in a tone of righteous anger. "You might crack it."

"Ohhhh, I'm not going to 'crack' it."

"Don't do it!"

He immediately stopped that thoughtless habit even as, ironically enough, Orpita herself took it up. She found that it was a lot easier to walk into the house and throw her keys onto the god's finger, where she would always find them, rather than spend five minutes rifling through her cluttered pocketbook for them.

"So you can do it and I can't, is that it?" Sandesh asked her when he realized she was doing exactly what she had demanded he not do. Even though he smiled as he asked this his tone was biting, accusatory, carrying a vein of irritated anger.

She knew that he was right. She knew that she was doing precisely what she had told him not to do. But she also knew that she was, for all her apparent deference to him as her husband, the real and ultimate head of the household;—the wife who ruled the roost; and so the "rules" could always be bent a little for her, never for him.

"Don't worry about it," she said, with a little appeasing laugh. "I'm not like you. I do it carefully. I'm not going to break anything."

A few weeks later, Sandesh was driving a client that he had picked up at JFK International Airport to Staten Island. The man was old and didn't look healthy. His face was bloated, his complexion was red and splotchy, and his eyes bulged a little too prominently. Whenever he was not coughing lightly or swallowing hard he was breathing heavily as though there were some obstruction in his throat. His business suit of fine material and cut did not make him look especially sharp, for it could not disguise the unflattering proportions—the sunken chest, the wide hips—of his ageing body. An ill-knotted, crooked silk tie around the open collar of his white shirt added an additional touch of expensive sloppiness. No doubt he was exhausted, for he had just gotten off an eighteen hour flight from Shanghai to New York. His name was Eli and he was in the garment industry.

They were riding along the Belt Parkway, along that scenic edge where old Brooklyn meets New York Bay, gateway to the Atlantic, and atop whose blue-gray, white-tipped waters great ships, standing stately oceanward, seem serenely still. Along the cement walkway close to the water people jogged, walked their dogs, or stood as lovers hand-in-hand as seagulls wheeled and cawed above them in the salted breeze. And ahead in the near distance appeared the sight that, no matter how many times Sandesh came upon it, always inspired him with a sense of power and glory and beauty: the great Verrazano-Narrows bridge, rising up from the earth with gargantuan majesty, its two great, heaven-reaching arches upholding with imperturbable grace the span that connected two distant points on earth in a single, breathless, winging sweep. It was hard to believe that men, individually so small and weak, had raised up this mighty, earth-defying, earth-uniting structure of concrete and steel. It was a testament to the people who had conceived and planned and built it, and somehow it made one proud to be a part of America. On this day of clear sky and bright sun the bridge looked especially grand, for it stood out in all its pale blue sublimity. Sandesh heard his passenger remark:

"Amazing, isn't it?"

"Yes!" Sandesh said, smiling and nodding, as they hurried toward the ramp at a speed far greater than the speed limit signs demanded; but then, this was New York—people didn't have time to obey speed limits.

"I remember when it was being built," Eli said, looking out the windows to the left and right as the car rounded the ramp and then evened out to a straight course on its way to the upper roadway. "Just a boy then. My father and I would drive out now and then to watch the construction. He had been a construction worker—liked seeing things built. He'd always said we needed a bridge here. He had this thing for bridges. Loved 'em. Liked the idea of them—you know, things to help you get over to the other side so that you weren't stuck where you were."

"How'd people get across before the bridge?" Sandesh asked.

"There used to be a ferry."

They were halfway across when Sandesh's cell phone rang. He glanced down at it on the passenger's seat and pressed the single button that answered it. It was Orpita calling him as she usually did during the day. He kept his voice low as he spoke, not wanting to annoy his passenger with his personal conversation. He heard the sound of running water and the clang of pots as his wife told him that everything was the same as usual except for the fact that Kirat had stayed home today from school because he hadn't felt well—he had woken up with a slight fever, probably had a little cold. He was in the living room watching television and she was in the kitchen making him some soup. They spoke for only five minutes, Sandesh ending the conversation with, "I'll talk to you later, okay? I'm just about to drop off someone." But he never called back.

At Sandesh's home meanwhile his son was touching his ear and wincing. "My ear hurts," he told his mother.

"Oh boy," Orpita said, looking at him both with mild perturbation and worry to think he had come down with an ear infection.

A week earlier her older son had been sneezing and complained of sore throat, though already he felt better. She was sure Kirat had caught his cold.

The boy hunched up his shoulders, turning his head into his right shoulder as he winced with pain, putting a hand to his ear and murmuring again that it hurt.

"Open your mouth—let me see your throat," Orpita said.

She peered into her son's mouth: it was pink, normal-looking. She placed the palm of her right hand against his face, however, and felt its somewhat excessive warmth. "You'll be alright," she said. "You just need to rest."

But two days of rest made no difference. The ache in the boy's ear subsided, but his temperature continued. And then on the third day an alarming symptom manifested itself: a swollen face. Actually it was not the whole face that was swollen but rather the area along the jaw line on either side of the head just before and below the ears: there, the flesh bulged out distinctly. Running her hands along her son's jaw, Orpita felt this strange swelling and grew alarmed, for she had never experienced this problem with her other son and did not remember it from her own youth. And then she noticed something else about him: tiny red splotches on his forearms.

She waited impatiently for nine o'clock when she called her family doctor, Dr. Rajani, and was able to speak with him. She told him about her son's swollen face and the small, strange, speckled bruises on the arms and legs. The doctor listened in silence and then said, with a strange authority that she was never to forget:

"I want you to take him to the emergency room at Circle Lane"—the hospital he was affiliated with. "I'll call ahead for you and we'll have some tests taken."

"What is it?" she asked. "What could it be?" Her heart pounded fast in her chest in anticipation of his answer.

"Well, it might be nothing," Dr. Rajani said, in an easy, re-assuring tone of voice. "It might be an infection of some kind. I just want to make sure, that's all."

When that morning she told Kirat to get dressed because he was going to "the hospital" for tests, he was afraid, resisted, and said he didn't want to go—didn't have to go. He hated doctors, whom he had only known as smiling but really ruthless strangers who in the name of "helping" you only hurt you by sticking you with needles, and seemed to do all they could, in the way of probing and palpating, to find something wrong with you so that they could stick you with needles. He was old enough to know that this wasn't true—that doctors and hospitals really were there to help you—but he feared them anyway.

"Get dressed now!" his mother told him, sternly, "I don't want to hear it! Hurry up! We don't have time!"

—And that was that. There was no refusing, no appeal, no possibility of negotiation. The law had been laid down and he must follow it. He was just a kid, after all.

Miserable with a sense of his powerlessness, of how often he was forced to do what he didn't want to do, and of how, now, he had to do something that downright scared him, he, as he dressed, morosely pitied and regretted his childhood. He would have given anything just then to be grown up. He would have stood his ground, then. He would have said, "No!"—and no one would have dared to try to overrule him, at least not without a fight, which he knew he would have won. He told himself that when he was grown up he would never let anyone mistreat him, never let anyone ever tell him what to do—ever.... But now he was just a kid.

Dr. Rajani had ordered several specific tests for which x-rays and blood were taken—the latter not without Kirat trembling for fear as he extended his arm and watched the nurse-phlebotomist prepare the preservative-infused collecting tubes, then tear open a sterile package containing a syringe. Even at the sight of it his whole body stiffened. "Don't look!" she said. It didn't matter. When the needle punctured his skin he let out a cry and wanted to run. The nurse had to use a lot of pressure to hold down his arm, saying sternly, "Don't move!"

"Ahhhhhhh!" he moaned, tapping his feet crazily, shuddering, as the blood was taken, his mouth pulled back into a taut expression of terror and pain. "Ahhhhhh!"

"It's almost done! Don't move! Don't look!"

Orpita was not in the room with him as his blood was being drawn, but stood just on the other side of the closed door, and at the sound of the boy's exclamation of pain she listened more intently, biting her lower lip.

Two hours later one of the doctors who had looked over the tests came out to her in the waiting room with a folder in his hands and, glancing at Kirat, said, "Perhaps your son could wait here just a few minutes. I'd like to go over a few things with you."

She followed him down the light-blue hallway to an office. As she followed him, hearing his and her heels clicking against the polished tile floor, she felt her heart beating fast with anticipation. Somehow she knew that what he was going to tell her was not good. That's why he had wanted to see her alone—he hadn't wanted Kirat to hear.

In a solemn, somehow analytical tone of voice, the doctor, opening the folder and scanning the test results, notified her that Kirat had leukemia. As though to obviate any extravagant or dramatic outburst on the part of the mother, he hastened to add that though the diagnosis was unfortunate and sounded bad, modern treatments for the disease were often very successful, and there was every reason to think Kirat would get better. "I've already notified Dr. Rajani of the results," he continued.

"He'll discuss with you the next steps you ought to take. I'm pretty sure they'll take care of Kirat at St. Francis of Assisi Hospital. They have an excellent pediatric oncology department; their doctors are all top notch." He paused for a moment and looked at her again in his sober way, but this time his voice softened a bit and he said, "I know it's difficult to hear all this. I'm sorry."

Orpita sat as still as a statue. A part of her refused to believe what she was being told. She kept telling herself that her son only had a cold, that what she was hearing had nothing to do with him, that he couldn't possibly have anything seriously— so seriously—wrong with him. The doctor was talking about something she had only heard of other children coming down with, not her child, not her little boy.

"I just don't understand," she said, her voice low, almost with a wondering quality about it, as though she were talking to herself, "how this could have happened?"

The doctor shook his head and said gently, "We're not sure why some people get it. It could be from exposure to radiation, or a virus, or harmful chemicals in the environment; then again, it might be none of those things. We think that genetics plays the largest role in it. But exactly why? We don't know. But as I say, and as I want you to keep in mind, there are very good recovery rates for this illness. Everything will be done so that he gets better."

When she came out of her meeting with the doctor, Kirat could see she that was upset about something, for her smile was strained and artificial, and her manner studied, duplicitous. This suspicion was confirmed when, after he asked her, "What did he say?" she did not directly answer him but only flashed an insincere smile and said, "Alright, let's go."

"What did he say?" he asked, again, following her.

"Well, there's a bit of a problem," she said, casually. "I have to talk to Dr. Rajani about it. But you'll be fine," she added, leading the way out of the hospital, hoping he wouldn't ask too many questions: for she didn't know what to say, how to explain to him what the diagnosis meant, what it might entail. He followed her in silence till they had gotten inside the car, then he turned to her and asked:

"Is it bad or something?"

"They're not sure yet, Kirat. They have to take more tests."

She didn't feel that she was lying to her son, for even as she spoke the words she told herself that it was possible, indeed probable, that a mistake had been made. Doctors and hospitals made mistakes all the time, and it was possible that they had made one in this instance also. In that case there was no point in scaring the boy. Before she would believe anything about her son having leukemia she would make sure it was absolutely proven.

When she got home and as Kirat was in his room resting, she spoke with Dr. Rajani on the telephone, and listened as he repeated the results of the test to her. When she ventured to say that perhaps the tests were mistaken, that a "second opinion" might be in order, he understood the fright which had propted her suggestion, and quietly told her that he was the second opinion, and that anyone, whether they looked at the test results a second, third, or tenth time, could interpret them only one way. He told her he knew that it was hard to accept and tried to calm the worst of her fears by mentioning—as the doctor at the hospital had done—how good the success rates for remission were "these days." He added that the sooner they "moved forward" on the treatments the better, and that he had already made the first appointment for her, which was to take place tomorrow. Orpita took down the information.

She hung up the phone and stood in her living room glancing about her with an ache in her heart and a sense of disbelief. She suddenly felt a terrible mysteriousness in human existence. How was it possible that such bad things could happen so suddenly? How was it possible that your life could be going along so well one moment and then, in the next, for no reason at all, be cast into an extremity of turmoil? Just last night her biggest "problem" had been running out of detergent with which to do the laundry; and now even the most frustrating, disappointing, or infuriating incidents of her past fizzled away in stature to the absolutely meaningless, to things which had never been worth giving a second thought to.

She thought of her husband who was going about his day as though it were any other, unaware of the sea change that had also just affected him. How was she going to tell him what had just happened? What words was she going to use? It would be strange to hear herself speak them. She wondered if she should wait till he got home, and give him at least a few more hours of relative peace, but then she thought that he would surely be angry if she didn't tell him at once. "What if he were to wait till I got home to tell me something like this ... how would I feel?" She knew that she would have been furious with him and would have held it against him for years, perhaps forever. And so, after taking a few minutes to compose herself, she dialed his cell phone number.

Sandesh had not been driving when she called. He had parked his car on the corner of 47th Street and Third Avenue and was standing beside the halal food cart of Ahmed Badu, a likeable, jolly immigrant from Saudi Arabia who had the gift of gab, always joked with his regular customers, and who for six hours a day stood behind his grill, flipping strips of lamb and chicken, sending up into the city's atmosphere curdles of gray smoke laden with odors of seared flesh and exotic spices. Like other livery drivers Sandesh occasionally stopped here to grab a bite to eat because the food was inexpensive yet tasty. He had bought a juicy, dripping, rather sloppy lamb sandwich from which he taken a second big bite and was chewing heavily, laboriously, then swallowing with a smacking of his lips. He kept his ears peeled to the sound of the two-way radio in his car, and was prepared to bolt over to it the moment he heard the dispatcher call out for him. Instead he heard the running, tinkling tones of his cell phone. Taking another bite of his sandwich, he stepped over to his car, reached into the open window for the phone lying on his seat, and picked it up and answered it.

"Hello," he said, his voice garbled with food.

As he listened to his wife speak, his quick chewing slackened, then stopped altogether, and he swallowed his mouthful of lamb only with reluctance or difficulty. He had been looking about him indifferently, but now his eyes settled on the sidewalk before his feet, and he stared at it, unblinking, unseeing, as the whole force of his mind was concentrated on what she was telling him. In only a minute the call ended. He called his dispatcher at the livery company and told him that he could no longer continue working that day—that a family emergency had come up and he had to get back home.

He drove to Second Avenue and down to the Queens Midtown Tunnel, and when he came out on the other side and impatiently passed the toll booth, he pressed the accelerator to the floor so that the heavy car revved loudly with power and shot forth on the Long Island Expressway. He constantly came up to and passed on the right even those cars that were flying along the fast, leftmost lane. A ride that should have taken him fifteen minutes wound up taking him less than eight. It was a wonder that he hadn't gotten a ticket.

When he got home he listened to his wife repeat what she had been told at the hospital and her conversation with their family doctor. Sandesh also felt, as she had, a terrible sense of catastrophe having descended on their lives. He went up to see his son, who was in the room he shared with his brother. He was lying in his bed, watching television. Sandesh saw that his son's face was rounder than usual—swollen along the jaw. He sat on the side of the boy's bed, asked him how he was doing and saw how the boy swallowed hard, uncomfortably, and indeed looked sallow. Sandesh only stayed a few minutes and when he left he patted Kirat's sheet-covered leg and said, "Okay. Rest up."

"What's going on?" Kirat asked his father before he could leave the room.

"We don't know yet. They have to take some tests on you tomorrow and find out."

"But I feel alright," Kirat lied, hoping to prevent another trip to the hospital.

"I know you do," Sandesh said, smiling encouragingly. "But we still have to check it out. Don't worry about anything."

So began the parents' charade of confidence and good cheer before their sick child. It was not something they consciously planned or plotted; it was merely the way they instinctively felt they had to be: careful to act normally, not to give any indication, either through worried looks or concerned tones of voice, that there was anything especially wrong with him. Henceforth their every move and expression would be, consciously or otherwise, calculated to ease any worries he might have. In whispered conversations the mother and father decided that sooner or later they would have to tell him what was wrong, that they couldn't keep it a secret. He could easily enough get on the Internet and learn about his illness and how dangerous it was.

Their job would be to reduce the frightening effects of any harrowing information he came across by filtering it for him into a more positive, hopeful interpretation.

The hospital of St. Francis of Assisi, just outside the city limits in Nassau County, was three-storied building of orange-gray brick with a facade of shiny, fluted aluminum siding that gave it a clean, ultra-modern look. It was led up to by a circular driveway in the center of which was a grassy plot full of flowering plants that in summer showed clusters of cheerful red, yellow, and purple blossoms; but by now these had fallen away and only greenth remained. Here also stood a bronze statue of the hospital's namesake depicted in a rope-waisted, hooded friar's robe, standing with a raised right hand on which a bird had fearlessly alighted.

Drs. Faber and Hampton were the resident pediatric oncologists at the hospital. To them had been forwarded Kirat's tests of the day before. Nevertheless they did their own, and confirmed the diagnosis. With Kirat, Orpita, and Sandesh sitting before them, they discussed the boy's illness and the typical treatment, which would consist of three phases: first, an "induction phase," by which an aggressive, month-long chemotherapy regimen would drive the leukemia into remission. The second, a "consolidation phase," would be much longer: six months. During this time the objective would be to destroy any cancer cells that might still be present in the body. Finally, there would be a "maintenance phase" comprising two years of outpatient chemotherapy, and if, after that time, there were no recurrences of the disease, the boy would be considered cured.

As the doctor spoke, the mother, inwardly dazed though outwardly attentive, reckoned up the time line: one month—six months—two years. The better part of three years? She wondered how she could possibly go on for almost three years not knowing whether or not her son was going to be well.

Kirat himself was thinking that two years was just about forever. But the most pressing concern on his mind was the one thing that the doctors had never mentioned. When Dr. Hampton, turning to him, asked him if there was anything he wanted to know, fear forced him to surmount his shyness and ask:

"Will it hurt?"

"Well ... sometimes, Kirat, some things might be a little uncomfortable," the doctor said.

The boy at once decoded the euphemism, and as though something too frightening even to look at had arisen before him, he shifted his eyes away from the man and looked down to the floor. He wanted to cry but he didn't dare, not wanting to seem weak, a baby, before this stranger, and embarrass himself and his parents.

"The thing to remember, Kirat," the doctor continued, smiling encouragement because he saw fright in the boy—the same kind of fright he sensed beneath the parents' outward calm—"is that you'll feel better afterwards. We're all here to help you and to make you feel better. You know that, right?"

He nodded, yes; though he did not know that.

"I'd like to admit him today," the doctor said, turning to Orpita and Sandesh. "Get him checked in, settled ... then later on we can do a bone aspiration and see where we stand."

"What is that?" the boy asked, suddenly tense, worried.

The doctor again saw the boy's fear and tried to reassure him. "It's nothing to worry about, Kirat. We just take a little bit of marrow from the bone so that we can test it. It's a very minor procedure. It doesn't take long and it doesn't hurt."

Even the admission process intimidated the boy. Wide-eyed and tense, as though with each step he were walking into danger, he followed his parents to the Admissions Office. There an obese woman took information from Sandesh and Orpita about who their doctors were, where they lived, their phone number, what job Sandesh had, and who their insurance company was— for this Sandesh producing a card, which he took out of his wallet and handed to the woman. She typed this information into a computer and printed out several sheets, some of which she stapled together with a quick slamming down of a stapler with her pudgy hand. She sorted through the other sheets, picking out several and handing them to Sandesh, saying, "These are for you, sir. Just take these up to the nurses' station on the fifth floor and they'll help you from there."

On the fifth floor, it seemed that the nurses were expecting Sandesh and his family. One of the nurses took the papers he had been given. She smiled at Kirat, who turned his eyes away, shyly.

Then a nurse, a woman in her late fifties, came out from

behind the counter and introduced herself by her first name to Sandesh, Orpita, and Kirat. She smiled at the boy, who, this time, managed to hold the stranger's eyes and return her smile with a faint one of his own: but he didn't like her. He didn't like anyone here. He felt terribly tense and helpless.

"Come with me," the nurse said.

The family followed the nurse. This was the pediatrics floor and on either side of the hallway were rooms whose doors were usually open and gave a clear line of sight to a bed within and whoever was lying on it: always a child; sometimes very young—no more than three or four years old; sometimes as old as Kirat, or older. These children lay on their backs looking at television, or on their sides staring out the door, or covered up to their necks in a sheet and sleeping. Most of them were attached to an IV unit or some kind of monitoring system. Often a grownup, a mother or father, could also be seen in the room, standing over the bed or sitting in an armchair beside it. Kirat wondered who these kids were and what they were sick with. Was it possible that they were all here because they had the same thing he had?

"Here we are," the nurse said, leading them into a room that was next to last at the end of the hall. The room was small, bright, and stark for its absence of color or decoration. It contained two beds, both unoccupied and severely made with sheets very white and fresh and stretched. Beside each bed was a large, comfortable-looking padded armchair, and two more lighter, thinner, less inviting chairs of plastic and steel stood against the opposite wall.

"Your name is ... Kirat?" the nurse asked, glancing down at a piece of paper she was holding. "Is that how you say it?"

Kirat, Orpita, and Sandesh nodded.

"Well, Kirat," the nurse said, "Just make yourself comfortable, dear. There's a gown there for you to put on," she said, nodding to something folded that lay on the foot of bed nearest the window. Turning to the parents, she said, "Dr. Faber should be up here soon to look in on him." —And with that she left.

Orpita took up the hospital gown, unfolded it, and shook it out to its full dimensions. It was so light and insubstantial that it floated in the air as she did so. She handed it out to Kirat, saying, "Here you go—put this on."

The boy took it into his hands and hardly knew what to make of it, and when his mother showed him how it went on he was mute with a sense of how shamefully he would be exposed in such a thing. Did they really expect him to go about in something that was wide open in the back, exposing his whole body? On top of everything else he felt as though he were being humiliated.

"You can go into the bathroom and put it on," Orpita said, seeing the way Kirat hesitated. "Go on," she prodded. "The doctor'll be here soon."

"I don't want to wear this!" he objected.

"Kirat, please!" Orpita said, with some irritation. "Just put it on. Go ahead!"

He didn't take off his underwear and socks: a sense of shame prevented him from stepping out into the world half-naked. When he came out of the bathroom he held his pants and shirt in front of him as though to protect himself against mocking stares, and asked, almost demanded of his parents:

"Why do I have to wear this? It's so stupid!"

"You'll be more comfortable with that on," Sandesh said.

That hardly made sense to the boy: how was he going to be more comfortable in something that humiliated him? He hated the hospital gown just as he hated everything that was happening to him. He got into the bed and pulled the sheet over himself as though to cover up his semi-nakedness.

Later that morning Dr. Faber came up to the room. He was more casual than had been earlier in the day and almost exuded a welcoming good cheer. He informed the parents of what was going to happen when Kirat was "taken down" for the bone aspiration; then he stepped over to the boy in bed, patted him on the shoulder, and spoke to him in a smiling, encouraging, fatherly way, telling him not to worry about anything—that it would all be over before he knew it. And there was in the man something so sure and authoritative, as though he had seen and done and knew everything, that one couldn't help placing one's confidence in him. Certainly he made Kirat feel a little less apprehensive.

But what really lessened the boy's apprehension was the pre-operative sedation. The same nurse who had escorted Kirat and his parents into the room came back with a small brown bottle and poured its red syrupy liquid into a plastic spoon which she held out to Kirat, saying, "Here you go, honey, take this!" Kirat swallowed the sweet cherry-flavored liquid, and only after swallowing it did he detect a medicinal taste. As the Versed entered his bloodstream and bathed his brain, his mood changed in a way he himself was pleasantly conscious of. His apprehensions, his anger and fear, subsided, nudged out of the way by an encroaching—happiness? Well, not quite that, perhaps; but at least something *like* happiness—an easy, somehow floating indifference. He was going in for an operation? Well, alright. Maybe it wouldn't be so bad after all. As he lay there he listened to his parents talking, sometimes directing their words to him, and a few times giggled at what they said, though he wasn't sure why. Even when two of the nurses came and placed an IV in his left arm he didn't squirm—at least not much—but rather docilely allowed them to do with him as they would, taking a kind of objective and by no means unpleasant interest in the procedure. And when one of them smiled at him and patted him on the shoulder with an encouraging, "There, all done!"—why, he had to admit to himself that hadn't been any big deal.

He was transferred to a gurney and wheeled out of his room. As he was wheeled down the hall he counted the fluorescent light fixtures that passed by overhead: one ... two ... three ... . four ... five ... six ... (a turn, that disorienting sensation of the world shifting to the left) ... seven ... eight ...

In the operating room the anesthesiologist put him into a twilight state of consciousness, something not quite sleep but not quite wakefulness either. He could hear the doctors and nurses shuffling about him. He heard their voices, and the blipping sound of monitors, and the clink of instruments metallically touching one another as they were laid on steel trays. At any one moment time passed with astonishing yet pleasant slowness: every single thing he heard reverberated so long in his consciousness that he seemed able to hold it in his mind and examine it at his leisure. All the while he told himself to be patient and still. He felt a pinch in his right upper leg as the biopsy needle pierced the skin, then felt rather than heard a crunching sound as it pierced through the bone and entered the marrow.

A lumbar aspiration was also done.

He heard a voice, a woman's—that of one of the nurse's—telling him:

"Don't move, honey. You're alright."

The resulting tests showed a high percentage of leukemic cells in the marrow, so much so that they had left little room for normal cells to grow and had emerged into the bloodstream, clogging up and enlarging the lymph nodes—such as those around the jawline, and which had caused Kirat's face to swell. The good news was that an aspiration of the lumbar region showed that the cells had not spread to the spinal column. As a precautionary measure methotrexate had been intrathecally administered to destroy any undetected cancer cells there. It was one of the standard chemotherapy drugs which targeted fast-reproducing cells such as those of cancer. It was powerful and effective, but its utility came at a price: when taken in large amounts or for long periods it severely affected the liver, lungs, kidneys, and other organs of the body.

During his bone aspiration he had also received his first bag of platelets, the cells which enable the blood to coagulate and the production of which had been crowded out in the bone marrow by the uncontrollably growing leukemic cells. It was for want of this blood component that petichiae, the red spots and blotchings on his forearms and legs, had occurred as blood leaked from subcutaneous capillaries. He received yet more platelets when he was returned to his hospital room.

Orpita and Sandesh remained with him all that first day at the hospital, from early morning when they had taken him there till late in the evening. Orpita little suspected that in this she had begun a pattern that she would follow for as long as her son was sick. For she could not bear the thought of leaving him alone, knowing that he was frightened by hospitals and doctors and the things that were happening to him.

When the boy received his first shot of a chemotherapy drug he yelled and screamed and floundered about at the approach of the hypodermic needle. His mother had to yell at him to stay still, and a nurse as well as a doctor had to hold him down. The drug was Elspar, which worked by depriving cells of asparagine, a substance all cells needed to live, but which can-

cerous ones could not make on their own. By inhibiting its production in all cells, those that were cancerous died first. All the
rest of the day the boy was tired and pale, and complained of
pain in his arms.

The doctors educated the parents about the drugs they
would be giving their son. They ran off a litany of chemical-
sounding names and how they would be used, as well as what
their side effects might be: chills, fever, nausea, diarrhea,
rashes, mouth sores, hair loss—to name just a few. They told
the parents that while not all of these things would happen,
some of them were bound to, though everything would be done
to minimize their severity. The parents only partially relayed
this information to their son, not wanting to frighten him; and
the little they did admit, they phrased in such a way as to
make it sound as though any discomfort would be minor and
quickly over. Neither of them detected in their son the suspicion he in fact felt about what they were telling him.

Kirat was again anxious and terrified when he learned that
in order for him to continue his treatments he would have to
undergo surgery to implant a port-a-cath: a bladder-like device,
with a circumference no larger than a quarter, stationed just
under the skin of the chest and from which a tube extended into
a major artery. It made the administration of drugs more efficient and safe because it obviated the search for veins and, on
account of its subcutaneous position, reduced the chances of becoming infected from bacteria atop the skin. It also made injec-
tions less painful because the skin could be numbed with
anesthetizing cream. But to think that they were going to put
that plastic and steel thing into his living self—how could it not
hurt to have it there, embedded in the sentient flesh? The doctor assured him that at most he'd be "a little sore" for a day or
two, and soon he wouldn't even know he had it. But he didn't
believe it. He didn't want it. On hearing what "they" were intending to do to him, his expression became overcast with terrified anticipation. He flashed several pale-faced, goggle-eyed
glances at his mother and father who were present as one of the
doctors explained the procedure to him. Though Orpita and
Sandesh saw and felt their son's terror they comported themselves indifferently for his sake, knowing that to do otherwise
would only enhance his fear. When the doctor left the room Ki-

rat turned to his parents and pleaded with them:

"I don't want that! I don't want to do it!"

"Kirat, you have to have it," his father said, and shaking his head a little and adding, in what he thought would be a comforting phrase, "It's nothing."

"I don't want it!" the boy said, tears coming to his eyes.

"It's only temporary, Kirat," Orpita said. "You only have it in for a little while, then they take it out."

"But I don't want it!"

"Well, what do you want them to do?" she returned, sounding impatient as the stress of the day began to catch up with her, "give you needles all day? 'Cause that's what they would have to do otherwise. And I know you don't want that. This is easier, and better for you. That's why they do it."

Caught between terror and helplessness, the boy almost panted with frustration and burst into tears. Crying before anyone, even his parents, humiliated him; he felt that he was being the most despicable of all things, "a baby"; but he couldn't help it; he was too miserable; and tears were the only outlet to his nervous fear and frustration. He asked himself why this was happening to him. He was tempted to ask this question of his parents but somehow he knew that it would have been pointless and immature to do so. If they had known they would have told him. Their own worry and anxiety, which he clearly enough saw in them, was proof enough that they were as lost and uncertain as he was.

Orpita and Sandesh also faced the prospect of informing their parents about what was happening. And yet Sandesh made it clear that he was not going to say anything to his mother and father "yet."

"There's no point in worrying them," he said.

"They're his grandparents, Sandesh. They would want to know what's going on."

But he shook his head and repeated that he didn't want to worry them. His parents were old and didn't feel well, and what good would telling them do anyway? It would only give them one more thing to worry about. He would tell them, he said, another time, and in his own mind this meant that he would tell them only after Kirat was well on the road to recovery.

Orpita wanted to press the point with him, but relented and did not do so: they were his parents, after all.

As for her parents, there was never any question in Orpita's mind that she would tell them. She called them in India on the evening before Kirat was to have his port-a-cath surgery. Her mother, Roopa, picked up the phone and exclaimed with joy to hear her daughter's voice, but soon enough started crying when she heard what was happening to her grandson. Roopa had not seen Kirat more than three times before on brief visits to New York, and the last time had been two years earlier, but her reaction was as immediate and sincere as if she had played a far fuller role in his life. Whatever she lacked in personal feeling for the boy was made up for by her instinctive sympathy for her daughter's anxious and broken heart. For twenty minutes the two women sorrowed with and then consoled each other. Orpita related to her mother everything that the doctors had said about the good chances Kirat had for recovery, and her mother picked up on this and echoed the hopeful prognosis, assuring her daughter that everything would be alright.

Orpita then spoke to her father. His voice was solemn, subdued, manly in its quiet, restrained, saddened way. He too assured his daughter that in the end things would work out for the best.

The next day Kirat was pale with fear at the prospect of another "operation"—a word that always held a special terror for him. As he lay in bed, his eyes constantly turning to the IV in his arm, he repeatedly asked his parents standing nearby why he had to have "that thing"—the port-a-cath—placed inside him, and for the umpteenth time, though now with a tired impatience, they explained the reason and brushed off his anxiety. As much as possible they tried to keep the atmosphere light and optimistic. They spoke in offhand tones of voice, with an air of complete assurance. "It'll be over before you know it," they told him. "In fact you won't even know it. You're going to be fine. And then you get to come home for a few days."

A nurse stepped into the room and brightly said to Kirat:

"How are we doing over there?"

He looked at her blankly, as though he didn't understand how she could be jolly at a time like this. She was carrying a syringe, which she poked into the tubing of the IV unit. She turned to his parents and explained:

"It's just something to make him relax a little before they send him down."

He almost didn't want anything to "relax," for it seemed to him that this was "their" way—they who did not listen to him, who never cared about what *he* wanted—of doing to him things against his will. As the nurse injected the sedative into his IV line the boy looked at his parents with an expression of the most urgently unhappy appeal they had ever seen. But they were too far removed from their own childhoods to regard their son's terror as anything other than a baseless, immature emotion to be glossed over, humored away, or (if all else failed) checked and overruled with imperious command.

Five minutes later, with a sedative circulating in his blood, Kirat was in a calmer state of mind. He was no longer fidgeting and lay in bed with a pleasant, patient expression. A few times he even smiled and spoke of going into surgery with a tone of eagerness to have it over with.

Two orderlies came by to wheel him down to the operating room. They were both young men in their early twenties and their easy, cheerful manner went far to make Kirat feel yet more at ease, for it was in the nature of his age to want to be ingratiating toward males not very much older than himself. His parents followed him downstairs and gave him a final few loving pats and words of encouragement before they were requested to go into the waiting room. The moment they turned away from their son, their faces became masks of solemn worry. They knew that the operation for placing the intravenous device was not in itself especially dangerous, but it seemed to portend so many things that were—was the first step in a process bleak and perilous, and always fraught with the threat of ... the threat of ... well, that was something they could not bear to think about.

During the operation they waited by turns sitting or standing. They said very little to each other. Now and then Sandesh glanced at his watch, though there was a clock on the wall. Orpita, feeling exhausted—having worn herself out over the last few days with worry—left her husband for a few minutes to get some coffee. She came back holding a white Styrofoam cup of the steaming liquid. She sat and sipped at it, holding the cup in the palms of both hands, often staring at the wall, her restless mind churning over one worried thought after another. She remembered again, as she had many times in the last few days, how the process of Kirat's eventual cure could take more than two years. She would bear it, of course—she would bear whatever was necessary for his sake. But two years ... so long ...

When Kirat emerged from surgery his parents saw him lying asleep in the ICU, where he was to stay for a few hours before they brought him back to his room. The surgeon who performed the implant said it had gone well and that Kirat had also received another unit of blood.

"He just needs to rest now," the doctor said. "If he doesn't have any complications from his treatments in the next few days we can send him home. A lot of it can be done on an outpatient basis."

Orpita was inclined to remain at the hospital for the rest of the day, but the doctor gently reminded her that her son would be under the effects of the anesthesia for some time yet, and afterwards would just need to rest. She might as well, he said, go home and come back tomorrow. Not without a sense of guilt she agreed.

On the drive home Sandesh and his wife spoke little for the first few minutes, then fell silent. After some time he heard her sniffling as she wept softly. He glanced at her, but her face was turned away from him as she looked out the window.

"It's gonna be alright," he said, feeling that subtle sense of panic, of urgency to take away the cause of upset, that a man feels on seeing a woman cry. "Don't worry."

Orpita rallied her emotions, hemming a little and managing to say, "I know."

They drove a few more minutes in silence. Then he said:

"I'm gonna have to go back to work tomorrow. I can't keep staying out."

She nodded, understanding. "It's alright."

"Are you gonna stay at the hospital all day tomorrow?"

She wondered why he even bothered asking. Still, she said, "Yes."

The objective of his question became clear to her when he further asked:

"What time does Anram get home from school?"

"Anram's not a little boy. He's sixteen years old."

"Sixteen isn't grown up, either," Sandesh said. "He still has to have dinner when he comes home."

"He can make something for himself. He's not helpless." But as though she felt guilty for saying that, she added, "I'll make him something and put it in the refrigerator. He can heat it up when he wants it."

From the corner of her eye she saw her husband shake his head in disapproval of what she had said. She understood why; again, she felt a little guilty for even having said such a thing and it occurred to her that another time, in other circumstances, she would have been appalled to hear herself or any mother talk about leaving a sixteen-year-old boy to fend for himself. But there had become for her a world of difference between twelve and sixteen years old.

A couple of days later Kirat developed a fever and was not released to go home. He remained in the hospital during his induction phase of the chemotherapy. He received cycled infusions of methotrexate, the negative effects of which were countered by the administration of another drug, leucovorin; then he was started on mercaptopurine, which inhibited cells from reproducing and therefore interfered first and foremost with rapidly-dividing leukemic cells. Almost at once he began suffering from side effects of these drugs. He was tired, lost his appetite, and was often nauseated. He was given Zofran for his nausea but he still had no appetite and the sight of food disgusted him. For breakfast he would take a mouthful of scrambled eggs and a few sips of warm coffee, then turn away from his food with revulsion. When lunch came the sight of it turned his stomach and he would push the tray away, saying, "I don't want it." And when, in the late afternoon, supper came, he would shake his head at it and say again, "I don't want it."

"You have to eat something!" Orpita would tell him.

"I can't. I don't want it."

"Well you have to try! Now don't be silly—here!" And she would cut his food for him into bite-size portions, or herself take up the fork or spoon and convey the food to his mouth as though he were a complete invalid; successful, at most, in getting him to swallow a few mouthfuls.

When no more serious side effects from his chemotherapy

seemed to occur, he was released from the hospital in which he had been captive for almost two weeks. The prospect of going home brought a light to his eyes. Orpita hoped that once he was home his appetite would return; she was determined to feed him continuously. But however grateful he was to be out of the hospital, his appetite remained suppressed. Even if he had had an appetite, the chemotherapy had caused sores in his mouth— tender blisters that hurt even when his tongue touched them, and which made the act of chewing painful. At most he would manage to eat a few ounces of food—wincing with pain as he slowly, carefully chewed—before protesting that he was "full." And when his father and mother pressed him to eat more, he would look at his food, feel a sudden surge of repulsion at the sight of it, and shake his head and say, "I can't, I'll throw up!"

One of the first things Kirat had done on getting home was to show Anram the place where the port-a-cath had been in- serted in his chest a few inches below his right shoulder. The older boy reached out and gingerly touched the tape-covered area, feeling the unnatural hardness. Anram had always made a show of his toughness but when he felt the object beneath his brother's skin a grimace of both wonder and disgust contorted his face, and with some alarm he looked at Kirat and said:

"Oh, man! Does it hurt?"

"Nope," Kirat said, feeling rather proud to say so to his older brother.

If there was indeed one good thing that came out of his ill- ness it was this new, better relationship with Anram. Over the last few weeks the older boy had taken silent counsel with him- self and reflected on his younger brother's serious illness, and what it would mean if he died. That he would be upset went without question: but he wondered if this was because he really loved Kirat or because it would upset the accustomed order of his life. In the end he decided they were really the same thing. One loved what one knew, what one had grown up with, what had been a part of one's life from as long as one could remem- ber. Kirat's absence would be so fundamental a change that it would be unpleasant, a kind of pain. And so it was clear to An- ram that he ought to be grateful for Kirat and make a conscious effort to treat him well—or at least as well as his very different, coarser personality would allow.

On his fourth day home Kirat had a setback. He developed another fever, his temperature rising to over a hundred degrees. Orpita called Dr. Faber and he suggested Kirat return to the hospital. A few days later a rash formed on his chest, and soon spread to his flanks and back; soon it covered most of his body. The red, inflamed skin itched horribly so that he couldn't resist the temptation to scratch, to claw at himself, sometimes so hard that he broke the skin. The danger in this was infection, which would be the more threatening on account of his weakened immune system. He was given Benadryl and analgesics to relieve the itching but these drugs helped only moderately during the day and hardly at all at night, when, for some reason, always, the itching became more severe, became maddening, irresistible, tormenting, as though a thousand little devils were pricking him with tiny pitchforks all over his body. He got no sleep for the painful tossing and turning. Sometimes he sat up in the darkness and cried out of sheer frustration. Thus added to his weakness on account of his loss of appetite was the exhaustion from lack of sleep. A dermatologist was called in to examine him and prescribed hydrocortisone cream to be applied four times a day. The doctors started him on a couple of antibiotics to prevent the development of infection from all his scratching, and quietly approved the administration of morphine if his discomfort at night became unbearable.

His mother was always with him in the hospital. She would leave her house in the morning as soon as Anram was off to school and get to Kirat no later than nine thirty or so. She often assisted the nurses who attended to her son. When he was thirsty, she poured him water and held the cup to his lips. When he wanted to get out of bed, she helped him out of it, and when he walked she stayed by his side with a hand ever-ready to reach out and hold him steady if he faltered. When his meals came she especially went into action, for nothing seemed to her more important than getting him to eat. She would receive the tray of his food from an orderly and, in order to stimulate his appetite, lift the covers over the various dishes with exclamations of how delicious each one looked. (In fact she found the food more horribly bland than American food usually was.) She would go so far as to hold up a first spoon- or forkful of food for him to take in hand, saying, "Here, Kirat, come on, start eating—just a few bites!" Sometimes for the sake of appeasing her he made an attempt to eat, but most times he couldn't even bear the sight of the food because of a mild but persistent nausea. He received more Zofran for his nausea, and nutrients through the IV.

Though she spent most of the day and much of the night at the hospital, Orpita did not and could not stay overnight; nor, she realized, had she the strength to do so. She was physically and, more than this, mentally exhausted at the end of the day, so much of which she had spent tamping down her own worries and sadness in order to maintain a cheerful, positive attitude for her son's sake. But the boy often saw the tiredness in his mother's eyes, and he felt bad about putting her out so, day after day. "You should go," he would tell her, sometimes as early as two o'clock in the afternoon. "You don't have to stay here. I'll be alright. Besides, I'm tired. I'll just watch TV or something ..." Whenever, on his prompting, she left early, he was glad to think that he had made her life a little easier by sparing her the effort of sitting in his room watching and waiting on him. But a few hours later, especially if he began to get a headache or his arms or legs hurt, or if, worst of all, his rashes flared up and a maddening itch developed on his chest or back, he would wish his mother were back, if only as a distraction from the subtle torment of his condition. Yes, he could and would call a nurse, and she might or might not do something to make him more comfortable, but after a few minutes she would leave and he would be left alone again to grapple in solitary silence with an infernal discomfort or downright pain. The prospect of spending the whole night like that would fill his soul with a leaden despair and he would feel his throat tighten and he would want to cry. Even when eventually he got to sleep he was sure to waken throughout the night, opening his eyes to the darkness and realizing, in the next few seconds, that he had a throbbing headache or pain in his joints. He would ring for a nurse. She would do what she could to ease his pain. "What time is it?" he would ask her, and she would tell him;—and his spirit would sink to learn it was still rather early in the evening, and there were hours and hours to go before the next day came.

The worst of these symptoms and reactions lessened as his

chemotherapy went forward. After several days of absolute misery, the boy was relieved to find himself feeling a little better. He was much more relieved when he learned that, so long as he remained without fever or any serious side effects he could be released from the hospital. Throughout the day, and especially at night when he lay quiet and alone in his bed, he prayed that even if he wasn't "getting better" he would at least *look* as though he were so that he could go home. He missed what had been the routine of his life before he had gotten sick. Even what he used to regard as unpleasant things, such as having to wake up early to go to school, or his older brother's contemptuous dismissal of him, seemed to him now desirable.

As though his prayers had been answered, there were no further complications to his chemotherapy and he was released. His treatments were to continue on an outpatient basis. And yet however relieved he was to be back home, he could never really enjoy it because he never felt well. Even when he wasn't nauseated or his legs or joints weren't sore he had little energy and would spend his time listlessly watching television or playing games on his computer for a few minutes at a time. He slept often. His appetite remained suppressed and he never took more than a few bites before saying that he felt "full." No proposal of ice cream, chocolate, puddings, cakes, pies, potato chips, popcorn, or other junk food could rouse his appetite to its former insatiable craving for them. In nearly four weeks he had lost fifteen pounds. His face had become gaunt, his cheekbones disturbingly prominent and the eyes sunken and darkly large. Orpita herself almost didn't realize how much weight he had lost till she happened to see a picture of him as he had been only a few months earlier. The picture was set, along with others, on the bureau beside the enameled and gilt statue her mother had sent her. One afternoon she happened in passing to catch sight of it, and stopped before it, and looked at it, hard. So ... that was Kirat as he had been. *That* was her son as she knew him in her memory, as she felt him to be in her heart. Would she have that son back? It was in order to get him back that she endured.

A week passed. One evening Kirat complained that he had a headache and that his knees and elbows were sore, and he looked paler than usual. A few hours later he developed a high fever and Orpita and Sandesh took him back to the hospital. A blood test showed that he had contracted an infection; how or why it was hard to say, though it was known that the methotrexate therapy, in addition to its other side effects, vitiated the immune system. He was started on antibiotics and would have to remain at the hospital. After two days the fever subsided.

The boy was always more sensitive to the chemotherapy drugs than most children who received them. He always experienced the worst side effects. He often had headaches. Often he felt pain in his chest or abdomen. Rashes continued to appear and torment him, especially at night, and neither Benadryl nor hydrocortisone cream relieved the symptoms for long. And then his hair began to fall out, for the same drugs designed to attack and eliminate cancerous cells by targeting and inhibiting their quick division likewise affected the hair follicle cells whose nature was also to divide quickly. He had been told by his doctors and his parents that loss of his hair was a "possible" side effect, and he had feared it, for it was one thing to be sick but quite another to look it: and when it began to happen, it alarmed and distressed him utterly. He would run his hands through his hair to find several, then dozens of strands coming away in his fingers. In the morning little tufts of hair lay on his pillow. The lack of pain associated with this loss was itself distressing. Ordinarily it had hurt to pull out a single hair; now whole clumps of it were coming away without any sensation as though a part of his body had become dissociated from the rest of him. Every morning he would look at himself in the bathroom mirror and see his scalp more clearly. In a little over a week most of his hair had fallen out, and not just on his head but all over his body—what little hair had been there. The transformation struck him as monstrous. It was as though, in addition to everything else he had had to endure, he also had to look revolting to the world and therefore to himself. To think that he looked so bad, so odd, so weird, filled him with despair that nearly brought him to tears. How could anyone possibly like him, the way he looked? His parents and the doctors and nurses constantly made light of it all, assuring him that it was only a passing phase, that in time his hair would come back as completely, as full as ever. But he reckoned that even if it started to grow again immediately—at this moment—it would still take months before it was all back, and during that long interim he would continue to feel and look strange. The only thing he could be thankful for was that he was no longer in school, for the stares and whispers of the other kids would have been too mortifying to bear.

Four weeks after he had been diagnosed with his illness Kirat went in for another bone marrow aspiration and biopsy to determine the effectiveness of the therapy he had received. The news was bad: the bone marrow still showed a high percentage of leukemia cells.

"We'll give it another couple of weeks," Dr. Faber told Orpita and Sandesh. "If he's still not responding, he'll need a bone marrow transplant. I'd like to have blood drawn from you and your older son to see if one of you might be a good match."

He went on to explain to them what the transplant entailed. He laid out the process step-by-step. The parents, who on first hearing the term had supposed it was some ultimate cure, listened with hopes that wavered, and then sagged, as the doctor frankly disclosed the risks.

"We condition him for the transplant with high doses of chemotherapy and radiation so that the cancerous bone marrow throughout the body is destroyed. Unfortunately, in destroying the bad cells we also destroy the good ones, and during this time he'll have no immunity, which means he'll have to remain in the hospital where we can control his exposure to things. You can't bring him any more food or gifts from outside, since they might carry bacteria or fungi, and we don't want to risk that kind of infection, and everyone, including you, will have to wash your hands with antiseptic soap and wear a protective gown and gloves and masks when you're around him. He'll often feel nauseated and have fever and diarrhea. He'll be extremely weak; and not just for a day or two at a time, but for whole weeks. He might not even have the strength to sit up very much, let alone walk or watch television. Because we'll be using high doses of radiation there may be secondary complications, such as damage to his liver and thyroid, GI tract sores, and down the road perhaps new cancers. His salivary glands might swell and he might come down with pneumonia. He will become sterile. In the short-term he might also be affected mentally, and experience some confusion, which might frighten him. As for actual physical pain, well, we can control a lot of that with pain killers, but I don't need to tell you that there's always a danger of over-sedating him. The transplant procedure itself is pretty easy and painless: we transfer the donated marrow through the IV line and it circulates in the bloodstream. In two to four weeks the new cells will begin to engraft—embed themselves in the bones and start producing new and healthy blood cells. Only then can we start taking him off the antibiotics. But as you can see," the doctor said, feeling again—as he always did when he saw the agonized faces of a mother and father—the terrible burden of his knowledge and expertise, "it's not an easy process. The first few weeks are very tentative and very hard."

"And if he doesn't do it he'll die?" Orpita asked.

She asked the question calmly, plainly, without undue emotion. She was surprised at herself for having done so: surprised at how far she had come toward accepting the possibility of her son's death. She was aware just then of how much Death had become a part of her life, walking at her side during the bustle of the day, and sleeping beside her in the watches of the night: a dark, lowering presence so often with her that she had come, almost, to accept its presence.

"No one can say what the future brings," Dr. Faber said, wisely enough. "If he doesn't have the bone marrow transplant will he die? I can't presume to tell you with absolute certainty what will happen. But," he added, lest the parents begin to grasp at straws, which he would have considered it a dereliction of his duty to allow them to do, "in my experience patients in his position don't make it without a transplant. Even then you should know that it isn't a guarantee of cure. There's a 25% risk of death in the first 100 days after transplant, and a 35% risk in the following one to five years—mostly in the first year. The five-year survival rate is no more than 40%. Of course, those are just statistics—averages. For all we know Kirat might be on the high end of that scale—might have an 80 or 90% chance of five-year survival, or even a total cure. You can never tell. But the thing to remember is that if it *does* work, and he begins to feel better, he'll be glad he did it.

"There is one more thing I should tell you," Dr. Faber continued. "You should understand that it's a serious procedure—

it's very hard on the body. Kirat's already been through a lot, but this means he'll go through a lot more—and maybe at times even worse. We'll have to keep him on the chemo till he's had his transplant—that's the only way to keep the disease suppressed. For two weeks after the transplant he'll feel increasingly bad until the new marrow takes. Given all that, I think you'll agree with me that he's the one who should make the decision about whether or not he wants to do it. I know you probably think he isn't competent to make that kind of decision, but he's a bright boy, he knows what's going on, and he's the one who has to go through it all, so he has every right to be part of this decision. So I would like you discuss it with him and let him decide."

On some level the parents resented having to consult their twelve-year-old son about whether or not he would go through with a treatment that alone might save his life. They had always taken it for granted that it was their right and responsibility to make important decisions for him; after all, he was just a child who had to be led, coaxed, and, when necessary, forced to do things he might not want to do but which were in his best interest; and now they found that this prerogative of theirs had been overturned and annulled, and in the most important matter of all. On the other hand even they had a sense of the obscene immorality in denying Kirat the ultimate decision in undergoing a process that they themselves might be unwilling or unable to endure. It is one of the bizarre peculiarities of human beings that parents often do not extend toward their own children the kind of basic respect they would, without a moment's hesitation, accord a stranger.

They explained to him what his situation was. Though they tried to be completely honest with him they nevertheless found themselves minimizing the fearful negative possibilities of the transplant lest the boy be too afraid to go through with it. Yet the very quickness with which they glossed over these things was seized on by him as the proof of their terrible existence. "Why do I have to do all that?" he asked. "I don't want to do it if all that's gonna happen to me!" His parents assured him again and more energetically than before that it wouldn't be as bad as he thought; that the side effects they mentioned were only possibilities, not certainties; that he had nothing to be afraid of and would get better if only he did this. More prevarications; more lies; more keeping out of his sight what he knew to be lurking in the sinister future. How could he make them understand that he didn't care about anything but being let alone! He knew he couldn't make them understand—ever. And so he began crying, softly at first, then more impulsively: out of fear and then out of frustration that again—again!—he was a cipher in this world simply because he wasn't an adult. "I don't want it!" he cried miserably. "I don't want any more operations or anything! I don't *want* the radiation!"

"But Kirat, you have to," Sandesh said, slapping his hands against his sides in sheer nervousness and heartbroken irritation at his son's recalcitrance. "It's the only way you can get better."

"I'm never going to get better!" the boy burst out, raising to his father a face flushed red with anger and grief.

"That's not true," Sandesh said; quietly because he had been taken aback by his son's passionate outburst. "You *will* get better ... you will, if you do this."

"Nooooo!"

—And there was something so desperate and impulsive in that denial, so pleading for an end to all the pain and fear, that the father could not bring himself to counter it with another demand or imperious suggestion, and so relented, shaking his head and looking to his wife as though she would take up where he had left off, would carry on the argument to convince their son of what he had to do. But she, who had watched at her son's bedside for weeks at a time, and seen and felt every inch of his terror and pain, understood that there were some things even she could not ask of him.

"Kirat, listen," Orpita said, in a way that put the boy at ease, for at once he heard in her voice and saw in her manner that she had already given way to his will, "you don't have to do anything you don't want to do from now on. Alright?"

"Orpita, what are you talking about?" Sandesh asked, in a tired, irritated tone of voice. "He has to have the transplant."

"No, he doesn't," she said, shaking her head and looking at her husband in such a way, with such an overwhelming sense of the rightness of her position that her smile itself had something disconcertingly adamantine about it. In that expression of hers he saw that no matter what he said or did or tried it was she who would prevail between them. She turned her eyes back to her son and said, "Listen, darling. We know it's hard. We know it's very hard. But the doctor says that the transplant might help you a lot—that you might finally get better with it. Of course there might be compli-cations, and sometimes you're not going to feel too well, but you're pretty tough—you know? You're very tough and strong and I think you can do it. And it might work—you know? And you would get better. And you could finally be away from this hospital forever. Wouldn't *that* be great? But this time, sweetheart, *you* make the decision— okay? We want you to make the decision, because we know it's not easy, and you're old enough to make up your own mind. If you don't want to do it, you don't have to. Your father and me will do what you want. Just ... don't make the decision right now. Alright? *Think* about it for a while. Just remember that it might be hard to go through ... that sometimes it *will* be tough ... but it really might work and you'd get better, and then it would all be worth it, and you'll be glad. So you really have to think about that, Kirat. Okay?"

He said nothing and glumly, resentfully, turned his watery eyes away from his mother and looked at the sheet covering his extended legs. "I don't want it," he mumbled; but both he and his parents understood that he had spoken out of fear and ill-humor, and that it wasn't a final, definitive answer.

Later that night he lay in bed and thought about how afraid he was to die. Since he had been in and out of the hospi-tal with his treatments, he had thought a hundred times about the possibility of dying. He had sometimes tried to figure out what death was; what it must be like to be dead. Somehow he could never quite imagine it: it never quite made sense. The more he concentrated on the matter the more his thoughts be-came lost among foggy depths of uncertain analysis. Now he concentrated on it so long and hard that the next thing he knew it was morning—he had fallen asleep and woken up to another day, and only hours afterwards did he recall what he had been thinking about so intently the night before. But whatever death was, maybe it wasn't so bad. People never said very much about it, after all. Whenever someone died they just said "He died" or "He passed away"—and maybe they mentioned *how* he had died, but almost never said anything about death itself. In the end the only things Kirat were that he didn't want to die and that if he did his parents would be terribly hurt. He could just imagine how much they would cry—yes, even his father, whom he had never seen cry once. When he thought of how his mother and father worried over him, looked after him, for whole days at a time, he felt bad about having put them through so much and making them so unhappy, though of course it wasn't his fault. He told himself that if he died it might even be better for them. Sure, at first they would be upset—that was only natural—but after a while everything would get back to normal, whereas worrying about him every day, day after day ...

Oh, but he didn't want to die! That was the thing. He wanted to live. There were so many things he liked to do, such as watching movies, playing computer games, eating pizza (in the days when he had been able to eat it), and listening to music—hard rock and heavy metal, which his older brother had introduced him to and which he had found so exciting and waiting to be explored. He knew that he was thinking this way, about all the things there were to live for, because at the moment he wasn't feeling especially bad, and that when things began to hurt again he would probably change his mind. It was hard to want to live when your whole body was burning with a rash, or when your mouth hurt from painful sores, or when you were nauseated and bowed over a plastic bowl dry retching. The only thing you wanted then was for it all to end. His parents had told him that once he began the new treatment he would be sick all over again, and somehow he knew that he would be sicker than ever. The prospect of all that was just too terrible to think about. Oh, why did he have to make that kind of decision! Why should he have to make it? He didn't know what he should tell his parents. He knew he didn't want to die, but he knew he didn't want to be sick again.

"Why did this have to happen to me?" he thought, as he so frequently did. "Why me? It's so unfair."

He recalled the good times in his life, the birthday parties he had had, the pranks he had played on friends in school, the way he had built snowmen in winter and gone swimming in summer—so many wonderful things; and was he never to do any of them again? But of course that's what death was: you never did things again. You never did anything. Not to do—not to be—anything, ever? It somehow seemed impossible.

"Alright," he told himself, as though something more powerful than himself was forcing his hand. "I'll do it. But if it gets really bad ... really bad ... I'll just stop, that's all. They can't *make* me to do something I don't want to do—not if I really don't want to do it."

When he told his parents that he would do the transplant, their joy and relief were visible, and he was glad to have made them happy. His mother put a hand around his face and with quiet pride and said, "I knew you would ... you'll see, everything is going to be fine!"

Days passed without further complications. He wasn't feverish, his rashes subsided, and, though his legs ached, the doctors decided he could return home again. He was very glad of this, as he always was. He hoped that this time he wouldn't have to come back to the hospital till his radiation treatments began. That wouldn't be for some time yet because a suitable bone marrow donor first had to be found. Orpita, Sandesh, and Anram had their blood drawn to see if one of them was suitable, but none of them was.

Orpita was always eager to get him out of the house for an hour or two at a time if only for the therapeutic change of scenery and the exercise of a walk;—a walk that was now as slow and unsteady a shuffle as an old man's. After ten or fifteen minutes he would have to sit down to recruit his strength. Kirat always felt an initial eagerness to go on these outings, representing to him, as they did, a return to normal life; but his pleasure was always negated by the way people stared at him in his surgical mask, which he had to wear as some protection against the innumerable germs of the everyday world, and the wool cap or hat he wore to hide his baldness. He felt especially embarrassed when kids his own age stared at him. His was not an outgoing personality: he did not like to be looked upon, scrutinized; he quailed at the thought of being negatively judged. After accompanying his mother twice into the outside world he afterwards declined, saying that he didn't feel up to it, and never let on that he was just ashamed to look so odd.

"But you have to get out a little, Kirat!" Orpita would say. "You need some fresh air!"

"I'll just take a walk in the back yard later," he would say. And he would do just that: carefully descend the three cement steps from the back door and step out onto the grassy area that was no more than twenty feet wide and forty feet long, and walk back and forth a few times before going inside, exhausted.

For the next two months the boy's life seesawed between a hopeful progress toward health and unexpected, discouraging setbacks. As Dr. Faber had told Orpita and Sandesh, their son had to continue his chemotherapy drugs in order to keep his disease suppressed—and he continued to experience their side effects. Drugs that he had received with minor or no complications might suddenly, on their next administration, cause an unexpected and severe reaction. For instance one day at the outpatient clinic he was given a shot of etoposide and in a few minutes his face turned red, he felt hot all over, and his throat dried and constricted. "I can't breathe!" he gagged, panicking. "I can't breathe!" The anaphylactic reaction was brought under control with anti-inflammatory drugs but for the rest of the day he had a sore throat. His rashes flared up again; in places his skin was so dry it cracked, opening up pathways for bacteria he was less able than ever to resist. Every other week he developed a fever, which would soar (especially at night) so that his parents would have to take him back to the hospital for observation, and as a precautionary measure he would be given antibiotics. Then there was the issue of nerve damage. He began feeling what he called a "tingly" sensation in his lower legs and feet. This was the first telltale sign of yet another side effect of some of the drugs he was receiving: a degeneration of the protective myelin sheath of nerve cells in his lower extremities, in effect short-circuiting them. This led to his developing "foot drop," a condition in which the nerves leading to one or both of the feet become so damaged that the foot droops downward and is unresponsive as though the muscles controlling its movement are atrophied. Unable to turn his ankle and toes upward, he would stumble when he tried to walk. During this time he would lay in bed (the bed either in the hospital or at home) and look at the peaks of the covers made by his feet and try to move his toes, commanding them, "Move! ... move! ... move!"—but they would not move. He was fitted for foot braces made of hard plastic and designed to keep the foot in a fairly level position.

They enabled him to walk again but made his steps stiff and mechanical.

The one thought and prayer of the parents was that a suitable marrow donor would be found in time. As week after week, then month after month, passed, and one crisis after another with Kirat's illness arose, was met, and kept at bay, the parents despaired of finding a donor in time. In their quiet, urgent thoughts Orpita and Sandesh would think, "Please, God, let there be someone ..." Kirat was still alive thanks to his chemotherapy, but this could not last forever; eventually the boy would grow too weak to survive it, or perhaps some unforeseen and especially severe side effect would kill him. There would come a point when his spirit itself would fail him and he would lose the will to live.

Then Orpita and Sandesh received a phone call that a donor had been found. For the first time since their son had become sick, Orpita and Sandesh thought themselves "lucky." The parents announced the news to their son with an air of joyful relief, expecting him to be enthusiastic. And so he was: but not nearly so much as they had hoped he would be. He reminded them of what they themselves had told him about the odds of survival in the first year.

"Oh, you silly!" Orpita burst out, perhaps (she was conscious of this) a little too quickly. "That's not going to happen to *you!* You're going to be fine!"

"Well," the boy said, "even if it works out in the first year ... still the odds aren't good. Remember?" he asked, looking to his mother in a way that seemed to dare her to contradict him, to lie to his face.

Orpita sidetracked the issue entirely, saying, "Kirat, nothing is perfect. Everybody knows that. But just because there's a chance that something might happen doesn't mean it will. Especially with you! You've had a few setbacks, but you're doing pretty well so far."

The boy wondered how she could even say such a thing. Chemotherapy had been harder for him than for most, having caused in him especially severe complications. Then again, he knew that his mother had spoken as much for her sake as for his own, and he didn't want to say anything that would upset her.

In order to prepare the body for a marrow transplant the native marrow, and consequently its capacity to produce cancerous cells, has to be destroyed. Total body irradiation and drugs achieve this. Until the new marrow has engrafted, the body is without defense against infection, since the capacity to produce white blood cells has also been destroyed. Any preexisting infection will then have a greater opportunity to grow, and therefore where one is known or suspected it is dealt with prior to the radiation treatments. One place where it is suspected as a matter of course is in the mouth. Questionable oral health or decayed teeth must be taken care of lest the bacteria that causes it flares up dangerously in the absence of the body's immune system.

But if there was one thing the boy despised almost as much as doctors, it was dentists. His parents had always had a hard time forcing him to go even once every few years for a checkup. He couldn't keep still as instruments or strange fingers probed his mouth, and this time, with a suction tube hanging from his lower lip and an ultrasonic cleaner screeching against his teeth, his legs jittered, his hands frantically held on to the arms of the chair, and finally, no longer able to stand it, he gurgled out a shout of protest and bolted upright, pulling the tube out of his mouth, coughing hysterically, and choking out, "I can't breathe!" This happened ten times so that a procedure that should have taken fifteen minutes took almost an hour, and he looked more wan and wasted than usual. But his reaction was still more violently intolerant when the dentist tried to fill the first of his five cavities. At the sound and sight of the drill, Kirat's whole body trembled, and the moment the drill touched his tooth he all but jumped out of the chair with a scream.

Quietly frustrated, the dentist turned off the drill and returned it to its holder. In his low seat he pushed away from the boy, stood up, and shook his head, removing his mask with an air of exasperated resignation. To Orpita, who had been standing in the doorway watching, he said, "I'm sorry, I can't work on him like this. He's gonna have to be sedated for the fillings, and I don't do that here."

Orpita looked at Kirat with angry eyes. The boy hung his head shamefully at having not lived up to the expectation of a parent: and yet he knew that he hadn't been able to help it and wondered why his mother couldn't understand this. Would she have been able to sit there with a drill buzzing away in *her* mouth? And even if she could, well, that didn't mean *he* could!

The dental surgery had to be scheduled at a hospital. Sandesh hurriedly submitted to his insurance company a claim for the expenses that would be involved: $5,600 for the use of an operating room; $2,900 for an anesthesiologist; $4,100 for the dentist; and $1,356 for a single day's recovery in a hospital room. A few days later he learned the claim had been denied. He was sure that this was an error—it had to be—and so he called his insurance company's customer service phone number. The woman who answered his call introduced herself as "Helen." She said she was a "Health Coordinator" and asked if she could "be of assistance" to him.

He explained why he was calling and when he had finished she politely asked him to hold on the line while she looked up his records. For the next eight minutes Sandesh listened to Muzak and when the Health Coordinator came back on the line—she excused herself for having taken so much time and thanked him for his patience—she told him that his claim had been denied because the procedure he had filed for was not covered under his policy.

"But it's necessary for the treatment," Sandesh said. "He can't go through with the transplant till he has his teeth fixed."

There were a few clicks of a keyboard on the other end of the line as the woman looked up records. "Yes sir, I understand your concern," she said with an easy politeness, and proceeded to quote from his policy a few sentences from a restrictive clause by which "ancillary" and "optional" procedures were not covered.

"But that's ridiculous. This isn't elective. He *has* to have his teeth fixed before he can continue with his treatments. And he couldn't go to a regular dentist because ... well, I put down all the information when I submitted the claim. Just look at what was submitted and you'll see—it's all corroborated by the doctors involved. They've all signed off on it. If you don't believe me, call them."

"I understand that, sir, but all these are regarded as ancillary procedures not covered by your policy."

"But I just told you it *has* to be done! Listen, this is ridicu-

lous," he said, irritated first by what had already become a circular argument, and secondly by the woman's oleaginous pose of
helpfulness that was no help at all.   "Could I speak to someone
else there—a supervisor or something?"

"Hold on please, sir," the woman said, in as cool a voice as
ever.   As a "Health Coordinator" she had gone through this
same conversation hundreds of times before, and had learned
that there was no point in taking personally the frustrations
and anger of policyholders who discovered that their insurance
was not quite the safety net they had expected, that there were
things—tremendously expensive things—that had been exempt
from coverage.

Sandesh tapped his foot with impatience as he held the
phone against his ear.   Again, Muzak.   "'Ancillary procedures'!"
he mumbled to himself, shaking his head.   "Bullshit!"

When the supervisor got on the phone he politely introduced himself as Mr. Allan the "Managing Director" of "Health
Coordinating Services" and asked how he could help Sandesh.
In fact in the nearly five minutes that had intervened before he
had picked up on the call he had been notified about what the
issue was, and had arrayed on his computer screen all the pertinent information.   Nevertheless he heard Sandesh out, often
murmuring "Yes" or "I see" as though he were hearing previously undisclosed information that altered the nature of the
case.   At one point he expressed his sympathy that Sandesh's
child was sick.   But when the moment came for him to make a
decision, to give a different answer from the one the Health Coordinator had given, he repeated the same things she had said
almost word for word.   It was not, he said, a matter of interpreting the policy.   The policy was clear in what it did and did
not cover. Kirat's dental surgery, and any costs associated with
it, were not covered and would have to be paid out of pocket.

"But don't you realize I can't afford that?" Sandesh asked,
and began quoting the fees required by the dentist, the hospital,
the anaesthesiologist.   "That's almost $14,000.   I don't have that
kind of money."

"I understand your disappointment, sir," Mr. Allan said, in
the same even-toned, superficially sympathetic, "professional"
tone of voice that had been used by the Health Coordinator, and
which is never more steadily assumed by the bureaucrat than

when he must harden his heart for the sake of the way he makes his living. "I can only go by what your policy stipulates, and as I say, those things are not covered. I'm really sorry about this. Have you spoken to someone at the hospital about perhaps making a payment plan?"

"That's not the point! The point is that this should be covered. It's *necessary.*"

"I'm sorry, sir, but there's nothing we can do for you in that area."

Angry now, Sandesh was about to demand to speak to someone else—another supervisor, someone yet higher in authority, someone with some common sense, some basic human decency, who would understand what was happening; but he realized that it was not going to be of any use. No matter what he said the insurance company would fall back on its policy, on what, according to it, was and was not covered. It was a business. It knew nothing of pity. The end and aim of its existence was to make a profit, and it did this best by denying and preventing as many expenditures as possible.

Thus did Orpita and Sandesh come face-to-face with the stark reality of how, in the country they had adopted and loved, medicine and extortion went hand-in-hand; a miserable state of affairs bound to happen when a profession is regarded as a road to riches and thus attracts purely mercenary characters, who color it with the dark hues of their single-minded and heartless greed. But the parents did not give way to their anger or disgust; there was no time for that; the only thing that mattered to them was the life of their son, and to ensure it, to prolong it, they would have done whatever was necessary: endured any hardship, absorbed any humiliation, been reduced to the most abject poverty. If they had had to sell their house and live in the street, then they would have sold their house and lived in the street.

When Sandesh had told the man at the insurance company that he didn't have the money for his son's dental work he had not been quite honest. For in fact he had accumulated a nest egg of some twenty thousand dollars. It was a sum to which he had been contributing for years and with which he had planned to send his sons to college so that they would get good educations—good jobs—and not have to struggle the way he had.

Wasn't that part of the greatness of America, of the "American Dream"—that if one worked hard, if one sacrificed and planned, one's children would do better than oneself ? But the dream had shattered with a single stroke. Now most of that money would have to be spent. His disappointment was only mollified with the relieving thought that at least he *had* the money to spend when it was so absolutely necessary.

Kirat's dental work took place under complete sedation in a hospital operating room. When he awoke he was nauseated from the anesthesia and only felt better several hours later, though even then he complained of headache and a painful throbbing in his lower jaw, where most of the dental work had been done. The next day he was allowed to go home in order to rest before his radiation treatments began. It was always hoped that there, in the comforting familiarity of home, his mental and physical condition would improve, would grow stronger in preparation for the taxing therapy he was to undergo; and in fact he *did* seem more content, if not more healthy. Getting him to eat, to put back on some of the weight he had lost, was always a priority for the parents. Aware of how the younger boy always emulated the older in all things, Orpita had taken Anram aside and told him, "Do what you can to make your brother eat. He'll listen to you." And so at the dinner table Anram, shoving food into his mouth as though it were going out of style and munching away happily, would tell Kirat "C'mon, you scarecrow, eat!" or "You're crazy if you don't like this!" or "This is the best stuff! Why don't you have some? Go on—try it!" And driven by an irresistible urge to imitate his brother, Kirat would first poke at his food, then begin eating it slowly, determinedly, almost in spite of himself. Each time he swallowed, Orpita felt a little surge of gratitude. But he never took more than a few mouthfuls before he put down his fork or spoon, shook his head, and said he had had enough.

In the meantime Kirat was fitted for a body mold that would ensure he remained immobilized during radiation treatments. It was created from what was essentially a large plastic bag filled with quick-setting foam: as he was laid down into it, with legs and arms slightly separated, the foam hardened beneath and around him. In getting up from it, he left behind a perfectly-customized, indented contour of his body. He also had to have his port-a-cath removed and a Hickman line implanted, the latter being deemed more antiseptic because a needle did not have to pass through the skin each time a drug was given; and now that his immune system would be systematically and completely destroyed, every possibility for infection had to be reduced. Again, Kirat quailed at the thought of the operation. He had grown quite used to the port-a-cath, that hard lump under the skin on the upper left side of his chest, even though it had required routine cleaning and re-dressing. He didn't see why it had to be taken out so that he could have (as he realized he would have) tubing coming out of his body as though he were some kind of half-mechanical creature. Again his parents had to use all kinds of blandishments, euphemisms, and forced good cheer to belittle and try to coax away his resistance, but the only thing that really worked was the sedation he took just before surgery.

On the day before Kirat was to return to the hospital for his radiation treatments Orpita informed her husband, "My mother's coming to stay with me for a while." She didn't say "us" because she knew that her husband was not fond of her mother and would not have regarded her visit as welcome for his own sake, so she made it clear that it was for hers.

"How long is she staying?" was his first question.

Orpita saw his displeasure, which rather irritated her, so that even though she knew that her mother was only going to stay for a couple of weeks, she answered:

"My mother can stay as long as she wants."

Sandesh's jaw tightened. In normal times he might have gotten into a fight with Orpita about the prospect of an unlimited stay by her mother: but in light of his son's illness, it hardly seemed so important—was unwelcome, to be sure, but in the larger scheme of things nothing more than a minor irritation.

Tests were carried out on Kirat to ensure that his heart, lungs, kidneys and other vital organs were at a certain level of functionality and could withstand the trauma of the transplant. The tests resulted in the judgment that he was "strong enough." The true meaning of this phrase was not lost on Orpita; she understood it to mean that her son met only some minimum requirement. It caused her to look on her son's external condition with a new objectivity. She compared him with other boys his age whom she saw in the street, and the comparison would leave her in wonder at how a child so thin and frail could have the strength to continue to receive the harsh drugs that were keeping his disease at bay. She realized that he had also become a different person. His illness and suffering had changed him. Gone was the mischievous liveliness of which he had been so delightfully, sometimes exasperatingly full. Gone was the curiosity, the almost impatient expectation in his eyes when a subject about which he knew nothing was mentioned in his hearing, as though he couldn't wait for it to be explained to him. The happy, wondering vitality of the child for whom the world is still full of facts to be learned and mysteries to be explored had disappeared. Orpita told herself, "He'll be that way again when he gets better."

To Orpita and Sandesh the radiation therapy and transplant had come to represent the definitive cure. It wasn't that they had forgotten about the possible setbacks, complications, or even uninspiring survival statistics; they both remembered these things quite well. But they had convinced themselves that this ultimate of all treatments would be the one that would work.

The boy was to undergo radiation treatments twice a day for five days, after which he would receive an intensive round of chemotherapy. Kirat was quiet with nervous apprehension on the night before his treatments were to begin. Six months had passed from his initial diagnosis; during that time he had been in the hospital so often that he had quite lost his fear of it—if anything, it had become like a second home. But he had never lost his fear of painful side effects and complications from his chemotherapy, and he was especially nervous when he remembered (as he did very well) the additional complications that could arise from the radiation. Even the procedure itself he was wary of. The doctors and nurses had told him that it wasn't painful at all—no more so than taking an X-ray; but of course you couldn't trust them when it came to telling you the truth about such things. He imagined all sorts of sharp pains he would feel. But he also remembered the vow he had made to himself of refusing to do anything he didn't want to. He renewed that vow now, telling himself that if it hurt too much he was going to stop it, and no one would be able to make him continue. No one.

The first time the boy was ushered into the radiation therapy room he was wondrously impressed with the size, bulk, and somehow space-age sleekness of the linear accelerator, the great machine that would shoot its cell-destroying rays into his bones and destroy the marrow. The body-holding form he had helped to make a few days earlier was atop the sliding table beneath the machine. The radiation oncologist helped him into it. She was a brisk, chatty young woman who had a way of making the process seem as normal and benign as combing one's hair. Once she had laid him down into his form, she moved the table into position under the overhanging part of the machine, then covered his chest with a lead-lined shield. Kirat felt this rest upon him with a somehow reassuring weightiness.

"Now here's what I want you to do for me," she told him, smiling pleasantly and putting a warm caring hand on his arm. "I want you to try to stay as still as you can, okay? You don't have to hold your breath or anything—just breathe normally— but try not to move too much. I'm going to go into the next room where I work the machine, but I'll be able to see you with those cameras—see them?—there and there? I'll be able to see you and hear you, so don't worry, you're not alone. Understand?"

He nodded, yes, grateful for her smiling kindness.

"Now when we get started, the machine's going to start making some noise and then you'll see it moving. It's going to move over you and around you. Just try to relax. And if for some reason you need something, or you need us to stop, you just say so and I'll be able to hear you. Alright?"

Again he nodded yes. He watched her as she walked around him a final time, giving little pressing pats to his legs and arms as she said, "Good ... good ... good," as though she were going through some sort of checklist.

"Looks great!" she said. "Just relax. I'll see you in a few minutes."

He watched her go with a feeling of loss; each click of her retreating heels increased in him a sense of desertion. She was a nice lady; she made him feel good and protected. She made him feel as though everything would be alright.

A little while after she had left the room he heard a noise— a strange buzz and clicking as though something mechanical were coming to life; and sure enough there followed a low hum, as of a motor revving up. The great machine above him began to move, to rotate, to the left. A fascinated Kirat followed it with his eyes. His boyish fancy imagined it as some alien Cyclopean robot curiously examining his puny, helpless human self. The motor hum ceased and the gigantic eye became still, locked into place, followed by a few seconds of a buzzing sound that ended with a click. Again and again, from one part of his body to another, the machine positioned itself with computerized exactitude, sending out beams of radiation so finely guided that if necessary they might have edged the head of a pin. Though he had been apprehensive at first about what would happen to him—about what he would feel—he noted with relief that he felt nothing at all.

Orpita stood behind the radiation oncologist in the control room, watching her son on the table as the machine passed over various parts of his body, intermittently stopping before moving on. From the distance at which the monitoring cameras were placed, and their relatively low quality, she couldn't make out his features very well and consequently he might have been any boy lying there beneath the machine—a circumstance that enabled her to watch the process somewhat objectively. "Such a big machine," she thought, looking at the relatively small body in its clutches. "It's amazing how such machines exist, how people have built them. God bless the people who know how to make them."

And so began the therapy in which the boy's bone marrow was methodically destroyed, and with it the capacity to create diseased cells—as well as healthy ones. The irradiation itself was painless, and for the first time, Kirat noted to himself, the doctors and his parents had not lied about the matter. After the first session he felt only a comfortable warmth throughout his body, which reminded him of those wintry nights when he had lain his bed and a nearby, steam-driven heater had emitted waves of caressing, comforting heat. But an hour or so later he would feel the first stirrings of a nausea that would that grip him painfully for hours. After the second day of treatments the glands in his neck swelled up; his throat was sore; his saliva thickened and it was hard for him to swallow. He had no appetite and couldn't eat. He was always exhausted. He never wanted to get out of bed; he didn't even want to sit up. Indeed whether or not he "wanted" to do something was irrelevant, for the issue was not one of volition but of lack of energy: a leaden inertness weighed down his limbs as though all vitality had been drained from them. His psychological state was consonant with this exhaustion: he was content to be silent for hours at a time, or at most talk quietly with his ever-present mother in a voice barely above a whisper. It was sometimes hard for her to hear him because she had to sit several feet away from him and wear a mask as a precaution against spreading germs to his increasingly vanishing immune system. These side effects changed his attitude toward the radiation machine itself: what had impressed him with its gleaming technology now struck him as subtly, covertly evil: a contraption that assumed an aura of benignity in order the more completely work its hurt and harm. He resisted having his last two treatments, but his parents explained to him that he had no choice but to continue: that he had to go through with them: the transplant had been planned—everything had been arranged—that if he backed out now he would die for sure. To hear his own parents tell him this, to hear them mention his death when they had always tried to hide that possibility from him, was a benumbing blow to the boy; silenced him, stripped away his will to resist; rather in the same way that a military leader, on the eve of great battle, on finding himself abandoned by his allies and betrayed even by his closest lieutenants, is left standing alone, in embittered, immobilized resignation to defeat.

He was also started on the aggressive chemotherapy that was to suppress the last of the viable cancer cells in his body. The drug used, Cytoxan, had the side effect of causing hemorrhagic cystitis, or bleeding of the bladder, against which possibility high rates of IV fluids were given to flush out that organ. He was also given Mesna, an "adjuvant" or counteracting drug meant to lessen the side effect of the Cytoxan. The lining of his mouth threatened to burst into new sores, and when he didn't feel the ache of nausea he felt stabs of pain in his stomach. Whenever possible a drug was introduced into his IV line to counteract these effects. When he finished with the Cytoxan treatments he was left weak and feverish. He lay in bed with his eyes either closed or languidly open, becoming more ani-

mated only when he felt another bout of pain or nausea to
which he didn't even have the energy to react strongly. One
night, flush with a slight fever, sweaty, dry-mouthed, sleepless
as he lay in bed in the dark, he made up his mind that he
wasn't going to do the transplant after all. He was sure that he
had made the wrong decision in agreeing to it. What was the
point of it? It hurt too much. If he had died already he
wouldn't have known any of this. All the next day he intended
to tell his mother. But just when he had screwed up his
courage to do so (she was sitting there, in the corner of his
room, looking at a magazine, and it had been some time since
they had spoken to each other), he saw the way she looked up
at him in anticipation of his saying something, and her expression was so pleasantly curious, her smile so warmly encouraging, that he couldn't bring himself to say anything that would
upset her, as though that would have been impossibly unfair to
her, a cruel ingratitude toward someone who had been with him
every day, who had watched over him every second, and patiently abided his sometimes nervous tantrums, and who was, in
short, doing everything it was possible for one person to do to
help another short of giving her own life. And yet that too—
wouldn't she have done even that if it could have ensured his
getting better? He knew that she would have. He looked away
from her. He held his peace. It occurred to him that even if he
didn't want to go through with the transplant, he ought to do it
for her sake, as a kind of repayment for all she had done for
him, for all the days she had stayed with him and worried over
him. He knew how much trouble and sadness he had caused
her and his father, and he wanted to make it up to them, even
if that meant feeling terrible all the time.

   "Are you okay over there?" she asked him. "You want anything?"

   Not looking at her, he shook his head, no.

   —Yes, he would go through with it. Perhaps he really
would be alright, the way everyone kept assuring him. Surely
he shouldn't give up now, after all he had gone through and
when it was just a matter of receiving the transplant.

   With the destruction of his bone marrow, his platelets and
red and white blood cells dropped. He received blood products
to sustain him and a steady stream of antibiotics to keep infec-

tion at bay. He often had low-level fevers. His appetite was in-termittent. When it returned, even a little, his mother was sure to find food for him. But it often happened that by the time the food came he had lost his initial, passing inclination for it, and turned away his face at the sight of it. Despite Orpita's pleading and demands that he eat, he would never take more than a few bites, the very last of which, after chewing with revulsion, he would spit out, saying, "I can't!" Nearly all the nutrition he re-ceived was delivered intravenously.

—So passed the terrible first week after the radiation ther-apy; the worst so far.

In the meantime Orpita's mother arrived from India. A woman of medium height, she had grown stout with age. Streaks of deep black ran among her mostly graying hair, which she wore swept back and close to her head. The skin around her eyes was a little darker than that of the rest of her face so that she had a sad, tired, or spectral cast to her expression. When she came off the plane at JFK Airport she was wearing a maroon sari, gold bracelets, and small gold earrings. She met her daughter at the exit gate and they fell into each other's arms and hugged and kissed each other, their eyes filling with tears of joy;—with tears of sadness, too, which came from the unspoken acknowledgment of their mutual worry. After these initial embraces the mother put her hands on her daughter's cheeks, looked into her face more carefully, and saw the toll her son's illness had taken on her.

She went to see her grandson the day after she arrived in New York. The sight of his wasted condition shocked her but she gave no hint of this and went toward the boy with exclama-tions of cheerful joy though her smile was hidden behind her surgical mask. Kirat found her greeting and ebullient manner a bit overwhelming—and rather artificial, for, with that strictly logical view children have of their relationships with adults, he didn't understand how she could love him so much when she hadn't seen him more than a few times in his whole life. She was his grandmother but she might have been a stranger to him. Nevertheless he was old enough to know to be gracious, and he did his best to seem happy to see her. He was especially grateful when she gave him a wrapped present (Orpita had had to ask permission from the doctors to bring it), handing it over to him as she said:

"I saw this in the airport and bought it for you! I think you'll like it!"

"What is it?" the boy asked, taking the package into his hands and, despite his weakness, his child's heart taking light at the notion of a gift.

"You'll see!"

The boy unwrapped the box, and when he had done so he gazed upon it, at the glossy picture of the object it contained, and wasn't sure how to react because he didn't know what it was. He looked up to his grandmother uncertainly.

"You'll see!" she said. "Take it out! I'll show you!"

It was a Newton's cradle. Five chrome-shiny balls depended from two parallel steel bars; five balls in a row, each hanging indifferently against the other. Roopa bade her grandson set down the object on the table beside his bed, and when he had done so she reached out and pulled out one of the balls on the end, and then let it go. It struck the first stationary ball, and yet not this ball but the one all the way at the other end of the row sprang outward and upward, as though it itself had been hit

The effect delighted the boy. It was magical, wonderful: to think that what happened at one end of the row of balls effected something all the way at the other, while everything in between remained the same. He himself pulled out the first or last ball, raised it, and let it drop; and saw with new delight how the energy of its impact traveled invisibly through three intervening balls to cause the fourth to jump up nearly as high as the first one had been lifted.

"How's it do that?" he asked.

Roopa only shook her head and smiled—shook her head because she wasn't quite sure herself, and smiled with gratification at having given her grandson something that took his mind off his troubles, even if it were only for a few minutes at a time.

In fact it would take his mind off his troubles for much longer than that, for he played with the mechanism often. All the while his grandmother had visited him he had put the cradle into motion, the sharp click-clack, click-clack of the striking balls filling the room. And later that night, after everyone had gone and he was by himself, he reached out to it again and lifted one of the balls on one end and let it drop; and watched how not the one it had hit, but the one at the opposite end of the line, sprang up. Click-clack, click-clack; back-and-forth, back-and-forth; inexplicably, magically, somehow necessarily.... How he stared at the thing! How it made him wonder! How it engaged something deep inside him, which he couldn't explain.

Though Sandesh had been less than enthusiastic about his mother-in-law's visit, her presence proved beneficial in a way even he couldn't deny. She picked up on the cooking and cleaning that Orpita, almost always at the hospital with Kirat, had let lapse. When he came home from work there was always a hot meal waiting for him. She kept the kitchen and bathroom spotless. She did the laundry, always ironing and folding the clothes neatly, then putting them away in everyone's dressers or closets. Her manner toward her son-in-law was entirely passive—quiet, demure, consciously deferential. She seemed determined to keep out of his way, to avoid the possibility of conflict, and whenever he was in the house she pretty much kept to her room. When Sandesh realized how much she was doing for him and his family, and yet was walking on eggshells on account of him, he felt guilty. He began to understand that whatever her faults were they weren't any worse than his own or anyone else's. And so whatever resentment or dislike he had harbored toward her quickly dissolved. One night when he came home from work and Roopa, as usual, quietly and efficiently served him his dinner and started to leave the kitchen, he stopped her departure with, "Where are you going?"

"Oh ... I have some things to do."

"Like what?"

"Oh ... just some things."

"They can wait. Why don't you sit down? Why don't you eat with me?"

"I already ate."

"Then sit down. Let's talk."

The older woman hesitated and regarded him cautiously as though his invitation were a prelude to a criticism or comeuppance, but then she detected in his eyes and expression a kindly encouragement, a note of reconciliation, and took a few steps to the kitchen table and sat down at it.

"Thanks for making dinner," he said. "I appreciate it. It's

very good."

She smiled with gratitude. "I'm glad you like it."

"I do." He hesitated a moment before adding, "I just want you to know ... I appreciate your helping out. It's helped a lot, your being here." Despite himself the tone of his words was such as to show they came from the heart.

Whatever reservations or caution Roopa had at that moment disappeared. She sat back in her chair and smiled at her son-in-law, grateful for his recognition that she had come in all humility to help.

"It's a pity Kirat can't eat this," she said, looking at the food with its fragrant, rich, turmeric-orange cream-sauce.

"There's a lot of things he can't eat. But I'm sure Anram liked it."

"Oh, he did," Roopa said, nodding, reflecting with satisfaction on how her other grandson came home from school and gobbled down her spiced cooking until he was full to bursting.

"Maybe you can bring some to Orpita when you go to the hospital."

"No, I can't. They don't want us bringing any outside food into Kirat's room."

"Oh ..."

There was a somewhat uncomfortable pause between them. Then Sandesh asked:

"So what did Anram do today?"

"Same as usual. Came home from school and went into his room and turned on his stereo. Oh, that music he listens to!" she said, shaking her head. "Horrible. All screaming and shouting! Why are they always shouting? I don't understand."

Sandesh almost chuckled as he said, "That makes two of us. But that's what the kids like here."

Roopa shook her head as though she would never understand such a thing, and Sandesh smiled sympathetically. Sandesh continued eating and a few minutes passed in which they sat silently before each other.

"By the way, is there anything you need?" he asked. "Do you need to go to the store or something? I'll drive you."

"The stores are all close here. I walk to them. I went today and did some food shopping."

"Well ... if you ever need to go anywhere, just let me know."

She smiled and nodded. Then, "Orpita doesn't look so good."

"I know."

"She's at the hospital all day."

"She always is. I told her she didn't have to be—that she shouldn't be. Kirat doesn't even want her around sometimes. But your daughter's very stubborn."

Partly in order to defend her daughter, partly in order to try to make Sandesh understand (in case he didn't) what Orpita, as a mother, must feel, Roopa said, "Well, she can't help it."

"Yes," Sandesh said. "I know."

"Are you going tonight?"

"Yes, later on."

Sandesh knew he ought to ask his mother-in-law if she wanted to accompany him, but unless she asked to go along he was not going to make the offer. The thickest of the ice between them might have been broken, but he preferred she not be present when he visited Kirat. Her presence at the boy's bed-side always somehow brought in the chilling element of the out-sider. Kirat himself was uncomfortably shy in her presence. Besides, Roopa had already been to the hospital several times with her daughter, so it wasn't as though he were depriving her of seeing her grandson.

The marrow transplant itself proved to be rather anticli-mactic. Dr. Faber personally administered the procedure. He set up the new IV bag with the marrow in it (it looked like any other bag of blood, only cloudier), and just before he connected it to Kirat's Hickman catheter he smiled reassuringly at him, pat-ted him on the shoulder, and said, "Just relax." For the next two hours the marrow dripped into the boy's bloodstream. In the middle of it complications occurred. His fever soared; he trembled with chills; and a few times his nausea was so strong that he retched. But worst of all was the increase in his blood pressure. At one point it rose dangerously to 190/140, and this was the more hazardous because if he had a stroke his low platelet level would make it impossible for the blood to clot. Dr. Faber administered one drug after another to alleviate these re-actions. Each time he ordered another substance, and filled a sy-ringe with it and injected it into the line inserted into her son's body, Orpita grew more agitated. She had always questioned the doctors about what drugs they were giving her son, but lately she asked these questions more frequently and with some apprehension and even with an air of disapproval, for it seemed to her that however efficacious they might be in reducing side effects they neverteless added to the overall, cumulative toxic load. But always the doctors answered her with an air of calm wisdom and certainty, and she couldn't bring herself to contradict or question them further. After all, what did *she* know? She wasn't a doctor. She hadn't gone to school for a decade, and then spent thirty years in medical practice, as many of these doctors had. They had to know what they were talking about. They had to know what they were doing. One had to trust in them.

The next day, after a drug-induced sleep, the boy felt better, though he complained of dull, insistent, throbbing headaches, which the doctor attributed to the high doses of antibiotics.

It was now just a matter of waiting for the new cells to engraft and begin producing healthy cells. But even during this time there were dangers, primarily the possibility of GVHD— Graft Versus Host Disease, a condition in which the new, donated cells see the body as foreign and launch an immunological attack against it. "Actually, we want some of this to happen," the doctors explained to the parents. "We want the new cells to target any leukemic cells that still exist. But there's a possibility that the new cells will see the whole body as foreign. We'll have to watch out for that."

In the next few days the main problem became neutropenic fever: stripped of its white blood cells—the new bone marrow not yet having engrafted—the body was defenseless against germs. At one point Kirat's temperature soared to 104° and he had to be cooled down with wet cloths and ice packs. An hour afterwards, however, he might be trembling with cold and correspondingly opposite efforts would be made to keep him warm. Blood was drawn to test for the specific infection and he was started on another antibiotic, which was known to be so hard on the kidneys as to cause renal failure, but the doctors assured the parents that their son would be given a conservative dosage and his condition would be closely monitored.

Over the next couple of days the fevers subsided. The ef-

fect was debilitating. Kirat wanted to lie in bed all day, which
however he could not do lest he develop pneumonia; he had to
get off his back and get some physical exercise. A stationary bi-
cycle was placed in his room and he was encouraged to get on it
and peda, if only for a few minutes at a time. But even when
his will overcame his weakness it could not overcome his pain.
His legs hurt him. The chemotherapy drugs which had affected
the nerves in his legs, which had first made them only tingle,
then caused foot drop, by now had done serious damage. The
pain was so great that it kept him up at night, prompting the
doctors to authorize a morphine drip, only for the morphine to
affect his ability to urinate. At one point his bladder filled and
he was unable to empty it; and then it began to hurt him so
much that he had to undergo a painful and embarrassing penile
catheterization. At the end of a particularly hard day, after his
mother had left to go home, he lay in bed, in the dark, not
sleeping, miserable, thinking:

"I knew I shouldn't have done it. I knew it ... knew it ..."

He still had very little appetite. Now and then, for a few
minutes at a time, he would say that he was hungry, but when
food was brought to him—even food he had specifically requested—he would take a few bites of it and push the rest away, or,
as sometimes happened, no sooner see and smell it than feel
nauseated. His treatments had even altered his sense of taste
and smell, so that food either lost its aroma or assumed a
strange or bad odor. He had become as wasted as a scarecrow.
His face was strikingly gaunt. There was an alarming, spectral
sharpness to his cheekbones and nose. His eyes seemed to have
grown immensely large; and they would, when he was medicated for pain, expand into large glassy pools like the huge eyes
of some starved, nocturnal creature.

It was the changeableness of Kirat's illness that kept the
parents on an emotional roller coaster. Two weeks after the
transplant, when he seemed to have plumbed the depths of
physical decline, he began to rebound, and hope for recovery and
cure sprang up anew. The latest blood work showed that the
white blood cell count had risen, auspiciously indicating that the
new marrow had engrafted and was starting to produce healthy
cells. He continued to receive blood and platelets, and pain-
killers for his neuropathy. But day by day he grew stronger. A

proper sense of smell and taste returned; and with it something
of an appetite. He no longer pushed away most of his food; he
made an effort to eat as much as he could; and his interest in
sweets returned, for the sweeter the food the more he liked it.
To see him take a few bites of some rich dessert with its hundreds of calories made Orpita's heart soar with delight. He
even began getting out of bed and wanting to walk around.
Even his hair had started to grow back—a dark fuzz that grew
blacker, thicker by the day. Each morning he shuffled into the
bathroom and looked into the mirror to see if it had grown any
more. Of all the bouts of "progress" he had ever made, it was
this one—the regrowth of his hair—that most relieved and satisfied him, since it seemed to him the visible, incontrovertible
pledge of a return to health.

Of his progress generally Dr. Faber told Orpita and
Sandesh, "It looks good. If he keeps on like this for a week or
two, he can go home."

That news made Kirat break out into a smile and become
excited. "Yesssss!" he said, making a fist and triumphantly
pounding the side of his bed.

Two weeks later, on the morning of his son's release from
the hospital, Sandesh drove the family car up to the hospital entrance and called his wife on her cell phone saying, "I'm downstairs!" During the few minutes that it took for his son and
wife come out of the building he stared at the closed glass doors
with a sense of intense expectation and relief ; and gratitude.
He was grateful for the doctors who had saved his son's life, and
he was grateful to God, Whom he had secretly so often and so
passionately appealed to. In his heart of hearts he knew that
from now on everything was going to be alright. For the first
time in months the "future" regained much of its old, quietly
comfortable perspective.

It was a great excitement for the boy to leave the hospital
where he had been living for weeks. All of his treatments were
over. The worst that could be done to him had been endured
and surmounted. When he stepped outside he felt an upsurge
of joy to feel again the wind against his skin, to see overhead
not a fluorescent light but the cheerful, vaulting sky. The moment he stepped out of the front doors he felt as though he
were "free." He was wearing regular clothes. Orpita was carry-

ing a small suitcase in which she had put his "hospital clothes"—mostly pajamas—and the other, miscellaneous possessions he had accumulated. However there was one thing he carried in his hands: his Newton's cradle. His father and mother gently guided him into the back seat of the car—"Watch your head," Sandesh said, placing his hand over his son's head as though to protect it from the steel frame of the car.

Even the act of getting into the car again, of sitting in it, made the boy happy. It was good to know again the vinyl smell of that interior, the subtle roar and shake of the engine starting, the sight of his father behind the wheel and of his mother sitting to the right of him. As the car became a part of traffic he was excited and happy to be again in the real world—the world of regular, everyday life: of people walking on sidewalks, of trucks making deliveries, of police cars whizzing by with blaring sirens. He experienced all these things not only with a kind of happy nostalgia but with a downright love of them. He had missed them more than he could have imagined. He told himself that he would never ignore them again now that he knew how wonderful they were. After a while he idly played with the Newton's cradle again—letting one of the balls drop and watching how they idly click-clacked back and forth.

"Hey, Kirat, look what's over there!" Sandesh said, happily, nodding to the right-hand side of the windshield, to the near distance where the golden arches of a fast-food restaurant peeped up behind a billboard. "How 'bout a nice hamburger! Would you like that?—huh? A big one! With lots of ketchup! How 'bout it?" In hopeful anticipation of his son agreeing to the proposal, Sandesh slowed down the car and prepared to turn off into the street where the restaurant was located, but glancing in the rearview mirror he saw his son shaking his head and heard him say:

"No, that's okay."

"Are you sure? It's good!"

Kirat shook his head, no, no, no. He was playing with his Newton's cradle, which went click-clack, click-clack, click-clack.

Orpita turned around in the front seat to her son. She glanced at the toy in his hand, then raised her eyes to his face, smiling as she gazed upon him. "I'll make you something good when we get home, alright?"

He nodded, yes, in part to appease her, in part hoping that he really might be able to eat something his mother made for him. But on another, deeper level he wondered why she, who of all the people in the world knew that sometimes he couldn't eat no matter how much he wanted to—why she was acting as though he could eat on command. Yet in the next moment he told himself that he would try—really try—to eat whatever she made for him.

As he neared his home, and saw familiar streets and buildings, he grew increasingly pleased and vital. He sat up a little straighter and turned his head to the left and right quickly, greedily taking in the sights of sweetly familiar things. Once again he realized how much he had taken them for granted and missed them. When his father turned into the driveway of their house, Kirat felt the quiet gratitude of profound fulfillment. How he loved his house!

Sandesh had just shut off the engine when his neighbor, Mr. Jeffries, stepped out onto his front steps and turned around to lock his door. Over his shoulder was the long, narrow, canvas case enclosing his shotgun. He was apparently going on another trip upstate to his "cabin." Mr. Jeffries had of course known for some time that his neighbor's son was sick and had asked after him whenever he had seen Sandesh or Orpita. He now assumed that because Kirat was home it meant he had gotten better. He came striding over to his neighbor's property, smilingly, happily calling out, "Well, well!"—intending to shake hands with Kirat and welcome him back home. Sandesh hurriedly got out of the car and stepped up to Mr. Jeffries to block his progress and politely informed him that he had to keep his distance because the boy's immune system was fragile.

Mr. Jeffries obligingly stepped back several paces—much more than was necessary—and from this new, more distant vantage point accosted Kirat, who was just getting out of the car. "Good to see you back, son!" he called out. "We missed you! Hope you're feeling better—eh?" He had spoken ardently, cheerfully, but in fact he was shocked to see how thin and fragile the boy looked. His sunny, breezy greeting had been forced; a reflex of that social instinct by which, whenever we see someone who is obviously sick or disabled, we make an especial effort to seem "normal," even inordinately friendly and good-humored, and so put him at his ease and thereby make his life a little easier or, we hope, help him to recover.

Kirat had never thought twice about Mr. Jeffries, the "old guy" who lived next door, but now he was pleased at his neighborly expression of goodwill. He didn't know what to say in return and just smiled shyly and nodded.

"If you guys need anything," Mr. Jeffries said, turning his attention to Sandesh with a concerned, solemn smile, "please just let me know. If you need me to get anything for you, or ... whatever!"

"Thank you, we will," Sandesh said.

"We appreciate it," Orpita said, putting her arm around her boy and leading him into the house.

Kirat looked forward to doing again the things he used to do, such as going into the back yard or basement to play, or sitting at his computer and surfing the Internet; but he would engage in these activities for only a few minutes at a time before becoming too tired to continue with them, whereupon he would sit or lie on the couch in the living room, watching or rather languidly staring at the television. In time he no longer played with his Newton's cradle (even the most fascinating toy loses its appeal in time); it stood still and unused on the hallway bureau—there among the small framed pictures and the large statue of Vishnu. But he happened to find the cheap plastic toy he had once gotten out of a cereal box. For a half hour at a time he would give his whole attention over to it, flicking the little plastic tab that sent the enclosed steel pellet flying up into the convex top and falling among the staggered channels to miss or be caught up in numbered indentations. And as he again played with this toy it occurred to him that it wasn't a game of chance at all. There were reasons why the pellet fell this way and not that. The forcefulness with which it was propelled forward, the angle at which the toy was held, every smallest movement of his hand or arm or body—they all influenced the course of the pellet. He understood that if one could only control all of these factors one could always ensure a perfect score; only, how could anyone control them all?—how could anyone even know them all, what with their dizzyingly innumerable interrelationships? You might be able to think of one or two or a dozen, but you just couldn't keep track of them all, and yet even the least among them had, ultimately, a decisive influence.

He was pleased at the way his older brother continued to be uncharacteristically kind to him. They watched television and played board games together. More importantly Anram began opening up about all the things he and his friends did. And what neat and sometimes deliciously illicit things these were! They smoked cigarettes and drank beer; they snuck into movie houses, or at least tried to; they climbed onto billboards with cans of spray paint and left their marks—Anram's being a big "A" with the right leg of the letter extending downward then shooting upward to the right and ending in an arrowhead. They went to the stores in Manhattan and looked at the newest computers and clothes, and "checked out the chicks—but only the hot ones." And speaking of girls, Anram, with a knowing leer, related any number of jokes and jingles of the most fantastically titillating kind—they often made Kirat laugh aloud. Once after Anram had sung quickly under his breath a rather obscene ditty about "riding down the mountain going ninety," Kirat laughed so loud that his mother, happening to pass her boys' room, knocked on the door, opened it, poked her head inside, and asked, "What's so funny in here?"—only to hear the boys say almost at the same time, "Nothing!" as they looked back at her with expressions that couldn't have been guiltier if they had just robbed a bank.

How good it had been to see him laughing like that! Orpita pulled away from the room, closed the door, and herself smiled widely with a heart full of peace and joy. Kirat was laughing!— a good, hearty, robust bout of laughter of the sort that only a healthy child, who feels good and is carefree, could produce. She thanked God for it! Her prayers had been answered. She had her son back. He had suffered enough, almost more than he or she could bear, but the pendulum of their lives was once again on the upswing.

It was a testament to how far that pendulum had swung in the dreadful direction that she, and indeed Sandesh and Kirat himself, regarded as positive their new circumstances, which by any objective standard were still so burdensome, still so often painful, and still fraught with potential disaster. Kirat had come away from the hospital with a prescription for fifteen medications, most of them to be taken daily. The dressing on his

Hickman catheter had to be changed once a day. His temperature had to be taken twice, and his blood pressure three times, a day. Twice a week he had to visit a lab to draw blood, and once a week he had to check into the outpatient clinic for an examination. The doctors told him that, in time, as he got better, as his new marrow produced better blood, the number of medications he had to take would be reduced and he would not have to be so closely monitored.

But he still continued to suffer side effects of the radiation and chemotherapy he had undergone, as well as from the drugs he was continuing to take. He grew swollen from fluid retention; his belly bulged as though he were pregnant (how odd it looked, that big bulge on a boy otherwise as thin as a scarecrow!), and his feet and ankles were puffy, the skin around them stretched taut. He was prescribed a diuretic to take each morning to help relieve this symptom.

He had been out of the hospital for three weeks. During one of his routine visits to the outpatient clinic, the doctor who examined him pressed the diaphragm against the boy's chest, first here, then there, all the while listening intently, saying, "Okay, Kirat, breathe in ... hold it ... breathe out ... breathe in again, deeply ..." This went on a little longer than usual. All the while the doctor, as he listened, looked off into space with especial concentration as though trying to understand what he was hearing. When he took the stethoscope out of his ears, he looked to Orpita and said:

"Well ... it's okay, but I do hear some crackles."

"Crackles?" she asked.

"Yes, little crackling sounds. It's from the alveoli in the lungs not opening quickly enough during respiration."

Orpita shook her head; she didn't understand. The doctor explained:

"The lining of the lungs is composed of little sacks or pockets, called alveoli. They're lined with fine blood vessels that absorb oxygen from the air. When you breathe in they open up, and when you breathe out they compress. Kirat's alveoli aren't quite opening up as easily as they should."

"How bad is that?" she asked.

Even Kirat, at the question, turned his eyes to the doctor, apprehensively.

"Well, it's not something we want to hear. From what I can tell it's pretty slight, but we certainly don't want it to get any worse. I'll let your doctor know. In the meantime, he should do some breathing exercises with a spirometer ..."—and the doctor produced the plastic mechanism with its graduated markings that measured the volume of air exhaled into it by way of a mouthpiece. He showed Kirat and his mother how to use it, what measurement he ought always to aim for, and prescribed that the boy do the exercises three times a day for at least ten minutes at a time.

In doing these breathing exercises, as in everything else that was prescribed for him, whether it was taking his medications, engaging in physical exercise, or keeping his appointments at the outpatient clinic, Kirat was meticulous as though he himself had become determined to overcome his illness, to beat the odds against him and regain his old life. Knowing that his immune system would be fragile for another year, he became intensely aware of how germs teemed in the world around him. He conscientiously washed his hands every time he touched something commonly used, such as a doorknob or a remote control or even his own computer keyboard. "I only have to be careful for a year," he told his mother, who was pleased to see that he was taking his own health so seriously and was already anticipating a return to normalcy. He forced himself to eat. He wanted to gain his weight back. As never before it struck him as desirable, even attractive, to be fat. How he wished he were fat! And so even when the sight of food repulsed him he would make a conscious effort to ignore that reaction, telling, commanding himself, "I can take one bite—one little bite—it won't hurt me"—and so bring the food to his mouth and chew it and swallow it. With all his willpower he would ignore the sudden surge of nausea that succeeded. A few minutes later, when that sickening feeling had subsided, he would again brace himself to take another tiny bite and hold it down.

—His parents, watching him, goading him on, would beam with pleasure to see how well he was doing.

One night he was watching television with his parents and brother. He was sitting on the couch with his legs folded beneath him. He had been coughing lightly all day, and now he had another bout of coughing, which was louder and sounded rougher than anything previously. His mother turned to him from across the room and said:

"Are you okay over there?"

Kirat shook his head, yes.

"You want some tea or something?"

The boy shook his head, no, and said, "I'm alright."

Orpita got up and went over to him. She put a hand against his cheek, asking, "You don't feel warm, do you?" She knew that at this point in the boy's recovery she still had to worry about infection and fever. But he didn't feel warm, and he had stopped coughing.

Still later in the evening, after Kirat and Anram had gone to their room, the parents remained in the living room to watch what was, for them, the last television program of the day: a news broadcast from India, to which they subscribed. The anchors were located in Mumbai and spoke in Hindi. They reported on politics in New Delhi, business trends in Calcutta and Bangalore, the state of the tea crops in Assam province, an exceptional cricket team from Gujarat, and farmers in Greater Noida who were protesting governmental land acquisition. Then one of the anchors announced a special report and warned his viewers that some of the scenes they were about to see were "graphic." It was about the Gadhimai festival, which happens once every five years in Bariyapur in southern Nepal and lasts for a month, and in which "upwards of 300,000 animals are brought to be sacrificed to the goddess." For as far as the eye could see a line of people were traveling down a dirt road, leading or carrying domestic animals to sacrifice. In one instance a young girl, wearing a red shawl and carrying a small white goat in her arms, proudly told the reporter how she was bringing her sacrifice for the first time. Then the scene switched to the killing fields. Hundreds, perhaps thousands of goats, cows, and other animals lay dead on the ground, the blood from their slit throats or severed heads having formed into red pools around their inert bodies. In the midst of this carnage a dark sweaty man stood looking into the camera with a proud smile. He had slaughtered many of the animals, and was about to slaughter yet another one: with one hand he was holding fast a small goat who, terrified with a sense of danger, was struggling to free itself, while with his other hand he held aloft the blood-stained machete he was about to bring down on the panic-stricken creature, and snuff out its life. But the report did not actually show the killing.

While growing up in India, Sandesh and his wife had so often heard or read of such things, of such strange regional customs, that they had never thought twice about them. But now something in the pit of their stomachs twinged. Perhaps they had been living in the United States too long;—perhaps all such "festivals" had grown uncomfortably strange to them;— whatever the reason, they shared the same immediate, repulsed reaction, summed up by Orpita who, in a low, even tone of voice, murmured:

"Horrible."

Sandesh, not looking at his wife, said only, "Stupid peasants."

That night Orpita had what started out as a good dream. It was set in the future. She was much older (though she didn't look or feel it) and Kirat was all grown up, a young man, perhaps in his late twenties or early thirties. In his handsome features she proudly saw the face of the boy she had known; and much more than pride, she felt relief. She remembered how a long time ago he had been very sick and how much she had worried about him. She told herself, "Those days were so terrible!"—and just as soon pushed the thought away, not wanting to dwell on bad memories. Kirat had brought her a present. It was in a large heavy box. She opened it and saw that it contained—water; but not just ordinary water; rather, a water so blue and clear and pure that it sparkled as though diamonds were floating on it. On the one hand she didn't understand why her son would give her a box of water but on the other she saw that it was beautiful and was grateful for its value as the finest of its kind. "It's very nice," she told him, by way of thanking him. Kirat grinned, and as he did so he began to look more boyish even as his features, which had been blooming with health, became drawn, and his eyes took on an air of distress. He began coughing. Her happiness subsided and a darker emotion filled her soul. Her heart raced with alarm as he coughed still more loudly and then, horribly, his eyes bulged out of his head and his tongue dangled obscenely from his mouth and—

she awoke with a jolt.

She sat up in bed, shaking with nervous fear, the reality of the terrible dream still upon her. Her sudden awakening roused Sandesh who had been sleeping beside her. He turned over to her, murmuring, "What?—what?" Then she heard it: coughing— actual coughing. It was Kirat. The coughing was loud, fast, and struggling.

The parents rushed to their son's room to find him standing up by his bed, coughing violently, clutching at his chest, with Anram, alarmed and sleepy-eyed, standing beside him, patting him on the back and, asking him—in a whispered, frantic voice—if he wanted water or something to drink.

It was five o'clock in the morning.

His parents rushed him to the hospital where he was given oxygen. X-rays were taken of his lungs and the resulting image—largely solidly white—showed that they were severely congested. He had to be put on a ventilator. He was sedated with Demerol and Ativan, and his hands were tied down to the bed so that he wouldn't try to pull out the respirator tube inserted down his throat.

It was a sudden and serious setback to his recuperation, but the cause of it wasn't exactly known. When infection was ruled out the doctors theorized that it was the result of his radiation treatments. In some instances the lungs received enough radiation that they were damaged and became inflamed.

"But he had a radiation shield on his chest," Orpita returned, almost defiantly, becoming a little aggressive in the face of what seemed an impossibly unfair turn of events.

"Some radiation still reaches the lungs," the doctor said.

When Kirat's sedation had worn off enough that he was conscious, his parents explained to him what had happened and told him that he must not touch or try to remove the tube that was helping him to breathe. He listened and nodded as though he understood, but this was only seeming, for the moment he came to himself a little more he began to panic at the sensation of the foreign object filling his mouth and reaching down his throat, and tried again to remove it. His arms had to be restrained and he was sedated again.

For the next two days he improved, was conscious, talking, seemed stronger; then had a relapse, at one point violently coughing up blood, choking, unable to breathe—upon which he was again heavily sedated, his lungs were suctioned, and the ventilator re-secured. Then for a whole morning he would be "stabilized"—his vital signs steady, though weak. A few hours later his vital signs would improve slightly; only for another set-back to occur....

It was always one step forward, two steps back.

By the hour or the day the parents veered between hope and despair. They were always emotionally exhausted. At ten or eleven o'clock at night they would leave the hospital. In the car on their way home they rode mostly in silence. Each of them tried to be strong and stolid for the sake of the other. Yet each of them also direly needed comfort; and though they might have given this to each other, especially at night, in bed, they could not bring themselves to do so, sensing it to be somehow inappropriate to feel any pleasure—even the vague, distant one an arm around one's shoulder as one slept—while their son was lying in a hospital room miles away and fighting for his life.

Sandesh no longer went to his job. He couldn't work any more, what with his head filled with uncertainty about his son's and therefore his own future. He knew he was "losing" a great deal of money and that sooner or later his remissness in this matter would come back to bite him; but he didn't—because he couldn't—care. At one point he told Orpita:

"I wouldn't be able to concentrate. I'd only get into an accident or something. I can't afford that."

On the morning of his fourth day back in the hospital Kirat's condition drastically worsened; again he started coughing up blood. Again his lungs were suctioned. As this procedure was carried out his distress broke through the veil of his sedation so that he gagged and coughed; his color paled, turned blue; his body squirmed and twisted and arched painfully. It took three hours to stop the bleeding, only for him to develop an equally dangerous condition caused by the blood drying in the lungs and making them stiffen. To compensate for this the volume of air from the ventilator had to be increased at the risk of collapsing his lungs altogether.

Throughout the whole course of Kirat's illness the doctors who had treated him had maintained an air of professionally quiet optimism. Even when they had been frank in conveying possible complications and inauspicious statistics regarding cure, there had been about them an air of confidence in their ability to treat his disease. Whenever Kirat had taken a turn for the worse they had met the challenge through an expert application of drugs or mechanical technology, and had managed to pull him through. But now the attending physicians were solemn with an air of defeat—the almost humiliating knowledge that every ministration their expertise could summon up was doomed to failure. They ruefully informed the parents that they didn't think their son could survive this latest setback. The lungs were compromised; the heart was weak; the kidneys had all but shut down; and his liver was enlarged. Of course they would continue to do all they could to treat him, but there was only so much that could be done.

On hearing this dismal prognosis Sandesh lowered his head and somehow he knew that he had lost his son.

One of the doctors added, "We'll keep him sedated and he won't feel any distress. He won't be in any pain."

Not much later, when Kirat's primary oncologist, Dr. Faber, examined him, he came to the same conclusion. His voice was calm and, despite its message of gloom, strangely comforting in its imperturbable objectivity. He said, "in all honesty," that he didn't think Kirat could pull through this time. After he had delivered this information he apologized for it, waited a few moments, then continued:

"His heart is very weak. There's a possibility that it might stop ... if so, I need to ask you if you want us to make the effort to revive him."

"Of course we do!" Sandesh said.

But Orpita put her hand on her husband's arm as though to quiet him and said, "No."

"What?" Sandesh asked, turning to her; and yet even in the next second he realized that his initial impulse was wrong. He looked away from his wife, to the doctor, then down. His expression, which had been one of anger, changed to one of quiet pain.

"I also need to ask you something else," the doctor continued. "I'm sorry if it seems inappropriate, but there's never really a good time to ask it. In the event Kirat doesn't make it ... we'd like your permission to do an autopsy. It can be valuable in research and might help other children in the future."

"Absolutely not," Sandesh said, decisively. He looked at the doctor as though he were out of his mind—as though he had said something preposterous. He turned to his wife with an air and expression that anticipated her equally offended reaction to the suggestion. But instead he saw that she was passive and silent, and when she turned her eyes to her husband they had about them a sad, leaden sureness. She turned back to the doctor and said only:

"We would have to talk about it."

"There's nothing to talk about, that's ridiculous," Sandesh said. "Kirat's going to be alright."

"Of course we all want that, sir," the doctor said.

"That's right. And he *will* be!"

—But Sandesh understood that he had spoken reflexively rather than reflectively, and he held his peace. But even after he and Orpita were by themselves, he spoke to her in the astonished, whispering tones of someone who cannot believe what he has just heard, because what he had just heard was his own wife saying, in effect, that if Kirat died his body ought to be hacked apart—dissected, desecrated.

"Are you crazy?" Sandesh asked.

"No, I'm not crazy," she said, quietly. "If he dies, this might help others."

"It's not right!"

"Don't tell me what's not right," she said. "This whole thing isn't right. Everything that's happened to him isn't right. But I know what he's gone through with all this, and what I've gone through, and what you've gone through: so don't tell me I don't know what I'm talking about. I know."

"And you want them to do that to him? To open him up like that, like he's a ... a nothing!—a piece of meat!"

"No that's not what I want. I want him to get better. I want my son back. But if he's going to die, I want to make sure it's not for nothing. I want some good to come out of it. I want to be able to help another child who's sick. Maybe *we're* in this position because too many people were like you and said 'no.' Think about it!"

Despite his air of continued anger, of repressed agitation and a retort that seemed to be on the tip of his tongue, Sandesh held his peace, for Orpita's last words had struck him with all the muting impact of incontrovertible logic: if everyone, always, said no, how could things get better for others? He continued to look at her with hard, reproving eyes, but his silence proclaimed his defeat and concession; and in the end he merely spluttered out, "It doesn't matter ... he'll be alright!"

But Kirat got worse with each hour as one organ after another failed. The left lung collapsed; his liver subsided to a fraction of its normal capacity; his kidneys shut down; his heart, which had been struggling to pump life through a failing body, began to beat irregularly, its rhythm unsteady, threatening to stop—bound sooner or later to stop, said the doctors and thought the nurses, who had seen the end of a life played out like this many times. Kirat knew nothing of it. He was heavily sedated, unconscious, a small, frail body with a ventilator tube still reaching into his throat and an IV line still dripping a cocktail of drugs into his now sluggish bloodstream. Orpita and Sandesh stood over him silently. Their faces were pale, their expressions somber, their sorrow ineffable. At one point they both thought the same thing, and not without gratitude: "At least he's not in pain." For it comforted their hearts to see their child lying still and no longer in distress. If he couldn't be saved, if he had to die, at least let him die peacefully, unconscious of when the end had come.

The heart monitor whose illuminated green line had shown a steady, if faint, spike per beat now showed two close together, followed by an unwonted long pause, followed by a slight peak, then another long pause.

A nurse came in to check on Kirat's vital signs. She did not look at the parents who were standing over their son's bed. Her movements were swift and silent and minimal as though she were embarrassed to be here at such a time.

Orpita leaned in to Sandesh and whispered something in his ear. He pulled away from her a little, looking at her with an expression in which surprise and then objection was held in check only by a stronger force of sympathy. He watched her as she turned away from him and walked out of the room. Then he turned back to the figure of his son and amid his dull grief arose the wondering sense that even after all these years he didn't know his wife.

Fifteen minutes later Kirat's heart stopped.

Standing beside his son's bed, Sandesh took big gulps of air, wrestling with the throbbing ache in his soul.

Several minutes later, after many clearings of his throat, gulpings for breath, and determined buckings up of his strength and spirit, he had composed himself enough to leave the room and seek out his wife. His legs felt so weak that he thought he might stumble as he walked; he had to make a conscious effort to put one foot before the other. In his chest, deep in the center of it, something hard and leaden had formed, and it at once weighed him down and depleted his vitality.

Orpita was standing at the end of the hallway, a few feet away from the nurse's station, leaning against the wall, looking down at the floor. She had come out into the hallway because, as she had whispered to her husband, she had not been about to stand at her son's bed and watch him die. At the sight of her something in Sandesh steeled his own determination to tamp down his emotions, to be steady and strong.

She raised her eyes to him as he approached and, when he stopped before her, scanned his face and read there what she knew she must discover. Her expression was pale and blank as she continued to watch him. For a few seconds it seemed that he would reach out to her, hold her and comfort her. Instead he continued to look into her face with all the sorrow and pity and understanding one distraught human creature can convey to another without words. Orpita's eyes began to tear over. Sandesh gave the faintest of nods and looked away as though in unbearable embarrassment; then—again consciously bucking up his fortitude—walked over to the nurses at their station to let them know it was over.

Several days later the funeral took place. The funeral parlor was not far from where Sandesh and Orpita lived. It was an unassuming, low, red-brick building with a U-shaped, paved driveway leading up to its front door. Over the years, when walking or driving by it, Sandesh and Orpita had seen any number of automobile queues lined up to its front door, dropping off darkly-dressed mourners. Now it was they who were the mourners.

In stepping into the building one entered a large foyer that reminded one of some sedate professional office, perhaps that of

an expensive law firm.   There were large, comfortable armchairs, thick-framed paintings, and papered walls against which
stood tables of dark wood upholding shaded lamps. To the left,
the right, and straight ahead were the entrances to the actual
funeral parlors. The one in which Kirat's service was held was
similarly muted in its color, decoration, and ambience, having
maroon carpeting, dark green drapes over the windows, and
walnut tables against the walls. Four rows of cushioned chairs
had been set up for relatives and guests, and faced the front of
the room where Kirat's closed coffin rested on a bier. A spray of
white flowers spread over the top of the coffin. To either side of
it easel-like stands supported flowered wreaths. Beside the one
on the right another stand upheld an enlarged, flower-garlanded
photograph of Kirat. There he was, looking out on the world
with his happy, impish grin, just as he had been in the healthy,
happy time of his life. His larger-than-life-sized face projected
his presence into the room so strongly that at times he seemed
to be there in the flesh.

Sandesh sat beside Orpita and Anram in the front row
along with their relatives who had flown in from India: her parents and two sisters, and his mother and brother. (His father
had not been feeling well and could not come.) They were
dressed in traditionally white or light-colored clothing, as were
friends and acquaintances who had inquired about the Hindu
custom and respectfully followed it. But two attendees, ignorant
of this, had showed up in dark suits. Their faux pas was noted
by the other mourners, who, however, excused it—after all, people in America couldn't be expected to know what was appropriate. One of these men was Alejandro, the driver who had once
complained to Sandesh about a reduction in the pay for drivers
of the company that employed them both. The other was Mr.
Jeffries. Both these men had entered the funeral parlor a little
nervously, not quite sure what to expect; then, seeing Sandesh
and his wife, had walked over to them, shaken their hands, and
offered low-toned condolences so deeply felt that their own eyes
welled up a little. The bereaved parents accepted their condolences with whispered gratitude and bade them have a seat if
they wished. They both wound up sitting in the back row only a
few chairs apart from each other. After having quietly introduced themselves to each other, they watched what transpired

before them from their room-encompassing vantage point.

Sandesh stared at his son's coffin for minutes at a time. The last couple of days had been harder on him than even the moment of his son's death, as though it had taken that long for him to become fully conscious of his loss. His eyes never got more than moist, for he had already shed many tears in private, in the solitude in which alone he felt comfortable to give way entirely to his grief, but he heaved great silent sighs, and sometimes his pursed lips trembled when he let out his breath. His wife and other relatives cried freely, or sniffled when they weren't crying, or sat swollen-eyed and pale when they weren't sniffling.

A Hindu priest had come to speak at the service. He was a middle-aged man dressed in a traditional robe. He stepped to the front of the room and, folding his hands before him, began offering what comforts he could to the bereaved. He quoted verses from scripture, the import of which was that all that is living is born to die and that grief for the dead, though natural and in some ways necessary, was owing to our not seeing far enough into the nature of the world. For death, he said, was not the end of existence but rather another phase of it. We should not be overly frightened or saddened by it, for it was but the return to the state in which we existed before our birth— that state out of which we and all living things came forth, and would come forth again, eternally. And did we ever, while alive, worry ourselves about where or what we were before our births? Of course not. So then why should we grieve so much about a return to that same state after our lives were over? Our individuality is necessarily short-lived, he said; the older we get, the more we understand how our longest life is but a blip of consciousness flashing across the unimaginable expanse of Eternity. Yes: Death hurts us by taking from us those we love; but if we will only see death in its truer perspective our grief cannot be long. "In the Bhagavad Gita," he said, "Lord Krishna tells us that the body, like a garment, is worn by the soul until it wears out, and then it assumes a new garment, a new body, to invest: and so what was old becomes young—what was sick becomes healthy—what was dying becomes newborn. Let us understand that we never really die. We only change. We are eternal. When our present existence is over we will come back yet again, in some place or in some way, until wisdom enables us to become one with God and we are no longer susceptible to the cycle of birth and death. But even in an everyday, mundane sense our individual existence continues. Kirat's greatest gift to us was the joy and promise he brought into the world. That joy and promise is not lost. We will carry it in our hearts and minds all the days of our lives, and it will influence our own actions for the good, which in turn will have their own good consequences throughout all time. For everything we do and think in some way influences the world around us. Our actions are never only of the moment: they have consequences through all time. The good things that Kirat brought into the world will live after him, influencing the world for the better. In our grief let us try to remember that. We will always be grateful that he was with us for as long as he was."

Beautiful words; beautiful sentiments; spoken earnestly; meant to comfort and inspire. Orpita listened deferentially, yet her heart was left hollow and aching. Despite her temperamental disposition to religiosity, she was too much a product of her ruthlessly scientific age to believe genuinely in the hocus-pocus of traditional faith; or perhaps, just now, she was too human. For even if it were true that her son continued to exist somewhere, a disembodied spirit or soul on some rarefied plane, imperishable, immortal, sure to return in some way, at some time, in either this world or some other—what was all that to her, or indeed to him? She would never again hear his voice and see his face; never again take joy in his presence; and he—could he, as he had been, speak or laugh or feel the sun? The swords of grief that pierced her heart beyond comforting had also shorn away the naiveté on which the comforts of faith rely. No religion or priest could have explained to her why someone so young and good and innocent as Kirat had had to die so terribly. There was no justice in the world if things like that could happen. No justice at all.

The priest turned to the spray-decorated casket and intoned prayers. His voice droned on for fifteen minutes. Sometimes he stopped and stood there silently for some minutes with a bowed head before continuing. When he finally finished he turned back to the mourners and glanced at them with a sober expression that conveyed a sense of completion, of the thing done that he had been summoned to do.

There was yet one more stage to the funeral to be completed: the cremation of the body. The funeral parlor did not have its own cremation facilities and the mourners had to follow a hearse to a crematorium. They did not see the casket again. It was taken into a different entrance to the facility and loaded into a cremation retort, a large, boxy, industrial-looking unit of gleaming stainless steel. When in operation it emitted a low whooshing sound as flames furiously filled its firebrick-lined interior. But from where the mourners sat on the other side of a concrete wall there was nothing to be heard except the occasional weeping of the mother, of one of the grandmothers, or of a guest.

The day had started gloomy and overcast, but throughout the morning the skies had cleared so that by the time Orpita and Sandesh left the crematorium in the early afternoon every trace of the day's initial inclemency had passed, giving way to a sky of amazing brilliance and clarity and calm. The mourners could not but remark to themselves on the irony of such a lovely day as this forming the backdrop to an event so lugubrious. It made some of them shake their heads to reflect on the cruel injustice of the universe—on how it could look down on so much suffering, and be so indifferent to it all.

CORRESPONDENCE

I can't believe that you haven't gotten a computer yet so that you can send email, and are still writing by hand! It must be on purpose. That's what it is—right? You are purposefully torturing me by making me write back in kind. But really, don't you get it? No one writes letters any more. I don't. You're forcing me into this one. Don't you think I have other things to do? I tried calling you last week to talk, to tell you that if you want to come visit me you're welcome to do so; but no one picked up. You don't even have an answering machine! And you said in your letter that you never pick up the phone because you "don't know who's calling"! Great reasoning! What is wrong with you? Are you turning into a hermit or something?

Anyway, your letter was dated July 3, postmarked July 20, and received by me on August 18;—which tells me two things for sure: you are a terrible procrastinator, and the post office in our country is as slow as ever. So, it took you nearly a month to write two pages! That's rather amusing. I can just see you sitting at home of an evening with a notepad on your lap and scratching out a sentence—then resting, thinking—then scratching out another sentence—then resting, thinking some more— then putting down a few more words—then sighing as though with exhaustion—then putting the pad aside and telling yourself you'll write a little more "later," which translates into the next day or the next week. My friend, let's face it: you are lazy. You always were. It's in your genes. I will never forget how, when you were a kid, you once told me that you would "always rather do nothing than something"—surely the quintessential credo of laziness. And you're also stubborn and you hate being told what to do. Which no doubt is why they threw you off the staff of that newspaper that you had finally, after years of trying, been hired by. As I recall you couldn't tolerate your editors giving you assignments to write about and then editing your work so that it fit in with the needs of their publication. Apparently it never occurred to you that that's what editors did. It also apparently did not occur to you that if you refused to write on your assigned subjects or to have your work changed you were going to get fired. But then, what did you expect them to do?— pay you to sit in an office and dream up pieces that they couldn't use? You told me that you were giving them "better stuff than they ever had in their lives." Maybe. But it wasn't for you to make that decision. I admit to admiring you a little for that unyielding element in your character that would rather risk a job than (as you undoubtedly take it to be) compromise your talent. There's a certain nobility in being able to say to the world: "This is the way I am so take it or leave it!" Unfortunately, as you now know, the world usually replies: "I'll leave it." And then where are you? No, you must learn to be flexible. You must learn to give way a little, and sometimes a lot. You were not born into wealth and you will have to make your living, and this will entail doing many things you don't want to do. Make peace with it; resign yourself to it; accept it as a necessary evil. The best way to do this is to resist the inclination to think the moment is everything—that what you are doing at this minute or during this hour or day undermines the rest of your life, when in fact it is just another span of time as ultimately unimportant as the majority of those that went before it. In short, don't make the mistake of missing the forest for the trees. Remember that even if you must give many hours over to working for your living there is *still* time to do any good work that is in you. It will be more difficult, but it will still be possible. Also remember that talent can only thrive when the necessities of life are met, and does still better with a few luxuries thrown in along the way. If you must work for those luxuries, work for them—the time is not ill spent. —And so enough of this.

You began your letter by reminding me that I had been gone for ten years and wondered when I was going to come back "home," as though it were a foregone conclusion that I would. Well, guess what? I am not you. I don't have any especial nostalgia for our homeland. I may now and then look back a little wistfully at the rural, slow-paced charm of our little town, but for all that I know very well that I wouldn't last there more

than a week before I'd start pulling out my hair. Maybe I
would go back for a visit, but not to live; at least, not for a long
time. And then you asked me how I liked it here. Well, like every other place, there is good and bad about it. Then again, it's
not as though I've seen a lot of this country. Since I've been in
America I've only made excursions to three other states—Vermont, Pennsylvania, and Florida; otherwise, I've lived exclusively here in New York City. You said in your letter that you
wanted to come to visit me here because you wanted to see what
America was about. Well, if you come here you will only see
what a certain few hundred square miles of this country is
about, for while this city is many things it is decidedly *not*
America. However, it is a window into the future of the country. What happens here creeps out, tentacle-like, to the other
cities and states by slow or fast degrees, for this is the media
center of the country and consequently sets a certain tone and
viewpoint unconsciously imbibed by a hundred million others via
the opinion-forming vehicles of radio and television. So come
here and see it and you will see what the country will be in fifty
or a hundred years. At first you'll undoubtedly be pleasantly astonished at the energy, changefulness, and endless variety of the
place—the "excitement" of it all. Of course that is the lure for
tourists, and that is their first impression. And like those
tourists you will think during your first or second day, "How
wonderful! I wish I could live here!" But by the end of the first
week your excitement will begin to flag; by the end of the second
week, you will begin to think you've had "enough for a while";
and if you should stay here a month, do you know what will
have replaced your first enthusiasm?—one great itch to run
away. And lucky you!—you will have that option.

Nearly everyone who lives here has that itch to get away.
There is nothing more common among New Yorkers than the
dream of leaving the city. Even when they say they love living
here, should they come into money—real money, the kind that
gives you independence from having to work for a living—the
first thing they are likely to do is buy a home in the country,
where the fields are green, the air pure, and people few; and
which only goes to show how their once vaunted pride in the
place was merely the sacrifice pride made to poverty. That also
goes to show you how often an easy hypocrisy runs rampant

among these people. How refreshing it is when I come across
someone who is honest and frankly confesses, "I can't stand the
place—but my job is here."

Still, come and see for yourself. In the meantime, perhaps
you'll allow me to offer you my own observations and opinions
about this city and country and people. After all despite our
differences in age and temperament we come from the same
place—were brought up in the same way—have certain, fundamental similarities of outlook; and as I see things now you probably would too, in time.

The first thing you should know about Americans is that
they are essentially kind; and depending on where they live this
is more or less the case. In the cities generally they are less so
because life there is harried by a hundred petty annoyances and
inconveniences which have a way of shortening one's temper.
Nevertheless even there they are generally true to type, and
kind, if at first more or less suspicious. But you must always
keep in mind that their brand of kindness is unlike our own.
With us, our likes and dislikes are transparent and aboveboard:
those whom we like we genuinely befriend, and those whom we
dislike we simply don't bother with. Americans on the other
hand will often deal with people they don't like because they
consider this to be "polite." Now I can't express to you enough
how important this notion of "politeness" is to Americans. Ultimately it is the reason why you really can't trust them, for in
their case it is less a matter of refinement than of camouflage, a
pleasant veneer for less generous sentiments. Americans *say*
they value honesty and goodness, but they value far more the
appearance of them. This makes them inclined to deception and
therefore difficult to befriend: you never really know what
they're thinking of you. Their warmest smiles may hide a cold
indifference. Thus they may ask you over for dinner, or volun-
teer to show you around town, while in their heart of hearts
they would prefer to be let alone. Perhaps they will even invite
you to spend a few days at their home, but before those few
days are over they will be impatient to be rid of you because
you will have interrupted the routine in which they derive a
sense of security; and when they bid you farewell with expressions of regret at your departure, and close the door behind you,
their first thought will be, "Thank God that's over!" In short, in

most cases, don't trust them. Unless you know him for many years and there is a history of proven affection and trust, regard any American you meet, even the most congenial of them, merely as an acquaintance. Given this national characteristic you may be sure that what is true the world over is especially true here, namely, that those with the most virtue in their mouths have the least in their bosoms.

I would bet that at least a part of your interest in coming here has been stoked by a lifetime of watching American movies and television shows, which have led you to think of the American as the noble maverick—the heroic champion in the fight for truth and justice against overwhelming odds. Do yourself a favor and put all that nonsense out of your head forever because it is not true. It is all a kind of propaganda, or rather and more accurately an American self-delusion. Oh, how these people romanticize themselves! What lovely, inspiring, soaring images of themselves they create and broadcast to the world! But live here a while and you will see the squalid reality of their actual, daily lives. Americans might have started out as high-minded, fire-breathing revolutionaries but let me assure you that they have become, especially over the last sixty years, the most low-minded of shopkeepers. Their heroes on television or in the movies are always tough, visionary men willing to put themselves in harm's way for the sake of forwarding some noble ideal or championing the just cause; but in the real world their admiration is reserved for fat-bottomed bankers, flabby entrepreneurs, and flashy politicians. Their current ideal always has a commercial taint to it. It is not freedom or liberty or justice they are concerned about so much as it is wealth, or—as they call it here—"success."

Now whatever decline this country has undergone or will undergo is owing to a combination of factors epitomized in that one word, "success." The transformation that the meaning of this word has undergone here is no less remarkable than if the word "black" had come to mean "white," or "down" "up," or "left" "right." Its real meaning of course is accomplishment, achievement, the satisfactory completion of some usually noble endeavor. But in the American language of today it means only—wealth. Is a man "successful"? Then he must have a lot of money. Is he not successful? Then he must be poor, or even middle-class. It was not always so. There was a time when an American might be a baker, a grade school teacher, a post office clerk, a fireman, or a house painter, and still have been regarded as successful, for he made his living, was independent, raised his family (with whatever close economy necessary), and was another cog, small perhaps but necessary and therefore valuable, by which the great machinery of society continued to run. His fellow citizens held him in esteem and respect. Certainly he was not made to feel as though he had failed in life because he had not become rich. But all that is changed. All this would be merely laughable if its consequences to the country weren't so destructive. But to gauge the value of a man on the expensiveness of his car rather than on the quality of his mind, on the sumptuousness of his house rather than on his contribution to the culture of his nation or the world, is the very sign and signal of social degradation. It bespeaks a people who have lost all bearing on what is and is not important. According to this miserable standard some of the greatest artists, scientists, and philosophers in history have been failures, whereas of course even the least of their works often outshines what Americans laud as the "successes" of so many of their current well-heeled heroes. But even on a less obvious level, the danger of this degraded ethos should be apparent to you: for at a stroke it devalues the majority of the population for whom "success" of the financial kind must necessarily be elusive, wealth being remarkable precisely on account of its uncommonness. Thus a majority are burdened with a sense of inadequacy, and there circulates through the body politic the poison of general discontent.

You will probably ask how it is possible that Americans have come to believe in, and to go after so completely and passionately, this shadow of a substance, this reflection of a falseness. The answer is the most obvious one: they are stupid. Such a backward notion could not have been so entirely accepted by them otherwise. Really, when one ranks the intelligence of different peoples one finds the Americans very near the bottom. They buy into the propaganda they're fed every day, and, what's worse, they pass it on to their children, especially in this matter of what it means to be a success. For there isn't a parent here who doesn't, either by outright pronouncements or a

hundred intimations, nurture her child into believing that the
end and aim of life is to become as wealthy as possible. Without
a blush of shame Americans will admit they send their children
to school not to enrich their lives with the adornments of learning but rather to "get a good job." The consequence is that each
year American high schools and universities churn out morons
by the millions—with just enough education to be taught some
specialized robotic skill in a mule-headed workplace. Perhaps
you will tell me that now I am changing my story; that just a
minute ago I was telling you how important it was to concede to
the workaday world and make your living, and now I am saying
that you ought to be above such concessions; but that is not
what I am saying. First and foremost you must always make a
living. But having done that, you must never lose sight of the
fact that what is commonly regarded as doing "enough," or even
doing "well," is, in fact, doing nothing at all, and that your real
potential (if you have any) lies in another, very different direction. For the great majority of conventional jobs require no more
intelligence than that possessed by an orangutan;—and surely
we were meant to do more than what an orangutan could do?
More to the point, human existence is so uncertain and changeable, so liable to dips and shocks, that unless one has developed
some internal resource with which to meet and resist them life
is bound to become an accumulation of embittering dissatisfac-
tions, a burden of resentment and sadness. Against that the
only real indemnification is education: the excitement of acquir-
ing knowledge, the joy in the ability to experience Art. To some
degree these things even offer some protection against the worst
of all evils, ill-health. But that is precisely the kind of education
that is withheld from Americans.

Yes, I say "withheld" from them—purposefully. It is no coin-
cidence that the American notion of success has arisen in proportion to the takeover of its government and institutions by
hugely moneyed and therefore powerful corporate interests. Consequently the educational system here has been refashioned to
ensure it produces mentalities which as much as possible shall
find all their contentment and expression in the world offered by
corporate culture;—that is to say, no culture at all;—which is
further to say that young men and women shall believe that
they have fulfilled their potential as human beings by one day

becoming glorified *shopkeepers.* For it would hardly be in the interest of the corporate powers that are really running this country to have it populated with genuinely intelligent people. The first thing an intelligent population understands is the brevity of life, of the short time given to men to enjoy life or produce something meaningful, and people who have that understanding and ethos would work to live but never—as the American construct now has it—live to work, especially at the kinds of jobs they are given to work at. They certainly would not believe that the "success" of their lives depended on the amount of money they made; on the contrary, they might think it depended on something very different from that! They would reject the notion that they ought to be grateful to spend the rest of their lives in alienating labor—to be one of the hive, one of the nest, trudging away day after day for years on end, for decade after decade, till they grow old and are too infirm to go on, or drop dead. They might begin to perceive that where that has become the definition of a normal life then nothing more is expected of them than a pismire existence the end and aim of which is the raising up of the next generation of insect laborers. Yet how much the norm has this appalling situation become! I have come across any number of people who tell me that they have not one but two or even three jobs and "only sleep four hours a night"—and then look at me with wide-eyed expectation, as though I ought to compliment them or they deserved some kind award. I always answer these fools in the same way: "And what books have you read lately? —At which their smiles fade and they aren't so friendly toward me! They know what I mean by that, and in their innermost hearts they know I'm right, and that's why, though they may smile back at me, the twinkle in their eye is the glance of a dagger.

Just how saturated these people are with the shopkeeper mentality is further seen in how they identify you by your job. They do this as surely as a rancher might identify a steer by a tag stapled into its ear or a brand burned into its rump. It's as though they can't figure out who or what a person is outside the status of an employee. In our country no one would ever ask a stranger on first meeting him what he did for a living—how he made his money. We would naturally consider such a question out of bounds—rudely personal, or rather rudely *im*personal.

But Americans ask this as a matter of course. After only a few minutes' conversation they will have no qualm even about asking you how the rest of your family make *their* living! If you come here you would do well to think about what you will say when they ask about your job. If you want to be well thought of, don't tell them that you're unemployed (as you now are). Instead mention some lucrative career. Tell them you're a lawyer (Americans dislike lawyers as a class, but they respect them individually and face-to-face as people who must be making a lot of money), or you could tell them you're a doctor (another profession that makes a lot of money). Or you could tell them you're the owner, the "President" or "Chief Executive Officer," of a business—any business, as long as you make out that it's large and profitable. Also, if you can, bring good clothes. Americans are suckers for anyone who dresses well. The sight of a snappily-tailored suit makes them drunk with respect. Remember, these are a stupid people, easily impressed with tinsel and show.

Whatever you do, do not tell them that you are an artist or have any ambition in that way. I know you consider yourself one, and are proud of it, just as I know your family and friends hope you really have found your calling and will excel in it. But you must understand that while in our country a dedication to the arts is seen as high-minded, here, in this country of shopkeepers, it is very different. Unless you have become "successful" at your art—unless you have made a lot of money at it, or at any rate a fair living—you will not be taken seriously and usually you will be despised. Americans say they are fond of art but in fact they are only fond of it when it has gained the imprimatur of widespread recognition and profit; otherwise they ignore it and sneer at anyone who pursues it as an eccentric, a perverse underminer of the normal order, at the very least as a slacker who would do better exerting himself in a more profitable goal—say, selling shoes. No matter that they stagger home at the end of each demoralizing workday and wearily plop themselves down onto a couch to watch movies or listen to music, and so consume the art without which their lives would be drab indeed; still, so far as they are concerned, art is not something that the mature, commonsensical, self-respecting man spends any significant time pursuing.

This city, New York, is supposed to be the capital of the

arts in America, and I suppose it is, but that doesn't mean you'll meet many artists here. What you *will* find here, in swarming, choking profusion, are a great many *frauds*. It is safe to say that artistic frauds are to this city what farmers are to the rural countryside. Let me give you an example. In my apartment building here in Brooklyn there are a hundred apartments; out of these, twenty are occupied by people who have introduced themselves to me as artists. In every instance in which these people allowed me to see or hear their "art," as they called it, I wanted either to laugh or to throw up. They had about as much talent as the dead and decaying pigeon I came upon on my way to the subway this morning. The question is, why are there so many of these frauds? Think about the American character as I have already described it to you and it won't be so hard to understand. A people so obsessed with appearances are frantic for cachet and need to believe, and more importantly need *you* to believe, that they are more than just accountants, waiters, bankers, cab drivers, receptionists, computer programmers, dental assistants, pizza makers, trash collectors or lawyers. Thus they arrogate unto themselves the title of artist and start painting, singing, writing, or acting; and if they find that they are no good at any of these things, why, rather than concede there is nothing extraordinary about themselves, they buy cameras, start taking pictures of trees or buildings, and call themselves "potographers"—and so in one smug, arrogant stroke again assume the ennobling mantle of Art. Quite apart from the fact that photography is less art than artifice, even here, in this bathetic-pathetic sphere, their true, inartistic nature shows through: their photographs are low, vulgar, inane, or simply indifferent. I don't pretend to be a photographer, or know a thing about cameras or exposure settings, but let me tell you something: compared to some of the "professional" photographs I've seen, mine are better even when my camera has gone off by accident.

They have also, these frauds, been motivated by America's glamorized, false representation of the artist. For the only artists they ever see, the only ones who have ever made an impression on their thick skulls, are those popular ones who have risen to prominence in a glitter of wealthy celebrity: of the obscure and in many instances better sort they know nothing, nor wish to know. It is really this dream of wealth that they hope to emulate. Note that even fame does not motivate them; at least, not in itself. Reputation means nothing to them except insofar as it coincides with the "success" (that word again!) that they have been taught is the goal of life. In short they regard art as just another potentially lucrative profession, but one which, they are sure, will not take nearly so much hard work to excel in—a notion that again shows their complete misunderstanding of the matter. If they knew from the first that as artists they would spend every waking hour either doing or thinking about their art, and that despite this enormous, all-consuming, superhuman dedication they still would gain neither recognition nor remuneration enough to make a bare living;—that all their lives they would work and struggle, and struggle and work, and then work and struggle some more in exhausting, frustratingly self-critical labor whose only result would be anonymous poverty;—that they would not even have the comfort of friendship because people would perceive their dedication as odd, as strange, as indicating some kind of "problem," and thus be toward them politely sociable, perhaps, but never intimate, so that in addition to all their other difficulties they had to bear an onerous and sometimes crushing lonesomeness;—if they knew that all *this* was really the artist's lot, why, the great majority of them would at once drop their pretensions as easily as they had assumed them, and with cockroach swiftness run for the cover of the most-respectable, best-paying job they could find. But compare that with the attitude and reaction of the real artist. Through every apparent failure, through all the years of continued poverty, indeed even after conceding to himself that he will win neither wealth nor fame from his work—he continues in it. He could not give it up even he wanted to. He will continue in it to the bitter, disastrous end. And he will do this not because he loves money less than anyone else (he probably loves it more, recognizing, as he does, its ability to provide him with the leisure and comfort in which to do his work), and not because he is stubborn (though in the end an artist must be), but because he cannot help being what he is: because, *despite* himself, he *must* fulfill his nature. The moment he goes against that the world is wrong with him; everything is wrong, intolerable; he simply cannot endure it. He finds that he cannot live in any other way but *his*. And that is why he is the real thing and others are not. This is also why, even though artistic skills can in some degree be taught, those so schooled never produce works as vigorous or powerful as those which arise from a genuine artistic temperament or character, which is inborn and beyond all teaching.

Nevertheless the frauds and poseurs in this city, as in the world generally, sometimes achieve notoriety even as the real artist wallows in anonymity. This is bound to make him hopeless, especially in his youth when his understanding of the world is limited. But in getting older and wiser he will take heart. He will then see that the success of undeserving contemporaries is only seeming: a freak of luck or of fashion, as changeful as the wind and no more substantial than it. The lionized artists of the day are often ignored a decade later; and in forty or fifty years might just as well have never existed. For each generation produces its own enlightened minority who review what has been done, and separate the wheat from the chaff. It is they who discover or revive what was really good, and sing the first praises of what becomes the general, long-standing chorus of recognition. As for the endless procession of artistic frauds I continue to meet? When they ask me if I would like to see their work, I nod in acquiescence and politely smile at their ghastly abortions—and hurry away as fast as possible.

If you think about the matter still more you will come to see why New York couldn't possibly have as many artists as you might have been led to believe. Its very atmosphere is antagonistic to such temperaments. At first there may occur to you the names of a dozen famous American artists who lived here; but so what? A swallow does not a summer make; nor do several dozen; nor do even a hundred; and the fact is that for every dozen artists who managed to do good work here there were a thousand whose talents were slain by this city. The point is that if some artists did good work here they did it *despite* the indecencies of the place. They forged ahead through all the degrading filth, noise, and congestion surrounding them. They kicked and clawed their way to their goal through all the defiling muck of this city's brainless bustle. They worked well, too, and most importantly, because even while they lived in the midst of this maelstrom of vulgarity they managed to isolate themselves from it, either physically or emotionally. They were New Yorkers in name only: *among* the masses, but never *of* them. And why should any of this surprise you? What is an artist after all but a *refined* soul—whether or not he creates? But a refined soul craves beautiful things, he flourishes on them, and he is pained by and declines in their absence; and by any objective standard New York City is ugly. It is all lifeless glass and steel and asphalt and cement—with a plant or a tree or a verge of grass thrown in along the way so as just to relieve it from being an unendurable nightmare. (There is Central Park, of course, and it is very pleasant, but it is not a part of New Yorkers' everyday lives.) Moreover this city is very expensive, and as artists are generally poor they would here only be poorer than they need be—they who, of all people, need comfort and security to do their best work. No, let me assure you that the "arts" in New York are, like so many things about it, more a matter of myth than of reality. If you want to find real artists in this country you must go into the distant, isolated parts of it where they have betaken themselves to work and live in healing silence and with some modicum of physical comfort; where they at least have greenth around them, a blue sky above them, and can take a breath of clean air into their lungs. I gather from knowing you over the years that you're averse from crowds, cringe at loud noises, and cannot stand clutter: all good indications that your talent is genuine. You can always tell a dolt by his need for company and his ability to tolerate noise.

In your letter you said how there is always some mention of America in our country, especially now that the presidential elections are soon to take place here. You asked me which of the two candidates I like. What if I were to tell you that I despise both of them?—and that not only I despise them but a great many Americans also do? What if I were to tell you that this government is as corrupt, and is as far from working in the people's interest, as ours was before our revolution? As used to happen in our country, so here, it hardly matters which of the two major parties assumes power: their competition is only seeming: both ultimately are controlled by the moneyed interests that have insinuated themselves into power and whose real allegiance is not to this country—nor to any country—but only to the "bottom line," only to profit, only to cash. They are the puppet-masters that pull the strings of the present and would-be President. This should surprise you the less when you understand that running for the office costs an enormous amount of money, which only the largest companies, or people associated with the largest companies, are likely to have; and businessmen do not reach so deeply into their pockets out of the goodness of their hearts. They expect their interests to be promoted, or at least guarded. They also hedge their bets by funding both of the two main political parties, so that no matter who loses, *they* always win. An average fellow seeking to buck this pernicious state of affairs by running for the Presidency outside of the major parties? He would have better luck jumping to the moon. For owing to lack of means he could not get his name or platform known about any further than he could shout them out. Even if he managed to gain some small exposure, or if somehow his campaign began to catch fire and aroused a general interest, the major media, owned and guided as they are by large corporations, would lose no time in paring him down to size; in discrediting, belittling, perhaps vilifying him; perhaps yanking some very blanched skeletons out of his closet, and so ensuring that the momentum of his campaign came to a grinding halt. Would Americans see through the conspiracy? No. At least, they never have. They always complain that their leaders are not like them and so cannot really represent them, yet the moment someone like themselves arises as a potential leader they are easily enough convinced that he is not a "viable candidate"—and so prove once again how little they *deserve* real democracy.

Perhaps you are wondering how the corporate powers controlling this country are able to use to their ends political entities so apparently divergent as the right and the left, or what are known here as the "Republican" and "Democratic" parties. How could political points of view apparently so different, at times antagonistic, possibly do the bidding of the same masters? It is easy: through the cyclic nature of politics in this country. Sooner or later the people grow tired or disgusted with the nonfeasance or corruption of the party in office and, clamoring for "change," vote the other party into power. Thus it goes, back and forth, back and forth, as predictable as the sunrise and sunset: and so one party carries out one half of the corporate agenda, and the other party, when it's in power, carries out the other half; and in time the *whole* agenda gets implemented. Let me give you a few examples of how each party has worked for purely moneyed interests and to the detriment of the American people.

Recently there was a big debate here about health care. You may know that America has never had a national health care system. That has always been one of the miserable failings of this society. Most civilized peoples understand that health care ought to be a shared responsibility, first because it is so expensive that it would otherwise be out of the reach of the poor and many in the middle class, and second and more importantly because a nation's true wealth is not in its stocks of gold or production of goods but in its people, in their intellect, creativity, industry, and contentment;—the prerequisite for all of which is physical health. Certainly Americans are taxed at a high enough rate to expect at least so much. Instead if they cannot afford expensive private insurance and are stricken with severe illness they can expect to lose their savings, their homes, all they have worked a lifetime for in an effort to pay for medical treatment. Even when they *have* insurance it is sometimes insufficient to cover the expenses incurred. Now, the so-called "conservatives" here excoriate national health care and brand it as "socialist." Indeed they are quick to slap that label on any program or person they don't like as though it were some proof of vicious intentions, though of course "socialism" means nothing more than a society's sense of shared responsibility—*such* an ignoble thing, eh? Also, how odd, even ridiculous, that so patriotic and even jingoistic a notion—that countrymen should have a sense of shared responsibility toward one another—is denigrated by the political party that prides itself on patriotism! The question of course is: Why would the right *not* want national health care? How comes it that any group of Americans would *not* want to see their country more secure because more healthy and content? You need only follow the money. Who would have most to lose? The health insurance companies. These are multi-billion dollar entities. They are not about to sit idly by and watch themselves be put out of business—lose all that enormous profit. The miserable men and women in charge of these companies have no qualms about placing their own welfare above the good of their country. In this they are guilty of a kind of treason and ought to be punished accordingly—put into prison for life or, better yet, lined up against a wall and shot. But they aren't punished because, through means direct or circuitous, they have bought their way into political power. Having also the means to manipulate the media, they can convince a stupid public to protest against proposed laws that would be in its interest.

Again: the "right" here are intensely pro-military. They always seem to want to expand the armed forces. Now, I am not against a strong military. On the contrary it is one of the things I believe in unexceptionably. Given the aggressive nature of mankind, it is always in the interest of a country to be stronger than its enemies, and even stronger than its "friends," whose friendship is usually based more on their awe of might rather than out of any respect for an alien people and culture. (The Americans themselves have come to see how many of their international "friends" in fact despise them—something they would see a hundred times more clearly if they ever lost their status as a superpower.) No, my problem with the right's avid pro-military stance is that it comes from no real desire to protect American interests so much as to ensure the profitability of corporate sponsors. They want to keep awash in taxpayer money the entities that fund their campaigns or reside in their districts, and which just *happen* to build and maintain the guns, tanks, ships, planes, and hardware of the military. How do I know this? It's pretty obvious. Here they are, these powerful Americans, with all their unstoppable armadas of aircraft carriers, with all their million-dollar jet aircraft and guided missiles, their billion-dollar submarines, their even more expensive black projects of still greater lethality, one or all of which could level a city in an instant—and yet they won't even drop a $5 stick of dynamite on the house of some two-bit Somali pirate! As they say here in New York, "Gimme a break, will ya?" What is the point of having a powerful military machine if you are not going to use it? Perhaps you will tell me: "But they are using it— have used it often, even too often, in the last decade, invading countries at the opposite ends of the earth and remaining in them for years." Well, in the first place, they used it only after an atrocious attack against them was committed, and even then not without controversy among themselves; and in the second place it is their "remaining there" that is the crux of the matter—the question that ought to arouse your suspicion. They remain in these countries because it is not profitable to the industries supplying the military if a war is fought and won and done with.   These companies only continue to make money when materiel is lost and needs to be replaced, or used and needs to be maintained, and when soldiers must be continuously supplied. Again, perhaps you'll tell me: "No, they are remaining in these places because if they go away their enemies will return." In that case, have they "won" these wars at all?   It seems to me that when you win a war there is no question about your enemy coming back, at least any time soon. Even if you don't destroy him utterly, you bloody his nose well enough so that he's not likely to want to repeat the experience. America needs to relearn that war is a dirty business and cannot be won with a too-tender conscience. Either fight to win or don't fight at all. And as harsh as that might sound, it's in fact the humaner mode of warfare, getting the dirty business over as quickly as possible rather than allowing it to drag out for years on end with a hundred times more suffering on all sides concerned.

What also disturbs me about the right in this country is their too-cozy association with religion, or rather fanatical religion. Somehow they have come to be bound up with people who are sure all the answers to life and the universe can be found in the Bible. The Bible of course has its literary and historical and spiritual value: but it was also written by people who today would be categorized as scientific imbeciles, so entirely ignorant were they of the physical realities of the universe and the physiological and psychological realities of humankind;—people who believed the earth was flat, a woman could turn into a pillar or salt, and the dead could return to life. It's all well and fine to believe such things if one wants to; there are no laws against being foolish or gullible; but such nonsense should never have anything to do with the framing of civil legislation. But in America people who believe such things would like to see a government run according to Biblical tenets, or at least to their interpretation of them. Abortion, for instance, they want to see made illegal everywhere and in all circumstances. Even when the child would be severely mentally or physically handicapped, it *must* be born. Is it not wonderfully "Christian" of them to want to impose on another, who can have no say in the matter, the kind of miserable life they would not want for themselves? Again, they are clamorously anti-homosexual. They base their prejudice on a few references by the Biblical writers who had no understanding of genetics and human sexuality, and who assumed therefore that everyone was naturally heterosexual. But that their antagonism in this matter is more a matter of prejudice than of piety may be seen in the fact that while they never tire of assailing this and several other specific "sins," they blithely overlook the hundred others the Bible no less vehemently decries, and which they themselves daily commit. Really, if their preachers were honest about calling out and cursing sinners, nine-tenths of their congregation would slink away before the sermon was over—and never come back. On the other hand don't think that in saying all this I am against religion. On the contrary I think the moderately conventional kinds of it are a great benefit to the individual and society. You, who are much younger than I am, will perhaps disagree with me. Perhaps you believe it a mark of sophistication in yourself to believe that the major religions, based as they are on the miraculous and supernatural, are absurd, unnecessary, even degrading to the human intellect. At your age I thought the same thing. But in time you will come to see that their value lies not in their "truth" but in their social utility: they may not make men any wiser about the next world, but at least they help keep them under control in this one. For the police cannot be everywhere at all times, and as the overwhelming majority of people are coarse and impulsive, they would too often give way to their ferocious, marauding, even murderous impulses without the internal restraints imposed on them by religious training. In fact I think that some basic form of it ought to be mandatory— that as a matter of law children ought to be inculcated with the belief that some Daddy-in-the-Sky who is watching their every move and is sure to punish them if they harm others. Just think about it! This kind of training would probably largely empty the prisons in a single generation. It is certainly the main reason why in our country we have so few prisons and so few people in them.

I have spoken about the right-wing in this country. Now I will tell you about left-wing, who have done no less harm and are equally corrupt in doing the bidding of the plutocrats. In the matter of national health care, for instance, they recently managed to pass certain legislation that was supposed to "overhaul" the system. It came in the form of a document that was (are you ready for this? are you sitting down?) nine-hundred pages long. Its absurd, obscene, unacceptable length was far from the worst of it; the worst of it was its content—or rather its sinister obscuration of content. I tried to read some of it. I only managed to get through three pages of it before my eyes rolled back into my head, the room began to spin, and I felt like toppling over as though in an epileptic fit. Such sulphur-clouds of semi-literate legalese! Such heaps upon heaps of drily moronic corporate-speak! Such divided, sub-divided, and then sub-sub-divided rules and counter-rules and references and counter-references! I am telling you no such document with its power to confound and addle an intelligent creature's brain ever existed before in this galaxy! From what I understand the insurance companies were allowed to "give their input" to this legislation—helped to draft it; which certainly goes far in explaining its stultifying incomprehensibility. For, as I have told you, those companies are not about to see themselves legislated out of existence. Before that ever happened they would assassinate a President, or drown twenty Senators at a time. But they didn't have to resort to such extreme measures, given the lack of honor among the politicians in this country: they needed only to apply a sufficiently thick layer of grease on various palms, which resulted in the linguistic fogs of this legislation and which have but one purpose: to hide from public view the guarantees of continued immense profits to insurance companies. But once again who is really and ultimately responsible for this kind of shenanigans but the American people themselves? Had they been a people of any minimum degree of common sense, they would have risen en masse against such legislation, telling their leaders, "No way! We will not accept nine-hundred pages of gibberish in something that concerns us so closely! If you cannot tell us what you intend to do with us in one hundred or fewer pages of plain English—then out with you all, you scoundrels and misfits!" —Yes, that is something an intelligent and united people would have said and done. But again, these are not intelligent or united people. Their attention was once again successfully diluted and diverted by the "left-right" paradigm; and as they bickered among themselves there continued apace the greatest plunder yet of their personal and collective wealth.

But the left has done the bidding of corporate interests in still more sinister and destructive ways. It is they, after all, who have relentlessly promoted "diversity." If you come here you are sure to hear or read this word a dozen times a day. It is always presented in the most positive, glowing way. But it means nothing less harmful than this: the systematic ingathering of peoples, even the most backward and benighted, from all parts of the world, of all races, creeds, values, beliefs, and intentions, and plopping them down within the borders of one country, and expecting them all to live together as one big happy family. Given the tribal nature of mankind, could anything be more absurd? Could anything be more destructive to the cohesion of a society? Is there anyone who, with a single, most slender sliver of a working brain in his skull, could think this a good, a rational idea? It's as though one should gather up every odd rock and stone along the road, shove them all into a tumbler, and expect them to glide over one another in lubricious silence and without a moment of friction—without a grind or roar, without a chip or scrape, or a ghost of dust. When I first came here I didn't understand how anyone could possibly take this idea seriously. Every time Americans proudly announced to me their faith and pride in "diversity" I would counter with my disdain for it, and forthrightly proclaim the madness of thinking that by Balkanizing a country one improved it. You should have seen their faces! Surprise— shock—horror! How *dare* anyone pipe up and declare that the emperor had no clothes! I would try to explain how their notion of "diversity" flew in the face of human nature, and as such was socially harmful. If even the most homogeneous countries are sometimes fractured by internal discord, I would ask them, how much more likely is this to happen where the population is increasingly composed of divergent and disparate peoples? But they didn't want to hear it. They refused to hear it. They shook their heads and looked at me askance, and sneered.

You may wonder how any people, even one so stupid as

Americans, could have been suckered into something so patently preposterous, so clearly detrimental to themselves, something that even a schoolboy in our country would know better than to take seriously.   You can certainly in part chalk it up to the machinations of the moneyed elite, to the shrewdness of the super-rich who were and are running this country. Having come to love money more than honor, even patriotism no longer restrained their greed, and in order to increase their wealth they sold out their country and countrymen.   They advocated for a free-for-all immigration that would in effect import poverty and so bring down the cost of labor, which, like any other commodity, is priced according to its availability.   The only obstacle to this plan was of course the resistance of the American people, who, however, were easily enough swayed into believing that any resistance they might have about it—about this fundamental change in their country, and even (as it was) this violation of their Constitution—arose from a shameful closed-mindedness, a "selfish" pride in their history and culture. They were, in effect, *psychologically terrorized* into silence and submission.

They are more psychologically terrorized than ever.   Nothing better proves this than the illegal immigration issue here. Over the last three or four decades America has been overrun by tens of millions of alien peoples in a way that has never happened in the history of the world outside of a catastrophic military defeat. Most of these people are from second- and third-world countries; many of them have no education, indeed are ineducable; and represent the worst of their countrymen—the liabilities of their lands. Who could possibly benefit from this tidal wave of the benighted but companies wanting cheap physical labor? But did not America have its own share of grunt workers? Yes, of course. But the homegrown variety demanded at least a liveable wage; believed that as "Americans," as citizens of a wealthy, first-world country, they should at least be able to afford a home, a car, and the means to bring up a child or two. But rather than provide wages that would ensure so much, Benedict A. Corporate wagged his greedy-admonitory finger before their uppity working-class faces and said, "I'll show you!"— and opened the floodgates.   In came the impoverished millions who were willing to work for less and less, and less and less, till in only a few decades Americans were reduced to working for

survival wages;—which is exactly the sorry state that they are
still in, and out of which, so far as I can see, nothing short of
some kind of revolution will get them.

One wonders why Americans still haven't reached that
bursting point and revolted. Again, it is due to careful, calculated indoctrination. Once they were taught to be proud of their
revolutionary heritage, to be ever suspicious of government, ever
vigilant against its usurpations; now they are taught about the
merits of "good citizenship"—of how their system, the "best in
the world," can only work when people "follow the rules" and
"work together." They are taught that "revolution" is somehow
"un-American," something only foreign peoples must trouble
themselves with because they are not blessed with democracy.
But they—Americans? They are above all that; are too politi-
cally evolved ever to fill the streets as enraged mobs and demand change on threat of violence against their elected do-
nothings. That is not the American way! Rather, if they are
upset about something, they need only politely write or call
their representative in Congress and "express their views," or go
to the polls and "vote for change." Well, the blockheads have
been expressing their views and voting for change for the last
forty years—with what results I for one clearly see!

But a day of reckoning is coming to those who placed
profits above patriotism—who thought that they, in their high
and mighty positions, would themselves never experience the
kind of adverse consequences their greed caused to their countrymen. They mistakenly thought that because their wealth
had always insulated them from the unpleasant aspects of society it would always do so. They could not see that in changing
the provenance of the people of their land they were bound to
change its culture. But surely even they, now, are beginning to
sense the ominous shift in mindset around them, namely, how
great wealth is regarded less as something to venerate or emulate than as an unfairness needful of redress. And when so
much of this country's wealth has come to be in so few hands,
such a change in attitude is inevitable and just. At any rate,
the "new Americans," as they might be called, increasingly have
the power to change this country through their vote, and have
already put into power people determined to chip away at huge
personal fortunes for the sake of the general weal. Oh! I can't

begin to tell you the warm delicious feeling I get all over when I think about that!—about how the wealthy "liberals" who were so eager to promote these changes in their society, who felt so superior and sophisticated in advocating them, will one day have their fortunes confiscated on account of them! It shows me that there is a kind of justice in this world after all—if only of the poetic kind.

Yes, all these things I am telling you about I have seen or considered with the objective clarity of the outsider. And though I used to talk to Americans about them, I no longer do so. Why not? Because they don't want to hear what I have to say. Their indoctrination is complete: they absolutely despise anyone who doesn't believe as they do. Besides, I am reminded of a precept by Voltaire: "Never tilt against the ruling superstition unless you are powerful enough to withstand it, or clever enough to escape its pursuit." I am neither. I am just someone who came to this country and report what I see. Besides, the truth is often shy: expressing itself best when there isn't a hostile audience to intimidate it. But I am confident that history will bear me out. Hundreds of years from now insightful historians will conclude that the major factor in America's decline was this fragmentation of its population and dilution of its culture.

On the other hand no one need wait a hundred years, or even one, to see how the seeds of decay have germinated here. To my mind it was evidenced clearly enough in the catastrophe of 9/11 and in the events immediately succeeding it. As you know, I was living here when it occurred. Every face and voice around me betrayed a stunned disorientation at the brutality of the attacks, as though people suddenly found themselves in a new, incomprehensible world. And so they were. For the rose-colored glasses that Americans are wont to wear had been suddenly torn away from their eyes, and they saw a world much more harsh, violent, and hateful than any they had been taught about or supposed. With disbelief, with shock, they saw that the life they extolled as "free," and which they had been happily advocating and exporting all over the world, was in some places so reviled and despised that in order to attack it men were willing to kill themselves in the commission of unthinkable atrocities. Above all the happy platitudes about the "benefits of diversity," which by then had become a secular article of faith in

America, had been exposed for the lethally dangerous thing it was. For the attackers had come from the most divergent, un-American backgrounds imaginable; had been welcomed into the country, nurtured by it, and partaken of its liberties; and yet had—struck at its heart. But it was in the incessant, elaborately-staged mourning ceremonies that succeeded the attacks that the new degeneration of the country was most evident to me. Rather than be roused at once to a united fury against their enemies, Americans turned for relief to spectacle. Religious services with bands and orchestras, honors for the dead presided over by speechifying politicians, the singing of hymns by opera and popular singers, masses of people engaged in communal weeping and wailing—on and on it went, on the radio, on the television, everywhere and inescapable, day in and day out, for weeks, for months, till, really, one was a little bewildered by it all, and only pity for the victims and their families enabled one to hold one's peace against so much wasted, misdirected energy; but that it was misdirected and wasted there could be no doubt to any clear-thinking mind. I remember how an old neighbor of mine, who came from a different time in this country, bristled at all this endless, exhausting wailing and impotent hand-wringing. "What are they *singing* about!" she fumed. "They keep singing and praying and making speeches and then singing and praying again! For God's sake!—start *bombing!*" Certainly sixty years earlier, in her generation, in her America, it had been a different story. Then, another attack had taken place against America, and the nation—when it had really *been* a nation—knew at once what it had to do; its President declaring, outrightly, war; at this declaration, a Congress roaring approval; and a united people setting out to win that war in as determined a way as any has ever done. *Then* a sleeping giant leapt into action, furious, clear-sighted, single-minded, and had helped defeat the greatest, most sophisticated military power that the world had yet seen. But now it was quite different. Now the giant had to medicate itself before stirring. Even after it stirred, even after it was fully roused and focused on its goal, it was distracted by the shrieking doubts of faction, which caused hesitation just when resolve was most needed, and thus cost its war effort more blood and treasure than necessary. More than once, in the very fire of battle, this greatest superpower in the world hesitated, held back, was ineffective, and this before a ragtag collection of fifth-world moronic misfits and human scum—and all so that it might not "look bad."

Since those days Americans have plucked back up their rosy spectacles and jauntily perched them on the bridge of their noses. Again to a dangerous degree they have begun to see the world not as it is but as they wish it to be. They have continued to import into their borders still greater numbers of alien peoples, some of whom have nothing but the worst intentions toward them—who are just waiting for the right moment to wreak havoc. And what makes me afraid, what it pains me to think of, is that it may take another disaster, even greater than that of 9/11, for Americans to be shaken out of the comfortable idealistic stupor they have largely been petted back into. Who knows but that even *then* they will be so far along in their dilution of nationhood and culture that, as they gaze on the flaming shambles of what once was a thriving city or region, they will begin casting blame on the various factions among themselves rather than directing a united anger toward the obvious internal or external enemy? —Which is in a nutshell the rot permeating this country: that its people, increasingly composed of such different kinds, can no longer see with the clarity of a single vision.

What could save this country? Well, as we are in an election cycle here the first thing that comes to my mind is a strong, clear-sighted President—a true leader, not one of the fake, phony kinds that have been parading about as such for the last forty years. Such a man would take advantage of corporate powers only insofar as they would enable him to attain power, but which, once he had it, he would use not in their but in the people's interest. For this he would have to be willing to risk his life, since he would be a marked man. Very likely he wouldn't succeed unless he had the help of highly-placed, like-minded people throughout the government. Yes, it would have to be carefully planned out and calculated by many people; a kind of conspiracy of integrity. —A fantasy on my part, I admit. But can't one dream a little? And yet even if this dream were realized, if somehow a cadre of genuine patriots were able to take back the government of this country, I fear that Americans, in their present degraded state of mind and character, would be easily enough manipulated to oppose their saviors, and buck and kick against them, and eventually tear away from themselves the very hands that would have held them back from falling into the Abyss.

In your letter you mentioned your concern about being "safe" here—you mentioned the high crime statistics of the country. Believe me, you'll be fine. There is certainly a lot of crime here—the murder rate *is* high—but it's a very large country and just as a matter of odds you are a thousand times more likely to be safe than otherwise. Of course here as well as anywhere else in the world you must avoid thugs when you see them; the only difference being that in New York you'll see a lot of them. You must also stay out of the "bad neighborhoods," as they call them here;—a euphemism for the places having the highest density of especially stupid and violent people. (More clearly than ever I see the connection between low intelligence and violent crime.) Still, there's no denying that there's a much higher crime rate here than in our country. We would never tolerate what Americans put up with—which is why we don't have to. It's another mark of their stupidity that Americans haven't grasped that most commonsensical of all concepts: that a people only endures the level of crime they are willing to tolerate. In our country when someone commits a violent crime the punishment is proportional and immediate; justice is served; and, having been served, fulfills the duty of the State to protect its citizens. But here they often coddle criminals, and the most heinous criminals—murderers—they tend to coddle most of all. A murderer about whose guilt there is no question will be put into prison for years, for decades, while his case is appealed, and then appealed again, and then appealed yet again by lawyers who, sometimes, do not even pretend to be pursuing justice but who are exerting themselves in this way because they "do not believe" in the death penalty and are determined to block or undermine it. —Thus the victims of these crimes are victimized again, and (what makes it so disgusting) by the very profession from which they ought to have gotten relief. And as though to rub the rag of filthy injustice still more vigorously into the public face, these criminals, these scum, these lowest of the low, are kept alive, are fed and housed and given medical attention at the taxed expense of the poorest, most law-abiding citizens! I am telling you, all this is a kind of madness here.

What hope is there for a society when it can't even decide to punish a scoundrel?

By the way, those in favor of abolishing the death penalty use the same arguments here that they have tried to use in our country; namely, that it is "inhumane." It never occurs to these numbskulls that the real inhumanity lies in abetting an injustice by allowing someone to keep his life after he has forfeited it by taking away another's. Or they say that capital punishment is not a deterrent, when common sense tells you that it is, since there will always be people for whom the fear of their own death prevents them from committing murder. At the very least it ensures that those who have been tried and punished for killing someone in cold blood cannot do it again. But the main argument they use here against capital punishment is the prospect of putting an innocent person to death. But this is like saying that because people die in highway accidents no one should be permitted to drive or ride in a car; or that because planes crash, the airline industry should be outlawed; or that because hundreds of people die from food poisoning each year, agriculture ought to stop;—it is an absurd argument because it presupposes that unless something is perfect it ought to be abolished. Thus for sake of preventing a handful of injustices over the course of a century, hundreds take place yearly by allowing monsters to live out their lives—and at the expense (one can never stress this too often!) of even the poorest of the citizenry.

Your question about crime was probably also prompted by all the violent American movies and television shows you've seen. And it is true that here you can hardly go to a movie without seeing someone, or rather several dozen people, strangled, beaten, knifed, shot, raped, or otherwise left bleeding and screaming in agony. Movie posters here are full of beautiful movie stars—holding guns. I am not sure how to account for all this kind of sick psychology unless it is this: to the degree that people are reduced to clockwork automatons—to the degree their lives are filled with boring routine—to the degree they have degenerated into shopkeepers—they seek out extravagant stimulations, and these progressively desensitize them so that in time only the grossest exhibitions of violence or suffering can arouse their excitement. In ancient Rome a jaded populace enthusiastically crowded into the Colosseum to watch people hack one another to pieces or be eaten by lions.

You also said in your letter that if you do visit New York it won't be till winter, perhaps as late as December. That is a good idea—better than you can know! You *do not* want to be here in the summer. Despite the relatively high latitude of this city, the summers here are tropical. From the end of July through the end of September it is hellishly uncomfortable. The sun beats down mercilessly on the streets and buildings, which absorb and then radiate back the heat so that it seems to come at you from all sides as though you were in giant oven. Only, an oven has dry heat, and the heat here is humid, oppressive, suf-focating. You can scarcely walk a block without your skin be-coming disgustingly clammy and your shirt darkening with damp spots; and if you persist in physical exertion you are soon dripping with sweat. People who ordinarily walk at a clip are reduced to trudging along like decrepit old people, breathing hard, growing tired quickly, their damp hair plastered against wan, glistening foreheads. The thick air is discolored with the thousand poisons of car exhaust. As for using the subways to get around town or to get to work, as the great majority of peo-ple here must do—well, in the summer the subways become tunnels of the damned. In any season they are demoralizing, filled as they are with gloom, noise, and bipedal pigs who have no qualms about throwing their trash or half-eaten food on the floor, or coughing up gobs of mucous and spitting it out for ev-eryone else to look at or step in. But in the summer, in addi-tion to all these disgusting things, there is the unrelenting, throbbing heat. The already hot tunnel-enclosed air is made hot-ter by trains throwing off steamy air from engines and air con-ditioners. Thus the temperature in the subway can be ten or twenty degrees higher than it is above ground. While you wait and wait for the next train you feel beads of sweat trickling down your armpits and chest and back. No amount of fanning yourself can make you more comfortable. No quantity of cold drink can sufficiently cool you down. I have seen people waiting in this panting environment for no more than ten minutes be-fore they begin to wobble, become unsteady on their feet. A cer-tain number of people every year faint away—fall to the filthy floor and have to be carried out on stretchers. Last year there was even the case of a poor soul who was overcome by the heat, fell onto the tracks before an oncoming train, and was chopped in half. The officials in charge of the public transportation system here are wont to boast of it, to talk up its extensiveness, its versatility, its relative inexpensiveness. But it is really one of the filthy realities of this city which adds its own large measure to the hardship of life here. I am certain that on account of it alone a certain percentage of people give up living here, having come to the practical conclusion that no benefit this city offers could possibly be worth the stress and demoralization of having to take a subway twice a day to get to and from work, especially in summer. For let's face it: one shouldn't have to *work* to get to work—one shouldn't have to suffer to go to a job.

So if you do come here, come in December, and at least you will be physically comfortable. You will also get to experience Christmas here. You will like that. It's one of the few times when New York City can be pleasant. It is very festive then. There are lights everywhere. Store windows glitter with displays. Christmas carols happily play in public places. In my neighborhood the streets are festooned with glittering snowflake ornaments. In Rockefeller Center they put up the famous Christmas tree. (It is very large but its lighting is always predictably bland—no doubt the unimaginative "creation" of some corporate functionary.) For the space of two or three weeks the New Yorker loses a little of his hard, dark, hurrying, suspicious nature, and into his murky spirit a refreshing crystalline beam of sweetness and poetry enters—the child's delight in sparkling things and the hope of magic.

The spirit of Christmas is so pervasive here that one might almost think Americans are religious. But they really aren't. Though out of a hundred Americans ninety-nine will tell you that they are of this or that religion, they keep few of the injunctions and tenets of their avowed faith, and rarely go to a church or temple on a regular basis. It's obvious that in their heart of hearts they don't *really* believe in God—that is to say, in the conventional, Daddy-in-the-Sky variety of it. Even *they* can't bring themselves to believe in that. Many of them will tell you that they aren't religious but "spiritual," that is to say, they believe there exists some grand, timeless, ineffable force permeating the universe and which is responsible for the world's and their existence. This always *sounds* insightful, though ultimately it is nothing more than turning into an article of faith the obvious limits of human knowledge;—and perhaps, as such, is nothing to sneer at. Nevertheless most Americans, in any casual conversation, will label themselves as belonging to this or that conventional religion, and if they have children they will raise them up in it because, after all, "They have to believe in something." Oh!—there it is again, that excruciating American need to keep up appearances! I am telling you, there never was a people who talked so proudly about "individualism" and who were so concerned about what everyone else thought!

Well, enough ... enough. Have you ever received a letter like this? Weren't expecting it, were you? Come to think of it, neither was I. Looking at it now—at all these pages piled up on my desk—I shake my head and think, Whew!—who knew I had so much to say? At the very least it will be a lesson to you about writing letters to *me!* Anyway, my hand is so tired, so sore now, that I have to stop.

—Or rather, wait. There *is* one more thing.

Maybe I shouldn't mention it. I have a sense that it's something you don't want me to know about, otherwise you would have told me about it yourself. But you should know that you are not the only conduit of information that I have regarding what goes on back home. I have always kept in touch with people there. And they tell me things. I found out, for instance, that you had "gotten involved" with someone. From all accounts she was a great beauty, and you were very taken with her. Everyone noticed the change in you. They said you were very happy. But things didn't "work out," and you were very upset.

"Upset"!

As the saying goes, I might have been born at night but I wasn't born *last* night. I know that in this instance the word "upset" speaks volumes. I am the more sure of this because you have written to me out of the blue saying that you want to come here for a visit—you who always hated to travel and have never even left our hometown. At least part of your desire to come here must have something to do with trying to forget something, or someone.

Now, you don't have to tell me anything if you don't want to. It's not even necessary. Believe it or not but I wasn't always the slow, cynical, and sometimes grumpy old goat you probably think me. Once I too was young; once I too got "involved" with people. And if I think back, very hard, I can sometimes, for a few seconds at a time, recapture those faces;—those beautiful faces;—one face in particular, more perfect and beautiful than any other face that has ever been;—and feel again some distant vibration of the wonderful, exhilarating, glorious, dark, horrible, destructive thing I felt then, in those years when I was so different, and so much more hopeful, and no doubt so much better a human being than I am today. So don't think that talking to me about such things would be like talking to a wall. This wall might just surprise you.

Well, that really *is* it. If you do make plans to come here, make sure you let me know about them well in advance, at least a couple of weeks. And my dear boy—*call*, don't write.

www.ingramcontent.com/pod-product-compliance
Lightning Source LLC
Chambersburg PA
CBHW020641110726
47901CB00001B/5